SELECT EDITIONS

Selected and Edited by Reader's Digest

SELECT EDITIONS

Selected and Edited by
Reader's Digest

 New York · Montreal

FROM THE EDITORS

Sometimes the stars align in mysterious ways. In the universe of tough-guy crime-fighting heroes who aren't afraid to seriously bend some rules/laws for the greater good, the stars have indeed aligned for this volume of Select Editions. That's just a fancy way of saying that something really cool happened.

We are delighted to include titles that feature beloved heroes Jack Reacher and James Bond. While Bond creator Ian Fleming passed away in 1964, bestselling British author Anthony Horowitz has taken up the Bond mantle and penned a prequel to *Casino Royale*. In *Forever and a Day*, we learn how a young Bond earned his license to kill.

And Jack Reacher? He's appeared many times in our pages, and a Lee Child book is always a treat to read. What can we say except that Reacher, like Bond, truly is one of a kind. While very different, both characters are iconic crime fighters who always deliver the page-turning goods.

Rounding out the volume are two titles that feature softer but equally compelling stories. First there's *Hope on the Inside* by Marie Bostwick, which examines how we can help ourselves by helping others. It also has quilting, family, midlife crises, and prison reform, all wrapped in one cozy package. Our final selection is *The Last Road Trip* by Gareth Crocker, an adventure story that's also a paean to senior citizens and their wisdom, energy, and courage. It's a lovely tale that can inspire all of us, no matter what our age.

We hope you enjoy these stories as much as we did!

Inside
SELECT EDITIONS

6 Past Tense

Lee Child

Old family secrets and new unexpected troubles greet Jack Reacher when he visits the tiny New Hampshire town where his father was supposedly born.

178 Hope on the Inside

Marie Bostwick

"Whatever comes your way, find the happiness in it." Hope received this advice from her mother decades ago. But with so many changes in her life, can she find the strength to follow it?

322 Forever and a Day

Anthony Horowitz

Just how did James Bond earn his license to kill? A spy is born in this explosive 007 prequel to Ian Fleming's *Casino Royale*. This is how the legend began.

466 The Last Road Trip

Gareth Crocker

Four senior citizens in a retirement community decide they still have a lot of living to do. Undeterred by skeptics, they embark on the South African road trip of a lifetime.

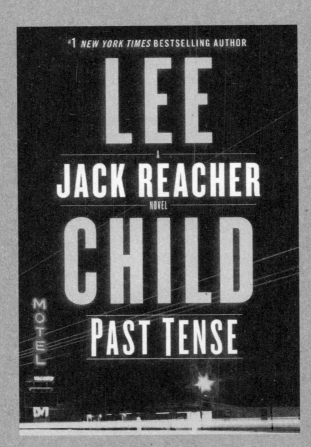

Chapter 1

JACK REACHER CAUGHT the last of the summer sun in a small town on the coast of Maine, and then, like the birds in the sky above him, he began his long migration south. But not, he thought, straight down the coast. Not like the orioles and the buntings and the phoebes and the warblers and the ruby-throated humming-birds. Instead he decided on a diagonal route, south and west, from the top right-hand corner of the country to the bottom left, maybe through Syracuse, and Cincinnati, and St. Louis, and Oklahoma City, and Albuquerque, and onward to San Diego. Which for an army guy like Reacher was a little too full of navy people, but which was otherwise a fine spot to start the winter.

It would be an epic road trip, and one he hadn't made in years.

He didn't get far.

He walked inland a mile or so and came to a county road and stuck out his thumb. He was a tall man, more than six feet five in his shoes, heavily built, all bone and muscle, not particularly good-looking, usually a little unkempt. As always most drivers took a look and then kept on going. The first car prepared to take a chance on him came along after forty minutes. It was a year-old Subaru wagon, driven by a lean middle-aged guy in chino pants and a crisp khaki shirt. Dressed by his wife, Reacher thought. The guy had a wedding ring. But under the fine fabrics was a workingman's body. A thick neck and large red knuckles. The slightly surprised and somewhat reluctant boss of something, Reacher thought. The kind of guy who starts out digging postholes and ends up owning a fencing company.

Which turned out to be a good guess. Initial conversation established the guy had started out with nothing to his name but his daddy's framing hammer, and had ended up owning a construction company. This was an organized guy, full of notions and maxims and cast-iron beliefs, one of which was that at the end of summer it was better to stay away from both Route 1 and I-95, and in fact to get out of Maine altogether as fast as possible, which was sideways, on Route 2, west into New Hampshire. To a place just south of Berlin, where the guy knew back roads that would get them down to Boston. Which was where the guy was going, for a meeting about marble countertops. Reacher was happy. Nothing wrong with Boston as a starting point. From there it was a straight shot to Syracuse. After which Cincinnati was easy. Reacher had been in worse places. Mostly in the service.

They didn't get to Boston.

The guy got a call on his cell, after fifty-some minutes on the New Hampshire back roads. The phone was hooked up to the car radio, and a name came up on the navigation screen, with a photograph of a red-faced man wearing a hard hat. Some kind of a foreman on a job site. The guy at the wheel touched a button, and phone hiss filled the car, from all the speakers.

The guy at the wheel said, "This better be good news."

It wasn't. It was something to do with a buildings department inspector and a metal flue liner above a fireplace in an entrance lobby, which was properly insulated, up to code, except that couldn't be proved visually without tearing down the stonework, or ripping out the custom walnut millwork in the dining room on the other side of the chimney, or the millwork in the closet above, which was rosewood and even more complicated, but the inspector was being a hard-ass about it and needed to see for himself.

The guy at the wheel said, "Which inspector is it?"

The guy on the phone said, "The new one."

The guy at the wheel glanced at Reacher, and then faced front again and said, "Did you offer him money?"

"Five hundred. He wouldn't take it."

Then the cell signal ran out. The sound went dead.

"I have to go back," the guy said. "I'm sorry. I'm going to have to let you out here. Is that okay?"

"No problem," Reacher said. "Whose is the rosewood closet?"

"His."

"Cut a big hole in it and show the inspector. Then give the client five reasons why he should install a wall safe. Because a guy who wants a fireplace in his entrance lobby wants a wall safe in his bedroom closet. That's for damn sure. You'll make a profit. You can charge him for the time it takes to cut the hole."

"Are you in this business, too?"

"I was a military cop."

The guy said, "Huh."

Reacher opened the door and climbed out and closed the door again behind him. The guy swung the Subaru around and took off back the way he had come, with a brief good-luck wave.

Reacher turned back and continued walking south.

Two miles later the road curved left, and a new road split off to the right. A classic Y-shaped junction. Both options ran out of sight through trees so mighty in places they made a tunnel.

A tilted arrow to the left was labeled Portsmouth, and a tilted arrow to the right was labeled Laconia.

Laconia, New Hampshire.

A name Reacher knew. It was his late father's place of birth, and where he was raised, until he escaped at age seventeen to join the marines. Such was the vague family legend. Escaped from what had not been specified. But he never went back. Reacher himself had been born more than fifteen years later, by which time Laconia was a dead detail of the long-ago past. No one in the family ever went there. The grandparents died young and were rarely mentioned. There were apparently no aunts or uncles or cousins or any other distant relatives. Which was statistically unlikely, and suggested a rift of some kind. But certain things were not discussed in marine families. Much later as a captain in the army Reacher's brother Joe was posted north and said something about trying to find the old family homestead, but nothing ever came of it. Probably Reacher himself had said the same kind of thing from time to time. He had never been there, either.

Reacher stepped right, and chose the road that led to Laconia.

AT THAT same moment, nearly thirty miles away, heading south on a different back road, was a worn-out Honda Civic, driven by a twenty-five-year-old man named Shorty Fleck. Next to him was his twenty-five-year-old girlfriend, Patty Sundstrom. They were both born and raised in Saint Leonard, a small town in New Brunswick, Canada. Patty worked in a sawmill. Shorty was a potato farmer. And he wasn't particularly short. Maybe he had been once, as a kid. But now he was an average-looking guy.

They were trying to make it nonstop from Saint Leonard to New York City. They had something to sell in the city, and saving a night in a hotel would maximize their profit. They had planned out their route using back roads to avoid the summer people, and figured it was feasible.

Except they had gotten a late start due to the aging Honda overheating. It had needed nursing along below fifty miles an hour for an extended spell.

They were tired. And hungry, and thirsty. And frustrated. The Honda was overheating again. There was a grinding noise under the hood. All the dashboard lights had been on continuously for the last two and a half years.

Shorty asked, "What's up ahead?"

Patty said, "Nothing."

Her fingertip was on a wandering red line on the map, which was shown running north to south through a jagged shape shaded pale green. A forested area. Which matched what was out the window. Nowhere likely to have a mechanic or a lube shop or radiator water. The best bet was about thirty minutes ahead, some ways east of south, a town called Laconia.

She said, "Can we make another twenty miles?"

"Maybe," Shorty said. "If we walk the last nineteen of them."

Patty rubbed her fingertip forward on the map. There was a spiderweb vein coming up on the right. Then up ahead she saw the mouth of a narrow road, right on time. But more like a tunnel than a road. The trees met overhead. At the entrance on a post was nailed a board, on which were screwed ornate plastic letters, and an arrow pointing into the tunnel. The letters spelled MOTEL.

"Should we?" she asked.

The car answered. The temperature needle was jammed against the stop. The whole engine bay was baking.

"No choice," Shorty said, and turned into the tunnel. They saw a second sign, identical, facing drivers coming the other way.

They drove over a wire laid across the road. A fat rubbery thing, not much smaller than a garden hose. Like they had at gas stations, to ding a bell to get the pump jockey out to help you.

Shorty said, "How bad can it be? The sign was nice."

"I agree," Patty said. "It was."

They drove on.

THE trees cooled the air, so Reacher was happy to keep up a steady four miles an hour. He did thirty minutes, two miles, and then he heard sounds behind him, and turned around to see an ancient pickup coming toward him. Reacher stuck out his thumb.

The truck stopped. An old guy with a long white beard leaned across inside and wound down the passenger window.

He said, "I'm going to Laconia."

"Me, too," Reacher said.

"Well, okay."

Reacher got in. The old guy pulled out.

"Why are you going to Laconia?"

"I was passing by," Reacher said. "My father was born there. I want to see it."

"What's your last name?"

"Reacher."

The old guy shook his head. He said, "I never knew anyone in Laconia named Reacher."

The reason for the previous Y-shaped fork in the road turned out to be a lake. Reacher and the old guy shuddered along the right bank. The view was stunning, and the sun was less than an hour from setting. Then came the town of Laconia itself. It was bigger than Reacher expected. Fifteen or twenty thousand people. A county seat. Brick buildings and neat old-fashioned streets.

The pickup truck stopped at a downtown corner. The old guy said, "This is Laconia."

Reacher thanked the guy and got out. Then he walked random blocks, getting a sense for what might be where, in particular two specific destinations for the next day, and two for immediate attention that evening, the first being a place to eat and the second being a place to sleep.

Both were available. He ate at a narrow bistro, because a waitress smiled at him through the window. He ordered some kind of salad with roast beef in it, which was the menu choice he felt would be most nutritious. But when it came, it was tiny, so he asked for two portions and a bigger cup for his coffee.

Afterward he tracked back to lodgings he had seen, on a side street near the city offices. There was room at the inn. He paid a premium price for what the innkeeper called a suite, but what he called a room with a sofa and way too many floral patterns and feather pillows. He shoveled a dozen off the bed and put his pants under the mattress to press. Then he took a long hot shower, and climbed under the sheets, and went to sleep.

THE tunnel through the trees turned out to be more than two miles long. Patty Sundstrom traced its curves with her finger on the map. Under the Honda's wheels was pitted blacktop, the finish completely washed away in places, leaving potholes. Shorty was going slow, to save the shocks and nurse the motor.

Then the canopy thinned, like they were arriving somewhere. What they saw was the road ahead coming out of the trees and running in a straight line through a couple acres of flat grassland. Its destination was a group of three wooden buildings, laid out on a curve, maybe fifty yards between the first and the last. All three were painted dull red, with bright white trim.

The closest building was a motel. It was long and low, with a pitched gray roof and a red neon OFFICE sign in the first window, and then a louvered door for storage, and then a repeating pattern, of a broad window with an HVAC grille and two plastic lawn chairs under it, and a numbered door, and another broad window with the same grille and the same chairs, and another numbered door, and so on, all the way to the end. There were twelve rooms in total. But there were no cars parked out front of any of them.

Shorty stopped the car. In the distance on the right they saw the second building was shorter, but taller and deeper from front to back. Some kind of barn. But not for animals. The concrete ramp to the door was clean. It was a workshop of some kind. Out front were nine quad bike ATVs lined up in three ranks of three.

"Maybe these guys would know how to fix the car," said Patty.

On the end of the line, the third building was a regular house with a wraparound porch that had rocking chairs set out on it.

Shorty rolled the car forward and stopped again. The blacktop was about to end. Ten yards short of the motel's empty lot. He was about to bump down onto a surface that his expert potato-farmer eye told him was made up of equal parts gravel, mud, dead weeds, and live weeds.

The end of the blacktop felt like a threshold. Like a decision.

"Okay?" he said. "I think it's this or nothing."

Patty said, "Let's take a look."

They parked outside the office. Shorty thought a second and shut the motor down. If it didn't start up again, too bad. It was already near enough where it needed to be. They had one huge suitcase, full of the stuff they planned to sell. It could stay in the car. Apart from that, they didn't have much to haul.

They got out of the car and stepped into the office. There was a guy behind the reception counter. He was mid-twenties, maybe a year or two more. He had short blond hair, combed neatly, and a good tan, and blue eyes, and white teeth, and a ready smile.

Patty told him they needed a room, and that they wondered if whoever looked after the quad bikes could take a look at their car, or failing that, they would surely appreciate the phone number of a good mechanic. Hopefully not a tow truck.

The guy smiled and asked, "What's wrong with your car?"

Patty said, "It's overheating and making banging noises."

The guy smiled again and said, "Sounds low on coolant, and low on oil. Both of which are easy to fix, unless something is leaking. If so, we know some good mechanics. Either way, there's nothing to be done until it cools down. Park it outside your room overnight, and we'll check it in the morning."

Patty asked, "How much is the room?"

"After Labor Day, let's call it fifty bucks."

"Okay," she said.

"We'll give you room ten," the guy said. "It's the first we've refurbished so far. In fact, we only just finished it. You would be its very first guests. We hope you will do us the honor."

Chapter 2

REACHER WOKE UP a minute after three in the morning. All the clichés: snapped awake, instantly, like flicking a switch. He didn't move. He just lay there, listening hard, concentrating.

What woke him? Not sight or touch or taste, because he had been alone in bed. Sound, then. He had heard something.

He waited for a repeat. He heard nothing. So what woke him?

He slid out from under the covers and listened at the door. Heard nothing. He lifted the drapes and checked the window. Nothing on the street. Pitch-dark. All quiet. He got back in bed and smacked the pillow into shape and went back to sleep.

PATTY Sundstrom was also awake at one minute past three. She had slept four hours, and then some kind of subconscious agitation had woken her up. She didn't feel good. The fifty bucks for the room was on her mind. Plus the car might cost a fortune. If parts were required. Cars were great until they weren't. Even so, the engine had started when they came out of the office. The motel guy didn't seem too worried about it.

But still, she didn't feel good. She didn't know why. The room was pleasant. It was newly refurbished. The AC was cold and quiet. There was a flat-screen television. The window was an expensive unit, with two thick panes of glass sealed in thermal gaskets, with an electric roller blind set in the void between. You didn't tug on a chain to close it. You pressed a button. Only problem was, the window itself didn't open. Generally she liked a breath of night air in a room. But overall, it was a decent place.

But she didn't feel good. There was no phone in the room, and no cell signal, so after half an hour they had walked back to the office to inquire about using the motel's landline for pizza delivery. The guy at the desk had smiled a rueful smile and said he was sorry, but they were way too remote for delivery. No one would come. Then the guy said, "But hey, we've got pizzas in the freezer down at the house. Why don't you come eat with us?"

Which was a weird meal, in a dark old residence, with Shorty and the guy and three others just the same. Same age, same look, with some kind of same-wavelength connection between them. There was something nervous about them. After some conversation, she concluded they were all maxed-out investors in the same new venture. The motel, she assumed. She assumed they had bought it and were trying to make a go of it. Whatever, they were all extremely polite. The guy from the reception desk said his name was Mark. The others were Robert, Steven, and Peter, who said he looked after the quad bikes.

They walked back to room 10 and went to sleep, except she woke up again four hours later, agitated. She didn't know why.

She wanted air. She slipped out of bed and padded barefoot to the door. She turned the knob.

But the door was stuck. It wouldn't move. She tried the knob both ways, but nothing happened. The door was jammed. Maybe it had swelled with the summer heat.

She crept back to bed and stared at the ceiling.

REACHER WOKE AGAIN AT eight in the morning.

He showered and dressed and walked out in search of breakfast. He found a place he figured might have good food hiding under layers of faux-retro irony. The basic idea seemed to be someone's modern-day notion of where old-time lumberjacks might have dined, on whatever it was that old-time lumberjacks ate, which seemed to be interpreted as one of every fried item on the menu. In Reacher's experience, lumberjacks ate the same as any other hard-working person, which was all kinds of different things. But he had no ideological objection to fried food as such, especially not in generous quantities, so he went in and sat down.

The food was fine, and the coffee kept on coming, so he lingered, watching out the window. Then he paid his check and walked two blocks toward the place he guessed he should start. Which was the records department of the city offices. Which had a suite number on a directory, outside a brick multipurpose government building, which because of its age and its shape Reacher figured had once contained a courtroom. Maybe it still did.

The suite turned out to be one of many small rooms opening off a mezzanine hallway. The doors were half glass, with the department name painted in gold. Inside the door was a room with a waist-high inquiry counter and an electric bell push screwed to the counter. A sign said IF UNATTENDED, RING FOR SERVICE.

Reacher rang for service. A minute later a woman came through a door in the rear wall. She was maybe thirty, slim and neat, in a gray sweater and a gray skirt. She stepped up to the counter and cranked up a warm and welcoming manner.

He said, "I need to ask you about an old real estate record."

"Is it for a title dispute?" the woman asked.

"No kind of dispute," he said. "My father was born here years ago. He's dead now. I was passing by. I thought I would stop in and take a look at the house he grew up in."

"What's the address?"

"I don't know. I've never been there."

"You didn't visit?"

"No."

"Perhaps because your father moved when he was young."

"Not until he joined the marines when he was seventeen."

"Then perhaps because your grandparents moved away before your father had a family of his own."

"I got the impression my grandparents stayed here the rest of their lives."

"But you never met them?"

"We were a marine family. We were always somewhere else."

"I'm sorry. But thank you for your service."

"My dad was the marine, not me. I was hoping we could look him up, maybe in a register of births, to get his parents' full names and find their exact address."

"You don't know your grandparents' names?"

"I think they were James and Elizabeth Reacher."

"That's my name. Elizabeth. Elizabeth Castle."

"I'm pleased to meet you," Reacher said.

"Likewise," she said.

"I'm Jack Reacher. My dad was Stan Reacher."

"How long ago did Stan leave to join the marines?"

"He'd be about ninety now, so more than seventy years ago."

"Then we should start eighty years ago, for a safety margin," the woman said. "At that point Stan Reacher would be about ten years old, living at home with his parents James and Elizabeth Reacher, somewhere in Laconia. Is that a fair summary?"

"That could be chapter one of my biography."

"I'm pretty sure the computer goes back more than eighty years now," she said. "But for property taxes that old it might just be a list of names, I'm afraid."

She turned a key and opened a lid in the countertop. Under it was a keyboard and a screen. She clicked and scrolled.

"Yes," she said. "Eighty years ago is just an index, with file numbers. If you want detail, you need to request the actual physical document from storage. Usually that takes months."

"Are there names and addresses in the index?"

"Yes."

"Then that's really all we need."

She clicked again, and scrolled. Finally she said, "No one named Reacher owned property in Laconia eighty years ago."

PATTY Sundstrom also woke again at eight in the morning. She sensed the space in the bed next to her was empty. She rolled over and saw the door was open. Shorty was out in the lot. He was talking to one of the motel guys. Peter, she thought. The guy who looked after the quad bikes. They were standing next to the Honda. Its hood was up. The sun was bright.

She slipped out of bed, showered, and dressed. The door was still open. Now Shorty was there alone. The other guy had gone.

She stepped out and said, "Good morning."

"Car won't start," Shorty said. "The guy messed with it, and now it's dead. It was okay last night."

"What did he do?"

"He poked around some. He had a wrench and a pair of pliers. I think he made it worse. Probably that's why they need nine bikes in the first place. To make sure they always have one that works."

She said, "Did you have a problem with the room door when you came out this morning."

"What kind of problem?"

"I wanted some air in the night, but I couldn't get it open."

"I didn't have a problem," Shorty said. "It opened right up."

Fifty yards away they saw Peter come out of the barn with a canvas bag in his hand. Tools, Patty thought. To fix their car. Peter clanked up to them with a smile.

She said, "Thanks so much for your help."

He said, "No problem at all."

"I hope it's not too complicated."

"Right now it's dead as a doornail. Which is usually electrical. Maybe a wire melted. We could splice in a replacement to bypass the bad part. First we need to find where it melted."

Peter ducked under the hood. He traced circuits with his finger, checking the wires, tugging things. He looked at the battery. He used a wrench to check the clamps were tight on the posts.

He backed out and said, "Try it one more time."

Shorty put his butt on the seat and kept his feet on the ground. He turned the key. Nothing happened. Dead as a doornail.

Patty said, "I think we better call a mechanic."

ELIZABETH Castle looked up from her screen. She said, "They were probably renters. Most people were. The landlords paid the taxes. We'll have to find them somewhere else. Maybe you should start with the census records. Your father should show up in two of them, when he was two years old and twelve years old."

"Where are they?"

"They're in the county offices."

She gave him the address of the place he needed, with directions how to get there, and he said goodbye and set out walking.

The building he was looking for turned out to be a modern structure built wide and low. He went in, and up to a reception desk. Behind it was a guy who looked like he was stationed there as a punishment. Reacher said hello and told him he wanted to see two sets of old census records.

"For where?" the guy asked, like he didn't care at all.

"Here," Reacher said. "Laconia, New Hampshire, USA."

"What years?"

Reacher told him, first the year his dad was two, and then the next census ten years later, when his dad was twelve.

"What is the reason for your search?"

"Family history," Reacher said.

"We have to see ID."

Reacher showed him his passport.

The guy wrote "Reacher" in a box on a form.

"Cubicle two, Mr. Reacher," he said, and pointed through a door in the opposite wall.

Reacher stepped into a hushed square space, with workbenches divided by upright partitions into separate stations. Each station had a tweed chair, a flat-screen computer, a pencil, and a thin pad of paper with the county's name printed at the top.

He sat down in cubicle 2, and the screen came to life. It lit up blue, apart from two icons in the top right corner. He was not an experienced computer user, but he had tried it once or twice.

He put the arrow on the left-hand icon and clicked twice, and the screen redrew to a gray color. In the center was a black-and-white image of the title page from a government report. At the top it said: "U.S. Department of Commerce, R. P. Lamont, Secretary, Bureau of the Census, W. M. Steuart, Director." In the middle it said: "Fifteenth Census of the United States, Returns Extracted for the Municipality of Laconia, New Hampshire."

Reacher skimmed the introduction, which was mostly about improvements made in methodology since the fourteenth census. Stuff you needed to know if you loved counting people.

Then came the lists, of plain names and old occupations, and the world of nearly ninety years before seemed to rise up all around. There were button makers, and hatmakers, and glove makers, and tin mill workers. There were blacksmiths and masons and engine hostlers and ladlers and smelter boys.

There were no Reachers in Laconia, New Hampshire.

Reacher opened up the right-hand icon, and he found the sixteenth census, different secretary, different director, but the same improvements since the last time around. Then came the lists, now just eighty years old instead of ninety, the difference faintly discernable, with more jobs in factories and fewer on the land.

But still no Reachers. Not in Laconia, New Hampshire, the year Stan Reacher was supposed to be twelve.

REACHER walked back to the records department, inside the city offices. The waist-high counter was once again unattended. He rang the bell for service, and Elizabeth Castle came in.

"Oh," she said. "Hello again. Any luck?"

"Not so far," he said. "They weren't in either census."

Elizabeth Castle said, "Huh. I guess every census misses people. They're forever trying to improve the methodology. There's a guy here you should talk to. He's a census enthusiast."

"What's his name?"

"Carter," she said.

"Where will I find him?"

"What time is it?" she said.

"Nearly eleven o'clock," he said. "Four minutes to."

"Seriously? You're not looking at your watch."

"I don't wear one," he said. "Like you."

"Then how do you know what time it is?"

"I don't know."

"For real?"

"Now it's two minutes and maybe fifty seconds before eleven."

"Wait," she said. She went back out through the door in the rear wall. A long moment later she came back in with her phone.

She said, "What time is it now?"

"Three, two, one, it's the top of the hour. Eleven o'clock exactly."

She pressed the button on her phone. The screen showed 11:00.

"How do you do that?" she said.

"I don't know," he said again. "Where will I find your friend Carter, the census enthusiast?"

"I didn't say he was my friend."

"Coworker?"

"Different department entirely. In the back office. Not part of the customer-facing ecology, as they say."

"Then how do I get to see him?"

"That's why I asked the time. He takes a coffee break at a quarter past eleven. Every day, for thirty minutes exactly, in the place across the light. In the garden, if the sun is shining. Which it might or might not be. We can't tell in here."

"What's Carter's first name?" Reacher asked.

"Carter is his first name," Elizabeth Castle said.

"What's his last name?"

"Carrington," she said. "Check back and tell me how it went. Don't give up. Family is important."

THE sun was shining on downtown Laconia. Reacher got to the coffee shop across the light at ten past eleven, five minutes ahead of schedule, and he got a seat at a table in the corner of the garden, where he could see the sidewalk from the city office door.

People came and went. Reacher ordered regular black coffee.

The garden was filling up, and pretty soon there were only three spare seats. One of which was opposite Reacher, inevitably. A fact of his life. People didn't find him approachable.

First in from the direction of the city office was a woman about forty. She said hi to a couple of customers and dumped her bag on an empty seat, not the one opposite Reacher. Reacher watched the sidewalk. In the distance he saw a guy come out of the city office and start walking down the block. He was tall and well-dressed. His suit was fine, and his shirt was white, and his tie was neat. He had fair hair, short, but a little unruly. He was tan, and he looked fit and strong. He looked like a movie star.

Except he walked with a limp. Very slight, left leg.

Another woman took one of the empty spaces. Which left the only spare chair in the garden directly across from Reacher.

Then the movie star guy stepped in. Up close he was good-looking, in a rugged kind of way. Tall, rangy, capable. Maybe thirty-five years old. Reacher made a small bet with himself the guy was ex-military. He was holding a go-cup of coffee and a paper bag slightly translucent with butter. He scanned the garden and located the only empty seat. He set out toward it.

Both the women called out, "Hey, Carter."

The guy said hey back, with a smile that probably killed them, and continued on his way. He sat down across from Reacher.

Who said, "Is your name Carter?"

The guy said, "Yes, it is."

"Carter Carrington?"

"Pleased to meet you. And you are?"

He sounded curious. He spoke like an educated man.

Reacher said, "Elizabeth Castle from the city records department suggested I speak to you. My name is Jack Reacher. I have a question about an old-time census."

"Is it a legal issue?"

"It's a personal thing."

"You sure? I'm the town attorney," Carrington said. "I'm also a census geek. For ethical reasons I need to be absolutely certain which one you think you're talking to."

"The geek. All I want is background information."

"How long ago?"

Reacher told him, first the year his father was two, and then the year he was twelve.

Carrington said, "What's the question?"

So Reacher told him the story, the family paperwork, cubicle 2's computer screen, the conspicuous absence of Reachers.

"Interesting," Carrington said. "Were you a marine, too?"

"Army," Reacher said.

"That's unusual. Isn't it? For the son of a marine to join the army, I mean."

"It wasn't unusual in our family. My brother did it, too."

"It's a three-part answer," Carrington said. "The first part is all kinds of random mistakes were made. But twice in a row makes that statistically unlikely. What were the odds? So we move on. And neither part two or part three of the answer reflect all that well on a theoretical person's theoretical ancestors. So you need to accept I'm talking theoretically. So don't get offended."

"Okay," Reacher said. "I won't."

"Focus on the count when your dad was twelve. Ignore the earlier one. The later one is better. By then we'd had seven years of the Depression and the New Deal. Counting was really important. Because more people equaled more federal dollars. State and city governments tried like crazy not to miss anyone that year. But they did, even so. The highest miss percentages were among renters, occupants of multifamily dwellings, the unemployed, those of low education and income levels, and those receiving public assistance. Folks on the margins, in other words."

"People don't like to hear that about their grandparents?"

"They like it better than part three of the answer."

"Which is?"

"Their grandparents were hiding from the law."

"Interesting," Reacher said.

"It happened," Carrington said. "Obviously no one with a federal warrant would fill out a census form. Other folks thought laying low might help them in the future."

Reacher said nothing.

Carrington said, "What did you do in the army?"

"Military police," Reacher said. "You?"

"What makes you think I was in the army?"

"Your age, your appearance, your manner and bearing, your air of decisive competence, and your limp."

"You noticed."

"I was trained to. I was a cop. My guess is you have an artificial lower leg. Barely detectable, therefore a really good one. And the army has the best, these days."

"I never served," Carrington said. "I wasn't able to. I was born with a rare condition. It has a long and complicated name. It meant I had no shin bone. Everything else was there."

"Your walk is close to perfect."

"Thank you," Carrington said. "Tell me about being a cop."

"It was a good job, while it lasted."

"You saw the effect of crime on families."

"Sometimes."

"Your dad joined the marines at seventeen," Carrington said. "Got to be a reason."

Chapter 3

PATTY SUNDSTROM AND Shorty Fleck sat outside their room in the plastic lawn chairs. They watched the mouth of the track through the trees and waited for the mechanic to come. He didn't.

Patty got up and took all their maps from the glove box of the Honda. She carried them back to her chair and spread them out on her knee. She found their current location, at the end of the inch-long spiderweb vein, in the middle of the pale green shape. The forested area, about five miles across, and maybe seven from top to bottom. There was nothing much beyond it, except the two-lane road they had turned off from, which wandered east and south, to Laconia, New Hampshire. Nearer thirty miles away than twenty. Her guess the day before had been optimistic.

She said, "Maybe the best bet is to forget the car and get a ride in the tow truck. Laconia is near I-93. We could hitch a ride to the cloverleaf. If we can get to Boston, then we can get the cheap bus to New York."

"Maybe the mechanic can fix the car," said Shorty. "It might be easy. Maybe there's a loose connection, simple as that."

They heard footsteps in the dirt. Steven walked toward them. He passed room 12, and 11, and came to a stop.

"Come to lunch," he said.

Shorty said, "When is the mechanic coming?"

"I'm afraid we haven't called him yet," Steven said. "The phone has been down all morning."

REACHER left Carrington in the garden and walked back to the city office. He pressed the record department's bell, and a minute later Elizabeth Castle came in through the door.

He said, "You told me to check back."

She said, "Did you find Carter?"

"He seems like a nice guy."

"He's Laconia's most eligible bachelor. What did he tell you?"

"That my grandparents were either poor or thieves, or poor thieves."

"I'm sure they weren't. Although I know both those things were frequent reasons. Would they have had driver's licenses?"

"Not if they were poor. Not if they were thieves, either. Not in their real names, anyway."

"Your dad must have had a birth certificate. He must be on paper somewhere."

The door from the corridor opened, and Carter Carrington stepped inside, with his suit and his smile and his unruly hair. He saw Reacher and said, "Hello again." Then he turned toward the counter and stuck out his hand. "You must be Ms. Castle."

"Elizabeth," she said.

"Carter Carrington. Really pleased to meet you. Thanks for sending this gentleman my way. He has an interesting situation."

"Because his dad is missing from two consecutive counts."

"Exactly."

"Which feels deliberate."

"As long as we're sure we're looking at the right town."

"We are," Reacher said. "I saw it written down a dozen times. Laconia, New Hampshire."

"Interesting," Carrington said. Then he looked at Elizabeth and said, "We should have lunch sometime. I like the way you saw the thing with the two counts. I'd like to discuss it more."

She didn't answer.

"Anyway, keep me in the loop," he said.

She said, "We figure he must have had a birth certificate."

"Almost certainly," he said. "What was his date of birth?"

Reacher paused a beat. He said, "This is going to sound weird. Sometimes he wasn't sure. Sometimes he said June, and sometimes he said July."

"Was there an explanation for that?"

"He said he couldn't remember because birthdays weren't important to him."

"What did the paperwork say?"

"July."

Carrington said nothing.

Reacher said, "What?"

"A child uncertain of its birth date is a classic symptom of dysfunction within a family."

"Theoretically," Reacher said.

"Anyway, birth records are in date order. Could take some time, if you're not sure. Better to find another avenue."

"Such as?"

"The police blotter, maybe. If nothing else, it would be nice to eliminate the possibility. And it won't take long to find out. Our police department is computerized back about a thousand years."

"Who should I go see?"

"I'll call ahead. Someone will meet you at the desk."

"How cooperative will they be?"

"I'm the guy who decides whether the city goes to bat for them when they do something wrong. They'll be plenty cooperative."

PATTY Sundstrom and Shorty Fleck went to lunch over at the big house. It was an awkward meal. Shorty was stiff. Peter was silent. Robert and Steven didn't say much. Only Mark really talked. He was bright and chatty. Very friendly. He apologized to them over and over about the phone. He said he was concerned people would be worried about them. Were there people they needed to call?

Patty said, "No one knows we're gone."

"Really?"

"They would have tried to talk us out of it."

"Out of what?"

"It's boring up there. Shorty and I want something different."

"Where do you plan to go?"

"Florida," she said. "We want to start our own business there."

"What kind of business?"

"Water sports, maybe. Like windsurfer rentals."

"You'd need capital," Mark said. "To buy the windsurfers."

Patty looked away, and thought about the suitcase.

Shorty asked, "How long will the phone be out?"

"They usually fix it in half a day. And the mechanic is a good friend. We'll ask him to put us first in line. You could be back on the road before dinnertime."

"Honestly, the best thing would be to just give us a ride to town."

Mark nodded, eyes down. "We're a little embarrassed at the moment, when it comes to rides to town. The investment in this place was enormous. Three of us sold our cars. We kept Peter's, because it was the oldest and least valuable. It wouldn't start this morning. Just like yours. I'm afraid we're all stuck here together."

REACHER set out for the police station. He found it right where Carrington said it would be. There was a civilian desk worker behind a mahogany reception counter. Reacher gave her his name and told her Carter Carrington had promised he would call ahead and arrange for someone to speak with him. The woman was on the phone even before he got through the first part of Carrington's name. Clearly she had been warned he was coming.

She asked him to take a seat, but he stood instead, and waited. Not long, as it turned out. Two detectives pushed through a pair of double doors. A man and a woman. They walked toward him, and the man said, "Mr. Reacher? I'm Jim Shaw, chief of detectives. I'm very pleased to meet you."

Shaw was a heavy guy in his fifties, maybe five ten, with a lined Irish face and a shock of red hair.

"I'm very pleased to meet you, too," Reacher said.

"I'm Detective Brenda Amos," the woman said. "Happy to help. Anything you need."

Her accent was from the south. She was ten years younger than Shaw, maybe five six, and slender. She had blond hair and cheekbones and sleepy green eyes that said *Don't mess with me.*

"Ma'am, thank you," he said. "But really, this is no big deal. All I need is some ancient history. From eighty years ago."

Shaw said, "Mr. Carrington mentioned you were an MP."

"Long ago."

"That buys you ten minutes with a computer. That's all it's going to take."

They led him back through thigh-high mahogany gates to an open area full of plain-clothed people sitting at paired desks. A cop shop. They turned a corner into a corridor. They stopped at the third office on the left. It was Amos's. She ushered Reacher in, and Shaw said goodbye and walked on. Amos followed Reacher inside and closed the door. The outer structure of the office was old, but everything in it was new. Desk, chairs, cabinets, computer.

Amos said, "How can I help you?"

He said, "I'm looking for the surname Reacher, in old police reports from the 1920s and '30s and '40s."

"Relatives of yours?"

"My grandparents and my father. Carrington thinks they dodged the census because they had federal warrants."

"This is a municipal department. We don't have access to federal records."

"They might have started small. Most people do."

Amos pulled the keyboard close and started tapping away. She asked, "First names?"

"James, Elizabeth, and Stan."

She typed some more, and clicked, and waited.

He said, "I'm guessing you were an MP, too."

"What gave me away?"

"First your accent. It's the sound of the U.S. Army. Mostly southern, but a little mixed up. Plus most civilian cops ask about what we did and how we did it. Because they're professionally curious. But you aren't. Most likely because you already know."

"Guilty as charged."

"How long have you been out?"

"Six years," she said. "You?"

"Longer than that."

"What unit?"

"The 110th, mostly."

"Nice," she said. "Who was the CO when you were there?"

"I was," he said.

"And now you're retired and into genealogy."

"I saw a road sign. That's all. I'm beginning to wish I hadn't."

She looked back at the screen.

"We have a hit," she said. "From seventy-five years ago."

She typed in a passcode, leaned forward, and read out loud. She said, "Late one September evening in 1943 a youth was found unconscious on the sidewalk of a downtown Laconia street. He had been beaten up. He was identified as a local twenty-year-old, already known to the police as a loudmouth and a bully, but untouchable, because he was the son of the local rich guy. Therefore I guess there would have been much private celebration inside the department, but obviously for the sake of appearances they had to open an investigation. It says here they went house to house the next day. They got an old lady who had seen the whole thing through binoculars. The victim started an altercation with two other youths, clearly expecting to win, but he got his butt kicked instead."

Reacher said, "Why was the old lady using binoculars late in the evening?"

"It says here she was a bird-watcher. She was interested in night-time migration and continuous flight."

Reacher said nothing.

Amos said, "She identified one of the two other youths as a fellow member of a local bird-watching club."

Reacher said, "My dad was a bird-watcher."

Amos nodded. "The old lady identified him as a local youth known to her, name of Stan Reacher, then just sixteen years old."

"Was she sure? I think he was fifteen in September of 1943."

"She seems to be sure about the name. I guess she could have been wrong about the age. She was watching from an apartment window above a grocery store, looking directly down the street. She saw Stan Reacher walking with an unidentified friend about the same age. They passed through a pool of light from a streetlamp, which allowed her to be confident in her identification. Then walking toward them in the other direction she saw the twenty-year-old. The three youths all met face-to-face. The bigger boy seemed to be demanding something. Then threatening. One of the smaller boys ran away. The other smaller boy stayed where he was; then suddenly he punched the bigger boy in the face."

Reacher nodded. Surprise was always a good thing. A wise man never counted all the way to three.

Amos said, "The old lady testified the smaller kid kept on hitting the bigger kid until the bigger kid fell down, whereupon the smaller kid kicked him repeatedly in the head and the ribs. Then he quit just as suddenly as he had started, and he collected his timid pal, and they walked away together like nothing had happened. The old lady made notes on a piece of paper."

"Good witness," Reacher said. "What happened next?"

Amos scrolled and read. "Nothing. The case went nowhere."

"Why not?"

"Limited manpower. The draft for World War Two had started. The police department was operating with a skeleton staff."

"Why hadn't the twenty-year-old been drafted?"

"Rich daddy."

"I don't get it," Reacher said. "How much manpower would they need? They had an eyewitness. Arresting a fifteen-year-old boy isn't difficult. They wouldn't need a SWAT team."

"They had no ID on the assailant, and no manpower to go dig one up."

"You said the old lady knew him from the bird-watching club."

"The unknown friend was the fighter. Stan Reacher was the one who ran away."

Chapter 4

THEY GAVE PATTY AND SHORTY a cup of coffee, and they sent them on their way, back to room 10. Mark watched them go, until they were halfway to the barn. Whereupon he turned around and said, "Okay, plug the phone back in."

Steven did so, and Mark said, "Now show me the problem with the door."

"The problem is not with the door," Robert said. "It's with our reaction time."

They crossed an inner hallway and opened a back parlor door. The room beyond it was painted black. The window was boarded over. All four walls were covered with flat-screen televisions. There was a swivel chair in the center of the room, boxed in by four low benches pushed together, loaded with keyboards and joysticks. Like a command center. Patty and Shorty were on the screens, live pictures, past the barn now, walking away from one bunch of hidden cameras, toward another.

Robert sat down in the chair. He clicked a mouse, and the screens changed to a dim night-vision shot.

He said, "This is a recording from three o'clock this morning."

The picture was room 10's queen-size bed, which had two sleeping people in it. It was the camera in the smoke detector.

"Except she wasn't asleep," Robert said. "Afterward I figured she slept about four hours, and then she woke up. But she didn't move at all. Not a muscle. By that point I was kind of laying back, frankly, taking it easy, because as far as I knew she was still asleep. But actually she was lying there thinking. Because, watch."

On the screens Patty suddenly flipped the covers aside and slid out of bed, controlled, neat, decisive.

Robert said, "By the time I got my finger near the unlock button, she had already tried the door. I decided to leave it locked, because it felt more consistent. I left it locked until Peter went up there to fix the car. I unlocked it then because I figured one of them would want to come out to talk to him."

"Okay," Mark said. "Is there a fix for this?"

"I guess we need to concentrate harder," said Robert.

"I guess we'll have to. We don't want to spook them too soon."

"How long before we make the final decision?" said Steven.

Mark said, "Make the final decision now, if you like. Why wait? I think we've seen enough. They're as good as we could ever hope to get. They're from nowhere, and no one knows they're gone. I think we're ready."

"I vote yes," Steven said.

"Me, too," Robert said.

"Me three," Peter said. "They're perfect."

Robert clicked back to the live feed, and they saw Patty and Shorty in their lawn chairs, on the boardwalk under their window, catching the wan rays of the afternoon sun.

"Unanimous," Mark said. "Send the e-mail."

The screens changed again, to a webmail page peppered with translations in foreign alphabets. Robert typed four words.

"Okay?" he asked.

"Send it."

He did. The message said: "Room Ten Is Occupied."

REACHER SAID, "I STILL DON'T get it. The bird-watcher lady supplied the ID on Stan, and Stan could have been leaned upon to ID his mysterious friend, surely. One extra visit to his house. Five minutes at most. That's no kind of a manpower problem."

Amos said, "Stan Reacher was listed as resident outside the jurisdiction. That's a whole lot of paperwork right there. Plus they must have figured he was likely to clam up, anyway. Plus they must have figured the mystery friend would be in the wind and out of the state by then. Plus they weren't shedding any tears for the victim, anyway. No doubt the easy decision was to let it go."

"Stan Reacher was a resident outside of what jurisdiction?"

"Laconia PD."

"The story was he was born and grew up here."

"Maybe he was born here, in the hospital, but then maybe he grew up out of town, on a farm or in a nearby village. He would put Laconia as his birthplace, because that's where the hospital was, and he would probably say he grew up in Laconia, too. Like shorthand for the general area as a whole."

"The Laconia metro area," Reacher said.

"Things were more dispersed back then. There were little mills and factories all over. Couple dozen workers in four-flats. Maybe a one-room schoolhouse. A church. All considered Laconia."

"Try Reacher on its own," he said. "No first names. Maybe I have cousins in the area. I could get an address."

Amos pulled her keyboard close and typed and clicked.

"Just one more hit," she said. "More than seventy years after the first." She read out loud, "About a year and a half ago, a patrol car responded to the county offices because a customer was causing a disturbance. Yelling, shouting. The uniforms calmed him down, and he apologized and it went no further. He gave his name as Mark Reacher. Resident outside the jurisdiction."

"Age?"

"Then twenty-six."

"He could be a distant nephew. What was he upset about?"

"He claimed a building permit was slow coming through. He claimed he was renovating a motel somewhere out of town."

AFTER THIRTY MINUTES IN the sun, Patty went inside to use the bathroom. On her way back she stopped at the vanity opposite the end of the bed. She looked in the mirror and blew her nose. She balled up the tissue and lobbed it toward the trash can. She missed. She bent down to correct her error. She was Canadian.

She saw a used cotton bud in the dent where the carpet met the wall. Not hers. It was deep in the shadows under the vanity. Imperfect housekeeping, no question, but understandable.

Except.

She called out, "Shorty, come take a look at this."

Shorty got up out of his chair and stepped in the room.

He left the door wide open.

Patty pointed. "Why is that there?"

"Someone missed the trash can. Happens all the time."

She said, "Go back to your lawn chair, Shorty."

He did. A long minute later she joined him.

He said, "What did I do?"

"It's what you didn't do. You didn't think. Mark told us this is the first room they've refurbished. He asked us to do them the honor of being its first guests. So why does it have a used cotton bud in it?"

Shorty nodded. Slow but sure. He said, "The story about their car was weird, too. Peter must be some kind of saboteur. When are they going to catch on?"

"Why would they lie about the room?"

"Maybe they didn't. Maybe a painter used the cotton bud. To touch up a last-minute ding in the wood stain."

"Now you think they're okay?"

"Not about the car, no. If theirs wouldn't start this morning, why hadn't they already called the mechanic, anyway?"

"The phone was out."

"Maybe not then. Maybe not first thing in the morning."

"Shorty, they're acting weird. What are we going to do?"

Shorty glanced around. "I don't know," he said. "Maybe we could tow the car with a quad bike. Maybe the keys are in them."

"We can't steal a quad bike."

"It would be borrowing. We could tow the car two miles to the road, and then bring the quad bike back again."

"Do we have a tow rope?"

"Maybe there's one in the barn."

"I don't think a quad bike would be strong enough."

"Maybe we could use a quad bike to haul just the suitcase. I think they have a platform on the back," he said.

"It's a possibility," Patty said. "I suppose."

"Let's wait until after dinner," Shorty said. "Maybe the phone is back on and the mechanic will show up and everything will work out. If not, we'll take a look at the barn after dark. Okay?"

Patty didn't answer. They stayed where they were, slumped down in their lawn chairs. They left their room door wide open.

FIFTY yards away in the command center in the back parlor, Mark asked, "Who missed the cotton bud?"

"All of us," Peter said. "We all checked the room, and we all signed off on it."

"Then we all made a bad mistake. Now they're agitated."

"He thinks it was the painter. She'll believe him eventually. She doesn't want to worry. She wants to be happy. They'll calm down."

"You think?"

"Why would we lie about the room? There's no reason for it."

Mark said, "Bring me a quad bike."

PATTY and Shorty heard an engine start up in the distance, deafening like a motorcycle, and they got up and walked to the corner to look. They saw Peter riding a quad bike back to the house.

"First turn of the key," Shorty said. "I hope they're all like that."

"Way too noisy," Patty said, disappointed. "We can't do it. They would know."

Peter parked at the distant house. He killed the engine, and silence came back. He got off and went inside. Patty and Shorty went back to their lawn chairs.

Shorty said, "The land is pretty flat around here. We could push the quad bike. With the engine off. With the suitcase balanced on it. We could use it like a furniture dolly. They can't be that heavy."

"Two miles there and two miles back? Which would leave the suitcase by the side of the road, and us back here. So then we would have another two miles to walk. Altogether six, four of them pushing a quad bike. It would take a good long time."

"I figure about four hours. We should time it to finish at dawn. Maybe we might see a farmer heading to market. There has to be traffic sometimes. So we should start in the middle of the night."

"It's a possibility," Patty said. "I suppose."

They heard the distant quad bike start up again, fifty yards away, then closer. It sounded like it was coming toward them.

The machine roared around the corner, with Mark riding it, scattering dirt. There was a cardboard carton strapped to the rack on the back. Mark braked to a stop and shut the motor down. He smiled his master-of-the-universe smile.

"Good news," he said. "The phone is back on. The mechanic will be here in the morning. We were too late to get him today. But he knows what the problem is. He's seen it before. There's an electronic chip close to where the heater hoses go through the back of the dashboard. The chip fries when the water in the hoses gets too hot. He's bringing a replacement chip he got from a wrecker's yard. He wants five dollars for it. Plus fifty for labor."

"That's great," Shorty said.

Mark said, "And I'm afraid I want another fifty for the room."

There was silence for a second.

Mark said, "Guys, I would love to tell you just forget it, but the bank would kick my ass. This is a business, I'm afraid."

"Come take a look at this," Patty said.

Mark climbed off the quad bike, and Patty led the way inside the room. She pointed down into the void under the vanity.

He looked. He saw. "Oh, dear."

He bent down and came back up with the cotton bud.

"I apologize most sincerely," he said. "This is unforgivable."

"Why did you tell us we were the first guests in this room?"

"You are the first guests in this room. We hired a photographer to take pictures for a brochure. He brought a model with him, and we let her do her makeup in here. I thought we cleaned up after her. Obviously we didn't succeed completely. I apologize."

"So do I," Patty said. "I guess. For jumping to conclusions. How did the pictures come out?"

"She was dressed as a hiker. Very big boots and very short shorts. The motel was behind her. It looked pretty good."

Patty gave him fifty of her hard-earned bucks.

He put the fifty bucks and the cotton bud in his pants pocket. Then he said, "I have something for you."

He led the way out to the lot again, back to the quad bike, to the carton strapped to its rack.

He said, "You are invited to dinner tonight, of course, and breakfast tomorrow, but equally all of us would understand if you preferred to eat alone. We put together some ingredients for you. Either join us at the house or help yourselves from the box."

He undid the straps and hefted the box in his arms. He half turned and slid it into Shorty's waiting hands.

"Thank you," Patty said.

Mark just smiled, and climbed aboard the quad bike, and started up its ferocious engine. He headed back to the house.

REACHER walked back to the fancy county office with the census scans and the million-dollar cubicles, and he found the same guy on duty at the desk. Once again Reacher asked for two censuses, the first when Stan was two, and the second when he was twelve, but this time for the whole county.

"Cubicle four," the guy said.

Cubicle 4 was the same as cubicle 2. It had the same tweed chair, and a flat screen, and a pencil, and a pad of paper with the county name at the top. The screen was already lit up blue, with two icons already top right, the same as before. Reacher double-clicked on the first, and saw the same title page saying all the same things he had seen before, except for the center line, which said this time the returns were extracted for the county.

He went straight to the R section. And there they were. James Reacher, male, white, twenty-six, a tin mill foreman, and his wife

Elizabeth Reacher, female, white, twenty-four, a bedsheet finisher, and their only child Stan Reacher, male, white, two years old.

Two years old in April, when the census was taken. Which would make him three years old in the fall, which would make him sixteen years old late on a September evening in 1943. Not fifteen. The old bird-watching lady was right.

Reacher said, "Huh."

He read on. Their address was given as a number and a street in a place named Ryantown. Their home was rented, at a cost of forty-three dollars a month. James had been twenty-two and Elizabeth twenty when they married. Both could read and write.

Reacher double-clicked on the tiny red traffic light at the top of the document, and the screen went back to the blue wash with the two icons. He double-clicked on the second of them, and the census from ten years later opened up.

The Reachers were still there. James, Elizabeth, and Stan, in that April thirty-six, thirty-four, and twelve years old respectively. James had changed his employment to laborer on a county road grading crew, and Elizabeth was out of work altogether. Their address was the same. James and Elizabeth were still listed as literate, and Stan was in daily attendance at school.

Reacher wrote the address on the top sheet of notepaper, which he then tore off and stuck in his back pants pocket.

MARK parked the quad bike back at the barn and walked on down to the house. The phone rang as soon as he got in the door. He picked it up and said his name, and a voice told him, "There was a guy here, name of Reacher, checking out his family history. A big guy, pretty rough. So far he's looked at four different censuses. I think he's searching for an old address. Maybe he's a relative. I thought you should know."

Mark hung up without replying.

REACHER walked back to the city office. He went up to the records department and pressed the bell. A minute later Elizabeth Castle came in.

"I found them," he said. "They lived beyond the city limit, which is why they didn't show up the first time around."

"Where did they live?"

"A place called Ryantown."

"I'm not sure where that is."

"That's a shame, because I came here especially to ask you."

"I'm not sure I ever heard of it."

"Can't be far, because his bird-watching club was in town."

She took out her phone and did things to it, with spread fingers. She showed him. It was a map, expanded. No Ryantown.

She started over with her phone. This time typing. Maybe a search engine, or a local history site.

"It was a tin mill," she said. "Belonged to a man named Ryan. He built worker accommodations and called the place Ryantown. The mill closed in the 1950s, and the town died. Everyone left, and the name fell off the map."

"Where was it?"

"Supposedly north and west of here," she said. She dabbed the map back on her phone and moved her fingers around.

"About here, possibly," she said.

There was no name on the map. Just a gray shape, north and west of Laconia, maybe eight miles out. Between ten and eleven on a clock face. The road that passed it by meandered north and west, ten or more miles, and then another ten through a wood, and then onward. A back road. He could picture it.

He said, "I guess there won't be a bus."

"You could rent a car," she said. "There are places in town."

"I don't have a driver's license."

"I don't think a cab would want to go out there."

Eight miles, he thought.

"I'll walk," he said. "But not now. It would be dark as soon as I got there. Tomorrow, maybe. You want to get dinner tonight?"

"What?"

"Dinner," he said. "The third meal of the day, generally eaten in the evening. Can be functional, or social, or sometimes both."

"I can't," she said. "I'm having dinner with Carter Carrington."

SHORTY CARRIED THE cardboard carton into the room and placed it on the bed. Then he sat with Patty, side by side in their lawn chairs, through the last of the afternoon sun. She was thinking. He knew the signs. He guessed she was processing the information she had received, examining it until she was satisfied.

Patty said, "Let's not go to the house for dinner."

"Works for me."

They got up and stepped inside the room. They left the door wide open. Shorty lifted the flaps of the box. Inside there were cereal bars and power bars, and bottles of water, and packets of dried apricots, and boxes of raisins. Everything was arranged in a pattern that repeated twelve times over. Like twelve identical meals, neatly laid out. Each one had a bottle of water.

There were also two flashlights in the box.

"Weird," Patty said.

"I think this place is for hikers," Shorty said. "Like in the photograph they took with the model. I bet they give this stuff out as box lunches. It's the kind of thing a hiker likes to carry."

"What are the flashlights for?"

"I suppose in case you're out late and have to eat in the dark."

"He said they put some ingredients together. They didn't put this together. It's prepackaged. Why does he make such grandiose statements?"

"They're weird," Shorty said. "But kind of helpful, too."

REACHER ate dinner alone in Laconia, at a greasy hole-in-the-wall. He didn't want to risk a fancier place, in case Carter Carrington and Elizabeth Castle picked the same spot. He didn't want to disturb their evening. Afterward he spent an hour walking random blocks, looking for a grocery store with an apartment window above it, that faced east down the length of a street. He found one possibility. The apartment was now an attorney's office. The store now sold pants and sweaters. He looked down the street. He saw a patch of night sky in the east, and below it the blacktop, lit up here and there by widely spaced streetlamps.

He walked the same direction the twenty-year-old had walked.

He stopped thirty yards out. He turned around and looked up at the old lady's window. Now he was the smaller boy. He imagined the big guy in front of them, threatening. Technically no big deal. For Reacher himself, anyway. At sixteen he had been bigger than most twenty-year-olds. He was fast, and nasty. He knew all the tricks. He had invented some of them. Stan had been a normal-sized person by comparison. Maybe six one, maybe 190.

Reacher imagined his father's footsteps, inching backward, and then turning and running.

PATTY and Shorty ate outside in their lawn chairs. They took meal number one and meal number two, which left ten in the box, and they dutifully drank their bottles of water. Then it got cold, and they moved inside. But Patty said, "Leave the door open."

Shorty said, "Why?"

"I need the air. Wedge it with your shoe."

Shorty kicked off his shoes, and wedged one between the outer face of the door and the jamb, and he bent the other into a pliable shape, and propped it against the inner face, to push back against gentle nighttime breezes. Potato-farmer engineering, he knew, but it looked like it might work.

STEVEN called to Robert, who called to Peter, who called to Mark. They were all in different rooms. They got together in the back parlor and stared at the screens.

"It's a pair of shoes," Steven said. "In case you're wondering."

"Why did they do it?" Mark asked. "Did they say?"

"She wants air. It's consistent behavior. She's mentioned it before. I don't think it's a problem."

Mark nodded. "I told her a story about a supermodel doing her makeup. I think she believed it. I told her a mechanic will be riding to the rescue in the morning. I think she's calm now. Doesn't matter about the door."

"We need to lock it pretty soon."

"But not tonight. Let sleeping dogs lie. They're relaxed now."

Chapter 5

REACHER PREFERRED TO move on whenever possible, so he found a new place to sleep, one street away from the previous night. It was a bed-and-breakfast, in a house built of brick. He got a top-floor room, through a low door at the head of a steep and doglegged stair. He took a long hot shower, and fell asleep.

Until one minute past three in the morning.

Once again he snapped awake, instantly, like flicking a switch. The same thing exactly. Not touch or taste or sight or smell. Therefore sound. This time he got out of bed immediately, and he pulled his pants out from under the mattress and dressed fast. He headed out through the low door and down the stair to the street.

The night air was cool. He stood still. A minute later he heard feet scrape on the sidewalk. Ahead and left. Not going anywhere. Just shuffling in place. Maybe two people. Nothing visible.

Another minute later he heard a muted yelp. A woman's voice. Maybe joy. Or ecstasy. Or maybe not. Maybe outrage or anger.

He moved left, and saw a gap between a bag store and a shoe store. It was pedestrian access to an alley that divided two buildings. The alley had doors on both sides for apartments above the stores. A man and a woman were standing next to one of the doors in a full-on clinch. Like wrestling standing up. The guy was young and big and solid. The woman was a little older. She had blond hair, and she was wearing high heels and a short black coat, which was getting rucked up by the wrestling.

Good or bad? Hard to tell.

Then the woman squirmed her face away and said, "No," in a sudden low tone, like spitting, as firm as talking to a dog, but also with what Reacher took to be feelings of shame and embarrassment and disgust. She tried to get away. The guy wouldn't let her.

Reacher said, "Hey."

They both turned their faces toward him.

He said, "Take your hands off her, kid."

The boy said, "This is none of your business."

"I heard her say no. So step back."

The kid turned. He was wearing a sweatshirt with the name of a famous university. He was maybe six three, and 220 pounds. Maybe an athlete. He was rippling with youth and excitement. He had a look in his eye. He thought he was a hell of a guy.

Reacher looked at the woman and said, "Miss, are you okay?"

She asked, "Are you a cop?"

"I was once upon a time, in the army."

She didn't reply. She was close to thirty, Reacher thought. She looked like a nice person. But sad.

"Are you okay?" he asked her again.

She pushed away from the boy and stood apart. She didn't speak. But she looked like she didn't want Reacher to leave.

He said, "Did this happen last night, too?"

She nodded.

"Same exact time and place?"

"It's when I get home from work."

"You live here?"

"Until I get on my feet."

Reacher looked at her heels and her hair and said, "You work in a cocktail bar."

"In Manchester."

"And this guy followed you home? Two nights running?"

She nodded again.

The boy said, "She asked me to, man. So butt out."

"That's not true," the woman said. "I did not ask you."

"You were all over me."

"I was being polite. That's what you do when you work in a cock-tail bar."

Reacher looked at the boy. "Sounds like a classic misunderstanding," he said. "But easily fixed. All you need to do is apologize sincerely and then go away and never come back."

"It's her who won't come back. Not to that bar, anyway. My father owns a big chunk of it. She'll lose her job."

Reacher looked at the woman. "What happened last night?"

"I let him," she said. "He agreed one time only. So I got it over with. But now he's back for more."

"I'll discuss it with him, if you like," Reacher said. "Meanwhile you go inside if you want. And think no more about it."

"Don't you dare go inside," the boy said. "Not without me."

The woman took her keys from her bag, and unlocked her door, and stepped inside, and closed her door behind her.

The boy in the sweatshirt stared at Reacher. Who jerked his head toward the mouth of the alley and said, "Run along, kid."

The boy stared a minute longer, apparently thinking. Then he walked out of the alley and turned right. Which made him right-handed. He would set up his ambush so Reacher would walk face-first into a right hook. Which pretty much defined the location. About three feet around the corner, Reacher thought.

But speed was under Reacher's control. The kid would trigger the hook at the first glimpse of him coming around the corner. Any kind of normal walking pace would bring it home good and solid.

Therefore nothing would be done at normal speed.

Reacher stopped six paces short of the corner, and waited, and then he took another pace, a slow, sliding step. And then another long wait, and another slow step. He pictured the kid around the corner, tensed up, his fist cocked. Getting all cramped and shaky.

Reacher took another step, long and slow. Now he was six feet from the corner. He waited. Then he launched fast, at a run, his left hand up, palm open. He burst around the corner and saw the kid confused by the change of pace, so that his right hook was a feeble squib, which Reacher caught easily in his left palm. The kid's fist was big, but Reacher's hand was bigger, so he squeezed, not hard enough to crush bones, but hard enough to make the kid concentrate on keeping his mouth shut, so no whines came out, which obviously he couldn't afford, being a hell of a guy.

Then Reacher squeezed harder. Mostly as an IQ test. Which the kid failed. He used his free hand to claw at Reacher's wrist. The wrong move. Always better to use your free hand to hit the squeezer in the head. Then Reacher added a twist to the squeeze until the kid got so lopsided he had to take his hand off Reacher's wrist and hold his whole arm straight out for balance.

Reacher said, "Want me to hit you?"

No reply.

"It's not a difficult question," Reacher said. "Yes or no."

By that point the kid was huffing and gasping. He said, "Okay, I got her signals wrong. I'm sorry, man. I'll leave her alone now."

"What about her job?"

"I was kidding, man."

Reacher clamped down harder. "Want me to hit you?"

The kid said, "No."

"No means no, right? I expect they teach you that now, at your fancy university. Kind of theoretical, I guess, from your point of view. Until now."

"Come on, man."

"Want me to hit you?"

"No."

Reacher hit him in the face, with a straight right, maximum force. The kid's lights went out immediately. He went slack, and gravity took over. Reacher kept his left hand rock-solid. All the kid's weight fell on his own locked elbow. Reacher waited. One of two things would happen. Either the strength and elasticity in the kid's ligaments would roll him forward, or they wouldn't.

They didn't. The kid's elbow broke, and his arm turned inside out. Reacher let him fall. He landed on the bricks outside the bag shop, one arm right and the other arm wrong. He was breathing. His nose was badly busted. Some of his teeth were out. His dentist's kid was going to be just fine for college.

Reacher walked away, back to his lodgings, back into bed. He punched the pillow into shape and went back to sleep.

AT WHICH MOMENT PATTY Sundstrom woke up. A quarter past three in the morning. Once again a pulse of subconscious disquiet had forced its way through to the surface. What were the flashlights for? Why two of them? Why not one, or twelve?

Maybe they were just shoved in there as afterthoughts. She kept her eyes closed and pictured the scene when they opened the box. She had slit the tape with her nail, and Shorty had lifted the flaps. What had been her impression?

Two flashlights in the box, crammed in among the food.

Crammed in. Therefore added later. Why?

Two flashlights for two people. They had each been given a flashlight and six subsistence meals. Why?

She flipped the covers back and slid out of bed. She padded over to the dresser, where the carton sat in front of the TV screen. She took out the first flashlight. It was big and heavy. She switched it on. It had a cluster of tiny LED bulbs.

She looked back in the box. The other flashlight was rammed between lunches nine, ten, eleven, and twelve. Some of the granola bars around it were cracked. Added later, for sure.

She padded toward the door, and she nudged Shorty's bent shoe aside with her toe, and opened a gap wide enough to slip outside. The flashlight cast a bright beam of light. She minced toward the Honda, with bare feet on the stones. She opened the passenger door. The hood release was where her shin would be. A black lever. She tugged on it. The hood sprang up an inch.

She walked around to the front of the hood. She raised it up and propped it with the bent metal rod that fit in the hole. She worked in a sawmill. She knew her way around machinery. She ducked her head, until she could see what she wanted to see.

The acid test.

He knows what the problem is. He's seen it before. There's an electronic chip close to where the heater hoses go through the back of the dashboard.

Patty identified the back of the dashboard easily enough. It was a bare panel, gray and dirty, partially covered by a thin sheet of sound-deadening material. All kinds of wires and pipes and tubes went through it. Mostly electrical, she thought. The hot water for the heater would be in a thick hose, clamped to a port on the engine block, which was where the hot water came from. And obviously it would be twinned with an identical black hose, for the return feed. Circulation, around and around.

She craned her neck and moved the flashlight beam.

She found two black hoses connected to the engine block. She followed them with the flashlight beam. They passed through the bulkhead into the passenger compartment very low down. Directly behind where the floor console was, with the gearshift lever. The heater was right above it.

The heater hoses go through the back of the dashboard.

No they don't, Patty thought. They went nowhere near the back of the dashboard. They went through level with the bottom of the footwell. Much lower down. And there was nothing near them, anyway. Just thick metal components, all caked with dirt. No wires. Nothing that would fry from excessive temperatures. Certainly no black boxes that might contain electronic chips.

She backed away and straightened up. She looked at the house. All quiet. She killed the flashlight beam and minced back to the room. She stepped to the bed and nudged Shorty awake.

He said, "What?"

She said, "The heater hoses don't go through the back of the dashboard. They go through real low down, about level with the bottom of the gearstick."

"How do you know?"

"I looked," she said. "With one of the flashlights they gave us."

"Why?"

"I woke up. Something is not right."

"Okay, maybe the mechanic got it wrong," Shorty said. "Maybe Hondas are different in Canada."

"Or maybe the mechanic doesn't exist. Maybe they never called one. Maybe they're keeping us here."

"What? Why would they? You mean, like an occupancy thing? Because of the bank? They want our fifty bucks?"

"I don't know why."

"Hell of a way to do business. We could go on TripAdvisor."

"Except we can't go on anything. There's no Wi-Fi and no cell signal and no phone in the room."

"They can't just keep people here against their will. Someone would miss them eventually."

"We as good as told them no one knows we're gone."

"We also as good as told them we're broke," Shorty said.

"We have to get out of here. We have to do the thing you said with the quad bike. So get dressed. We have to go."

"Now?"

"This minute. They're asleep now. We have to do it now."

Shorty said, "Why did they give us flashlights?"

Patty said, "I don't know."

"It's like they knew we might want to leave in the dark."

"How could they?"

Shorty got out of bed. He said, "We should take some food."

They got dressed, in the half dark, with nothing but moonlight coming in the open door. They packed their stuff by feel and put their bags outside near the car.

They walked down to the barn on the grass, not the dirt, because they felt it would be quieter. They were cautious across the last of the gravel, to the bike Peter had driven away for Mark to use. Its engine was still faintly warm. Shorty wanted that one because it was closest. He clicked the lever to neutral and pushed back on the handlebars. The machine rolled back obediently.

"This is not too bad," he said.

He dragged the machine to a stop and took up a new position and pushed it forward again. Patty joined in on the other side, and they pushed together and got up to a decent speed, steering along the center of the track toward the motel building. They pushed on, breathing hard, around room 12's corner, and onward to the Honda, outside room 10. They stopped the bike right behind the car. Shorty popped the hatch.

He bent forward and heaved up the suitcase at the front, until it rested at an angle on the lip of the hatch. He grabbed the handle and hauled, intending to balance the case weightless on the lip, so he had time to change his position and adjust his grip, ready for the clean and jerk, and the turn toward the bike.

But the handle tore off the suitcase.

Shorty said, "Damn."

"Proves we couldn't have carried it, anyway," Patty said.

"How are we going to get it on the bus?"

"We'll have to buy a rope. We could wrap it around a couple of times and make a new handle. So we need a gas station or a hardware store. For the rope. First place we see."

Shorty stepped forward again and bent down and got his fingers under the case. He grunted and lifted and set it down on the bike, lengthways, the top corners resting on the handlebar, the bottom edge digging into the padded seat. He nudged it and got it balanced. It ended up pretty solid.

He shut the Honda's hatch, and they strapped their overnight bags on the bike's rear rack. Then they took up position, Shorty on the left and Patty on the right, each of them with one hand on the handlebar and the other hand close to it, partly pushing, partly juggling a flashlight. Getting started required a full-on effort, and then keeping going afterward required nearly as much, although it got better when they bumped up out of the stony lot and onto the blacktop, at the end of the road through the trees.

They entered the tunnel. The air was cool and smelled of rotten leaves. Through trial and error they learned it was best to keep their speed as high as they could bear. They kept on going, just grinding it out.

"I need to rest," Patty said.

They let the bike coast to a stop. They huffed and puffed, and eased their necks.

Shorty said, "How much farther?"

"About a mile and a half to go," Patty said.

"How long have we taken so far?"

"Maybe twenty minutes."

"Damn, that's slow."

"You said four hours. We're about on schedule."

They took up their positions again, and forced the thing to roll. They did another half mile, and rested again. And another. A whole hour had gone by.

They passed through the section where no trees grew.

"Getting close," Patty said.

Then she said, "Wait," and she hauled back on the handlebar and dug her heels in, like a kid stopping a homemade cart.

Shorty said, "What?"

"There was a wire. Like at the gas station. For ringing a bell. Laying across the road. It probably rings in the house."

Shorty remembered. He searched ahead with his flashlight. They saw nothing. They rolled on, half speed.

A hundred yards later they saw it lying across the road.

They stopped four feet short.

Patty said, "How does it work?"

"I guess inside there are two metal strips. Somehow held apart. But when a wheel goes over, they get pressed together and a bell rings. Like a push switch."

"So we can't let a wheel go over."

"No."

Which was a problem. Shorty couldn't lift the quad bike.

Patty ducked down and eased her fingers under the fat rubber wire. She lifted it. It came up easily, an inch, a foot, as much as she wanted.

"Get ready," she said.

She lifted it up on open palms, head high. Shorty ducked and pushed the bike under it. She held it until he was clear.

"Okay," Shorty said.

She laid the wire back down. They pushed on, energized. Their flashlight beams bounced, first showing nothing but trees, but then a different kind of void loomed up ahead. The two-lane road.

Patty said, "We need to find a place to hide the suitcase."

They let the bike slow to a stop where the mouth of the track widened out to meet the road. The last yard of shoulder was thick with underbrush. Although maybe a little thinner where the frost-heaved posts were set. Maybe there was a hole behind one.

Patty went to check. The right-hand hole was better than the left. They huffed and puffed and got the bike as close as possible. Shorty lifted the suitcase off the bike and dropped it in the bushes, where it came to rest pretty well hidden. Patty walked up the road a spell and said she saw nothing much. She was satisfied.

Then her voice changed, and she said, "Shorty, come here."

He went. Together they looked along her flashlight beam, which was centered back on the frost-heaved post.

He said, "What am I looking for?"

"Think," she said. "What did we see when we turned in?"

He thought. He visualized. What had he seen? He had seen a frost-heaved post, on which was nailed a board, on which were screwed ornate plastic letters, and an arrow pointing into the woods. The letters had spelled out the word MOTEL.

Now there was no board. No letters, no word, no arrow. Now there was just a post. Nothing on it. Same both sides of the track.

"Weird," he said.

"You think? We have to get out of here."

"We are. First car that comes."

"After we take the bike back to the barn."

"We don't owe them that," Shorty said. "We don't owe them diddly. Not anymore. We should dump the bike here and let them come get it themselves."

"They get up with the sun," Patty said. "If there's a bike missing, they'll know right away. But if it's back in its proper place, they might not think about us for hours. It could buy us a lot of time. They'll come looking for us as soon as they find us gone. We need to be miles away by then."

Shorty said nothing. He looked along the dark and silent road.

Then he said, "Okay, we'll take the bike back to the barn."

"As fast as we can," Patty said. "Now it's all about speed."

They unstrapped their overnight bags from the rack and stashed them close to the suitcase, and then they got the bike pointed back down the track. They took up their positions. They set off. The same two-plus miles, in reverse. They didn't stop or rest.

It took them a fraction more than thirty minutes to push the two-plus miles. They rolled to a stop where the track came out of the trees. The motel was dark and quiet. The barn, dark and quiet. Five thirty in the morning, by Patty's watch.

They pushed on, as quiet as they could, straight toward the barn. They could see eight ghostly shapes, neatly parked, and the ninth slot empty. They cut the last corner across the grass and rolled on the parking area's gravel. Putting the bike back in place was easy. Just a question of lining it up and pushing it in. Job done. Perfect. They walked back to the track, where they stood for a second and took a breath.

Behind them a door opened. Over at the house. Relatively distant. A faraway voice called out, "Hey guys, is that you?"

Mark.

They stood still. A flashlight beam lanced beyond them.

"Guys?" Mark called again.

They turned around.

Mark was walking through the dark toward them. He was fully dressed. His day had already begun. He was keeping his flashlight low, and so were Shorty and Patty, all three beams acting polite, trying to illuminate, but not dazzle.

Mark arrived. He said, "This is the most amazing coincidence."

Along with the flashlight he was carrying a blank sheet of paper and a pencil.

Patty said, "Is it?"

"I'm sorry, I should have asked, is everything okay?"

"We're fine. Why is it a coincidence?"

"Because literally at this very moment I have the mechanic on the phone. He starts work at five. This morning he remembered we had mentioned you drove down from Canada. He realized that you might have a Canadian-spec car. In which case you would have the mandatory winter package, which back then was a different heater and no AC. In which case his diagnosis was wrong. In Canada it's the starter motor relay that fries. He needs to know which part to pick up at the scrapyard. He literally just sent me out to get the ID number off your windshield."

He held up the paper and pencil, as if in proof.

Then he said, "But obviously it will be a lot quicker for all concerned if you come in and answer his questions yourselves."

Shorty looked at Patty. She looked at him.

Mark said, "We could make a pot of coffee. We could ask the guy to call us back when he's actually got the part he needs. I feel at this point a little reassurance is in order. You folks have been messed around with enough already."

He held out his hand, in a courtly *After you* gesture.

Patty and Shorty walked toward the house. Mark walked with them, ushering them in at the kitchen door. He flicked on a light and pointed ahead to the inner hallway, where the phone receiver was lying on the seat of a chair. On hold, the old-fashioned way.

Mark said, "His name is Carol. Probably spelled different. He's from Macedonia."

Patty picked up the receiver. She said, "Carol?"

A voice said, "Mark?"

"I'm Patty Sundstrom. My boyfriend and I own the Honda."

"Oh, I didn't mean for Mark to wake you up. That isn't polite."

The voice had an accent that sounded Eastern European, she thought. His voice was friendly. Helpful and full of concern.

She said, "We were awake, anyway."

"Listening to your voice, I'm guessing you're Canadian."

"So is our car."

"Yeah," the voice said. "I made an assumption and thereby nearly made a mistake. I apologize. But let's be certain. Have you ever had cause to change out the heater hoses?"

"I know they go low down," Patty said.

"Okay, that's Canadian for sure. Good to know. I'll pick up a starter motor relay. Then I got to pay the bills. I'll head out to the highway for a spell. Maybe I'll get lucky with a wreck. If not, I'll get to you all the sooner. Call it two hours minimum, four hours maximum."

"You sure?"

"Ma'am, I promise I'll get you on your way."

Then the call went dead, and Patty hung up the phone.

Mark said, "The coffee is ready."

Patty said, "He'll be here between two hours and four hours from now."

"Perfect."

They heard a vehicle on the track outside. They looked out the window and saw Peter parking a battered old pickup truck.

Shorty said, "Whose truck?"

"His," Mark said. "He gave it another try last night. He got it going. Now he's been down to the road and back, to charge it up. He can give you a ride to your room, if you like."

They said they didn't want to impose, but Peter wouldn't take no for an answer. His truck was a crew cab, so Shorty rode in front and Patty sat in back. Peter parked next to the Honda. Room 10's door was closed. Patty was sure they had left it open.

They got out of the truck. Peter watched them to their door. Patty turned the handle and opened up. She went in first. Then she came straight back out again. She pointed at Peter in his truck, and she yelled, "You stay there."

She stepped aside. Shorty looked in the room. In the center of the floor was their luggage. Back again. Their suitcase and their two overnight bags. Their suitcase was now tied up with rope. There were complicated knots and an improvised handle.

Patty said, "What the hell is this?"

Peter got out of his truck. "We sincerely apologize," he said. "We are very embarrassed that you should get caught up in it."

"In what?"

"It's the time of year, I'm afraid. College semesters are starting. Undergraduates are everywhere. Their fraternities set them challenges. They steal our motel signs all the time. Then they started a new thing. Some kind of initiation rite. They had to steal everything out of a motel room while the guest was temporarily absent. I found your stuff down by the road. Please let us know if anything is damaged. We're going to make a police report."

Patty said nothing. Shorty didn't speak.

Peter got back in his truck and drove away. Patty and Shorty went inside. They stepped around their luggage and sat down together on the bed. They left the door open.

Chapter 6

THE BREAKFAST PART of Reacher's bed-and-breakfast deal was located in a pretty room that was half a story below the street but level with the small rear garden. Reacher took an inside table at a quarter to eight in the morning, ready for coffee. He was the only person in there. He was showered and dressed and looked respectable, all except for a cut knuckle. From the kid in the night. His teeth, no doubt. Not a serious injury. But a distinctive shape. Reacher got up and stepped out to the garden. He scraped his right hand on the brick of a flower bed wall. Just enough to make the tooth mark one of many. Then he went back to his table.

Five minutes later Detective Brenda Amos stepped into the room. She was writing in her notebook. At her shoulder was the bed-and-breakfast's manager. Reacher heard him say, "This gentleman is the only guest still on the premises."

Amos glanced up from her notebook, and glanced away again. Then she looked back. A classic double take. She blinked.

She said to the man in the suit, "I'll talk to him now."

"May I bring you coffee?"

"Yes, please," Reacher called out to him. "A pot for two."

The guy nodded politely. She sat down at Reacher's table.

She said, "As a matter of fact, I already had coffee this morning. I think Dunkin' is spiking it with LSD today. Or else this is the biggest déjà vu in history."

"How so?"

"Yesterday we dug up an old case, in which a youth was found unconscious on the sidewalk of a Laconia street. He was a local twenty-year-old, already known to police as a bully, but untouchable, because he was the son of the local rich guy. Remember?"

"Sure," Reacher said.

"When I got to work, I was told that a youth had just been found unconscious on the sidewalk of a Laconia street, identified as a local twenty-year-old, known to the police as a bully, but untouchable, because he was the son of the local rich guy."

"Seriously?"

"And I walk into the hotel across the street and here you are."

"Clearly such crimes happen all the time."

"Seventy-five years apart is all the time?"

"I'm sure there were many similar incidents in between. All rich bullies get a smack sooner or later. Are you going house to house for witnesses?"

"That's what we do."

"Did anyone see anything?"

"Did you?"

"I'm not a bird-watcher," Reacher said.

"Did you hear anything?"

"What time?"

"The kid was still unconscious at seven. Call it no earlier than five o'clock."

"I was asleep at five," Reacher said.

"The kid also has a broken arm," Amos said.

"That can happen," Reacher said.

A waitress came in with two pots of coffee and two fresh cups. Reacher poured, but Amos didn't. She closed her notebook. He asked her, "How is this investigation viewed in the department?"

She said, "We have low expectations."

"Who was the kid?"

"The kid is a lout and a bully and a predator. The kind who gets the best of everything, including victims and lawyers."

"Doesn't sound all that complicated to me."

"We're worried about what happens next."

"You think he's going to get up a posse?"

"The problem is his father already has a posse."

"The local rich guy? Who is he?"

"He's really from Boston. But he lives in Manchester now."

"And what kind of posse does he have?"

"He makes financial arrangements for clients who can't risk paper trails. In other words, he launders money. I imagine he could borrow pretty much any kind of posse he wants. And we think he will. Someone attacked his family. This guy can't look weak. That's why it's complicated."

Reacher poured another cup of coffee.

Amos watched. She said, "How did you hurt your hand?"

"I punched the garden wall."

"That's an odd way to put it."

Her phone dinged, and she read a message.

She said, "The kid woke up but doesn't remember a thing."

"That can happen," Reacher said again.

"He's lying. He knows, but he's not telling us. He wants to tell his father instead. I hope whoever did it knows what's coming."

"I'm sure whoever did it will leave town. Just like seventy-five years ago. Déjà vu all over again."

"What are your own movements today?"

"I guess technically I'm leaving town. I'm going to Ryantown," Reacher said. "If I can find it."

HE BOUGHT a paper map at an old edge-of-town gas station. It showed the same kind of vagueness as Elizabeth Castle's phone. Certain roads headed in certain directions, but none had names anymore. He wasn't sure what kind of geographic setting a tin mill would require. He guessed heat was involved. Fires and furnaces. Maybe a steam engine, to drive belts and tools. Water would be necessary, to make the steam. He looked at the map again, for roads, and rivers, and streams.

There were two possibilities. One was eight miles out, and the other was ten. Either spot would fit the bill. Except the road in and out of the ten-mile place curved north. Away from Laconia. Whereas the road in and out of the eight-mile place curved south. Toward Laconia. Reacher pictured a boy on a bike, rattling eagerly away from home, his binoculars around his neck. From the eight-mile place he would be heading straight toward the heart of town. Which boy would say he lived in Laconia?

Which was good. Eight miles, not ten, would save an hour on the round-trip. He set out walking.

He got a mile beyond the old edge-of-town gas station, around a long New England curve through deep woods. Then behind him he heard tires on the blacktop. He stopped and turned around.

He saw a dark sedan. Medium in size and crisp in appearance. There was a sprung antenna on the trunk lid. An unmarked squad car. In it was Jim Shaw, chief of detectives. The guy from the Laconia police station, the day before, with Brenda Amos. The red-headed Irish guy. He let his window down.

Reacher walked closer. He said, "Can I help you?"

Shaw said, "Brenda told me you were headed this way."

"You going to offer me a ride?"

"If I do, it will be back to town."

"How so?"

"The house-to-house turned up a woman who lives in the alley. She works in a cocktail bar in Manchester. Which is half owned by the folks the kid's father works for. She told us what happened last night. Everything except a physical description of her savior. She claims she was so stressed her mind has gone blank."

"That can happen, I guess," Reacher said.

"She's lying. She's protecting someone who did her a favor. But we have other evidence. The kid looks like he was run over by a freight train. Therefore we're looking for a big guy. Probably right-handed. Probably woke up with damaged knuckles."

"I scraped my hand on a wall," Reacher said. "Just one of those things."

"A smarter man than me might start putting it all together. The woman from the cocktail bar gets home in the middle of the night, at a predictable time, and the kid is waiting there for her, so she yells for help, which wakes a guy up, within a certain narrow radius, who then gets out of bed and goes to check, and who ends up dragging the kid away and smacking him around."

"You told me she already said all that."

"The interesting part is the narrow radius. The guy asleep had to be close by. Maximum one block, we think."

"I'm sure there are many variables," Reacher said. "Maybe it's all down to how well people hear and how fast they get dressed."

Shaw said, "A woman's cry for help would be heard through windows over the street. On a one-block radius. The house-to-house lists only six such rooms as occupied last night. We had six people to look at. Five were ruled out, two for being women and three of the men for age and infirmity and slightness of build."

"I was asleep at five o'clock," Reacher said.

"Brenda told me. And because once upon a time you were a brother cop, we believe you. And because the kid was a scumbag, we don't care, anyway. Except Brenda also told me she told you the scumbag's father is obliged to react."

"She did."

"That's my point. They'll be looking for a big guy with a damaged hand. They're going to send whoever it takes to get this job done. We don't want trouble here."

"Has the kid called his father yet?"

"First he called his lawyer. No doubt the lawyer called his father. By now burner phones are burning up in more than one state. They'll be arriving soon. Better if they didn't find you here. Better if you took a look at the old homestead and then kept on walking. Better if you didn't come back."

"Relax," Reacher said. "I'll keep on walking. It's what I do. Assuming I find Ryantown first."

"I'm serious. I don't want trouble in my town."

"Ryantown ain't yours."

"It's all Laconia to guys from Boston. They'll be here tomorrow, asking around. Anyone seen a big guy with a banged-up hand?"

Reacher said, "Tomorrow?"

"They won't let this go."

"But until tomorrow walking on county roads is still pretty much a legal activity."

"That's the problem. You could be walking forever. Those old places are nothing more than holes in the ground now. So do me a big favor, okay? Find any old hole in the ground, call it Ryantown, and then get the hell out."

Reacher nodded, and turned, and walked on. Behind him he heard the sound of tires rolling away, back to town. He kept up a steady pace, four miles an hour. He checked his map as he passed a left turn that led to a place with gray shading but no water. It was right where it should have been. He was on track.

PATTY and Shorty were sitting on the bed long after dawn. They had stared for hours at their luggage, as if hypnotized. The sudden reversal of its hard-won voyage was hard to process.

Patty said, "Do you think the story about the undergraduates is true?"

"Are you crazy?" Shorty said. "You know we took it down there ourselves."

"I don't mean this time. I mean undergraduates ever doing that."

"I don't know," Shorty said. "I guess it could be true."

"It doesn't matter, anyway. What matters is what he said. And what he said was weird. He said students steal their motel signs all the time. That means over and over again, year after year."

"I guess."

"Except everything else they've said makes this feel like a brand-new start-up. Like this could be their very first season."

Shorty was quiet a long moment.

Then he said, "But you spoke to the mechanic."

"Yes," Patty said. "He sounded bright and wide awake and on the ball. Friendly but courteous. He asked mechanic questions."

"Total worst case?" Shorty asked, like a ritual between them.

"We'll know soon enough," Patty said.

AFTER another mile the woods stopped and the vista opened out to a patchwork of fields. Reacher walked on. Coming up ahead on his left he saw his general target area. Ryantown was in there somewhere. He checked the map. The road he wanted was a shallow left turn about a mile ahead. Some distance short of it was a thinner spur. Same direction, but shorter and narrower.

He walked on and took the turn into the narrow track. It led to a pleasant split-level, about as old as he was. The house had sensible plants around the foundation, neatly trimmed. It had a carport, shading a pickup truck. It had a white picket fence.

Behind the fence was a pack of six dogs.

All mutts, all scruffy. Not barking yet. They came close and stood inside the picket gate. He was going to have to wade through them. He wasn't scared of dogs. He didn't plan to bite them. Why assume they planned to bite him?

He opened the gate. The dogs sniffed around him. They followed him down the path. He found the front door and pressed the bell. A long minute later the door opened and a man appeared behind the screen. He was a lean person, with buzzed gray hair. He was wearing jeans and a gray T-shirt. He was old enough to get a discount at the movies, but a long way from needing a cane.

The old man said, "Yes?"

Reacher said, "Sir, I'm sorry to disturb you, but I was passing by, and I have a question about some real estate north of here, and I wondered if you might fill in the gaps in my information."

"Are you from the government?"

"No, sir."

"Okay," the guy said.

He opened the screen door to shake hands.

"Bruce Jones," he said.

"Jack Reacher."

Jones closed the screen again.

He said, "What real estate?"

"Where the next road on the left meets the stream." Reacher pointed west and north. He said, "Maybe a mile or two from here. The abandoned remains of a tiny industrial hamlet."

"Industrial?"

"Small-scale," Reacher said.

"Would it have had something to do with pollution?"

"Possibly. It was a tin mill."

"You better come in," Jones said.

The screen door creaked open. All six dogs came in, too. Jones led Reacher to an alcove off an open-plan kitchen and dining room. The alcove was in use as a home office area. Jones opened a file drawer and thumbed through a folder. Then he stopped.

"Here."

He pulled out a faded sheet of paper. Reacher took it from him. It was a photocopied newsletter, dated eight years previously. Clearly one of a sequence of several, covering an issue in feverish detail, with a clear assumption of some prior knowledge. But it was easy enough to follow. The issue was Ryantown.

A little prior history was referred to, with the first appearance of the mill in the historical record, and then much later its period of peak production. The narrative cut to the then current chase, which seemed to be equal parts political, legal, and deranged. Apparently it was not yet proved that the decomposition of Ryantown's ancient mineral run-off had harmed anyone's groundwater. But it surely would be proved, and soon. Therefore readiness was everything. In which connection there was splendid news. Old Marcus Ryan's long chain of heirs had finally been untangled, and it was now certain that the remaining stock in his company was technically in the hands of a mining corporation based in Colorado. At last the Ryantown ecological disaster had an identifiable owner. The lawsuits were typed up and ready to go.

At the bottom of the newsletter was a call for all concerned citizens to attend a meeting. Below that was an obvious pseudonym as the writer's name, and an e-mail address.

Reacher handed the paper back to Jones.

He said, "What did you think of this at the time?"

"There's nothing wrong with our water," Jones said. "Never has been. I remember at first I figured this guy was a lawyer. I figured he had identified a big corporation to go after with a class action suit. But I never heard about it again. I guess he never got his proof. Which he couldn't, anyway, because the water is fine."

"You said at first you thought he was a lawyer."

"Later someone told me he was just a crazy old coot about five miles north of here. Then I met him, and he seemed harmless enough. He's not looking for money. He wants them to acknowledge their wrongdoing. Like a public confession."

"You didn't go to the meeting?"

"Meetings are not my thing."

"Pity," Reacher said. "One very important fact about Ryantown was not in the newsletter. Where it is."

"I thought you knew. You said the side road and the river."

"That was a best guess. A guy who wants to build a mill would need the road and the water. Is there anything else he'd need?"

"Where the river meets the road would make sense. Look for a stand of trees with straight edges. The neighbors would have wanted safe grazing and would have railed off the falling-down buildings. The copse will have grown the same shape as the fences. Usually it's the other way around."

"Thank you," Reacher said.

"Good luck," Jones said.

The screen door creaked open ahead of him, and slapped shut behind him.

He walked away. All the dogs followed him to the gate.

PATTY and Shorty had moved out to their lawn chairs. Patty looked at her watch.

She said, "Why is it when someone says between two hours and four hours it's always nearer four hours than two hours?"

"How much longer has he got?"

Patty looked at her watch again, and did a sum in her head.

"Thirty-three minutes," she said.

They watched the track. The sun was higher, and the front rank of trees was lit up bright. Solid trunks, packed together.

Shorty said, "How long has he got now?"

"Twenty-four minutes," Patty said.

And he came.

They felt it before they saw it. There was gradually a deep bass presence in the air, in the distance. Then it resolved into the throb of a giant diesel engine. Then they saw a red tow truck drive out of the trees. A huge one. Industrial size.

Patty stood up and waved.

The truck bumped down off the blacktop into the lot. The guy's name was written on the side, a foot high. It was Karel, not Carol.

"Wow," Shorty said. "Finally we're out of here."

"If he can fix it."

"We're out of here either way. He doesn't leave here without us. Okay? Either he fixes our car or he gives us a ride. Deal?"

"Deal," Patty said.

The truck came to a stop behind the Honda. Up high the door opened, and a guy used one step of the ladder and then jumped the rest of the way down. He was medium-sized and wiry, with a shaved head. But he was smiling. He had a twinkle in his eye.

"Ms. Sundstrom?" he said. "Mr. Fleck?"

Patty said, "Call us Patty and Shorty."

He said, "I'm Karel."

She said, "Thank you so much for coming."

He pulled an object from his pocket. It was a black box the size of a deck of cards, with stubs of disconnected wires coming out.

He said, "We got lucky with a wreck. Same model as yours."

Then he smiled and shooed them toward their door.

"Go pack your stuff," he said. "This is a two-minute job."

"We packed already," Patty said. "We wanted to be ready."

"Have you not enjoyed your stay?"

"We're anxious to get going. We should be somewhere else by now. That's all. Your friends have been very kind to us."

"No, I'm the new guy. They're not my friends. They're clients," he said. "Nine quad bikes and five cars. Guaranteed work."

"Five cars?"

"As of now. Plus a ride-on lawn mower."

"They told us one car," Shorty said. "An old pickup truck."

"That's the beater they use around the property. On top of that they got Mercedes-Benz SUVs, one apiece, in the barn."

Shorty said nothing.

Patty said, "Please fix our car now."

"That's why I'm here," Karel said.

He opened the Honda's hood with practiced movements. He leaned forward and held the new black box down low, as if trying it for size. Then he extricated himself and stood up straight.

He said, "Actually your relay is in good shape."

Patty said, "Then why won't it start?"

"Must be a different problem."

Karel put the black box back in his pocket. He shuffled around the fender and approached from a different angle.

"Try the key one more time," he said. "I want to hear how dead it is."

Shorty got in behind the wheel and flipped the key, on, off, on, off, *click, click, click.* Karel said, "Okay, I get it."

He shuffled to the opposite fender, and he bent down again, where the battery was bolted into a skeletal cradle. He twisted his neck so he could see underneath. He felt with his fingertip. Then he backed out and straightened up and stood still for a second.

He said quietly, "Did any of these guys work on your car?"

"Peter did," Shorty said. "He said he looked after the quad bikes, so we asked him to take a look."

"He doesn't look after the quad bikes."

"Did he screw it up?"

"He cut the main positive feed coming out of the battery."

"How? By accident?"

"Not possible by accident," Karel said. "It's a pure copper wire thicker than your finger. You would need a big pair of pliers with a wire-cutter blade. It would be an act of deliberate sabotage."

"Peter had a pair of pliers. Yesterday morning. I saw him."

"It's like disconnecting the battery. Zero electrical activity. The vehicle is paralyzed. Which is exactly your symptom."

"I want to see," Shorty said.

"Me, too," Patty said.

Karel said, "Look underneath."

They took turns. They saw a black wire chopped in half.

Karel said, "I don't know what to tell you. I don't know these guys very well. I have to assume this was their idea of a practical joke. But it's a stupid one. It won't be cheap to fix. You have to remove a whole bunch of other components just to get near it."

"Don't fix it," Patty said. "Just give us a ride right now."

"Why?"

"It wasn't a practical joke. They're keeping us here. They won't let us leave. We're like prisoners."

"That sounds pretty weird."

"But it's true. Everything they tell us is lies. They said we were the first guests in this room, but I don't think we are."

"That's totally weird. There were people in this room a month ago. I know, because I had to bring a tire to a guy in room nine."

"They said you were their good friend."

"That was the second time I ever met them."

"They said their phone was out yesterday. But I bet it wasn't. They just wanted to keep us here."

"But why would they? This is very weird," Karel said.

He stood there, uncertain.

"Please give us a ride," Patty said. "Please. We have to get out of here. We'll pay you fifty bucks."

"What about your car?"

"We'll leave it here. We don't care what happens to it."

She stared at him. He nodded slowly.

"Okay," he said. "Time to arrange a jailbreak. So let's think for a minute. We don't know how they're going to react to this. Therefore it's better if they don't see it happening. Agreed?"

"Much better," Patty said.

"So you guys stay out of sight, while I turn the truck around, so it's facing in the right direction, then grab your bags and hop on board, and away we go. Okay?"

"We're good to go," Shorty said.

Karel looked in the door at the suitcase.

"That's pretty big," he said. "Can you lift it? Want me to come back and help?"

"I can do it."

"Show me. A delay could screw this up."

Patty went in first. She picked up the overnight bags and stood out of the way so Shorty could get to the main attraction. He wrapped both fists around the new rope handle and hauled the case into the air. Karel watched from the doorway, as if judging.

He said, "How fast can you move with it?"

"Don't worry," Shorty said. "I won't screw up."

Karel looked at the two of them standing there side by side in the space between the bed and the AC. He said, "Okay, wait there, and don't come out until I get turned around."

"Sounds good," Shorty said.

Karel leaned in the doorway and grabbed the knob and closed the door on them. Through the window they saw him climb the ladder to the cab. They heard the engine roar and saw the truck jerk into gear and move slowly away, right to left, out of sight.

They waited. It didn't come back.

No sound, no movement. Nothing.

Shorty said, "Maybe he got hung up for a minute."

"He's been gone longer than a minute," Patty said. She stepped closer to the window. She craned her neck and peered out.

"Can't see anything," she said.

Shorty stepped to the door. He turned the knob and pulled. But the door was stuck. It wouldn't move at all. Patty stared at him.

"They locked us in," Patty said.

"How?"

"They must have a button in the house. Like remote control. I think they've been messing with it all along."

"That's completely crazy."

"What isn't here?"

They stared out the window. The Honda, the lot, the grass.

Then the window blind motored down in front of them, and the room went dark.

KAREL stepped into the back parlor, and the others crowded around and whooped and hooted and slapped him on the back. Steven pattered at a keyboard, and the video on the screens rewound, three jerky figures racing around, doing everything backward. He put on a TV voice and said, "Folks, let's ask the man of the hour how it felt to hit that big grand slam."

He changed to forward motion and normal speed, and on the screens Karel was seen smiling encouragingly and shooing Patty and Shorty toward their door. The audio caught him saying, "Go pack your stuff. This is a two-minute job."

Mark said, "That was a masterpiece of emotional manipulation. They were worried all morning, then suddenly filled with intense hope, which then increased to actual euphoria, as they stood there, waiting to go, and now they're suddenly sick with defeat."

Steven clicked to a live feed. Patty and Shorty were sitting on their bed, in the dark, not moving at all.

"It works better this way," Karel said. "It marinates their brains. It makes them more fun later, cross my heart."

Then he said, "I'll see you soon," and walked out the door.

Chapter 7

REACHER SAW THE LEFT TURN coming up a hundred yards ahead. It met the main drag at an oblique angle and curved gently away. Then it ran onward through apple orchards. He walked on toward it. When he was halfway there, a giant red tow truck blew by. He watched it go. Then he walked on again and took the turn.

The side road was narrower than the main drag. On either side in the orchards the apple trees were bending over with heavy fruit. He could smell it in the air.

Then, half a mile after its turn away from Laconia, the road turned again, due west. After that it ran through more apple orchards, toward a small shiny dot, which Reacher figured might be a parked car. As he got closer, he saw the dot was indeed a car. Eventually he saw it was a Subaru. It was parked head-on against a wooden fence that ran side to side where the blacktop ended. Beyond the fence was another acre of apple orchard, and then another fence, beyond which were wild trees with bigger leaves.

There was a guy in the Subaru sitting behind the wheel. Reacher could see the collar of a blue denim jacket, and a long gray ponytail. The guy was just staring ahead through the windshield.

Reacher walked the length of the car on the passenger side and stopped with his back to the guy and his hips against the fence. The next fence was a hundred yards away.

Behind him he heard a car door open, and a voice said, "You're the man who talked to Bruce Jones."

Reacher turned around and said, "Am I?"

The guy was reedy, maybe seventy years old, tall but cadaverous. Under his jacket his shoulders looked like a coat hanger.

He said, "He showed you the newsletter I wrote."

"That was you?"

"The very same. He called me. He thought I might be interested that you were interested. I was, so I came out to meet you."

"How did you know where?"

"You're looking for Ryantown," the guy said.

"Have I found it?"

"Straight ahead. Those trees thin out in the center."

"Sure I won't get poisoned?"

"Tin has the potential to be dangerous. More than a hundred milligrams of tin per cubic meter of air is immediately injurious to life and health. What's worse is when tin bonds with certain hydrocarbons to make organotins. Some of those compounds are more lethal than cyanide. That's what I was worried about."

"What happened with that in the end?"

"In the end, the corporation in Colorado banned me from trespassing on what I insisted was their land. They took out a restraining order to keep me away. I can't go beyond this fence."

"Pity," Reacher said. "You could have shown me around."

"What's your name?"

"Reacher."

The guy said an address. A street number and a street name. The same name and the same number Reacher had seen in cubicle 4, on the screen, from the census when his father was two.

"It was on the ground floor," the guy said. "Some of the tile is still there. In the kitchen. It was there eight years ago, anyway."

"You haven't been back?"

"You can't fight city hall."

"Who would know?" Reacher said. "Just this once."

The guy didn't answer.

"Okay," Reacher said. "Maybe I'll see you later."

He swung his legs over the fence and stepped in the orchard.

"Wait," the guy said. "I'll come with you."

The guy performed a maneuver similar to Reacher's. They walked together past shiny green eye-level apples, all of them bigger than baseballs. A hundred yards later they arrived at the second fence, where ahead of them were trees of a different kind. They were thinner and unhealthier dead ahead, because there they were growing through where the old road resumed, without the benefit of either a bulldozer or planting.

"How long before we see anything?" Reacher asked.

"Right away," the guy said. "Look down. You're walking on the old road. Nothing has been done to it, except by nature."

Which was plenty. They climbed the fence and pushed through thin trunks and half-hearted bushes. Soon the road could be traced ahead, curving toward where Reacher could hear water. The stream. Maybe the mill was down there.

The guy with the ponytail started pointing things out. First up on the left was a rectangular foundation. The church, the guy said. Next up on the right was the nub of a stone foundation, just inches high. This was the schoolroom, the guy said. All the kids could read and write. Teachers were respected then.

"Were you a teacher?" Reacher asked.

"For a time," the guy said. "In an earlier life."

The mill was where the road met the stream. It had been built half in and half out of the water. All that was left was a complex matrix of blocky foundations made of mossy stone.

The workers' housing was across the street, in two buildings laid out in a line. Just the foundations remained. Both would have had a central lobby with stairs, with left-hand and right-hand apartments up and down. Two four-flats. A total of eight residences. Ryantown, New Hampshire.

The guy said, "The Reacher address would have been the right-hand ground floor apartment. Nearest the mill. Traditionally the foreman lived there. Your grandfather, perhaps."

"For a time he graded roads for the county. But his address didn't change."

"The mill was idle for a couple of years late in the Depression. No point throwing him out in the street. It wasn't like they needed his house. It was World War Two that got it going again."

Reacher looked up at the sky. It was full of bird life. He wondered how it was back in the fall of 1943, with the mill running night and day, and the sky full of smoke.

The guy said, "I better get going. I shouldn't be here. Stay, if you want. I'll wait in the car. I could give you a ride, if you like."

"Thanks," Reacher said. "But don't wait any longer than you want to. I'm always happy to walk."

The guy nodded, and slipped away through the trees, back the way they had come. Reacher walked over to the right-hand four-flat. The hallway floor had three trees growing through it. Beyond them were low lines of smashed brick, showing where the rooms had been. Two bedrooms, he thought, plus a living room and a dine-in kitchen. All small. No bathroom. Maybe out back.

Then he heard a sound, way off to his right.

It was a yelp. A man's voice. Definitely not joy or ecstasy. Just pain. Distant. About where the orchard was, on the way back to the car. Reacher picked his way over the tumbled stones as fast as he could, following the old road back to the fence.

Where fifty yards away he saw the old guy with the ponytail, halfway across the orchard. Another guy less than half his age and twice his weight was standing behind him, twisting his arms.

Reacher stepped over the fence and set out toward them.

He kept his strides long and his shoulders loose and his hands away from his sides. He kept his head up and his eyes hard on the guy. A primitive signal, learned long ago.

The big guy turned to face him. He wrestled the old guy around in front and used him like a human shield.

Reacher stopped six feet away. "Let him go."

Just three words, but in a tone also learned long ago, with extra paragraphs hidden in the dying vowel sound at the end of the phrase. The big guy shoved the old guy aside and stepped into Reacher's space, not more than four feet away. He was twenty-some years old, dark-haired and unshaven, more than six feet and two hundred pounds, tanned and muscled by outdoor labor.

He said, "This is none of your business."

Reacher thought, What is this, Groundhog Day?

But aloud he said, "You were committing a crime on public land. I'd be failing in my duty as a citizen if I didn't point it out."

The guy glanced away to the south, and back again.

He said, "This ain't public land. This is my granddaddy's apple farm. And neither of you should be here. Him because he ain't allowed and you because you're trespassing."

"This is the road," Reacher said. "Your granddaddy stole it from the county forty years ago."

The guy glanced south again, but this time he didn't glance back. Reacher turned and saw another guy approaching, walking fast. He looked the same as the first guy, except a generation older. The daddy, perhaps. Built the same, but fifty-something.

He arrived and said, "What's going on here? Who are you?"

"Just a guy standing on the public road asking you a question."

"This is not the public road."

"That's the problem with denial. Reality doesn't care what you think. It just keeps rolling along. This is the road. Always was. Still is."

"What's your question?"

"I saw your boy assaulting this older gentleman. My question is how well you think that reflects on your parenting skills."

"In this case, pretty damn well," the new guy said. "What are our apples worth if people think our water is poisoned?"

"That all was eight years ago," Reacher said. "It came to nothing, anyway. So get over it."

The old guy with the ponytail said, "They have a contract with the corporation in Colorado. There was a rider on the restraining order. It said they get paid if they can prove I was here."

"How do they prove it?"

"They just did. They texted a picture. That's where he went. No cell signal, except up on the rise."

"Law and order," the daddy said.

"Except for stealing the county road to grow more apples."

"I'm getting sick of hearing you say that. Why were you in the woods, anyway?"

"None of your business," Reacher said.

"Maybe it is our business. We have a relationship with the landowner."

"You can't text a picture of me."

"Why not?"

"You would have to take your phone out of your pocket. Whereupon I would take it away from you and break it. You should call for reinforcements. But oh dear, you can't. No cell signal, except up on the rise."

"You're a cocky son of a bitch, aren't you?"

"I prefer realistic," Reacher said.

"Want to put it to the test?"

"I would have an ethical dilemma. It might scar the boy for life to see his daddy laid out in front of him. Equally it might scar you to see your boy laid out. After being unable to protect him."

The guy didn't reply.

Reacher said, "Wait."

He looked south, where the orchard came down the slope.

"You were on your way back," he said. "The text was already sent, from the top of the hill. The photograph must have been taken some moments before that. So why was our mutual friend still here, with his arms behind his back?"

The guy with the ponytail said, "I was to get a beating. So I would learn my lesson. At that point they didn't know you were in the woods, too."

Reacher looked at the daddy, and then at the son.

He said, "Time is wasting, guys. Give him his beating."

No one moved. Reacher looked at the young guy.

He said, "It's okay. He won't hurt you. He's old."

The guy moved his head, like a dog sniffing the air.

"Or maybe it's conscience trouble. You don't want to hit an old guy. But hey, I could help you out. You could give me a beating first. That way you would feel you had earned it, when you start in on the old guy. It might make you feel less troubled."

No response.

Reacher stepped in close. If the kid was dumb enough to throw a punch, it was better to smother it early. Which would be easy enough. If the kid was dumb enough. Reacher was thirty pounds heavier and three inches taller and five inches longer in the arm.

The kid was dumb enough.

His shoulder jerked back in what Reacher took to be the early-warning stages of what was no doubt intended to be a short clubbing right to his face. So Reacher jerked his head sideways and let the short right fizz past his ear, in all its glory, and then he waited for the kid to drag his fist back unrequited, and then he hit the kid under the chin with a solid right-hand uppercut. The kid collapsed backward on the grass. His head lolled to the side.

Reacher gave the guy with the ponytail a *Let's go* nod.

Then he looked at the kid's daddy.

"Parenting tip," he said. "Don't leave him lying in the road. He could get run over."

"I won't forget this."

Reacher said, "I already have."

He caught up to the old guy, and they walked the second fifty yards together, back to the Subaru.

EVENTUALLY Patty got up off the bed. She walked to the door, where the light switch was. Three steps. Through the first she was certain the power would still be on. Through the second she was sure it would be off. If they could lock the door and shade the window by remote control, surely they could kill the electricity.

She tried the switch.

It worked. The lights came on. She tried the door. Still locked. She tried the buttons for the window blind. Nothing. Shorty sat

still and watched her. She looked all around the room. At the furniture. At their bags, still where they had dropped them when the
truck didn't come back. At the ceiling. It contained nothing except
a smoke alarm and a bulkhead light, both above the bed.

Shorty said, "What?"

Patty looked back at their bags.

She said, "How well were they hidden in the hedge?"

"Pretty well," Shorty said. "You saw."

"And then Peter got lucky and got his truck started and took it
down the track to warm it up. There and back, real quick. Yet he
had time to spot our luggage. He had time to make a rope handle.
Using rope he just happened to have with him," she said.

"What are you thinking?"

"Why did they make a rope handle?" Patty said.

"I thought they were maybe helping us."

"Are you kidding? They were taunting us. We talked about getting a rope to make a handle, so that's exactly what they did. They
got a rope and made a handle. To demonstrate their power."

"How could they know what we talked about?"

"They're listening to us. There's a microphone in this room."

"Where is it?"

"Maybe in the light."

They both squinted at it, hot and yellow.

Shorty said, "Mostly we talked outside. In the chairs."

"Then there must be a microphone out there, too. That's how
Peter found our luggage. They heard us talking. They heard the
whole plan."

"What else did we say?"

"Lots of things. You said maybe Canadian cars are different, and
the next thing we hear is, hey, Canadian cars are different. They
were listening all along."

"What else?"

"Doesn't matter. What matters is what we say next."

"Which is what?"

"Nothing," Patty said. "We can't even plan what to do. Because
they'll hear us."

REACHER AND THE GUY WITH the ponytail climbed the fence and walked to the Subaru. The guy said, "You were pretty rough there."

"Not really," Reacher said. "I hit him once."

"His father meant what he said. He won't forget. That family has a reputation to keep up. They'll have to do something."

Reacher stared at him. Déjà vu all over again.

The guy said, "They won't want people laughing at them behind their backs. So they'll have to come looking for you."

"Who?" Reacher said. "The granddad?"

"They offer a lot of seasonal work. They get a lot of loyalty in exchange."

"How much more do you know about Ryantown?"

The guy paused a beat. He said, "There's an old man you should talk to. I was debating whether to mention him at all. Because honestly I think you should get going instead."

"Where is the old man I should talk to?"

"You couldn't see him before tomorrow. It would have to be arranged."

"How old is he?"

"I guess more than ninety now."

"From Ryantown originally?"

"His cousins were. He spent time there. I interviewed him about the tin. I asked him about kids who got sick. He came up with a list of names. But they were just regular childhood ailments. Nothing conclusive."

"Why tomorrow?"

"He's in a home in the countryside. Visiting hours are limited."

"I would need a motel tonight."

"There's a place twenty miles north of here. It's supposed to be good. But it's deep in the woods. No bus. Too far to walk. You would be much better off in Laconia."

Reacher said nothing.

The guy said, "Better still if you moved on altogether. I could drive you somewhere, if you like."

"Drive me to Laconia," Reacher said. "Then make the arrangements with the old guy."

REACHER GOT OUT ON A downtown corner, and the guy with the ponytail drove away. Reacher looked left and right and got his bearings. He took a side street, where he had seen an inn. It was another narrow three-floor building. He paid for a room and went up to take a look at it. The window faced out back. Which he was happy about. He might get a quiet night.

Then he went out again, because he was hungry. He had skipped lunch. He found a coffee shop a block away that offered all-day breakfast. He went inside. There were five booths. Four were occupied. The first three by what looked like out-of-town shoppers refreshing themselves after an exhausting spree, and the fourth by a familiar face. Detective Brenda Amos.

She was deep in a salad. No doubt a long-awaited meal much delayed by ongoing chaos. Reacher had been a cop. He knew what it was like. Eat when you can, sleep when you can.

She looked up.

At first she looked surprised, and then she looked dismayed. He shrugged and sat down on the bench across from her.

He said, "Shaw told me I'm legal until tomorrow."

She said, "He told me you agreed to move on."

"If I found Ryantown."

"Didn't you?"

"Apparently there's a guy I should talk to. A very old man. Same age my father would be. An exact contemporary."

"Are you going to talk to him today?"

"Tomorrow."

"This is what we were afraid of. You'll be here forever."

"Look on the bright side. Maybe no one is coming. The kid was an ass. Maybe they think he deserved it."

"No chance whatsoever. They'll mobilize before midnight. They'll be here by morning. The distances are not great. They'll have your description with them. Therefore Shaw is going to dial it up to eleven before first light. He's going to treat this place like a war zone. Where does this old man live?"

"In a home out of town. A guy I met is going to pick me up."

"At an agreed-upon time?"

"Nine thirty on the dot. Something about visiting hours."

"Okay," Amos said. "You're authorized to do that. But you'll do it my way. You don't leave your room at any point, and at nine thirty in the morning you run straight to the car. And you drive away. And you don't come back. Or we run you out now."

"I already paid for my room," Reacher said. "Running me out now would be an injustice."

"I'm serious," she said. "This is not the O.K. Corral. This is collateral damage just waiting to happen. If they miss you, they'll hit two other people instead. We are not going to allow drive-by shootings in our town. And with respect, Major, you should support our position. You should know better than to put innocent bystanders at risk."

"Relax," Reacher said. "I support your position. I'll do everything your way. Starting tomorrow. Today I'm still legal."

"Start when it gets dark tonight," Amos said. "Play it safe."

She took out a business card and handed it to him.

She said, "Call me if you need me."

Chapter 8

PATTY TOOK OFF HER SHOES, because she was Canadian, and stepped up on the bed, and stood upright on the bouncy surface. She shuffled sideways and tilted her face up toward the light.

She said loudly, "Please raise the window blind. I want to see daylight. What harm could it do? No one ever comes here."

Then she climbed down and sat on the edge of the mattress.

The blind stayed down.

"Good try," Shorty mouthed silently.

"They're discussing it," she mouthed back.

Then the blind rolled up, and afternoon light came spilling in.

Patty glanced up at the ceiling. "Thank you," she said.

At first she felt good. She'd established a line of communication. But then she felt worse, because she realized she had given them leverage. She had told them what she feared to lose.

REACHER did it Amos's way. He went to his room and holed up for the afternoon. Except dinner was going to be a problem. The place with the all-day breakfast was only a block away. But the wait staff had already seen him at lunchtime. Which was not good. Yes, they could say, he's in here all the time. Which would focus any subsequent search on the immediate neighborhood.

Not good. Better to go farther afield. He recalled a storefront bistro, with a half-curtained window. Six blocks away, he thought. He could zigzag through the side streets. Safe enough.

He went downstairs and stepped out to the fading light and set out walking. His mental map worked well enough. The bistro came eight blocks out, not six. Farther than he thought.

On the sidewalk outside the bistro he stood up tall on tiptoes, so he could see inside over the half curtain. There was an empty two-top in the far rear corner. The room was about half full. Six people eating. All good. Except that two of the six people eating were Elizabeth Castle and Carter Carrington.

A second date. He didn't want to ruin their evening. They would feel obliged to ask him to join them at their table.

But he owed Amos. *You don't leave your room at any point.* How much more walking around could he do?

In the end, the decision made itself. Elizabeth Castle looked up and saw him. She waved, an eager *Come join us* gesture.

He went in. Carrington stood up to shake hands. Elizabeth Castle leaned across and scraped out a third chair. Carrington held out his palm toward it, like a maître d', and said, "Please."

Reacher sat. He said, "I don't want to wreck your evening."

Elizabeth Castle said, "Don't be silly."

"Then congratulations," he said. "For your second date."

"Fourth," she said. "Dinner last night, coffee break this morning, lunch, dinner tonight. And it was your predicament that introduced us. So your passing by is like a good omen."

"I found Ryantown," Reacher said. "It all matched up with the census. The occupation was listed as tin mill foreman, and the address was right across the street from a tin mill."

Carrington nodded, and said nothing, in a manner Reacher thought deliberate and reluctant.

Reacher said, "What?"

"Nothing."

"I don't believe you."

"Okay, something. We were just discussing it. We can't pin it down. We looked at the original documents. They're both lovely censuses. You develop a feel. You see patterns. You can spot lies. Mostly about reading and writing for men, and age for women."

"You found a problem with the documents?"

"No," Carrington said. "They were beautifully done."

"Then it sounds pinned down pretty good to me."

"Like I said, you develop a feel. You're in their world. You become them, through the documents. Except you know what happens next, and they don't."

"And?"

"There's something wrong with the story you told me."

"But not in the documents."

"Some other part. Can't pin it down."

Then the waitress came by and took their orders, and the conversation moved on to other things. Reacher ate a main course only, and got up to go. He wanted them to have dessert on their own. It seemed the least he could do. They didn't object.

He stepped out the door and turned right. Traffic was light. The stores were all closed. A car came by from behind, and it drove on ahead. Nothing to worry about. The center of normal.

Then he saw something that wasn't.

Headlights, coming toward him. A large vehicle.

Reacher was pinned by the lights. They washed over him, and then they slid past him. He turned and saw a pickup truck, high and shiny, with two rows of seats and a long, long bed, and big chrome wheels turning slow, just rolling along, relaxed as can be.

It was on the inside where the action was happening.

Five faces were swiveling toward him. Five pairs of eyes were locked on his. Five mouths were open. One of them was moving.

It was saying, "That's him."

The guy with the moving mouth was the daddy from the apple farm. He was in the second row, behind the driver.

The other four were a generation younger. Not so different from the kid in the orchard. Same kind of build, same kind of muscle, same kind of tan. The same human species. But poorer.

The truck squelched to a stop, and all four doors opened. Five men jumped down. Two guys came around the hood and formed up shoulder to shoulder with the other three, with the older guy right in the middle.

The guy from the apple farm said, "You need to come with us."

Reacher said, "Do I?"

"Best to come quietly."

Reacher said, "Are these new boys any better? I sure hope so."

A ripple ran down the line. Sharply drawn breaths rustled arms against chests, and jabbed glares jerked heads above shoulders.

Reacher looked at the four younger guys.

He asked, "Where were you born?"

None of them answered.

"You should tell me," he said. "It's important to your futures."

"Around here," one of them said.

"And then you grew up around here?"

"Yes."

"Not Southie or the Bronx or South Central LA?"

"No."

"Any military service?"

"No."

"Any secret clandestine training by Mossad?"

"No."

Reacher turned back to the guy from the apple farm.

"See the problem?" he said. "You can't deliver. Not with this crew."

Obviously Reacher knew they would all react, which was exactly what he wanted. The kid to the left started forward, enraged by the derision, so Reacher lined him up and threw his punch. His fist hit the kid in the face, and then Reacher snapped it back fast and stood upright and easy, like nothing had happened.

The kid fell down.

Fifty yards away, Elizabeth Castle and Carter Carrington stepped out of the bistro. He said something, and she laughed. The guys from the truck turned to look.

Fifty yards away, Carrington took Elizabeth Castle's hand, and they turned together and set out walking. Head-on. Approaching. Reacher turned to the farm guy and said, "The city attorney is coming. A credible witness, if nothing else."

The guy from the farm said nothing.

"I'll make it easy for you," Reacher said. "I'll make sure we meet again. Tomorrow or the next day. Keep an eye out for me."

He walked away. He didn't look back. Behind him he heard muttered commands and scuffling feet, and the truck backing up. He heard a door slam. Then he turned in on a side street, and heard nothing more, all the way back to his room. Where he stayed the rest of the night, and where he slept soundly.

Until one minute past three in the morning.

Reacher snapped awake instantly. Same reason. A sound.

He padded naked out of bed and checked the alley through the window. Nothing. A quiet night. Except apparently not.

He heard Amos's voice in his head: *They'll mobilize before midnight. They'll be here by morning.*

Reacher pulled his pants out from under the mattress and put them on. He buttoned his shirt. He collected his toothbrush from the bathroom, and he put it in his pocket. He was good to go.

He walked downstairs to the lobby, and waited inside the street door and listened. He heard nothing. He stepped out. He saw no one. He walked to the corner. Nothing there.

He heard a car. Behind him, in the distance. The faint hiss of its tires, the breathing of its engine. Three blocks away, he thought.

He turned back toward the inn. He walked through cones of yellow light. Once he stopped in the shadows and listened. He could still hear the car. Rolling slow. Still three blocks away. Turning right every now and then, going around and around.

A giant map-sized spiral. A search pattern. But a lazy one. Maybe a lay-of-the-land reconnaissance.

The car turned right, two blocks behind him.

He stopped walking. He strolled to the corner and waited. The street was deserted. Still the dead of night. All good.

Except right then the car chose to step in another block closer. Way early, compared to its previous pattern. It came rolling down the cross street on Reacher's left, with its bright lights on, sweeping both sidewalks at once. Reacher was lit up like a movie star. The car stopped fifteen feet away. A door opened.

Behind the light a voice said, "Laconia Police Department. Raise your hands."

"I can't see you," Reacher said. "Kill the lights."

Which was a test. A real cop might, and a fake cop wouldn't.

The lights went out.

Reacher blinked, and the yellow nighttime glow came back. The car was a Laconia PD black-and-white. The guy behind its open door was in a patrolman's uniform. His nameplate said DAVISON. He was maybe in his middle twenties. Bright and alert. For once a routine night patrol had turned out interesting.

"Raise your hands," he said again.

"Not really necessary," Reacher said.

"Then turn around and I'll cuff you."

"Officer, I don't see a lot of probable cause here."

Davison said, "None is required. You're a person of interest. You were mentioned in the start-of-watch briefing. A sketch was distributed. You're not supposed to be seen in public."

"Who conducted the briefing?"

"Detective Amos."

"What else did she say?"

"Report immediately if we see a Massachusetts license plate."

"Did you?"

"Not yet."

"She's taking it seriously," Reacher said.

"She has to. We can't let anything bad happen. Sir, you need to come with me."

"Am I under arrest?"

"Sir, Detective Amos informed us of your prior service in the MPs. We're happy to extend every courtesy."

"Yes or no?"

"You're about an inch away," the kid said, bright and alert.

Reacher thought about coffee. No doubt an ever present fixture in the police station.

"An arrest won't be necessary," he said. "I'll ride with you of my own free will. But in the front. Call it a rule."

They got in the car and set out in a direction that Reacher recognized led to the station. A straight shot. About half a mile.

Davison pulled in outside the lobby doors. He got out. Reacher got out. They went inside together. Davison explained the situation to the night guy. Who was unclear on only one point.

He said, "Until nine thirty, do I need to lock him up?"

Davison looked at Reacher. He said, "Does he?"

"Not really necessary. All I want is coffee."

Davison turned back to the night guy. He said, "Find him an office to wait in, and get him a cup of coffee."

Then ahead of them the double doors swung open and Brenda Amos walked through.

"We'll use my office," she said.

THE first arrival happened well before dawn. He lived in northern Maine, in a wooden house in eighty square miles of forest, all of which he owned. He drove an old Volvo wagon fitted with fake Vermont plates. His phone told him where to turn. He saw the mouth of the track, and the blacktop, and the fat rubber wire. Which rang a bell somewhere, to scare up a welcome.

Which was offered in the motel office by Mark. Mark offered him room 3. Mark watched as he parked the wagon. Watched him as he carried his bags inside. He was wondering which bag held his money, the new guest assumed. He set his stuff down near the closet and stepped outside again, to the predawn darkness. He couldn't contain himself. He crept past room 4, past 5, toward a dead-looking Honda Civic. He stepped out into the lot and looped around behind it, so he could take in room 10 from a distance. It was currently blank and quiet. The window blind was down. There was no light inside. No sound.

The new guest walked back to room 3.

Chapter 9

REACHER TOOK COFFEE from the squad room pot, and then Amos walked him back to her office.

She said, "I asked you to play it safe, for my sake."

He said, "Something woke me up. I went out to take a look. Nothing doing, except an excellent performance from Patrolman Davison. With which I had no problem. I'm happy to wait here. All good. Except I'm sorry you had to get up early."

"Yeah, me, too," Amos said. "You also went out for dinner."

"How do you know?" he asked.

"Carter Carrington told us," she said. "You walked eight blocks to the same bistro he was in. That wasn't playing it safe. You should have called me. I would have brought you pizza."

"Why did you ask Carrington about me?"

"We didn't. We needed a legal opinion. Your dinner plans came up in the subsequent conversation."

"What kind of legal opinion?"

"Who we can detain, before they've actually done anything."

"And what was the answer?"

"These days, practically anybody."

"I'll be out of here at half past nine. They'll find me gone."

"I sincerely hope what you just said is true. We got some news. Slightly encouraging for us. Not so much for you."

"What is it?"

"Current thinking has downgraded the risk of drive-by casualties.

Chief Shaw was on the phone with the Boston PD. They think the attempt will not be made here. Their preferred tactic will be to get you in their car, so they can drive you back to Boston, where they'll throw you off an apartment building. That's what they do. Like a signature."

"I won't get in the strange man's car," Reacher said.

Amos didn't reply. Her door opened, and a head stuck in and said, "Ma'am, we have reports of a Massachusetts plate incoming from the southwest, on a black Chrysler 300 sedan, which according to Mass DMV seems to be registered to a freight forwarding operation based out of Logan Airport, in Boston."

"Where is it now?"

"Still south of downtown. With a squad car right behind it."

Amos said, "Stay with him. Make it obvious. Show the flag."

The head ducked out, and the door closed again.

"So," Amos said. "Here we go."

"Not yet," Reacher said. "Not with this guy. It's a big black sedan with tinted windows. It's immediately traceable back to Boston. It's owned by a freight forwarding company at a major international airport. It might as well carry a neon sign. It's a decoy. They want you to follow it. It's going to drive around all day. It's going to signal every turn, and you can bet its taillights are in working order. Meanwhile the real guy is in an electrician's van. Or a plumber. Or whatever. The real guy is going to slip into town sometime today, and no one is going to notice. But hopefully after half past nine in the morning. By then I'll be long gone."

"We're basing a lot on your friend from yesterday actually showing up again. What if he doesn't? You'll be here all day. That's the scenario I promised Shaw I wouldn't let happen."

Reacher nodded.

"I don't want to put you on the spot," he said. "I'll give my guy thirty minutes. If he doesn't show by ten, you can drive me to the city limit yourself. Then I'll be outside the jurisdiction."

"It's a line on the map. You could be followed. Electricians go from job to job. Also plumbers and flower delivery."

"But the county will be stuck with the paperwork, not the city."

"You shouldn't stick around."

"I don't want to," Reacher said. "I like to keep moving. But on the other hand, I don't like to be chased away. Especially not by people who plan to throw me off a building."

"Don't let ego get in the way of a good decision."

"I won't," Reacher said. "I'll be gone in a day. Life will move on. Hopefully I'll be somewhere warm."

Amos didn't answer.

Her door opened again; the same head stuck in. "The black Chrysler is now cruising downtown, with no apparent destination, obeying all traffic laws, and the squad car is still behind it."

The head withdrew, and the door closed.

"Decoy," Reacher said.

"When will the real guy get here?"

He didn't answer.

THE second arrival had more moving parts than the first. Peter drove his Mercedes SUV to a small hobby airfield near Manchester. No tower, no log, no reporting requirements at all. He parked inside the fence. Five minutes later a twin-engine Cessna came in low and landed. Peter flashed his lights, and it rolled toward him.

It was an air taxi, out of Syracuse, New York, booked by a shell corporation on behalf of a passenger who had an Illinois driver's license in the name of Hogan. He had arrived in Syracuse moments earlier in a charter Gulfstream out of Houston, Texas, booked by a different shell corporation, on behalf of a passenger with a California license in the name of Hourihane. Neither license was real.

He climbed down from the plane, and Peter helped him put his stuff in the Mercedes. Three soft bags and two hard cases. The money was in one of the soft bags, Peter assumed.

The plane blared down the runway and into the air. Peter drove out the gate and along the back roads. The new arrival sat beside him. He looked excited. He was sweating a little. He wanted to say something. Peter could tell.

He said, "What are they like?"

"They're perfect," Peter said.

Dawn came up bright and clear, and a patrolman came by to take breakfast orders, from a diner down the street. Reacher chose a fried egg sandwich. Ten minutes later it arrived. Protein, carbohydrate, grease. All the food groups. He got more coffee from the squad room. No one was in there. Day watch was an hour away.

There was a feed from the radio room playing through a speaker on someone's empty desk. Reacher went closer and listened. A dispatcher was talking to two separate squad cars. One of them seemed to be right behind the Chrysler, and the other seemed to be tracking them both, from a block away.

A voice that could have been Davison's broke in and said, "Now he's in the drive-through lane for coffee."

"That's good," the dispatcher said. "It means sooner rather than later he'll need to take a leak. Maybe you can get a look at him."

Then a new voice said, "The cameras at the highway cloverleaf show a Massachusetts plate heading our way. On a dark blue panel van. A Persian carpet cleaning company out of Boston."

"Back burner," the dispatcher said. "We're going to get plenty of clutter. FedEx and UPS and all kinds of things."

Reacher knew Persian carpets were expensive. Cleaning them was a delicate matter, and experts were few and far between. So it was plausible that a customer in Laconia would need to send to Boston for service. Pickup and drop-off included. All good.

Except.

He topped up his coffee and headed back to Amos's office. She was at her desk, with her hand on the phone.

He said, "I heard the radio in the squad room. The decoy is getting coffee. And a blue van came off the highway."

She nodded

"Got an opinion?" Reacher said.

"It's a van. I can think of a hundred reasons why it's okay."

"Ninety-nine. How many Persian carpets have you seen?"

"A few. An old lady we used to visit. In a big old house."

"Exactly. An old biddy. What's the earliest time of day such a lady would be prepared to receive tradespeople at her door?"

Amos said nothing.

"The van is too early," Reacher said. "That's what's wrong. It's just after dawn. It's not making a customer call in Laconia."

She thought for a moment, and then she picked up the phone. She said to whoever answered, "Keep eyes on the blue van from the carpet cleaner. Let me know where it goes."

AN HOUR later the workday was fully under way. The new watch was in. The station was bustling. Reacher heard a patchwork of news, some of it from the radio feed. The decoy in the Chrysler was still driving around. But they had lost the blue van. Opinion was divided between two theories. Either the van had parked in a hidden location, which made it suspicious, or else it had driven straight through town and exited to the northwest.

Amos said, "It's nearly time for you to go. I'm going to drive you. No one would be dumb enough to attack a police vehicle."

"Are you worried about me?"

"Purely in an operational sense. I want you out of here."

She made a couple of arrangements on the phone, and then she led Reacher out to the lot, where she chose a black-and-white. The keys were in it. Reacher rode in the front. He gave her directions to the corner before the side street where the inn was. There was a late rush hour jam at one of the lights. Amos lit up her roof bar and slipped through in the wrong lane.

And there dead ahead was the Subaru. Waiting at the curb. On the right spot. At the right time. Amos pulled up behind him.

"Thanks for everything," Reacher said.

He got out of the car and walked ahead. He tapped on the Subaru's passenger window. The old guy glanced back at the flashing lights. He was confused. He didn't understand.

Reacher opened the door and got in the car.

"She gave me a ride," he said. "That's all."

The old guy said, "Why would a cop give you a ride?"

"Protective custody," Reacher said. "The folks from the apple farm were in town last night."

The explanation seemed to settle the guy. He nodded.

"I told you," he said. "That family doesn't let things go."

He said nothing more. He drove on. They seemed to be heading north and west. Toward Ryantown.

Reacher said, "Did you make the arrangements?"

"They're expecting us. Visiting hours start at ten. The old man's name is Mr. Mortimer."

"Great," Reacher said.

They found the main drag out of town, and two miles later turned left. They followed the road west, through woods, past fields. In the distance came the orchards, and Ryantown itself, overgrown and ghostly.

Two miles later on the left Reacher saw low buildings, laid out in a field. There were crisp blacktop roads with white markings. There were newly planted trees. The buildings were bland stucco. There was a sign at the entrance. Something about assisted living.

"This is it," the old guy said.

The clock in Reacher's head hit ten exactly.

THE third arrival was as stealthy and self-contained as the first. The man in question drove himself from a small town in rural Pennsylvania. Initially he was in a car reported scrapped in western New York four months previously. He had two overarching aims. He didn't want to be caught, and he didn't want to be late.

The plan was about anonymity and untraceability. Stage one was to drive in the paperless car to a friend's place just west of Boston. He knew the guy from a different community. A different shared interest. A tight, passionate group of guys. What a fellow member wanted, a fellow member got. No questions asked.

The friend's day job was trading commercial vehicles. He bought them at auction, after they came off lease. On any given day he had a couple dozen around. On that particular day he had three clear favorites. All panel vans, all ordinary, all invisible. No one paid attention to a panel van.

The best example was dark blue with gold signwriting. It had come in as a repo, from a bankrupt carpet cleaner in the city. Persian rugs. The man from Pennsylvania loaded his stuff in it and started it up. He set the GPS on his phone. He drove north. The route took him to a small town named Laconia.

Where he got scared. He saw two cop cars, clearly eyeballing everyone coming in from the south. Searching. Staring at him. He panicked and pulled over in an alley. He checked his e-mail. His secret account, on his secret phone. There was no cancellation message. No warnings, no alerts.

He backed out of the alley and drove on. He was quickly out of town. He didn't see the police cars again. He relaxed. He drove through woods and past fields. He kept on straight, ten more open miles, and then the woods came back. The van rushed along.

Then his phone told him the final turn was fast approaching, in half a mile on the left. He took it, and thumped onward over blacktop missing some of its surface. He ran over a wire, which he figured rang a bell somewhere.

Two miles later he came out in a clearing. The motel was dead ahead. There was a Volvo wagon outside of what must have been room 3. There was a guy in a lawn chair outside of room 5. Outside of room 10 was a blue Honda Civic. Foreign plates.

He met Mark in the office. For the first time, face-to-face. They had corresponded, of course. He got room 7. He parked the van. He put his bags in the room, and then he stepped back out to the light. He nodded to the guy in the lawn chair. But he strolled the other way to room 10. Important. His first look. At nothing much, as it turned out. Room 10's window blind was down.

REACHER thought the old people's home was a cheap but sincere attempt to provide a decent place to live. He liked it. They were welcomed at the reception desk by a cheerful woman.

The woman pointed and said, "Mr. Mortimer is waiting for you in the dayroom."

Reacher followed the guy with the ponytail down a corridor to a set of double doors. Inside was a circle of armchairs. In one of them was a very old man. Mr. Mortimer, Reacher assumed. His hair was white and wispy, and his skin was pale. His ears were big and full of hearing aids. His wrists looked like pencils.

There was no one else in the room. The guy with the ponytail walked over and stuck out his hand. "Mr. Mortimer, it's good to see you again. I wonder if you remember me?"

The old man took his hand. "Of course I remember you. I would greet you properly, but you warned me never to say your name. Walls have ears, you said. There are enemies everywhere."

"That was a long time ago."

"Do you need my help again?"

"My friend Mr. Reacher wants to ask you about Ryantown."

Mortimer nodded. His gaze tilted up and stopped on Reacher. He said, "There was a Reacher family in Ryantown."

"The boy was my father," Reacher said. "His name was Stan."

"Sit down," Mortimer said. "I'll get a crick in my neck."

Reacher sat down. Up close Mortimer showed some spark. Any weakness was physical, not mental.

"I had cousins there," he said. "We lived close by. We visited back and forth, but my memories of Ryantown might be patchy."

"You remembered which kids got sick."

"Only because people talked about it all the time. It was like a county-wide bulletin, every morning. Someone's got this, someone's got that. You had to know who to stay away from."

"Did Stan Reacher get sick?"

"The name was never listed in the county-wide bulletin," he said. "But that doesn't really mean I knew who he was. Everyone had cousins in and out all the time. I remember Mr. Reacher the mill foreman. He was a well-known figure. But I couldn't swear which of the kids was his. We all looked the same. You never knew exactly where anyone lived. They all came running out the same four-flat door. About nine of them from the foreman's building, I think. One of them was a good ballplayer. I heard he went semipro in California. Would that be your father?"

"He was a bird-watcher."

Mortimer was quiet a beat. Then he smiled. "You know, I had forgotten about the bird-watchers. How extraordinary that you should remember and I didn't. What a memory you must have."

"Not a memory," Reacher said. "It's a later observation. I know he was a member of a club by the age of sixteen. But you said bird-watchers. Was there more than one?"

"There were two," Mortimer said. "I got the impression one of them was someone's cousin and didn't live there all the time, and one of them did. But they were together plenty. Like best friends. One of them must have been Stan Reacher. I can picture them. I got to say, they made it pretty exciting. I guess, truth to tell, the first time I ever met them I was probably ready to stomp them for being sissies, but first of all, I would need to bring an army, because they were the best fighters you ever saw, and second of all, pretty soon they got everybody doing it, quite happily, taking turns with the binoculars. We saw birds of prey. One time we saw an eagle take something about the size of a puppy."

"Stan had binoculars?"

"One of them did. Can't say for sure which one was Stan."

"I'm wondering how he afforded binoculars."

"I assumed they were stolen. No offense," Mortimer said.

"None taken."

"We were all nice enough kids. We wouldn't break into a store. But we wouldn't ask too many questions, either. Not if something came our way. I suppose the thought of anything worse would have been in our heads because of his father. We all thought Mr. Reacher the mill foreman was a bit dubious."

"What kind of dubious?"

"Everyone was scared of him. He was always yelling and throwing punches. Looking back on it, I suppose he drank."

"Do you remember when Stan left to join the marines?"

Mortimer shook his head.

"I never heard about that," he said. "I was already drafted."

"Where did you serve?"

"New Jersey. They didn't need me. It was the end of the war. They had too many people already. They canceled the draft soon after that. I never did anything. I felt like a fraud."

Reacher said, "Any other memories of Ryantown?"

"Nothing very exciting. It was a hardscrabble place."

"What about Elizabeth Reacher? James Reacher's wife?"

"She would be your grandmother."

"Yes."

"She sewed things," Mortimer said. "I remember that."

"Do you remember what she was like?"

"She was a hard woman. Cold. I never saw her smile or say a nice thing. They deserved each other, that Mr. and Mrs."

Reacher nodded. "Anything else you can tell me?"

"I remember one time there was a big hoo-ha about a rare bird. First time it was ever seen in New Hampshire. The bird-watching boys wrote it up for the bird-watching club. For the minutes of the meeting. One of them was club secretary by then. The report was about all the things going on that might influence the bird being there, or not. It was impressive. I believe it got picked up for a hobby magazine."

"What bird?"

"I don't remember, but you could find out. Because of the bird-watching club. Their old ledgers are in the Laconia library."

"The downtown branch of the library?"

"That's the only branch there is."

THEY left old Mr. Mortimer in his armchair and walked back to the desk. The cheerful woman accepted their departure with grace and equanimity. They walked back to the ancient Subaru.

Reacher said, "Do you know the library in Laconia?"

"Sure," the guy with the ponytail said.

"Can you park right outside?"

"Why?"

"So I can get in and out real fast."

"No," the guy said. "It's a big building in a parcel all its own. It looks like a castle. You have to walk through the gardens."

"How many people will I see in the gardens?"

"On a nice day like this, there could be a few."

"How far is the library from the police station?"

"Sounds like you have a problem, Mr. Reacher."

Reacher paused a beat. "What's your name?"

"The Reverend Patrick G. Burke, technically."

"You're a priest?"

"Currently I'm between parishes."

"Since how long?"

"About forty years. Tell me about your problem."

"The apple farming folks aren't the only ones mad at me. Apparently I upset someone in Boston, too. Different type of family. Different type of likely reaction. The Laconia Police Department doesn't want its streets shot up like the Saint Valentine's Day Massacre. I'm supposed to stay out of town."

"What did you do to the people in Boston?"

"I have no idea. I haven't been in Boston in years."

"Who are you exactly?"

"I'm a guy who followed a road sign. Now I'm anxious to get on my way. But first I want to know what bird it was."

"Aren't you worried about the people from Boston?"

"Not really," Reacher said. "It's the cops I'm worried about. I kind of promised I wouldn't come back. I don't want to let them down. One in particular. She was an army cop, too."

"But you want to know about the bird."

"Since it's right there."

"I never saw a police officer in the library gardens," Burke said. "Chances are they would never know you were there."

Reacher said, "Just make sure you park as close as you can."

Twenty miles to the north, Patty Sundstrom once again took off her shoes, and stepped up on the bed, and spoke to the light.

She said, "Please raise the window blind. As a personal favor to me. And because it's the decent thing to do."

Then once again she climbed down and sat on the edge of the mattress, to put her shoes back on. Shorty watched the window.

Nothing happened. The blind stayed down.

Then the TV turned on. All by itself.

The picture lit up bright blue, with a line of code. Then it was replaced by another picture. A man.

It was Mark.

The screen showed him head and shoulders, like an at-the-scene reporter. He was standing in front of a black wall, staring at a camera. Staring at them.

He said, "Guys, we need to discuss Patty's latest request."

Patty said nothing. Shorty was frozen in place.

Mark said, "I'm happy to raise the blind. But I'm worried you won't enjoy it as much the second time around. It would help me ethically if I could double-check your positive consent."

Patty stood up. Put her hands to her shoes.

Mark said, "You don't need to get on the bed. I can hear you from there. The microphone is not in the light."

"What do you want from us?"

"Right now all I need is your positive consent to raise the window blind. Up or down?"

"Up," Patty said.

The TV turned itself off. The screen went blank.

Then the blind came up, with warm sunlight pouring in. The view was the same. The Honda, the lot, the grass, the wall of trees. But it was beautiful. The way it was lit. Patty put her elbows on the sill and her forehead on the glass.

She said, "The microphone is not in the light."

Shorty said, "Patty, we're not supposed to be talking."

"He said I didn't need to get on the bed. How did he know I got on the bed? They have a camera in here. They're watching us. They've been watching us all along."

Shorty looked around. "Where is it?" he said.

"I don't know," she said.

She sat down next to Shorty. She didn't want to move.

Then right in front of her a man peeked in the window.

He was on the boardwalk outside, craning around. Peeking in, one eye. Then he stepped more into view. He was a big guy with gray hair and a rich man's tan. He stood square on and stared. At her. At Shorty. Then he turned away and waved. And beckoned. And spoke. Patty couldn't hear what he said. The window was soundproof. But it looked like he said, "Their blind is up now."

Another man stepped into view. And another.

All three men looked in the window.

They were staring, and judging, and evaluating.

They were pleased by what they saw.

Patty said, "Mark, I know you can hear me. Who are these people?"

His voice came out of the ceiling.

"We'll discuss that very soon," he said.

Chapter 10

THE LIBRARY WAS a handsome construction, built of red-and-white stone. As promised, it was surrounded by landscaped gardens. Reacher took a paved path from a gate near where the Reverend Burke parked the Subaru. Inside there were people strolling, and people sitting on benches. No police anywhere.

Up ahead on the street beyond the building was a white panel van. Parked at the curb. Diametrically opposite the Subaru. The other side of the square. It had ice-blue writing on the side. An air-conditioning repairman. Reacher walked on. So far four people had passed him by on the narrow winding path.

He went up the steps and in through the door. The lobby had the same red-and-white stone inside as outside. He found the stair to the basement. He came out in a big underground room with shelves like the spokes of a wheel. The reference section.

A woman at a desk looked up and said, "Can I help you?"

"The bird-watching club," Reacher said. "Someone told me you have the old records."

The woman pattered on her computer keyboard.

"Yes," she said. "We have those. What years?"

Reacher gave the woman four consecutive years, from when Stan was fourteen up to when he left home to join the marines.

"Take a seat," she said. "I'll bring them to you."

He sat down at a study carrel, one of many in the center of the room. Three minutes later the woman brought him the records.

The records were in four large ledgers with maroon marbled covers. Inside, the pages were numbered, and lined, and covered in neat fountain pen handwriting, gone pale with age.

He opened the first ledger. It continued from where the last ledger must have left off. The year Stan was thirteen. The first page jumped right in with the minutes of the next meeting. Stan Reacher was not listed as present. Much time was taken up debating whether to change the club's name. Currently it was the Society of Laconia Birdwatchers. A faction thought the Laconia Audubon Society would be better. Much discussion ensued.

Stan Reacher was not present at the next meeting, either.

Reacher put the first ledger aside and tried the second. He opened it at random, in the middle. Where he found a handwritten essay about hummingbird migration, written by someone named A. B. Smith. It was like a scholarly article.

He tried the third book and found the meeting where his father was elected secretary. Right there. Stan Reacher. Stan slowly got control. The meetings got faster. There was more talk of birds than binocular repairs. The writing was neat. But not Stan's. He must have delegated the clerical duties. But the content sounded like him. "The secretary ruled immediately that it was an inappropriate subject for discussion. . . . The secretary set a two-minute time limit on discussion of the motion." In other words, shut up, and hurry up. Like later in life. Why the Corps invented captains.

Reacher turned the pages. Another meeting, and another. And then a report on proceedings. There were maps and pictures and diagrams, done in colored pencils. There were columns of text, done in ink. The title, carefully lettered, was "An Historic Sighting over Ryantown, New Hampshire." The article was submitted by S. Reacher and W. Reacher.

The bird-watching boys. Both Reachers. Cousins, probably.

The bird was a rough-legged hawk.

It was thought to be gone, but it came back. There was no issue with the identification. It was a hard bird to mistake. The question was why it came back.

The answer, according to S. and W. Reacher, was vermin. Settlements like Ryantown attracted rats and mice like magnets, where they were poisoned, so either the hawks got nothing to eat or they died from consuming toxic flesh. Naturally the few survivors went elsewhere, not to return until years later, when the government started commandeering items for the war, including steel and rubber and aluminum, of course, but also other things. Such as rat poison. The military needed it all. For unspecified reasons. The result was the rats and mice in Ryantown grew plump and healthy. So the hawks came hustling over from wherever they had weathered the chemical storm, and they got back to work.

W. Reacher was not listed as present at the next meeting. Or the meeting before. Reacher flipped through the pages, forward and backward, and never saw the name. Not once.

Reacher closed the book.

The woman at the desk said, "Did you find what you needed?"

"It was a rough-legged hawk," Reacher said. "In Ryantown, New Hampshire."

"Really?" She sounded astonished.

"Because of no more rat poison," he said. "A new abundance of prey. I think it's plausible."

"No, I mean it's amazing because someone else looked at that exact same thing about a year ago. I remember. It was about two boys, right? They recorded the hawk and wrote an explanation. It was reprinted in an old magazine a month or so afterward."

She pattered at her keyboard.

She said, "Actually it was more than a year ago. It was an ornithologist from the university. He had seen the historic magazine reprint, but he wanted to see the original. We talked a little bit. He said he knew one of the participants."

"One of the boys?"

"I think he said he was related to both of them."

"How old was this guy?"

"Not old. Obviously the boys were from a previous generation. Uncles or great-uncles or something. The stories were clearly passed down. Some of them were pretty interesting."

"Which university?"

"New Hampshire," she said. "Down in Durham."

"Can you give me his name and number?"

"Not without a good reason."

"We might be related, too. One of those boys was my father."

The woman wrote out the name and the number. Reacher folded the paper and put it in his back pants pocket.

He thanked her and went back up the stair to the lobby. He was all done in town. He had nothing more to see. On a whim he crossed to the main staircase, which was inside a wide tower, just like it would be in a castle. He went up as far as the second-floor windows for a last look around. He saw the Subaru, patiently waiting, about sixty yards away. He crossed the hall, and in the opposite direction he saw the air-conditioning truck. Still there.

Plus three guys standing next to it. Sixty yards away. They were wearing some kind of one-piece jumpsuits. The jumpsuits looked tight. Short in the arms. The men looked impatient.

Reacher crossed to the left-hand window.

Trees, bushes, a quiet street. With a cop on the sidewalk.

The cop was crouching in the unmistakable stance of an armed man holding himself back from a corner. Until ordered to advance. Which implied a degree of coordination. With whom?

Reacher crossed to the right-hand window.

A mirror image. Trees, flowers, a quiet street, and a cop holding, ready to roll his shoulder around the corner and take aim.

He went back to the center window with the view of the truck. The three guys were probably surrounded. But not by an over-whelming force. Solo guys on the left and right flanks implied no more than two more anyplace. Four people, max. A light force.

He crossed back to the left-hand window. The cop was inching toward the corner. No doubt his earpiece was counting him down. He crossed to the right-hand window. Same story. Still a mirror image. Synchronized. Seconds to go. It was a very bad plan.

On the right the cop rolled around the corner.

Reacher hustled across the hall.

Same thing on the left. A very bad plan.

He crossed back to the center window just in time to see the air-conditioning guys step into the library gardens and keep walking. Behind them the cops on foot sprinted back the way they had come, to retake the flanks. Way back two more cops were running up. Then fanning out. Staying on the street. Establishing a cordon. One cop per side of the square. Because common sense said the three guys would have to come out sometime.

But for the moment they kept on walking straight. Now they were very close to the library.

Reacher backed away to the top of the stairs and watched them enter the lobby. They were obvious phonies. Their jumpsuits were too tight. Borrowed for the occasion. Along with the van.

They were each about six two, and broad, with big hands and big feet, and wide necks. They might have been in their early forties. Not their first rodeo. Two had black hair and one was gray.

They stopped dead in the center of the lobby.

We don't want trouble here. Better to nip it in the bud.

Reacher came three steps down. The three guys looked up. At first surprise, and then wary recognition.

Reacher held up his right hand. Knuckles out.

All around them people melted away. Ancient instinct. Suddenly the lobby was empty. No one was there. Except the four interested parties. Three downstairs, and one halfway up.

They had left their guns in the truck, Reacher thought. Their overalls were tight. Any heavy metal objects would stand out in their pockets. Clear as day.

They took another step. Reacher saw inspiration in their eyes. He knew why. For them he was two birds with one stone. He was a civilian hostage, to guarantee their passage out of town, and he was also the prize their bosses had demanded in the first place.

But then they hesitated. Again Reacher knew why. They had left their guns in the truck. They had to execute an unarmed capture. The nearest guy would get kicked in the face. Missing teeth, a busted jaw. Who wanted to be the nearest guy? They waited.

Reacher helped them out. He came down one more step. Still higher, still bigger, but closer. Maybe close enough to swarm.

Which might have worked, if Reacher had stayed down a step. But he didn't. They charged, and he stepped back up to where he was before, and he kicked the nearest guy in the face. And then he twisted and hit the left-hand guy with his elbow, and twisted again and hit the right-hand guy with the same elbow coming back. Gravity and New Hampshire granite finished the job. All three guys went down backward in a slack tangle and rattled their bones and cracked their heads.

Then the lobby door opened and Brenda Amos walked in.

Amos was in plain clothes, obviously, being a detective, but more than that she was acting a part. She wasn't a cop, creeping in slow. She was a regular person, breezing in without a care in the world, coming in undercover. She was carrying a purse. In it would be her badge and her gun. But on the outside she was just a lady who'd come to borrow a book. She was bright and cheerful.

Then she wasn't. She stopped.

Reacher said, "I guess this seems like a coincidence."

She didn't speak. He knew why. She didn't know which feeling was uppermost. Was she mad or glad? Both, of course.

"I apologize," Reacher said. "I needed to find out about a bird. I'm going now."

"You need to. Next time they'll send someone better."

"I got what I need," he said. "I'm out of here."

"How?"

"In the Subaru. It's waiting for me."

Amos looked at the guys on the floor. Then she got on the radio and ordered all four of the street cops to head for the library.

Then to Reacher she said, "And you go get in the Subaru, right now this minute."

"And get out of town?"

"By the fastest possible route."

He stepped over an arm and a leg and went out the door he had come in through. He crossed the sidewalk to the Subaru. He tapped on the glass, politely, and then opened the door and got in.

Burke asked, "Did you find what you were looking for?"

"It was a rough-legged hawk," Reacher said.

"I'm glad you know now."

"Thank you."

"I'll drive you to the highway now, if you like."

"No," Reacher said. "I'm going back to Ryantown. One last look. You shouldn't come with me. You can let me out at the end of the road. You shouldn't be involved."

"Neither should you. They'll be waiting."

"I would hope," Reacher said again. "I more or less promised I would come. I like to be taken as a man of his word."

Burke didn't answer. He started the car and made a turn that Reacher thought was right for Ryantown. Reacher settled in. He felt paper in his back pants pocket. The note from the librarian. The ornithologist. His name and number. From the university.

He fished around and pulled it out.

He said, "Do you have a cell phone?"

"It's an old one," Burke said.

"May I borrow it?"

Burke handed it over. Reacher dialed the ornithologist's number. An assistant answered. The guy was in a meeting. Reacher left a message. Ryantown, the hawk, the rat poison theory, and how S. Reacher was his father. He said the number he was on might be good for another hour or two.

He clicked off and gave the phone back to Burke.

Who said, "Why would the government take the rat poison?"

Reacher said, "The military foresaw sooner or later it would require immense storage facilities, literally hundreds of square miles in hundreds of countries, full of food and bales of clothing, all the things that rodents like, so someone ordered ahead."

They drove on, past the first of the horse fields.

THE fourth arrival involved private air transportation. Which at a certain level was still as anonymous as hailing a cab. Ironically not at the top, with the glossy Gulfstreams and Learjets, but down on the bottom rung, with grass fields and short-hop prop-driven puddle jumpers, which flew below a certain altitude, literally, where there were no logs or reports or flight plans or manifests.

Three or four such rides could be chained together to cover long distances in total secrecy. Which was the strategy the fourth arrival had employed. He landed for the last time at a flying club near Plymouth, New Hampshire. Steven drove out to meet him, and the first thing he saw was the bag with his money.

It was a soft leather duffel. The guy had two more pieces of soft luggage, matching, and then two hard cases. Steven helped him unload. The guy was a rangy character, tall and solid, maybe sixty years old, with snow-white hair. He was in jeans and battered boots. From somewhere out west, Steven thought.

They packed the stuff in the Mercedes, and Steven drove south. The guy didn't talk. Thirty minutes later they turned in at the mouth of the track. Ten minutes later the guy was putting his bags in his room. Then he stepped back outside to cast an eye over a small group of other guys, who were gathering nearby.

There were three of them so far. First they all nodded, by way of introduction. Then they started talking. They were partly secretive and partly what-the-hell friendly. One said he had driven down in a Volvo wagon. He implied most of the year he lived in a house in the woods. He was a pale, wiry man, maybe seventy. He was from Maine, the fourth arrival thought.

The second guy didn't say where he was from, but he offered a long story about charter flights and phony licenses. He was about fifty. He was a solid guy, polite as a salesman. But excited, too.

The third guy was handsome and built like an athlete, loose and rangy. He said he drove up in a car that didn't exist, and did the last lap in a van. He pointed to it. Persian carpets.

The fourth man asked, "Have you seen them yet?"

The second guy said, "Their blind is up. But right now they're hiding in the bathroom."

"What are they like?"

The man from Maine said, "They're both twenty-five years old. They're both strong and healthy. They seem to have a close relationship. We looked at some tapes. She gets impatient with him from time to time. But he catches up in the end. They solve problems together."

The second guy said, "She's the brains, no question."

"Are they good-looking?"

"Plain," the good-looking guy said. "Not ugly. They both have muscles. He's a farmer, and she's a sawmill worker. They're Canadian. I have to say, I was very pleased when I saw them."

"Me, too," said the man from Maine.

"How many more players will there be?"

"Two more," the guy said. "For a total of six. If they make it."

The fourth man nodded. Rules were rules. If you got there late, you got there never. *Room Ten Is Occupied*. The clock was ticking. There was a cutoff point. No excuses. No exceptions.

He said, "Why is there no window in their bathroom?"

"Don't need one," the second man said. "There are cameras in there. Go over to the house and take a look."

THE Reverend Patrick G. Burke insisted on driving as far as his restraining order would permit, which was all the way to the fence, beyond which the road no longer ran, anyway. He said he would wait there. Reacher insisted he turn his car around. Nose out, not in. Ready for a fast getaway.

Reacher further insisted Burke keep his engine running. Burke agreed. Then Reacher insisted he feel free to take off without him. At any time at all, whatever his gut or his instincts told him.

"Don't second-guess it," Reacher said. "Don't overthink it."

Burke agreed.

Reacher got out of the car. He set out walking.

He made it all the way to the second fence. Undisturbed. All around was peace and quiet. Nothing was moving. Straight ahead the leaves were darker and the smell was ranker.

He climbed over the fence. Ryantown, New Hampshire.

He walked down Main Street, like the day before, passing the remains of the church, and the school. He picked his way onward, to the four-flats. To the right-hand foundation. To the remains of the kitchen, in the far back corner. He pictured his grandfather yelling and throwing punches and knocking people down. Probably drinking. He pictured his grandmother, hard and cold. Never smiling. Never saying a nice thing. Always looking cross.

He pictured his father, crawling around on the floor. Or not. Maybe sitting quietly in a corner, staring out the window.

Your dad joined the marines at seventeen, Carter Carrington had said. *Got to be a reason.*

He stood there for a long moment more, and then he said his goodbyes to the place. He retraced his steps out the door.

He walked back up Main Street. He got back to the fence. Ryantown's city limit. Ahead of him was the orchard. A straight shot, a hundred yards, to the Subaru. Which was still there, visible in the distance. Between it and him were two points of interest. The more distant was Burke himself. He was standing on the safe side of the fence, and he was jumping up and down, waving his arm.

The second point of interest was fifty yards closer. Halfway across the orchard was a line of five men.

Reacher climbed the fence. He walked between orderly lines of trees. Up ahead the five men stood still. The guy in the center was bigger than the others. Reacher was pretty sure he hadn't seen him before. Also he was pretty sure the older guy was standing on the big guy's right. The other three were the same as the night before. Minus the one that got popped.

He walked on.

The guy in the center of the line of five was tall and wide. He had a small head set on a thick bull neck. He looked young, and fit, and strong. He was a wrestler, Reacher thought.

Twenty yards to go.

The wrestler was staring dead ahead. He had tiny eyes set back deep in his tiny head. Not much expression. Altogether passive.

Fifteen yards to go.

The older guy was glancing left and right at his troops. He looked mostly excited. He was about to see some real good fun.

Ten yards out.

The older guy looked ready to shout orders. Which made him a legitimate target. Even though he was fifty-something and soft. He was a commander in the field. Rules of engagement.

Reacher figured the other three would run away. Loyalty had its limits.

Five yards to go.

Reacher believed in staying flexible, but also having a plan. On this occasion the plan was to never slow down, to arrive at full speed, and to head-butt the wrestler mid-stride. Which would check all the boxes. Surprise, force, general shock and awe.

But it turned out flexibility was better. Because of the wrestler. He dropped into some kind of combat stance. He looked like a fat kid pretending to be a grizzly bear. Stubby arms, like claws.

So Reacher modified the plan. On the fly. West Point would have been proud of him. Instead of head-butting the guy, he kicked him in the balls. A vicious upswing, a dead-on connection.

A football would have left the stadium.

It came out both good and bad.

The good part was it put him exactly where he should be. Ready for a left hook. Which he delivered to the old guy. *Bang*. Daddy went down. His command influence was terminated.

The bad part was the wrestler was wearing an athletic protector. A cup. Smart kid. Even so, he had taken a heavy blow. But he was still on his feet, stumping around, breathing hard. Which meant the other three guys didn't run away. Instead they crowded in a step, a blocking maneuver, to let their quarterback recover.

Reacher thought, Damn. The vagaries of chance. He wanted to back off a pace, to reset the geometry, but instead he hit the guy crowding nearest. A solid shot to the gut. Which doubled the guy over, puking and gasping, so Reacher hit him again, with an elbow chopped down hard against the back of the guy's head, which planted him face-first in the grass. Game over right there, so Reacher stepped left and lined up the next guy. No delay.

But the next guy was barged out of the way. By the wrestler coming through the line. He shoved another guy out of the way. Then he planted his feet. He crouched. Like the start of a bout. He glared.

Reacher thought, Okay, then.

In the distance Burke was still waving his arm.

The wrestler moved. His body turned like a single rigid unit, and he thumped his right foot down, just ahead of where it had been before. Then he turned the other way, just as rigid, and he thumped his left foot down. Like sumo. Now he was half a step closer. He was a big solid guy. That was for damn sure.

Reacher decided to stay clear of his arms. Wrestling was all about grabbing and grappling. The guy was probably good at it. Fortunately his arms were not long. Something could be done.

But what exactly? For once in his life Reacher wasn't sure. The head butt was a possibility, but risky. Body shots could be delivered, fast right-left-right combinations, but the guy was built with the kind of slabby construction that would feel like punching a bulletproof vest. With about as much effect.

The wrestler moved again. The same dramatic maneuver. Again like sumo. Now the guy was a whole step closer.

Too late Reacher realized what the guy was going to do. Which was to barge forward, leading with his stomach, again like the sumo on the television. Reacher wasn't moving at all, which meant the other guy had all the momentum, which meant Reacher was about to get hit hard. Like getting run over by a tractor tire.

He ducked and twisted and flung a Hail Mary right hook into the guy's side, which landed hard, and therefore took some momentum out of the equation, but the guy's barreling bulk was basically unstoppable, and Reacher was spun around and bounced away, and then he had to twist again to avoid a bear claw swinging out toward him. He staggered backward, flailing his arms.

The wrestler charged again. He was nimble, for a guy built like a walrus. Reacher launched a straight right to the guy's face, which was like punching the wall of a rubber room, and then he ducked away, low down under the bear claw's swing, and came back up and twisted and got a hard left hook into the guy's back, before bouncing away out of range.

Now the wrestler was breathing hard. The two surviving guys from the night before were creeping nearer. They formed up and fanned out, a step ahead of the wrestler. Flank support.

The wrestler dropped down into his combat stance. Reacher waited. The wrestler charged. Same as before. A low-down swarming thrust off bent and powerful legs, and a high-speed waddle, leading with the stomach, aiming to use it like a battering ram.

Reacher swayed left, but his foot caught in an undulation and the guy hit him a glancing blow with his charging shoulder, which felt like getting run over by a truck, twice, first with the original impact and then immediately again as he hit the ground.

The guy came straight back. Reacher rolled away, but not fast enough. The guy got in a kick that caught him high on the back and rolled him faster. A rare position for Reacher to be in. But not unknown. Rule one was get the hell up. So was rule two. He waited until he rolled facedown and then sprang upright.

The wrestler dropped down into his combat stance again. And Reacher saw what he should have seen before.

He waited.

The wrestler charged. A low-down swarming thrust off bent and powerful legs. Reacher stepped in and kicked him in the knee. The result was spectacular.

The kneecap shattered, and the guy went down like his strings were cut, and then the same rule one instinct bounced him upright again, immediately, howling, standing on one leg, waving the bear claws for balance. The two surviving guys stepped back a pace.

From that point on Reacher opted for brutal efficiency. The wrestler threw a despairing bear claw at him, and Reacher caught it and jerked him off balance, and he went down again, whereupon Reacher kicked him in the head until he went still.

Reacher stood up straight, and breathed out, and in, and out.

The two surviving guys stepped back another pace. They raised their hands, palms out. Surrendering.

Reacher asked them, "Where did you find this tub of lard?"

The kid on the right said, "He came up this morning."

"From where?"

"Boston. He lives there now, but he grew up here. We knew him in high school."

"Get lost," Reacher said.

They ran south, at a sprint. Reacher watched them go. Then he walked on through the orchard. Burke was waiting at the fence. He held up the hand he had been waving. In it was his phone.

"It kept trying to ring," he said. "But there's really no service here. So I walked to where I got half a bar. It was the ornithologist. He was returning your call. He said it was his only chance to talk, because he's tied up the rest of the day. So I ran back here and tried to attract your attention. He left a message with me."

Reacher nodded.

He said, "First I need to call Amos at the Laconia PD."

Chapter 11

THE FIFTH ARRIVAL WAS as unobtrusive as the first and the third. In the back parlor, Mark and Steven and Robert heard the bell ring, from the wire across the blacktop. They watched the screens.

In five minutes, they saw a pickup truck come out of the trees. It was a Ford F-150. Single cab, long bed. Dirty white paint.

Robert tightened the shot some more, to check the license plate. It said Illinois, which they all knew was bull. The guy was from New York City. His office ISP was unbreakable, but his home Wi-Fi was wide open. He ran a fund on Wall Street.

They watched him drive into the motel lot. They saw him stop outside the office. They saw Peter come out to greet him. Peter gave him a key and pointed. Room 11.

Robert tapped keyboards and arranged the screens so they could see just about everything at once. They saw the Wall Street guy park his truck beyond the dead Honda. They saw him detour for a look in room 10's window. Nothing doing. He walked back. He looked like Wall Street. Decent haircut, fit from the gym, tan from a lamp. His luggage was two hard cases and a nylon duffel.

Plus, last of all, from the passenger seat, a plastic bag from a New York deli, stuffed with either potatoes or rolls of money.

Meanwhile the first four arrivals were gathering, getting ready to talk. Male bonding. Robert turned up the sound. There were hidden microphones all up and down the length of the motel. Consumer feedback was important, Mark said.

They listened. The voices were tinny. There were guarded greetings, and the same war stories from the road, about getting there undetected, and the same description of Patty and Shorty themselves, in terms of health and strength and general appeal.

Then the consumer feedback turned a little negative. A small schism had opened up. Arrivals number one, two, and three had actually seen Patty and Shorty through their window. After their blind went up. Arrivals number four and five had not. By then Patty and Shorty were hiding in their bathroom. If everyone was starting out equal, level playing field, and so on and so forth, then raise the damn blind like a ceremony. With everyone lined up to witness it.

"They're right," Robert said. "We should have left the blind down until everyone got here."

"Relax," Mark said. "What's done is done."

"Never too late to fix a mistake," said Robert.

"How?"

"You get on the mike with Patty and Shorty and say we decided to close their blind again. And we do, right away. They'll hear it. They'll come out of the bathroom. Meanwhile we apologize to arrivals four and five, and we tell them we'll have a proper ceremony later. Maybe as the sky goes dark. We could suddenly raise the blind and light up the room both at the same time. I bet we would catch them right there on the bed."

Mark was quiet a long moment. Then he glanced at Steven.

Who said, "I guess."

Mark nodded. "Okay."

Robert clicked a switch labeled ROOM TEN, WINDOW BLIND, DOWN.

His voice came out of the ceiling. In the bathroom it was just as loud as it had been in the main room. He said, "Guys, the blind is down again now. I'm sure you'll be more comfortable that way."

Patty said, "What do you want with us?"

"We'll discuss that before the end of the day." Then there was a small electronic pop and the ceiling went quiet again.

Shorty got up stiffly from his spot on the floor and opened the bathroom door a crack. There was no bar of daylight. Just gloom.

"I'm going through," he said. "It's uncomfortable in here."

"They're going to raise it again."

"When?"

"Probably when we least expect it. They're messing with us."

Shorty stood at the door for a moment. Then he went through. He was sore from sitting with his butt on cold tile. He lay down on the bed and stared up through the dark at the ceiling. Somewhere there was a camera. It was probably in the smoke alarm.

He stared at it. He imagined smashing it with a hammer.

He got up off the bed again and went back in the bathroom. He closed the door. He set the faucet running in the sink. Patty watched him from her spot on the floor. He bent down low, close to her ear, and he spoke in a whisper. He said, "I was thinking, suppose I had a hammer, what would I do?"

"What?"

"I would come in here. This is the back of the building. Maybe no one is watching the back. The wall is nothing but a skin of tile, then half an inch of wallboard, then a six-inch void between the studs, maybe packed with insulation, and then cedar siding nailed on sixteen-inch centers."

"So?"

"If I had a hammer, I would bust my way through."

"Then it's a shame you don't have a hammer."

"I figure we could use the suitcase on the tile. Like a battering ram. We could swing it, with the new rope handle. I bet the tile would come off. Then I could kick the rest of the way through."

"You can't kick through cedar siding."

"All I need is to pop it off the studs from the inside."

"How wide of a gap would there be?" said Patty.

"About fourteen inches. We could step through sideways."

"With the suitcase?"

"Something we got to accept," Shorty said. "We need to be realistic. The suitcase stays here until we capture a vehicle."

Patty whispered, "Capture a what?"

"Some of these guys peering in the window must have driven here. Which means there must be cars in the lot now. Or maybe they all got picked up in a Mercedes SUV. In which case it's still out there. If we can't find it, no matter, because there are plenty more in the barn. I bet all the keys are hanging on a little board."

"So first we destroy their property, and then we steal their car."

"You bet your ass we do."

"How long would it take to kick through a wall?"

Shorty said, "One minute, maybe."

Patty said, "That's pretty good."

"If the tile comes off all in a sheet."

"What if it doesn't?"

"We would have to bust off every piece separately. Just hope it comes off all in a sheet."

She said, "Are we really going to do this?"

"I vote yes."

"When?"

"I say right now. We could run straight for a quad bike."

Patty was quiet another long moment.

"One step at a time," she said. "First we'll test the suitcase on the tile. We'll see if it comes off in a sheet. If it does, then we can go ahead and make a final decision."

Shorty opened the bathroom door and went to get the suitcase. He strolled over, and hefted it up, and strolled back. He put it down and closed the door.

They picked their spot. To the left of the sink. A blank patch of wall. No outlets. No pipes inside, either. Perfect.

They pulled the suitcase into position. They lifted it six inches and set it swinging, gently, back and forth, back and forth.

"Ready?" Shorty said. "On three."

They swung once, and twice, and on three they stepped in toward the wall and accelerated the weight as hard as they could.

The case smacked against the tile.

Half a dozen tiles shattered into pieces. Some of the broken bits rained down on the floor. Others stayed up on the wall, still solidly glued to separate coin-sized daubs of adhesive. But the wallboard itself hadn't flexed at all.

They put the suitcase down. Shorty pressed his thumbnail in the space between two surviving fragments. Then he pressed harder, with his fist. The wallboard didn't yield. It felt solid.

"Weird," he said.

"Should we try again?" Patty asked.

"I guess," he said. "Real hard this time."

They backed off as far as the width of the room would allow, and on three they smashed the case into the wall.

Same result. A couple more orphan fragments fell off the wall. Nothing more. It was like hitting concrete.

They dragged the case out of the way. Shorty tapped on the wall, experimentally, here and there, in different places. The sound it made was strange. Not exactly solid, not exactly hollow. Somewhere in between. He stepped back and kicked out hard. The whole wall seemed to bounce and tremble as a single unit.

"Weird," he said again.

He picked up a jagged shard of tile and used it to scrape at the skim coat. He made a long furrow, and deepened it, working back and forth, stabbing and scraping. Then he made another furrow, and another, in a wide triangle. Then he stepped back and kicked out again, hard, aiming carefully. The scored-around triangle of skim coat flaked off and fell to the floor. Under it was revealed the papery surface of brand-new wallboard. He attacked it with the shard of tile, hacking and gouging. Then he stepped back and kicked in a frenzy of frustration. He kicked the wallboard to fragments and powder. He pulverized it. He reduced it to nothing.

But he didn't kick his way through it. He couldn't. It was backed by some kind of thick steel mesh. Which came into view as the wallboard was destroyed. It was a net, with steel filaments as thick as his finger running up and down and side to side.

He used the shard of tile to cut more wallboard away. He found a place where a green ground wire was soldered to the back of the mesh. Like an electrical connection. A yard away he found another. Then he found a place where the mesh was welded to a prison bar.

There was no doubt about it. He knew from the size, and the shape, and the spacing. There were floor-to-ceiling prison bars built inside the wall. The mesh was spot-welded to it, here and there, like a curtain. He knew why it was there. It made the room a Faraday cage. Room 10 was an electronic black hole. Any radio signal trying to get in would splinter every which way through the mesh, and then drain away to ground, through the many soldered wires. Same thing for a signal trying to get out. Cell phone, satellite phone, pager, police radio, whatever, it wasn't going to happen.

A signal couldn't get out because of the mesh.

A person couldn't get out because of the bars.

Patty looked over his shoulder and said, "What is that stuff?"

Shorty didn't answer.

BURKE and Reacher drove back south toward Laconia, far enough to get bars on Burke's old phone. They pulled off on the shoulder. Reacher took out Amos's business card and dialed her number. It dumped to voice mail. He tried again, this time with her cell number. It rang five times, and then it was answered.

Her voice said, "Interesting. You're calling on the Reverend Burke's phone. You're still with him. You're still in the vicinity."

"How did you know this is the Reverend Burke's phone?"

"I saw his license plate this morning. I checked with county. Now I know all about him. He's a troublemaker."

"He's been very nice to me."

"How can I help you?"

"Something made me think about guys getting drafted in from Boston. Did anyone show up yet?"

Amos didn't answer.

Reacher said, "What?"

"Chief Shaw is talking to the Boston PD again. They're calling in some favors. The word on the street is five guys are working out of town today. It's a reasonable assumption they've been sent our way. In which case we know all about the first four. They were the guy in the Chrysler and the three in the library. It's the fifth guy we need to worry about. He left Boston much later than the others. We assume he's their cleanup hitter."

"Has he arrived?"

"I don't know. We watch what we can, but we're sure to miss something."

"When did he leave Boston?"

"Long enough ago to be here by now."

"With my description," Reacher said.

"That doesn't matter anymore," Amos said. "Does it?"

Then she paused.

Then she said, "Don't you dare tell me you're coming back to town. Because you ain't, Major. You're staying away."

"Relax, soldier," Reacher said. "Stand easy. I'm staying away."

"Then don't worry about your description."

"I was wondering exactly what it said. I was thinking back to what the kid can have seen. It was the middle of the night, and most of the time he was mad as hell and then he was unconscious. Therefore his grasp of detail is not likely to have been impressive. So what would a kid in his position say afterward? Just the basics, surely. A big guy, with messy fair hair."

"Okay."

"Except at one point I spoke to the cocktail waitress. She asked if I was a cop. I said I was once upon a time, in the army. The kid might have remembered. So actually I think he must have said a big guy, messy fair hair, used to be in the army. That's what the guys in the library saw. A simple three-point checklist."

Amos said, "Why does any of this matter?"

"I think the description fits Carter Carrington, too. He's bigger than the average guy. His hair is all over the place. I thought he was army. Turns out he wasn't, but I would have sworn."

Amos said, "You think we should warn him?"

"I think you should put a car outside his house."

"Seriously? Protecting him would be a huge diversion of resources."

"I would hate to see anything happen to him. He's an innocent bystander. He's also the guy who goes to bat for you."

"I think he would refuse on principle. Precisely because of that. He'll say he can't accept special treatment. He won't do it."

"Then tell him to get out of town."

"I can't just tell him. Doesn't work that way."

"Tell him there's something wrong with the story."

"What does that mean?"

Reacher paused a moment to let a truck roar past on the road. A huge tow truck. It was bright red and spotlessly clean. He realized he had seen it before. It growled away into the distance.

Reacher put the phone back to his ear.

He said, "Carrington will know what I mean. Tell him he could take a short vacation. Somewhere romantic."

"He has a job," Amos said. "He might be busy."

"Tell him I'm happy to listen to him about census methodology. He should listen to me about staying-alive methodology."

Amos said, "I was feeling good until you laid this on me. We have a bad guy in town, okay, but the bad guy has no target. Now you tell me he does have a target, sort of."

"Call me if you need me," Reacher said. "I would be happy to come back to town and lend a hand."

"Do not come back to town," Amos said.

"Never?"

"Not soon," she said.

Reacher clicked off the call.

LUNCH hour was long gone, and Burke said he was hungry. He said he wanted to go get something to eat. Reacher offered to pay, as a way of saying thank you for all the driving around. So they headed east toward a lake, where Burke knew a bait shop that had sandwiches, at the head of a trail that led to the water. It was a decent drive, and at the end of it the destination was as advertised. It was a shack with a deli counter, with a choice of chicken salad or tuna on white bread plus a bag of potato chips, plus a bottle of cold water, all for three dollars.

Burke got tuna, and Reacher got chicken. They ate outside, at a government-brown picnic table near the head of the trail.

"Now give me the message," Reacher said. "From the ornithologist."

Burke said, "Obviously it's you he wants to talk to. He seems excited. He said he was completely unaware that Stan had kids."

"Who is he, exactly? Did he tell you?"

"You know who he is. He's a professor at the university."

"I mean how is he related?"

Burke took a drink of water. "The short version is you count back four generations on your father's side. Your great-great-grandfather was one of seven brothers. Who had children, grandchildren, great-grandchildren, and great-great-grandchildren. Apparently you and the professor are both in there somewhere."

"Plus about ten thousand other people."

"He wants to talk to you about Stan. He wants to meet face-to-face. He has an idea he wants to discuss. He was very insistent."

"Did you like him?"

"I felt pressured by him. In the end, I took the liberty of telling him in my estimation you would likely move on very soon, in which case it might prove very difficult to arrange a face-to-face meeting, simply because of scheduling issues alone."

"But?"

"He's coming tomorrow."

"Coming where?"

"I was unable to suggest an exact rendezvous. In the end, he offered a suggestion. I'm afraid I took the liberty of accepting on your behalf. I felt rushed. He put me on the spot."

"What was his suggestion?"

"Ryantown. He knows where it is. He was there for research."

"What time tomorrow?"

"He said he'll be there at eight o'clock in the morning."

"Did you like him?" Reacher asked again.

"Does it matter?"

"I'd like to hear your opinion. You got a sense of the guy."

Burke was quiet a long moment.

Then he said, "If you meet with him, he'll tell you something upsetting. I felt not everything he said made sense. At first I wasn't sure he was getting it straight."

"What wasn't straight?"

"He kept referring to Stan in the present tense. He was saying, Stan is this, Stan is that. At first I assumed that ancestry buffs talk that way. In the end, I asked him why he was talking that way."

"What did he say?"

"He thinks Stan is still alive."

Reacher shook his head. "That's crazy. He died thirty years ago. He was my father. I was at his funeral. He was buried in Arlington Cemetery. My mother wanted that for him, because he fought in Korea and Vietnam. She thought he deserved it."

Burke said nothing.

Reacher said, "What?"

"Coincidence, I'm sure," Burke said. "The professor said the family story has it that Stan Reacher was working away from home for a very long time, completely out of touch, but then finally he retired, and he came back to live in New Hampshire."

"When?"

"Thirty years ago," Burke said.

"That's crazy," Reacher said again. "I was at the funeral. The guy is wrong. I should call him back."

"You can't. He's tied up the rest of the day."

"Where is this old guy who came back to New Hampshire supposed to be living now?"

"With the granddaughter of a relative."

"Where exactly?"

"You can hear it from the horse's mouth first thing tomorrow."

"I'm trying to get to San Diego. I need to get going."

"Are you upset about what he said?"

"Not upset at all. Just not sure what to do. I don't want to waste time talking to an idiot."

Burke was quiet a moment.

"My only worry was emotional strain," he said. "In its absence, I suppose you could give the professor the benefit of the doubt. It might be an innocent error. You might still enjoy talking to him."

"I'd need a motel," Reacher said. "I can't go back to Laconia."

"There's a place north of Ryantown. About twenty miles. I told you about it. Supposed to be good."

"Deep in the woods."

"That's the one."

"If I gave you fifty bucks for gas, would you drive me there?"

"Fifty bucks is too much. I would take twenty."

"Deal," Reacher said.

They climbed out of the picnic table and walked to the Subaru.

KAREL was the sixth and final arrival. He worked the morning as normal, starting early, out at the highway. After he had clocked off and was heading north, he saw an old Subaru stalled on the shoulder. But it turned out to be nothing. Two guys in it, admiring the view, one of them talking on the phone.

Twenty miles later he turned left, into the narrow opening. Into the mouth of the track. The wire was up ahead. The warning bell. He wanted all three axles to ring it separately. That was the code. *Bing, bing-bing.* Hence the low speed.

He rolled slowly over the wire. And stopped. He shut down the engine. He opened his door against the press of the foliage and dropped his bags ahead of him. Then he squeezed out sideways and locked the door from below. His truck was jammed in.

It was a perfect roadblock.

Four minutes later Steven showed up in his black SUV. The Mercedes. Karel loaded his bags. Steven backed up to a hole in the trees and turned the car around. They drove on.

Peter was in the office. Karel got room 2. He put his bags inside. He said hi to the other guys. They were gathering, swapping stories. Karel made out like he had never been there before.

Then Peter stuck his head out the office door and called down the row to say everyone was invited to walk over to the house, for an introductory briefing, and a look at the video highlights from the last three days. So they all wandered over, just strolling, feeling good. Starting to believe. The party was complete. All six of them were present. It was real. It was happening.

Chapter 12

Burke and Reacher drove west toward Ryantown. Reacher watched the bars on Burke's old phone. When they dropped from three to two, he asked Burke to pull over on the shoulder so he could call Amos again. She answered on the third ring.

She said, "Where are you now?"

"Don't worry," Reacher said. "I'm still out of town."

"We can't find Carrington."

"Where have you looked?"

"His home, his office, the lunch places he goes."

"Does he have a cell phone?"

"He's not answering."

"Try the city records department. Ask for Elizabeth Castle. She's his new girlfriend. Maybe he's hanging out over there."

He heard her call across the room, Elizabeth Castle, city records.

He asked, "Any sign of the guy from Boston?"

She said, "Nothing yet."

"Want me to come back to help?"

"No," she said.

He heard someone shouting a message.

Amos said, "Elizabeth Castle is not at work, either."

"I need to come back to town."

"No," she said again.

"Last chance," he said. "I'm about to head north to a motel. I'm going to lose cell service."

"Do not come back to town."

"Okay. But in exchange I need you to do something for me. I need you to look at ancient history on your computer again. Check the files after that thing with my father, seventy-five years ago. The next twenty-four months, until September 1945."

"What happened then?"

"He joined the marines."

"What would I be looking for?"

"Something unsolved. I'll call you back as soon as I can."

THEY passed the wandering turn that led away through the orchards to Ryantown. Up ahead were miles of fields, and then more woods, far in the distance. Burke said he thought the motel entrance was about five miles in. On the left side. He remembered the signs, one each way. They said MOTEL in plastic letters painted gold. They were mounted on old posts.

Five minutes later they drove into the trees. The air felt cooler. The trees grew thicker. Like a tunnel. Burke said he was pretty sure the turn was coming up. But they saw no signs. Just a pair of twisted old posts and the mouth of a track.

"I'm pretty sure this was it," Burke said.

Reacher hitched up and pulled his map from his pocket. The one he had bought at the old edge-of-town gas station. He unfolded it and found the back road. He showed Burke. He said, "This is the only turn for miles around."

Burke said, "Maybe someone stole their signs."

"Or they went out of business."

"I doubt it. They were very committed. They had a business plan. I heard they got in a fight about a permit."

"Who did?"

"The people developing the property. They said the county was unreasonably slow with the permit. The county said the developer had started work without permission. They got in a fight."

"When was this?"

"About a year and a half ago."

A patrol car responded to the county offices because a customer was causing a disturbance. He claimed a building permit was slow coming through. He claimed he was renovating a motel somewhere out of town. He gave his name as Mark Reacher.

Reacher said, "I really need to go take a look at this place."

Burke turned in, over broken blacktop that was missing whole patches. Branches dipped in close, some of them broken, still fresh, as if a large vehicle had brushed by not long ago.

They found the large vehicle thirty yards later. It was stopped up ahead, blocking the track completely.

It was a tow truck. Huge. Red paint, gold stripes.

"We just saw this," Reacher said. "I also saw it yesterday."

A yard behind its rear tires was a wire, laid across the road. It was fat and rubbery, the kind of thing they had at gas stations.

Burke stopped the Subaru six feet before the wire. Reacher opened his door. He got out and walked forward. He stepped over the wire. Burke followed him. Reacher made sure Burke stepped over the wire, too. He didn't like wires on roads. Nothing good ever came of them. Best case surveillance, worst case explosions.

The truck had a short sturdy crane and a giant tow hook. Reacher squeezed down the driver's side, leading with his left shoulder, keeping his left elbow high, keeping the twigs away from his face. He slid past the owner's name, which was Karel, proudly painted in gold letters. He stepped up on the bottom rung of the ladder and tried the driver's door. It was locked. He stepped down again. Ahead of him the track ran on through the woods. There were tire tracks, some of them ancient, some of them recent. Twenty yards farther on there was a hole in the trees. It had brand-new tire tracks. Two tight V shapes. Like a car had backed in to turn around. Which made some kind of sense. Because the tow truck driver didn't seem to be around anymore.

Reacher said, "I'm going to go take a look up there."

"How?" Burke said.

"I'm going to walk."

"Your map showed this track is more than two miles long."

"I need a place to sleep. Also I'm curious. I think the guy who got in the fight about the permit was a kid named Reacher. It was in the police computer. A squad car had to go calm things down."

"Are you related?"

"I don't know."

"Do you want company? I guess now I'm curious, too."

They set out together. Two miles would have taken Reacher

thirty minutes, but they took Burke forty-five. They came out of the trees together, and they saw the track run on ahead, through a couple of grassy acres, to a dirt parking lot in front of a motel. It had an office at the left-hand end, and a station wagon and a panel van and a compact car and a pickup truck, all parked at intervals outside the rooms. They set out walking toward it.

THEY were instantly detected. Steven was watching the right screen, as part of a disciplined rotation through the points of the compass. He saw two men step out of the shadows.

He said, "Mark, look at this."

Mark said, "Who the hell are they?"

Robert zoomed the camera all the way. Two guys were walking toward the lens. Head-on. One guy was small and old. Denim jacket, gray hair. The other guy was huge. As wide as a door. Hair sticking up all over. A face like the side of a house.

Peter buzzed from the office. His voice came out of the intercom speaker. He said, "They walked two miles past the roadblock."

Mark said, "Damn."

Then he said, "Keep everyone inside the house. Show them another video. Keep the doors closed. Make sure no one leaves."

BURKE and Reacher stepped off the last of the blacktop onto the dirt of the motel lot. Up close the panel van parked second in line from the motel office turned out to be dark blue. Enhanced by curls of gold writing. Persian carpets. Expert cleaning. A Boston address. A Massachusetts license plate.

The biggest déjà vu in history.

Except not exactly, because he hadn't actually seen the van before. He had only heard about it on the radio. It had been caught by the cameras, coming off the highway, too early for a residential customer. Whereas he had actually seen the tow truck before. Two separate times. That really was déjà vu all over again. He slowed half a step, thinking. Burke walked on ahead.

Beyond him Reacher saw that the station wagon parked first in line was a Volvo, with a Vermont plate. The small compact was blue, with a plate he didn't know. The pickup truck was dirty white. It had an Illinois plate. It was last in line. It was outside of what would be room 11. The Volvo was outside of 3, and the carpet van outside of 7. The small blue import was outside of 10. Ten's window blind was down.

They walked on toward the office, which had a red neon sign. They went in. There was a guy behind the counter. In his late twenties, maybe, with dark hair and pale skin. He had an air of intelligence. He was educated. He was healthy and fit.

Reacher said, "I need a room for the night."

The guy said, "I'm sorry, but the motel is closed. I took the signs down at the entrance. I hoped I would save people a trip."

"There are plenty of vehicles here."

"Work people. Plumbers and electricians. I'm way behind with the maintenance."

"You got Persian carpets?"

"They're organic jute, actually. I'm trying to be sustainable."

Reacher asked, "What's your name?"

"Tony."

"Tony what?"

"Kelly."

"Mine is Reacher."

The guy looked blank for a second, but then he said, "I bought this place from a family called Reacher. Are you related?"

"I don't know," Reacher said. "When did you buy it?"

"Nearly a year ago."

"Why did they sell?"

"A grandson took it on, but I think he found it wasn't for him. He got in trouble with permits, I think. So I bought him out. I'm really sorry about the wasted trip," the guy said.

Then he stopped.

"Wait. How did you get here? You can't have driven. I just realized. The wrecker is stuck."

"We walked," Reacher said.

"I am so sorry. The last guest I had before I closed abandoned a broken-down car. Apparently it wouldn't start, so he called a cab and disappeared. Naturally I wanted the car towed, and today was supposed to be the day, but it turned out the tow truck is so huge it got jammed in the trees."

Then he stopped again, struck by another new thought.

"Let me drive you back. At least that far. I assume your car is parked behind the truck. It's the least I can do."

Reacher said, "What was wrong with the abandoned car?"

"I don't know," the guy said. "It's pretty old."

"What's the plate on it?"

"Canadian," the guy said.

"Okay," Reacher said. "You can drive us back."

"Thank you," Burke said.

The guy ushered them out of the office, and locked the door behind them, and asked them to wait in the lot. Then he jogged away, toward a barn, maybe thirty yards distant. It was a blunt square building, with nine quad bikes parked outside.

A minute later the guy drove out of the barn in a black Mercedes SUV. It stopped beside them. Burke climbed in the front, and Reacher got in the back. The guy sped through the meadow.

He said, "You should head east toward the lake country. You'll find plenty of options there, I'm sure."

They reentered the woods through the same natural arch they had come out of. The guy drove fast. The two miles took the Mercedes three minutes. The guy stopped nose to nose with the tow truck. The truck was in firm contact with the surrounding vegetation, certainly. But it wasn't stuck. The guy was worried about his paint. Understandable. It must have cost a buck or two.

The guy apologized again for their wasted trip, and Burke said thank you, and got out, and Reacher followed him. Burke squeezed down the side of the truck, and Reacher went after him, elbow high, but then he turned around to watch. The Mercedes backed up smartly, and the guy reversed into and drove out of the natural hole in the trees, neatly, crisply, and fast. As if he had done it before. Which he had. He had picked up the truck driver.

Reacher stood for a second more, and then blundered his way back to where Burke was waiting next to the Subaru. They got in the car, and Burke backed up to where the track met the road.

"East to the lakes?" he said.

"No," Reacher said. "South until your cell phone works. I want to call Amos. I want an update on Carrington."

"You asked a lot of questions at the motel. Like you were suspicious."

"I'm always suspicious."

"Were you happy with the answers?"

"The front part of my brain thought the answers were fine. They were all plausible. The back part of my brain didn't like that place. It's a sense. Like smell."

"But you can't pin it down."

"No."

They drove south. Reacher watched the phone. Still no service.

AFTERWARD Peter nearly collapsed from tension. He let the two men out, and then he hustled home as fast as he dared. He drove straight to the house. He ran through to the parlor. The others crowded around him and burst out in fist-pumping triumph.

Peter said, "Did the customers see anything?"

"Nothing at all," Mark said.

"When are we going to explain the situation to Patty and Shorty?"

"Do you have a preference?"

"I think we should do it now. The timing would be right. It would give them enough hours to make some choices, and then start doubting them. Their emotional state will be important."

"I vote yes," Steven said.

"Me, too," Robert said.

"Me three," Mark said. "One for all and all for one. We'll do it now. We should let Peter do it himself. As a reward."

Peter said, "First let me get my breath back."

PATTY and Shorty were sitting on the bed. The blind was still down. They had skipped lunch. They couldn't face it. Now they were hungry. But eating would be an act of will. The last two meals from the carton. The last two bottles of water.

The TV turned on. All by itself.

The same as before. The same bright blue picture, with the

same line of code, like the screen you weren't supposed to see.

It was replaced by a man's face. Peter.

The weasel who had screwed with their car.

He said, "Guys, you've been asking what's going to happen, and we think now is the time to bring you up to speed. Later this evening your door will unlock. You will be free to walk away. But I mean that literally. No vehicles of any kind will be available. Except of course your own, but your car doesn't work. All the other vehicles here are too new to hot-wire. You'll be walking. Are you with me so far?"

"Yes," Patty said.

Shorty said, "I guess."

"All around this piece of forest is what looks like a firebreak. It's a hoop about sixty feet across, with no trees growing. It runs all the way around."

"So what?" Shorty said.

"You walk all the way there, through the woods, and you step out in that gap, in any location, and you've won the game."

"What game?"

"Think of it like a game of tag. You have to make it all the way to the break without getting tagged. Simple as that. Walking, running, creeping along, whatever works for you."

"Tagged how?" Patty said. "By who?"

The TV turned off. All by itself.

Because it was their natures, they thought on it for a while. Engage brain. Think before you speak. Begin at the beginning.

Patty whispered, "Obviously they're tricking us somehow. It must be impossible to get to the break in the trees."

"It can't be impossible."

"It must be."

"Against how many people?"

"We've seen three. There are twelve rooms, less this one. Nine quad bikes. Pick a number."

"You think they'll use the quad bikes?"

"I'm sure they will."

"Call it nine people, then. They can't cover it all. It's huge."

"I saw on the map," Patty said. "It's about five miles across, and about seven from top to bottom. This place is about half a mile off-center, toward the east. It's about equal north and south."

"Then it might be possible. There would be one of them every forty degrees of the circle. They could be a hundred yards apart. If we got in the space behind them, we'd be home free."

"It can't be possible," Patty said. "Because then what? We make it to a road, we get a ride, we call the cops and the FBI, because of the kidnapping and the false imprisonment, and they pay a visit, and they see the prison bars and the locks and the cameras and the microphones. Peter and his buddies can't afford for us to get out of here. They must be totally confident we won't."

Shorty didn't answer. They sat side by side in the gloom.

Then all at once the room lit up bright, and the motor whirred and the blind rolled up in the window. Outside they saw a line of six men. An inch from the glass. Staring in. Karel was one of them. The weasel with the tow truck.

The six of them stared. Openly, frankly, no inhibition at all. They were judging, and evaluating, and assessing. There were nods of approval. There were gleams in eyes, of enthusiasm.

Then on some unspoken cue they raised their hands and clapped, long and loud, a standing ovation, as if they were a respectful audience saluting star performers.

But somehow in advance.

Ten minutes later Reacher dialed Amos again. She answered. She sounded out of breath.

He said, "What's up?"

"We still can't find Carrington."

"Did you find Elizabeth Castle?"

"Her, neither."

"I should come back to town," Reacher said.

"No," she said. "We think Carrington is still in the area. Allegedly he was seen entering the county offices. But no one else remembers him, and he isn't there now."

"Was he alone, or with Elizabeth Castle?"

"It was hard to say who was with who. It was busy."

"Did you get a minute for ancient history?"

She paused. "It was longer than a minute," she said.

"What did you find?"

"I need advice before I tell you. From Carrington, ironically."

"Why?"

"You asked for unsolved cases. I found one. It has no statute of limitations."

"You found an unsolved homicide?"

"Therefore technically it's still an open case."

"When was it?"

"Within the dates you specified."

"Who was the victim?"

"You know who the victim was."

"The kid?" Reacher said.

"Correct," Amos said. "Last seen facedown on the sidewalk, late one September evening in 1943. Then later he shows up again, now twenty-two years old, just as much of an ass as he was before, and he gets killed. The two files were never connected. I guess there was a lot going on back then. They didn't have computers. But today's rules say the first file makes a material difference to the second file. We can't pretend we haven't seen it. Therefore we're obliged to reopen the homicide as a cold case."

"How did the kid get killed?"

"He was beaten to death with a pair of brass knuckles."

Reacher said, "Why wasn't it solved?"

"There were no witnesses. The victim was an ass. No one cared. Their only suspect had disappeared without a trace. It was a time of great chaos. It was right after V-J Day."

"August 1945," Reacher said. "Did the cops have a name for the suspect?"

"Only a kind of nickname. The bird-watcher."

"I see."

"Wait," she said.

He heard the rustle of paper. A message.

He heard a step, and a door, and on the phone she said, "I just got an alert from the license plate computer." She went quiet.

"Not what I thought it was," she said. "No one left town. Not yet. Carrington is still here."

"I need you to do something for me," Reacher said. "A professor at the university told me that thirty years ago an old man named Reacher came home to New Hampshire after many years on foreign shores. As far as I know, he has been domiciled here ever since and lives with the granddaughter of a relative. I need you to check around the county to see if you can find him."

"What is the old man's first name?"

"Stan."

"That's your father. You told me he was deceased."

"I know. I was at the funeral."

"The professor is confused."

"Probably."

"What else could he be?"

"The funeral was thirty years ago. Which was also when the guy showed up in New Hampshire after a lifetime away. It was a closed casket. Maybe it was full of rocks. The Marine Corps and the CIA worked together from time to time. I'm sure all kinds of secret squirrelly stuff was going on."

"That's crazy. It's like a Hollywood movie."

"Based on a true story."

"One in a million."

"Agreed," Reacher said. "One in a million. But that's my point. The odds are better than zero. Which is why I want you to check. You're about to reopen a cold case with no statute of limitations, with a one-in-a-million possibility your main suspect is still alive, living in your jurisdiction, and is related to me. I figured I should clarify things beforehand. In case I need to call him. Hey, Pops, get a lawyer, you're about to be arrested. That kind of thing."

"That's crazy," Amos said again.

"The odds are better than zero," Reacher said again.

"Wait," she said again. "This is a weird coincidence. Our new software counts who enters and who leaves, using license plate recognition technology. But apparently it's running a couple layers underneath. It's looking for outstanding warrants."

"And?"

"The van we saw this morning was illegal. The Persian carpet cleaners. It should have been showing dealer plates."

"Why?"

"Because its current owner is a dealer. The carpet cleaner went out of business. The van was repossessed."

Chapter 13

PATTY AND SHORTY SAT side by side on the bed, facing away from the window. They didn't care if the blind was up or down. They whispered to each other, short and quiet, using hand signals, discussing things as privately as they could. They knew more, but understood less. Clearly the six men who had looked in the window were the opposition team. Their task was to win a game of tag. In thirty square miles of forest. Presumably in the dark.

Thirty square miles. Six men. In the dark. Yet they were confident of success. They couldn't afford to fail. The quad bikes would help. Much faster than running. But still. Thirty square miles was ten thousand football fields. All empty, except a random six, and each of those with just one man. In the dark.

They didn't get it.

Shorty whispered, "Maybe they have night-vision goggles."

Which sparked a cascade of gloomy thoughts and many questions. Including the biggest question of all. What kind of tag would it be? Six men. Quad bikes and night vision. Not good.

Which led to the biggest decision of all. Stick together or split up? They could go different directions. It would double their chances. More than. If one of them got caught, the other would benefit from the diversion. One of them might get away.

REACHER SAT IN THE SUBARU on the wide gravel shoulder. The back part of his brain was worried about the organic jute carpets. The guy showed up in an SUV with a V8 motor. And he drove it pretty fast. Not like a guy who would use organic jute. That guy would drive a hybrid car. Or electric.

If the organic jute wasn't true, then nothing was true. The tow truck wasn't there for an abandoned car. Not the way the story was told. Amos said taxis wouldn't drive out that far. The abandoned car was invented. It was part of a fantastically elaborate story. Along with the alleged plumbers and electricians.

The tow truck was a roadblock.

Burke said, "What are you thinking?"

"I'm wondering where the people were. We saw one guy, but there were four vehicles parked. So I'm thinking something weird is happening up there. Possibly bad things. But I lose the phone if I go up there. And I want to hear about Carrington. And Elizabeth Castle. It's my fault they're together. And I think Amos is going to call me. Sooner or later she's going to want me back in town."

"What could you do there?"

"I could walk around. They have my description. I'm the real thing. Carrington is a pale imitation. It would take the pressure off him. Now the bad guy would be coming after me."

"Doesn't that worry you?"

"He wants to take me back to Boston. He wants to throw me off a building. That would be a long and complicated operation. I don't see how it could end well for him."

"What kind of bad things could happen at a motel with a roadblock?"

"Your guess is as good as mine," Reacher said.

THE last of the day was fading, so the outside lights were on, up and down the boardwalk. The six men were starting to lay out their gear. All six doors were open. Guys wandered in and out, holding bits and pieces. There was an element of display involved. Not that there was much latitude for showing off. The rules were tight. Everyone started equal. Everyone got a randomly issued quad bike. Everyone used the same night vision. Clothing and footwear were not restricted, but everyone dressed the same. Nothing in the soft bags was worth a second look.

The hard cases were a different story. Strange, suggestive shapes. Again, not restricted. A personal choice. Anything was permitted. Or any combination. Recurve, reflex, self, long, flat, composite, or takedown. Everyone had a favorite. There were plenty of sideways glances when the hard cases came out.

THE view from the gravel shoulder was dimming and going gray. In his mind Reacher replaced it with the motel. The office on the left, the Volvo wagon outside of 3, the fake carpet van outside of 7, the small blue import outside of 10, and the long-bed pickup truck outside of 11. Plus room 5's lawn chair.

Burke said, "What?"

"It's a back-of-the-brain thing," Reacher said. "What do they need to make a bad thing happen?"

"There could be many things."

"They need a victim. Maybe it's a young girl."

"You think it's porn?"

"It could be a lot of different things. But all those things require a victim. Somehow captured and held there."

Burke said, "On the premises where?"

"Room ten was different," Reacher said. "Two separate ways. First the car. The only foreign plate. Also smaller and cheaper and worn-out. Therefore probably a young person's car. Possibly far from home and vulnerable. Secondly the bedroom window. The blind was down. The only one out of twelve."

Burke said, "You should go take another look."

Reacher said nothing. He dialed Amos's number.

It rang four times.

She said, "Nothing yet. Rush hour is over. Downtown is quiet. We have eyes most places they need to be."

"Would it help if I was there?"

"Honest answer?"

"On a scale of one to ten."

"Then a one," she said.

"Okay, good luck," he said. "I'm going out of cell phone range. I'll check in when I can."

ONCE again the TV turned on by itself. This time it was Mark.

He said, "Guys, this is a follow-up session, for questions and answers. So here we are."

Patty said, "Tell us about the tags."

"Come sit on the end of the bed. We'll have a full discussion."

Patty shuffled around. Shorty followed.

Mark said, "Patterns of consumption are changing. Aspirational expenditures are no longer limited to bigger and better physical objects. Now people buy experiences. Some of them pay to act out their fantasies. Some of them are harmless. Some of them are sick. They gather on the Internet. They find secret message boards. That's where we advertise."

"What message boards?" Patty said. "Who are these people?"

"You've met Karel," Mark said. "The other five come from one website. It has a fascinating ambiguity in its name. Is it describing its members, or the activity it promotes to its members?"

Patty said, "What's the name of the site?"

"Bowhunting People."

"What?"

"Which I hope answers your question about the nature of the tag. The game places no restriction on the type of bow. Except no mechanical draw and no crossbows. Probably they'll use composite recurves and broadhead arrows. If they see you early, they might track you for a spell. Then they'll shoot to wound. They want you to last all night. They paid a lot of money."

"You're insane."

"Not me," Mark said. "I'm just catering to the grubby end of the market. Their desires are their own business."

"You're talking about murdering us."

"No, I'm talking about giving you the chance to get away from here. I'm your best friend right now. I'm trying to help you."

"Do they have night vision?"

"Well, yes."

"And quad bikes."

"Which mean you can hear them coming. Don't you see? You're not completely helpless here. Choose your direction carefully, stay alert, listen hard, try to predict from the sound which way the bikes will go, and then slip in behind them after they're gone. It might be possible. It's only two miles by the shortest route. Straight down the track. But I would advise against. Too obvious, surely. Someone would be lying in wait."

No one answered.

Mark said, "More advice, if I may. Check your door from time to time. The clock starts ticking as soon as it unlocks. It's your responsibility to know. When it opens, I suggest you depart immediately. Give it your best shot. Look on the bright side. It's a big woods. Bowhunters like to get within forty feet. Shooting arrows in a forest is hard. There are always trees in the way."

No one spoke.

Mark said, "More advice, if I may. Please don't plan to sit in your room. It never works. As soon as they realize what you're doing, they'll have you surrounded. You'll have six guys at your door. They'll be disappointed. They'll take it out on you."

No one spoke.

Mark asked, "Did you talk about splitting up and going solo?"

Shorty looked away.

"I know," Mark said. "Tough choice. The percentage play would be go for it. Problem is, you would never know what happened to the other person. In their final moments, I mean."

BURKE drove north. The phone died bar by bar. Reacher laid down the law. Burke was to let him out at the mouth of the track and then go home and stay home, safe and secure. That was the deal. Burke agreed.

They drove into the trees. It was already full dark under the canopy. The twisted posts showed up five miles later. Burke stopped the car. Reacher got out. Burke drove away. Under the trees was darkness. Reacher set out walking.

Two minutes later he arrived at the tow truck. He felt for the fat rubber wire and stepped over it. He forced his way along the side of the truck, getting pelted and scratched with twigs and leaves. He came out at the front and set out walking. Two miles to go.

PATTY and Shorty heard the quad bikes start up. The distant shriek of a starter motor, the fast and anxious idle. Then all of them, growling and rumbling, turning toward the motel.

Patty tried the door. Still locked.

The bikes formed up into what sounded like single file. They drove through the lot. Shorty watched out the window. A procession. The bikes drove by, one by one. The riders were all dressed in black. They all had bows slung across their backs. They all had quivers full of arrows. They all had weird one-eyed night-vision goggles strapped to their heads. Then they all rode away.

Patty tried the door. It opened.

She pulled it all the way open and stood staring out.

"This is crazy," she said. "I don't want to go."

"We aren't safe here," Shorty said.

Patty said nothing. She put her hand out the door. She opened her fingers. She felt the air.

"We'll go to Florida," Shorty said. "We'll have a windsurfer business. Maybe Jet Skis, too. We'll sell T-shirts. That's where the money is. Patty and Shorty's Aquatic Emporium."

Patty looked back at him.

"Okay," she said. "Let's go to Florida."

They took nothing except the flashlights. They hustled out and tracked around room 12, and came back on the blind side, along the back wall, to where they guessed their bathroom was. West was dead ahead. They heard nothing, and they saw nothing.

They held hands and set out walking. Fast, but not running. Soon they were out in the open. They fixed their eyes on the dark horizon. The wall of trees. They ran the last fifty yards.

They slipped between the first trunks and stopped dead, bent over, breathing hard, with primitive joy at having survived. They stood up again. They listened. They heard nothing. They moved deeper into the woods. They didn't risk the flashlights. Not yet.

Five minutes later Patty said, "We should turn south now."

"Why?"

"They could have been watching. They saw us heading west, so now they think we're going to continue heading west."

"Okay, we should make a left turn," Shorty said.

So Patty turned what she hoped was ninety degrees. Shorty followed. On and on. The same slow progress. Grabby vines, and saplings. Sometimes fallen boughs, propped diagonally across their path. Which meant a detour, and a long look back to make sure they hadn't gotten turned around.

Way far in the distance they heard a bike. Maybe a mile away. It rode a minute, and it shut down again. Repositioning, maybe. For what? Patty stopped walking, and Shorty bumped into her.

"We should turn southwest now," Patty said. "I think from here it would be the fastest way to the break in the trees."

"Okay, we should head half a turn to the right."

"If we're really heading south right now."

"I'm pretty sure," Shorty said. "More or less."

Patty said nothing.

Shorty said, "What?"

"I think we're lost in the woods. Which is full of archers who want to kill us. I think I'm going to die surrounded by trees. Which I guess is fair. I work in a sawmill."

"Hang in there. Turn half right, keep on going, and we'll reach the clearing."

They did all those things. They turned half right, they kept on going, and they reached the clearing. But it was the wrong clearing. They were behind the motel again. They were coming out of the woods about twenty yards from where they ran in.

REACHER heard motorcycle engines in the distance. First a swarm, then individual machines about a mile away. The quad bikes, he assumed. There had been nine, neatly parked in front of the barn. Now they were out and about.

Hunting, said the back part of his brain.

Okay, said the front part. Maybe a protected species. A bear cub, or something. Highly illegal. Maybe that was the victim. Except a cub didn't drive an import or hide with the blind down.

He shuffled off the track and stood six feet in the trees. Way up ahead he heard a bike. Not moving. Idling in place. Waiting. No headlight. Then it shut down. The silence became total again.

Reacher moved up through the trees, following the track, six feet from its edge.

PATTY sat on the ground with her back against a tree. She stared across at the motel. Where they had started.

Shorty sat down against the next tree.

He said, "We'll get better at it."

"No, we won't," she said. "Not without a compass."

"What do you want to do?"

"I think the track is the only way. Alongside, in the trees. So we don't get lost. Any other direction, we could wander all night."

"They know that."

"They always knew. They knew sooner or later we'd have to try the track. We should have known, too. We were stupid. Thirty square miles with six guys was always ridiculous. But it isn't thirty square miles. It's a narrow strip either side of the track. That's where all the action will be. They're waiting for us there."

Shorty was quiet for a long moment. Then he said, "I want to try something. Follow me."

IN THE back parlor, Steven tracked the GPS chips inside their flashlights. Currently they were moving from the forest toward the back of the motel. Walking in a straight line, which was in stark contrast to their previous navigational performance, which had been chaotic. They had been staggering south of west from the get-go, in a curling line they evidently thought was straight. Their final turn brought them back to where they had started.

He watched. They made it to the motel's back wall. Then they retraced their earlier steps exactly. They tracked back around the end of the building. Around room 12. Into the lot. Past room 11. Then they stopped outside room 10.

SHORTY RAISED THE HONDA's hood and felt around under the battery. The stiff black wire, chopped in half, the cut ends like new pennies. He backed away and walked through room 10 to the bathroom. He grabbed all the towels and carried them outside. He dumped them on the gravel near the Honda's rear wheel.

"Check the other doors," he said. "Get more if you can."

Patty started with 11. The door was unlatched. She went in. Shorty went back to 10. He picked up the suitcase. Both hands, around the rope. He staggered out with it all the way to the grass on the far side, the meadow before the woods. He made it thirty yards, and dropped the case, and laid it down in the grass.

Then he walked back. Patty had gotten towels out of 11, 7, and 5. Altogether they had four piles. He went back to 10's bathroom and came out with a jagged shard of tile. He dropped it on the towels near the Honda's rear wheel.

He asked, "Which room had the most stuff?"

"Seven," Patty said. "Lots of clothes. Lots of potions in the bathroom. That guy takes good care of himself."

Shorty walked down to 7. He found what he wanted. A nail clipper. Metal. He put it in his pocket and walked back to the Honda. He put the shard of tile aside. He laid the towels one on top of the other, like a thick quilt. He shuffled it into position, flat on the gravel, under the Honda's rear end. He did the same thing with the towels from 5, 7, and 11, under the Volvo, the Persian carpet van, and the pickup truck respectively.

He went back to the Honda and lay down on his back. He squirmed into position. He stabbed the shard of tile into the bottom of the gas tank. Again and again. He felt the tip go in.

He widened the hole, and a minute later he had about five gallons soaked into the towels. He did the same thing under the truck and the van and the Volvo. He pulled out the dripping wads one by one and piled them on the boardwalk. All apart from one small towel, which he took with him. Soaked in gasoline. He slid it under the Honda's battery. He draped it over bolts and brackets.

Then he backed away and shook his hands to dry them. He got in the driver's seat and put the key in the lock. He clicked it on. He clicked every switch he could find. Heated rear windshield, lights, wipers, radio. Whatever. He wanted maximum load.

He got out. He took the nail clipper from his pocket and unfolded the file. It was maybe two inches long and a quarter inch wide, made of metal, with a curl on the end, good for scraping.

He put one arm under the hood and slid the tip of the file into the severed space between the two halves of the stiff black wire. Between the two copper pennies. He twisted the file. He completed the circuit. Metal to metal to metal. There was a furious cascade of sparks, and the gas-soaked towel went *whoomp* and burst into flames, and Shorty dropped the nail clipper and ran back and forth to the boardwalk, grabbing more towels, lighting them on fire, tossing them into rooms, into 11, into 10, on the bed, on the floor, into 7, into 5, the last few anywhere, on the boardwalk, on a plastic lawn chair, outside the office door.

They walked backward across the lot. Already flames were curling out of doors and windows.

Shorty said, "They can't afford to look at it. Not with night vision. It would fry their eyeballs. All we have to do is keep it directly behind us, and they won't see us coming."

Patty nodded and said, "That's pretty smart, Shorty."

They walked east through the meadow, with the fire plumb behind them, and the mouth of the track dead ahead.

REACHER found a quad bike parked on the track. It loomed up in gray filtered moonlight. The bike was stopped on a diagonal, facing toward the motel. No sign of a rider.

Hunting, said the back of his brain.

Okay, said the front. But where? Up ahead, surely. Which meant Reacher was currently behind him. A good place to be.

Reacher moved up in the trees. He saw the rider. But only just.

The guy was standing in the middle of the track, almost invisible in the moonlight gloom. He was half turned away from something up ahead. He was dressed in tight black clothes, like athletic gear. He had an archery bow slung across his back. He had a quiver of arrows. Strapped to his head was a one-lens night-vision device. Like a cyclops eye. U.S. Army. Second-generation. Reacher had used them.

A night hunt, said the back of his brain. Told you so.

There was a faint glow on the horizon. Slightly orange. Something was on fire, way far in the distance.

The guy was about eight feet away. He was a well-built individual. A nighttime bowhunter. Of what?

Reacher moved.

The guy heard. He took the bow off his back in one fluid motion. A split-second later he had an arrow in his hand. He nocked the arrow and half drew the string, and held the weapon half ready, pointing low. He looked all around. His night vision was still in the up position. Disengaged. The arrowhead was wide and flat. It was a decent chunk of steel. It would do some damage.

Then the guy raised the bow high, both hands, and used his forearm to knock his optical tube back into place. Now he had vision again. He peered around, his head moving slowly.

Reacher stepped back and left. He lined up the trees. He wanted a sliver of view, but a narrow one. The narrower the better.

The guy turned to see what was behind him.

He looked straight at Reacher. The blank glass lens fixed right on him. The guy raised the bow and drew the string. Reacher swayed right. The arrow fired and buried itself in the tree in front of him with a ringing *thunk*. Like an ax, but harder.

The guy reloaded, taking an arrow from the quiver.

Reacher called, "Are you aware you're shooting at a human?"

The guy fired again, then the same *thunk* as it hit a tree.

Reacher thought, I guess I'll take that as a yes.

The night vision was a huge advantage. Reacher could see the gleam of the next arrowhead. It was tracking left, tracking right, trying to find a line through the trees. The guy was stepping in, trying to find his shot. Reacher started moving, swaying randomly, enough to need a new ballistic calculation every single time.

Reacher called out, "You need to come closer."

The guy locked on. The glassy end of the coffee can pointed straight at Reacher. Who saw only a sliver of the right-hand edge of the lens. Which in turn meant the guy saw only Reacher's right eye, and then a wide tree, and then maybe part of his left shoulder.

The guy was no doubt thinking things through. A small crowded space, with limited room for maneuver, especially with a bow. Tactically awkward, especially in terms of range. Anything more than arm's length, there was a tree in the way. But anything less than arm's length was game over. The bow could be grabbed, the night vision could be knocked off, and lethal weapons could be seized from the quiver. He wouldn't come in the trees.

Reacher moved to his left. The arrowhead tracked him. Still no clear shot. Nor would there be for three more steps. After which there was a tree missing. Which left a hole. Directly in Reacher's path. A room-size space.

Speed would be the critical factor. Arrows were fast, but not like bullets. The guy would have to shoot ahead of the target. He would have to fire the arrow in anticipation. He had to commit.

Reacher ran left, one stride, two, three, maximum acceleration, and the guy fired at where he was going to be, a cast-iron slam dunk grand slam, except Reacher jinked to the right, and instead of entering the treeless space, he came straight at the guy, who was caught fumbling his reload. He barreled into the guy, shoulder first. The guy went sprawling. Reacher kicked whichever part was nearest. Then he grabbed the bow, and pulled the night vision off the guy's head, and slid an arrow out of his quiver.

Then he froze.

Anything less than arm's length was game over.

They would know that. They would hunt in pairs.

He grabbed the guy by the collar and hauled him into the trees on the far side of the track. His bow clattered on the blacktop. It came to rest out in the open. Unfortunate. It told a clear story. Reacher stopped six feet in the trees. He hauled the guy upright. He made him stand in front, like a human shield. From behind he pushed the tip of the arrow up under the guy's chin.

Reacher whispered, "Who are you hunting?"

The guy breathed out like a sigh. Then the guy flipped his feet out from under his knees, and lunged forward and took his whole falling weight on the point of the arrow under his chin. Which sliced up into his mouth, through his palate, and into his brain.

Then Reacher let it go.

In the back parlor, Steven was losing screen after screen. Most of the cameras were on the motel, disguised as brackets for the rainwater gutters. As the motel burned, they burned. Also all the comms hubs were in the roof space. All the radio antennas, and all the telephone links. The hidden satellite dish for the secret Internet account. They were alone in the world. They were cut off.

The GPS still worked, in the flashlights. Currently it showed Patty and Shorty heading for the mouth of the track. In a straight line. With the burning motel directly behind them, no doubt. Smart. Night vision or no night vision, they would be very hard to see against a bright moving glare directly behind them.

His final problem was customer number three's heart rate monitor. It was sounding an alarm. So far number three had displayed increasing excitement, with a recent huge peak, and then he had flatlined. According to his monitor, he was dead.

Chapter 14

Patty and Shorty held hands, and somehow the palm-to-palm contact was better than talking. One step they felt secure. The next step they felt they were walking the length of a gigantic airport runway, lit up by a thousand probing searchlights.

They didn't know which feeling was real.

They walked on. They waited for arrows. None came.

They anticipated sentries wide on the flanks. Impatient types, hoping for early contact. They planned to avoid them by coming in centrally, with the fire behind them. But then at the last moment they planned to veer off course, just as far as the edge of the blaze would cover them. Then they would work around in the woods and pick up the track's direction a little farther down.

Also they planned to split up. Just by ten yards or so.

"Close enough to help," Patty said. "Far enough not to make one big target."

In the distance behind them the motel's roof fell in. A huge cloud of sparks rose up. The fire was brighter than ever.

"Now," Patty said.

They went south. To their right. They skipped along sideways, glancing back at the fire, trying to stay covered by its glow, going as wide as they dared. Then Shorty ran for the woods first, as agreed. He made it. Patty waited. No shouted warning. She went after him, squeezing between the same two trees, aiming to head around the same quarter circle, back toward the track. She could hear him up ahead. She was close enough to help. She was far enough to get away. Would she?

She walked on.

Then two things happened fast. Too fast to see. Except Shorty was suddenly standing in front of her, and a guy was lying on the ground. Then came a painful slow-motion replay, like a mental reaction. In her mind she saw a guy looming up, a nightmare vision. All in black, tight nylon, a bow, an arrow, a hideous one-eyed face. The bow aiming low, at her legs. *They'll shoot to wound.* Then the string drawing back, then out of nowhere Shorty was behind the guy, swinging his long metal flashlight, hitting the guy full-on behind the ear. The guy went straight down. Dead, she was sure. The sound alone told her. She had heard enough cows killed to know.

"Thank you," she said.

"I busted my flashlight," he said. "It doesn't turn on anymore."

"You can have mine," she said. "It's the least I can do."

"Thank you. Keep mine for a weapon," he said.

They traded flashlights. An absurd little ceremony.

"They must have known we would play it like that," she said. "I think their obvious solution would be to hunt in pairs."

A voice said, "Damn right about that, little girl."

They turned. Another nightmare vision. Glistening black nylon tight to the skin, a complicated bow, a steel arrowhead as big as a serving spoon, a cyclops stare through a glass circle.

The nightmare vision shot Shorty in the leg.

The bowstring thumped, the arrow hissed, and Shorty screamed and went down. The arrow was stuck in his thigh. He was hauling on it, and jerking his head side to side, screaming into separate rapid-fire gasps of agony, *ah ah ah*, like a racing heartbeat.

Patty was calm. She heard herself in her head, saying, Sure, Shorty's bad, but he won't get any worse in the next three seconds. So feel free to take care of the other thing first.

Which was the guy with the bow. Who was old, she saw. Stooped and sparrow-chested. He was slow with his reload. He tried to compensate by scrabbling for the arrow early. He fumbled it. Patty breathed in.

Keep mine for a weapon, Shorty had said.

She did it beautifully. Despite very little prior experience. She sensed every compound flooding her brain. Some were complex emotions. Mostly about Shorty. Primeval feelings. Much stronger than she expected. They gave her strength, and speed, and cunning, and ferocity. She danced across the space, shuffling her stride to perfection, swinging the flashlight ahead of her, accelerating it hard, keeping it low, the cyclops eye coming down to track it, then whipping it up in a savage U-shaped curve, into the narrowing angle between the dropping chin and the arching neck.

It hit with a crunch she felt all the way to her elbow. The guy went down like he ran into a clothesline. He landed on his back. She grabbed his bow and threw it away. His night vision was bound to his head with thick rubber straps. She tore it off. He was a thin, pale, sour man, about seventy years old.

His mouth was opening and closing, like a goldfish.

He pointed to his throat. "Can't breathe," he mouthed.

Tough, she thought.

Later she knew she would have no defense, if a lawyer asked her, sternly, "Did you in fact beat the victim to death with the flashlight?" Damn right she did. With every ounce of her strength.

Then she crawled back to Shorty. Who was quiet.

He had seen.

First things first. She got her hands under his arms and dragged him deeper into the woods. She got him sitting against a tree. She got his legs straight out in front. Then she ran back to the guy she had killed. She took his night-vision device. She strapped it on.

Now she could see. Luminous green, in fantastic detail. It was better than daylight. She felt like Superman.

She ran back to Shorty and got to work.

Reacher took the dead guy's night-vision device. He strapped it on and adjusted the buckles. The world went bright and green. He took the whole quiver of arrows. Better than nothing.

He moved deeper into the woods. The track was still visible through the trees, even though it was now thirty yards to his left.

He moved up four paces and stopped. He figured the second guy would be close, but not too close. Within earshot, certainly.

He turned a long slow circle. No sign of him.

Reacher checked the other side of the track. He moved back and forth, to see through the trees. Fifty yards away, easy. Perfect detail. Better than daylight.

He saw the guy.

Leaning on a tree, about six feet from the edge of the track. Skintight clothing, dark in color, bow in his hand, looking mostly forward up the track, but glancing back all the time, down the track, behind him. He was anxious. He couldn't hear his partner.

He was forty yards from Reacher. Which implied some cautious stalking. For one of them, anyway. Reacher stood still. Sometimes he believed in letting the other guy do the work.

First he took a second arrow from the quiver. One in each hand. Then he chose a thick tree. He ranged away a step and squatted down. He used the arrow in his right hand to beat and batter and scythe through the undergrowth, big sweeps of his arm, intended to replicate the sound of a staggering man falling over.

Then he straightened up and stood sideways behind his tree.

He waited. Two whole minutes. Then he heard him. Close by.

Quiet. He was a good stalker. He was probably right-handed. Therefore the bow would be in his left. The bow would be thrust forward, half ready. The string would be halfway back. He would be leading with his left shoulder, walking half sideways.

Reacher waited.

The guy called out in a whisper, "Hey, Three, are you there?"

Reacher didn't move.

The guy said, "Where are you, man? We need to get moving. We got something on fire up there."

Reacher kicked the brambles at his feet.

The guy said, "Three, is that you? Are you hurt?"

As a reply Reacher made a sound in the back of his throat. He guessed the nearest word would be air, said long and breathy.

The guy crept closer.

He came around Reacher's tree, leading with his far shoulder, looking through a tube, which was a technical marvel with only one significant negative, which was a lack of peripheral vision. Which meant the guy came a step too far around the tree. Before he saw. Reacher stabbed him with the arrow, a vicious uppercut high in the stomach. The guy pitched forward on his face. The arrowhead punched out his back.

STEVEN had lost one of the flashlights. The GPS had blinked off and never returned. An impact, possibly. Currently the surviving flashlight was sixty feet in the forest, sixty yards from the track. It had not moved for many minutes. He didn't know why.

But his bigger worry was the heart rate monitors. Now four had flatlined. Four of their customers were technically dead. Which had to be an equipment fault. But maybe someone should go take a look. The GPS showed Peter and Robert widely separated, on the flanks, at the edge of the forest. Still in neutral mode, there only if called upon. Mark was moving, in a wide loop back toward the buildings, either walking or riding slow on his bike. Too slow. He needed to tell them. But he couldn't. The radio hub had burned up. Their earpieces were useless. They were hearing nothing.

Then the surviving flashlight started to move.

SHORTY'S PANTS LEG WAS soaked with blood. Patty couldn't tear the fabric. Too wet, too slippery. She ran back and got an arrow. She used the edge of its head to widen the slit the first arrow had made. She took a look. The wound was vertical. The arrow had come in with one tang up and one tang down, and it had hit above his knee, about a third of the way up his thigh. It had speared through muscle and hit bone. Through the quadriceps to the femur. Ninety degrees from the femoral artery. Not even close. He wasn't going to bleed to death. They had been lucky.

Except she was pretty sure the arrow had broken the bone.

She felt around. There was a ledge-shaped lump on the back of his leg. Like a displaced fracture. His hamstrings were pushed out of place. He was gasping and groaning, partly with pain, partly with fury. He was pale green in the night vision. In shock, but not all the way. His heartbeat was fast, but steady.

She studied the arrow she had used to cut the cloth. The head was a simple triangle. Two wicked edges came together at the point. The edges were like razors. They would slice through anything. But there were no barbs. The edges would slice right back out just as easily. No further damage.

Except Shorty's muscle had spasmed and clamped down hard. It was gripping the arrow like a vise.

She said, "Shorty, I need you to relax your leg."

He said, "I can't feel my leg."

"I think it's broken. I need to get you to the hospital. But first I need to pull the arrow out. Right now you're gripping it. You need to let it go."

"I got no control. All I know is it hurts like hell."

She said, "I think we really need to pull it out."

"Try rubbing the muscle," he said. "Like I had a cramp."

She rubbed. He groaned and gasped. She squeezed both sides of the wound, inching the web of her thumb closer and closer to the arrowhead, gaping the wound. Blood welled up, and spilled out in little green rivers, some one way, some the other.

"Tell me where we're going," she said.

"Florida," he said.

"What will we do when we get there?"

"Windsurfers."

"What else?"

"T-shirts," he said. "Where the money is."

"What kind of design?"

He paused, thinking, and she gripped the arrow's shaft and jerked it sharp and hard. The arrow came out, and Shorty shrieked.

"Sorry," she said.

He gasped and he panted.

She slipped off her jacket and used the clean arrowhead to cut off the sleeves. She tied them together, end to end, with a generous knot. She folded the body of the jacket into a tight pad. She pressed it down on the wound and tied it on with the sleeves. A pressure dressing on the front, to stop the bleeding, and a splint of sorts on the back. The big knot would hold things steady for a while.

"Wait there," she said.

She ran back to the first nightmare figure. The one Shorty had hit behind the ear. She pulled off his night-vision device and took another arrow from the quiver. She ran back to Shorty. She gave him the headset to wear and the arrow to hold. For security.

"Now I'm going to find us a quad bike," she said.

She took the working flashlight in one hand and the clean arrow in the other. She ran back to Shorty's guy. She stood where she had stood before. She replayed the scene in her mind. The guy had loomed up ahead of her. He'd been coming from the north.

She stepped over the guy and moved on to where the voice from the dark had spun them around. *Damn right about that, little girl.* They had turned and seen him. He had been coming from the north, too. They were a pair. Common sense said they would have left their bikes behind them and then ranged ahead on foot.

She stepped over her guy and set out walking, north.

MARK saw her go. He WAS all set to follow, but then at the last second he saw what she was stepping over. A dead man. Two dead men. Which put things in a whole different perspective. Burning the motel was bad enough. It was insured, ironically. But obviously he wouldn't risk a claim. The cops would come and sift through the wreckage, and they would find all kinds of weird stuff. But rebuilding with cash would eat up half of what they were making that night. Which would be a severe blow.

Were there alternatives? Suddenly he thought so. Why rebuild at all? The motel was a dump. It was a junk part of some weird old title passed down from a dead guy he never knew. Then and there he decided to leave it in ruins. It would be much cheaper to convert a single room in the main house, to change the signs from MOTEL to B&B. A different kind of invitation. Should work fine.

But dead people were a whole different category. The dead people would be missed, questions would be asked, data would be traced. If Robert could find people, so could the government.

He thought, Time for plan B.

He walked back to his bike and rode it slowly to the house. The motel had burned to the ground. Only the metal cage around room 10 was still standing. He rode to the house, gunned the bike up the steps, and parked it on the porch. He went straight to the parlor. Steven said hello without looking up. He was watching the GPS. He knew Mark was in the house.

Mark looked over Steven's shoulder at the GPS screen. Only one flashlight was showing. Peter and Robert were static on the flanks. Steven said, "Four of the heart monitors failed."

"Four now?" Mark said.

Steven switched screens and showed him the data. It was laid out as four separate graphs. Heart rate versus time. All of them showed basically the same thing. First elevated and consistent excitement, then a brief plateau of extreme stress, then nothing.

"Might be an equipment fault," Steven said.

"No," Mark said. "I saw two of them dead already."

"What?"

"Their heads were bashed in. By Patty and Shorty, I guess. Who are clearly better than we thought."

"What happened to the other two?"

"I don't know," Mark said.

Steven switched back to the GPS screen. The surviving flashlight was moving down the track, in the trees, close to the edge. Peter and Robert were still stationary. In a separate window the two surviving customers were showing elevated but consistent heartbeats. Excited. But no sudden spikes. No contact yet.

"Which ones are they?" Mark asked.

"Karel and the Wall Street guy."

"Can we tell where they are?"

"We know where their bikes are. They seem to have taken up a middle position. Who got the back two?"

"I don't know," Mark said again.

"This changes everything. What do you want to do?"

"Plan B. Watch carefully where the flashlight goes."

Steven kept his eyes on the screen.

Mark pulled a boxy black handgun up and out from under his jacket. His elbow went high, because the gun was long, because it had a suppressor attached. He shot Steven in the back of the head.

He took the bags of cash from the closet and set them down on the hallway floor. He opened the closet's back wall and took out his escape kit. Cash, cards, a driver's license, a passport, and a burner phone. A whole new person, zipped in a plastic bag.

He threw Peter's and Steven's and Robert's on the closet floor.

He carried the bags of cash outside and set them down a distance away. He came back to the porch and opened the front door wide. He removed the gas cap of the quad bike and threw it away. He squatted down like a weight lifter and toppled the bike on its side. Right next to the open door. Gas gurgled out of the open tank.

Mark threw a match, and backed away, and grabbed the bags, and ran to the barn. He put the bags in his Mercedes. He backed it out and parked it a distance away. He ran back to the barn and hustled over to the shelf where the gas cans were kept. Five of them, filled every time someone drove to town.

He emptied the cans on the floor, under Peter's Mercedes, under Steven's, under Robert's. He threw a match and ran to his car. He set the hazard flashers going. For Peter and Robert to see. A panic signal. They already knew their radios were dead. They were looking at two brand-new fires. They would come running.

He drove toward the mouth of the track at a stately speed, past the glowing ruins of the motel, flashing orange all the way.

He stopped in the center of the meadow.

Robert zoomed in from the right, flattening the meadow grass under four fat tires. He maneuvered next to the passenger side. Mark buzzed the far window down and shot him in the face.

Mark buzzed the window back up. Peter was approaching on the left-hand side. The same wide swooping curve through the meadow. Aiming to arrive at the driver's window.

Mark buzzed his window down.

Peter maneuvered alongside. Face-to-face.

The gun was too long. Because of the suppressor. Mark couldn't maneuver it. It snagged on the door.

Peter stopped his engine. He said, "How bad is it?"

"Couldn't be worse," Mark said. "The motel burned down. The house and the barn are on fire. And four customers are dead."

"We should get out," Peter said. "Right this minute.

"I need to open my door to stretch my legs," Mark said. Peter checked. "You have plenty of room," he said.

Mark opened his door. But he didn't get out. Instead he stopped the door as soon as the handle moldings were clear of the suppressor, and where Peter was still nicely framed in the window. He shot him in the chest, in the throat, and in the face.

Then he closed his door again, and buzzed his window up, and turned off his hazard flashers, and drove on, down the track.

REACHER got through the next section of forest pretty quick, because of the night vision. He stayed six feet off the track. He made no attempt to be quiet. He relied on the mathematical randomness of tree distribution to save him from arrows.

At one point way far away he heard four separated pops. The back of his brain said those were suppressed 9-millimeter rounds, fired in the open air, about a mile away. The front said maybe they were something cooking off, possibly aerosol cans, in the fire. Which was getting brighter again, as if more was burning.

He stopped. Up ahead on the left he saw two quad bikes parked side by side. No riders nearby. Presumably they were up ahead.

He moved on, quieter than before.

He stopped again. He saw a guy up ahead. On the other side of the track, about thirty feet in the trees. Clothes like a scuba diver, a bow, a cyclops eye.

No sign of his partner. Some signs of anxiety, Reacher thought. The guy was tall and substantial, and his head was up, but he wasn't comfortable. Reacher had seen his type before. No doubt the guy was a big-deal alpha male at whatever it was he was good at. But right then he was out of his depth.

Reacher moved up quietly through the trees, on the other side of the track, to where he was level with the guy. Reacher was six feet in the trees. Then came the track. The guy was thirty feet in on the other side. A straight line. But not a clear shot in a forest. The guy had boxed himself in. He had no natural avenue of attack.

Reacher walked across the track, dead on line, a hundred random trees between him and the guy. He stepped back into the woods on the other side and worked his way through, now twenty feet from the guy, still dead on line. The glow in the sky winked and danced through the leaves. Up ahead the guy was looking down. Maybe the sparkle bothered him.

Reacher moved on. As always he believed in staying flexible, but as always he also had a plan. Which in this case was to stab the guy in the neck with an arrow. But flexibility intervened. Up close, it was clear the guy was worried in a particular kind of way. An elemental way. Like a billionaire whose car gets in a fender bender in the wrong neighborhood. Maybe ready to make a deal.

Reacher rushed him, and the guy reacted by jerking his bow up. Reacher scythed his arrow down, slashing the guy's left knuckles. The guy howled and dropped the bow, and Reacher stepped close, their optical tubes colliding, and kicked the guy behind the knees, so that he fell over on his back, whereupon Reacher flipped the guy's night vision up with his foot, and then jammed the same foot on the guy's throat, and forced the tip of the arrow between his lips.

"Want to talk?" he whispered.

The guy couldn't answer because of the arrow jammed against his teeth. Instead he kind of nodded with his eyes.

Reacher withdrew the arrow. "Who are you hunting?"

The guy said, "This is not what it seems. I came here to hunt wild boar. I was deceived."

"And what are you hunting instead?"

"People," the guy said. "Not what I came for."

"How many people?"

"Two. A young couple. Their names are Patty Sundstrom and Shorty Fleck. I was told wild boar. They lied to me."

"Who lied to you?"

"A man named Mark. He owns this place."

"Mark Reacher?"

"I don't know his last name."

"Why are you nevertheless stalking around in the dark with your bow and arrow?"

No answer.

"Wait," Reacher said.

He heard a car up ahead. He saw bright shards of light coming through the trees. A big vehicle with its headlights on. He flipped up his tube. The world went dark, all except for the track, thirty feet to his right. It was all lit up. Twin high beams were punching forward. A black Mercedes SUV rolled by. Then it was gone.

Reacher dropped his tube back in place. The world went green again. He shifted his foot on the guy's neck. To make room for the tip of the arrow. He exerted modest downward pressure.

The guy said, "I didn't know what I was getting into. I swear. I'm a banker. I'm not like these other guys. I'm a victim, too."

"You're a banker?"

"I run a hedge fund. These other guys are nothing to do with me. I didn't know they were hunting people."

"I think you did," Reacher said. "I think that's why you came."

He leaned harder on the arrow until it pierced the skin, and drove down through the neck, clipping the spine, and out the other side, pinning the guy like a dead butterfly against the forest floor.

Then he moved on through the trees.

Chapter 15

MARK STOPPED HIS MERCEDES nose to nose with the tow truck. He had run the numbers. There was a maximum of four people still unaccounted for. Karel and the Wall Street guy, plus Patty and Shorty. Plus hypothetically a fifth person, if the outside pair had been victims of a third party. Of the big guy, perhaps, come back again. Because he had spotted something. Because he had been unconvinced.

Four people. Or five. All up ahead. He needed three short minutes. He needed to reverse the tow truck out to the road, then sprint back and hop in his car and blast off. To anywhere.

He ran the scene in his mind. It was a loud diesel engine. Everyone would hear it in the distance. At first the customers would assume the perimeter was being loosened. An on-the-fly in-game adjustment. None of them would be suspicious.

Except Karel. It was his truck. He would know something was going on. He might be more than three minutes away. He would need to thread his way through the forest, back to wherever he parked his bike. That could be three minutes right there. Or not.

Overall, Mark figured there was a good chance of success. Either Karel would let it go or he wouldn't, multiplied by either he was close by or he wasn't. Two coin tosses in a row.

He left the Mercedes running, and he left the driver's door open. He squeezed between the trees and the truck's enormous hood. He battled his way to where the cab towered above him. He grabbed the handles and climbed the ladder. The door was locked.

Which he had not foreseen. At first he was angry. Karel was stupid to leave the truck without the door open and the key in. Who the hell would do that? It was insane. Flexibility was everything. They might have needed to move the truck at any time.

Then he got worried. Where was the key, if not in the truck? The best case was bad enough. The best case said the key was in Karel's pocket, which meant finding the guy and taking it from him. Which would create a delay. Not good.

But it was better than the worst case. Karel's pockets were tight. Stretch fabric, shiny black. Would he want to carry a key? The worst case said Karel had left the tow truck key on room 2's dresser. Now ashy, melted, twisted out of shape.

Mark climbed down the ladder and forced his way along the hood to his car. He reversed ten yards, and turned around in the hole in the trees, and drove back the way he had come.

PATTY saw him pass by again. She had seen him leave minutes before. If it was really him. She was only guessing it was Mark in the car. Running away, she thought, the first time he passed. But evidently not, because he came back again.

She couldn't find the quad bikes. She didn't think they would be deep in the trees, so she searched near the edges of the track. But she found nothing. She stopped walking and looked ahead carefully. She was growing accustomed to the night vision. She turned around and looked behind her. The glow in the sky was bright again. Too bright to look at directly. She turned back around.

There was a man in front of her.

Out of nothing. Just suddenly there. With a bow held ready. The string was drawn back. The arrow was aimed.

The nightmare vision spoke. "We meet again," it said.

She knew the voice. It was Karel. The weasel with the tow truck. Karel asked, "Where's Shorty?"

She didn't answer.

"Didn't he make it? Or maybe you don't know. Maybe you went your separate ways. He ain't up ahead, because I checked. He can't be behind you, because that would be neither use nor ornament."

She looked away.

"Interesting," Karel said. "Is he back there for a reason?"

She didn't answer.

He smiled under his glassy snout. Wide and delighted.

He said, "Is he wounded?"

No reply.

"This is exciting," he said. "You're out gathering roots and berries, to make a potion to heal your man. You're worried. This is a delightful situation. You and I are going to have so much fun."

"I was looking for a quad bike," she said.

"No point," he said. "My truck is parked in the way. No one gets out of here before me. I ain't dumb."

"No," she said.

"No what?"

"Yes, Shorty was wounded. I think his thigh bone is broken. Now I need to get back to him."

"Shame," Karel said. "The game says freedom of movement depends on not getting tagged."

"Please, I don't like the game. It has gotten way out of hand."

"No, I think it has gotten to the good part."

Patty didn't speak again. She just stood there, with her flashlight in one hand and her arrow in the other. It was the working flashlight, not even the weapon. The arrow would be good for slashing or stabbing, but the guy was ten feet away. Out of range.

He drew back the string an extra inch. The bow curved harder.

It was the working flashlight.

All in one movement she dropped the arrow and found the switch and lit up the beam. She aimed it right at the guy's big glass eye. He flinched away, and his arrow fired low and thumped in the ground. He ducked and squirmed. She chased him with the beam of light, like a physical weapon, aiming always for his face. He fell to the ground and rolled over and tore the machine off his head.

She switched off the flashlight and ran. She knew running would turn out either smart or dumb, depending on whether Karel caught her or not. Simple as that. At first she was hopeful. She was running well, and she figured he might be slow to get going.

Then, bad news. She heard crashing feet behind her. Getting closer. She darted right. Up ahead in the bouncing night vision she saw the track. She was running toward it at an angle. She burst out on the track. Karel burst out after her. He raised his bow.

They were lit up by headlight beams. Amplified twenty thousand times. Karel flipped up his tube. Patty tore the whole apparatus off her head. The world went dark, except the car. The black Mercedes. All lit up. Slowing down. Mark at the wheel. He came to a stop. He opened the door. He got out.

Karel raised his bow and aimed the arrow at Patty.

But he spoke to Mark.

He said, "What's on fire up there?"

"Everything's on fire," Mark said. "We're in a whole new ball game now. People have died. We should get out. Just you and me."

"Just you and me?"

"You're my number one draft pick. The others are useless. They're a burden. You know that."

Karel didn't answer.

"We need to move your truck right now. A tactical adjustment."

"We don't need a tactical adjustment. Not anymore. Shorty is wounded, and I got Patty right here. The game is over."

"Okay, shoot her and then let's get going."

"I would want to go finish Shorty first."

"Do you even have the key to the truck?" Mark said.

"I got the key right here," Karel said. "It's in my pocket."

"Good to know," Mark said. He moved the long black gun out from behind his leg, and he shot Karel four times. Karel went down on the track, in a heap, with the crack of his head on the blacktop.

Mark turned the gun on Patty. "Get the key out his pocket."

Patty got right to it. The key was no bigger than the Honda's.

"Throw it over here," Mark said.

She threw the key. It landed at his feet.

He said, "How bad is Shorty? Can he move?"

"His leg is broken."

"I think you and I might be the last two standing," Mark said. "Purely as a matter of interest, how long do you think he would survive?"

"Let me go help him."

"No, I think he should be left on his own right now."

"Why do you even care? The other people are out of the picture now.

So you're done. Move the truck and get out of here. Leave us alone."

Mark shook his head.

"Shorty burned my motel," he said. "That's why I care. Forgive me for feeling a tiny bit vengeful."

"You made us play the game. Starting a fire was a valid move."

"And leaving him to die is a valid response."

Patty looked away. At Karel, lifeless on the blacktop.

"Let me see to Shorty. Come with me. Do it there. Both of us."

"That's romantic," he said. "Where is he exactly?"

"A ways back."

"Too far. I need to get going. Let's do it here. Just you."

He aimed the gun. She saw it clearly in the headlight spill. A Glock, she was sure. She breathed out. Patricia Marie Sundstrom, twenty-five, two years of college, a sawmill worker. Briefly happy with a potato farmer she met in a bar. Happier than she ever expected to be. She wanted to see him again. Just one more time.

Something moved behind Mark's left shoulder.

She saw it in the corner of her eye. In the deep shadows beyond the headlight beams. A flash of something white. Ten feet back. Suspended in the air. Eyes, she thought. Or teeth. Like a smile. She listened. She heard nothing. Just the car's idling engine.

Mark asked, "Ready?"

"I'm glad your motel burned down," she said. "I just wish you had been in it."

"That's not nice," he said.

She looked back at him. There was a man right behind him. A giant. In his left hand was a single arrow. On his head he was wearing a night-vision device with the tube flipped up. He was six inches taller than Mark and about twice as wide. He was huge.

He stepped up right behind Mark's back, not more than a foot away. He reached around with his right hand and closed it over Mark's wrist. He eased Mark's arm sideways, keeping it straight, until the Glock was aimed sideways at nothing. He reached around with his left hand and clamped a bent elbow over Mark's upper body and crushed him to his chest. He touched the point of his arrow to the hollow of Mark's throat. Neither man moved.

The big man said, "Drop the weapon."

A deep voice, but quiet. Almost intimate. As if intended for Mark's ear alone. In tone it sounded more like a suggestion than a command. But with a bleak implication behind it.

Mark didn't drop it.

Patty saw muscles bunching in the giant's right forearm. There was no expression on his face. She realized he was crushing Mark's wrist. Slowly, steadily, inexorably. Mark jerked and thrashed.

The big man kept on squeezing. Mark dropped the gun.

"Good choice," the big man said.

But he didn't let go. He said, "What's your name?"

Mark didn't answer.

Patty said, "His name is Mark."

"Mark what?"

"I don't know. Who are you?"

"Long story," the big man said. His muscles bunched again.

Mark squirmed.

"What's your last name?" the big man asked.

Bones clicked and creaked and moved.

"Reacher," Mark gasped.

A HUNDRED yards back, Reacher had seen the woman light up the hunter with the flashlight beam and then run like hell. He had seen the hunter chase after her. He had chased after both of them. He caught up in time to see the Mercedes arrive. He crossed the track in the dark way behind it and crept up on the far side. He heard most of the conversation. He had heard the guy say he thought he and the woman were the last two standing. Her name was Patty Sundstrom, according to the banker, just before he died. Shorty would be Shorty Fleck. Canadians. Stranded.

"I got money," Mark said. "You can have it."

"Don't want it," Reacher said. "Don't need it."

"Got to be some way we can work this out."

Reacher said, "Patty, pick up his gun. Very carefully. Finger and thumb on the grip."

Patty came close and grabbed the gun and scuttled back. Reacher bent Mark's arm more, until his forearm was folded back on his upper arm, and his hand was touching his shoulder.

Reacher took his arrow away from Mark's throat, and his elbow off his chest, and Mark dropped gratefully to his knees, to relieve the pressure on his arm. Reacher changed his grip. He let go of his wrist, bunched his fist in his collar, and twisted.

Then he looked at Patty and said, "Do you want to do it, or should I?"

"Do what?"

"Shoot him."

"Who are you?" she said again.

"Long story," he said again. "I needed a motel for the night."

"We should call the police."

"Were you headed somewhere?"

"Florida," she said. "We wanted a new life."

"Doing what?"

"Windsurfer rentals. Maybe Jet Skis and T-shirts, too."

"Sounds great."

"We thought so."

"Alternatively you could spend three years living in a chain hotel somewhere in New Hampshire, talking to really obnoxious people, half the time bored to death, and the other half scared to death. Want to do that instead?"

"No."

"That's what will happen if we call the police. You'll be talking to detectives and prosecutors and lawyers and psychiatrists, over and over again, including some pretty tough questions, because they'll do the math the same way I have. So far I caught up to four of them. I'm guessing there were more, originally."

"There were six originally."

"What happened to the first two?"

She didn't answer. Just breathed in and breathed out.

"You would win in the end," Reacher said. "Probably. Some kind of justifiable homicide, or self-defense. But nothing is certain. You need to think about this carefully."

She said nothing. Mark started to struggle.

Reacher said to Patty, "He wanted to leave Shorty to die."

She paused, then looked down at the gun in her hand.

"Come around," he said. "So you're pointing it away from me."

She came and stood next to him.

Mark struggled and thrashed until Reacher hauled him upright and punched him hard in the solar plexus, and lowered him down again, momentarily incapable of voluntary muscular control.

Reacher said, "Stick the tip of the suppressor hard in his back, between his shoulder blades. The safety is a little tab on the front of the trigger. It clicks in as soon as your finger is in the correct position. Then all you do is squeeze."

She stood still for what felt like twenty seconds.

She said, "I can't."

Reacher let go of Mark's collar, and sent him sprawling with a push. He took the Glock from Patty. "I wanted you to have the opportunity. That was all. Otherwise you would have wondered all your life. But now you know. You're a good person, Patty."

"Thank you."

"Better than me," he said.

He turned and shot Mark in the head. Twice. A fast tight double tap, low in the back of the skull. What the army schools called the assassination shot. Not that they would ever admit it.

THEY used the Mercedes to go get Shorty. First Reacher dragged the tow truck guy into the trees on one side of the track, and then Mark on the other. Out of the way.

Patty drove. She got turned around and headed back with high-beam headlights. She came out of the mouth of the track. Up ahead and two acres away the motel was a low pile of glowing embers. The barn was burning fiercely. The house was burning harder.

Two quad bikes stood abandoned near the center of the meadow. There were two humped shapes on the ground next to them.

"There were four altogether," Patty said. "Mark, Peter, Steven, and Robert."

"I heard gunshots," Reacher said. "Suppressed 9-millimeter rounds. I think Mark just dissolved the partnership."

"Where's the fourth guy?"

"In the house, probably. I wouldn't have heard a gunshot from there. There won't be much left behind."

They watched the flames for a minute more, and then Patty turned left and drove across the bumpy grass close to the edge of the woods. She slowed down in two separate places, and took a long hard look, but both times she drove on. Finally she stopped.

She said, "It all looks the same now."

Reacher asked, "How deep in is he?"

"I can't remember. We walked a bit, and then I dragged him farther. To where I thought he was safe."

"Where did you go in?"

"Between two trees. I think it was here."

They shut down and got out. Without headlights the world was pitch-dark. Patty put her headset on again, and Reacher dropped his tube down in place. Infinite green detail came back.

They pushed into the forest. Patty led the way. They walked a slow curve, east and north. Vines and bushes clawed at their ankles.

Patty said, "I don't recognize anything."

Reacher called out, "Shorty? Shorty Fleck?"

Patty called out, "Shorty, it's me. Where are you?"

Nothing. They walked on. Every ten paces they stopped and called and shouted and yelled. Then they stood still and listened.

Nothing. Until the third time they did it.

They heard a tiny sound. Distant, quiet, metallic, slow. *Tink, tink, tink.* Due east, Reacher thought, maybe forty yards away.

He called out, "Shorty Fleck?"

Tink, tink, tink. They followed the sound.

They found him slumped against a tree. Exhausted with pain. He had night vision on and an arrow in his hand. He was tapping it against the optical tube. *Tink, tink, tink.* It was all he could do.

REACHER carried him back and laid him out across the rear seat of the Mercedes. His leg was busted bad. He had lost a lot of blood. He was pale but hot. He was damp with sweat.

Patty said, "Where should we take him?"

"Probably better to get out of the county," Reacher said. "You should go to Manchester. It's a bigger place."

"Are you not coming with us?"

Reacher shook his head. "Not all the way. I have an appointment in the morning."

"They'll ask questions at the hospital."

"Tell them it was a motorcycle accident. They'll believe you. Hospitals believe anything about motorcycles."

"Okay."

"Get him set, and then go park the car somewhere quiet. Leave the doors unlocked and the key in. You need it to disappear quick."

"Okay," she said again.

She got behind the wheel. Reacher got in the passenger seat, half turned around to keep an eye on Shorty. Patty turned a wide slow circle over the lumpy ground. Shorty bounced and jostled and gasped. Patty turned in at the mouth of the track.

Shorty slapped the seat beside him, weak and feeble.

Reacher said, "What?"

Shorty opened his mouth. He whispered, "Suitcase."

"We had a suitcase in the room," Patty said. "I guess it burned."

"I took it out," Shorty whispered.

Patty stopped the car. "Where is it?" she said.

"In the grass," he said. "Across the lot."

She turned around and set out across the meadow. Past the abandoned bikes and the bodies.

She stopped in the lot. They could feel the heat through the windows. Reacher saw the metal cage, sticking up out of the carpet of coals. Steel bars and steel mesh. Room 10. Shorty moved his forearm back and forth, just once, weak and limp. *From there to there.* Reacher got out and walked to the edge of the grass. He dropped his night-vision tube in place.

He saw the suitcase immediately. It was a huge old leather thing tied up with rope. It was lying flat in the grass. He stepped over and picked it up. It weighed a ton. He struggled back with it, lopsided. Patty opened the trunk for him.

He said, "What the hell have you got in here?"

"Comics," she said. "More than a thousand. All the great ones. Lots of early Superman. From our dads and granddads. We were going to sell them in New York, to pay for Florida."

There were two duffel bags already stashed in the trunk, zipped and bulging. Reacher took a look inside. They were both full of money. Bricks of cash. Maybe a million dollars in total.

"You should keep the comics," Reacher said. "You should use this instead. You could buy all the windsurfers you want."

"We can't," Patty said. "It isn't ours."

"I think it is. You won the game. You earned it," Reacher said.

She said nothing. Then she asked, "Do you want some?"

"I have enough to get by," Reacher said. "I don't need more."

He hefted the suitcase up and slid it in the trunk.

"What's your name?" Patty asked. "I would like to know."

"Reacher."

She said, "That was Mark's name."

"Different branch of the family."

They got back in the car, and she drove through the meadow, into the woods, all the way to the tow truck. Reacher took the key and climbed up and let himself in. He was a bad driver, anyway, and the controls were unfamiliar. But after a minute he got the lights turned on. Then he got the engine started. He found the gear selector and shoved it in reverse. A screen on the dashboard lit up, with a rearview camera. A color picture. It showed an ancient Subaru, parked right behind the truck, just waiting.

Reacher climbed down from the cab, and gave Patty a *Wait one* signal, which he hoped she understood. Then he squeezed and slid down the side of the truck, to the rear, and out to the air.

Burke met him right there. He had his hands up, in a kind of placatory *I know, I know* gesture. Apologizing in advance.

He said, "Detective Amos called. She said I should find you and tell you 10-41. I don't know what that means."

"It's a military police radio code," Reacher said. "It means immediate callback requested."

"There's no cell service here."

"We'll head south. But first move your car so I can move the truck.

We got someone else also heading south. They're in a bigger hurry."

He squeezed back to the cab, and gave Patty what he hoped was a reassuring wave from the ladder. He got the selector back in reverse. He saw a live picture of Burke backing up, so he backed up after him and parked backward on the opposite shoulder.

The black Mercedes nosed out after him.

He climbed down from the cab. The Mercedes stopped beside him. Patty buzzed the window down.

He said, "I'm getting a ride from the guy in the Subaru. It was nice meeting you. Good luck in Florida."

She craned up in her seat and looked down at the road.

"We're out," she said. "At last. Thank you. I feel we owe you."

"You would have figured it out," Reacher said.

"Thank you," she said again. "I mean it."

"Good luck in Florida," he said again. "Welcome to America."

He crossed the road to where the Subaru was waiting. She drove away, south. She raised a hand through her open window, like a wave, and then she kept it there a hundred yards, fingers open, feeling the rush of nighttime air against her palm.

Chapter 16

BURKE DROVE SOUTH on the back road. Reacher watched the bars on the phone. One bar came up, then a second, then the wide gravel shoulder they had used before. Burke pulled over. Reacher dialed. Amos answered right away.

She said, "The Boston PD called to tell us the cleanup hitter got home in the middle of the evening."

"Does he have Carrington?"

"They're making inquiries."

"What about Elizabeth Castle?"

"Both are still missing."

"Maybe I should go to Boston."

"You have somewhere else to go first. I found Stan Reacher. He showed up thirty years ago. He lived on his own for a long spell, and then he moved in with a younger relative. He's registered to vote, and he still has a driver's license."

"Okay," Reacher said.

"I called his house. He wants to see you."

"When?"

"Now."

"It's late."

"He has insomnia. He says you're welcome to come over."

"Where does he live?"

"Laconia," she said. "Right here in town. Chances are you walked right by his house."

It turned out the closest Reacher had previously gotten was two streets away, in his second hotel. He could have made a left out the door, and a right, and a left, to neat three-story town houses.

Stan lived in the house on the left.

Amos met them in an unmarked car at the entrance to the alley. She shook Burke's hand and said she was pleased to meet him. Then she turned to Reacher and said, "This could be very weird."

"Not very," he said. "Maybe a little. I think I figured most of it out. There was always something wrong with the story. Now I know what. Because of something old Mr. Mortimer said."

"Who is old Mr. Mortimer?"

"The old guy in the old people's home. He said back in the day from time to time he would visit his cousins in Ryantown. He said he remembers the bird-watching boys. He said he was drafted near the end of the war. He said they didn't need him. They had too many people already. He said he never did anything."

Amos said nothing.

They all went to the door together. Like delivering a death message, Reacher thought. Two MPs and a priest.

He rang the bell. Through a pebbled glass pane set high in the door he saw an old man shuffle into view. Stooped, gray, slow, unsteady. He got closer and closer, and then he opened the door.

The old man was about ninety. He could have started out six one and 190, at his peak. Now he was bent over like a question mark. His skin was slack and translucent. His eyes watered. He had strands of gray hair, as fine as silk.

He wasn't Reacher's father.

Not even thirty years older. Because he wasn't. Simple as that. Also forensically, because no broken nose, no shrapnel scar on his cheek, no stitch mark in his eyebrow.

The old man held out a wavering hand.

"Stan Reacher," he said. "I'm pleased to meet you."

Reacher shook the old man's hand. It felt cold as ice.

"Jack Reacher," he said. "Likewise."

"Are we related?"

"We're all related, if you go back far enough."

"Please come in."

Amos said she and Burke would wait in the car. Reacher followed the old guy down the hallway to a nook between the living room and an eat-in kitchen. It had two armchairs, set one each side of a lamp with a big fringed shade. Good for reading.

Old Stan Reacher waved his hand at one of the armchairs, like an invitation, and he sat down in the other. He was happy to talk. He confirmed he grew up in Ryantown, in the tin mill foreman's apartment. James and Elizabeth Reacher were his parents. He said it never occurred to him to wonder whether they did a good job or not. Bird-watching had given him a whole other world to live in.

Reacher asked, "Who introduced you?"

"My cousin Bill," Stan said.

"Who was he?"

"Back then, any kid's best friend was likely his cousin. Bill was mine, and I was his."

"What kind of cousin was he?"

"Neither one of us could count high enough. All we knew was I was Stan Reacher and he was William Reacher, and way back we both had the same ancestor in the Dakota Territory. I suppose the truth is Bill was a waif and stray. He seemed to be based up on the Canadian border. But he spent a lot of time in Ryantown."

"How old was he, the first time he came?"

"I was seven, so he was six. He stayed a whole year."

"Did he have parents?"

"We supposed so. He never saw them. But they weren't dead or anything. He got birthday cards every year. We thought they must be secret agents, undercover in a foreign country. Later we thought they were more likely organized crime."

"Was he already a bird-watcher at the age of six?"

"With the naked eye. Which he always thought was best of all. He wasn't good at explaining why. Later we understood. After we got binoculars. You get a bigger picture with the naked eye. You don't get distracted by the close-up beauty."

"How did you get the binoculars?"

"That was later. Bill would have been ten or eleven by then."

"How did you get them?"

The old man looked down for a second.

"Did he steal them?"

"Not exactly. They were spoils of war. Some kid with a stupid vendetta. Bill ran out of patience. We had been reading old battle poems. He said he felt he should seize something. The binoculars and thirty-one cents were all the kid had."

"You wrote about the rough-legged hawk together."

"We sure did," the old man said. "That was a fine piece of work. I would be proud of that today."

"Do you remember September 1943?"

"I guess a few things. It was a long time ago."

"Your name comes up in an old police report, about an altercation on the street. Late one evening. In fact, not far from here. You were seen with a friend."

"There were altercations on the street all the time."

"This one involved a local bully who was beaten to death two years later."

Stan Reacher said nothing.

"I'm guessing the friend you were seen with that night in

September 1943 was your cousin Bill. I think he started something that took two years to finish."

"Tell me again, who are you exactly?"

"I'm not exactly sure," Reacher said. "As of right now, I'm thinking maybe your cousin Bill's second son."

"Then you know what happened."

"I was a military cop. I saw it a dozen times."

"Am I in trouble?"

"Not with me," Reacher said. "The only person I'm mad at is myself. I guess I assumed this was the kind of thing that happened to other people."

"Bill was a smart boy. Streetwise. But he knew other stuff, too. He was good at his books. He knew a lot of science. He loved his birds. He was a nice person, back when that meant something. But you better not mess with his sense of right and wrong. He had a rule. If you did a bad thing, he would make sure you only did it once. He was a good fighter, and he was brave as a lunatic."

"Tell me about the kid he killed."

Stan shook his head. "I would be confessing to a crime."

"No one will bust you. The cops filed it under NHI. No human involved."

Stan nodded. "I could agree with them. That kid was every kind of bully. He was the kind of kid who hung around four years after high school, doing the same old things to younger and younger victims. But in a nice car, because his daddy was rich. He became perverted. He started interfering with little boys and girls. He was making them do disgusting things. At that point Bill didn't know about him. Then he came back to town and found out, that night."

"What happened?"

"Bill showed up in Ryantown, like he often did, out of nowhere, and we came down here to the jazz lounge. There was a band we liked. We were walking back to where we hid our bikes, and then all of a sudden the kid came walking toward us. He ignored Bill and started tormenting me. Because he knew me. He was probably starting up again where he left off the last time. But Bill was hearing this stuff for the very first time. He took the kid apart."

"Then what?"

"Then it became different. The kid put out a kind of death warrant. Bill started carrying brass knuckles. There were a couple of incidents. A couple of would-be friends, trying to make their bones. Bill kept the emergency room busy. He sent the would-be friends their way. Then it was a background thing for a while. Bill was in and out of Ryantown. Then it blew up again. One night they ended up all alone, face-to-face. The first I knew about it was Bill showing up later, asking for a favor."

"He wanted to borrow your birth certificate, to join the marines."

Stan nodded. "He needed to bury the name William Reacher. He needed the trail to go cold. It was a homicide, after all."

"And he needed to be a year older than he really was," Reacher said. "That's what was wrong with the story he told. He said he ran away and joined the marines at seventeen. No doubt that's true, in and of itself. But he couldn't have done it if the marines knew he was seventeen. They wouldn't have taken him. Not then. It was September 1945. The war was over. They wouldn't want a seventeen-year-old. Two years earlier, sure. They were fighting in the Pacific. But not anymore. On the other hand, an eighteen-year-old was always entitled to volunteer. So he needed your ID."

Stan nodded again.

"We thought it would make him safe," he said. "And it did, I guess. The cops gave up. I left Ryantown soon afterward. I went bird-watching in South America and stayed forty years. When I got home, I had to sign up for all kinds of things. I used the same birth certificate. I wondered what would happen if the system said the name Stan Reacher was already taken. But it all worked out fine."

"Thank you for explaining," Reacher said.

"What happened to him?" Stan said. "I never saw him again."

"He became a pretty good marine. He fought in Korea and Vietnam. He served in all kinds of other places. He married a Frenchwoman. Her name was Josephine. They got along. They had two boys. He died thirty years ago."

"Did he have a happy life?"

"He was a marine. Happy was not in the field manual. Sometimes he was satisfied. That was about as good as it got. But he was never unhappy. He felt he belonged. He kept on bird-watching. He loved his family. Sometimes we thought he was crazy. He wasn't sure of his birthday. Now I understand why. Yours was July, and his was originally June. I guess sometimes he got confused. But he did fine with the name. I never heard him slip. He was always Stan."

They talked a while longer. Reacher asked about the motel, and their theoretical relative Mark, but Stan had no information beyond a vague family story about some distant cousin getting rich during the postwar boom, and buying real estate, and then having a cascade of offspring, all kinds of children and grandchildren and great-grandchildren. Presumably Mark was one of them.

Then he said he needed to nap for an hour. That was how it went, he said, with his insomnia. He took hour-long naps whenever he could. Reacher shook his hand and let himself out of the house. Dawn was coming. Burke and Amos were sitting in Amos's car. Burke buzzed his window down, and Reacher bent down to talk.

He said, "I need to go to Ryantown."

Burke said, "The professor won't be there for hours."

"That's why."

Amos said, "I need to think about Carrington."

"Think about him in Ryantown. It's as good a place as any."

"Do you know something?"

"We should be looking for Elizabeth Castle as much as Carrington. They're very romantic. They counted their morning coffee break as their second date. They're almost certainly together."

"Sure, but where?"

"I'll tell you later. First I want to go to Ryantown again."

THEY went in Amos's unmarked car. She drove, and Burke sat beside her. Reacher sprawled in the back. He told them everything Stan had told him. They asked how he felt. He said nothing had changed, except a minor historical detail. His father had once been called by a different name, long ago. Same guy. If you did the right thing, he left you alone. A good fighter, and brave as a lunatic.

"Did your mother know?" Amos asked.

"Great question," Reacher said. "Probably not. It turned out she had secrets of her own. Maybe that's why they got along."

On their right the sky was streaked with dawn. The car was filled with low golden light. Amos found the turn to Ryantown. The gentle left, through the orchards. She stopped at the fence.

"Five minutes," Reacher said.

He got out of the car and stepped over the fence. He walked through the orchard. The dawn light was on his back. He stepped over the next fence. The Ryantown city limit.

He walked down Main Street like before, past the church, past the school. After that the trees grew thinner, and the sun crept higher. Dappled sunbeams twinkled in. The world was new.

He heard voices up ahead.

Two people talking. Lightly and happily. About something pleasant. Maybe the sunbeams.

He called out, "Hey guys, officer on the floor, coming in, make yourselves decent and stand by your beds."

He waited. Nothing happened. He walked down to the four-flats and found Carter Carrington and Elizabeth Castle standing side by side on the ghost of the road, halfway to the stream. Beyond them were two mountain bikes, leaning on trees. Beyond the bikes a tent was pitched, where the mill foreman's living room used to be.

Carrington said, "Good morning."

"You, too."

"It's always good to see you," Carrington said. "But is this purely a coincidence?"

"Not exactly," Reacher said.

"You were looking for us."

"Something came up. Turned out to be nothing. It's all good now. But I thought I should drop by, anyway. To say goodbye."

"How did you find us?"

"For once I listened to the front of my brain. I guess I remembered how it felt. Just when you think it's passing you by, boom, you meet someone. You do all the sappy things you thought you were never going to get a chance to do. You celebrate the thing that brought you together. Some people do really weird stuff. You do Stan Reacher. You were tracing Stan's birth record. You wanted to do it properly, every step of the way. You got the last known address. Elizabeth already knew where it was, because she and I worked it out together, on her phone. So you went to find it."

They smiled and held hands.

Reacher said, "I'm glad you're happy."

Elizabeth Castle said, "Thank you."

"And it shouldn't make a material difference."

"What shouldn't?"

"In the interests of full disclosure, I have to tell you it turns out Stan Reacher was not who I was looking for."

"He was your father."

"Turns out he was just a borrowed birth certificate. I hope that doesn't put a jinx on your relationship."

"Who borrowed the birth certificate?"

"An obscure cousin. A blank space on the family tree."

"How does that make you feel?"

"Absolutely great," Reacher said. "The less I know, the happier I get."

"And now you're moving on."

"It was nice to meet you. I wish you both the best of luck."

Carrington said, "What was the cousin's name?"

"William."

"Would you mind if we looked into him? It could be interesting. It's the kind of thing we enjoy."

"Knock yourselves out," Reacher said. "In exchange for a favor. Come say hello to a friend of mine. Just a five-minute walk. I'm sure you know her. Detective Amos, from the Laconia PD."

"Brenda?" Carrington said. "Why is she here?"

"Theoretically there might have been a threat against you. She won't believe it's over until she sees for herself."

"What kind of threat?"

"You slightly resembled the target of an attempted gangland killing. Detective Amos's thoroughness made it a concern."

"Brenda was worried about me?"

"You're the guy who goes to bat for them. They seem to like you. It's a sign of weakness. You need to be tougher in future."

They walked up Main Street together. Past the school. Past the church. Out to the sunny orchard. Amos and Burke waited at the far fence. There were handshakes across the top rail. Assurances were given. Explanations were made. Vacation, no cell service, apologies. No problem, Amos said. Just following up.

Carrington and Castle walked back.

Reacher watched them go. He climbed the fence and stood with the others. He said, "I decided to skip the professor. Maybe you could give him a call."

"Sure," Burke said.

"Back to town now?" Amos asked.

Reacher shook his head. "I'm going to San Diego."

"From here?"

"Seems appropriate. My dad started out from here many times. This was one of the places he lived. A year, when he was six."

"You want us to leave you in the middle of nowhere?"

"I'll get a ride. I've done it before. You guys get going. It was a pleasure to meet you. I mean it. I appreciate your kindness."

They all stood for a moment. Then they all shook hands, kind of sudden and awkward. Two MPs and a priest. All buttoned-up.

Burke and Amos got in the car. Reacher watched them drive away. The low morning sun boiled around them. Then they were gone. He set out walking in the same direction. Through the same gentle curve. The sun was in his eyes all the way. He made it to the north-south back road. He picked a spot, and stood in the gutter, and stuck out his thumb.

AfterWords

Past Tense is Lee Child's twenty-third Jack Reacher novel, and the author is still going strong. In this entry, Child tapped into the current genealogy fad and decided to have Reacher dig into his roots by way of a tiny town in New Hampshire. But along with old census reports and unexpected intel on his parents, Reacher finds trouble, too, just as naturally as he'll find a ride to the next town in the next book.

As usual, Child did not use an outline for this story, nor did he have any real plan for where it would go. He simply started the first sentence on September 1, as is his annual habit, and wrote a few lines. "I wrote that first paragraph and realized I used bird-watching-type imagery about the migration of birds," he recalls. "And about the only thing we know about Reacher's father from previous books is that he was a bird-watcher. So I thought, Why have I done it that way? Well, this is obviously going to be a book about his father." And so book number twenty-three was launched.

The Jack Reacher series is one of the most successful brands in publishing. Reacher books have been published in forty-nine languages and in 101 territories. With over a million books sold, the series has garnered more than a billion dollars in sales.

There are rumors circulating about negotiations for a possible Reacher series on Netflix, so stay tuned with fingers crossed.

MARIE BOSTWICK

NEW YORK TIMES BESTSELLING AUTHOR

Hope on the Inside

Chapter 1

On most days, Hope Carpenter was early to rouse but slow to rise.

It was a habit she had developed while a young and happily harried mother of four, including one set of twins, with a to-do list that would have required a twin of her own to complete. Setting her alarm to go off before the rest of the family stirred, Hope woke before dawn and lingered in the cocoon of covers for fifteen minutes, relishing the luxury of stillness and unstructured time.

Even now, with her children grown and gone, she still cherished those few precious, predawn moments of peace and quiet. When her cell phone began to hum on a Friday in November that seemed like any other, Hope stirred and stretched in the dark before shutting off the alarm. Careful not to wake Rick, she plumped her pillow, smiling to herself when she caught the scent of lavender.

Hope was acutely sensitive to smells. Whenever she smelled boxwood, she was instantly brought back to her grandmother's tidy garden where she played hide-and-seek with her little sister, Hazel. When Hope smelled motor oil, she was suddenly sitting on the concrete floor of the garage, handing tools to her dad as he worked on his 1969 Boss 429 Mustang.

Thirty-four years before, Hope had made her own wedding

bouquet—white roses, dusty miller, and fragrant French lavender. Moments before the church doors opened, she was hit by a sudden jolt of nerves. Taking a deep breath, she smelled lavender and felt suddenly brave and sure. Ever since, Hope believed that lavender imparted courage. That was why she sprinkled a little lavender oil on her pillow each night; it helped her embrace the day to come.

Most scents summoned up happy memories for Hope. But not always. The hospice where her mother died had an herb garden with a huge rosemary bush. An avid and skilled cook, Hope enjoyed the scent of most fresh herbs. But since her mother's death, just five months after Hope's twenty-first birthday, Hope associated the smell of rosemary with ominous news.

Though Hope was wide awake on that early Friday morning, the sun still wasn't up when the phone rang.

Reed, born seventeen minutes after his twin brother, Rory, was calling from Philadelphia. He'd just been offered a full professorship in the English department and was so excited to share the news that he forgot about the three-hour time zone difference between Oregon and Pennsylvania.

Five minutes after Reed hung up, McKenzie phoned. She and Zach had just landed in Seattle, returning from their Hawaiian honeymoon. As usual, McKenzie had dialed Rick's cell phone, but Hope, who was getting dressed for work by then, eavesdropped on the conversation.

When Rick said, "Yes, kitten, she's right here. Hang on," Hope was surprised. Usually, Rick had to prompt their only daughter to talk with her. That day McKenzie was eager to talk to her, sounding truly happy, almost giddy.

McKenzie, who never sought her mother's advice, asked Hope to e-mail her famous goulash recipe.

"Not the noodles," McKenzie clarified. "Just the sauce. I'll put it over macaroni."

"Sure. That'll work," Hope said. It was good to hear McKenzie so happy. Zach turned out to be the right man for her after all.

After her daughter's two broken engagements, Hope could be forgiven for having dragged her feet when it came to making wedding arrangements. When Hope realized her daughter was serious, she kicked into high gear. She oversaw the menus, hand-calligraphied place cards, and stitched sachets as favors for the wedding guests. Hope had wanted to sew the wedding dress as well, but McKenzie was dead set on wearing Vera Wang.

Hope's mother had been an excellent seamstress. She'd often talked about making wedding dresses for Hope and Hazel when they grew up. But by the time Hope was engaged, it was too late. She was losing ground against the illnesses she'd battled for so long and no longer had the strength to sew.

Instead, Hope made the gown. When it was finished, Hope brought the dress to her mother's room and sat on the bed while she and her mom stitched the hem of the huge, flouncy skirt. As they sewed, Hope's mother imparted every piece of marital advice in her arsenal, barely pausing between subjects. It was a long talk.

At the end of it, she took Hope's hands in her bony grasp and said, "Make up your mind to be happy, Hope. Whatever comes your way, find the happiness in it. That's the real trick of life."

Thirty-four years later, Hope still tried to follow that advice.

The conversation with McKenzie went so long that Hope was nearly late to work, sprinting from the faculty parking lot and through the door of the high school just before the first bell.

After a nearly three-decade hiatus to raise her children, this was only Hope's second year back in teaching. Things had changed a lot in that time. Home Ec was now called FACS, Family and Consumer Science, and the curriculum was completely transformed.

During her first year back in the classroom, she often felt overwhelmed. Staying one step ahead of her students required her to burn a lot of midnight oil. But now, three months into her second year, Hope had a handle on things. The glowing review she received from her principal that day confirmed it.

She tried calling Rick to share the good news, but he didn't answer his phone. However, since it was Friday, she got to tell Hazel all about it when the sisters met for happy hour.

"It's funny, isn't it?" Hope said, taking the last piece of cheese.

"What is?" Hazel said.

"How things work out. I only went back to teaching because Liam got into film school at UCLA. If we hadn't needed the extra tuition money, I might have quit after a month. But now I love it."

"Why do you sound so surprised? You're a natural born teacher. I mean, you raised four amazing kids. Well, five, if you count me." Hazel grinned. "What's motherhood besides a two-decade long teaching gig?"

"Oh, it's way longer than that," Hope said. "Doesn't matter how old your kids get, you never stop being a mom."

When the waitress approached with the check, Hope nipped it quickly, earning an exasperated look from her sister.

"Come on," Hazel said. "At least let's split it."

Hope gave the waitress a stern look. "Trust me. You don't want my sister's money. She's a well-known counterfeiter."

The waitress laughed, and Hope and Hazel got up from the table.

Hope held the door open, then followed Hazel onto the sidewalk. It was chilly and wet—typical for November in Oregon.

Hazel looked down at her phone as she scanned through her text messages. She stopped, frowning.

"Oh no. Hang on, Sis. I need to call the office." Hazel punched a number into the phone, switching to her all-business voice when her assistant answered. When Hazel said, "We are not going to lose a two-million-dollar transaction because Stan failed to read the contract," Hope realized Hazel was going to be a while.

If Hope had to sum up her sister in three words, they would be *loyal, honest,* and *single-minded*. Only twenty-eight years after closing her first real estate deal on a charming Victorian—a fixer-upper that Rick and Hope were *still* fixing up—Hazel was the owner of Hazelnut Realty, with fifty employees and three offices.

Hope glanced at her watch, then squeezed Hazel's shoulder in farewell. Hazel mouthed a goodbye and went back to her call.

Hope stopped by the market to pick up ingredients for goulash, thinking it would be nice to surprise Rick. He had been working late for months, ever since his engineering firm had been bought by another firm.

But when Hope got home, she was surprised to see Rick's car in the garage. It had been months since he'd left the office early. Rick kept telling her that his crushing work schedule was just temporary, that things would settle down once people quit feeling like they had to prove themselves to the new management.

Maybe his prediction had finally come true? Hope carried the groceries to the house, humming a happy tune.

But that was before Hope opened the door, sniffed the air, and felt her stomach clench like a fist.

Rosemary.

Rick Carpenter stood six-four and weighed two hundred twenty pounds. He had blue eyes, short gray hair that matched his beard, and muscular shoulders. He had played for the senior division of the Portland Rugby Club into his early fifties. Even now, at age fifty-eight, he looked like he could kick the butts of guys half his age.

Rick inherited his love of rugby from his dad, an Irish dockworker turned welder who emigrated at age twenty with ninety dollars in his pocket and died from complications of an industrial accident when Rick was just fourteen.

His deceased father loomed large in his life. Rick was the stubborn son of a stubborn man, a man whose boyhood had been cut short and who had pulled himself up by the bootstraps.

But the influence of Rick's mother, Ruth, was also strong. She instilled him with a reverence for education and a belief that hard work would not go unrewarded. And when Rick's temper started getting him into fights at school, Ruth taught him to bake.

It was just what he needed.

Whereas other men might handle anxiety by pounding a speed bag at the gym or heading to the nearest bar, Rick pounded his frustrations into a mound of warm bread dough.

When Rick got home that day, around noon, he'd gone directly into the kitchen. He went to work, furiously chopping olives and rosemary before mixing them into the sticky dough. By the time he'd kneaded it a second time, he had formulated a plan and felt much better.

The only thing he had to do now was deal with Hope. She'd be upset at first, like he'd been, but Hope was nothing if not sensible. Once she got past the emotional part, she'd realize that nothing had changed.

He just had to break the news gently.

"Hey," Rick said, giving her a peck on the cheek before lifting the hot loaves from the baking pan to a cooling rack. "Got home early and thought I'd surprise you. Don't they smell great?"

Hope looked surprised. She was carrying a grocery bag in one arm and clutching the neck of a wine bottle in her hand.

"What's wrong?" Hope asked, ignoring his grin.

"Nothing."

Hope shook her head. "Something's happened. You only make rosemary olive bread when something's gone wrong and you're trying to break it to me gently."

"Hope, it's only bread. Nothing's wrong. Really." Rick searched for a corkscrew, avoiding her eyes. "There is a . . . well, a situation. But it's not bad," he said quickly as he took two wineglasses from the cabinet. "In fact, it's good. I'm retiring."

"What?" Hope stared incredulously. "Retiring? You're only fifty-eight years old. You love being an engineer!"

Rick poured wine into the first glass. He did love being an engineer. He'd worked harder than anyone he knew to become one.

When they first married, Hope was still teaching, supporting them both so he could go to school full time. Then the twins came. For seven years, Rick worked construction during the day, studied and went to class nights and weekends. When he finally finished, Hope, Hazel, Rory and Reed, two-year old McKenzie, and his mother were all there to see him receive his diploma. Ruth said it was the proudest moment of her life.

And now he was retiring? No wonder Hope didn't believe his story. The doubt in her voice made him doubt himself.

"You mean . . ." She hesitated. "You mean they fired you?"

"No," he said, and handed her some wine. "They did *not* fire me. They offered an early retirement package to me and a few of the other senior engineers. And I decided to take it."

"*You* decided?" she snapped. "Without even discussing it with me? Haven't we talked about this?"

They had, more than once. The last time was when Hope came

home from a weekend with Hazel and found a brand-new SUV parked in the driveway. The argument that ensued was heated.

"You said you wouldn't make any big decisions without—"

"I didn't decide! They decided for me! All right?" Rick roared. "They decided! Are you happy now?"

Hope stood silent. Rick knocked back his wine, gulping it down without tasting it, trying to swallow back the catch in his throat.

"These people are vultures," he said. "They gave me two options, retire early with severance or wait to be fired." He put down his glass. "What else was I supposed to do?"

The anger in Hope's eyes melted. She laid her hand over his.

"Babe, I'm so sorry. Are you okay?"

"I'm fine," he said, his throat still tight. "Glad to be out of there. It's been miserable since the buyout."

"It has," Hope agreed. "You've been killing yourself."

"Yeah. Well. Not anymore."

He topped off his glass and tilted it in her direction. Hope touched the rim of her glass to his, returning his smile. Somehow Rick felt renewed. And forgiven.

"What would you say to Christmas in Hawaii?" he asked.

"Hawaii?" Hope said, laughing a little. "This doesn't seem like quite the time for a vacation, does it?"

"It's the perfect time. You'll have a break from school, and for the first time in forever, my calendar is totally open."

Hope smiled. "A real vacation? Very tempting. What about Hazel? We can't desert her over the holiday."

"Tell her to come along," Rick said. "The more the merrier. I'll look for a condo we can rent."

"Well . . . okay. Let's do it," Hope said, her face splitting into a grin. "Assuming you haven't found another job by then. You're not really planning on retiring. Are you?"

"Of course not."

Rick sliced into one of the loaves, smiling at a job well done.

"Don't worry," he said. "I have a plan. I'm going to spend the next few weeks working on the house. Thought I'd start by replacing the roof on the sunporch."

"Really?" Hope said, her face lighting up.

"Really. Then we'll fly to Maui for an amazing Christmas before I come home and start sending out résumés."

"But," Hope said, "are you sure you want to wait that long?"

"Nobody will be hiring until January. I might as well take a little time off while I can." He handed her a piece of the bread. "Honey, we're fine," he said, seeing the wheels turn behind her eyes.

The two of them had grown up poor. Pinching pennies was a hard habit to break, harder for Hope than Rick.

"The package they offered me is pretty decent. It won't take long for me to find another job. After all, who engineered half the buildings in downtown Portland?"

"Let me think . . ." Hope said, giving him a smile. "Was it you?"

"Damn straight, it was. I'll find a new job by St. Patrick's at the latest," Rick declared. "Then we'll bank the severance. Or pay off the second mortgage we had to take out for Liam's tuition."

Hope's eyes widened a bit. "Do you really think we could?"

He nodded, thinking how beautiful she was and what a good team they made. He was nothing when they met, a part-time student and full-time drywall contractor. He'd given her the hard sell, explaining that someday he would become the man she deserved.

With Hope by his side, it had happened. "You know something?" Rick said. "I think this is going to turn out to be a good thing." He laid his arm over Hope's shoulders, kissed the top of her head. "Everything's going to be fine. You'll see."

Chapter 2

A YEAR AND A HALF LATER, everything *was* fine.

They weren't homeless or hungry. They had their children and health, which, as Hope often reminded herself, was what mattered.

In the big picture, everything was fine. But it was also different. Hope was angry. But not for the reasons you might think.

At first, things were actually pretty terrific. Rick spent weeks before Christmas replacing the porch roof and refinishing the dining room floors. When they first bought the house, they tackled those kinds of projects together. But as his responsibilities at the office increased, Rick had less time for home repair.

That was all right. Hope understood.

When the kids were young, she always felt they were working toward the same goal—building a strong family. She didn't earn a paycheck, but she worked just as hard as Rick did. Hope scheduled play dates, field trips, and game nights. She was the den mother, room mother, troop leader, and bus chaperone. Every kid in the neighborhood wanted to hang out at the Carpenter home.

Hope and Rick approached the job of child-rearing much the way their parents had, dividing the work along traditional gender-specific lines. Hope understood it wasn't the only good way to raise a family, but it worked for them.

Rory, the oldest twin, was a doctor. Reed was a professor. McKenzie worked as an IT professional for the state of Washington. Liam, the baby, attended UCLA film school. Whenever Hope looked at her children, she thought, *Yeah. We did good.*

On that first Monday after Rick's forced retirement, Hope came home and discovered that Rick had torn the shingles off the porch roof. He'd also made dinner. Rick was so talkative, excited about the possibility of a new career challenge. It reminded Hope of the old days, when they were both bursting with plans for the future.

For a while, everything went according to plan.

Their Hawaiian Christmas was truly the trip of a lifetime. When they got home, Rick turned the dining room into his "Career Change Command Center" and started sending out résumés.

That's when the plan started to fall apart.

Hope didn't blame Rick. He sent out scores of résumés, went to dozens of networking luncheons, and applied for every job posting that vaguely matched his skills. For seven months, Rick made looking for work his full-time job. Nobody could have tried harder.

Then Ruth died. She caught pneumonia and was gone in a week.

At first, it seemed like Rick was taking it pretty well, considering how close he'd been to his mother. Yes, Hope caught him crying more than once, but why shouldn't he? Hope cried too. Ruth had been a wonderful mother-in-law and grandmother. They all missed her. Still, all things considered, Rick seemed okay.

Then something changed. Rick spent less time in his Command Center and more time in the kitchen baking and eating. When he wasn't doing that, he watched the Food Channel.

For a while, Hope let him be. He was entitled to his grief, and they were okay financially. Between Rick's severance and her salary, they were getting by. Then in August, Hope's principal called. Due to budget cuts, they were cutting the FACS department, not just at her school, but at all the schools, statewide.

That's when Hope started to get scared. She looked for another job, but with only two years of classroom experience, she wasn't going to get hired to teach anytime soon. She looked for other work, finally taking a job at a discount store. The hours were terrible, but at least she was bringing in a little money. She thought Rick would be happy, even proud of her. He wasn't.

Two days after Hope started working at the store, they fought.

It started because Rick made a batch of sourdough starter and left it on the counter. Thinking it was a baking experiment gone wrong, Hope threw it out. But, of course, it wasn't really about the sourdough.

Rick snatched a beer from the refrigerator and slammed the door. "Hey! If you're sick of me hanging around the house all day, then come out and say it. Do me a favor and be honest for once."

"Rick," she said through clenched teeth, "I have no idea what you're talking about. I came in from work. I was tired. I was cleaning, and the dough smelled funny, so I threw it away. I didn't realize you wanted to keep it. It was a mistake, not a criticism."

"Right," he said, making a show of nodding his head. "*You* were working all day. *You* were tired. No criticism there. Uh-uh. Why don't you come out and say it? Just ask me the question you're dying to ask instead of throwing out all the jabs and hints!"

"What question? Rick, I have no idea what you're talking about."

"Yes, you do. You're just too busy pretending to be understanding and supportive to say it." He cracked open the beer can and made his voice a nasally whine. "Poor hardworking Hope, slaving over a hot cash register all day long while her deadbeat husband stays home and bakes cookies. Please," he said, tossing back a gulp of beer. "You know what the question is! You want to know what the hell I do here all day while you're out working so hard!"

"Well?" she shouted. "What *are* you doing? From where I'm sitting, it looks like nothing. It looks like you've given up!"

Rick spewed a string of curses and got right up in Hope's face.

"Do you have *any* idea how many résumés I've sent out? What do you expect me to do? Keep pounding my head into the wall?" he shouted. "Or maybe you want me to learn from your example, take some crap job ringing up bags of stale chips and bottles of generic shampoo. Would that make you happy?"

"Hey!" Hope cried. "At least I'm making an effort. Don't you get it? When the severance runs out, we could lose everything!"

Rick let out a snarling laugh.

"Well, well. Look who just woke up and realized that it takes money to live. You're about thirty years late getting to the party, but, hey, I guess I should be grateful you showed up at all, right?"

Angry tears spouted in Hope's eyes. "Stop it, Rick. You know that's not what I was—"

"When I need a lecture on financial reality, I'll let you know, okay? In case you hadn't noticed, while you were staying home and playing house, *I* was the one providing for this family, not you!"

That was what Hope was angry about.

For over thirty-four years, she thought of them as a team, different in their responsibilities but equal in their contribution. This was the belief she'd based her entire life and marriage on.

If Rick saw himself as an island and Hope as a millstone around his neck, then what *was* their marriage? What was her life?

What had they been playing at all these years?

HAZEL was sitting on the sofa in her pajamas, holding a glass of red wine, thinking about the phone conversation she'd had with her niece, wondering what, if anything, she should do about it.

When the doorbell rang at ten o'clock, Hazel was surprised to see her sister standing on the stoop. But not that surprised.

"If you've come for a drink," she said, raising her almost empty wineglass, "you're almost too late."

"Rick and I had a fight."

Hope told her sister all about the fight, how it started (stupidly), where it headed (downhill quickly), and how it ended (badly).

"He punched a wall?" Hazel's eyes widened in disbelief. She knew her brother-in-law well. After all, he'd partly raised her.

Two years after Hazel and Hope's mother died, their father fell while repairing the roof, hit his head, and died four days later. Hazel was sixteen. Hope and Rick took her in without hesitation.

Hazel understood that Rick had a short fuse, but he wasn't a violent man. Things must be even worse than McKenzie said.

"I grabbed the car keys and ended up here," Hope said. "Do you mind?"

Of course she didn't mind. Hazel poured her a glass of wine, then made her tell the whole story again, but more slowly.

When Hope was done, Hazel offered to lend them some money. Hope refused.

"No," she said firmly. "Besides, this isn't just about the money. It goes a lot deeper. After tonight, I'm wondering if I know Rick at all. Or if he knows me."

Hope put down her glass and buried her face in her hands.

"Oh, Hazel. The things we said to each other . . ."

"You didn't mean it. Neither did he. You and Rick love each other, always will. But, Hope, you're tired, and worn out—"

"And broke. Or about to be." Hope lifted her head. "My job at the store covers groceries and gas but that's it. We've got to come up with a plan before the severance money runs out. But what?"

"Well," Hazel said, "I've been doing some research. Do you know what your house is worth in today's market?"

Hope didn't, so Hazel told her.

"Really? That much?"

Hazel nodded. "House prices in Portland are skyrocketing. If you sell, you'll have enough to pay off the mortgages and then some."

"Enough to buy another house in our neighborhood?"

Hazel shook her head.

"Oh," Hope said, her face falling. "Well, what about—"

Hope started listing neighborhoods. Hazel kept shaking her head, finally explaining that the price hikes that would allow them to pay off their mortgages had also priced them out of Portland.

But Hazel had a plan.

"Olympia?" Hope said, sounding confused. "No. There has to be another solution. I've lived in Portland my whole life. So has Rick. All our friends are here, everybody we know. *You're* here."

Hazel put down her glass. "McKenzie and Zach love Olympia. And they'd love having you closer."

Hope frowned. "You already talked to McKenzie about this?"

"Olympia is a great town," Hazel said, ignoring Hope's question. "And it's not like we'll never see each other. I can drive up there in two or three hours, tops. And you can come visit me."

"I was born here," Hope said. "My roots are here. So is my house. I painted walls, put up wallpaper, tore out that awful linoleum . . ."

"Hope," Hazel said. "You said it yourself. You need a plan."

"You're right," Hope said softly, looking at her sister with wet and shiny eyes. "But can't I have a different one?"

"Hope. It's just a house. Rick is your—"

"I know." Hope took a deep breath. When she spoke again, her voice was steady. "You talked with McKenzie? You called her?"

"She called me," Hazel admitted. "I guess she's been talking to Rick. She's worried. And she'd love to have you closer."

Hope nodded, lifting her glass to her lips. "It might be good for Rick, having Kenz closer. She's always been his favorite."

"You're his favorite," Hazel countered.

"Mmm," Hope murmured absently.

"You *are*," Hazel insisted.

Hope put down her glass and looked into her sister's eyes.

ONCE the decision to sell the house and move to Olympia had been made, the plan to make it happen unfolded with almost disorienting speed. Most disorienting of all was how quickly Rick embraced the idea.

He was asleep when she got home from Hazel's that night. But sometime during Hope's shift at the discount store, Hazel talked to McKenzie, who talked to Rick. When Hope got home from work, she found him in the bedroom, pulling out shirts and sweaters from his side of the closet and tossing them into an empty box.

"What are you doing?"

"Getting rid of things I don't need. No point in paying money to move stuff I don't want anymore, right?"

The next day, Hazel showed up with her assistant and started staging the house, a process that primarily involved taking down and packing away anything that might remind potential buyers that actual human beings lived there.

They even got rid of the pen marks on the kitchen doorway where, year after year, Hope had marked the kids' heights on the first day of school. That was her low point.

Her mother had a rule when Hope was growing up: everybody is entitled to feel sorry for themselves but not more than once a day and not for more than ten minutes.

Hope went into the garden shed, set a timer on her watch, and bawled for ten minutes. When her watch beeped, she wiped her tears, went outside, and started raking.

By the end of the open house, they had two solid offers. The one they accepted was six thousand over asking but stipulated that they close in thirty days.

Hope felt like somebody had punched her in the stomach. Rick seemed jubilant, at least to Hope's eyes. But on their last night in the house, Hope realized she'd been wrong.

He stood in the front entry, at the foot of the grand oak staircase, staring up toward the dim corridor and empty bedrooms.

"Remember McKenzie's prom? She came down the stairs wearing that green dress. All grown up. Just like that," he said, his voice low. "That boy she was going with, what was his name?"

"Justin Striker."

"Justin. Justin Striker," Rick murmured, as if trying to burn the name into his memory. "The look on his face when she came downstairs . . . His jaw actually dropped. Do you remember?"

"No. But I remember how you made him sign a contract swearing he wouldn't speed, drink, or do anything to endanger or disrespect your daughter and would have her home by midnight." Hope laughed softly. "Poor Justin. McKenzie was mortified."

Rick smiled but only for a moment. He turned to face her.

"I'm sorry."

Hope almost said, "For what?" but stopped herself. She knew what he meant.

"You're not failing anybody, okay? Especially me. You never have."

Hope placed her hands on his rugged face. She looked into his weary eyes, seeing creases that hadn't been there a year before.

"This is going to be good," she said. "A fresh start for us both."

"You think?" Rick asked.

"Absolutely."

Her tone was so confident that she nearly convinced herself.

THE condo was on the fifth floor.

It had three bedrooms, two bathrooms, a dedicated parking space, wood floors, a so-called chef's kitchen with stainless steel appliances, and walls of windows with jaw-dropping views of Budd Bay and Mt. Rainier.

"This unit was totally renovated just last year," said the Realtor, Marcia. "You wouldn't need to do a thing."

She was right about that. Everything was pristine.

Maybe that's what bothers me about it, Hope thought. She walked slowly toward the kitchen with the shiny new appliances and countertops that had never known a spill. She was aware that Marcia and McKenzie were looking at her expectantly.

"Are there any other units for sale in this building?" Hope asked. "One that hasn't been updated?"

McKenzie laughed incredulously. "Mom. Why would you want a fixer-upper when you could have this?"

"I just thought we might save some money by doing the work ourselves. Besides, I like putting my own stamp on things."

McKenzie rolled her eyes. "So paint a wall or something. Hang some pictures. Why go through the work of remodeling if you don't have to? Did you see the price? You can afford this, no problem."

"It *is* well-priced," Marcia said. "The owners were transferred overseas and want a quick sale. It's the only unit for sale in this building. I'll be amazed if it isn't sold by the end of the week."

McKenzie bobbed her head. "Lucky thing we saw the open house sign. There's not another building like it in Olympia."

"You can't beat the views," Marcia added. "Or the location. Just minutes from downtown, so it's a really easy commute."

"My dad is retired," McKenzie said. McKenzie was speaking for Rick more and more. Hope didn't like it.

She appreciated McKenzie and Zach's kindness in letting them stay with them this last month. Hope was anxious to get out of the kids' place as soon as possible. But buying a home was a big decision. Was *this* the right place for them?

"There are lots of retired couples in this building. You'd fit right in," Marcia said with a smile that irritated Hope. "The unit is all on one level, so there are no stairs to climb. Also, the hallways are wide enough to accommodate a wheelchair, and the master bathroom is handicapped accessible."

Hope's jaw went slack. Marcia seemed to mistake her expression for confusion and clarified her comments.

"It's something a lot of retired people are looking for, somewhere they can age in place."

"Age in place?" Hope choked out a laugh. "Thanks but wheelchair-width hallways aren't at the top of my must-haves list."

"Not yet. But, you know . . ." McKenzie said, then shrugged.

When she thought about it later, Hope didn't quite understand what had gotten into her. But something had been bubbling inside her for days. And when McKenzie shrugged, as if to indicate that, in her opinion, the days of her parents' dotage were fast approaching, the bubbles fizzed, sputtered, and spilled over.

Without stopping to think, Hope executed a perfect cartwheel, sticking the landing right in front of Rick, who let out a laugh.

"Whoa! What was that about?"

Hope didn't know.

"Mom! Are you crazy? That dining table is made of glass! What if you'd crashed into it?"

The horror on her daughter's face brought Hope back to herself. Before Hope could answer, she felt Rick's arm around her waist.

"But she didn't. Good job, babe. Nice landing."

Marcia clapped her hands together and said, "Well, it's a very special home. Whatever your stage of life."

Rick nodded. "How much are homeowners association dues?"

The figure she named wasn't insubstantial. When Rick raised his eyebrows, Marcia said, "But that includes everything—maintenance, landscaping, insurance, and garbage."

Homeowners' fees were among Hope's objections to buying a condo. Convenience came at a price. And it wasn't like they didn't have time to deal with household maintenance themselves. Since coming to Olympia, they had nothing but time on their hands.

Hope needed meaningful things to do. So did Rick. She wasn't going to let McKenzie turn him into an old man before his time.

Initially, Hope thought that spending time with McKenzie would be good for Rick. But rather than help him shake off his depression, it seemed to Hope that McKenzie was encouraging him to lean into it. McKenzie barely let Rick do anything, even get up from the table to pour his own coffee. Rick needed to get away from McKenzie's coddling, and soon.

"How soon are the owners planning on moving?" Hope asked.

"Already gone," Marcia said. "You can move in as soon as the paperwork is finished. Have you been prequalified for a loan?"

Hope started to answer, but McKenzie beat her to it.

"Yes. They're working with EBA Mortgage," she said, turning to her father. "What do you think, Daddy? It seems perfect—"

"Excuse me," Hope said, addressing Marcia and interrupting McKenzie's interruption, "but would you mind giving us a minute? I think Rick and I need to discuss this, alone."

Marcia excused herself and went down the hallway. McKenzie followed but not before shooting her mother the sort of look Hope hadn't seen on her face since McKenzie was a teenager.

"Well? What *do* you think?" Hope asked when they were alone. "Do you want to put in an offer?"

"That depends. Do you think you could be happy here?"

"Could *you?*"

"I like that it's move-in ready and within our budget. I like that it's close to the kids. And I love this view."

That was the nearest thing to enthusiasm Hope had seen from him in months.

Rick took hold of her hand. The warmth of his skin felt like a promise, or a down payment on one. Maybe he *could* be happy here. And if he could, then she could too.

Chapter 3

MCKENZIE CHOKED SO HARD that she practically spat ginger ale into her pasta.

"Real estate?" she laughed, her eyes wide. "You?"

"Yes. Me," Hope said. "Is that so impossible to imagine? Hazel's done really well with it." Hope stabbed her salmon with her fork.

"Well, sure. Hazel," McKenzie said, her tone making it clear that her aunt's success in business didn't mean it ran in the family.

Hazel shot McKenzie a look. "If your mother decided she wanted to be a Realtor," Hazel said, fixing McKenzie with a laser-beam gaze, "then she'd be a brilliant one. Best in the business."

McKenzie shrank in her chair. Hope took a momentary pleasure in her sister's defense, then quickly regretted it. McKenzie was her only daughter. Why were they always at loggerheads?

"*Is* that what you want?" Hazel asked, turning toward Hope. "To become a Realtor?"

"Well, I . . . I like houses," Hope said, realizing she had spoken without really thinking things through. "I like fixing them up."

"You're good at that," Hazel agreed. "Selling them is different, though. But if you're really interested—"

"I'm not," Hope admitted. "I just want to do . . . something."

Hazel tipped her head to one side and waited.

"I thought things would be different here. With Rick, I mean." Hope sighed. "He's just as miserable in Olympia as he was in Portland. Apart from watching cooking shows and staring out the window, all he does is bake bread. And eat bread. I bet he's gained ten pounds since the move. I know I have," Hope said.

"Oh, you have not," Hazel said. "You look just the same."

"At *least* ten pounds," Hope said. "I don't care about his weight so much as his attitude. Before he was morose; now he's angry. Last week, I saw a listing for a discussion at the library on a book about the rivalry between Thomas Edison and Nikola Tesla and asked if he wanted to go. He jumped down my throat for suggesting it."

The waitress came by, proffering a basket filled with the last thing she needed—more bread. Hope waved her off. Hazel took another brioche.

"Maybe you need to try another approach, find something Rick is more interested in," Hazel said. "I saw that they're looking for new contestants for *Cake Wars*. Maybe Rick should audition."

When Hope snorted a laugh, Hazel looked happy to have brought a little levity to what was supposed to be a fun girl's day out but had quickly become a downer. Hope laughed again, deliberately this time. She hadn't seen Hazel in a month. She didn't want to spend what little time they had together complaining.

"Anything but *that*," Hope said. "Bread is bad enough. If Rick starts baking cakes, I'll get so big we'll have to remodel the whole condo—make the doors bigger, widen the hallways."

"Hey"—Hazel shrugged—"if that's what it takes to reignite his interest in engineering—"

"What is *wrong* with you!" McKenzie practically shouted. "Daddy lost his job and almost his whole identity, and you sit here making *jokes?* He's depressed! Don't you get it?"

Hope glared at her daughter.

"You think I don't know that? I've been married to your father for thirty-four years. I think I know him at *least* as well as you do. Possibly even a little better."

"If you do," McKenzie hissed, "why don't you help him instead of making fun of him? Why don't you try being there for him?"

"McKenzie, I've left a home and a life I love to be there for him. But I can't help him if he's not willing to help himself."

"What about counseling?" Hazel asked, looking at her sister.

Hope shook her head. "Rick will never go to a therapist."

"How do you know that?" McKenzie said.

"Because I asked him. About two hundred times." Hope put down her fork. "McKenzie, I would do almost anything for your father. But I will *not* sit in that condo day after day, twiddling my thumbs and watching him bake yet another loaf of bread.

"I've got to find something to do," Hope said, sounding almost desperate, turning toward Hazel. "I'd like to teach, but it's no better here than it was in Portland. No openings. But I need a job."

"How do you think that would make Daddy feel?" McKenzie interjected. "If you find a job when he can't? If you need something to do, why not volunteer work?"

"Because we also need money."

"But I thought things were fine now," McKenzie countered, her worried frown giving Hope the sense that she was finally listening. "I thought you guys had enough to get by."

"Just enough," Hope said. "If we're careful. I don't mind forgoing the extras, but I do mind forgoing insurance at our age."

"Insurance? I thought you got it through Dad's old company."

Hope shook her head. "They had to keep him on the company policy for a while but not forever. They'll boot us from the plan at the end of next month. Private policies are way out of our budget. I need to find a job. Not just for me. For us."

Their conversation was less heated after that. McKenzie grew quiet. Hazel asked the waitress for a go-cup of coffee for the drive back to Portland. They paid the check and got up from the table.

Hazel needed to visit the ladies' room before leaving, so McKenzie and Hope stood in the lobby of the restaurant, waiting to say goodbye to her. "I shouldn't have yelled like that," McKenzie said.

"No, you shouldn't," Hope agreed. "But it's okay. You were just trying to be protective of your dad. So am I. When it comes to your father, I've got a pretty good idea what works by now."

McKenzie nodded. "It's not easy, is it?"

"What? Dealing with your dad?" Hope asked.

"Being married."

"No. Not always," Hope said slowly, dipping her head, trying to look into her daughter's eyes. "Kenz? Is there something—"

Just then, Hazel exited the restroom. She had a big, dark stain on her blouse.

"The stupid top came off the stupid cup," she growled. "And the stupid towel dispenser is empty. And the blouse is brand new."

"Don't move," Hope said.

Hope found their waitress, who got her a handful of wet paper towels. When she returned to the lobby, McKenzie was gone.

"She bounced out of here in a hurry," Hazel explained. "She got a text and realized she was late for a conference call. She said to tell you she'd see everybody this weekend."

"Oh, good. Liam's coming home for a few days, so I'm cooking a big dinner on Sunday. I don't suppose you can make it?"

"Wish I could," Hazel said. "I'm hosting an open house."

Hope nodded, trying to mask her disappointment.

"So," Hazel said as they were leaving, "how are things with McKenzie? Did you two make up?"

"I think so," Hope said. "Though, when it comes to me and McKenzie, you never really know."

The next day, Hope phoned McKenzie at work. Several times.

McKenzie didn't answer until the fourth call and sounded very annoyed, especially after Hope said that no, nothing was wrong. She just wanted to confirm that she and Zach would be coming over the following weekend, for Liam's welcome home dinner.

"Of *course* we're coming. I told Hazel to tell you we were."

"Just wanted to make sure."

"It's over a week away. I've got to go. I'm late for a meeting."

Hope didn't get it.

Kids liked her, always had. From grade school on, McKenzie's girlfriends would show up in Hope's kitchen with their worries in tow, and Hope would listen, advise, and encourage. So why was it so impossible to have a conversation with her daughter?

It didn't make sense. Apart from McKenzie, everybody on the planet seemed eager to share their life story with Hope. Rick joked that she could go through a tollbooth and come out with a relationship. People were always telling Hope their stuff.

It happened again on Friday morning in Starbucks.

Hope went to fill out a job application. Barista wasn't quite the career path she'd planned on, but she heard they offered insurance, even to part-time employees. The manager, a young woman named Beth, looked harried but was nice enough to sit down and give Hope an interview. Somehow they got around to the topic of Beth's teething baby, how hard it was for working mothers, and how guilty Beth felt about wanting time to herself.

Hope assured her that a crying baby didn't mean Beth was a bad mother. Then Hope suggested frozen peaches as a means of soothing sore infant gums and a neighborhood babysitting co-op as a means of soothing jangled mommy nerves.

"Thank you," Beth said. "I think I really needed to hear that." She smiled and looked down at Hope's application.

"I wish I had an opening for you. I really do. You'd be a good addition. But we're completely staffed up right now. I'm sorry."

"That's all right," Hope said, trying to hide her disappointment. Beth scanned the application again. "You were a FACS teacher? That's the same as Home Ec, right?"

"More or less. The curriculum has changed a lot."

"So why would you want to work here?"

Hope was used to people spilling their guts to her. But it wasn't a reciprocal arrangement. Other people talked. Hope listened. But there was something about Beth's eyes. She looked like she cared.

Hope told her everything. When she was finished, Beth said, "That sucks. You really got a raw deal," which wasn't much in terms of advice but helped more than Beth knew.

Hope blew her nose into a Starbucks napkin. "Sorry."

"Don't be," Beth said. "I just wish there was—" She stopped abruptly and reached for her phone. "Hang on a second."

"Why?"

"Just hang on. I need to call my cousin," Beth said, and punched some numbers on her phone. "Nancy? Hey, it's Beth. Remember that job you were telling me about? For the craft teacher?"

Hope felt a flutter in her chest. Somebody was looking to hire a craft teacher? That would be perfect!

"Yes," Beth said, nodding in response to whatever it was her cousin was saying. "But they're still accepting applications? Oh. That many, huh? Wow."

Hope felt her stomach sink. Obviously, she wasn't the only person who thought teaching crafts was a dream job.

"Well, I'm sitting across from a lady I think would be perfect," Beth said. "She used to teach Home Ec. Exactly. That's what I thought too. Okay, I'll tell her. Thanks, Nancy."

Beth ended the call and looked at Hope.

"The job is open. They're taking applications for another week."

"But they've had a lot of response?"

"Over two hundred applications so far," Beth said, then clucked her tongue in response to Hope's fallen expression. "Don't get discouraged. It won't hurt to try. But you're going to have to get creative, find some way to make your résumé stand out. I mean, assuming you even want the job."

"Are you kidding? Teaching crafting is completely up my alley."

Beth slurped the last drops of her mocha. "You might change your mind after you find out who you'd be teaching. And where."

"Cut!"

Liam chopped the air with his hand before lowering his camera. Hope made a sputtering sound.

"Again? What's wrong this time? The lighting? The angle?"

Liam laid his camera down on Hazel's kitchen counter next to the supplies for the sashiko embroidery project Hope was supposed to demonstrate. Assuming they ever got that far. After fourteen takes, Hope still hadn't gotten through her introduction.

"Lillabet was about to walk into the shot," Liam said, plucking Hazel's cat from off the counter, "but that's not why I stopped. It's the emotion. You're not making me believe you."

"Oh, Liam, please." All Hope had managed to do so far was give her name and that she'd like to be considered for the craft teacher job in a women's prison. "What's not to believe?"

"Mom, the reason we're filming your application is to help you stand out from the crowd, right? You've got to show them what's special about you—your passion, commitment, who you are *inside*."

Liam pressed his hand to his heart for emphasis, and Hope rolled her eyes at her darling and oh-so-dramatic youngest child.

"Honey, we're making a video, not an artistic statement."

"I make films, not videos. And films *always* make an artistic statement."

Liam twisted his lips.

"The lighting in here is the *worst*. Are you sure we can't do this back at the condo? That would be ideal, all those windows, so much natural light."

"No," Hope said. "I don't want Dad to know about this."

"Well," Liam said, "if you get the job, you'll have to tell him."

"Yes. If, by some miracle, they actually pick me, then I'll tell your dad about it. After all the drama over my last job, I don't see any point in stirring the pot unless I have to."

Liam gave Hope a considering but slightly worried look.

"Are you guys okay?"

"Of course we're okay. Your dad and I have been married for about a thousand years. Now and then, you have to expect some of those years to run through a rough patch."

"Okay," Liam said slowly. "But if you two keep shutting your-selves off and each other out, it's not going to end well."

"What are you trying to say? That I shouldn't apply for this job?"

Liam groaned. "Of course not. I think this is a really neat op-portunity for you. But you and Dad need to talk and quit keeping secrets from each other. You should tell him what you're up to."

"Liam," Hope said, "I know you mean well, but I don't have the energy to argue with your dad about a job I didn't get."

"But if you *do* get it?"

"Then I'll tell him. But the chances of that happening—"

"Are excellent," he interrupted, picking up his camera. "You are a very talented woman who gave birth to a very talented son who is going to use those talents to show those people at the prison how truly fabulous you are. Now, are you ready for another take?"

"Okay."

Liam placed the camera back on the tripod, then got two of Hazel's dining room chairs and placed them near the camera.

"We're going to try something different. Take a seat," he said, motioning toward the chairs. "We're just going to talk for a while."

"Talk? About what?"

"About you. What's the first thing you ever made?"

Liam sat in the other chair. Hope laughed nervously.

"The very first? It was a stuffed elephant made with pink and gray velveteen and plastic googly eyes, the kind you glue on."

"How old were you?"

"Seven."

"Sounds like a pretty complicated project for a seven-year-old. Did somebody help you?"

"Oh, yes," Hope said. "My mother. It was her idea. We'd gone downtown to run some errands, and I saw a plush stuffed elephant in the display window of a toy store. It was just like the one that MaryAnn Traynor had brought to school for show-and-tell. I was obsessed with it," Hope said, shaking her head.

"I asked Mom to get it for me, and she said it was too expensive. I cried during the entire bus ride home. When we got to our stop, I started crying even harder. I was sure Mom was going to punish me when we got home. Instead, she took me into her studio."

Hope hadn't thought about that day for a long time. But even now, after so many years, her mother's studio was vivid in her mind, and the memory of it made her smile. Even as a little girl, she'd understood that her mother's studio was her sanctuary. Until the incident on the bus, Hope had never been allowed to enter.

That day, her mother took her by the hand and led her inside.

"She dug through a box," Hope said, smiling, "pulled out a piece of pink velveteen, handed it to me, and said, 'Hope, you need to make peace with the fact that life isn't fair. Nobody gets everything they want or think they want. But the sooner you learn to make the most of what you have, the happier you'll be.'

"Then she shoved a pile of stuff off the table, took out a piece of butcher paper, and sketched out an elephant pattern. I took over from there. Mom stood over me while I worked, showed me how to thread the sewing machine and made sure I didn't cut myself. But I did about ninety percent of that project on my own.

"I called my elephant Pamela Pachyderm. I took her to school and told everybody that I'd made her myself. Everybody made such a fuss, my teacher especially. It was like they'd noticed me for the first time. Strange as it sounds, in some ways it felt like the first time I'd noticed myself as well, realized I had something to offer."

Hope's voice trailed off as she thought about that moment.

Make the most of what you have.

Her mother's motto became her own.

"So that was a big moment, right? A turning point?" said Liam.

"It was," she said, talking to her son and not the camera. "You know, people spend a lot of time trying to figure out their purpose in life. In the details, it's different for everybody. But at the broadest level, I believe we're created to be creators ourselves, to leave our mark by making the most of what we have.

"That is what's always excited me about teaching. When I teach somebody to make something they feel proud of, something beautiful and useful that they've crafted with their own hands, I am really teaching them who they are and what they're capable of.

"That's why I'm *here*," she said. "Because I—"

Lillabet chose that moment to leap onto the kitchen counter, knocking over Liam's tripod and camera in the process.

Startled by the sudden flash of fur, Hope cried out. Liam dove for the camera and managed to catch it before it hit the ground.

"*You* are a very bad kitty," Hope scolded when it was all over, lifting the cat from the counter. Hope put her back on the floor and turned to Liam, who was checking over his camera.

"Is it okay?"

"It's fine. No worries."

"Well, it was a good save. You know," Hope laughed, "I really did forget it was there after a while. Should we go again?"

Liam shook his head. "No, we're good. I got what I needed."

Chapter 4

HOPE SLIPPED OUT OF BED and tiptoed into the bathroom to dress. She was pretty sure Rick was only pretending to be asleep, but she was quiet just the same and left the house without saying goodbye.

At precisely eight, Hope was standing at the prison gate as instructed, holding a heavy cardboard box. A grizzled and gray-haired guard with a paunch hanging over his belt approached.

"Hope Carpenter?"

When Hope nodded, he pressed a button to unlock the gate, holding it open as she walked through, a gentlemanly gesture at odds with the scowl on his face. "Not that way," he growled when Hope started walking toward a beige brick building. "We're going to medium. The superintendent wants to see you."

The medium-security building definitely looked like a prison. It was tall and formidable. The gray brick exterior was the color of spent fireplace cinders. The upper story had only one window. The lower floors had no windows at all.

The guard's scowl deepened.

"All right, put your box down on that bench; then go over and talk to Cindy. She'll give you a locker and get you checked in."

"A locker?"

"For your purse. You can't bring it or anything else inside. Didn't you read the e-mail they sent you?"

"Sure, yes. The purse isn't a problem," Hope said, glancing down at the box. "What about the rest of my—"

"You can't bring anything inside. That's policy. You got a problem with that, take it up with the superintendent," he said.

"Right. Sorry. Thanks for your help."

The guard sniffed dismissively, then turned on his heel and marched out the door. Hope set her box down and approached the other guard, a woman in her midforties with dirty blond hair.

"Don't mind Wayne," she said. "He spent four years in the Marines and never got over it. I'm Cindy," she said as she searched Hope's purse.

Hope smiled. "Cindy, what's it like to work here?"

"Not bad. The hours are regular, and the pay is decent. Good benefits. I like the people I work with. Mostly." She grinned as she glanced toward the door Wayne had walked out of.

"And you're never . . . you know, scared?"

"You mean of the inmates?" She shook her head. "Not really. Just follow procedure, you'll be fine."

The door opened, and a petite young woman, just over five feet tall, with cappuccino-colored skin and a fringe of black, blunt-cut bangs above her dark eyes, came in carrying an armload of books. She set them down on the counter without a word. Cindy started flipping through the pages, one after the other.

"How you doing, Mandy?"

The younger woman shrugged. Cindy picked up another book, shaking her head as she riffled the pages. "You sure read a lot."

"I've got a lot of time for it."

"Not too much longer, though. Seven months?"

"And four days," Mandy replied.

"Not that you're counting, right?" Cindy smiled, closing the last book. "Okay, you're good to go. See you next week."

Mandy picked up the books and cast a glance at Hope before leaving the lobby. Hope watched her walk toward the beige building, wondering what she'd done to end up in this place.

"That girl, Mandy Lopez?" Cindy said. "She's doing five years on a drug charge because she was dealing for some worthless man." Cindy clucked her tongue. "After what I've seen here, I'm staying single. Forever."

Cindy handed Hope her purse and pointed to the bench. "Leave it over there for now. We'll give you a locker later."

"But my box," Hope protested. "I need it."

"Everything you brought needs to be inspected and approved before it comes inside. We'll get it to you later. Right now, I just need you to walk through the metal detector. Hands down at your sides. That's it," Cindy said, waving Hope through.

The machine started to bleep. Hope's heart leapt like a startled gazelle, but Cindy wasn't a bit perturbed. She pressed a button to turn off the alarms, then told Hope to take off her earrings and shoes and try again. The result was the same.

"Let me guess," Cindy said. "You wearing an underwire bra?" Hope nodded. "Didn't you read the e-mail they sent you? The one with the list of what you can and can't wear?"

Hope had read the e-mail. There were a lot of rules about clothing. You couldn't wear blue jeans because that was what the prisoners wore, no hats, no gang colors, no sunglasses, no metal jewelry.

She had taken all these things into account when choosing her outfit—khaki trousers, pink blouse, brown jacket, and moccasins with rubber soles. What she had not taken into account was the impact of underwear on metal detectors.

"Sorry, I must have missed that part."

"Just pop into the ladies and take it off. But hurry up, okay? Superintendent Hernandez isn't a guy you want to keep waiting."

Hope stood there for a moment. Was Cindy serious?

"But . . . why? Are brassieres lethal weapons now?"

Cindy's smile disappeared.

"This is no joke. The rules and procedures in this prison are here for one reason—to keep everybody safe, including you. If we get slack and metal gets smuggled inside, trouble comes with it."

Hope's cheeks went pink. For the first time, it occurred to her that she might be out of her depth. In the grand scheme of things, she had lived a very sheltered, very safe life.

Sitting in the hard metal chair that seemed to have been deliberately placed at a distance from the desk of Superintendent David

Hernandez, it occurred to Hope that being bereft of undergarments wasn't the only reason she felt awkward and vulnerable.

"If you're going to work here," he said, looking over the top of his black-rimmed glasses in a way that made it clear this was still a very big if, "it's not enough to read the procedures; you have to follow them. To the letter. Understand?"

"Yes. Absolutely," Hope replied, before adding a final, "sir."

This seemed to mollify him but not much.

"This program wasn't my idea. I want you to know that."

Hope nodded. Message received.

"It's a waste of resources," he went on. "Why are we trying to turn felons into artists when we could be using that money to teach them something useful? Something that might help them earn a living so at least a few of them won't end up back here?"

He shook his head and glanced down at one of the many pieces of paper on his desk. This particular piece of paper, Hope realized, was her résumé.

"Well, sir, I can understand that argument. It's certainly something I've run across before, when I was teaching. Especially in an era of limited budgets, emphasis is placed on teaching skills that will help students get into the job market. But I believe there's another argument to be made.

"The reason to teach crafts isn't because we're looking to create artists. I want to impart broader concepts—self-confidence, problem solving, and the ability to stick with a difficult project. Those skills help people succeed in whatever work they end up doing."

Hope leaned in a bit, warming to her subject. "You see, if you can teach students the skills to—"

"Inmates, Mrs. Carpenter." He paused, glowering at her. "These aren't a bunch of giggly teenage girls. They're felons. They're drug addicts and dealers, burglars, prostitutes, and child abusers. The women in our custody have skills, plenty of them. But not the kind that a housewife from Portland can probably relate to."

He released his grip on Hope's résumé. The paper fluttered to his desktop, like a dead leaf falling from a tree.

"How many years did you teach?"

Hope's jaw tightened with irritation. He already knew the answer because he'd just read it on her résumé. She refused to be cowed.

"Four total—two before I had my children and two more after they left home."

"Four whole years of professional teaching experience," he said. "None of it in a correctional setting. Until today, I bet you've never set foot inside a prison." He tapped her discarded résumé with his index finger. "Do you honestly believe that a résumé like this qualifies you for this job?"

"That's not for me to say, Mr. Hernandez. But since I received a letter saying I was hired with instructions to report for work today, I have to assume that someone thought so."

"Someone. But not me. I was out of the office for three months, came back this week and discovered that, in my absence, the program had been approved and you'd been hired as the teacher."

Three months? Hope could only think of one reason for a person to be excused from work for such an extended period of time—they were on medical leave. That could explain the yellowish tinge to his otherwise swarthy complexion and the loose fit of his suit.

"You must be glad to be back," Hope said, feeling more compassionate toward him as she tried to imagine what might force such a relatively young man—Hope guessed he was in his forties—to take such an extended leave of absence. "I hope you're feeling better."

"I was," he said. "Until I came in on Monday and found out that, in my absence, the associate superintendent, Jodie Whittaker, who conducted your phone interview, and the chaplain, Nancy Hendricks, made a hiring decision based primarily on a video of you telling a sentimental story about your mother."

He turned his head away and mumbled something. Hope was pretty sure she heard the words *women, incompetent, soft,* and an expletive linked together in a way that wiped away her momentary sympathy.

"Excuse me?"

"You can't run a prison on sentiment," he snapped. "Look, Mrs. Carpenter, I'm sure you're a nice person. And I'm sure you did a perfectly fine job teaching a bunch of privileged, college-bound teenagers in the suburbs—"

"My district was in the city," she said calmly, "and my students came from a variety of backgrounds."

He shook his head while she was speaking, making it clear that he wasn't listening. "I don't care where you taught before. You're not qualified to teach *here*. If I'd been here to make the decision, you wouldn't be sitting here today. I'm sorry if that hurts your feelings, but I believe in being up front."

"I'm glad to hear it because I believe in being up front too. The fact is, Mr. Hernandez, I *am* sitting here today. I received a letter of employment from your office. If you are trying to rescind that offer on my first day, without legal justification . . ."

Hope sat up straighter in her chair and smiled sweetly.

"In any case, and in spite of your reservations, I'm glad to be here. I'm going to try my best to do the job well and earn the respect of the inmates and staff, including you."

The superintendent pushed up his glasses.

"Well, we'll see, won't we?"

"Yes, we will," Hope said stoutly. There was a knock on the door. Hernandez left off frowning long enough to bark, "Come in!"

The door opened halfway. A woman's head popped through.

Her short, salt-and-pepper-colored hair was gelled into stiff spikes on her head. She wore a black shirt with a white clerical collar. The blue rims of her enormous eyeglasses matched her blue eyes, which lit up when she spotted Hope's face.

"Ah! There you are! *So* sorry I'm late," the woman said in a British accent. "I wanted to be here to greet you, but I was counseling a new arrival— Anyway, doesn't matter."

She waved her hand dismissively before grabbing Hope's and pumping it enthusiastically.

"Delighted to meet you, Hope! As soon as Jodie and I saw that video, we knew you were the right woman for the job!"

Hope's face lit up. At least somebody was glad to see her.

"You're Nancy, right? Beth's cousin."

"Yes, and the chaplain here. I'm so happy that you and Beth ran into each other. And even happier that Beth didn't have an opening for you!"

Nancy let out a laugh, then clapped her hands together and looked at the superintendent and Hope in turn.

"So? How goes it here? You two getting on?"

RICK was sitting at a Thai restaurant, drinking hot chai and wondering where McKenzie could be.

The waitress came over for the third time to see if he was ready to order. McKenzie was often late, but not this late. He decided to give her another ten minutes.

"How about . . ." Rick glanced up at the waitress. "Some spring rolls to start. We'll decide on entrées once she gets here."

The appetizers arrived about a minute before McKenzie.

"Sorry I'm so late, Daddy," she said, bending down to give him a peck on the cheek. "My meeting ran long."

"It's all right. You're here now."

Rick caught the eye of the waitress and ordered. After she'd left, McKenzie apologized again for being in such a rush. "Don't worry about it, kitten. I get it. I used to be the busiest man on the planet, remember? How's work?"

He took a sip of tea, smiling to see how she attacked the spring rolls. She must have been starving, Rick thought. Probably rushed out of the house without eating breakfast.

That was McKenzie. Always in a hurry but always late.

Hope was three weeks past her due date when McKenzie finally decided to make her entrance. Hope's labor had gone so quickly that Rick had to pull the car over and deliver his baby daughter by the side of the road, two miles short of the hospital. It was the most terrifying and most exhilarating ten minutes of his life.

After the baby was born, he pulled off the sweater he'd been wearing, wrapped her up in it, and laid her in her mother's arms. Hope, lying on the backseat of the minivan, looked down at her daughter, then up at her husband, and said, "My hero."

Though he didn't realize it until just that moment, these were the words he'd always wanted to hear from her. He'd spent every moment since trying to live up to them.

"It's good," McKenzie said. "It's just a lot of hours. I always feel like I'm playing catchup. But it's good," she assured him.

"Good. And how's Zach?"

"Fine. Still waiting to hear about that promotion. Between his schedule and mine, we barely see each other," she said.

The waitress arrived, apparently just in time. McKenzie practically fell on her food, shoveling noodles into her mouth. "So. How're things with you and Mom? I know you've been upset about her going to work."

"Not true," Rick said. "I just don't like her working in a *prison*, that's all. Why would I? I don't think it's safe."

"Where is safe these days?" McKenzie asked. "You didn't have a problem with her working in a public high school. If you think about it, prison might actually be safer. Besides, Mom's smart. She knows how to look out for herself."

Rick shook his head. "Your mother is too trusting. And she gets *way* too involved. First it was the kids in the neighborhood, then her students at the high school. Gets herself so worked up over a bunch of strangers that she doesn't have time left for her family."

He looked up and saw McKenzie staring at him with an expression he couldn't quite read.

"What. You don't agree?"

"Well," she said slowly, "I did until now. But hearing you say it out loud made me realize I was being kind of a jerk about it."

Rick didn't know what to say.

"Sorry, Daddy. I wasn't saying that you were a jerk, just that *I* was. Trying to juggle job, house, and husband is making me appreciate Mom more. I don't know how she did it. I drop into bed exhausted every night, and I don't even have kids yet."

At the mention of kids, Rick shifted his eyes from his plate to McKenzie's face, hoping this might be the precursor to an announcement, but none was forthcoming. "So, listen. Daddy. I heard about this job opening for an engineer with the planning department. It's only part-time, but I was thinking that—"

Rick lifted his hand to stop her.

"Thanks, Kenz, but no. I'm done."

"But, Daddy—"

"No," he said firmly. "I'm not going through all that, not again. I'm retired. I'm happy. I'm fine," he said. "End of story."

"Okay," McKenzie said, sounding defeated. "I was just trying to help. I really think you should get out of the house more."

"I'm thinking of taking up golf."

"Really? That's great!" McKenzie glanced at her phone. "Oh, shoot. I've got to run. Same time next week?" she asked, popping up from her chair. "Unless, of course, you're out on the links."

"More likely stuck in a sand trap," Rick said, getting to his feet and returning McKenzie's squeeze.

After she left, Rick paid the bill. When the waitress brought back his change, a man walked over to his table.

"Hey, I couldn't help but overhear your conversation with your daughter. A friend of mine works at a pro shop. If you're in the market for a set of clubs, I'm sure he'd give you a nice discount."

"Thanks. But I don't play."

The man frowned a little. "But you told your daughter you were thinking of taking up golf?"

"Yeah," Rick said. "I think about a lot of things. But that's not the same as doing them, is it?"

Chapter 5

"David *is* gruff," Nancy admitted to Hope a few minutes after the two of them left the superintendent's office for a tour of the facility. "And bitter. Harbors an *intense* distrust of women."

"No kidding," Hope said. "Why is that?"

"I think it has to do with his mother. From what I can gather, she was involved in some nefarious activity when he was young. She was convicted, and David was shipped off to foster care.

"Hard to know for sure but I'm guessing that this is his way of punishing her," Nancy said, sweeping out her hand as they walked through the noisy dayroom, crowded with tables and women, including a petite girl with dark hair who Hope thought might be the same one she'd encountered at the guard station.

Yes, Hope realized as they got closer, it was the same girl. She had the same stack of books and, in spite of the chaos surrounding her, seemed completely absorbed in reading one of them. What was her name? Mandy? Yes, that was right. Mandy Lopez.

Leaving the dayroom and cafeteria, Nancy and Hope moved into a long and far quieter corridor, lined with blue metal doors that Hope supposed must open onto cells.

"But if he hates women so much, why stay here?" Hope asked. "Why not transfer to a men's facility?"

"Because," Nancy said, "he doesn't *hate* women. He distrusts us. And not entirely without reason. His wife walked out on him not long after his diagnosis."

"That's terrible. She left him because he got sick?"

"Oh, I doubt it," Nancy said. "But that's what *he* thinks."

"That's got to be hard. Is he going to be all right?"

"Chemotherapy is never a picnic, but testicular cancer is highly treatable if it's caught early enough. My husband's an oncologist," Nancy said, responding to the question in Hope's arched brows. "David should be fine."

Hope liked it that Nancy, though far from blind to his flaws, liked the cranky superintendent. But Hope suspected Nancy felt that way about everybody.

Nancy stopped walking and turned toward Hope. "Against all odds, a few of these women *do* manage to successfully turn their lives around. Now that you're here, maybe you'll be able to tip the odds a bit farther in our favor?"

Nancy looked Hope up and down.

"Yes, I think you might. Your name alone means something. Perhaps Hope will be the one to bring hope to the inside?"

Hope smiled. "I don't know about that. But I'd like to. That's part of why I wanted to work here."

"Most of us feel that way at some level," Nancy said. "Even David. Who knows, Hope on the Inside? Perhaps you'll resurrect David's faith in the rest of us."

Hope laughed, and they started walking again. "At the moment, I'd settle for getting through my first day without him firing me."

"No worries there," Nancy said. "You've got a verified letter of employment. To fire you, David would have to build a case against you, which would take at least six months. Unless, of course, you do something to give him cause—insubordination, blatant policy violation, dating an inmate—that sort of thing."

Nancy gave Hope a concerned look, as if she'd just remembered something. "You're married, right?"

"Very. To Rick."

The chaplain let out a relieved breath.

"Good. No worries about fraternization then. You're not permitted to have social or personal contact with inmates, you know. That would be cause for immediate termination."

Hope shook her head. "Everybody around here is always talking about policies. There sure seems to be a lot of them."

"Because there are," Nancy said. "You've got to keep on the right side of them. Otherwise, David can and *will* fire you. But, apart from that, you've got six months to change David's mind about the crafts program. Ah! Here we are!" Nancy exclaimed as they rounded a corner and approached a wooden door. "Your classroom."

Nancy opened the door, allowing Hope to enter first.

The space was narrow, about ten feet wide by sixteen feet deep. Long, narrow tables and orange plastic chairs ran along both walls, leaving a center aisle just wide enough to walk down.

At the far end of the room, Hope found a gray metal cabinet with a lock and a small table and chair. The cardboard box she'd had to leave outside the guard station was sitting on the table.

Hope peered into the box and frowned.

"Hey. Some of my stuff is missing." She started digging through the box. "A *lot* of my stuff is missing."

"Really?" Nancy came over and stood beside her. "Like what?"

"My scissors, my rotary cutter, my pins, knitting needles, the mason jars I use for mixing paint colors, acetone I use for cleaning brushes, and my glue!" Hope slapped her hands against her sides. "Why would anybody steal glue?"

"It wasn't stolen. It was removed," Nancy said. "Hope, none of those kinds of items are permitted inside a prison. You can't bring in anything sharp or anything with a blade. Acetone is highly flammable and the glue—I'm guessing it was model glue?" Hope nodded. "We have a lot of addicts in here."

"Okay, I get it. But . . . mason jars?"

"To you and me, a jar is a jar. But if somebody steals it and breaks it, the jagged edges or shards can become a weapon."

"Fine. So I'll keep them in there when I'm not using them," Hope protested, gesturing toward the gray metal cabinet, keys dangling from the lock. "Nobody will steal them."

Nancy laid a hand on Hope's shoulder. "You don't know that. Let me be clear. I love these women. So will you when you get to know them—they're such wounded birds. But they're here for a reason. Theft is second nature to some of them, so is violence. You can't turn your back on them. You can't bring supplies into your classroom that might be a temptation to some or cause harm to others."

"Well, that's just great," Hope said. "How am I supposed to teach a craft class with no craft supplies?"

Nancy smiled and patted her shoulder. "You'll figure something out, I'm sure. You've got a whole hour."

"An hour? Wait. Are you saying—"

"Your first class is coming in right after lunch," Nancy said cheerfully as she walked toward the door. "Don't worry. There's only eight in this first group. We didn't want to overwhelm you on your first day."

"Gee. Thanks."

"Good luck!" Nancy called out.

AFTER his lunch with MacKenzie, Rick got into the car, turned on the ignition, and sat there watching the windshield wipers swish back and forth, trying to figure out what to do for the rest of the day. He probably should go buy some new pants. His old ones were so tight he could barely button the waistbands. But the thought of going to the mall was too much. Ultimately, he pulled out of his parking space and headed back toward the condo.

About a mile along his route, he saw a sedan pulled over by the side of the road, tilted in a way that suggested a flat tire.

Rick slowed down to avoid splashing water onto the driver, who was bending down to examine the tire. Just as his car was pulling parallel to the sedan, the driver straightened up, turning briefly toward the road, allowing Rick to catch a glimpse of her face.

For a moment, he forgot to breathe.

Rick found a place to pull over, then jumped out of his car and ran back toward the stranded sedan and its elderly driver, who was, once again, bending down to look at the tire. His shoes crunched over the gravel, alerting the driver to his presence.

When she stood up and looked toward him, Rick felt a wave of disappointment wash over him. "Well! That was pretty quick after all!" the old woman exclaimed. "Are you from Triple A?"

"No, ma'am. I just saw your car pulled over and thought . . ." Rick wiped the rain from his forehead. "Do you need help?"

"I do," she said. "But I don't want to bother you. Triple A said they'd have somebody here in about forty-five minutes. I was just trying to see if I could figure out how to take care of it myself. My husband used to handle this sort of—" She stopped mid-sentence and frowned. "Are you all right?"

"Yes, I—" Rick took in a breath and let it out. "You just reminded me of somebody, that's all."

"Oh, yes. I get that a lot. It's this Irish face of mine," she said with a laugh. "I look like everybody's mother, or aunt, or long-lost cousin Colleen."

Rick wiped his face again.

"Ma'am, why don't you get inside your car out of the rain while I change this tire for you?"

She shook her head. "Thank you but no. I couldn't ask you to do that. You'd get soaked. The tow truck will be along soon."

"Well, I'm already soaked," Rick observed. "So are you. I might as well change this tire so you can be on your way."

The woman twisted her lips a bit, considering this.

"All right. But only if you let me watch you so I can learn to do it myself. Age and sex are no excuse for helplessness."

Rick smiled. She didn't just look like his mother; she sounded like her too. Not just in what she said but in the way she said it.

"Do you have a spare?" he asked.

"It's in the trunk. There's a compartment under the carpet." She walked toward the rear of the car. Rick followed her.

"By the way," she said, "my name is Kate, Kate McGahan."

The tire didn't take long to change, even with Kate "helping" by loosening the lug nuts while Rick looked on. However, once Kate got behind the wheel, the car refused to start.

"I'm guessing it's a transmission problem," said the tow truck driver, who had arrived after the tire had been changed. "But we won't know until the mechanic takes a look. Is there a garage you want to use?"

"Peterson's Auto," Kate said. "Ask for Joe."

The tow truck driver pulled out his phone.

Kate turned to Rick. "How much do new transmissions cost?"

"Maybe it's just the fluid," Rick said, though he was pretty sure it wasn't. "Can I give you a lift somewhere?"

"Oh, no. Thanks. I'll just ride along in the truck. I'm sure one of the boys from the garage can take me home."

The tow truck driver took the phone from his ear. "Joe says they're swamped but, since it's you, to bring it over and he'll try to take a look at it first thing tomorrow."

Rick arched his eyebrows. "Sure I can't drop you off at your house?"

"Oh, I couldn't," Kate replied, looking defeated. "I shouldn't take up any more of your time. I'm sure you've got lots to do."

"Not really," Rick said. "Not one single thing."

DEEDEE, a skinny, wiry, twenty-two-year-old with ebony skin and close-cropped hair, pinched the pink paper between her fingers and picked up the object, examining it from all sides.

"What is it?"

"A crane," Steph said, rolling her blue eyes, then taking a corn chip from a bag. "I told you before, a paper crane."

"Yeah. I know what you said it was," Deedee replied. "But really, what *is* it? Looks like a piece of folded paper to me."

"It is a piece of folded paper, stupid. It's origami. Some kind of Chinese paper-folding thing."

"Japanese," Mandy said without looking up from her book. "Origami is a folding-paper technique that originated in Japan."

"How would you know?" Steph asked irritably. "You didn't even take the class."

Mandy tapped her book with her index finger.

Another woman, Nita, who had also attended Hope's hastily thrown together origami class, crossed the room and sat down at the table. She was about thirty, broad shouldered and heavyset, and wore her light hair in a single thick braid down her back.

"Was that a joke or what?" she said, filching one of Steph's chips. "It was like something you did in kindergarten."

"I know," Steph huffed. "Mine looked like a sick chicken. How did yours turn out?"

"Didn't finish it," Nita said. "Didn't even try. I'm just taking the class to kill some time. Need to look busy around here or they sign you up for kitchen duty. Making kindergarten cranes is better than scrubbing pots. But not a lot better."

"That teacher," Steph said. "Where did they find her? Could she be any greener?"

"Uh-uh," Nita laughed. "Did you see the look on her face when we all trooped in? Deer in the headlights. I bet you anything she's never been on the inside before today."

"Got that right," Steph said. "She won't last long."

"Maybe a month. Two, tops." Nita grinned. "Hey, you want to bet on it?"

"On what? That she'll quit?"

"Uh-huh. I will bet you four bags of Fritos that Deer-in-the-Headlights-Craft-Lady will quit within a month."

"With your help?" Deedee asked.

"Could be," Nita said. "What do you say? You in?"

"Too rich for my blood," Deedee said. Nita looked at Steph.

Steph thought it over for a minute.

"Deal," she said finally.

"Baby," Nita hooted, "I am going to win this thing, no problem. Only downside for me is that I've got to wait a whole month to collect. Tell you what, let's add a side bet."

"Like what?"

"One bag of Fritos says that, within a week, she breaks down crying in class."

"A week?" Deedee said. "I'll take some of that action."

"Me too," said Steph.

Nita started laughing. Steph and Deedee joined in, the three women chortling about how delicious victory would taste.

Mandy, who had been reading with both elbows propped up on the table to cover her ears, glared at the trio.

"Do you mind? I'm trying to study here."

"So? If you don't like it, you can move," Nita said.

"So can you. I was here first."

Nita glared back at her for a moment. "Fine," she said finally. "Why're you such a grouch today?"

"Because I'm trying to study and there's so much noise in here I can hardly hear myself think!" Mandy covered her eyes with her hands. After a moment, she lowered them. "Sorry. Maybe I should take a break."

Deedee leaned forward to see the cover of Mandy's book.

"Advanced algebra? No wonder you're stressed. You don't think you're ever actually going to need that, do you?"

"Probably not. But I need it to graduate. You can't get a decent job on the outside if you don't have at least a high school diploma, so I've got to earn mine before I get out of here. If I can't get a job, I can't take care of Talia."

"How is she? You got any new pictures?"

Mandy smiled and reached into the pocket of her prison-issue khakis and pulled out a photo. "My mom just brought this one; Talia's first-grade picture."

The women cooed and aahed in response.

"Is she a sweetie or what?" Deedee asked. "Those eyes? Just like her momma. She's gonna be a heartbreaker."

"Can't believe she's already in first grade. And losing her baby teeth," Steph said, shaking her head. "Time sure flies."

"Everywhere but here," Nita said. "But that is one adorable kid. Your ex sure makes cute babies."

"Yeah. That's about all he knew how to do," Mandy said. "Besides dealing drugs and beating the crap out of me. But Talia makes up for a lot. All I want to do with my life is get out of here, get my kid back, and be a good mom. That's it."

"How much longer till you get your diploma?" Deedee asked.

"Hopefully within seven months and four days," Mandy said. "I'm still short two credits to graduate."

"Two credits of what?" Nita asked.

"Anything," Mandy said.

"Well," Steph said, "what about taking this craft class?"

Mandy frowned. "What craft class?"

"The one we've all been talking about!" she exclaimed. "Don't you hear anything when you've got your head stuck in a book?"

"Not really," Mandy said. "So, this craft class would count as a credit toward high school graduation?"

"I think so. The lady in charge used to teach Home Ec at a high school, so she must be a real teacher. See if you can get an art credit or something. It's got to be easier than algebra, right?"

"That's for sure," Mandy said. "Okay, thanks. I'll check it out. You know, I think I saw her when she was coming through security this morning. Brown hair, pink top, looked nervous?"

"That's the one," Nita said with a grin.

Mandy left the common room and went searching for Hope, without success. On her way back to the common room, Mandy passed the chaplain and asked if she knew anything about the new craft class and if it was being offered for credit.

"That's brilliant," Nancy said. "Hope is a licensed teacher, so I can't think why not. I'll discuss it with her when she comes in."

"She's already gone?" Mandy asked.

"Yes. She had a bit of a headache, so she left a few minutes early. No worries, she'll be back tomorrow."

"So? How was your first day?" Cindy asked when Hope came back through the security check to retrieve her jacket and purse.

"Not bad. Could have been worse."

Cindy laid a hand on Hope's shoulder. "Hey. Around here, any day that *could* have been worse is a win. See you tomorrow?"

Hope forced a smile but didn't speak, lifting her hand in farewell as she walked out the door. Wayne was manning the outer gate. Hope didn't look at him as she walked through the gate and into the parking lot and climbed into her car.

When the prison fences disappeared in the rearview mirror, Hope turned onto a side road and pulled over. Then she turned off the ignition, checked the time on the dashboard clock, laid both her arms on the steering wheel, and began to cry.

Ten minutes later, she wiped her eyes and drove home.

THE condo was empty when Hope got home.

She dumped her purse on the sofa, poured herself a glass of Syrah, and carried it out to the balcony.

She welcomed the chance to think through this awful day before Rick got back, read the defeat on her face, and started to crow.

She didn't need Rick to tell her that she was in over her head. She was supposed to be the teacher, but those women had definitely taken her to school.

It wasn't that they'd been unruly; she'd have known how to handle that. But these women were just so . . . quiet.

It didn't help that she'd had to wing her first project with less than an hour's notice. But no matter the project, she was sure it would have been the same. From the moment the women filed through the classroom door until the moment they filed back out, Hope felt their eyes on her. They watched her every word, move, and gesture, as if sizing her up and finding her wanting.

She'd tried joking around with them, but her attempts at humor had fallen flat. Like everything else. The only hours in her life that felt longer than her first hour teaching in prison were those she'd spent in childbirth and her second hour teaching in prison.

Going home early felt like defeat, but she didn't think she could keep it together through a third class; better to fall apart in her car than melt down in front of the inmates. It felt like that's what they were waiting for, even hoping for—to see if she'd burst into tears, run from the room, and never return.

One of the ones from the first class, Nita, looked at her in such a way that Hope gained a new understanding of the phrase "daggers in her eyes." But it was the silence that really got to her. Maybe because she'd been getting so much of the same from Rick. Where was Rick anyway? McKenzie said they were meeting up for lunch at noon. It was almost five.

"He said he was going to buy some new pants," McKenzie reported when Hope phoned. "Maybe he's still shopping?"

Hope shook her head. "He hates shopping, only goes when he absolutely has to."

"You know what?" McKenzie said. "I bet he stopped by a golf course. He told me he's thinking about taking up golf."

"Really? That doesn't sound like him. But if it gets him out of the house and away from the loaf pans, I'm all for— Oh, hang on," Hope said when she heard a key turn in the lock, "I think he's coming in now. Do you want to talk to him?"

"That's okay," McKenzie said. "I've got at least two more hours of work before I can get out of here. Tell him I said hi."

Hope started to tell her not to stay too late, but McKenzie hung up before she could. Rick came into the kitchen sans shopping bags, still wearing his old chinos.

"No luck at the mall?" Hope asked. When Rick looked at her blankly, she said, "McKenzie said she thought you were going to buy some new pants."

"Oh. Right. Changed my mind. I'm going to try to lose some of this weight instead."

"And golf is part of that?"

Rick gave her another blank look.

"McKenzie said you mentioned something about taking up golf?

I wasn't sure where you were, and she said you might have gone to check out a golf course."

"Yeah, I'm thinking about it. So. How was your first day?"

"Good. Lots to learn but, you know . . ."

Under normal circumstances, Hope and Rick would have picked up on each other's white lies. As it was, they sat down at the table and had a conversation, of sorts. Mostly they talked about the weather. But it was more conversation than they'd had in many days, and so they played nice, avoiding unnecessary inquires, anxious to maintain their uneasy truce, each unaware that they weren't the only one who was being less than honest.

Chapter 6

DAVID HERNANDEZ FOLDED his hands into a church and rested his hands on the steeple.

"Needles? You want to bring needles into your classroom."

"Yes," Hope said firmly, holding up a long metal needle that was bent at the top, creating a small handle. "Felting needles."

"Felting needles," David said, his tone flat. He shook his head. "You can't bring sharp objects into the prison. We've been over this more than once. So why are you bringing it up again?"

"Because I was hired to teach crafting classes, and I can't do the job unless the students have access to crafting supplies," Hope said. "These are grown women, David. But because of the restrictions placed on me, I'm left with no options but to teach them projects that would be dull to the average fourth grader. It's no wonder they're acting out. They're bored!"

"Look, if you can't manage your classroom—"

Hope raised a finger and pointed it straight at him. "Hold it right there! Yes, this is a challenging environment. And yes, after nearly a month on the job I am still finding my way. But I am an *excellent* teacher. And I am *not* giving up. So, unless you're prepared to have this same conversation, week after week, I suggest you and I start acting like adults and reach some kind of compromise."

Hope held her ground, staring at David with silent indignation. She was done being nice. She'd said her piece, stood up for herself and her students. If there were consequences, so be it.

Finally, after a long, tense silence, David narrowed his eyes, took in a breath, and then let it out in a long, slow whoosh.

"A compromise. What exactly did you have in mind?"

Hope took a breath as well, taken aback both by the question and David's, if not conciliatory, at least non-combative, tone.

"Every week, I'll submit my projects to you or Jodie in advance. I'll tell you what I want the students to make and the tools they need to do so. I'll do my best to keep anything that could be potentially dangerous to a minimum. For example, for the felting project, all they'll need are these needles. I'll count them before class, distribute one to each student, collect them at the end of the period, and count them all again. No one will be allowed to exit the classroom until every needle is accounted for. Between classes, I'll keep them locked in the supply cabinet."

David leaned back in his chair, fixing Hope with a steely glare. He hated her; she was sure of it. She was also sure that the next words out of his mouth would be "You're fired."

David pressed his lips together. "Lesson plans to be submitted one week in advance. Only one potentially dangerous piece of equipment allowed per project. Nothing with a blade longer than four inches. All equipment to be checked in and out as you described. Inmates will be patted down by a guard before exiting the classroom. Inmates will not be allowed to bring anything, with the exception of fully completed projects, in or out of the classroom. Those are my terms. Agreed?"

Hope swallowed before answering. "Agreed."

"Good. Now, if you'll excuse me, I have work to do."

Hope rose from her chair, more than ready to leave.

"By the way," he said. "If anything goes wrong, I'm holding you responsible. One incident, one injury, one missing tool and you'll be out the door the same day. Are we clear on that?"

"Perfectly."

David nodded again. Hope didn't wait to be asked to leave. As soon as she stepped out into the hall, she leaned back against the wall to catch her breath. Her heart was pounding.

Hope had never been afraid to lock horns with Rick, not when she knew she was in the right. But, apparently, it was one thing to pick a fight with her husband and entirely different to pick one with her boss. Which made sense. After all, no matter how heated the argument, Hope knew that Rick loved her. With David, it was just the opposite. He hated her. She was sure of it.

But it didn't matter. She'd gotten her way. She'd won.

Hope walked toward her classroom, feeling like a champion.

THE feeling didn't last long.

Hope might have won over David Hernandez, but the women were much harder nuts to crack.

In the nearly four weeks that had passed since Hope began working at the prison, she had yet to see a single one of her students so much as crack a smile. There were one or two bright lights in her classes, but not many. Mandy Lopez was one of them. She'd joined the class in the second week, after Hope had agreed to come up with a curriculum that would make her program qualify for credit as a high school art elective. Mandy was as subdued as the rest of them, but Hope never felt anything approaching hostility from Mandy. She kept to herself, worked quietly, and did good work. She did a particularly good job with the macramé bracelets. For a moment, while she was weaving in the beads, Hope almost thought she saw Mandy smile. But she couldn't be sure.

If only the rest of the women were as cooperative as Mandy, Hope's job would have been, if not a joy, at least tolerable.

But they weren't.

Though the women rarely made eye contact with her, Hope could feel hostile gazes boring into her when her back was turned.

And though the projects were, for the most part, embarrassingly elementary, the finished projects of most of her students were poorly executed, almost as if they were trying to do bad work. Most of the women were either just going through the motions or trying to sabotage their own projects. Why? She couldn't figure it out.

That Friday, things changed. But not for the better.

Of all the projects she'd presented thus far, Hope thought this one was kind of fun. They were making little, desktop-sized trees out of old books. It was something that Hope remembered doing with her mother when she was little. And since nothing was required beyond an old paperback book, some paste, an empty wooden thread spool, and scraps of ribbon or buttons, it was an ideal project for her students—nothing sharp or dangerous involved. The finished products could be pretty, even elegant.

Picking a book from the pile of paperbacks, Hope demonstrated the technique required to create the correct angle on the tree. When she was done, she looked up and said, "That's all there is to it. When you're finished folding, you just glue the tree on the spool, which is like the trunk. Then you can glue on buttons or ribbon for decorations. Any questions?"

To Hope's surprise, Nita, the inmate whose eyes seemed to carry a greater grade of loathing than the others, raised her hand.

"Yeah," she said. "I've got a question. Where did you get your teaching degree? A Cracker Jack box? Because these crafts you keep bringing in are kid stuff, complete crap."

The women snickered and exchanged glances, laughing at Hope's expense. The only exceptions were Steph, who was sitting quietly at her table, looking somewhat guilty, and Mandy.

Hope, embarrassed as well as angry, felt her cheeks begin to flame but quickly recovered her composure.

"Well, Nita, you had quite a lot of trouble with all the other projects. If you're able to complete this one with a little more skill, maybe you'll be able to move on to something more complicated."

There was another round of snickering. Nita stood up, looking at Hope with loathing.

"What are you doing here, anyway? Slumming? Seeing how the poor folks live? Or were you just bored?"

"What I'm trying to do is teach," Hope said. "But it's difficult when I keep being interrupted. Sit down, Nita."

"So you think you're better than us," Nita said, keeping to her feet. "Is that it? You thought you'd come and rescue us?"

"Nita, sit down."

Nita stepped out from behind the table and took two steps forward. "That's it, isn't it? You think you're going to rescue us. Rich lady thought she'd come down here and civilize the poor savages, teach 'em how to fold paper cranes and sit with their hands in their laps and behave themselves. Isn't that right?"

With all eyes on her, Hope took a step forward.

"No, that is not right. I'm here because I'm a teacher, one who thinks that all people are born with a creative spark and that tapping into that can make life more meaningful, no matter where we come from. I'm here for one simple reason, to teach."

"Oh, I see," Nita sneered, taking another step forward. "So you're here because you're a teacher? Well, I think you're a lousy one. I think you ought to—"

Steph, who apparently *did* have something to say and couldn't keep it to herself any longer, jumped to her feet and stood in the aisle, becoming a roadblock between Nita and Hope.

"Knock it off, Nita! Seriously, that's enough."

Nita spat, pursing her lips and flinging phlegm on Steph's sneakers. "Mind your own business."

"She's all right," Steph countered. "She's just trying to help. So leave her alone already. It's the last day, Nita. Face it, you lost."

Before Hope had time to wonder what Steph meant by that comment, Nita lunged forward, grabbed Steph's hair, and pulled her to the ground. The two women began to tussle, spitting curses, landing blows and receiving them.

"Stop!" Hope yelled. The women yelled, too, some urging them to stop, some cheering them on. Hope slammed her hand onto a red button on the wall behind her desk.

Within seconds, she heard the sound of pounding feet. Wayne

ran into the room, breathless and red and brandishing a billy club. Cindy was right behind him.

On Saturday morning, Hope and Hazel left for their annual road trip. They called it their "Thelma and Louise weekend."

They took turns choosing the location and itinerary. This year, Hazel proposed a road trip to Idaho's Sun Valley region for the Trailing of the Sheep, an annual festival of all things sheep—everything from knitting, felting, and yarn dyeing classes to an elegant farm-to-table dinner and sheepdog trials.

"This," said Hope, when Hazel picked her up at six o'clock on a chilly morning in October, "is without a doubt the absolutely coolest Thelma and Louise weekend in the history of the universe. You rock, Hazel. Do you know that?"

"Actually, I do. Now get in the car. I want to get there in time for the 'Secret Life of Sheep Ranchers' lecture."

Hope closed the door and buckled her seat belt. "I checked the maps app on my phone, and it'll take ten and a half hours."

"Pfft," Hazel sputtered. "Amateurs."

Hazel slammed her foot on the gas pedal so hard that the tires left rubber tracks on the pavement. Hope clutched at the door handle, laughing and squealing at the same time.

Two hours later, Hope was still smiling as she poured Hazel some coffee from the Thermos she'd brought along and handed her a homemade muffin.

"Thanks again for doing this," Hope said. "I really needed to get away. These last four weeks have been really tough."

As Hope told her sister about the frustrations, roadblocks, and the fight, as well as the self-doubt she'd been dealing with since taking the job, the frown lines that pleated Hazel's forehead got deeper. Finally, she interrupted Hope's litany.

"Hang on. You get into your car every day after work and *cry?* Every. Single. Day. Hope . . ." Hazel took her eyes off the road long enough to look at her sister pointedly.

"I know," Hope sighed. "But I never cry in front of anybody, and I never let myself cry for more than ten minutes a day."

"Ah, Mom," Hazel said, shaking her head "She may be gone, but her spirit lives on. Still, maybe this isn't the job for you."

"I can't quit, Hazel. I *can't*. I won't give Rick, or the inmates, or David Hernandez the satisfaction."

"So that's why you're going to stay in a job that makes you cry every single day? Out of stubbornness?"

"Don't knock stubbornness," Hope said. "It's spurred me on to conquer all kind of obstacles. And you too."

"It *is* kind of the family inheritance," Hazel admitted. "Let's talk about your real life. How's the family?"

"Good," Hope said. "Liam called a couple days ago. He made it to the second round of some contest. He was pretty excited."

"Good for him. I would be too. And the twins?"

"They're good too."

"And Rick?" Hazel asked. "What's he up to?"

"Believe it or not," Hope laughed, "he's taken up golf."

"I *don't* believe it," Hazel replied. "Football, rock climbing, *that* I could believe. But golf? Rick's always been such a macho man."

"A macho man who bakes bread and adored his mother," Hope reminded her. "Rick's part caveman, part Julia Child."

"Now there's a mental image," Hazel said, shuddering. "Golf, huh? Well, if it gets him out of the house—"

"That's what I keep saying. He's lost about ten pounds, has gotten a little bit of a tan, and seems a lot less miserable. He plays nearly every day, usually doesn't get home until after me. What?" Hope asked, feeling Hazel's eyes boring into her.

Hazel shifted her gaze back to the road. "Nothing," she said.

Hope rolled her eyes. "What? I know that look, Hazel. Spit it out. Say whatever it is you're trying so hard not to."

"No, no," Hazel protested. "It's nothing. It's stupid."

Hope let out a frustrated sigh.

"Okay, fine," Hazel said. "It's just that . . . doesn't it seem weird to you? A month ago getting Rick to leave the house practically required setting it on fire. Now he's a dedicated golf nut? Playing every day and not getting home until after you do?"

Hazel turned toward her sister, searching her face.

"Hope. Nobody hits golf balls in the dark."

"Not in the dark," Hope said. "In the afternoon. It's cheaper."

Hazel's expression was unchanged.

"Hazel. Rick is *not* having an affair. Come on!" she laughed. "You *know* him. We both do. Rick is the most monogamous man on the planet."

Hazel frowned thoughtfully for a moment, then nodded. "You're right," she said finally. "I mean, it's Rick, right?"

"Exactly," Hope said with a smile, her sister's more convinced tone quelling her momentary flutter of anxiety.

Hope reached into purse, pulled out her phone, and dialed Rick. He'd been asleep when she left, so she hadn't said a proper goodbye.

"No answer?" Hazel asked.

Hope lowered the phone from her ear. "He's probably asleep. Or in the shower."

"Probably," Hazel agreed. "It's still pretty early."

Hope slipped her phone back into her purse. Spotting a gas station, Hazel pulled in and then hopped out of the car to fill the tank. "I'm going to zip into the bathroom. You need anything?"

"Nope. I'm good. I'll stay here and keep an eye on the tank."

Hope watched her sister cross the parking lot toward the service station. As soon as Hazel was inside, Hope pulled out her phone and dialed Rick again.

Still no answer. Where *was* he?

KATE came around the side yard, carrying a mug of hot coffee and a plate of freshly baked homemade oatmeal cookies to Rick, who was nailing treads onto the wobbly stairs he was replacing.

"They look wonderful!" Kate exclaimed.

Rick took a step back to admire his handiwork.

"They're not going anywhere, that's for sure," he said. "Come back in fifty years, and these steps will still be here."

"I'll have to trust you on that. At this point in life I'm on the twenty-year plan," Kate said.

Rick flapped a hand. "What are you? About seventy?"

"Seventy-four."

"Well, you can't tell by looking at you. I'm betting you'll live to be at least one hundred."

"Thank you. It's nice to know that, when I do go, it won't be in a porch step collapse," she said. "I can't thank you enough for all you've done—replacing these steps, fixing the railing, replacing the grout in the kitchen." Kate's smile became wistful. "With Lyle so sick those last few years, I guess I didn't realize how much things had deteriorated. Anyway, I'm so lucky to have met you. I've come to think of you as my guardian angel."

Rick chuckled. "Trust me. I'm no angel. Just ask my wife."

"Well, then, she must be an angel, letting you spend so much time over here," Kate said. "Are you sure she doesn't mind?"

"Nah," he said. "Like I told you, she's at work all day. Working on your place keeps me out of trouble. I forgot how much I like fixing and making stuff. Feels good to get to the end of the day and know I actually accomplished something real, something I can see and touch, that will last."

"I'm glad. But are you sure you won't let me pay you?" Kate asked. "At least a little? You've done so much for me, and all you've gotten in return is lunch and a few cookies."

"Hey, don't discount the value of those cookies. Just like the ones my mom used to make. She was famous for them. She shared all her recipes with me except that one. Always joked she would but not until she was on her deathbed. And then. Well . . ."

"You miss her," Kate said.

"Yeah," Rick said, his voice hoarse. "I think I always will."

"As it should be. She was worth missing." Kate laid her small hand over Rick's big, calloused paw. "I'll always miss my Lyle. And aren't we lucky, you and I, to have someone we loved so dearly and miss so much? There are lonely people all over who would give anything to be able to say that."

Rick nodded and drew his mouth upward into a ragged smile.

"You know something? I just figured out how I can repay you. That cookie recipe? It's been my secret, too, for fifty-five years. I always assumed I'd pass it on to my children. But since we never had any," she said, "I'm going to pass it on to you."

"Well . . . thank you. I'd like that."

Kate smiled. "I'll go inside and copy it down for you."

Rick grinned and got back to work.

AN HOUR and a half later, with a sore right arm and an index card of cookie ingredients and baking instructions in his back pocket, Rick got into his truck and headed home, feeling better than he had in a long time. But the feeling was short-lived.

As he pulled into the parking lot, Rick saw McKenzie's car in his spot. McKenzie was standing in front of the car, her backside resting on the hood and her arms crossed over her chest.

He parked in one of the visitor's spots, hopped out of his truck, and walked toward her.

"Kenz? Everything okay?"

McKenzie uncrossed her arms and shook her head.

"I'm waiting for you. I've been waiting for you for three hours. Where've you been? Playing golf? That's what you told Mom you were going to do. Where are your clubs?"

Rick's expression hardened into indignation.

"Did your mother put you up to this?"

"No," she spat. "Mom called and asked if you were with me. She was worried. Said she'd called your cell but you never called back."

"Guess I had the ringer on silent," he muttered.

"So? Where were you?" McKenzie repeated, her chin jutting toward his. "I went upstairs when I got here, wanted to make sure you hadn't had a heart attack or something. Your clubs are sitting in the foyer. Where've you been, Dad?"

"What I do," he said, his voice low and sharp, "and where I go is nobody's business but my own. You're way out of line here, Kenz."

"Dad. How could you?" McKenzie's voice cracked. "You and Mom have always been—"

"McKenzie, I don't know what you're thinking, but I don't have to explain myself to anybody. Certainly not to you."

He pushed past her, striding toward the lobby doors. "You're in my parking spot. Don't let it happen again."

Chapter 7

TALIA WAS GETTING SO BIG that supporting her weight made Mandy's leg go numb. But she wouldn't have removed the child from her lap for anything. Instead, Mandy shifted Talia to the other leg and squeezed her even tighter.

"This is amazing," Mandy said, scanning Talia's most recent report card. "I'm so proud of you, baby. So proud."

Talia looped her arm around her mother's neck.

"I'm proud of you, Mommy. You had a good report card too."

"Well, not as good as yours," Mandy said. "I barely squeaked by on my algebra midterm, but as long as I get my diploma, that's good enough for me. After I graduate, get out of here, and find a job, we'll be together all the time. How does that sound?"

"Good," said Talia, nestling her head on Mandy's shoulder. "How much longer?"

"Not long now. About six months."

Mandy's mother, Lola, who accompanied Talia to the prison every two weeks and had been sitting in a folding chair on the far side of the room, glanced at her watch and coughed.

"We should get going."

Mandy looked at the clock that hung on the wall of the visitor's room. "We've still got five minutes."

"I know," Lola said, picking her purse up off the floor, "but I need to get Talia to her soccer game. Come on, Talia."

Talia hopped off Mandy's lap.

"It's our turn to bring the snacks—orange slices and Rice Krispie bars. I'm playing goalie today!"

Every minute spent with Talia was precious to Mandy. She

wanted to protest their early departure but decided to hold her tongue. Why upset Talia by starting an argument?

Besides, it looked like her mother had problems of her own. She sat in her chair without speaking, fiddling with her charm bracelet, the way she always did when something was bothering her. Mandy figured that something was probably her dad.

She hadn't seen it when they first got involved, but Marcus was so much like her dad. Both were impatient, demanding, and controlling and were one hundred percent certain that they were right, always. Enrique, Mandy's father, was less reckless than Marcus. He didn't use or sell drugs and didn't hit women. But he knew how to wound without ever striking a blow.

When she got out of prison, Mandy intended to be a much better person. She might as well start practicing now by giving her mom a break. After all, if Lola hadn't been willing to make the bimonthly trek to prison with Talia, she would hardly ever have seen her daughter. Enrique had never come to see her, not once.

"So, which are you more excited about?" she asked Talia, kneeling down to zip the little girl's jacket. "Eating Rice Krispie treats or playing goalie?"

Talia tipped her head to one side and opened her mouth into a wide, gap-toothed smile as she considered the question.

"Uhh . . . Rice Krispie treats!"

"Thought so."

Mandy gave Talia one more kiss, then got to her feet and hugged her mother and kissed her on the cheek.

"Thanks for coming, Mami. I really appreciate it."

"Yes. Okay."

Lola felt stiff in her arms. Mandy examined her face.

"Mom? You okay?"

Lola bobbed her head. "Yes, fine. It's just . . . we need to get going. The traffic will be terrible. Talia, say goodbye to Mami now."

"Bye, Mami."

"Bye-bye, chiquita. Be a good girl, okay? Oh, wait. Hang on a second," Mandy said, reaching into the pocket of her khakis. "I almost forgot. I've got something for you."

Talia's face lit up. "What is it? A present?"

"Uh-huh. Hold out your arm."

Mandy tied the present, a small bracelet of blue beads woven together with white cording, onto her daughter's slender wrist.

"Do you like it?" she asked. "I made it for you in my arts and crafts class."

Talia stared down at the bracelet with shining eyes. "It's beautiful, Mami. Did you get an A?"

Mandy laughed. "Yeah, I did. Guess I'm better at art than algebra, huh?"

"Talia, we have to go."

Lola took the child's hand, opened the door, and nodded to the guard who was waiting to escort them off the grounds. Mandy stepped out into the corridor to watch them go.

It never got easier. In fact, the closer she came to her release, the harder it became. But as the chaplain had reminded her only the week before, she was winning the battle against time. All she had to do was keep her head down, stay out of trouble, and wait. She was close now. So very close.

Soon Mandy would be walking down the corridor, through the gates, and into the free, fresh air. Talia would be standing outside, waiting for her, and they would never be separated again.

Thinking of this, Mandy swallowed back tears and forced a smile. Just before turning the corner, Talia looked over her shoulder and raised her hand over her head.

"Bye, Mami. Thanks for my pretty bracelet. I love you."

"I love you too, baby."

On Monday morning, Hope dumped a bag of soft, lusciously colored balls of wool out on the center table and told the women they could pick whatever colors they wanted.

She didn't need to say it twice.

Within seconds, they were gathered around the table, comparing colors, giggling like girls as they squeezed the balls of roving tight into their fists. Just like that, everything changed. Hope didn't understand it, but she felt so happy she could have cried.

"What is it? Where did you find it?"

"It's wool roving," Hope replied. "My sister and I went to a sheep festival in Idaho over the weekend. One of the vendors was selling it. Isn't it gorgeous? Hand-dyed."

"Mrs. C?" Deedee asked. "What's a sheep festival?"

"Well"—Hope paused, trying to think how to explain it—"it's a celebration of all things sheep and the ranching lifestyle. There were demonstrations on dyeing and spinning yarn and a bunch of other crafting classes. There was also a farm-to-table dinner."

"Farm to table?" Tonya asked. "What's that mean?"

"Farm-to-table dining is very popular right now," Hope explained. "People have started to realize that fresh food, produced locally, is healthier for you. And tastes a lot better too. This dinner was a chance for sheep ranchers to educate people about how to use the food that can be made from their herds—meat, cheese—"

"Cheese?" Deedee asked. "What does sheep cheese taste like?"

"It comes in a lot of different flavors and textures," Hope said. "But the kind I had was crumbly and tasted a little bit sharp. They put it in a salad, served with garlic mashed potatoes and tiny, tender lamb chops grilled over hickory smoke."

The women, who were practically salivating by this time, issued a collective groan of longing that brought a smile to Hope's face.

Though she'd been working at the prison for a month, she knew that food was a hot topic of conversation. Inmates spent hours talking about the dishes they missed most, reciting the recipes that they, their mothers, or their grandmothers used to make and dreaming aloud about the first thing they would eat on the outside.

"What about dessert?" Mandy asked. "What did they have?"

"They brought everybody a plate with five different desserts."

"What kind?" Deedee asked. "Pie? Pudding? Cobbler? I need specifics here."

Hope stepped back from the table. "Tell you what. Before I do, what if everybody picks out three colors of roving they like and I'll demonstrate how we're going to use it to make one of these little felted birds, okay?"

Hope held up a felted cardinal, vermillion red with a bright yellow beak and beady black eyes that she'd made the night before. The women murmured again, this time with the cooing that accompanies the sighting of a newborn baby. Hope grinned.

"It's so cute. You really think I can make that?" Steph asked.

"I *know* you can. Now, come on, everybody. Pick out your colors and let's get to work."

WHAT should have taken five minutes—simply choosing their materials—took nearly twenty. Once every student had made her choice, Hope was finally ready to begin teaching.

Hope showed them how to immerse the balls of wool into bowls of water, squeeze out the liquid to make them smaller and more dense, and stab the wool with their felting needles, over and over and over again, to work the wool into the correct shape.

"Hey, make sure you stab the wool and not each other," Hope cautioned. "These felting needles are small, but I had to get special permission to bring them in. If anything goes wrong here, you're all back to origami cranes. Got it?"

For the first time since Hope had begun teaching in the prison, her students laughed at one of her jokes. She savored the sound.

For a few minutes, the room was quiet but comfortably so. This was the peaceful, contented silence that occurs when women enjoy what they're doing and the presence of their sisters. But then, as inevitably happens, one woman cast an admiring glance at the work of her neighbor and followed up with a compliment that was soon returned. Then someone asked for an opinion and there was another question, and soon the room was humming with companionable conversation and soft, pleasant laughter.

Deedee held up her completed bird, a bright yellow canary, and asked if it wasn't the cutest thing ever. After receiving a round of affirmation from the room, she asked Hope if she could make another one. Hope looked up at the clock, surprised to see that there were only ten minutes left in the class.

"Not today. We're out of time." She clapped her hands together. "All right, everybody. We need to wrap up. If you didn't finish your bird, leave it on the table for next time. Let's start cleaning up and handing in your supplies. Mandy, would you mind collecting everybody's felting needles and giving them to me? There should be fifteen. Nobody can leave until we have an accurate count."

"Only fourteen. You've got the fifteenth needle," Deedee said, pointing at Hope's hand. "Nita isn't here, remember?"

"That's right. I almost forgot," Hope said, wondering if Nita's absence might account for the about-face in the students' attitude.

"She'd have dropped out anyway," Steph said. "She only hung on because of the bet."

Hope frowned. "What bet?"

Steph clamped her lips closed, but Deedee, who had a habit of engaging her mouth before her brain, was happy to answer for her.

"Nita bet Steph four bags of Fritos that you'd quit before you finished your first month."

"She what?"

"Oh, yeah," Deedee said. "But that was the second bet. The first was that you'd start to cry during class, but that only paid out if it happened during your first week. Tell you the truth, I really didn't think you'd last, but I'm sure glad you did. You turned out to be way cooler than I thought." Her tone was marked with admiration as well as surprise.

"Well. Thanks. I guess." Hope turned to look at Steph, who was staring down at the tabletop with flaming cheeks. "And what about you? Did you win or lose?"

"I won," she said sheepishly. "It's not as bad as it sounds . . ."

"No?" Hope arched her brows. "Because even if you were hoping I'd stick it out, betting on whether or not a person could be so mean and behave so badly that it would make another person cry or quit her job *sounds* pretty bad."

Steph lifted her eyes to meet Hope's gaze.

"Sorry."

"So am I. Don't do it again. To anybody."

Steph nodded, then got up from her seat and lined up with the others next to the door. Mandy handed the needles to Hope, saying they were all accounted for.

"Thank you," Hope said as a guard who would escort the women back to the dayroom knocked on the door. "Hey, can you stay behind for a minute? I'll let the guard know I'm walking you back. I want to talk to you about something."

"Okay," Mandy replied.

Hope spoke to the guard, then said she'd see everybody on Thursday before walking back to the front of the room with Mandy, who was studying her with a somber expression.

"Am I in trouble?"

"You?" Hope let out a surprised little laugh. "You're the least of my problems. I just wanted to thank you for . . . well, for everything. Up until today, I've felt like you were the only one who was actually on my side in all this. Now I think I know why."

"I wasn't part of the bet, if that's what you're asking," Mandy said. "I didn't know anything about it."

"Mandy, tell me something. Why would they have done that? Who bets on the misery of somebody they don't even know?"

"Oh, man. You really don't have this place figured out yet, do you? You know what the worst part about prison is?"

Hope shook her head.

"That." Mandy pointed to the wall clock. "Time moves slower here than anyplace in the world. You do what you have to do to make it pass. It wasn't personal, them betting to see if you'd cry or quit. They were just trying to fight off the boredom."

Hope took a seat at the table, motioning for Mandy to do the same.

"You're not like the others, are you? Most of them are doing just what you said, killing time. But you seem to be making the most of it. You're working toward your diploma, reading every book you can get your hands on, taking parenting classes. So what's the difference between you and the others?"

"Well, first off," Mandy said, "I'm not the only one. Plenty of us are trying to make the best of our time here. They don't get noticed as much because they're like me, just trying to keep their heads down. It's safer that way. Smarter too." She shrugged. "Look, I can't answer for anybody but myself, but I know what keeps me going. It's Talia, my little girl.

"When I first got here, I was convinced that I'd permanently screwed up my life. I was so depressed that they had me on suicide watch. But then Nancy came to see me and kind of kicked me in the butt. She said I was overselling myself and that a person had to be way more dedicated to leading a life of crime than I was to screw up their entire life at twenty-one."

"Did she honestly say that?" Hope asked, laughing.

"Yeah." Mandy grinned. "Anyway, she convinced me that it really wasn't too late to turn my life around and that I had a very good reason to try—Talia. My daughter is my hope, my reason for waking up every day. I want to build a good life for both of us."

"Looks like you're heading in the right direction."

Realizing that she needed to escort Mandy back before her next class started, Hope got to her feet. Mandy did the same.

"Hey," Mandy said as they neared the dayroom, "I wanted to thank you for something. Those macramé bracelets we made last week? I gave mine to Talia, and she loved it."

"Oh, good! I'm so happy she did."

"It was the first time since I got here that I'd been able to give her anything. My mom buys her stuff and *tells* her it's from me."

Mandy's eyes started to fill. Knowing what she was trying to say but couldn't, Hope felt tears in her own eyes.

For a mother, there is nothing quite so heartfelt and instinctual as the desire to give gifts to her children. Helping Mandy fulfill that long-denied desire was a gift to Hope as well.

Suddenly, an idea popped into Hope's mind. The moment it did, she knew exactly why she was here, among these women.

She also knew what she needed to do about it.

Chapter 8

"QUILTS." NANCY'S EYES WIDENED, as if she wasn't quite certain she'd heard Hope correctly. "You want them to make quilts?"

"Yes," Hope replied.

"Right," the chaplain said. "Why? I mean, couldn't you just stick with the macramé bracelets? Or crocheting?"

Hope clutched the edge of Nancy's desk. "Think about a child— let's say a little girl. Her mother is locked away behind a wall and can't come out, can't tuck her in at night, can't comfort her when she wakes up in the dark crying after a bad dream.

"Now think about what it would mean to that same child to get into bed at night and fall asleep under a quilt her mother made with her own hands. She knows that her mommy picked out all those fabrics just for her, stitched every seam with her own hands.

"Think about what that means to a child who's never been convicted of anything but has been punished just the same, sentenced to separation from her mother. But when she falls asleep under her quilt, it's like her mother is there with her, keeping her warm and safe, reminding her that someday they'll be together again.

"Now think what it means to the mother who makes that quilt, a woman who wakes up every day feeling guilty, hopeless, and ashamed because of the mess she's made of her own life—"

"She'd feel like she had something meaningful to offer," Nancy said, finishing Hope's thought in a quiet, almost introspective voice. "It would be a chance to tap into the best part of herself and share her love and creativity, maybe for the first time."

Nancy took in a deep breath and let it out slowly.

"Oh, Hope. I don't know. I understand the value in this. But . . .

quilting. Are you sure there isn't some other way to accomplish the same thing? A craft that doesn't involve sharp objects?"

"Nancy," Hope said, "any craft I teach them is going to involve a certain amount of risk. We could take precautions—check out tools and equipment, count them before anyone is allowed to leave, limit participation to inmates with records of good behavior.

"Think about the benefits," Hope urged. "I've heard you say it— the root reason most of these women ended up here is because they feel worthless. This program could change that."

"Just by making a quilt?" Nancy asked.

"Well, actually . . ." Hope cleared her throat. "I was thinking about three quilts. And a nine-month program."

"Three! Are you planning on opening a factory?"

"Hang on," Hope said. "Just hear me out. Making three quilts will give them that opportunity to really master the skills involved. Very few of them know what it means to take on a difficult task and see it through to completion. When they finish their quilt, they'll feel proud of themselves, especially after they see how that hard work can bless the lives of another person."

"So, the quilts will be gifts for family or friends?" Nancy asked.

"No," Hope said. "The first two, which will employ more basic techniques, will be given away to charity. My hope is to help them start envisioning themselves as contributors to society."

Nancy nodded deeply. "So many charities could make good use of quilts—shelters, nursing homes, programs for foster kids."

"Exactly." Hope smiled. "The third quilt would be their masterpiece. They'd choose all their own colors and fabric. They can either keep it or give it as a gift. I want them to make something they truly feel proud of, an heirloom that will last a lifetime."

Nancy nodded again. "Okay, I'm sold. But as I'm sure you're aware, there's only one vote that matters here and that's David's."

"I know," Hope murmured. "And it's not as if I'm on his list of favorite people. I was kind of hoping you'd present the idea to him."

"Me?" Nancy laughed. "What makes you think I'd have any better luck than you would?"

"Nancy, I *know* this program could make a difference. But if I'm the one presenting the idea, David's going to shoot it down. If you bring the idea to him, we might at least have a chance."

"Hope, I'd have to be the greatest peddler on the planet to get David on board with letting you bring pins, scissors, and rotary cutters into his prison. Unless you're friends with the kind of person who could sell ice to Eskimos, I don't think you've got a prayer.

"Although," Nancy continued with a shrug, "that's not nothing. If you want me to pray about it . . ."

Hope slumped in her chair. When it came to getting David's approval, Nancy had been her Plan A. She didn't have a Plan B—not until Nancy started talking about ice and Eskimos.

Why hadn't she thought of that before?

Hope jumped up. "That's a great idea," she said as she headed for the door. "You pray. I'm going to call my sister."

David Hernandez was a very busy man.

So busy, he informed Hope when she dropped by his office seeking an appointment to discuss a curriculum proposal, that he didn't have an open spot during office hours for at least a month.

"What about after work?" Hope asked. "How about a drink on Thursday? The Dockside Bistro is nice."

Much to her surprise, he agreed.

"One drink," he said. "I've got a conference call with a blue ribbon commission on prison reform early on Friday, and I need to finish reading the report."

"Just one drink," Hope promised. "We'll get to the point."

"We. Let me guess," David said wearily. "You're bringing Nancy and Jodie along to gang up on me about something."

"Nope," Hope said. "Just me. And my sister, Hazel."

"Your sister?"

"She's visiting from Portland."

"And she's joining us for a drink so we can discuss this thing you refuse to tell me about in advance?" David pushed his glasses up the bridge of his nose. "I'm not in the market for a girlfriend."

"No! Lord, no!" Hope exclaimed, aghast.

"Lord, no?" He arched his eyebrows. "I'm not that bad, am I?"

"No, no," Hope said, laughing nervously. "Not at all. I just meant, 'Lord, no' I would never do such a thing. Set you up, I mean. Clearly, if you wanted a girlfriend, you would have one by now. Probably several. Not at the same time or anything. I just—"

Hope was never so grateful to be interrupted as when David said, "I barely have time to get a decent night's sleep, let alone date. Besides, it's only been a year since my divorce. Too soon to start dating, don't you think?"

Hope stood there for a minute. Was he asking her opinion?

"Not too soon," she said. "Not if you feel ready. Or lonely."

David sniffed enigmatically and picked up his pen.

"So. Thursday, you said? At the Dockside."

Hope nodded. "Right after work."

"Okay," he said gruffly, and started writing. "One drink."

"Great. See you Thursday," Hope chirped, and then backed out the door before he could change his mind.

To Hope's complete shock, one drink became two and was followed by crispy Point Judith calamari, beef tenderloin skewers, and then coffee and a slice of key lime pie with three forks.

An hour and forty minutes into what Hope had assumed would be a half hour meeting, David still hadn't embraced the idea of letting Hope teach quilting. But neither had he given a definitive no.

After outlining the basic idea, Hope let Hazel take over. "You set the hook," Hazel said when they'd discussed strategy over the phone. "I'll reel him in." It had definitely been a good call.

Hazel, a world-class debater if ever there was one, continued to match him objection for objection and argument for argument. "Look, ask Hope if you don't believe me," Hazel said. "Teaching the women to quilt isn't just about giving them warm fuzzies. These are hard skills they can put to use after they're released."

"Such as?" David asked, his skepticism evident.

"Well," Hope said, "basic math for one thing. Reading a pattern and constructing a quilt involves addition, subtraction, multiplication, and an understanding of fractions—as well as a lot of geometry. It also reinforces reading comprehension and the ability to decode and follow instructions. When I taught high school, my lesson plans were all designed to help support and reinforce the concepts taught in the core educational classes. There's no reason we couldn't do the same thing with the quilting program."

"See?" Hazel said. "What she said."

David's expression softened. Hope almost thought he was going to smile. Then something even more surprising happened.

Hazel grinned and stuck out her tongue, making a "so there" face, and David cracked up. Hope had never even seen him smile, let alone laugh. Until that moment, she didn't know he could.

"Okay, okay," David said, spreading his hands. "So they'll learn something. But we've got classes for that already, and I don't have to bring blades and sharp objects into the building to teach them."

"But we already talked about that," Hazel protested. "Anything that could pose a potential danger could be kept in a locked cabinet in Hope's locked classroom. Tools and equipment could be checked in and out at the beginning and end of each session. No one would be allowed to leave until everything had been accounted for right down to the pins. You could have the guards do a pat down if you want. Heck, you could even bring in a metal detector."

David shook his head slowly, but he was still smiling.

"Do you have any idea how much an extra metal detector would cost? Speaking of money, where am I supposed to find the funding for all of this? As I'm sure your sister can tell you," David said, giving Hope a wry but not completely unfriendly glance, "she's already overspent her budget. I can't just write a blank—"

"I'll raise the money myself!" Hope interjected, so buoyed by David's good humor that she spoke before really thinking it through.

David's smile faded. The look of skepticism returned.

"How?"

"I'll contact local businesses, fabric and craft shops. I'll write grant requests. A project like this could be a good match for all kinds of charities and foundations."

"You think so?"

"Yes. Absolutely."

Hope had never written a grant request in her life. Nor did she know of any foundations whose mission focused on prisons or prisoners. But they had to be out there, didn't they? And if they were, she'd find them. Somehow.

"See?" Hazel said, as if Hope's hasty response settled all doubts. "And what about that blue ribbon commission?"

"What about it?" David asked.

"You said the commission had tasked you with creating new programs particular to the needs of a female prison population that would help increase educational levels, support societal integration and family reunification, and decrease recidivism."

"You left out the best part," David said. "I get a whole year and not one extra dollar to accomplish this impossible feat. Governor's commissions," he mumbled. "It's all about looking good and holding on to their jobs. Do you know what they—"

Hazel interrupted, waving her hands to get his attention.

"Hey. Don't you get it? Hope's program actually fits all of the criteria the commission handed you—education, societal integration, family reunification, and recidivism," Hazel recited.

David twisted his lips in a grudging but respectful smile.

"Okay, sure," he replied. "Potentially, Hope's program could have a positive impact in those areas. Potentially. But you don't actually know that because you don't have any proof."

"So get some proof," Hazel countered. "Make it a pilot program. Start with a small group and see how it goes. No matter what happens, you'll be able to fulfill the mandate of the commission."

"A pilot program? Huh."

David sniffed and narrowed his eyes. Finally, after a minute that felt like a hundred, he looked Hope squarely in the eye.

"Okay. We can try it. Twelve inmates, twice a week for two hours. For nine months—a pilot program. When it's over, we'll assess. Does that work for you?"

"Yes! Totally!"

Hope clinked her cup of lukewarm brew against Hazel's mug; David, too, lifted a cup and joined in the unspoken toast. There was no end to the wonders of this day.

"Twelve inmates means twelve sewing machines, right?" David asked. "You sure you're going to be able to get all that?"

"Absolutely," Hope said, her voice radiating confidence she felt not at all. "Won't be a problem."

Out on the street, after saying good night to David and watching his car drive off, Hope threw her arms around her sister's neck.

"You did it! You actually won him over. You made him smile. And laugh! I always knew you were an amazing saleswoman. But I didn't know you were a curmudgeon whisperer."

"Oh, stop," Hazel said. "He's not so bad. Is he married?"

"Was. His wife left him and— Wait a second! You're not actually attracted to him, are you?"

"Why wouldn't I be? He's kind of cute. Seems smart too."

"He is. But he's . . ." Hope paused. "He's just so inflexible. And humorless. Until today I've never seen him laugh. Not even once."

"Well, maybe he hasn't had much reason to laugh. Maybe he's hurting. You know, Hope, not all wounded birds are women. Not all of them are trapped inside the walls of a prison, either." Hazel paused, fixing her sister with her eyes. "How's Rick?"

"Oh, crap. Rick! I told him I'd be home in time to make dinner. Hope he didn't wait for me. He'll be starving."

Hope pulled her phone out of her pocket and dialed the house. When Rick didn't answer, she dialed his cell phone. There was no answer there either.

"He must still be at the golf course," Hope said as she shoved her phone back into her purse.

Hazel cocked an eyebrow. "What's going on with you guys?"

"Nothing. I mean, nothing more than you already know about."

"Hope, this is *me* you're talking to. You know I won't judge. So, tell me the truth: are you thinking of leaving him?"

"Leaving Rick? How can you even ask such a thing?"

Hazel said nothing in response to her sister's aghast expression. Instead, she arched her brows and crossed her arms over her chest, her posture an echo of the question Hope had yet to answer.

Chapter 9

IN THE WEEKS SINCE he'd first rescued her from the side of the road, Rick had tackled seven years' worth of deferred maintenance on Kate's cozy craftsman bungalow. By now, he knew every inch of the house. He knew nearly as much about Kate herself and her late husband, Lyle, a civil engineer, and how, for more than forty years, they had lived, loved, and cared for each other.

And Kate had gotten to know Rick pretty well too. Well enough so that Kate felt she could ask him some personal questions, including one that came so completely out of the blue that Rick choked on his coffee before he was able to answer.

"Thinking of leaving Hope? Never. Why would you even ask?"

"Because," Kate said, "from where I'm sitting, it looks like you already have."

"What? I'm not fooling around, if that's what you're asking. When would I have time?" he asked in a teasing tone, hoping his smile would convince her to abandon the inquiry. "I come here in the morning, hammer nails all day, and go home every night."

"Engineers," Kate sighed. "Why do you all have to be so literal? Do you think it's cute or something? Because it's not."

"What?" Rick said again, feeling genuinely perplexed.

"You want me to spell it out for you? Fine. There are plenty of ways to leave your wife without actually walking out the door. You can, for example, leave her emotionally. You can cut off conversation and congress. You can move your lips but say nothing, limiting your discussions to the weather and the passing of the salt. Or you can say everything without uttering a word. Reproach and simmering resentment are best communicated through ponderous silence."

Kate shook her head at him.

"Don't pretend you don't understand what I'm talking about, Rick. Two people can occupy the same home for months, or even an entire marriage, yet live lives that are entirely separate. And lonely. That's what you and your wife have been doing.

"Why else would you spend every day fixing broken steps and installing smoke alarms in the home of a poor old lady you picked up on the side of the road?" she asked. "Because you don't know what to do with yourself. You come here because your home echoes with punishing silence you're too stubborn to break.

"And you come here," she said more gently, "because I remind you of someone you miss terribly. Because, for weeks now, you've been waiting for me to tell you what she would have told you, that you're a stubborn ass of a man who needs to quit punishing himself and his wife and get on with it."

Rick laughed again, more hoarsely this time, then rubbed the corner of his eye with the back of his hand and blinked.

"How did you know?" he asked.

"At first, I didn't know," Kate said. "I just thought you were a nice man with too much time on his hands. But I figured it out after a while. My cookies are good, but they're not that good."

Kate smiled and squeezed her fingers around Rick's clenched fist. Her grip was surprisingly strong and strangely familiar. So were her words and the no-nonsense way she delivered them.

Quit being a stubborn ass. Get on with it.

That's what his mom would have said. How he missed her. And Hope. He had only himself to blame for that. For so many things.

"There's no point in beating yourself up about it," Kate said, as if reading his mind. "Nothing's so broken it can't be repaired."

Rick lifted his eyes. "You sure about that?"

"I'm sure," Kate said. "Not for a man who loves his wife as much as you do. Angry as you are with Hope, with life, with everything—there's a spark in your eye whenever you speak of her. Talk to her, Rick. Go make things right with your wife."

"How? What do I say?"

"Start with 'I was wrong and I'm sorry' and take it from there."

Rick smiled. Kate pushed back her chair and got to her feet.

"Now, if you'll excuse me. I hope you don't mind letting yourself out. My poor old kidneys can't handle as much coffee as they used to—" Kate was interrupted by the sound of the doorbell. "Oh, bother. Who could that be?"

"I'll get it," Rick said.

The doorbell rang again, twice, in quick succession. Whoever was on the other side of the door was very insistent. "Hang on a second," Rick called out irritably when the bell rang yet again.

He fumbled with the lock he'd installed the week before. Finally, the bolt clicked over and Rick opened the door. When he saw who was standing on the other side of it, Rick's jaw went slack.

"Kenz? What are you doing here?"

McKenzie crossed her arms over her chest and glared at him.

"You first," she said.

McKenzie stepped over the threshold without invitation, pushing past Rick and walking into the middle of Kate's living room. She turned in a circle, taking in the decidedly feminine surroundings.

"Well?" McKenzie snapped. "Who is she?"

"Kenz. It's not what you think—"

"Isn't it? I've been sitting outside for five hours. What could you possibly be doing in another woman's house for *five* hours?"

"Hang on. How did you know I was here? What have you been doing? Tailing me?"

"No! Of course not! I drove up to the condo just as you were driving away and—" McKenzie screwed her eyes shut and raised her hands. "You know something? It doesn't matter. I don't care who she is. And I already know what she is." Opening her eyes, she let her hands flop against her sides. "How could you? How?"

"Okay, Kenz. Stop right there. You're not only out of line, but you're also really confused."

"*I'm* confused? What about *you*? Seriously, how confused do you have to be to get involved with a woman who has such terrible taste in decorating? This whole place looks like something straight out of 1974!"

"Actually, the last time I redecorated was 1982," Kate said as she entered the living room. "But your point is well taken. It's due for an update."

McKenzie's jaw dropped. Kate's eyes crinkled, and her mouth bowed as she stuck out her hand.

"You must be McKenzie. Your father has told me so much about you."

IF THE flames on McKenzie's cheeks hadn't made her mortification abundantly clear, the multiple apologies she offered after Kate enlightened her to the depth of her mistake would have.

The fifth time McKenzie said she was truly sorry, Kate nodded and said, "It's all right, McKenzie. I understand. You were just trying to protect your family. As I said before, apology accepted. But if you'll forgive me for sticking my nose into things that are probably none of my concern, I think your father is the one you should be apologizing to, not me."

"You're right," she said softly. "Daddy, I—"

Seeing tears in her eyes, Rick lifted his hand to cut her off. "It's okay, Kenz. Don't worry about it. It's getting late. We should get out of Kate's hair. Come on. I'll walk you to your car."

After saying goodbye to Kate at the door, Rick and McKenzie descended the porch steps and walked toward the street.

Stopping at the curb, McKenzie turned to look at him.

"Dad? I really am sorry."

"It's okay, sweetie. I get it. You were just trying to protect your mother. And the family. Something I should have been doing all along. But don't worry, okay? I will from now on."

McKenzie shook her head.

"I don't understand," she said. "Why didn't you just tell Mom what you were up to?"

"I don't know," he said, taking McKenzie's arm as they crossed the street. "Because I was acting like an idiot, I guess. And because, even when you love somebody as much as I love your mother, marriage is tougher than it looks."

"Tell me something I don't already know," McKenzie muttered, clicking her remote to unlock the doors on her hatchback.

Seeing McKenzie's car, Rick's brows lifted with fatherly disapproval. The hatchback was stuffed with suitcases and boxes piled so high there was no way that McKenzie could see out the rear.

"What's all this?" he asked. "Did Zach finally decide to clean out the man cave? Why didn't you ask me to come over and give you a hand? I'd have brought the truck."

"I know," said McKenzie. "That's why I drove over to the condo today. I wanted to ask if you'd help me. It's not Zach's stuff, Daddy. It's mine. I'm moving out. Zach's been cheating on me."

"What? Oh, baby . . . Zach? Are you sure?"

Rick couldn't bring himself to believe it. What kind of guy would be stupid enough to cheat on a woman like McKenzie? But when McKenzie stared at him, her eyes filled with pain, and she slowly nodded her head, Rick knew it was true.

"Oh, Kenz."

Rick opened his arms. McKenzie walked into his embrace.

"Would it be okay if I moved back in with you and Mom for a while? Just until I get myself sorted out?"

"Sure. Of course you can. For as long you need to."

"Thanks, Daddy."

"Zach," Rick muttered, "that lying son of a . . . That day when he came over to tell me he was going to propose, I said if he ever hurt you, I'd track him down and kill him. The way I'm feeling right now, I'd have no problem carrying through on that threat."

"I know, Daddy. Me too. But we can't."

"Why not?" Rick growled.

McKenzie lifted her face toward her father's.

"Because I'm pregnant."

Chapter 10

Two months later

LIKE MOST OF THE OFFICES in the prison, Nancy's was cramped and windowless. But it was private and quiet, which was why Hope and Nancy had fallen into the habit of meeting there on Monday afternoons to eat lunch and catch up.

This week, there was a lot to catch up on. Nancy had just returned from a two-week trip to England, where she had visited her parents in Suffolk and spent five days trekking in the Cotswolds with her husband, John.

"I'm glad you got to go home for a while," said Hope. "It seems to have done you a lot of good."

"It did," said Nancy. "I love my job, but it's good to spend time on the outside. How are things with you? All well?"

"Oh, yes. Liam was offered a summer internship he's all excited about. McKenzie is doing as well as can be expected. She found a new apartment, five minutes from our place, and plans to move in after the holidays. The divorce papers have been filed."

"No hope for a reconciliation?"

"Zach moved in with the other woman."

"Oh, dear. Poor McKenzie. But the baby's doing well?"

"The doctor says everything's fine."

"How wonderful," Nancy said. "By the way, I ran into Mandy and Deedee this morning. They were bubbling with praise for you and excitement about the quilting program. Oh, and I understand that Rick's friend Kate got volunteer clearance to come in and help you with the program?"

Hope nodded. "She's my friend too, now. If she hadn't smacked

Rick upside the head when she did, who knows how long it would have taken for us to start talking again. I owe her."

Nancy laughed. "And so you repaid her by letting her volunteer at the prison?"

"I know, right? But she was looking for meaningful ways to fill her time. She's so funny and cheerful. Everybody just loves her."

"Deedee certainly does. She went on and on about both of you. And Mandy told me she's nearly finished with her first quilt top?"

Hope bobbed her head.

"She'll be released in March, so I'm letting her skip the second charity quilt and move right on to her personal quilt. She wants to make a quilt for Talia."

"What a good idea," Nancy said. "It would be good for her to keep her mind occupied."

"Well, the block pattern she wants to use—Dove in the Window—should do the trick. It's kind of advanced for a beginner, but Mandy's up to it. If she works hard and stays focused, she should finish the quilt in time for her release."

"And Deedee?" Nancy asked with a knowing smile. "Is she catching on quickly as well?"

"Oh, Deedee." Hope laughed at the mention of her most affable and most bumbling student. "Don't ask me how but yesterday she sewed her quilt block to her sleeve. Twice." Hope laughed again. "I'll make a quilter of her yet. Just see if I don't."

"Oh, I believe you," Nancy said earnestly. "Any woman who can make the rounds of local businesses and quilt clubs and, in two weeks' time, come away with twelve sewing machines and fabric and supplies is someone to be reckoned with."

"It wasn't nearly as hard as I thought it would be," Hope replied. "Once I explained what I wanted the supplies for, I was flooded with donations."

"Thanks to you, some of our wounded birds are beginning to believe that they have something worthwhile to give. And because you've shown that you think they're worth taking a chance on, they're starting to believe it themselves."

Hope rolled her eyes, and Nancy clucked her tongue.

"You just can't take a compliment, can you? Fine. If you don't believe me, maybe you'll believe our esteemed superintendent."

"David?"

"Uh-huh. He dropped by this morning to welcome me back. He thinks you're doing an amazing job with the women and that, thanks to you, he's going to have something of substance to say when he writes his report for the Governor's Commission."

"Well . . ." Hope said slowly. "I'm glad he feels like that. And it brings up something I've been thinking about."

"What's that?"

"Inviting David to Christmas dinner. When Hazel came up from Portland to help me try to convince David to green-light the quilting program, I noticed a definite spark between the two of them."

"Oh, really?" Nancy said. "Do tell."

"There's nothing to tell, yet. But I was thinking, you know, maybe get the two of them in a room and see if the spark—"

"Becomes a flame? Brilliant idea."

"Also, I'm sure you already have plans and loads of invitations, but if you and John did happen to be available, we'd love it if—"

"Join you for Christmas dinner? Thought you'd never ask. We'd be thrilled to come. And as long as we're issuing invitations, why don't you come to services on Christmas morning? It's going to be a first-rate sermon. I know this because I'll be delivering it."

"Oh. You're sweet to ask. But I'll be pretty busy that day. Besides, I haven't been to church since . . . well, not for a long time. The stained glass would probably shatter the second I walked in." Hope laughed, hoping to convince Nancy to drop the subject.

Instead, Nancy regarded Hope with a confused expression.

"Stained glass? Oh, no!" Nancy exclaimed. "I didn't mean *church* services. I was talking about chapel."

"Chapel. You mean here? At the prison?"

"Yes. We do it every year, right in the cafeteria. It's a sunrise service, five o'clock, and only lasts forty minutes. It's a beautiful service, Hope. It would mean so much to the women if you came. Deedee is singing a solo. Say you'll come."

Hope bit her lip. After a moment's thought, she opened her

mouth, prepared to say no. But then, for some reason, she didn't. "All right. I'll come."

WHEN she began serving her sentence, Mandy was just twenty-one, and, in spite of all the things she'd seen and done since her dad had thrown her out of the house at sixteen, still a little green. She learned quickly that the way to survive on the inside was to make herself as unobtrusive as possible. For five years, she kept her head down and made no enemies. But she hadn't made any friends either, not until she started taking Hope's quilting class.

For the first time since she'd passed through the prison gates, Mandy felt like she had friends.

That's why, when Deedee told Mandy that she was going to sing a solo at the sunrise service on Christmas and asked if she would come, Mandy said she would.

Cindy gave her a poke in the shoulder at twenty minutes to five and whispered, "Merry Christmas." Mandy lay in her bunk for a couple of minutes and nearly fell back asleep. When she heard quiet rustling from a handful of other inmates who were getting dressed in the dark, she got up and did the same. Yawning, Mandy shuffled through the dark dormitory and down the hallway.

The cafeteria was dark, too, which surprised her. The only light in the room came from a single candle, set on a silver lamp stand. Nearly every seat was filled, and no one spoke a word. In a prison housing more than a thousand women, silence was a rare and precious commodity. Its presence filled Mandy with a sensation so far distant from her memory that it took her a moment to identify it—peace.

Nancy entered the room at the stroke of five, dressed in a splendid flowing robe and a clerical stole. Two inmates walked in front of her, one carrying a Bible with a gold cover, the other a shallow gold plate. After the women took their seats, Nancy greeted everyone.

Debby Harper stood up and read the nativity story from the Book of Luke. After a moment, Mandy stopped listening and started wondering. She wondered if Talia was awake yet. She wondered if she'd opened the present that Mandy had "bought" for her, courtesy of a charity that supplied gifts to the kids of inmates. She wondered how she was going to live through the months until her release. And if she would finish Talia's quilt before she left.

Chaplain Nancy stood up and gave a sermon on the subject of unpaid debts, a concept her audience understood only too well. Every woman in that room was there because she had incurred a debt and society had demanded repayment. That was the way of the world. But heaven wasn't like that. According to the chaplain, God came down to show what heaven *was* like and to pay humanity's uncollectible debts, to serve the sentence of the guilty, invite them to dwell in his home as family, forever and ever. Amen.

It was a good sermon. But Mandy wasn't in heaven. She was on the inside, counting the days until her release even as she worried about what would happen after she was released. Would she be able to find a job? Would her job pay enough for her to support Talia? Would she be able to find an apartment they could afford, in an area that was safe, and a landlord who was willing to rent to a felon?

The sermon was over.

Mandy gazed to the front of the room where Deedee stood, hands folded in front of her. Deedee took a deep breath, opened her mouth, and then, without accompaniment, started to sing.

The beautiful sound that came from Deedee's body took Mandy's breath away. She had no idea Deedee could sing like that. When Deedee got to the second verse, Mandy's eyes began to flood.

> *"Let not your heart be troubled," His tender word I hear,*
> *And resting on His goodness, I lose my doubts and fears;*
> *Though by the path He leadeth, but one step I may see;*
> *His eye is on the sparrow, and I know He watches me.*

Mandy felt like Deedee was singing just to her. Deedee couldn't possibly have known that this song, these words, were exactly what Mandy needed to hear right now. But someone must have.

It was like what Hope said about the quilt Mandy wanted to make. She'd been attracted to one called Dove in the Window because of the name. That was what she felt like right now—a trapped bird, peering out the window to the world beyond, heart thrumming with fear and anticipation for that thrilling but terrifying moment when the window would open and she would fly free.

But that quilt . . . it had so many pieces and looked so complicated. Mandy thought it was beyond her.

Hope disagreed.

"The reason it looks hard is because you're trying to take it all in at once. If you look closely, you'll see that it's based on one block, made in different sizes, and that the block is just squares, rectangles, and triangles. You can do this, Mandy. I'll be there to help you at each step. Trust me. You won't be in this alone."

Trust me. You won't be in this alone.

The path ahead was steep and winding. She couldn't see the end of it, but she didn't have to, because she wasn't alone. All she had to do was trust and take one step. Then the next. And the next.

It would be all right. She wasn't in this alone.

Cleansing tears coursed down Mandy's cheeks. She wasn't the only one. All around her women were crying.

When Deedee reached the final chorus, she held out her hands. The moment she did, every woman in the room sprang to her feet, eagerly accepting the invitation, and joined in the song.

I sing because I'm happy. I sing because I'm free.
His eye is on the sparrow, and I know He watches me.

They stood side by side and sang with one voice.
They sang because they were happy. And free.
In that moment, they were.

Chapter 11

McKenzie wasn't stupid. She understood exactly what her mother was up to and why. Hope worried too much. Considering the circumstances, it really wasn't a bad Christmas, or wouldn't have been, if every person she met hadn't been quite so in love.

Reed was head over heels for his girlfriend Pamela. Then there was Aunt Hazel and David Hernandez. They weren't as giddy as Reed and Pamela, but there was definitely something there. But of all the displays of affection that got under her skin during the holidays, none bothered her as much as that of her mother and father.

Which was stupid. Really, really stupid. And selfish.

She should be happy for them! And she was.

Except when she wasn't. Like at Christmas.

Even though McKenzie had tried as hard as she could not to let her troubles spoil Christmas for the rest of the family, she knew that her mother knew that she was sad and jealous of everyone who wasn't as alone as she was and probably always would be.

That was the real impetus behind Hope's urge to throw her baby shower in January, five full months before the baby would arrive.

When Hope tossed out the idea of a shower, McKenzie initially said no. Maybe later, she told her mother. Not when she was so far from her due date. And so depressed. McKenzie didn't mention this last part but she didn't have to. Hope already knew.

Which probably explained why she just wouldn't let it go. Hope wheedled and whined, lobbed arguments and counterarguments. Finally, McKenzie caved. But only after issuing her caveat.

"All right! Fine! You can throw a baby shower. But you have to promise to keep it simple, okay?"

"Absolutely," Hope said. "Just a nice little party to celebrate you and the baby. Nothing over the top." She totally lied.

Going behind McKenzie's back, Hope had called Zinnia, McKenzie's best friend from work, and got her to expand the number of office invitees from six to twelve. Hazel, Kate, and Nancy came, as well as Wanda, Zach's mother, who brought a huge basketful of baby gifts. Her dad was there as well, to serve beverages and help out in the kitchen.

The decorations were beautiful and, yes, totally over the top. Why had McKenzie even gone through the motions of asking her mother to tone it down? It was a futile request.

Even so, McKenzie couldn't help but smile when she opened the door and saw dozens of yellow balloons bobbing near the ceiling, each wrapped with a square of gauzy tulle with a pattern of tiny silver stars.

Each of the four tables was covered with a snowy white cloth overlaid with a topper of cheery yellow gingham and matching napkins. Hope had sewn the toppers and napkins herself and made the fishbowl centerpieces. Each fishbowl, filled halfway with water, had a bright yellow rubber ducky bobbing inside.

"What could be simpler than a bowl of water with a plastic duck floating in it?" Hope said with an innocent smile when McKenzie accused her of violating their agreement regarding simplicity.

Then there was the dessert. But McKenzie couldn't get on Hope's case about *that*. The dessert was all Rick's doing.

"Well, Kenz? What do you say? Do you like it?" Rick asked, crossing his arms as she admired the cake, all four tiers of it, iced with alternating layers of yellow and white.

"Oh, Daddy. I don't even know what to say. It's stunning."

"Whew!" Rick replied. "That's a relief. If you knew how many episodes of *Cake Wars* I've watched since you moved into your new apartment, trying to get this right—"

"Too many," Hope injected. "Then there were all the trial runs. I don't think I'll eat another slice of cake for as long as I live."

Rick raised his brows. "No? Not even if it was lemon poppy seed cake? With raspberry filling?"

"Well . . . maybe," Hope said. "Just a little piece."

"That's my girl," he said, kissing her full on the lips.

McKenzie stood there, watching them kiss, waiting to feel the usual twinge of jealousy and accompanying dose of self-pity. It didn't come. Instead, she felt happy for her parents and for herself.

Nobody's life is perfect, but it suddenly occurred to McKenzie that hers was way better than most and that she was very lucky.

"I love it. The cake, the food, the decorations. Just everything. Thanks so much. This is amazing," McKenzie said.

She looked down toward her swelling waistline, feeling that skittering sensation in her middle that signaled the baby's movement.

"It's going to be a great party, guys. The best ever."

It was. Everyone had a wonderful time, McKenzie most of all.

But it wasn't about the decorations, the gifts, the food, or even her father's spectacular cake. It was about how all of it made her feel—loved, special, cherished and anything but alone. For the first time since seeing that blue line on the pregnancy test, McKenzie felt fully alive and optimistic about her future.

When the party was over, McKenzie kissed Hope and Rick in turn, saying, "Until today, I was feeling scared, worried I'd make a mess of everything. But now I feel like maybe I've got this."

"You do," Hope affirmed. "You're going to be a terrific mom. And if you ever need help, we're just up the street."

"Yeah," McKenzie said, relief apparent in her sigh. "How lucky was I to find a perfect apartment less than five minutes from here? And how lucky will this baby be to have its own personal day care just up the street, right? It's going to make everything *so* much easier. Well, good night, guys. Thanks again."

McKenzie gave them each one more hug and headed down the hall toward the elevator, so blissfully happy that she didn't even notice the strange and somewhat stunned expression on her mother's face, as if she'd just been caught totally off guard.

"THAT. Is. Beautiful," Debby Harper said, enunciating each word as she leaned over Mandy's shoulder.

After much sewing and ripping and resewing, Mandy had completed eight of her Dove in the Window blocks. But until that morning, she hadn't been feeling that great about the quilt.

Each block was fine on its own, but when she tried to picture them joined in one quilt, it seemed like there was so much going on. There were only two months remaining until Mandy's release. Time was running short. She didn't want to spend it sewing block after block, only to put them together and realize that Talia's quilt was a big mishmash of colors and patterns. Hope said it saved time to finish all the blocks before putting them together, but finally, probably sick of listening to Mandy's worrying, she gave Mandy permission to stitch her blocks together. Mandy was so glad.

Her quilt was weeks away from being finished, but as soon as she joined those eight blocks, Mandy could see the pattern emerge.

And the colors! In spite of the range and variety—chambray, lilac, opal, berry, teal, deep gray, periwinkle—every color she'd chosen enriched and balanced the others. Her concerns about the patterns were likewise unfounded. It was going to be beautiful.

Deedee had caught a bug and wasn't in class that day. Eager to show her handiwork to her sick friend, Mandy asked if she could take her partially finished quilt down to the infirmary so Deedee could see it. Normally, their quilting supplies were kept in the locked cabinet between classes, but since Mandy was just talking about fabric, nothing potentially dangerous, Hope said she could.

Mandy had gone from class directly to the cafeteria, intending to visit Deedee in the infirmary right after lunch. But then Bonnie Glazier caught sight of the folded-up fabric and asked to see the quilt. Mandy obliged, spreading the quilt out on the cafeteria table. Within moments, they were surrounded by other inmates.

"Can I touch it?" Debby Harper asked. When Mandy nodded, she brushed her fingers across the blocks. "It's so soft. I love the colors."

"It's for my little girl," Mandy replied. "Purple is her favorite."

"Mine too," Bonnie said. "This must have taken you forever."

"Not forever. But, yeah, I had to put some time into it. Once you understand how the block goes together, it's not that hard."

"For you maybe." Bonnie shook her head. "I could never make something like that."

"How do you know?" Mandy asked. "I mean, look at Deedee. Who knew she could sing like that? People have all kinds of hidden talents."

"Yeah? Well, mine must be *really* hidden."

Bonnie's comment brought a murmur of laughter from the growing knot of women who had surrounded the table. Grinning, she delivered her next line in a louder and more expressive tone.

"I mean they are deep, *deep* down. Down where ain't nobody gonna find them."

The audience laughed again. But Debby, who had been listening carefully to the exchange, looked at Mandy and said, "You really think I could learn to make something like this?"

"Definitely. If you're willing to put in the effort, you can learn to do just about anything. Of course," she said, "having a good teacher helps. Hope is fantastic. You should put your name down on the waitlist for the quilting class."

"Really? Do you think I could get in?"

"Sure. I mean, there's no extra space right now, but the pilot program is going so well that I bet they'll expand it. Shouldn't be a problem, as long as your behavior record is clean."

"You mean, shouldn't be a problem as long as you're willing to suck up to Hopeless Carpenter."

Nita elbowed her way through the cluster of women until she was standing next to Mandy, Debby, and Bonnie.

"It's a stupid program," she said, addressing Debby. "Even if you didn't have to kiss Hopeless's ass to get in, it's boring. Total waste of time. That's why I dropped out of the crafting class."

"You didn't drop out," Mandy said. "You were kicked out."

Nita turned to face her.

"First off, you're full of it. I dropped out because the class was boring. Second, I wasn't talking to you." Nita uttered an expletive and followed it up by placing her hand on Mandy's shoulder and giving her a shove, enough to make her challenge clear.

Nita crossed her arms over her chest, staring at Mandy. The rest of the inmates stood, waiting to see what would happen.

Mandy unclenched her fist and got up from her chair. Nita took a step toward her, but Mandy stepped aside, pulling her quilt off the table before pushing her way through the crowd.

"Hey! Did you hear me?" Nita taunted, raising her voice. "I *said* I wasn't talking to you."

"I heard you. Fine with me. I wasn't talking to you either."

Mandy kept her eyes in front of her and her progress steady but purposely unhurried. She couldn't afford to look like she was running away. She had to appear tough and strong, like she couldn't be bothered to fight because Nita was simply beneath her notice.

It seemed to be working. Somebody in the crowd chuckled in response to Mandy's comment. A couple more people joined in. The laughter was light, but it was directed toward Nita, not her. Mandy found herself smiling. She shoved her hands in her pockets, slowed her pace even more, and started to whistle.

That was a mistake.

With Mandy less than twenty feet from the door, Nita pushed through the knot of bodies, following in Mandy's wake, lengthening her step with every stride and shouting.

"Did you hear me? Hey! You better turn around and listen because I'm talking to you. Did you hear me? I'm talking to you!"

Nita's shouting was growing louder. Mandy could tell she was practically on her heels. She stopped, ready to turn around and make a stand, but before she could do so, Nita lunged forward, shoving Mandy so forcefully that she stumbled and nearly fell.

"Hey!"

The shout was louder than Nita's and more reverberating, the shout of a man, an angry one. Regaining her balance, Mandy looked across the cafeteria and saw Superintendent Hernandez coming through the door opposite, eyes blazing as he strode across the room. The crowd of women parted before him.

"What's going on here?" He came to an abrupt stop in front of them. "Nita? What did you push her for?"

"I didn't. Everybody was hanging out, talking, and then Mandy got up to go, but she forgot her quilt. So I grabbed it and ran after her. I didn't shove her. I just tapped her on the shoulder, trying to get her attention."

"If you just tapped her, why did she trip?"

"Dunno." Nita shrugged, as if it were really none of her concern and he'd be better off asking Mandy. He did.

"Mandy?"

She raised her brows, attempting to appear somewhat but not overly surprised to hear him speak her name.

"Why did you trip?"

"Like she said, I didn't hear her coming. I was thinking about my algebra test next week. She tapped me on the shoulder, and it startled me, so I tripped."

Hernandez stared at Mandy long and hard, waiting for her to crack. She didn't. Finally, he relaxed his stance and said, "Okay."

Nita turned around and walked back toward the tables. When Nita took her seat, he turned toward Mandy.

"You on your way somewhere?" he asked.

"Well, I was just—"

"Walk with me."

They were halfway to the end of the corridor before he broke the silence. "Nice work," he said at last, glancing toward Mandy's quilt.

"Thanks."

"What's it doing out of Mrs. Carpenter's classroom?"

"Deedee's sick, and I wanted to show it to her, so I asked Mrs. C if I could bring it down to the infirmary and she said I could."

"She did?"

Mandy wished she had lied, told him she'd slipped it out of the classroom when Mrs. C wasn't looking. "I shouldn't have brought it to the cafeteria," she said. "That was stupid."

"Yes. It was."

Hernandez halted his steps and turned toward her. "Mandy, I remember when you first got here. I wasn't sure you were going to make it. I wasn't sure you wanted to. You've done an amazing job of turning yourself around. You also kept your head down, didn't make enemies. That's half the battle here. What were you thinking, bringing this in there?" he asked, grabbing the quilt and shaking it in her face. "It doesn't take much to make people jealous here. So why would you start showing off about things you get to do that others don't? Especially in front of somebody like Nita? She's the type that doesn't care how far she falls, as long as she brings somebody else down with her."

Hernandez shoved the quilt back in Mandy's direction, shaking his head. She rolled up the quilt and tucked it under her arm.

"You're right," she said, hanging her head as she realized exactly how right. "It was a stupid thing to do. I wasn't thinking."

"Well, *start* thinking. You're so close to release, Mandy. Don't do anything to jeopardize that. Understand?"

She looked up at him. "Mr. Hernandez? Don't be mad at Mrs. C. This was my fault, not hers. She didn't know—"

"Maybe not but she *should* know. But don't worry about Mrs. Carpenter. She's my problem. You just worry about you, okay? Worry about walking through that gate and back to your family."

"Yes, sir. Got it."

"Do you know he didn't even offer me a chair? He called me to the carpet and then literally left me standing on the carpet!"

Hope lifted her wineglass and tossed back another swallow, then shifted her phone to the other ear.

"He just sat there behind his desk, chewing me out like some kind of wayward sophomore he'd caught skipping out of third period. The nerve. It's January; has he already forgotten that we had him over for Christmas dinner? The man was our guest—"

"He's also your boss," Hazel said. "One doesn't preclude the other. If you thought it did, then you shouldn't have invited him."

"I was trying to be *nice*," Hope countered.

"Then keep being nice and admit you were wrong. You knew you weren't supposed to let students remove anything from the classroom. You promised to keep everything under lock and key."

"Well, sure," Hope said. "Scissors and pins and rotary cutters. This was just a little bit of patchwork. Not exactly hazardous."

"But it sounds like it could have been," Hazel said, "if David hadn't shown up when he did. Look, whether you like it or not, everybody has a boss. And whether you like *him* or not, David is yours. So learn from your mistake and move on."

"Hey, just because he's your boyfriend doesn't mean you have to take his side all the time. I'm your sister. I was here first."

"Okay, first, David isn't my boyfriend. David has a job in Olympia, and I own a business in Portland. I've done the long-distance thing before, too many times. It never works."

"Sure it does. If you want it badly enough, you make it work."

"Would you make up your mind?" Hazel said. "One minute you can't stand him; the next minute I should upend my life for him."

"Good point," Hope said. "I revert to my earlier position; I can't stand him. Unless . . ." Hope paused to take another drink. "Unless he makes you happy. If *that's* the case, then make it work."

Hazel laughed. "Wow. How much wine have you had?"

"Too much. It's been a rough week."

"So? Tell me what happened. Because I know this is about more than David chewing you out."

Hope told her what had happened at the end of the baby shower after the guests had departed, explaining how McKenzie had dropped the bombshell about her expectation that Hope would be providing full-time childcare after the baby was born.

"What?" Hazel gasped. "Why would she think that? She just expects you to quit your job to become a full-time babysitter?"

"Apparently."

Hazel's laugh was incredulous. "Well, that's interesting. What did she say when you told her it wasn't happening?"

Hope was silent.

"Oh, Hope. You're not really thinking about doing it. Are you?"

"I don't know. McKenzie needs me."

"And your students at the prison? They don't need you?"

Hope rubbed her hand over her forehead. She was so tired.

"What does Rick say about it?"

"Just that it was good the timing worked out so that I'd be able to get the first group of quilters through the pilot program before the baby came."

"So he just assumes you're going to walk away from all your students and the program you created?"

"Hazel," Hope said, speaking in a purposely calm and modulated voicing, hoping her sister would follow suit.

"No! This just *really* ticks me off. Why doesn't Rick stay home and take care of the baby? Now that he's retired from both engineering *and* golf, he's got time on his hands."

"Don't," Hope said. "If I asked, he would take care of the baby. I know he would. But I don't want him to. I didn't say anything yet because he asked me not to tell anybody, not until he's sure."

"Sure of what?"

"Well, you know he started volunteering at that housing charity, Many Hands, right? Somebody on the staff found out he's an engineer. Now it looks like they might offer him a job as the project coordinator. It would only be half-time, but he's excited about it."

"Well, that's great," Hazel said, her tone softening slightly. "I hope it works out."

"So do I. He needs this."

"What about your needs? You've got a career that you love. Unless the women—Mandy, Deedee, Steph, and all the others—don't mean as much as I thought they did."

"Don't be stupid," Hope snapped. "I love my job, and my students. I don't want to walk away from them. They need me."

"Doesn't it make you mad that McKenzie assumes you'll quit?"

"Yes!"

"Then why don't you *tell* her that? Tell McKenzie that you don't want to be her babysitter."

"Because I do!" Hope shouted. "Don't you get it, Hazel? I *want* to take care of my grandchild. And I want to take care of McKenzie too. I want to be there for her. I want to take care of Rick. And my students. And you. I want to take care of everybody!"

"But, Hope. You can't. Nobody can."

"I know!" Hope shouted again. "That's why I'm so mad!"

Hope pinched the bridge of her nose. Her headache was getting worse. Much worse.

"So?" Hazel asked. "What are you going to do?"

Hope sighed. "I don't know. McKenzie and I are getting together on Saturday. She wants me to help her pick out a crib. Hopefully, I'll figure it out before then. Or be kidnapped by aliens. Or drafted. Does the military accept women in their fifties?"

"Wow," Hazel said after a long pause. "You really are a mess."

"Tell me something I don't know," Hope said.

AFTER visiting several department stores and finding that prices for new cribs far outstretched McKenzie's budget, Hope suggested they check out consignment shops. At the second one, they found an inexpensive crib and changing table that were nearly identical to models that McKenzie had liked at the department store.

When they were finished shopping, they walked over to a storefront café. A waitress took orders at the counter, then delivered food to the table. Hope ordered a BLT, sweet potato fries, and an iced tea. McKenzie ordered a double cheeseburger, large fries, strawberry milkshake, and side salad with extra dressing.

After placing their orders and sitting down, Hope grinned at

McKenzie. "You should have just ordered the whole left side of the menu. It would have saved time."

"Oh, I thought about it. Believe me. Were you this hungry when you were pregnant?"

"I gained forty-five pounds when I was pregnant with you."

McKenzie's eyes went wide. "Forty-five pounds! Seriously? How long did it take you to lose it?"

"Who says I did?" Hope said, then laughed. "Actually, I'm down another five pounds. Since your father cut back on his baking, they keep melting away."

"Fine," McKenzie groused. "Rub it in, why don't you?"

"Honey. You're growing an entire human. Of course you're gaining a little weight. But don't worry, once the baby is born, you'll lose it in no time. You're planning on nursing, aren't you?"

"For as long as I can," McKenzie said. "Between maternity leave and my saved-up vacation days, I'll be able to stay home for two months after the baby is born."

The waitress arrived, carrying their lunch. When McKenzie's burger was gone, Hope took sip of iced tea and cleared her throat.

"So, Kenz. Speaking of maternity leave and you going back to work, we should probably talk about childcare."

"I know," she said. "I was wanting to talk to you about that. After I got home from the baby shower, I realized that I made it sound like I was signing you up for free babysitting for the rest of your life. But I want you to know, I'm planning to pay you—"

"Kenz," Hope said. "You don't need to do that."

"Yes, I do. It's only fair. And if you're worried that I won't be able to afford it, don't," she said. "I just found out that I'm getting a promotion to department head and a nice raise to go with it."

"Oh, McKenzie! That's wonderful. I'm proud of you."

McKenzie rubbed her stomach. "I haven't even laid eyes on this baby, but I already know how tough it will be to go back to work. Good thing I've got somebody who knows what they're doing to take care of her," McKenzie said with a grateful smile. "Really, Mom. Makes me feel so much better about everything."

The surge of love that Hope felt was accompanied by a smaller but palpable feeling of disappointment. But what could she do?

"I'm glad, Kenz. Happy I can help."

McKenzie's grin said that she was happy too.

"I mean, can you imagine what would happen if I had to raise this baby unsupervised?" she said. "We both know I'd find some way to screw up. I'm just glad this baby will have a *real* mother to look out for her, somebody who knows what she's doing."

A bell jingled as the door to the café opened. A man wearing a bomber jacket, Oakland A's baseball cap, and green tennis shoes with a weird faux alligator pattern walked up to the counter. Hope glanced at him briefly, then lowered her voice.

"McKenzie," she said, "you know I'm thrilled to be a grand-mother. But this baby can only have one mother, and that's you."

"No, I get that. But compared to you . . . Let's face it, I couldn't even keep a marriage together for more than two years. Just imag-ine the havoc I could cause in twenty years of parenting."

Hope was distracted by the movements of the man in the bomber jacket. Something about him bothered her.

Now he smacked the bell on the counter. The waitress came out from the back. The man tugged his baseball cap lower on his head, shielding his eyes, and leaned across the counter.

"McKenzie—"

"You know it's true," she said, talking over her mother. "I'm self-ish. But mothers can't be. That's why it'll be better if you can han-dle more of the mother thing. I'll be more like the dad. I'll pay the bills, start a college fund, that kind of thing. And then be around on weekends for the fun stuff—taking her to the park, or soccer games, or out for ice cream."

Hope wasn't listening. Her eyes were glued to the scene playing out at the register. At first, the waitress hadn't seemed to under-stand what the man was saying to her. When he leaned even closer, he said it again and grabbed her sleeve.

"McKenzie—" Hope said more urgently.

"Mom, I know what you're going to say. But you don't—"

The waitress let out a short, sharp cry. Hope saw fear in her eyes, a glint of steel from the man's pocket.

"McKenzie!" she shouted. "Kenz, get down!"

Hope kicked her chair backward and sprang across the table, pulling McKenzie to the floor with a clatter of dishware. She shoved McKenzie as hard as she could, pushing her under the table, then spread out her arms, making her body a shield between her daughter and unborn grandchild and the man with the gun.

Chapter 12

IT HAPPENED SO FAST that almost before McKenzie realized what was happening, it was over. Hope's shouts and the clattering dishware had distracted the gunman. He turned momentarily toward the sound, and the waitress snatched a vase from the counter and smashed it over his head. Later, the police officers said that she'd been lucky and should have just handed over the money.

They'd all been lucky. The man dropped the gun, grabbed his bleeding head, and fled on foot through the door. The police were called and arrived almost immediately, as well as an ambulance. McKenzie insisted that she was fine, but Hope was even more insistent. To appease her, McKenzie agreed to go to the hospital for a checkup and an ultrasound. The baby was fine. The police searched the area but were unable to locate the gunman. Later that afternoon, however, one of the officers who had been on the scene came into the emergency room on other business and noticed a man sitting in the waiting room. He was wearing a bomber jacket and greenish tennis shoes with a strange alligator pattern, and held a bloody Oakland A's baseball cap in his lap. No one was hurt, and the bad guy was caught.

To McKenzie, it still seemed kind of unreal. It was just so crazy. By the time she went over to her parents' place to share an extra-large pizza that evening, she was making jokes about it.

"Hey, Dad?" she said. "I advise you to tread lightly around your wife. One false move and boom! You could find yourself on the floor."

"I'll keep that in mind. Another good thing to remember," he said, "never wear alligator shoes to a robbery."

"Or really anywhere," McKenzie mumbled.

"And always root for the Mariners," Rick said. "Right, honey?"

"Right." The wooden tone of Hope's response caught McKenzie's attention. Rick laid his hand on Hope's shoulder.

"Hey. You feeling okay?"

"I'm fine," Hope replied, pushing her chair back from the table. "Just tired. I think I'll turn in early."

"Good idea," Rick said. "You had a crazy day."

Hope nodded. "I'm sure I'll feel better in the morning."

"Actually," McKenzie said, getting to her feet, "I should get going. I'm supposed to meet Zach for coffee in the morning."

Rick's brows came together into a single, disapproving line. "What's that about? He's not trying to get you to take him back?"

McKenzie choked out a laugh. "Definitely not. He probably just wants to discuss some of the financial stuff."

McKenzie walked over to her mother, wrapped her arms around her, and squeezed her tight.

"Hey. I thought what you did today was amazing. You're my hero," McKenzie said, realizing it was true.

"No," Hope replied. "Just your mother."

"Same thing, right?"

Hope returned McKenzie's smile.

"Sometimes. Depends on the day."

ZACH's eyes flew open, and his jaw dropped. "A gun! Like an actual loaded gun? My God, Kenz. Are you okay?"

"I'm sitting here talking to you, aren't I?"

"And the baby's okay?" he asked.

"Yes. I had an ultrasound at the hospital. Everything's fine. Now, what did you want to talk about?" she asked.

"I get that you're still mad," Zach said. "Maybe you always will be. And I know I deserve it, but with the baby coming, I was hoping that we could call a truce."

"Zach. If this is about custody—"

He shook his head. "I swear it's not. Yes, I want to be involved in her life, but I'm not cut out to be a full-time father. Or even a part-time one. I kind of envision myself as more of the fun uncle type, the one who takes her to Mariners games, or the water park, buys extravagant birthday presents. That's the part I'd be good at."

McKenzie cast her eyes down, feeling her cheeks grow hot.

"There's something else. I'd like to be there when she's born," he said. "In fact, I'd like to come to the birthing classes with you."

McKenzie blinked. She hadn't seen this coming.

"I don't know, Zach. That feels like it would be awkward."

"Only if we make it awkward," he said, his voice urgent, almost pleading. "Kenz, like it or not, you and I are going to be parents, so we're kind of stuck with each other. You can spend the rest of your life hating me if you want to. I could do the same. But for the baby's sake, for ours too, what if we tried to be friends?"

"Friends?" McKenzie scoffed. "Why? We never were before."

"I know. But maybe we should have been. We couldn't be any worse friends than we were lovers. Can we give it a try?"

ZACH stood outside the coffee shop watching as McKenzie climbed into her car. McKenzie nodded before driving away.

In the end, she'd said he could participate in the birth, but only if he showed up for all of the birthing classes that she'd signed up for. As for his other request, that they become friends, she hadn't given him an answer. Time would tell, she supposed. But the thing that was most on McKenzie's mind was Zach's description of the kind of relationship he envisioned for himself and their daughter, casting himself more in the role of playmate than father.

His words, or at least the attitude behind them, sounded embarrassingly familiar. Thinking about her mother and father made her realize that Zach had no clue.

Maybe she didn't either; not until today.

Being a parent, a good parent, wasn't a part-time proposition. You couldn't pick and choose the parts you liked. It wasn't about being popular or making your kid like you.

It *was* about doing your best, however imperfect. It was about sacrifice and putting your child first, always, no matter the consequences. It was, as her parents had demonstrated so clearly, about love—all-in, one hundred percent, never-take-a-day-off love.

Zach would probably never change. He didn't want to.

But McKenzie did. Very much.

IN SPITE of her assurances to Rick, Hope didn't feel better the next morning.

Though she'd fallen asleep quickly, her slumber was restless. She dreamt she was back in the café. In the dream, instead of getting beaned over the head and running out the door, the gunman pointed the gun right at them. Hope woke up gasping.

She lay in bed and took slow, deep breaths until her heart resumed a more normal rhythm. She forced herself to go back to sleep only to wake up twice more in the same condition. In the morning, she was so exhausted and anxious that she called in sick.

The pattern of nightmares and interrupted sleep continued. She called in sick for five days in a row. Days weren't much better than her nights. Rick was being kind and patient, but she found herself snapping at him over the littlest things. She felt anxious, too, nervous and unsettled, but couldn't figure out what was making her feel that way. The incident in the café was on her mind, of course. But she didn't think that was the root cause of all this. She tried to stitch the binding on the quilt she was making for the new baby. Then her hands started to tremble. She didn't tell Rick about it; he was worried enough about her already.

On Friday afternoon, when she was trying, unsuccessfully, to take a nap, Rick came into the room and perched on the bed.

He took her hand and lifted it briefly to his lips.

"Nancy called a few minutes ago. She said to tell you hello and that everybody misses you, your students especially. She wanted to know if you're coming back to work on Monday."

Hope pulled her hand from Rick's grasp.

"Oh. Well, it was nice of her to call."

"So are you?" Rick asked. "Going back on Monday?"

She'd been asking herself the same question for a couple of days now. She gave Rick the same answer she'd given herself.

"I don't know. I want to. But I don't know if I can. I feel so anxious and exhausted. I don't know what's wrong with me."

"Maybe you should talk to somebody," Rick said gently. "I mean, after what you went through, it makes sense that you'd be nervous about going back to the prison. Until now, I'm not sure it really sank in that your students were real criminals, that some of them might have been involved in things every bit as terrible as what you experienced in the café."

"No," Hope said. "That's not it. I always understood what I was getting into and who I was dealing with. But now . . ." Hope shook her head. "If I'm going to quit in a few months to help McKenzie with the baby anyway, would it be better to do it now?"

Rick frowned and shook his head. "I don't think so."

Hope frowned, surprised by his response. "Why not? You were never happy about me taking this job. So what's changed?"

"I know you," he said. "If you back out on the commitment you made to those women, you will hate yourself for it later."

"But if I'm going to end up quitting anyway—"

"To take care of the baby? I'm not sure that's a good idea," Rick said. "Let me clarify. I'm not sure *you* think it's a good idea. We haven't talked about it much, but I've got the feeling you're not convinced. If you want to quit working and take care of the baby, fine with me. And if you don't, that's fine too."

"Honestly, I don't know what I want right now."

"Hope. Are you sure you don't want to talk to somebody?"

She knew what he was saying and why—sleeplessness, anxiety, and irritability could all be signs of post-traumatic stress. And of course it all made sense. The incident *had* been traumatic.

In the moment, she hadn't thought about what she was doing. It wasn't until later, when she was watching a technician perform McKenzie's ultrasound, that she thought about what *could* have happened. A moment later, she experienced a trembling in her hands.

That was the first time. It had happened a few times since then. Sometimes it came on while she was thinking about the café, but sometimes it just seemed to come out of nowhere. Was the trauma of what had happened in the café at the center of it? She didn't think so, but on the other hand, what else could it be?

"I need a few days to think things through. I'll make up my mind by Monday. And if I can't . . ." She met Rick's worried gaze. "If I still can't, then I'll talk to someone. Okay?"

"Okay," he said quietly. "Whatever you decide is fine with me. I just want you to be happy. That's all I've ever wanted."

Hope rested her hand on the side of his face.

"My hero."

MANDY's hands were shaking as she inserted the phone card into the telephone kiosk, then punched in the number. While waiting for the call to be accepted, she took slow breaths, trying to hold it together. But the minute the call connected, she lost her resolve as well as her composure and started to cry.

"Hello? Mandy?"

She opened her mouth, but all that came out was a strangled sob.

"Mandy, are you all right? You shouldn't be calling me. I'm not supposed to have any personal contact with inmates."

"I know. I'm sorry," she said, swallowing back her tears as best she could. "It's just . . . I don't know what to do. My dad just left and he—Hope, what am I going to do?"

"Mandy, what's wrong? Your dad came to see you? And he had bad news? Is something wrong with your mom? "

"No, no," Mandy said. "It's about Talia. He came to tell me that they are going to court to try and get permanent custody. He said I'm an unfit mother—a thief and an addict. They're going to take my baby away. Please come back! I don't know what to do!"

Hearing the words from her own mouth brought it all back again. Even with her eyes screwed shut, she could see his face, the disgust and loathing in his eyes. He hated her.

If I get my way, you'll never get to see Talia again.

That's what he'd said. Mandy had no doubt that he meant it, just as she had no doubt that—unless someone helped her—he would get his way. He always had before.

"Please, Hope. I need help. There's no one here I can talk to."

"Mandy? Mandy, listen to me, okay? You've got to try to calm down. Is Nancy there today? Have you tried to see her?"

"No. I don't want to talk to her," she snapped. "She lied to me. She said that if I turned my life around, I'd get Talia back. And I was so stupid that I actually believed her! If I can't be with my daughter, then it was all for nothing, worthless. Just like my life."

"Mandy, your life is *not* worthless; do you hear me? You're not thinking of ending it, are you?"

"You can't end what's already over," Mandy said bitterly. "But Talia's been through so much already. I won't do that to her."

"Good," Hope said. "Now listen. You can't give up. Just because your father says something doesn't mean it's going to happen."

"You don't know what he's like," Mandy said, letting out a small, derisive laugh. "He always gets what he wants. Always."

"Not this time," Hope said. "You're not an unfit mother, Mandy. You *have* turned your life around. You can't let your father tell you who you are. You've got to fight him."

"I don't know how," Mandy said. "I never did."

"Well, you've got to now," Hope said. "For Talia's sake."

Mandy bobbed her head. She knew Hope was right.

"Where have you been? People are saying you're sick."

"I've been sick," Hope said. "Something bad happened to me and my daughter."

"What?"

"It doesn't matter. You just worry about you right now."

Something about the tone of Hope's voice worried Mandy.

"But you're coming back, aren't you?"

The answering silence from the other end of the line transformed worry into panic. If Hope deserted her . . .

"You've got to come back. My father—I can't fight him by myself, I just can't. Please! Please say you're coming back."

RICK walked into the kitchen just as Hope ended the call.

"Babe? Are you okay? Do you need to sit down?"

"That was Mandy," she said. "Her dad came to visit her today to tell her that he's going to court to try to have her parental rights terminated. He said she was unfit to be a mother.

"How can he say that about his own daughter?" Hope continued, throwing out her hands. "And how can her mother stand by and let this happen? She's brought Talia to visit the prison every two weeks for five years. She knows how hard Mandy has worked!"

Rick watched her pace back and forth across the kitchen.

"Mandy called? And you accepted the call? I thought you weren't supposed to have any personal contact with inmates."

"I'm not," she admitted. "But she wouldn't have called unless something was really wrong. What was I supposed to do? Tell the operator I wouldn't talk to her?"

Rick didn't speak, but the look on his face said that yes, that was exactly what she was supposed to do. "I couldn't just blow her off, Rick. Not when she needs help."

"I know," he said, a small smile tugging at the corner of his mouth. "You've never been able to say no to anybody who needs help. So? What are you going to do?"

"Go back to work," Hope said. "At least until the baby is born. I don't know if I can help Mandy. But at least I can be there. She needs to know that somebody cares. They all need to know that."

"Well, you're the one I care about," Rick said, putting his arms around her. "You're sure this is what you want?"

"I'm sure."

Rick nodded. "Then that's what I want too."

Chapter 13

"HEY! MRS. C!" Deedee exclaimed when she came through the classroom door on Monday morning. "I'm so happy you're back!"

"And I'm so happy to be back," Hope replied as the rest of the women filed into the room. Mandy brought up the rear. She looked simply awful. She sniffled and ducked her head.

Deedee put an arm around Mandy's waist. "Uh-oh. Don't go starting that again, Mandy. Mrs. C? Will you talk to her or something?" Deedee asked. "She was crying all night long. You won't let them take her baby away, will you? Tell her to quit blubbering. Everything's going to be okay."

Was it going to be okay? Hope's brief conversation with Nancy before heading down to her classroom left her wondering. From what Nancy told her, Mandy's father was already lawyering up, ready to fight and fight hard. Mandy, on the other hand, with no money and no connections, would have to represent herself.

Kate's arrival saved Hope from having to respond.

"Sorry I'm late," Kate said. "I had to go through the metal detector three times. Seems that my new shoes had metal in the heel. Fortunately, Cindy found these beauties in the Lost and Found."

Kate glanced down at her feet, which were encased in a pair of big, squashy white bedroom slippers. The women all laughed.

"Okay," Hope said, clapping her hands together to get the group's attention. "Let's get to work. Mandy? You and Kate can start checking out everybody's machines and equipment."

The women began lining up in front of the cabinet to receive their supplies. Hope walked up to the front desk but stopped a few paces short, suddenly feeling out of breath. She laid her hand on her chest; her heart was galloping. Kate came up behind her.

"Hope? Can I get the keys?"

Hope took a quick but deep breath. When she reached into her pocket for the cabinet keys, her hands were shaking.

"I'm fine," Hope said quickly, dismissing the concern in Kate's eyes. "I should have eaten more at breakfast."

Kate smiled, then took the keys and unlocked the cabinet. As each woman approached the table in front of the storage cabinet, Mandy found the cardboard box with the woman's name, checked the contents, even counting out the numbers of straight pins inside, and then reported the numbers to Kate, who checked off the information next to the inmate's name on her list.

Hope was glad she'd put Mandy in charge of the checkout process. Especially today, it was good that she had a job to do, something to distract her from her worries. It was good, too, that she was here with her friends.

After all the women had their equipment and were sewing, Hope pulled a bag filled with red, white, and blue fabrics out from under her desk. Those were the colors Tonya had requested for her personal quilt, which she intended to give to her son, who was halfway through his Army basic training. Helping Tonya choose her fabric was the first thing on Hope's list that morning. She knew she had to get to it before—

"Mrs. C?"

Hope looked across the room toward Deedee, who, yet again, had managed to sew her pinwheel block to her sleeve.

Hope sighed. "Hang on, Deedee. I'll get a seam ripper."

SOMEHOW Mandy had believed that simply having Hope back in the building, being back in Hope's classroom, would make her feel better. It was weird, how much this had come to mean to her.

Hope made her feel capable, smart, and trustworthy. In another place, being put in charge of distributing and keeping track of needles, pins, scissors, or rotary cutters wouldn't be a big deal. In here, it was. There were people who would give plenty to get their hands on some of those items. That's why making sure that every single item went back under lock and key at the end of class was a big responsibility. And Hope had entrusted it to her.

Since crossing the threshold into this small, safe, and supportive company, Mandy had started to feel like nothing was beyond her.

Then her dad showed up.

In the nearly five years of her incarceration, Mandy's dad had never come to visit her. She'd actually been excited when a guard came to tell her that her father was in the visitor's room. She thought he'd come to bury the hatchet between them.

Instead, he'd come to destroy the only dream she had left. And while he was at it, he made a point of reminding her that she was stupid, irresponsible, dishonest, untrustworthy, and unfit.

"You're just as worthless as you've ever been. I won't have you ruining Talia's life the way you ruined everything else," he'd snarled.

Twin tears dripped onto the block Mandy held in her hands. She felt a hand on her shoulder and looked up.

"You okay?"

Hope looked so pale. She'd seemed fine at the beginning of class, but now Mandy could see her teacher was tired and weak.

Mandy wiped her eyes and frowned at her.

"You should go home."

"No, no. I'm fine." Hope bent down to inspect Mandy's quilt block. "Let's see what you—"

Hope stopped in mid-sentence and opened her mouth wide, as if she was gasping for air. A moment later, her whole body started to shake. Hope clutched her hand to her chest.

Mandy let out a cry and sprang from her chair. Hope collapsed into her arms. Mandy looked across the room toward Kate.

"Kate! Kate, help!"

In an instant, the room was filled with exclamations of alarm and fear. Hope was conscious but still gasping and seemed unable to speak, her eyes wide and frightened. Mandy heard Kate's voice.

"Let me through," she demanded, and then, "Oh, my Lord."

For a moment, the old woman looked almost as weak and white as the teacher, but she quickly came to herself.

"Anita! Pick up the phone and dial 8. Tell whoever picks up that it's an emergency and we need an ambulance. Mandy, help me put her on the floor so we can cover her up with one of the quilts. We need to keep her warm until the ambulance gets here."

HOPE wasn't quite asleep when she heard a tentative tap on the bedroom door. Opening her eyes, she saw Rick standing at the threshold, looking apologetic.

"David Hernandez is here. I can tell him to come back another time if you're too tired."

"No, that's all right," Hope said, sitting up. "I'll put on a robe and be out in a couple of minutes."

"He brought flowers," Rick said.

"You're kidding," Hope said. "Well. In that case, I'll be out in thirty seconds."

David was sitting on the sofa, drinking coffee, when Hope came out of the bedroom. The bouquet he had brought, pink carnations and white daisies, was sitting on the coffee table.

"Thank you," Hope said, nodding toward the flowers. "You're very kind, but, honestly, I'm embarrassed over all the fuss."

"Sounds like you gave everybody quite a scare. They thought you were having a heart attack."

"So did I," admitted Hope.

"Do they know what caused it?"

"They kept me a couple of days and ran a bunch of tests. We don't have the results yet, but I'm feeling much better."

"That's good to hear," David said. He fell silent. The look on his face made Hope's stomach sink. "Hope, I . . ."

Hope licked her lips. "Ah. So this isn't a social call."

"I wish it was," he said. "All incoming and outgoing calls from inmates are recorded, so I know about the phone call between you and Mandy on Sunday. I'm sorry, Hope. I have to let you go."

"David. David, come on. We talked for about three minutes—"

"Four," he said. "And twenty-seven seconds."

"Okay, four. Fine. It wasn't like we were planning a breakout or jewel heist. She was overwrought, desperate, and sobbing. What was I supposed to do? Hang up on her?"

"What you were supposed to do was not accept the call. And you know that, Hope. I've told you before, every policy—"

"Is there for a good reason," she said, finishing his sentence for him. "I know. And you're right. It was a mistake. I was wrong and I'm sorry. It won't happen again. Give me another chance."

"I can't."

"David. Please. I know I deserve whatever happens to me, but the inmates are the ones who'll suffer, especially the women in the quilting program. They've been making such progress. They're calmer and more confident. And they're more responsib—"

David held up his hand. "Hope, you don't need to convince me. The inmates in your quilting program have made huge strides.

Even Wayne has noticed. Just last week he told me that the inmates in the quilting program are the best in the facility."

"See?" she said, throwing out her hands. "I know you're a stickler for the rules, but if even cranky old Wayne sees a difference . . ."

David looked at her. His gaze was clear, and his voice was firm.

"Hope, I'm shutting down the quilting program, permanently."

"What? David, you can't! Why? Why would you do that?"

David picked up his coffee mug and sighed heavily.

"I don't have a choice. Nita and Mandy got into an altercation in the bathroom, and a fight broke out. There was a razor blade involved. Nita got cut on her hand, nothing very deep. Fortunately Cindy broke things up quickly. But it could have been a lot worse.

"Nita admits that she was the one who started it. According to Nita, she was giving Mandy a hard time, made a comment about Mandy's father suing to remove her parental rights, saying it was a lucky thing for Mandy's little girl that he was."

David paused when Hope gasped, and then went on.

"Anyway, according to Nita, Mandy lunged for her. They tussled around for a bit, and then Nita says that Mandy pulled the razor on her. Mandy denies it, says that Nita was the one who pulled the blade, but . . . it was a round blade, Hope. Same kind as the ones you use in your sewing program."

"And you think Mandy stole it?" Hope's jaw went slack. "Never. She wouldn't do that, David. Mandy is the most responsible, hard-working student in my class. No matter what was going on between her and Nita, Mandy would never do that."

"A week ago, I might have agreed with you. I sent Nita back to medium for a month. I just cut back on Mandy's privileges and took back some of her good time, so she'll be staying with us a little longer. That's the best I could do."

He shook his head.

"This thing with her father has hit Mandy hard. She's not the same. She's distraught and desperate. She's also the only one who had access to the cabinet where you keep those rotary blades. When they were taking you to the hospital, Kate left her in charge. Cindy was supposed to do a pat down when the women left the room, just like always. But things were pretty confused, and those blades are small enough to conceal. Obviously, she missed something."

"No," Hope stated definitively. "I don't believe it. No matter how confused things were, there is no way that Mandy would take advantage of the situation just to settle a score with Nita."

"I'm not saying she took the blade because she wanted to hurt Nita. I think she had someone else in mind," said David.

Recalling Mandy's phone call, the desperation in her voice, Hope felt her stomach clench.

"No," she said slowly. "No. She wouldn't do that to Talia. Talia means everything to her."

"And now her father is trying to take her away." David tilted his head to one side. "Mandy has a history of depression. We had her on suicide watch when she first got here."

"That was years ago," Hope protested.

David put the cup on the table and got to his feet. "I'm sorry, Hope. You're fired. You're a good teacher, and the quilting program was a good idea. I wanted it to work. But my first instincts were right; it's too risky. I'm shutting down the program."

Chapter 14

THREE DAYS AFTER Hope was released from the hospital, McKenzie came to visit, bearing a plate of homemade cookies. Hope invited her to sit in the kitchen while she made a pot of tea.

"Wow. So he came over here specifically to fire you?" McKenzie said. "That's got to hurt."

"It does," Hope admitted, pouring chamomile tea into McKenzie's mug and then her own. "But I'm more sorry for the women than myself. It's just so unfair."

"Yeah, but . . ." McKenzie said slowly, "you can't really blame him, can you? I mean, if students are smuggling razors out of class . . ."

"*If*," Hope replied. "I'm not convinced that's what happened."

"Well, then where do you think the blade came from?"

"Not from any of my girls. I'm sure of it."

Hope rubbed her forehead. She'd felt a dull ache behind her eyes all morning. Whether her headache was caused by the stress of losing her job or anxiety over the uncomfortable conversation she needed to have with McKenzie was impossible to say.

"Anyway," Hope sighed. "It's done now."

"I'm really sorry, Mom." McKenzie laid a hand on her stomach. "On the upside, maybe it's good you have some time to recover?"

Just then the baby kicked, so hard that McKenzie's hand bounced. McKenzie laughed and then looked up at her mother.

"Did you see that? You'd better rest while you can, Mom. Because once your granddaughter makes her appearance, I think it'll take every ounce of energy you've got just to keep up with her."

Hope swallowed her tea and took a breath.

"McKenzie. Honey, there's something we need to—"

"Well, I'm off!"

Rick bounded into the kitchen, wearing jeans, a red and white flannel shirt, a brand-new pair of work boots, and a grin. He bent down to kiss McKenzie's head before looking up at Hope.

"It's only a half day today. Ben's just going to show me the ropes. I should be back by one. You'll be all right until then?"

"Yes," Hope said. "I'll be fine."

The news that Rick had gotten the job as a part-time construction coordinator for Many Hands Housing could not have come at a better time. He was like a kid again, bursting with enthusiasm. Rick grabbed his keys off the kitchen counter.

"You going to stick around for a while?" he asked McKenzie, who nodded. "Keep an eye on your mother. Don't let her overdo it."

Rick bent down to give Hope a goodbye kiss and then headed out the door, whistling a tune.

"Somebody's happy," McKenzie said, grinning.

"So happy. You have no idea. He's thrilled to be going back to work—especially for this organization, where he's building something more meaningful than corporate profits. You get to a certain point in life and you start to think seriously about your legacy, what you'll leave behind." Hope lifted the cup to her lips, smiling.

"It's funny," she continued, "I still miss Portland but not the way I used to. Back then, we thought we had it all, but somewhere along the way, we'd lost track of each other. Rick will work hard at this job, but he's got his priorities set straight now. We both do."

"So? You're never too old to grow up?"

Hope laughed. "Yeah. I guess."

"Well. That's a relief." McKenzie looked down at her belly. "You hear that, kid? Don't be discouraged. There's still a chance that, someday, your mother won't be a *total* train wreck."

"McKenzie, you are *not* a train wreck."

"I'm kidding!" McKenzie countered. "And I think you're right. Even grown-ups can still grow up. Or at least change. I think we've changed in the last few months, haven't we? You and me?"

"Yeah," Hope said, her voice a little hoarse. "I think so too."

McKenzie cleared her throat. "Right. Anyway. What were you saying before Dad bounced in here?"

"Saying?"

Hope felt her pulse quicken. She couldn't do it. Not now, anyway. For the first time in thirty years, they had the kind of close, cozy connection Hope had always longed for. How quickly would things change for the worse if Hope told McKenzie that she wasn't going to be a full-time babysitter for her grandchild?

"I didn't say anything. Or if I did, I don't remember."

"Sure you do," McKenzie said casually. "We were talking about how the evil David Hernandez fired you, and I was saying that maybe it wasn't all bad, you getting a chance to rest before the baby was born, and then you said you had something to tell me—"

McKenzie looked into Hope's pained face and turned pale.

"You're sick, aren't you? You said it was just something with your thyroid, but it's something else, isn't it? What? Your heart?"

"No, no," Hope said urgently, grabbing her daughter's hand. "It's exactly what I told you—my thyroid. Nothing else."

"You're sure?" McKenzie asked. "Because you looked really funny just then. Like you were trying to figure out how to share bad news."

"I was just thinking about . . . about getting fired. That's all."

It was true, at least partially.

"Okay," McKenzie said, her expression relieved but still tinged with suspicion. "And you're sure. It's nothing with your heart?"

"Nothing with my heart," Hope repeated. "All those things I was experiencing—anxiety, rapid heart rate, tremors in the hands—are symptoms of hyperthyroidism. The medication is already working; I'm feeling a lot better."

McKenzie broke her cookie into two pieces, took one for herself and placed the other onto Hope's plate. "There's something I've been wanting to ask you. But you have to promise not to get all— you know—the way you get."

"The way I get about *what?*" Hope said.

"The way you get when you are too happy about something small. The way you *get,*" McKenzie said, opening her eyes wider.

"Fine," Hope said. "I have no idea what you're talking about but—" Hope's face lit up. "Kenz! Are you having twins?"

McKenzie laughed. "No. I am *not* having twins. I wanted to tell you something else. Well, ask you really. Would you teach me how to crochet? I want to make something for the baby."

Hope clenched her fist and pressed it against her mouth.

"Oh no," McKenzie moaned. "I shouldn't have said anything. I should have just looked for a YouTube video or something."

Laughing, Hope wiped away her tears. "It's okay. I'm just happy, that's all. Yes, I would love to teach you how to crochet. But are you sure you wouldn't rather try quilting? I mean, I *can* crochet, but it's never been my strong suit."

"I know. That's the reason I asked. It's just that . . . I kind of want to figure it out for myself." McKenzie paused briefly. "Mom, if I tell you something, can you promise not to take it personally?"

Hope frowned. She wasn't quite sure where this was going.

"Well, I don't know if I can promise but I'll try."

McKenzie paused again. "You were an amazing mother. And ready or not, in another ten weeks, I'm going to be a mother. I know I won't be the kind of mother you were—and are. But I think that I can be, that I *have* to be, my own kind of mother. Right or wrong, I'm going to have to find my own way to screw up my kid."

"As every parent does," Hope said. "Including me."

"Nah. You did good. Anyway, the reason I came over was to ask you to teach me to crochet. But there's something else too."

McKenzie winced, almost as if she were anticipating a blow.

"Would it hurt you terribly if I found somebody else to be my babysitter? I know you were excited about it and you'd be amazing. But, Mom, even though they fired you, I think the work you were doing at the prison was important. You will be an amazing influence on the baby, but . . . I think you should spread that influence as far as you can. It's like you said, you get to a certain age and you start thinking about your legacy. You need to chart your own path, apart from just our family. And as a mom, I need to chart mine."

For a moment, Hope was unable to speak. But had she been able to, she'd have told her daughter that, as her mother, she had never been prouder.

She hadn't just raised a daughter; she had raised a woman. And should Hope's next breath be her last, she knew her legacy was already secure. And profound.

"LET me get the door. You're dropping stuff everywhere."

Hazel took Hope's key ring, unlocked the condo door, and then held it open for her sister. Hope carried her burden into the kitchen and set the overflowing box down onto the counter.

Hazel, who had been following in her sister's wake, picking up the objects Hope had dropped along the journey from the front door, put everything down on the counter next to the box.

"Thanks for coming up," Hope said.

"No problem. What are sisters for if not to help cheer you up when you hit a rough patch? Although, how this is supposed to help cheer you up, I have no idea." Hazel plucked a worn, circa-1950s copy of a Hardy Boys mystery from the box on the counter.

"I told you," Hope said. "I'm making junk journals—little scrapbooks made with recycled or vintage papers."

"Junk journals." Hazel shook her head. "Well, the name makes sense. You know that this book is missing half the pages, right?"

"But the cover is perfect. I'll use it to make a journal for Rory—he was always crazy about the Hardy Boys."

"Very nice. And these?" Hazel took swizzle sticks out of the box. "Are we planning on opening a tiki bar?"

"No," Hope said. "I'll use them as plant markers for my herbs."

Hazel shook her head. "Wow. You are so bored you hardly know what to do with yourself. You have *got* to find another job."

"Believe me, I'm looking," Hope said. "There's an opening at the Boys and Girls Club. I sent my résumé yesterday."

"Do you think you'll get an interview?"

"Maybe. Assuming David doesn't slam me if they call for a recommendation."

"He won't," Hazel said quietly.

"How do you know? Are you two seeing each other?"

Hazel shook her head. "We text sometimes. If we lived closer, I think that I *would* see him. But the distance, our jobs, our personalities . . . I don't think it would work."

"Maybe it won't work," Hope said to her sister. "But you never really know until you try. That's how you figure out what matters to you, and how much you're willing to sacrifice for it."

Noises started to come from the front foyer.

"Rick?" Hope called out. "If you've been at the job site, take off your boots, okay? I washed the floors this morning. Rick?"

"Already did," he said, entering the kitchen and setting down his bag of groceries before giving Hope a peck on the lips. "Hey, Hazel. What's all this?" he said, nodding toward the box.

"Treasures," Hazel said.

"Oh, good," he said. "Because we were almost out."

"Funny." Hope peeked into the bag. "Did you get steaks?"

"Yup. Oh, and there's a package in there too. I picked up the mail on the way in. Looks like it came from the prison."

"The prison?"

Hope reached into the bag and fished out a padded manila envelope, addressed to her. She ripped open the top. At the first glimpse of purple, gray, and periwinkle, Hope knew what it was and why it had come to her.

"Oh no," she murmured.

"What is it?" Rick asked.

"Mandy's quilt top."

"Her quilt top? Why would she send it to you?"

Hope pulled the fabric from the envelope and spread it out on the counter. As she did, another smaller envelope fell out.

Hope unfolded the letter she had taken out of the smaller envelope. Reading the scrawled and anguished words, Hope's heart clutched with shared anguish. Rick moved close, put his arm over her shoulder, and read along with her.

"What's it say?" Hazel asked. "Why did she send you the quilt? I thought she was making it for her kid."

"She was," Hope said, eyes still scanning the letter. "But now, since that fight with Nita, they're delaying her release. Not by a lot, just two weeks. But still . . ." Hope sighed heavily. "David and his stupid policies. Didn't he realize what would happen next?"

"What's David got to do with it?" Hazel asked.

"When inmates are involved in fights, they can have some of their time off for good behavior rescinded," Hope said. "Two weeks would be the minimum in this sort of case, which tells me that David was trying to be lenient. But Mandy's dad is using this as ammunition in his court battle to deny Mandy's parental rights. He's trying to paint her as violent and unreformed."

"That's terrible," Hazel said. "Can't her lawyer fight back?"

"Mandy doesn't have a lawyer. She's got to fight this all on her own and from inside a prison. And, honestly, I'm not sure she's got any fight left in her. That's why she sent the quilt, because she says she'll probably never get to see Talia again and so she's sending it to me so I can finish it for McKenzie's baby.

Rick, who was still holding the letter, read the final lines aloud: *"In a month I'll walk through the gate. They say I'll be free, but it's not true. No matter what I do in the future or how hard I try, I know I can't be free of the past. People never let you forget. I hope your granddaughter will like the quilt. It's nice to think that some little girl can use it, even if she's not mine."*

Rick stopped reading.

"She sounds terrible. How can her father claim she hasn't changed if he never even went to visit her?"

"That's what I say," Hope replied. "Mandy may have given up, but I won't. She's worked hard to turn her life around. She deserves a chance to be with her daughter."

"But how can you help? You're just her teacher," Hazel said.

"Not anymore," Hope corrected. "As an employee of the prison, I couldn't have any personal contact with Mandy. But now, as her friend . . ." Hope took her phone out of her bag and started dialing.

"Who are you calling?" Hazel asked.

"Kate. She's lived here her whole life, worked at the capitol, knows everybody. If there's a lawyer in town who'd be willing to take Mandy's case, Kate will know how to find them."

"You know," Hazel said, "I almost feel sorry for Mandy's dad. Making my sister mad? That was a big mistake."

KATE did know an attorney, Diane Waverly. She wasn't very encouraging.

"It's always a crapshoot in these situations," Diane said. "So much comes down to the judge. I'll be honest, the fact that Mandy was involved in a fight involving weapons is not good."

"But Mandy didn't start the fight," Hope protested. "Nita did. There is no way she would have stolen a blade from the supply cabinet, not in a million years. I'm sure of it."

"I know you're sure," Diane said. "But a judge can't just take your word on it. You're going to need proof. Do you have any? And if not, can you get any?"

Hope looked a question at Kate.

"I don't think *we* can," Kate said. "Hope is persona non grata at the prison right now. But maybe I could get in touch with somebody who could ask questions? Somebody who knows everybody's business?"

"Deedee?" Hope asked.

"It's worth a try," Kate said.

"Good," Diane said. "But even if you can prove that Mandy didn't instigate the fight or provide the weapon, there's still no guarantee that a judge won't terminate her parental rights. She's been convicted of two felonies. Plus, the child has been in the custody of the grandparents for the last five years. If I was the attorney for the other side, I'd argue that being separated from the grandparents and placed into the care of a woman she barely knows would cause the child emotional damage."

"But Talia does know her mother," Hope said. "She's crazy about her. Until Mandy's father got the court involved, they saw each other every two weeks. I thought that courts were supposed to lean toward family reunification whenever possible."

"They are," Diane said. "But 'whenever possible' is open to interpretation. Judges can also take the best interests of the child into consideration. And they should."

Diane leaned forward, looking Hope squarely in the eye.

"I do think Mandy is being treated unfairly; that's why I've agreed to represent her on a pro bono basis. But the least powerful person in this situation is Talia. So, before we go any farther down this road, are you sure Mandy will be a fit parent?"

"I'm sure," Hope said. "She'll devote every ounce of energy she has to being the best possible mother for Talia. She's already spent the last five years doing exactly that."

"I agree with Hope," Kate said. "Everything Mandy does, she does with Talia in mind. She's been a model prisoner."

Diane shifted her weight back in her chair.

"All right. Then I'll do everything I can to help Mandy. Even so, I can't guarantee the outcome. The best thing would be if this case never got in front of a judge at all. Any chance you can talk the family into changing their minds about bringing the suit?"

"I've never met Mandy's parents," Hope said. "But from what I hear, her father is adamant. He threw Mandy out of the house when she was sixteen, something about her using the car without permission and staying out after curfew. She didn't have anywhere to go, ended up living with a boyfriend who was older and a drug dealer. She got pregnant with Talia at age eighteen, was arrested at twenty, and incarcerated at twenty-one.

"I could try to talk to Mandy's dad, but he doesn't know me at all. And he doesn't sound like a person who listens to reason."

Diane glanced at her watch and got to her feet. "You never know. As a teacher, you might carry some kind of influence with him. And if not? Well, maybe you can find someone who does."

Chapter 15

RICK AND HOPE PARKED just down the street from a small but tidy ranch-style home with a gray front door and a well-tended lawn. "Maybe I should go in with you," Rick said.

"I don't think it's a good idea," Hope said. "Mandy's mother seems kind of shy. I think she'll be much more likely to open up in a one-on-one conversation, and to another woman."

"You're sure the dad isn't in there? I don't like the idea of you being around that guy."

"He should be at work by now," Hope said. "And Talia will be at school. Anyway, from what Mandy told me, he's not violent. He never hit her or her mother."

"Some guys can hit without throwing a punch," Rick groused. "Mandy's dad sounds like one of them. I hate a bully."

"Be right back." Hope leaned across the seat, kissed him on the lips, and then hopped out of the truck. Before closing the door, she turned back toward him. "By the way, I am very happy that I picked you to be the father of my children."

"Well, okay. Me too," Rick said, and gave Hope a lopsided sort of grin. "Good luck. If you need anything, I'll be right here."

Hope crossed a couple of lawns and climbed the front steps of the blue rancher. A few moments after she rang the bell, Lola, Mandy's mother, opened the door.

"Mrs. Lopez? You might not remember me, but my name is Hope Carpenter." Lola frowned but said nothing. "I was Mandy's teacher. We met at the prison?"

"Is my Mandy in trouble? I haven't seen her for weeks."

"None that you don't already know about," Hope said. "That's what I wanted to talk to you about. Do you have a few minutes?"

Lola looked left and right, then opened the screen door.

"Okay," she said. "I have to go pick Talia up for a dentist appointment in about half an hour. But, please. Come inside."

RICK sat in his truck, his eyes glued to the gray door his wife had disappeared through, waiting.

At long last, the door opened.

Hope stepped through. She wasn't smiling. A woman with gray hair and slight build followed her. They stood on the walkway talking for a moment; then the woman climbed into a blue sedan in the driveway and drove off. Hope retraced her path across the neighboring yards toward the truck.

"Well?" he asked after she climbed inside and closed the door. "How'd it go?"

"Honestly? I don't know." Hope paused, gazing up the street. "She was cautious about opening up to me, especially at first. She's got perfectly reasonable concerns about how this will impact Talia; she was so little when Mandy was sentenced that she doesn't remember another home. And, of course, Lola loves Talia. It must be hard to think about letting her go.

"Still, I think she's worried about what will happen when Talia gets older. Apparently everything was fine between Mandy and her dad until Mandy hit puberty, but then suddenly he didn't trust her; everything she did made him suspicious. Maybe he thought he was protecting her?"

Rick sputtered. "Maybe he was being a jealous jerk. I'm telling you, babe. The guy's a bully."

"Maybe. I think he's the one driving this. Lola knows Mandy has changed. But I think she's afraid to stand up to her husband."

Rick reached across the seat, grabbed Hope's hand, and then pulled it to his lips, placing a kiss on the ridge of her knuckles.

"You're an amazing woman, do you know that?"

Hope let out an unconvinced little laugh. "Thanks. But if I was really amazing, I'd have walked out of that house knowing that Lola was going to stand up to her husband."

"You never know, things still might work out."

"They might," Hope said. "I appealed to her as a woman and a mother. That's really all I can do. The rest is up to her."

"Well. Maybe," Rick said. "I've been sitting here thinking, and I'm not so sure about that."

Hope frowned. "What are you talking about?"

"When it comes to helping Mandy regain custody, I do think you've done everything you can. But the other inmates still need you. I think you should try to get your job back."

"Hang on. Did you just say you wanted me to go back to work at the prison? I thought you hated me working there."

"I did," he admitted. "But that was before I saw how much it meant to you and what a difference you're making there. Besides, even if you lose, sometimes you've got to stand up for what's right."

"But how? David wouldn't budge. Policy."

"So go over his head."

"How? It's not like I can complain to the supervisor; he *is* the supervisor. Of everything."

"Go *way* over his head. David enforces policy. Appeal to the person who actually makes it."

"Okay," Hope said slowly. "Sounds good to me but once again, I ask the obvious question—how? Do you have a plan?"

Rick sniffed and turned the key in the ignition. The old truck sputtered and complained for a moment, then roared to life.

"Not a plan exactly. More of an idea."

"An idea. Are explosives and pickaxes involved? Spies? Superhero capes? Because that's what I think it would take."

Rick shifted the gears. "I was thinking more along the lines of you, Kate, and a quilt," he said. "But capes would be a nice touch."

THE steady drizzle did nothing to dampen the enthusiasm of the crowd that was standing shoulder to shoulder in Seattle's Waterfront Park, waiting for the rally to begin.

Hope and Kate tried to squeeze their way to the front of the crowd. It was slow going.

"Now I know how salmon feel," Kate said, calling over her shoulder to Hope as they inched forward.

"Just keep moving!" Hope replied, shouting to make herself heard over the cheering and music and chaos.

When her progress was blocked by a huge man, Kate tapped him on the shoulder and said, "Excuse me, sir. Can my friend and I get by? We're trying to get up front to see the governor."

The man turned around, scowling. He wore a plaid shirt and a gray and red WSU Cougars baseball cap. "Lady, we're all trying to see the governor."

"Yes," Kate said, smiling, "but we drove all the way up from Olympia because we want to deliver a quilt to the governor."

"A quilt?" The mountainous man scowled again. "Why would you come up here to give the governor a quilt? You were already in Olympia. Why not just drop it off at the capitol? Or mail it?"

"We want to deliver it to Governor Russman personally, along with a letter. We're hoping that she'll intervene to help some friends of ours." Hope looked up at his hat and smiled. "Oh, are you a cougar? My husband went to WSU. Wonderful school."

"Sure is. I grew up near Pullman."

"Really? My aunt Marilyn was from Pullman."

After a couple minutes of small talk, Mountainous Man let them pass and Hope and Kate progressed a few more yards, until their path was blocked by someone else, only to be cleared by the finding of common ground a few minutes later. It went on like that for a good forty minutes, which was just about the time Governor Norma Russman arrived on the scene.

She was a good speaker. Hope and Kate were more focused on trying to work their way over toward the right side of stage, where the governor had entered and where they assumed she would make her exit, than on the speech itself. Even so, after the governor outlined a detailed plan to improve high school graduation rates, Kate said, "You know, I was thinking of voting for the other guy, but after listening to her, I've changed my mind."

As the governor thanked the crowd, bidding them farewell, Hope and Kate pressed forward toward a line of metal stanchions meant to separate the candidate from the crowd. Hundreds of others did the same. The governor slowly worked her way down the line of admirers, leaning out to touch as many hands as she could, stopping now and then to exchange a few words with people.

When Governor Russman was only a few feet away from them, nearly close enough to touch, four men in dark suits moved closer to the candidate.

The men formed a tight wall of protection around the governor and began to guide her to the left side of the stage, in the opposite direction from where Hope and Kate were standing.

"Governor!" Hope cried, leaning across the metal railing, the quilt in her arms. "Governor! I have something to give you!"

Hope shouted as loud as she could, but it was impossible to make herself heard over the crowd. The men in the suits closed ranks and whisked the candidate to a waiting SUV.

And then she was gone.

FIFTEEN minutes into what had been a largely silent journey back to Olympia, Kate said, "Oh, I forgot to tell you—I went to the prison on Tuesday and was able to talk to Deedee."

"And?"

"According to her, the rumor going around is that Mandy did steal the blade. They say that Nita started the fight but that Mandy had taken it because she was depressed, thinking of cutting herself, but then used it on Nita when she attacked."

"That's not possible," Hope declared. "She wouldn't do that. They did a count of the supplies afterward, and none of the blades were missing. Everything was accounted for."

"Some people are saying the count was off to start with."

"It wasn't," Hope said. "I counted them myself. There were four blades total. Even I can count to four."

"Well, maybe Deedee will come up with something. I gave her money to buy a few bags of Fritos. Maybe a few incentives will convince people to start talking."

Hope nodded but said nothing.

"At least we tried," Kate said after a long moment.

"I suppose."

"Oh, come on. Don't be so gloomy. Another two minutes and we'd have been able to talk with the governor. Next time, we will. There'll be other rallies."

"Maybe," Hope said. "But the governor doesn't have any public events on her schedule for the next ten days or so. Apparently, she's getting ready for a big trip to Japan, promoting trade."

Kate scowled. "Well, don't worry. We've got ten days to think of something else."

"True," Hope said. "We just need to come up with a new plan."

"Right," Kate said. "Any ideas?"

Hope paused for a moment.

"Not really. Except that a miracle would come in very handy about now. Who do I see about arranging one of those?"

Four days later, the much hoped and prayed for miracle had not appeared. Nor was Hope getting anywhere with her job search. After calling the Boys and Girls Club the day before to check on her application, she was told that the position had been filled.

She hadn't even gotten an interview.

"Why don't you come with me," Rick suggested as he was lacing up his running shoes after they finished breakfast. "It'd get your mind off things. Running's great for stress."

"I wouldn't run unless zombies were chasing me." Hope sighed. "I was thinking of painting an accent wall in the living room. At least I'll have accomplished *something* today."

Rick looked at her.

"Are you planning to spend the whole day feeling sorry for yourself?"

"Nancy called. They hired a new craft teacher at the prison."

Rick winced. "Ow. I'm sorry. Well, maybe you do get to spend the whole day feeling sorry for yourself."

Hope shook her head. "I told you; I'm going to paint an accent wall in the living room this morning. I'll spend the *rest* of the day feeling sorry for myself."

Rick smiled and bent down to give her a kiss.

"See you in an hour," he said.

In thirty-nine minutes, Rick was back. He was huffing and puffing so hard that he could barely speak.

"Honey! Are you okay? Do you need to sit down?" Hope asked.

"Had to tell you right away. I saw her."

"Saw who?" Hope said, shaking her head in confusion.

Rick stood up straight, grinning, and took one more big breath.

"The governor and two of her bodyguards. Down at Marathon Park. She's a runner, Hope. Runs almost every day."

HOPE's forehead was dripping with sweat. Her lungs felt like they were about to explode. But she'd made up her mind.

She was going to run a quarter mile even if it killed her. The footbridge was only a few yards ahead of her. Once she crossed it, she'd have reached her goal. At least she'd have something to show for the last five days of misery and aching muscles.

She shifted her burden to her other arm. Even though Hope had rolled it tightly into a tube shape before wrapping it in plastic, Mandy's quilt made an awkward baton. She was almost there. Another twenty yards. Fifteen. Ten.

Rick sped past her with long strides, then ran to the end of the bridge and a few yards farther before turning around and slowing his pace to a jog, meeting Hope at the end of the footbridge.

"Great job, babe! You did it!"

"That was absolutely miserable."

"But you did it," Rick said. "And without zombies. Good job!"

"Slow as I run, it's a good thing there weren't any zombies involved. Otherwise, I'd already be among the undead. How many times did we go around?"

"Twice. That's all I have time for. I've got to get over to the job site. The building inspector is due this morning. You ready to go?"

Hope looked to the left and right, scanning the horizon, looking for a redheaded woman about her age who, according to Rick, would be running between two fit men in their early thirties. She saw only individual runners. She looked at Rick.

"No sign of her on the other side of the lake?"

"You think I'd have kept it from you if I had? Honey, you tried. That's all anybody can do."

"I guess. It was always kind of a crazy plan," she said. "She's leaving for Japan tomorrow. Maybe I should have just mailed it."

"You still can. Just because you don't hand it to her personally doesn't mean she won't actually see it or read the letter."

"True. But if I could just talk to her, I could explain what happened and why the quilting program should be reinstated."

"You ready?" Rick asked.

Hope shook her head. "You go on without me. I'll walk home."

"It's a pretty long walk."

"I know," Hope said. "I want to stay a little longer. Just in case. And if I don't see her . . ." Hope shrugged. "Well, then I'll put it in the mail. You're right. All I can do is try."

Rick gave her a quick kiss. "See you tonight," he said before jogging off toward the truck.

"See you tonight."

CARRYING the quilt under her arm, Hope finished walking the upper loop of Capitol Lake. Either the governor wasn't running today or they'd missed her. Much as she hated giving up, it was time to admit defeat and head home.

Olympia Coffee Roasting company was less than a block away.

Hope went inside, ordered a small latte and a chocolate croissant, then sat down at one of the tables to enjoy a well-deserved treat. As Hope took a sip, the door opened. A middle-aged woman with red hair, flanked by two fit young men in their early thirties, walked up to the counter and ordered three iced coffees.

Hope almost choked on her coffee.

It wasn't possible. After all this time, all the miles she'd clocked, carting Mandy's quilt around the lake, hoping beyond hope that she might almost literally run into the governor of the state, she stumbled upon her in a coffee shop entirely by accident?

Hope retrieved the quilt from the chair next to her. The governor was still at the counter, joking with the cashier. Hope approached slowly, not wanting to interrupt. When there was a lapse in the conversation, Hope cleared her throat.

"Excuse me? Governor Russman? Do you have a moment? There's something I wanted to give you."

Still smiling, the governor turned around to face Hope. But the instant Hope pulled the plastic-wrapped, tube-shaped quilt from under her arm, the governor's smile fled. Almost as instantly, the two fit young men stepped in front of her.

"Step back, ma'am! Put the package on the floor and your hands up. Do it now!"

"The package?"

Seeing the look in those young men's eyes, realizing it was fear and that she was the cause of it, Hope did as she told.

"It's not a package. I mean, it is, but there's nothing dangerous inside. It's a quilt. I just want to give the governor a quilt."

A red head popped up over the shoulders of the two young men.

"A quilt? Somebody made me a quilt? Can I see it?"

Hope glanced at the two men, her eyes silently asking permission. The taller man frowned and gave a short nod.

Hope knelt down, ripped away the plastic cover, and then got to her feet again, unfurling Mandy's quilt with a purple and periwinkle flourish. The governor gasped.

"Oh, it's gorgeous! What's the pattern? My grandmother was an avid quilter, but I don't recognize this block. You made it for me?"

"It's called Dove in the Window. Most of the piecing was done by a young woman named Mandy. She's an inmate at the women's prison and I'm her teacher, or was, until a couple of weeks ago when the program was ended.

"There's a letter pinned to the back of the quilt," Hope said, placing the quilt in Governor Russman's arms, "but if you have a few minutes, I'd like to tell you about it."

"Governor?" One of the young men took a step forward. "Ma'am, you've got a final Japan briefing in forty-five minutes."

The governor then turned toward Hope. "What's your name?"

"Hope Carpenter."

"Nice to meet you, Hope. I'm Norma Russman." The governor extended her hand. Hope shook it. "And I've got five minutes."

"MR. HERNANDEZ? Please hold for the governor."

Though Governor Russman wouldn't be able to see him through the phone, David suddenly felt the need to sit up in his chair, straighten his tie, and square his shoulders.

When Steve Vincent, aide to the governor, called a couple of weeks before, David hadn't been surprised. They'd already chatted about David's forthcoming report on programming for the female prison population.

The surprising part was when Steve started asking questions about the quilting pilot program. David hadn't discussed it with him. But somehow Steve knew about it. Apparently, the governor did too and wanted to know more.

When David explained that the program had been suspended because of safety concerns, Steve said that the governor wanted a report anyway, along with any information about the other programs they'd been working on—the arts and crafts classes, the family preservation project, and the practical living initiative.

"Well, the arts and crafts classes had to be suspended along with the quilting pilot. But the new teacher came on board last week, so that's back on track. The practical living initiative is still in the idea phase," David explained. "We'd offer classes in basic life skills—budgeting, job interview techniques, basic meal planning—skills a lot of our population missed along the way."

"Sounds interesting. Got somebody in mind to teach all that?"

David paused, sighing inwardly. "Uh, no. Not right now."

"Well, sounds like something worth exploring. Anyway, I'd like for you to write all this up—especially the quilting thing. If you could send it over by ten o'clock tomorrow morning—"

"Tomorrow morning? What's the rush?"

"She's flying to Japan tomorrow, wants to read the report on the plane. Hey, David, gotta go. I'm late for a meeting. You on this?"

"Sure," David said. "You'll have it by ten tomorrow."

David e-mailed the report to Steve at 9:51 a.m. the next day. Six minutes later, Steve e-mailed back: THANKS, BUDDY. APPRECIATE IT. And then . . . nothing.

It was disappointing but not unexpected. This was far from the first time that David pushed to get something somebody said they absolutely had to have as soon as humanly possible and then never heard from them again. It was part of the job.

But now the governor was calling.

Once they got through pleasantries and her apology for taking so long to get back to him, it was clear that Governor Russman had not only read his report but had also spent a lot of time thinking about it. Her questions were insightful, and her commitment to prison reform was genuine.

"Well, I think the practical living program is definitely worth pursuing," the governor said, about fifteen minutes into the conversation. "We've only got room in the budget to fund a part-time position, but you might want to start thinking about staffing."

"Yes, ma'am. I . . . I do have someone in mind."

"Good. Now, let's talk about the quilting pilot program. As I understand it, the cancellation was specifically based on safety concerns. Otherwise, it had been very successful, is that right?"

David detailed the circumstances behind his decision.

"Uh-huh," the governor said. "I think that was a reasonable response. But it also sounds like you had strict safety procedures in place that, up until the incident, had been effective. And when it was looked into later, nothing was missing from the cabinet?"

"That's right, ma'am. All four blades were still in the cabinet."

"So, the weapon in question might not have come from the classroom at all, isn't that true? It's possible the blade used in the incident could have been smuggled in by some other means."

David wiped a sweating palm on his pant leg and coughed.

"We're very careful about screening and searches, but yes. That is a possibility. However, since we couldn't prove it one way or another, I thought it best to err on the side of safety."

"Agree completely," Governor Russman replied. "Safety has to take highest priority. But if you *could* prove that the blade was smuggled in by some other means, then I assume you would have no qualms about reinstituting the program? Or even expanding it?"

"No, ma'am. None at all. As a matter of fact, there have been some rumors recently that the blade might have come from the outside. Nothing I've been able to substantiate so far, but—"

"Is that so? Well, if you can find out if the rumors are more than rumors, I'd definitely like to know about that."

"Certainly, Governor. I'll get on it right away."

"Good. Thank you for your time. And keep up the good work."

TEN minutes later, David was striding down a corridor that led to the cafeteria. When he saw Nancy exiting the cafeteria, talking with a red-eyed recent arrival, he interrupted their conversation.

"Deedee?" Nancy said. "Oh, yes. I saw her a few minutes ago. She went out to the courtyard for a cigarette. I think Nita's out there too. She's back already. That month flew by, didn't it?"

"Thank you," David said, then continued on his way, exiting a pair of doors into the courtyard, which appeared to be empty.

However, the sound of voices coming from the northwest corner, behind a bed of roses, caught his attention and he began walking in that direction. When the volume of the voices increased and was followed by a shout of surprise and pain, he started running.

Though the faces and bodies were obscured by the rosebushes, he saw two female forms circling each other like prizefighters before a bout.

David ran as fast as he could, adrenaline flooding his body. When he was just a few yards away, the larger figure lunged and the smaller shrieked in anguish. David shouted as loud as he could. The figures froze for an instant, then turned toward him.

He saw the silver glint of steel and the sickening red of gushing blood. He heard another cry of pain, this time his own, as the larger figure lunged again, and he flung himself forward, putting himself between the smaller woman and the blade.

Chapter 16

IN THE MIDDLE OF MAY, spring finally seemed to make up her mind about staying. Hope, like every other resident of the Pacific Northwest, made the most of the sunny season.

Knowing it would be busy on a Saturday morning, she arrived at the coffee roasters early.

McKenzie waddled through the door just as Hope snagged a table. "Good! You got a seat by the window. It's such a pretty day."

Mandy arrived a couple minutes later. Hope caught her eye and waved her over. After introducing the two younger women, Hope hopped up from the table to place an order.

Mandy reached toward her purse, but Hope waved her off. "No, no. I've got it. This is your Coming Out party. You and McKenzie stay here and get to know each other. I'll get the food."

By the time she returned, the two young women were gabbing like girlfriends.

"Oh, I *know*," Mandy said, shaking her head in sympathy. "The last month before I had Talia the only thing I could fit into was flip-flops," Mandy laughed. "When are you due?"

"Three more weeks," McKenzie sighed. "I wish I could have her right now. Today."

"Not today," Hope said, passing out the beverages. "I need to get back over to your place and finish wallpapering the nursery."

"She means re-wallpapering," McKenzie said. "I tried to do it on my own and made a total mess of it."

"It wasn't that bad," Hope said.

"She's being kind," McKenzie said. "It was a complete disaster. You see, Mandy, the crafty gene seemed to skip me. Well, except for crocheting. As it turns out, I am pretty good at that."

"Much better than me," Hope said.

"Not true," McKenzie said. "At least not yet. But I'm getting better. I finished the sweater last night. Do you want to see?"

Responding to Hope and Mandy's eager assurances in the affirmative, McKenzie reached into her purse and pulled out a tiny pink cardigan. Seeing it, Mandy clutched her hand to her chest.

"Awww. It's so teeny and cute!" she exclaimed. "I could never make something like that."

"But you can sew," McKenzie said. "Mom showed me your quilt before she gave it to the governor. It was just gorgeous."

"Thanks. I had a pretty good teacher," Mandy said, looking toward Hope. "Any word on how that went?"

"With the governor?" Hope asked, shaking her head. "She promised she'd look into it when she got back from her travels. You never know. Something might come of it."

"I hope so," Mandy said, her eyes downcast. "I feel bad that the quilting program was canceled because of me."

"That wasn't your fault," Hope said firmly.

"Yeah, well . . ." Mandy mumbled.

McKenzie shifted her gaze to her mother, and then, reading Hope's silent permission to change the subject, she said, "So how are thing's going for you? Does it feel good to be out? Or weird?"

Mandy smiled a little. "Both, I guess. The halfway house is okay. I miss my friends. I spend a lot of my free time writing letters to the girls. My old friends are part of the reason I ended up getting into trouble, so I'm steering clear of them. And, you know, my parents and I aren't exactly on speaking terms."

"What about Talia?" Hope asked. "Have you seen her?"

"Not yet. Diane is petitioning to get me supervised visits. She says the best thing I can do to convince the court that I'm ready to take care of Talia is to find a job. So, I'm focusing on that."

"How's it going?"

"No luck so far. My counselor at the halfway house is going to set up an interview for me next week," she said, "with a landscaping company. They've placed a few people there. It'd only be for the summer, pulling weeds and stuff. But I like working outside."

Mandy lifted her head and gazed out the window onto the sunlit Saturday sidewalk.

"That's the good part," she mused. "Being able to walk out the door, go anyplace I want to go and do anything I want to do. Well, as long as it's legal and I'm back by eight. The halfway house is pretty strict about curfew.

"What about you?" she asked Hope. "Any luck with the job hunt?"

Hope shook her head. "Not yet. Life on the outside is tough."

"Got that right," Mandy said.

The three women chatted a bit longer, finished their coffee and pastries, and got up to leave. Before they parted, McKenzie gave a business card to Mandy.

"So, listen, a couple of my friends and I have decided to start getting together on Wednesdays after work, here at the coffee shop, to talk and crochet. If you'd like to come, give me a call."

Mandy looked up at McKenzie.

"Really?"

McKenzie nodded. "I'll probably only be able to come for a couple more weeks, until the baby comes. But I think it'll be fun."

"Wow. Yeah. I'd like that. But . . ." Mandy's eager expression faded. "I don't have any needles or yarn. And until I get a job—"

"Oh, don't worry," McKenzie said, flapping her hand. "Do what I do; shop in Mom's stash. She's got enough yarn to open a store."

"She's right," Hope said. "Honestly, Mandy, you'd be doing me a favor by taking some of it off my hands."

"You sure?"

"Absolutely," McKenzie said. "I was planning to follow Mom home and find something for my next project. I can pick something out for you too. You could make Talia a scarf."

"Okay," Mandy said, grinning. "That'd be great."

"Good," McKenzie replied. "See you on Wednesday."

WHEN they got back to the condo, McKenzie parked and then rode upstairs with her mother.

Hope opened the front door, then stopped dead in her tracks, sniffing the air.

"Oh no," Hope murmured.

"Dad's baking again?" McKenzie sniffed too. "What's wrong? Smells good."

Hope dropped her purse on the floor.

"Rosemary," she said, and strode straight to the kitchen.

When she entered, Rick was standing at the kitchen counter, slicing bread. Nancy was sitting at the kitchen table. Both of them looked up when Hope entered the room.

"Nancy! Oh, thank heaven," Hope said, shoulders slumping with relief. "I thought something bad had happened."

"Hope has a thing about rosemary," Rick explained to Nancy before putting his knife down on the cutting board. "I've got some work to do in the bedroom. So, I think I'll leave you two to talk."

He looked at McKenzie, who had entered the room shortly after her mother, with raised brows. McKenzie frowned for a moment, then said, "Right. Well, I'm going to go look for some yarn."

Hope kept her eyes on Nancy's solemn face as she took a seat at the table while Rick and McKenzie left the room.

"I was going to say I was happy to see you, but something tells me I shouldn't be. Not today."

Nancy tipped her head to one side, her somber expression softening into one of compassion. "Not today," she echoed. "It's not all bad news. But something happened at the prison."

Nancy took a deep breath, then began to speak.

"Deedee has been asking a lot of questions lately, trying to see if she can get any information about the fight between Nita and Mandy, and where those rotary blades could have come from if not the sewing supplies. It seems that she was making progress.

"One of the new girls, Rhoda, said she overheard one of the other prisoners saying that they'd heard that Nita had gotten close to one of the cafeteria workers and exchanged—shall we say, favors—to get him to smuggle some blades in for her.

"According to Rhoda, this prisoner said Nita wanted to get back at Mandy. Since Mandy was one of the only prisoners with access to the sewing cabinet and since rotary blades are so unusual, she reckoned she'd be able to pin everything on Mandy. And with

Mandy being so depressed about possibly losing custody of Talia, and having been on suicide watch in the past—"

"*Years* ago," Hope said. "Right after she arrived."

"Nita thought people would believe it," Nancy continued. "Apparently, Nita heard that Deedee was asking questions. On Friday, she found Deedee alone in the courtyard and attacked her."

"No!" Hope gasped. "Is she all right?"

"She will be. The doctors put twenty-two stitches in her forearms—she was trying to defend herself—but apart from the scars, they say she'll be fine. Nita pulled a blade on her. A round one."

Hope's mouth dropped open. For a moment, it felt like she'd forgotten to breathe or that her heart had skipped a beat. "So Mandy didn't steal the blades from the cabinet."

Nancy shook her head. "She didn't."

"This is *amazing* news," Hope said. "I've got to call Diane. No, wait. First I should call Mandy; then I'll call Diane. And David! The only reason he canceled the quilting program was because of the blades. Does he know about this?"

Hope put her hands against the table to push herself up from her chair. Nancy grabbed her around the wrist.

"Hang on, Hope. You didn't let me finish. David was in the courtyard when the fight broke out. He was the first staff member on the scene. When he put himself between Nita and Deedee, Nita started going for him instead. The other staff got there as quickly as they could but . . ." Nancy paused. "He was hurt pretty badly."

Hope sank back down into her chair. "How badly? Is he going to be all right?" she whispered.

"I don't know. I was with him when the ambulance arrived. He lost a lot of blood. And his face . . ." Two tears rolled down Nancy's cheeks. "Oh, Hope. His face."

"Oh my God." Hope shut her eyes. "Oh my God. Please."

Nancy closed her eyes as well and grabbed Hope's hand. "Oh, yes. Please. Please, God."

Hope sat clutching Nancy's hand, pleading for the life of a man who, until that moment, Hope had not realized was her friend.

After a time, her pleas were interrupted by the clunking sound of footsteps on the floor as McKenzie came up behind them.

"Mom? Are you okay?"

Hope wiped her eyes with the back of her hand. "I'm fine," she said, her voice stark. She rose to her feet. "Where's my purse?"

"Still in the foyer," McKenzie said. "You dropped it there when you smelled Dad's bread, remember?"

"That's right," Hope said, sniffling as she started to walk toward the door, where McKenzie was standing. "Okay. Good."

"Mom?" McKenzie said. "Are you going somewhere?"

"Yes," she said, pushing past her daughter. "To the hospital."

"Oh. Can I come with you? I think my water just broke."

"WELL, McKenzie, you're fully effaced and three centimeters dilated," the doctor said, pulling the sheet down over McKenzie's knees. "Looks like we're going to have a baby today."

McKenzie's eyes went wide. "Today? I'm not due for three weeks." She clutched at Hope's hand. "It's too soon."

"No, it's not," Hope said calmly. "You were early, too, remember? And you weighed seven pounds and were healthy as a horse."

"The baby is fine," the doctor assured her. "I'm not at all concerned about her being early or underweight. She's ready."

"See?" Hope said when the doctor left to go check on some other patients. "She wants to make an entrance, just like you did."

"She might be ready," McKenzie said. "I don't know if I am."

"Yes, you are. You are going to be a wonderful mother, Kenz. This is one lucky little baby." Hope squeezed McKenzie's hand.

"I love you, Mom."

"I love you too, baby."

Rick entered the room. "I called Zach. He's on his way."

"Good," Hope said. "What about Ted and Wanda?"

Rick shook his head. "They're on vacation in Florida, but Zach said they'll be flying home the day after tomorrow."

"Three birth coaches are more than enough," McKenzie said. "Hey, Mom, why don't you go and see how David is?"

Hope bit her lower lip, torn between the desire to stay by McKenzie's side and concern for her friend.

"It's okay," McKenzie said. "Nothing is going to happen for hours anyway. And even if it did, Dad's here."

"That's right." Rick put his arm over Hope's shoulders. "When it comes to birthing babies, I'm old hand. Remember?"

HOPE opened the door quietly. The form under the blanket stirred as she crept into the dimly lit room.

"What now?" asked a weakened but still familiar voice. "Can't you people just let me sleep?"

"It's me, David."

Hope stepped nearer, and David turned his head toward her. A pool of light from the wall sconce revealed a ravaged, almost unrecognizable face, swollen and purpled with bruises, his left eye covered with a thick white bandage, another on his throat.

Hope moved to the edge of the bed. To her surprise, he lifted his hand toward her. She took it in hers, blinking back tears.

"What are you doing here?"

"Seeing you. But my daughter is also in labor. It's going to be a few hours before the baby comes."

"Early, isn't it? The baby?"

"About three weeks. But the doctor says it should be all right."

"Good," he rasped. "I'm glad. A girl, right?"

"Yes," Hope said, her eyes tearing anew. "Maybe I can bring her by and introduce the two of you later."

"Oh, I don't know. One look at me could scar her for life. Scarred for life," he repeated, chuckling as if he'd just picked up on the irony of his statement.

"No, it wouldn't. You don't look that bad."

"Don't take up a life of crime, Hope. You're a terrible liar."

She smiled.

"But I'll be all right. I'm not planning to die, if that's what you're wondering." He released her hand. "Nita tried her best, but lucky for me, her aim was off."

"Lucky for all of us," Hope said.

David attempted a smile. "Wish you'd been in the operating

room. Stitches would have been a lot smaller. Stitches . . ." he murmured, his words trailing off and his eyes becoming heavy.

Hope patted his arm. "I'm going to let you get some sleep. I'll be back later, after the baby comes, to see how you're doing."

"Okay," he mumbled. "Sorry. I'm just so tired."

"It's all right."

"Hope? One thing. Did you take another job yet?"

"No, David. Not yet."

"Good," he mumbled. "Don't."

Chapter 17

HOPE POPPED OPEN THE TRUNK of her car, took out a large, cube-shaped bakery box, and carried it to the gate. Wayne, looking uncharacteristically cheerful, was there to greet her.

"Mornin', Hope. Big day, eh? You didn't bake any files into that cake, did you?"

"Not a one," Hope said. "You want to see?"

She lifted the lid of the box. Wayne peered over the edge.

"Well, that is just too pretty to eat, really. You baked that?"

"My husband did the baking, and I did the decorating. As hard as the girls have worked over the last few months, I wanted to do something special for graduation. I'm really going to miss them."

"It's not like most of them are going anywhere anytime soon," Wayne said. "Well, except Tonya. I hear she's getting out in a couple of months. And you've got a whole new class coming in next week, don't you?"

"*Two* classes. And a waitlist," Hope said, bending down carefully to retrieve her purse. "Is she here yet?"

Wayne shook his head. "They said to expect her around ten

fifteen. The wife pressed my uniform extra special." He grinned.

"Well, you look good," Hope said, and began walking toward the door. "I'll save you a piece of the cake."

THE governor actually didn't arrive until ten thirty, but she got there in time to help hand out the graduation certificates, present an award to Kate, and then give a short speech.

"The creativity and determination that you women have displayed is something you can be very proud of. But as all of you are aware, without the creativity and determination of some very remarkable people, this program could have ended before it began.

"Facing enormous obstacles, your teachers refused to give up. When Mrs. Carpenter tracked me down to try and convince me that this program should be reinstated, it was her obvious passion and commitment to all of you that convinced me to investigate further. Another woman, a lesser woman, would have given up. But as all of you know, your teacher is not a lesser woman—"

"That's right!" Deedee shouted. "Amen to that!"

"Yeah, Mrs. C!" whooped one of the other women, while another added, "You're the best!"

Grinning, Governor Russman went off script briefly to say, "She is indeed," nodding her agreement.

"And when I had the opportunity to read a previously unpublished report written by Superintendent Hernandez, the value he attributed to this program convinced me it should be saved, if possible. A lesser man, a man less committed to the job, might not have approved this program to begin with, might not have placed his responsibility for his charges above his personal safety."

"Yes, ma'am!" Deedee cried, shouting again.

"And a less determined man," the governor said, looking toward the front row, where David sat, "might not have endured the hard work of rehabilitation so he could be present to celebrate your accomplishments today. But, because David Hernandez is *not* a lesser man, I know that nothing would have prevented him from doing so. I trust that determination will carry him through the remainder of his recovery so he may continue his work here very soon."

More clapping and whooping greeted this pronouncement. Hope, who was seated next to David, clapped loudest of all.

"I want to remind you of something important. Though life isn't always fair, the determination that you have shown in completing this program can tip the scales in your favor. Though you will not always have control over the circumstances of life, you are always in control of how you respond to those circumstances.

"All of you have something meaningful to offer. The quilts that you have made, the hard work and creativity that you have put into them, have blessed the lives of others. I hope you will take that knowledge with you today and that you will continue to be a blessing to others, both within these walls and, someday, without.

"Congratulations, ladies. We are all very proud of you."

Applause broke out once again. Hope rose to her feet.

"Excuse me, everyone. But before we have our cake, we have one last presentation. Deedee?" she said, beckoning her forward.

"Actually," Deedee said when she came to the front, bringing along a paper grocery sack, "we have *two* presentations."

Deedee moved forward, standing directly in front of David.

"Mr. Hernandez, when I started this program, the thing I was most excited about was making a quilt for me. But if it wasn't for you, I wouldn't be here today. So I want to give you my quilt. Thank you for saving me. I hope you get done with all your surgeries and come back real soon."

Deedee pulled the quilt from the bag, a pattern of scrappy red and white bow-tie blocks on a creamy background, and laid it over his knees. Hope saw his Adam's apple bob as he swallowed.

"Well. This is amazing. I don't know what to say."

Deedee propped a hand on her hip. "Well, when somebody gives you a present, you're supposed to say thank you."

There was a murmur of laughter. David joined in it.

"Thank you, Deedee."

"You're welcome," she said. "Now, just one more present."

Kate stood up and came forward.

"Several weeks ago," she said, addressing the audience, "a group of students came to me and said they wanted to do something for

Mrs. Carpenter, to thank her for all she's done. All twelve of the original students contributed two blocks to a baby quilt for Mrs. Carpenter's new granddaughter, Leesha."

Kate reached beneath the podium, pulled out a folded quilt, then unfurled it so that everyone could see it, a cheerful pattern of brightly colored snowball blocks on a crisp white background, with white sashing and colorful cornerstone patches at the corners.

"Oh, it's beautiful!" Hope exclaimed. "But how did you manage to sew the blocks without me knowing what you were up to?"

"It was *not* easy," Deedee said in a dramatic tone. "We thought for sure you were going to find out. Miss Kate took the blocks home and finished the quilt for us. We hope the baby likes it."

"Well, if she doesn't, then Grammy might just have to steal it from her," Hope said, clutching the quilt to her chest.

Hope turned forward to face the audience.

"For a teacher," she said, "the measure of a student is how much she learns from them. That's why I mean it when I say that I will never, ever forget you. You're the best class I've ever had."

"This is good cake," David said.

"Glad you're enjoying it," Hope replied.

"No, I mean it. This is seriously good cake. Like biblically good." He bobbed his head as he chewed. He swallowed and pointed his plastic spork at the paper plate. "You made this?"

"Rick did. Now that he's settled into his new job, he's baking again. If he keeps this up, I may have to start running for real."

"So, Rick's liking his new job?"

"Loves it."

"And what about you?" he asked. "Liking your new-old job?"

"More than ever. The part-time schedule really is better for me. Rick and I get to spend our days off together, and we're available to help McKenzie with the baby if she needs a backup or a break. And the work itself?" Hope spread her hands to indicate that the answer should be obvious. "Apart from seeing my kids turn out so well, this is the most satisfying thing I've ever done in my life."

"In some ways, it's kind of the same thing, isn't it?" David said, casting his eyes around the room at the inmates who were still milling about, enjoying cake and each other's company. "We don't have as many success stories as I wish we did, but when they can leave here and make a new life for themselves on the outside? Well. There's something pretty great about that, isn't there?"

"Speaking of success stories," Hope said, "I saw Mandy a couple weeks ago. She had a summer job with a landscaping company, and they decided to keep her on over the winter. She's doing office work, mostly bookkeeping."

"Really? Good for her. Guess those math classes paid off."

"Best of all is that she and her parents called a truce. Well, it was her mother really. Apparently, Lola told her husband that if he kept up with his plan to rescind Mandy's parental rights, she'd leave him. He didn't believe her—until the moving truck pulled into the driveway."

"So the daughter is living with Mandy now?"

"They're working out a gradual transition of custody. Right now, Mandy just has Talia on weekends. That was Mandy's idea; she thought it would be better for Talia. And they're all going to family therapy. It sounds like they're working out some issues."

"Huh. I always thought Mandy had a lot of potential, if she could just get herself straightened out. Sounds like she has."

"On the road to it anyway," Hope said. "But how are you doing? You look great."

"Still the world's worst liar," he said. "I don't look great. But I definitely look *better*. After this next surgery, I'm hoping I'll look kind of . . . rugged. As far as when I'll come back—I might not."

"What?" Hope gasped. "Why? David, you were a *great* superintendent. Did you hear all that stuff the governor was saying about you? She told me the report you wrote about ways to better serve the female prison population is being shared with correctional superintendents all over the country. And you were just saying, not ten seconds ago, how satisfying this is—"

"I know, I know. And it *is* satisfying. Or was. But a lot has happened to me in the last few years, Hope. I got cancer; my wife left me. I never dealt with that. And now this?" He spread his hands. "It's starting to feel like God is trying to tell me something."

"Okay," Hope said grudgingly. "What are you going to do? Will you look for another job? Go work for another prison?"

"Actually," he said, "I was thinking of going back to school, getting my master's degree. In secondary school education."

Hope's eyes went wide. "You want to be a teacher?"

"Thinking about it," David said. "I'm going to start classes at Portland State in January, try a semester and see how I feel."

"Well— Wow." Hope blinked twice. "That's great, David. So you're moving to Portland. Need the name of a good Realtor?"

"No, thanks. Already got one."

The twinkle in his eye was so mischievous that, had he not had a patch over his eye, Hope would have sworn she saw him wink.

"In fact," David said, "I was just talking to Hazel the other day. We'd been texting a lot, before this happened."

"Yes, she told me."

"Right. Well, after I got hurt, I kind of cut it off."

"She told me that too," Hope said.

"Yeah. That was pretty stupid of me. But I had a lot going on and I thought, if she saw me like this . . . well. You know."

"I think Hazel really likes you, David. More than likes you."

David lifted his head to look at Hope.

"And I more than like her."

Hope nodded.

"So anyway," he said, then cleared his throat, "after I get this corneal transplant, I'm going to have to recover for a while and figured that I might as well do it someplace with a beach. I've rented a condo for a couple weeks down in La Jolla. I asked Hazel to come with me, and she said okay. Did she tell you that?"

Hope shook her head. "No. She didn't."

"Ah. Well. That okay with you?"

"David," she said, her lips drawn into a bow, "not only is that okay with me; it's the best news I've heard in a long, long time."

KNOWING Hazel and David needed to drive back to Portland that night, Hope had moved the meal a few hours ahead this year. So even though it was still early evening when she walked them to the door to say goodbye, the candles were beginning to sputter.

The remaining revelers—just the family at this point—were lolling on couches and chairs in the living room, apparently so bloated that they were unable to summon the energy to get up and say goodbye when Hazel said it was time they get going.

The nephews and nieces waved from their various places of collapse.

"See you, Hazel!"

"Bye, David!"

Hazel gave Hope another hug and kiss. "Thanks, Sis. Another amazing Christmas. I honestly don't know how you do it."

"I'm so glad you could come," Hope said, squeezing her sister one last time.

After giving Hazel and David a final wave, Hope went into the living room and started picking up abandoned and empty glasses. A moment later, Rick walked in.

"So. Who's ready for more pie?" he asked, and received a chorus of groans and protests in response.

"Maybe later," McKenzie said. "I couldn't eat another bite."

"Hey," Liam said. "Let's go find a pub, order a pitcher, and toast Reed and Pamela's engagement."

"I'm in," Rory said. "Kenz?"

McKenzie thought about it for a moment, then said, "I probably shouldn't. I have to get up early and drive to Bellingham. We're meeting Zach at his parents' and doing Christmas all over again. Besides, it's almost Leesha's bedtime."

"Oh, come on," Liam moaned. "One beer."

"You go on," Hope urged her. "Dad and I can babysit."

"Sure you don't mind?" McKenzie said, sounding hopeful.

"Mind?" Hope held her arms wide. "As if I could ever mind spending time with the cutest, smartest, most beautiful baby on the face of the earth. Come here to Grammy, you sweet little girl."

AFTER the kids left to toast the expansion of the family fold, Hope propped baby Leesha on her hip and carried her around the condo, showing her the sparkling lights of the Christmas tree and explaining the history and origins of the various ornaments.

"And that silver one? Your great-grandma painted that one.

"And see the cross-stitched ornament that says 'Baby's First Christmas'? Grammy did those, when your mommy and uncles were born. And see that funny reindeer with the red nose? Your mommy crocheted that one just for you! To celebrate Leesha's first Christmas! You come from a very talented family.

"And someday, when you're just a little bit older, Grammy is going to teach you all kinds of things so you'll be able to add *your* ornaments to the tree. What do you think about that?"

Leesha blinked and yawned. Hope laughed and carried her back into the living room where Rick was lying prone on the sofa.

"This one is getting tired," Hope said. "Can you take her for a minute? I'm going to get her pajamas."

"Absolutely. I was beginning to wonder if you were ever going to share," Rick said, holding out his arms. "Come here, baby girl."

Leaving the baby with Rick, Hope went in search of the diaper bag. When she returned a few minutes later, she found Rick still on the sofa with the baby on his chest, both sound asleep.

She stood there watching the rise and fall of Rick's breathing, the look on her granddaughter's face as she went along for the ride, an expression of contentment and utter peace that matched Rick's own.

Hope considered waking them but only briefly. She had lived long enough to know that such moments, though few and far between, must be treasured.

Instead, Hope lowered herself into a chair to keep watch, cherishing her life, and family, and home. And the knowledge it was exactly as it was meant to be.

All of it.

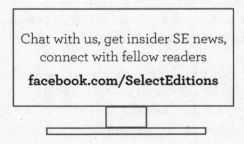

AfterWords

According to Marie Bostwick, *Hope on the Inside* was a "labor of love" many years in the making. It began seven years ago, when she attended an exhibit of quilts made by inmates. She recalls that "the quilts they produced were so honest, raw, and emotionally evocative that they truly rose to the level of art."

Bostwick immediately knew she wanted write a book that took place in a correctional setting. But when she attempted to write it, she says, "the story simply wouldn't come." Believing the lives of the characters were too far removed from her own experiences, she shelved the idea.

Then she moved to Oregon and stumbled across an article about the Coffee Creek Quilters, a quilting program operating inside the Coffee Creek Correctional Facility in Wilsonville, Oregon. Bostwick says her conversations with the program's volunteers "helped me to see that a tale about a woman at a crossroads, encountering this world for the first time, *was* a story I could tell." Newly energized by her encounters with the group, she set out to finish her stalled novel.

Bostwick currently resides in Oregon with her husband of thirty-five years. The prolific author, whose books include the popular Cobbled Court Quilt series, speaks at bookstores, quilt shows, and more. When not writing, she enjoys quilting, cooking, and spending time with family.

A JAMES BOND NOVEL

WITH ORIGINAL MATERIAL BY IAN FLEMING

FOREVER
AND A DAY

ANTHONY HOROWITZ

NEW YORK TIMES **BESTSELLING AUTHOR OF** *MAGPIE MURDERS*

CHAPTER 1

Killing by Numbers

"So 007 is dead."

"Yes, sir. I'm afraid so."

M took a last, fleeting look at the photographs that lay scattered across his desk and that had been sent to him by General André Anatonin, his counterpart at the SDECE, or the Service de Documentation Extérieure et de Contre-Espionnage, in Paris. They had been taken from different angles but showed the same bleak image. A dead man, lying facedown in dark, glistening water, his hands stretched out limply above his head, as if in one last futile attempt at surrender. Eventually, the police had pulled him out and laid him on the quayside so that closer pictures could be taken of his face, his hands, the three holes in the breast of his jacket where the bullets had penetrated. He had dressed expensively. M remembered him sitting in this very office only a month ago, wearing the suit that had been made for him by the tailor he liked just off Savile Row. The suit had kept its shape, M reflected. It was the man who was lying there, dripping wet and lifeless, who had lost his.

"Are we sure it's him, Chief of Staff?" The evidence seemed inescapable, but M asked the question anyway.

"I'm afraid so, sir. He was carrying no identity papers—no

surprises there. And he didn't have his gun. But the French have Belinographed his fingerprints, and there's no doubt. It's 007."

"And this was taken in Marseilles?"

"Yes, sir. The basin of La Joliette."

Bill Tanner was closer to M than anyone in the building, although the distance between them was incalculable. They had never eaten together, never inquired about each other's private lives. M despised small talk anyway, but it would not have occurred to either of them to discuss anything but current operations and the general work at hand. Even so, Tanner—previously a colonel in the Sappers until he had been sucked into the less formalized world of the Secret Intelligence Service—knew exactly what would be going on in the head of the older man. The death of an active agent was to be regretted. More important was to find out what had happened and to take immediate, quite probably permanent, countermeasures. It wasn't just a question of revenge. The service had to demonstrate that killing one of its operatives was nothing less than an act of war.

He actually had been with M in this very room when the idea of a Double-O Section had first been mooted, the cipher being as blank and anonymous as possible: It was literally nothing and nothing again. And yet it meant everything to the elite group of men who would at once be promoted to the front line of the country's war against its many enemies. Tanner still remembered the reaction of Sir Charles Massinger, permanent secretary to the Minister of Defense, when the proposal had first been put to him. His lip had curled in evident distaste.

"Are you serious? What you're suggesting here is tantamount to a license to kill."

It was the same old-fashioned thinking that had hampered the efforts of the Special Operations Executive at the start of the war. At first the RAF had refused even to provide planes to transport their agents, not wanting to dirty their hands with Churchill's "ministry of ungentlemanly warfare." And now, just five years after VE Day, how many of those same agents were to be found in the corridors of the tall gray building next to Regent's Park? Still ungentlemanly. Still, whatever the public might think, at war.

Tanner had listened as M quietly explained the point that the civil servant had missed. Hostilities had not come to an end in 1945. There were a great many people dedicating themselves to the complete destruction of Great Britain. You had to fight fire with fire, which meant that there was an urgent need for men and women who would be prepared to kill, if only in self-defense. And like it or not, there would be times when the service would have to strike first. M could not have his hands tied. The license was as much for him as it was for the people he commanded.

The Double-O Section had been kept deliberately small. In fact, after this recent loss it was down to just two men—008 and 0011. M had always rejected the idea of there being a sequence—001, 002, 003, and so on. Patterns are the enemy of counterintelligence.

"What exactly happened?" M reached for his pipe, which rested next to an ashtray made out of a twelve-inch shell base.

"We still don't have all the details, sir," Tanner replied. "We sent 007 to the south of France a little over three weeks ago. He was investigating the activity of the Corsican underworld in the area. Or rather, the lack of activity. Someone had noticed a sharp drop in the supply of drugs coming out of Marseilles, and the natural assumption was that they must be up to something else.

"These Corsicans are really nothing more than modern-day gangsters. But this silence is worrying. If they've managed to organize themselves, that could make them a danger not just to the immediate area but to the whole of Europe and—inevitably—us."

"Yes, yes." M had this information in the cavernous filing cabinet that was his mind and didn't need it paraded in front of him.

"007 went in undercover. We gave him a new name, new passport, and an address in Nice. He was an academic working out of University College, writing a history of organized labor. That allowed him to ask all the right questions without raising too many eyebrows. At least, that was the idea."

"Did he come up with anything? Before he was killed?"

"Yes, sir." The chief of staff cleared his throat. "It seems that there was a woman involved."

"There always is," M growled into the bowl of his pipe.

"007 mentioned her in what would turn out to be his last radio transmission. He referred to her as Madame 16."

"Sixteen? The number?"

"Yes, sir. It's not her real name, of course. You'll know her as Joanne Brochet—French father, English mother. She spent three years at Bletchley Park before she was selected by Special Operations, who trained her up and parachuted her into France under the code name Sixtine." Tanner spelled it out. "She was very highly regarded and provided us with useful intelligence in the buildup to Operation Overlord. She was captured and tortured by the Germans. We assumed that she had been killed. But she turned up again a few years ago, working in Europe. She called herself Sixtine or Madame 16, and she'd gone into business for herself."

"She was the woman who sold us the Kosovo file."

Tanner nodded. Both men knew what he was talking about.

The Kosovo file was a feasibility study that had been put together by a low-grade civil servant with too much time on his hands. It set out the strategy to incite an armed uprising in Albania, which had become a communist state after the war. There was never any chance that the plan would be given a green light, but the file had gone into minute detail, identifying local operatives. The Kosovo file should have been shredded the moment its existence was known. Instead, it had been photostatted and circulated, and then, unbelievably, a young man working as third secretary at the Prague embassy had left a briefcase with a copy under his seat one evening when he got off a tram.

"We never found out how Sixtine got her hands on it," Tanner went on. "But it was hardly surprising. By now she'd reinvented herself as an agent for hire. She contacted us and agreed to sell the papers back for £2,000."

"It was blackmail, pure and simple!" M made no attempt to hide his annoyance. "We should never have agreed."

"That may well be true, sir." Tanner drew a hand over his chin. It was always risky, answering M back. "But for what it's worth, our man in the Treasury thought she struck a remarkably fair deal. The Russians would have paid five times as much. It may be that she felt some loyalty toward us, left over from the war."

"And 007 met her in Marseilles," M said.

"We don't know that, sir. But he was certainly interested in her. The very fact that she was in the south of France indicated that she was up to something. We know for certain that she'd been talking to the syndicates. In the last transmission he made, a week before his death, 007 said he had concrete evidence."

"What sort of evidence?"

"Unfortunately, he didn't say. If 007 had one fault, it was that he liked to keep his cards close to his chest. In that same transmission, he mentioned that he had arranged to meet someone who could tell him exactly what she was up to—but once again he didn't tell us who it was." Tanner sighed. "The meeting took place at the basin of La Joliette, and that was where he was killed."

"He must have left something. Have we been to his house?"

"He had an apartment in the Rue Foncet, and the French police searched it from top to bottom. They found nothing."

"Perhaps the opposition got there first."

"It's possible, sir."

M tamped down his pipe with a thumb. "You know what surprises me in all this, Chief of Staff? How could 007 allow himself to be shot at close range in the middle of a crowded city? And why wasn't he carrying his weapon?"

"I was puzzled by that," Tanner agreed. "I can only assume he must have been meeting someone he knew, a friend."

"Could he have actually met with Madame 16 herself? Or could she have found out about the meeting and intercepted it?"

"Both those thoughts had occurred to me, sir. The CIA have people out there, and we've been trying to talk to them. The whole area is crawling with security services. But so far . . . nothing."

The heavy, sweet smell of Capstan Navy Flake hung in the air. M used the pipe to punctuate his thoughts. The lighting and the relighting gave him time to consider decisions that had to be made.

"We need someone to look into what happened," he went on. "I'm not having one of my best agents put down like a dog. I want to know who did this and why, and I want that person removed from the field. And if it turns out that this woman, Sixtine, was responsible, that goes for her, too."

Tanner understood exactly what M was saying. He wanted an eye for an eye. Somebody had to be killed.

"Who do you want me to send? 008 is still out of action."

"You've spoken to Sir James?"

"Yes, sir." Sir James Molony was the senior neurologist at St. Mary's Hospital. "It's going to be another few weeks."

"And 0011?"

"In Miami."

M laid down the pipe. "Well, then we're just going to bring forward this other chap you've been preparing. How is he doing?"

"Well, sir, he managed his first kill without any difficulty. It was that Kishida business. The Japanese cipher man."

"Yes, yes. I read the report. He's certainly a good shot, and he kept his nerve. At the same time, though, firing a bullet into the thirty-sixth floor of a New York skyscraper doesn't necessarily prove anything. I'd like to see how he works at closer quarters."

"We may very well find out," Tanner replied. "He's in Stockholm now. If all goes well, he'll be reporting back in the next twenty-four hours. I already have his fitness report, his medical and psychological evaluations. He's come through with flying colors, and for what it's worth, I like him personally."

"If he gets your recommendation, that's good enough for me, Chief of Staff." M frowned. "You didn't tell me his name."

"It's Bond, sir," the chief of staff replied. "James Bond."

Sitting in a corner of Restaurant Cattelin in the medieval district of Stockholm, stabbing at a bad filet mignon, James Bond thought about the man he had come to kill.

Rolf Larsen had had what is called a good war. Starting as the editor of a clandestine counter-propaganda newspaper, he had escaped from Norway in 1942, reaching England via Sweden. He had joined the famous Kompani Linge, where he had received paramilitary and parachute training, returning to his own country in time to play a key role in Operation Mardonius, an attack on

Oslo harbor with limpet mines delivered by canoe. He had finished
the war with a Distinguished Service Order from Great Britain
and a War Cross with Sword from the Norwegian government.

Almost immediately he had moved to Stockholm and made
millions exporting timber goods from Sweden's pine forests. He
married a Swedish heiress, and they had two young children together. Bond had seen the well-dressed, respectable family the day
before as their chauffeur dropped them off at Östermalms Saluhall,
the food market in central Stockholm. Rolf was in his forties now,
his expanding belly the signpost of a life well lived.

Except that it was all a lie.

It turned out that Rolf Larsen had been a double agent working
for the Nazis. He had been responsible for the deaths of dozens of
Norwegian agents. But that wasn't what had signed his death warrant. In 1944 a plan was put forward by the British for an assault
on northern Norway, with troops leaving the Shetland Islands on
fishing boats, penetrating the fjords under cover of darkness and fog.
Two men had been sent ahead to pinpoint a suitable landing position,
and Larsen had betrayed them both. They had been captured, tortured, and killed. Even before the war ended, the wheels had started
turning, and slowly the truth had emerged, the investigation closing
in on the young hero who was now the wealthy family man. It would
be six years before the final proof was discovered, and by this time a
new decade had begun. Dragging a twice-decorated man like Larsen
through the court system would benefit no one. Someone high up
had made the decision. This one could be dealt with unofficially.

As he pushed away his plate and called for a coffee, Bond considered what that meant. Nobody in Stockholm knew that he was
here: not the police; not the government; not Säpo, the Swedish
security service. This had to look like a straightforward murder.
Larsen was alone. Only that afternoon the man had put his wife
and children on the train to Uppsala, where they were spending
the weekend. Right now he was at the Stockholm Opera House
watching a performance of *Tosca*. There were to be no guns. Bullets came with a history that stab wounds did not. Larsen's family
home was spread over the top two floors of a building just around

the corner from the restaurant. A room upstairs was occupied by a manservant called Otto who had come out of Säpo. The entire house was alarmed. The kill had to be fast and, above all, silent.

And what then? Two little girls, ages five and three, would find themselves without a father. A plump, happy wife would become a widow. The newspapers would celebrate the life of a war hero. And, all being well, Bond would be awarded his Double-O number. He would have earned his license to kill.

It was something he had wanted from the moment he had entered the secret service. Why? Was it a hangover from the war, where killing the enemy had been taken for granted and where any talk of morality would have been seen as a sign of weakness? Or was it simply the desire to be the best at everything he did? That was it, really. There were only three Double-O agents, and they were respected like no others. He was going to be the fourth.

The steak was still sitting on his plate. He gestured at the waiter to take it away, then drew a cigarette, a Du Maurier, out of its signature red packet. He had no appetite, knowing what lay ahead. He glanced at his watch. Five past ten. The fat woman would be poisoning herself or whatever else she did in the last act of Puccini's masterpiece, and soon the audience would be on its way home.

And then . . .

Bond took his time with the cigarette. Finally, he called for the bill, paid, and left.

He found himself in a narrow street, with the Stockholm Cathedral rising up at one end. A light blinked out on the sixth floor of the Larsen mansion. Bond knew his moment had come. He stepped out of the shadows, glanced up and down the street, then withdrew a thin strip of plastic from his jacket pocket. The front door, with its Yale-style lock, offered no resistance. He climbed six floors to a hallway and another door. As Bond eased it open, the alarm mounted on the wall blinked but did not sound. The system had been imported from London, and the day before, two men had arrived to give it an overhaul. They had carried the necessary identification papers. Nobody had given them a second thought, and now the alarm slept, unaware of the figure slipping past.

Bond found himself in an expensive, old-fashioned apartment, its furnishings more German than Scandinavian, with heavy dark furniture, rugs, chandeliers. He made no sound as he climbed the stairs. He had studied plans of the building and knew exactly where he was going. He turned a corner and padded down a corridor with an antique mirror at the end. The third door opened into the master bedroom. Bond's hand clamped down onto the elaborate brass handle. Very slowly, deliberately, he squeezed it open.

Rolf Larsen slept in a king-size bed with a carved headboard. He had thrown off the blanket and was covered by a white muslin sheet. Bond could make out his silver hair, the rise and fall of his chest. He was aware of his own heart beating faster. When he had killed Kishida, he had felt less involved. His only concern had been that he shouldn't miss. But this was different. He could smell Larsen and easily make out the sound of his breathing.

Bond reached into the left sleeve of his jacket and pulled out a blade—seven inches long, with a Dunlop rubber handle. Larsen stirred in his sleep. The time had come. Using the edge of his knife hand, Bond flicked on the bedside light. At the same time, he leaned forward, his other hand clamping down on Larsen's mouth before he could call out for help.

Larsen's eyes opened, filling with surprise, understanding, and terror. He saw a man aged about thirty, clean shaven with black hair and very straight features; the nose, the mouth, and the eyes almost mathematical in their precision. A three-inch scar on the man's right cheek destroyed the symmetry. The man was wearing a dark suit, a white shirt, and a knitted tie. His hand was pressed against his mouth with unusual force, making it almost impossible for him to breathe.

"Larsen?" The man had only spoken a single word, but somehow Larsen knew straightaway that he was British.

Larsen nodded. The man's hand moved with him.

"I'm here for Bourne and Calder."

Bourne and Calder. The two men sent to the northern coast of Norway. The two men Larsen had betrayed. It hadn't been part of Bond's brief to extract any information from the traitor before he killed him, but he had to know for his own peace of mind.

"Do you understand?" he asked.

Larsen hesitated, then nodded very slowly. Bond had seen what he needed in the man's eyes: the acknowledgment of guilt. So be it. Without a second thought he drove the knife forward.

The moment of death, when it finally arrived, was anticlimactic. Bond removed the knife, wiped it clean, and returned it to its sheath. He looked around him, then took Larsen's gold cuff links, his Rolex Speedking, and a wallet containing 300 Swedish krona. It was hardly a reasonable motive for such a violent crime, but it would have to do. He then turned off the lamp and left. He climbed back down six flights of stairs and let himself out into the street. Crossing the Strömbron Bridge at the northern corner of the island, he dropped the objects he had taken into the water below.

The wallet went first, then the cuff links, and finally the silver watch. It hit the surface, and Bond saw the ripples, a series of circles—zeroes, perhaps—closing in on themselves and then vanishing as the evidence of what had taken place sank out of sight.

Chapter 2

First Day

Breakfast, for James Bond, was the one meal of the day that he considered to be indispensable. Lunch was a pleasure, dinner often a celebration, but breakfast had the solemnity of a ritual, a time when he could sit back and contemplate the day ahead. On the day after his return from Stockholm, he came down to the table in his Chelsea home and watched as his elderly Scottish housekeeper, May, came bustling in with a well-laden tray. "Good morning," she muttered. "Did ye have a good trip?"

"Yes. It went very well, thank you, May."

She continued setting the plates down. "I don' rightly ken what they're thinking, this business with the Koreans," she grumbled, handing over *The Times*. The headlines were full of the American attack on Chinju. "Ye'd have thought the werld would have had enough o' war." She sighed. "It's all the fault of these communists. Well, what will be will be, I suppose. . . ."

She left the room, and in the silence that followed, Bond enjoyed scrambled eggs, buttered toast, and several cups of coffee. It was only as he left that he acknowledged that he had been deliberately putting all thoughts of Stockholm and Larsen out of his mind.

Bond drove to work in a midnight-blue Jaguar XK 120.

He was aware that his current salary would never have afforded these luxuries: the car, the Regency house close to the King's Road, the housekeeper. His parents had died when he was just eleven years old, leaving behind a trust fund he had inherited when he was eighteen. He sometimes wondered if his life would have turned out differently if they had survived the climbing accident that had taken them. Not having the closeness of immediate family—had this in some way molded the man he had eventually become?

With these thoughts in mind, Bond came to a halt on the edge of Regent's Park and continued the last ten minutes to the office on foot. The doorman nodded at him as if he'd barely noticed him, though in fact he had a photographic memory and knew the names and the office locations of everyone who worked in the building.

Bond turned a corner and walked into the lift.

The liftman glanced at him.

"Which floor, sir?"

"The fifth, please."

There. He had said it, somehow making it a reality.

The liftman pressed the button, making no comment.

Usually, Bond went to the third floor reserved for Communications and Electronics Development, a name that disguised a multitude of clandestine activities. Bond had spent the past few weeks preparing the logistics for a black frontier crossing into East Germany, until Stockholm had come up. That assignment would now have to be handed to someone else.

He stood silently as the doors closed. Bond felt a certain nervousness in the pit of his stomach. Everything about the building looked different. But of course, it was he who had changed. Barely twenty-four hours had passed since he had taken a second life. In doing so, he had earned his license to kill, joining an elite force, just four of them in the entire organization.

Three of them. Bond had heard about the death in the south of France. He was a replacement, not an addition.

The lift doors opened, and he stepped out into a corridor. He found the number of the office he was looking for, knocked, and to the invitation of "Come!" went in.

The single occupant worked in a blank white box with a picture of the king on one wall and the prime minister on the other. "Commander Bond?" The man behind the desk looked up.

"That's right."

"Please, come in. Take a seat." Bond sat down, facing him.

The man smiled thinly. "Congratulations on your promotion, and welcome to your first day in the Double-O Section. We just have a few formalities to go through. It won't take long."

Paymaster Captain Troop, RN Retired, was the head of administration. He proceeded to describe Bond's new responsibilities in the driest of tones. He did not pause for questions. At the end of his speech, he drew out several sheets of paper from a drawer and tapped them with an authoritative finger. "Could you sign here, please, Commander Bond? And here?"

Bond did as he was told. The first document was a confidentiality agreement. The second provided him with statutory life insurance. The third was shorter and more brutal, giving his employers complete power of attorney over his affairs in the event of his being killed in action. Troop waited until he had finished, then swung the papers around with a satisfied nod.

"Thank you, Commander Bond. I'll show you up to your new office. Your secretary will take over from there."

He did not speak as he and Bond took the lift up to the eighth floor and then walked past a series of doors (no numbers here, Bond noticed), stopping at the last one on the right.

"This is where I'll leave you," Troop said. "Good luck." He turned and walked back the way he had come.

Bond knocked on the door. It was opened by a woman who was dark and slender, with the sort of beauty that was all the more alluring because it was so obviously out of bounds. Her manner was restrained, her eyes challenging him. But he could see within them the spark of humor that told him they were going to get on.

"Mr. Bond?" she asked.

"James."

She considered the name and smilingly accepted it. "I'm Loelia Ponsonby. Let me show you to your desk."

She turned her back on him, and he followed her into a small anteroom, enjoying the sway of her hips. Bond looked for a wedding ring, somehow knowing he would not find it. She walked over to a second door on the other side. This led into a larger room, with three desks and a window looking out onto Regent's Park.

"Loelia," Bond muttered. "I can't possibly call you that. Do you mind being Lil?"

She looked at him coolly. "As a matter of fact, I do."

"Well, I'm not going to call you Miss Ponsonby," he said. "It makes you sound like a schoolteacher." He went over to the window and glanced out. "So how does this work?" he asked. "I take it I don't have the office to myself."

"No. There are three of you." She gestured at one of the empty desks. "That's Bill's." She faltered. "I mean, 008. He only got back to the country last week, and he's resting." The final word had been carefully chosen, and Bond recognized the euphemism. "0011 sits here," she went on briskly. "But he's away."

She went over to the third desk. Bond noticed that a pile of brown folders had been neatly laid out for his attention. He swung the first of them around and opened it. He found himself looking at a black-and-white photograph of a dead man lying spread out on a quay. He knew at once that the image showed his predecessor. He closed it again without making any comment.

Loelia Ponsonby was standing by the door. "We were all devastated by the news," she said. "There have been reports coming in all week. I've put them on your desk with the most important ones on the top. You'd better start with them. M is going to want to see you later this morning and you'll need to be fully briefed."

Bond sat down in the leather-backed swivel chair. Suddenly he wanted to get this initiation over with. "All right," he said. "I'm going to need some coffee. Black, no sugar. I never drink tea, by the way, so please don't offer it." He briefly scanned the surface of the desk. "And I'd like an ashtray."

"Right." She turned to leave.

"I'll find out who killed him," Bond added, speaking more softly. She stopped and looked back. "I'm sorry it had to happen this way. . . . My arrival, I mean. I know it won't be easy, taking his place, but I'll do my best."

"Thank you." Bond saw the invitation in her eyes. She wanted to be friends. He opened the first of the files as she left.

Bond went through the details of the death in the La Joliette basin, part of the main seaport of Marseilles. He examined the photographs: one of the body floating on the water and one, taken from a wider angle, showing police cars and an ambulance parked in front of a dilapidated wall. He could make out part of a slogan painted on the brickwork—ARITÉ AUX MINEURS. There had been an autopsy. Three shots fired at close range into the stomach and chest. Death instantaneous. Body hurled into the water by the velocity of the 9-mm bullets. He moved on to the next file.

This one contained a longer, typewritten memorandum. It was titled: "A New Direction in Marseilles-based Criminality?" He began to read.

Background

For all the beauty of its beaches and boulevards, the strip of France known as the Riviera remains a cesspit of corruption and crime, with the spoils divided between the Corsican syndicates and the Sicilian Mafia. Torture and murder are commonplace, with running battles often taking place in the street. The local populace not only accept this "*grand banditisme*"—as it is known—but seem to admire it. Although there is evidence that the French authorities have managed to rein in some of the excesses of this criminal fraternity, it is unfortunately true that they continue to receive protection from police and government officials who frequent their bars and enjoy their patronage.

Marseilles has been described as the Chicago of France, and much of the traffic in drugs, prostitution, gambling, money laundering, racketeering, and extortion begins here. It has, however, spread rapidly along the coast. Note that Riviera criminality is as opportunistic as it is amoral—the Spanish Civil War, for example, saw a spike in arms trafficking, and it was at this time that Jean-Paul Scipio (see attached) came to prominence.

Narcotics were, until recently, the number one source of income to the criminal underworld, as well as being the greatest threat to the security of the Western world.

Marseilles is the point of entry, with supplies coming from Turkey and Indochina to be turned into the highest-quality No. 4 heroin by skilled Corsican chemists. Unlike the Mafia, Corsican syndicates tend to be small, less hierarchical, and family based. Laboratories are situated both in Marseilles itself and in surrounding villages and may be extremely rudimentary, contained in basements, unused kitchens, and garden sheds. They are highly mobile and can be dismantled and moved to a new location in a matter of hours.

At least three men, all wearing gas masks, are required for the processing, and conditions are extremely hazardous. If the morphine mix is heated beyond 230 degrees Fahrenheit, it is likely to explode. Even so, until the end of last year, gangs were moving an average of 600 pounds (272 kilos) of heroin each month to the United States, meeting the needs of an estimated 60,000 active users.

However, in the past eighteen months officers from the CRS (the Compagnies Républicaines de Sécurité, which has been leading the fight against the Mafia and the syndicates) have alerted security forces to a strange anomaly. There has been a massive drop in the production of heroin at both local and international levels. The immediate effect has been an outbreak of sporadic violence and murder as dealers/users around Marseilles find their supplies exhausted. There have also been many more hospitalizations and deaths as a result of the dilution of what product remains with flour, chalk, talcum powder, and powdered milk. This has been replicated in New York and London.

There is no good reason why the syndicates should have curtailed their most successful business. There has been no significant progress made by any government body that would have led them to retrench. This leads to the conclusion that the shutdown must be voluntary, and there is speculation that the syndicates may have turned their attention to some other, more lucrative activity.

There is also a real concern that any interruption to the drug flow may destabilize the political situation in both France and the so-called Golden Triangle of Burma, Thailand, and Laos. This could have serious implications for intelligence services in both the U.S. and Great Britain.

Footnote

(*Comment by C.C.*) It is impossible to examine drug trafficking in the south of France without taking into account the involvement of the CIA—a major error of judgment in the view of this author.

It has long been American policy to support warlords in Burma and areas close to the Chinese border, as these tribal armies have been seen as useful allies in the fight against worldwide communism. However, there can be no doubt that these warlords have taken advantage of U.S. largesse to branch into the cultivation and distribution of heroin.

It is to be regretted that the CIA also has decided to lend tacit support to the crime syndicates in the south of France with exactly the same justification. Here the enemy is seen to be the French Communist Party, and the prize: control of the French docks. There can be little doubt that the last two dock strikes in Marseilles were broken by the CIA working hand in hand with the Corsican underworld.

This may have helped the Americans to ensure the smooth running of imports/exports in relation to the Marshall Plan, but it also has exacerbated the sense of lawlessness in the area. Worse still, it has allowed the flow of drugs to continue with impunity. In 1945 there was a good chance that heroin addiction in the United States could have been eliminated. This is an opportunity that has been missed simply for short-term gain.

Loelia Ponsonby came into the office carrying a cup of coffee and an ashtray. She set them down on the desk and left without a word. Bond lit another cigarette, then turned to the next page.

Jean-Paul Scipio

Currently, Jean-Paul Scipio is one of the most powerful leaders in the Corsican underworld and certainly the most feared. He is known as "Le Boudin," French slang, which can be translated as "the fat man," a common nickname although appropriate in his case, as his girth is such that he is unable to fit into a standard car and is said to require a specially strengthened chair when he dines in restaurants.

His size is attributable to a vendetta that took place in 1915, ten years after his birth. It is believed that Scipio's father, an olive farmer, fell out with his neighbor over a land dispute and the entire family was subsequently attacked and a great many of them killed. The ten-year-old Jean-Paul had his throat cut (it was the practice to kill the sons to prevent them taking revenge for their dead fathers), and it is a miracle that he survived. However, his lymphatic vessels were ruptured and this was responsible for his subsequent weight gain.

Friends of the family smuggled him out of Corsica, and he grew up in Paris, where he became an early member of the Bande des Trois Canards, a vicious gang of racketeers. He moved to Marseilles at the end of the war and became a major player in the narcotics business. He now has control of eighty percent of the drugs entering the port. Although he enjoys a flamboyant lifestyle, with a prodigious appetite for food and alcohol, he is unmarried and has no interest in women, leading to speculation that he may be homosexual.

Remarkably, Scipio has never learned English or French and conducts all his business in the Corsican dialect of Pumuntincu. He is accompanied at all times by a translator.

The printed document was attached to a photograph of a man so enormous that he barely fit into the frame. Jean-Paul Scipio had enough flesh and muscle for two or perhaps even three human beings. He was wearing a dark three-piece suit, with a tie barely visible beneath the fourth of his chins. His hair was black, cut in the style of Napoleon, although it had the ill-fitting awkwardness of a wig. He was holding a crystal champagne flute.

Bond slid it to one side and opened the third file, this one marked JOANNE BROCHET, AKA SIXTINE, AKA MADAME 16. He turned his attention to the photograph that was also attached. This was less useful. She was wearing dark glasses, a beret, and a dark raincoat. There had been plenty of photos taken of her before the war, but it was impossible to get any idea of what she looked like now.

Bond began to read and had just reached the last paragraph when the telephone on his desk rang. He picked it up.

"James?" The voice at the other end belonged to Bill Tanner, M's chief of staff and a man Bond knew well. "I hope you've settled in."

"I think I'm finding my feet," Bond replied.

"Glad to hear it." There was a short pause, followed by words that Bond would hear many times again in the years to come. "I wonder if you'd mind coming up. M would like to have a word."

BILL Tanner was waiting for Bond outside the lift on the ninth floor. Theirs was a friendship that had begun in the last years of the war with a chance meeting in the Ardennes, but it had been firmly cemented after Bond was recruited to the secret service.

"Congratulations." That was Tanner's first word as Bond stepped out onto the thick carpeting that might have been purposefully designed to swallow any sound in this part of the building.

"Thank you, Bill. I'm sure you put in a good word for me."

"Not at all. You were next in line for promotion, and I'm only sorry it had to happen the way it did. How was Stockholm?"

"Bloody."

"Yes. I read your report. M has it, too." Was there a hint of warning in Tanner's voice? "Anyway, something's come up. You're not going to find it quite as straightforward as Stockholm. But it'll give you a chance to spread your wings, so to speak. I'll take you in, and maybe you and I can have lunch later on."

They had been walking down the corridor as they spoke, and now Tanner stopped in front of a green door, opened it, and went through. Bond hesitated, savoring the moment. He was entering the inner sanctum. He was actually going to sit opposite M, one on one, for the first time.

And what did Bond know of the man who ruled every aspect of the Secret Intelligence Service? Certainly not his name, although his initials were said to be MM. He came from a naval background. He was about sixty years old and tended to wear an old-fashioned three-piece suit. He was terse but never rude. And there wasn't a single person in the building who would not offer him their unswerving loyalty, even to the cost of their own life.

Bond stepped into a small outer office. A woman sat at a typewriter, but she had paused with her fingers over the keys. Bond knew Miss Moneypenny by sight and reputation. She was the undisputed leader of the coterie of young women who worked at the most senior level within the service. He was glad she was M's secretary and not his. She was, quite simply, too desirable, and he wouldn't have wanted that to get in the way of work.

"I'm James Bond," he said.

"Yes. I know who you are." Her eyes were examining him with interest, and he wondered how much she knew. "I'm sure we'll get to know each other better," she went on. "But not now, I'm afraid. M is waiting."

"Another time, then."

"You never know."

"I'll look forward to it." He made his way toward the double doors on the other side.

Tanner had already gone into M's office, and Bond followed.

M was sitting behind his desk with a report in front of him.

He examined the new arrival with gray eyes that missed nothing. "Come in, Bond," M said. "Take a seat."

Tanner was standing to one side. Bond sat down opposite the man who would now control his destiny.

"So how did Stockholm go?" M asked.

"I'd say it went very smoothly, sir," Bond replied.

"Well, the Statspolisen are treating it like a burglary, which is exactly what we wanted."

He tapped the report.

"I understand you spoke to this man, Larsen."

Bond nodded. He had been thoroughly debriefed when he got back, and he had described exactly what had happened. "Yes, sir."

"He was awake when you entered the room?"

"No, sir. I woke him up."

"I'm surprised you thought there was any need. What exactly did you say to him?"

"I mentioned the names Bourne and Calder."

"And why was that?"

"I suppose I wanted an acknowledgment of guilt, sir. I wanted to be absolutely sure that I was killing the right man."

It was what M had been expecting. When he spoke again, his voice was brusque. "Do you think I'd have sent you to kill the wrong one? If you're going to work in the Double-O Section, it might help to have a little more trust in this organization. Larsen was guilty. He was responsible for the deaths of at least a dozen people, and it was my decision to send an executioner. Not a lawyer."

Bond accepted the rebuke silently. M might have a point, but it hadn't been him sitting in the bedroom with the knife. He glanced at Tanner, who was looking away uncomfortably.

"Well, you did a good job," M went on, more pleasant now. "And you've certainly earned your promotion." He closed the folder. "Now I have an assignment for you. It connects with the man you've replaced. I want to know what happened to 007 and what exactly is going on in the south of France, particularly with regard to the Corsican syndicates and the supply of heroin. You might say it's good news that they seem to have stopped producing this muck, but 007 was onto something—and it got him killed.

"And then there's this woman—Joanne Brochet or whatever she calls herself—to investigate, too. It may well be that she was directly or indirectly responsible for his death. She must be in France for a reason, and we know she has been in contact with the syndicates. Our man was investigating her when he was killed. He went to a meeting to get information and ended up getting three bullets instead. And finally there's the manner of his death. It happened in a public place in daylight, and he wasn't carrying his weapon."

"Yes, I thought about that," Bond agreed. "It suggests that he was meeting someone he knew well. The bullets were fired at close range." He paused. "It could have been a liaison."

"Exactly."

"We have no idea what she's doing in the south of France?"

"No," Tanner said. "She's taken up with an American businessman, a multimillionaire called Irwin Wolfe. You may have heard of him or his corporation—Wolfe America."

"They make film," Bond said.

"That's right. Film—not films. He started out producing orthochromatic negative stock for the film industry, and he was one of the first manufacturers to move into color. He's opened a European plant on the Italian border. He's also branched out into luxury travel. He's got a brand-new cruise ship he's about to launch on its maiden voyage to America."

"Could he be involved in all this?"

"I doubt it. Wolfe is something of a national hero. Before the war he was an isolationist. He spoke out against America getting involved with the fight against the Nazis. Didn't think it was any of their business. But he had two sons who joined the army, and he lost them both on Omaha Beach. They were killed within minutes of each other. The Americans go for stories like that. He's been in and out of the White House many times since then. An adviser to Roosevelt and Truman. He's also getting on a bit. He must be well over seventy, and there are rumors that he's unwell."

"Did 007 mention him?"

Tanner shook his head. "Not a word."

"I want you to leave at once," M cut in. "Miss Moneypenny will arrange the air ticket for you to Nice. That was where 007 was based, and that's where I suggest you start."

"We sent 007 out under a false name," Tanner said. "But there doesn't seem to be any point doing the same for you. It clearly didn't do him any good. He called himself Richard Blakeney, working out of University College. He had an apartment, number twelve in the Rue Foncet. The French police have been in there, but it might still be a good idea to have a look around."

"Station F will provide you with everything you need," M said. "But I don't want you to contact the SDECE or any other French departments, and I haven't told them you're on your way. We can't be certain they're to be trusted, and until we know more, it might be safer for you to act as an independent agent."

"I agree, sir."

M reached for his pipe. "There is one more thing. You're going to need a number. You'll be working with 008 and 0011. I don't know why, but 009 sprung to mind. What do you think?"

Bond had been getting to his feet, but he sat down again. "If it's all the same to you, sir, I'd like to take over the 007 designation."

M raised an eyebrow. "Really? Why?"

"I suppose there are two reasons. The first is that I knew—" Bond named the man who had died. "I'd go so far as to say we were friends, and I'd like to keep his memory alive."

"And the second?"

"I think it sends out a message. You can take one of us down, but it changes nothing. We'll come back as strong as ever."

M exchanged a glance with his chief of staff, then nodded. "Well, it makes no difference to me. As long as you're not superstitious. Just make sure you take care of yourself. Good luck."

The following day, James Bond 007 left for France.

CHAPTER 3

"Hold it right there . . ."

THE SUN HAS ALWAYS BEEN a little in love with the south of France. It beats down, making the sea blue and the beaches welcoming. As Bond walked along the Promenade des Anglais, curving around the waterfront at Nice, he found it impossible to imagine the scene in the rain. What would happen to the sun worshippers, stretched out on the sand, or the smart set, drifting in and out of the fashion shops, sitting beneath the canopies with their *grands café crèmes?* He had arrived that morning and checked into the Hotel Negresco. He had quickly unpacked, and now, dressed in a dark-blue cotton shirt and white linen slacks, he looked no different from any of the other tourists making their way down the thoroughfare.

Only the .25 Beretta in his back pocket told a different story. He turned off, leaving the great sweep of the sea behind him. The Rue Foncet was a ten-minute walk away, a long, narrow street that ran in a straight line. The quiet of the seafront was punctured here by two sweating workmen digging up the road with a jackhammer. Bond went around them and continued past an old-fashioned tailor's and a flower shop. There were fewer people here and almost no traffic. The flat Bill Tanner had mentioned—rented by a university lecturer who went by the name of Richard Blakeney—was opposite a funeral parlor, which seemed to Bond unpleasantly prophetic. The main entrance to the building was open. Bond walked in and took the stairs to the fifth floor—as high as the building went.

There were two flats here, one at each end of a corridor that had seen better times. Bond quickly examined the door of number twelve, which had been secured with a simple lever tumbler lock. He drew a slim, silver tool from his pocket—a curtain pick—and after listening to make sure there was nobody inside, inserted the pick and manipulated it carefully until he heard the tumbler fall.

He opened the door and found himself in a two-bedroom flat. In the front room a well-worn rug covered a small area of otherwise bare floorboards. He glanced through a second door and saw a brass bed, unmade, the mattress still holding the shape of the man who had once slept there.

The SDECE had sent back the personal belongings of the dead man, but these had amounted to very little: his wallet, silver cuff links, a Cartier cigarette lighter. And yet he had been onto something. He had closed in on an international criminal, Madame 16, and claimed he had evidence she was in bed with the local underworld. What sort of evidence? Photographs? Letters? The French police had already searched the flat and found nothing. Why should it be any different for Bond? Never mind. . . .

He started in the bedroom. A few clothes hung in the wardrobe. Bond tapped the pockets, expecting to find them empty. They were. He went into the living room and searched the cupboards, feeling under the shelves. There was a grandfather clock in one corner of the room, a hideous thing. He opened it and rummaged through the workings. He studied every inch of the floor, searching for a board that might come loose. Thirty minutes later he was certain that the rooms had nothing to hide.

What else, then? A safe-deposit box in a local bank? No. If he'd got something, he'd have wanted to keep it close.

Bond took out a cigarette, lit it, then walked over to a glass door that opened onto a small terrace overlooking the street. A motorbike had just pulled in on the other side, an Airone Turismo. It was painted a firebox red. He could imagine the air-cooled engine propelling the rider along the French coast. That was what he would rather be doing, not shuffling about in this house of death.

He glanced down and noticed a dark footprint on the floor in front of him. Someone had stepped into an area of black asphalt or tar and left a faint imprint of their shoe. But there was something wrong. The footprint was facing into, not out of the room. If it had been the other way around, there would have been no mystery. You come in from the street. You go over to the window and open it. You leave a mark. But that wasn't what had happened.

Bond turned the handles, pulled open the glass door, and stepped onto the terrace. There was a metal table and two chairs. The floor was covered with a latticed metalwork, and there was nothing that could account for the footprint. He looked up at the balustrade that ran the full length of the building just above his head. He had an idea. Moving quickly, he climbed onto the table, then pulled himself over the balustrade and onto the roof.

All at once Bond found himself in a strange landscape of chimneys, skylights, and jutting dormer windows. In front of him, he noticed a whitewashed boxlike building, about the size of a garden shed. It was fastened with a padlock, and Bond examined it with interest. Although the paintwork was old and flaking, the padlock was brand new. Bond took out his Beretta and waited for the jackhammer to start up again. As the noise echoed down the street, he fired once. The lock shattered. Bond opened the door.

The shed was floored with black asphalt. It housed some of the machinery that operated the lights and the lift inside the building. Bond rummaged around without finding anything, then noticed a shelf above his head. Standing on tiptoe, he ran his hand along it. His fingers touched something soft, made of paper. He dragged it down: a thick envelope, unsealed, clean. It hadn't been there long.

Back in the daylight, he examined the contents: a gun, a wad of 10,000-franc notes (200,000 francs in total), two passports—one of them in the name of Richard Blakeney—an invoice of some sort, a postcard with a view of the sea, and several photographs. Bond knew at once that he had hit the jackpot. Pleased with himself, he slid them back into the envelope. The street was still empty, the bike parked opposite. He swung himself down and went back in through the open door.

He had taken two steps into the room when he felt something cold pressed against his neck. A voice said, "Hold it right there."

Bond froze. Out of the corner of his eye, he could see a man wearing a leather motorbike jacket, one arm outstretched, holding a gun. Inwardly he cursed himself. He had seen the bike, but it had never occurred to him that the rider might be on his way here.

"I'll have that, if you don't mind," the man said. He had a gravelly voice and an American drawl.

Bond was holding the envelope that he had found in his right hand. "And what if I do mind?" he asked pleasantly.

"Just hand it over."

"Sure." Bond turned, as if passing the envelope across, but he suddenly accelerated, slamming the package into the man's gun hand and at the same time ducking low. The gun blasted out its load, but its aim had gone wild, the bullet smashing into the grandfather clock. Bond sliced upward, driving his knuckles into the man's throat. The man slumped to the ground.

Bond stayed where he was, still holding the envelope. He took the gun—an M1911 Colt Service Ace, much liked by the U.S. government. He emptied it and laid it on a table, then quickly searched the unconscious man. He found an ID card that identified Reade Griffith as a member of the Central Intelligence Agency, helpfully adding that he was six feet tall, weighed 170 pounds, had blue eyes and brown hair. Bond would have added that he was clean shaven, built like a quarterback, and kept himself in shape.

The agent's eyes flickered open. "That hurt!" he said.

"You shouldn't have pulled a gun on me," Bond said mildly.

"I'll remember that next time. I don't suppose you could get me a glass of water. My larynx seems to have been crushed."

"Sure." Bond went over to the sink and filled a glass. He handed it to the agent.

"You've seen my ID." Bond had left it next to the gun. "Did you know it's a felony to assault an agent of the CIA when he's in pursuance of his duty?"

"And it's actually a capital offense to point a gun at a member of the British secret service when he's in pursuance of his."

"The British secret service? I sort of guessed that when I heard the accent." Griffith gulped down some of the water. He got unsteadily to his feet and held out a hand. "Reade Griffith," he said.

"James Bond."

"Nice to meet you, James Bond. And I sincerely apologize for trying to railroad you just now. Given what happened to the last occupant of this apartment, I figured it was best to play it safe." Griffith rubbed his throat. "When did you get into Nice?"

"This morning."

"Well, you certainly don't hang around." He glanced at the envelope. "Where did you find that?"

"There's a sort of service hut on the roof."

"That's smart. Smart of him to hide it there, smart of you to find it. So have you finished here, then?"

"I would say so. Yes."

"Then what say the two of us head out of here and get a drink?"

Bond smiled and handed the CIA man back his gun.

Ten minutes later they were outside a bar with parasols, wrought-iron tables, and haughty-looking waiters in white aprons. Griffith had made a telephone call before he had sat down, running a background check on Bond while Bond ordered the drinks: a Campari for himself and, for Griffith, a cold beer.

"Okay. It looks as if we're on the same side," Griffith said. "Welcome to the south of France. I guess they've sent you to find out what happened to your friend."

"Did you know him?" Bond asked.

"I met him a few times. He was pretending to be some sort of writer, but I soon found out why he was out here—the same reason as me. It would have turned out better if the two of us had worked together, but he preferred to play things solo."

"So what are you doing here?"

"Broadly speaking, my job is to keep an eye on things. I'm sure I don't need to tell you how important the French ports are to our interests—the Marshall Plan and all the rest of it. They're our gateway to Europe. You can think of me as an American outpost, James, fighting the good fight in my own little way."

"How long have you been here?"

"About eighteen months. I joined the CIA after the war. Actually, I didn't join them. They came for me. I was with the Marine Corps, working in intelligence. When the war finished, I went back to Harvard to study law. There was a knock on the door and the next thing I knew, I found myself over here in the Côte d'Azur. Nice place, by the way, if you look out for yourself."

Bond remembered the report he had read and the comment that the CIA had supported the crime syndicates. "Looking out for yourself. Does that involve cooperating with Corsican gangsters?"

Griffith laughed. "That was official policy two years ago, but we realized it didn't work. These people are animals. Monday they're your best friend. Tuesday they shoot your head off. Right now I've got no idea what they're up to. The supply of heroin seems to have fizzled out, and that doesn't make sense. I've been trying to figure out what's going on, and when your guy turned up dead, I guessed he must have stumbled onto something. That's why I went to his place. When you turned up, I assumed you must be up to no good."

It was a pattern that Bond recognized. Two intelligence agencies, operating from different sides of the world, had come to blows in a dingy Riviera flat. That was the trouble with the secret services. They didn't even trust their own allies.

"That was your bike?" he asked. "The Turismo?"

"Sure," Griffith said. "It wasn't easy getting the office to agree to that one, but I told them the traffic here stinks." He sipped his beer, then set the glass down. "So in the spirit of transatlantic cooperation, are you going to show me what's in that package?"

The envelope was on the table between them. Bond had barely glanced at the contents and still wasn't sure that he wanted to share them. At the same time, he had taken a liking to Reade Griffith. He took out the photographs first and laid them down flat.

They showed three people, a woman and two men, meeting over a bottle of wine. They were close together on the crowded terrace of a bar, with the old port of Marseilles behind. The name of the bar was printed on the canopy: LA CARAVELLE.

Griffith whistled. "Well, you're definitely onto something with this. That's Jean-Paul Scipio. The man with him is his translator."

The Corsican gangster was instantly recognizable. He was so fat that his shoulders and his head were some distance from the table. He was wearing a three-piece white linen suit and smoking a cigarette. The translator, sitting next to him, was completely bald and was dressed in a dark suit with round spectacles. The woman facing them was leaning back, a glass of wine in her hand.

Bond examined the long dark hair, the slim body, the folded legs. It was hard to match this photograph with the one he had seen in London, although he was almost certain they showed the same person. "Sixtine," he said.

"That's her, all right."

"You've met her?"

"No, I can't say I've had the pleasure, but I've seen the files and she's a piece of work. Last time I looked, she was number three on the CIA Most Wanted List, although we don't arrest her, because it's almost impossible to pin anything on her. She's too smart for that. She's a go-between, a buyer and a seller, but she always manages to keep her hands clean. At the same time, I could tell you a dozen people who've lost everything, thanks to her."

Griffith spun the photograph around. "So if this little tête-à-tête is anything to go by, it looks pretty certain that Madame 16 is in business with the drug syndicates. That's interesting. I wouldn't have said it was quite her style, but she goes where the money goes, and Scipio's certainly got big pockets. What else have you got?"

Bond went back to the envelope and drew out the invoice he had noticed earlier. The top of the page was printed with the letterhead and the name of a company—FERRIX CHIMIQUES—with an address in Marseilles. In the right-hand corner was the word INVOICE and a number: 82032150. This was the third, or even the fourth, carbon copy, stolen perhaps from the bottom of a pile. The typewriter keys had barely made it through, and although Bond could make out a few letters, the rest of it was illegible.

"Ferrix Chimiques," Bond said. "Do you know them?"

Griffith shook his head. "Never heard of them. Chimiques is French for chemicals, and it looks like someone paid quite a lot for whatever it was they bought." He pointed to the figure at the bottom of the page. "There are five zeroes. That's 100,000 francs."

"Presumably they'll have kept the original. We need to pay them a visit. But let's go in quietly." Bond picked up the invoice and folded it. "There must be a reason why this was kept hidden."

"I'll check them out with my people. See what I can find."

Finally, Bond took out the postcard. On the front there was a view of the French coast, possibly Cannes. There was a telephone number on the back and a name: Monique. He showed it to Griffith, who shrugged. "Why don't you give it a try," he said.

Bond went into the bar and called the number. A minute later he came back to the table. "No reply."

"So what are you going to do next?"

"I suppose it might be time to have a word with Sixtine."

Griffith finished his drink and called for the bill. "If you like living dangerously, that's probably a good idea."

"Any idea where I might find her?"

"Yeah. Sure. You need to head down to the casino at Monte Carlo. She's there most nights, usually on her own. She plays a few hands of blackjack. Then she disappears."

"Monte Carlo?" Bond couldn't help smiling. He had been there less than a year ago. "I'll look in tonight."

"I hope you don't mind if I don't join you." Griffith touched his neck. "I might turn in early. I seem to have a sore throat."

"Let's hope it's not catching," Bond said.

CHAPTER 4

Madame 16

BOND HAD NEVER BEEN particularly comfortable at the casino of Monte Carlo. There was something unashamedly vulgar about the decor—the crimson carpets, the theatrical curtains, the inevitable chandeliers. But even as he climbed the steps that led to the grand entrance, dressed now in dinner jacket and black tie, he felt the familiar stirrings of excitement known to every gambler. He didn't intend to take part in any serious gaming tonight, but it was against his nature to come here only as a spectator. The moment he arrived, he changed the 200,000 francs he had found at the Rue Foncet into plaques of 50,000. He had no qualms about playing with the funds of a dead man. On the contrary, this would be his memorial to an old friend. If he lost, they would have lost together. If he won, he would donate the winnings to one of the service's favorite charities. As he took his place at the roulette table, the *chef de partie* handed him the card showing the run of the ball since the last session had started. Bond noticed that zero had shown its ugly face twice in the last hour. He took comfort from the calculation that the chances of a third appearance might be considered infinitesimal. Two spins later the zero came up a third time and Bond was down 40,000 francs. He accepted this slap in the face and plowed on anyway. After a dozen more *coups*, he had doubled his original stake and left the table confident that the rest of the evening would go his way.

Walking slowly, he made his way over to the blackjack tables.

Blackjack—*vingt-et-un* in France—is one of the most popular casino games in the world. It is said that no other card game has earned so much money—for the casinos. Bond didn't have the patience to work out the strategies that would supposedly shift the odds in his favor. He preferred the roulette wheel, where the ball tumbling into a single pocket might make someone a millionaire.

He saw Sixtine almost at once.

She was sitting on the far side of the furthest table with four other players, and she had clearly been winning; the plaques were piled up in front of her. Her long, slender legs were tucked beneath her, and one elbow rested on the table. Her black hair hung luxuriously, framing a face that was serious and businesslike. Her eyes were brown and were focusing intensely on the game. She was wearing Christian Dior—a black shantung dress with a tightly fitting bodice and a full skirt. She was about ten years older than him, and he had to admit that she had been—and still was—a beautiful woman. Bond examined the other players. Nearest him was a man in his early thirties, perhaps a schoolteacher or an accountant, with his thick glasses and timid manner. Next came a plump businessman who chewed on his gold signet ring while he played. His wife, a little bored, sat beside him. On her right—between her and Madame 16—sat a man who reeked of inherited wealth. He was unshaven, with curly hair, and wore a white dinner jacket while everyone around him was in black. There was one seat free, but Bond didn't take it. He preferred to observe from a distance.

He watched half a dozen hands, noting at once that in this version of the game, the hole cards were being dealt faceup, which might be very much to the players' advantage, giving them a greater knowledge of what remained in the deck. Sixtine was a quiet, confident player who won more often than she lost. Was she playing a system? All the clues were there. She was drinking iced water. Most of the professional card players that Bond knew avoided alcohol. When she wanted another card, she tapped a finger impatiently, as if waiting to be proved right. She was playing a game of chance but gave every impression of being in control.

On the seventh hand, he worked out what was going on.

Sixtine's hole card was a ten, lying underneath her down card, which was carefully hiding its face. She lifted a corner and peeked at it, then immediately turned both cards. They were both tens, and she had decided to split them, doubling her bet of 15,000 francs. It was a strange move. Bond knew enough about the rules of *vingt-et-un* to know that you never split tens. Why risk a high score of twenty with two scores that have every chance of being weaker? The dealer dealt her a seven on one of her tens and a five on the other. Seventeen and fifteen: two mediocre hands had replaced one good one. Bond waited for her to lose.

The dealer was showing a queen. He turned a card. It was a six. With a score of sixteen, the rules forced him to draw again. The next card was another six. Twenty-two! He was bust!

He saw Sixtine smile. She had known what was going to happen. But how? There had to be an answer, and with a prickle of excitement, Bond realized what it was.

Vingt-et-un is the one casino activity where each game directly informs the next. The deck isn't shuffled until all the cards have been used, and it is possible for a player to make assumptions based on what has already happened. So if all four aces have already appeared, there will be no more "soft" hands—with the aces counting one or eleven—and no blackjacks. Bond had also noticed that the dealer was using a single deck of cards, which would give more skillful players a slight edge. More and more casinos were using two or even three decks to swing the odds back in their favor, which was perhaps why Sixtine had chosen to play here.

But it also means that a player with extraordinary powers of concentration might be able to memorize the whole deck. That same player might also be able to calculate exactly how many cards remain, simply by scrutinizing the thickness of the deck, the number of cards in the dealer's hands. Sixtine had perfected this technique. He was quite sure of it. It struck him that she had also chosen her position at the edge of the table deliberately. She was the last to receive her hand, allowing her to use all the cards that had so far been dealt to the other players in her own calculations.

When she had split the tens, she had known what cards were remaining in the deck. At the same time, she had worked out the odds of the dealer busting himself. She had decided to take the gamble, and she had won, making herself 30,000 francs. The dealer came to the end of the deck, shuffled thoroughly, and began again. Bond watched the next few hands. Sixtine won a couple of hands and lost a couple. All the time, her gaze remained fixed on the deck of cards, remembering everything that was dealt, turning over the odds, and waiting for the moment to strike.

Bond saw when that moment arrived. The dealer had reached the last ten or eleven cards. Suddenly there was a flicker of excitement in Sixtine's eyes, and before the dealer had time to collect all the cards and raise the deck for the next hand, she nodded slightly.

At once the other players left the table. The schoolteacher swept his plaques off the table, as if announcing that he was quitting while he was ahead. The plump businessman's wife muttered something to him, and with a little sigh and a shrug of his shoulders, he slid off his chair and walked away with her. The curly-haired man decided that he needed a drink and sauntered over to the bar.

What was going on? The dealer was as surprised as Bond, but since there was now only one player remaining, he had more than enough cards to go ahead. He glanced questioningly at the lady in front of him. She smiled. She was ready for the next hand.

The five players were a syndicate! The entire group was working in concert, and their departure had been carefully rehearsed. The idea was to leave Sixtine on her own at a specific moment. She knew the values of the remaining cards in the deck and had worked out exactly when it would work to her advantage to go head to head with the dealer. Right now the odds must be stacked in her favor, and she was preparing to make one last maximum bet.

The dealer leaned forward, but before he could begin the next deal, Bond had taken three quick steps and placed himself on the empty seat at the far end of the table, opposite Sixtine. He knew that his being there would change all the odds, and he was amused to see a slight narrowing of her eyes as she acknowledged his presence. Bond took out a plaque for 50,000 francs, the maximum bid, and laid it on the green baize. Sixtine glanced at him for a moment with just the hint of a frown. Then she did the same.

The cards were dealt. Bond had the eight of hearts. Sixtine had the seven of clubs. The dealer also had a seven—in spades. Bond's hole card was yet another eight, this one in diamonds. He wasn't at all surprised by so many identical values. Sixtine must have known that there were sevens and eights clustered together at the bottom of the deck and worked out her strategy accordingly. So what would she do in his position? Bond displayed both his cards, splitting them and placing another 50,000 francs on the table. The dealer dealt him two more cards. They weren't good: a nine of clubs and a five. Bond now had seventeen in one hand and thirteen in the other. Should he stand—or try to improve the lesser of the two hands? He glanced at Sixtine. She had engineered this situation. She had worked things out so that she would win. Yes, of course. Bond waved a hand. He was going to stand.

Now it was Sixtine's turn. Whatever she had, it wasn't a pair. She took one last peek at her concealed card and threw another 50,000 plaque onto the table, doubling down. This allowed her just one more card. The dealer turned it. The card was a queen of clubs. Bond knew at once that it was bad news. Scowling, Sixtine turned over her hole card. It was the five of hearts. With the queen and her original seven, she now had twenty-two. She was bust.

And what of the dealer? He left his seven of spades lying on the table and turned over its ugly sister, the eight of spades. He had fifteen, and according to the rules, he had to draw again. He did so. An ace! It still wasn't enough. He drew again, a knave of clubs, which busted him. Bond had four cards making up two indifferent hands, but they had still managed to win him 100,000 francs.

The miniature drama was over. Sixtine walked away without saying a word. Looking at the wreckage of what she had left behind, Bond could see why she was angry. If he hadn't imposed himself on the game, the distribution of the cards would have been very different. The 100,000 francs that Bond had won should have been Sixtine's. Scooping up his plaques, he nodded his thanks to the dealer, then followed her out of the room.

SHE hadn't ordered yet. Bond found her in the Bar Salle Blanche waiting for the barman when he walked over.

"I think I owe you a drink," he said.

Her dark eyes settled on him. "You don't owe me anything."

"I brought you bad luck," said Bond.

"I don't believe in luck."

"Bad timing, then."

"That may be true." She considered. "I don't see why I should refuse a share of your winnings. What do you propose?"

"A glass of champagne, perhaps? I can recommend the Taittinger Blanc de Blancs Brut '43."

"I'm not in the mood for champagne."

"A dry martini, then." She nodded, and Bond turned to the barman. "I'd like two martinis," he said. "Three measures of Gordon's, one of vodka, half a measure of Kina Lillet. It needs to be served ice cold with a slice of lemon peel. All right?"

"Of course, monsieur." The barman smiled and nodded.

"Wait a minute." Sixtine had stopped him before he'd turned away. "I'd like mine shaken, not stirred," she said.

The barman was about to argue, but then he fluttered his eyelids. "Whatever madame desires."

As he hurried away, Bond turned to her quizzically. "Does it really make a difference?" he asked.

"Oh, yes." She was quite serious. "My late husband used to say that if you shake a cocktail, you bruise the alcohol. Also, you melt more of the ice. Stirred not shaken was one of his mantras." She drew out a cigarette and allowed Bond to light it. "Ever since he died, I've made it a point of principle to do everything the opposite of what he told me." She glanced at the cigarette in her hand. "He didn't like me smoking, either."

"When did he die?" Bond asked.

"Not soon enough." She picked up her handbag and went over to a table. He sat down next to her.

"Do you often play here?" he asked.

"I prefer the casino at Estoril, in Portugal. It's more majestic. And I play at Crockford's when I'm in London."

"Always on your own?"

"What makes you think I'm on my own?"

Was this a tacit admission of the syndicate that had been playing alongside her? Bond wondered where the three men and the woman had gone. "You knew every card in the deck," he said.

"No. But the more cards that have been discarded, the easier it is to predict the odds. That's why I enjoy *vingt-et-un*. I saw you playing roulette. That seems to me to be a waste of time. Why should you pursue any activity over which you have no control?"

"Why gamble at all, then?" Bond asked.

"My husband was a gambler. He lost everything. I've made it my personal crusade to take a little back."

The drinks arrived at their table and with them a short, bald man in black tie, bristling with excitement. With a sinking heart, Bond recognized Émile Tournier, the general manager of the casino. The two of them had met before, and the smaller man could not contain his delight. "Monsieur Bond! What a pleasure to see you again!" he exclaimed in heavily accented English. "You should have informed us that you were coming. Please accept these drinks on the house."

"Thank you." Bond gave him a thin smile. In other circumstances the very mention of his name might have been a death sentence. As it was, the intrusion was annoying enough.

"It is my pleasure. It is the pleasure of the Casino of Monte Carlo. When I think what might have happened if it had not been for you. *Formidable!* Please let me know if there is anything that I can do for you, and I wish you both a most pleasant evening."

Bowing, he backed away. Bond and Sixtine were left with the drinks. "So now you know my name," Bond said.

"Oh, I knew it already," Sixtine replied. "You are James Bond of the secret service. You were recently elevated to the Double-O Section, which means you have a license to kill. It makes me wonder who in this building has made themselves your target. Me, perhaps? I hope not. I enjoy my life, and I don't think I've done anything recently that would put me on your assassination list."

So she had known about him all along. How was that possible? There were only a handful of people who knew about the Double-O Section, let alone his promotion to it. Bond was impressed. "In that case, you must know why I'm here," he said.

"No. Are you going to tell me?"

He picked up his glass. The liquid was slightly cloudy, a result of the treatment it had received, but when he sipped it, he could discern no difference in the taste. "A friend of mine was killed," he said. "You might have known him as Richard Blakeney."

"I didn't know him." She sounded bored. "Was it an accident?"

"He was shot three times at close range."

"Then he was careless."

"You say you didn't know him, but he certainly knew you."

"A lot of people claim to know me." She searched for an ashtray. Bond slid it toward her. "I never met Richard Blakeney or anyone else from British intelligence," she went on. "I assume he was one of yours? How are things in Regent's Park, by the way?"

"I'd be interested to know what you're doing here in the south of France."

"I'm sure you would. But I can't imagine why you'd think I'd have any interest in telling you."

Bond smiled. "Can I at least ask if it's business or pleasure?"

"My business *is* my pleasure. If it wasn't, I wouldn't continue." Her eyes leveled on his. "Do you take pleasure in killing people?"

Bond was completely thrown by the question. He ignored her. "Why did you meet Jean-Paul Scipio?"

She shook her head. "That's not how it works, James. Any information that I have is for sale or for exchange. Nothing is free. I'm interested to know what it feels like to be a young man with so much power. Who else can choose between life and death with no fear of retaliation? Only a secret agent or a psychopath."

"I certainly don't feel like a psychopath," he said. "And I have less power than you think. I merely do what I'm told. As to the rest of your question, I don't need to answer it. We've both been through a war. There are heroes and there are villains. You have to decide which side you're on and you go where that takes you."

It was enough—for the moment. "I have no interest at all in Jean-Paul Scipio," she said. "He's a drug dealer. His business and mine have nothing in common. Why would I want to meet him?"

"That's what I'm asking." Bond took one of the photographs out of his pocket and laid it on the table. The dark eyes glanced down briefly, then flickered away. "This was taken at La Caravelle bar in Marseilles," he said. "Why do we have to play games with each other? You might find it easier to tell me the truth."

"I didn't say I hadn't met him. I said I wouldn't want to—and that's true. For a start, he's repulsively fat. He has no manners."

"When was this taken?"

"How many people have you killed?"

Bond hesitated. "Two."

"In France?"

"One in New York. One in Sweden."

"I was at La Caravelle just over a week ago. It was a Tuesday, I think. Scipio invited me, and it seemed sensible to accept."

"What did he want?"

"My turn, James. How did you know I would be here?"

"I didn't know. But I heard you came here sometimes and I hoped to meet you."

She looked at him coldly. "You could have waited until I'd finished the game and introduced yourself then."

"On the contrary, I enjoyed playing cards with you. In fact, watching you was an experience in itself. I imagine it must help a great deal if you surround yourself with friends."

She didn't deny the accusation. "What did that man mean just now? The little man with the mustache? What was it that would have happened if it wasn't for you?"

Bond made a gesture with one hand. "It was nothing."

"Why don't you let me be the judge of that?" Now it was her turn to smile. "It seems to me that we may have common interests. You're in the south of France because you want to know what Scipio is doing. And what Scipio is doing might make a difference to the reason I'm here, too. I could walk out of here, and you might never see me again. Or we could keep talking and see where that takes us. Of course, if you find my company boring . . ."

"I don't find you at all boring," Bond said. "On the contrary, I was simply thinking that the story wouldn't be of any interest to you. But if you want to hear it, let me order a couple more cocktails . . . shaken, not stirred. It may take a while."

He signaled to the waiter, then began.

"It happened last year and concerns a ship, a Soviet cruiser called the *Aleksandr Kolchak*, making a propaganda trip, showing the flag around the Mediterranean. Its first port of call was here in Monte Carlo, and I was sent down to take a closer look."

"A look? Is that all?"

Bond lit a cigarette. "We'd been trying to intercept the signals it was sending back to Kronstadt, but we hadn't been successful, because we didn't know what wave bands it was using and we didn't have the schedules. So far, we'd been unable to pick up any transmissions. I was here to see if there was any way around that.

"It soon became clear that there wasn't very much I could do. The *Aleksandr Kolchak* was moored about half a mile out. It was a Chapayev-class cruiser, a six-hundred-footer with the usual range of guns. No visitors were allowed anywhere near. I tried to speak to some of the crew, but they'd been warned off talking to anyone.

Then I had a stroke of luck. One evening, I happened to see a fifty-year-old man, obviously Russian, coming into the casino with a rather attractive French tart. It was clear that she was having to cajole him to go with her. I knew at once who he was—none other than Captain Nikolai Stolypin, the man in charge of the *Kolchak*.

"I followed them in. Of course, the captain was bowled over by the casino. He cracked open his first bottle of champagne, and after a couple of glasses, the girl led him over to the roulette table and showed him how it worked. Russians are all gamblers at heart, and it wasn't long before Stolypin was placing bets. He was winning, too. He'd managed to stack up a pile of plaques, but over the next few hours I saw them dwindle and finally disappear. He was bust. At the same time, I knew it wouldn't stop him coming back."

"You're right about the Russians. They have no self-control. It comes from always being told what to do."

"You've had many dealings with them?"

"Don't change the subject. I want to hear more." Sixtine was clearly absorbed by the story.

"Stolypin came back the next night," he continued. "And the night after that. The *Kolchak* was due to leave in a week, and he seemed determined to make the most of his time. Every night, he'd play until his pockets were empty, but the following evening, he'd still come in for more. By the end of the week, he was obviously a desperate man, gambling fiercely and even insanely. The last time, he played until five o'clock in the morning. I noticed that he'd been looking at his watch from time to time, and exactly on the hour, he hurled his chair back and got up. He called for the manager—that was the man you saw just now—and the two of them went into his office with an anxious group of casino officials. As it happened, I'd already met Monsieur Tournier, and he had an idea that I was a policeman of some sort. He let me tag along, which was how I became a witness of what happened next.

"The Russian made an impassioned speech in pretty execrable French. He said that he had lost all his own money. Worse than that, he'd raided the cabin of the ship's paymaster and stolen more cash from the safe. The bottom line was that he was down one million francs. And then he announced his masterstroke. He was ruined, he said, but in revenge he was going to destroy the casino.

"Stolypin pointed out the window. It was all very theatrical. 'I gave orders that if I was not back on board at a quarter past five, my cruiser's main armament was to be trained on this casino,' he exclaimed. 'I have ordered my gun crews to fire at six o'clock whether you return the money to me or not. I shall die, but I shall have the satisfaction of knowing that this monstrous, capitalist enterprise will have been razed to the earth!'

"Tournier and the other officials rushed over to the window. The *Kolchak* had twelve six-inch B-38 guns mounted in Mark 5 triple turrets, and they were slowly swinging around. In about thirty seconds they were all aimed broadside. Tournier ran to a safe in the wall. He opened it and pulled out several packets of 100,000-franc notes, which he threw onto the table. But Stolypin had decided it was all over for him. He sat there shaking his head.

"It was half past five. Only thirty minutes remained until the balloon went up. Finally, the officials remembered that there were still a few people playing in the casino and decided to evacuate them. I persuaded Tournier to leave the room with all the others. So off they all went, and the two of us were left alone."

Sixtine sipped her drink. There was the rattle of a ball and then a cry of triumph from the salon next door.

"Stolypin spoke better English than French," Bond continued. "I laid it on pretty thick. If the guns actually opened fire, it might be the start of a world war. His entire crew would be massacred. The captain had to think of his wife and family in Russia and what would become of them. I asked him his wife's name.

"For a moment he stayed silent; then he burst into tears. 'Irma . . .' I put an arm around his shoulder and said, 'Irma is waiting for you now. Go home to her. Let's forget about this.'

"He nodded and got to his feet, tears streaming down his face. He began to scoop up wads of cash, stuffing them into his tunic. But at the last moment, I grabbed hold of him. He looked at me, alarmed. 'There is just one other thing,' I said. 'If I'm going to let you walk out of here, I'm going to need the answer to one question. Give it to me and you will be back on board your ship—with the money—in minutes. Otherwise, the casino will be evacuated. I'll report to London and they'll warn Washington. Whether war comes or not, you will have disgraced the Soviet navy.'

"A minute later Stolypin walked out of the room, past the officials on the other side of the door, trying to hold on to what little dignity remained. He didn't look back until he had left the casino.

"They all came rushing in, and I explained that I'd managed to persuade the captain to change his mind. It was true. Looking out the window, we saw the guns slowly settling back in their mountings. The clock was showing five fifty-nine."

"That was certainly worth a couple of free martinis," Sixtine said. "But what was the question that you asked him?"

Bond finished his drink. "The frequencies and times of transmission of his ship's radio, of course," he replied. "That was all I wanted, and to be honest, if he hadn't given it to me, the casino and Captain Stolypin could have gone to blazes."

Sixtine laughed out loud. Suddenly she had come to life, and Bond seized the moment to press home his advantage. "You were going to tell me about your business with Scipio," he said.

"Was I?" She sounded surprised.

"Did he want to talk to you about Ferrix Chimiques?" It was a long shot. But the invoice and the photographs had been in the same envelope. There had to be some connection.

"I don't even know what that is."

Bond regretted his direct questions. He knew that she was disappointed in him.

"Scipio wanted to know what I was doing here, and he tried to intimidate me. He didn't succeed. That's all there is to it."

Bond didn't know if she was telling the truth. "All right," he said. "But it seems to me that I've told you a great deal more about myself than you've told me about you. Why don't we meet again. There's a restaurant I know in Beaulieu."

She thought for a moment, and some of the humor returned to her eyes. "I'm not sure I'd trust myself alone in a restaurant with a British spy. But there's no reason why we shouldn't see each other again. I'm staying with a friend. His name is Irwin Wolfe."

"I know who he is," Bond said.

"He's having a party tomorrow night. He has a villa called Shame Lady above Cap Ferrat. Why don't you come. I'm sure he'd love to meet you." She stood up. "Thank you for the drinks. But as you didn't actually pay for them, you still owe me 100,000 francs." She looked at him curiously. "I may find a way to extract it from you."

"I might enjoy that."

"I wonder."

As she walked away, he called after her. "Shame Lady?"

She turned. "It grows in the garden. It's a plant." She paused. "I hope you weren't thinking it referred to me."

He watched her disappear into the crowd.

CHAPTER 5

Not So Joliette

THE BASIN OF LA JOLIETTE stretched out, sullen and sweltering in the August heat. The black water beside the jetties had the thick, noxious quality of melting tar. James Bond gazed around him at what should have been Europe's busiest port, but the midday sun was beating down on empty quays with piles of sacks, pallets, and oil drums left haphazardly, the shacks and walkways abandoned.

"Where is everyone?" Bond asked.

Reade Griffith laughed. "It's midday, James. You don't separate a French dockworker from his lunch, not unless you want the unions coming down on you like a ton of bricks."

Bond had hired a Citroën Cabriolet-Roadster in Nice. He and the CIA agent had made the three-hour journey together along the coast. During that time, Griffith had brought Bond up to date.

"I've had it checked out, and as far as I can see, Ferrix Chimiques is legit. It imports chemicals from all over the world and supplies different industries in France. I've arranged an appointment for us this afternoon with the managing director, Andria Mariani."

"Andria? That's a Corsican name, isn't it?"

"It might be, although the company is registered here in Marseilles. You're going to be Mr. Howard from Universal Export, looking for a European partner. I'm Bill Plover from Polygon Agrochemical Supplies, your international representative."

"I'm going to have to get into their accounts or wherever they keep their invoices."

"You got any idea how you're going to do that?"

"I'll find a way." Bond thought for a moment. "Before that I want to look at La Joliette . . . where the shooting happened."

"Yeah. I'd like to see that, too." Griffith glanced over his shoulder as he changed gear. "I never asked you. How did you get on with Mata Hari?"

"She's certainly an interesting character."

"Did she tell you anything?"

"We're meeting again tonight."

Griffith raised an eyebrow. "You've certainly made an impression, James. But I'd take care if I were you."

The section of the dock where the body had been pulled out of the water was closed off to the public with red-painted signs reading PRIVÉ and ENTRÉE INTERDITE. These seemed to have been ignored by two people fishing—perhaps a father and son—at the end of the otherwise empty quay.

A young, stocky French-African man with suspicious eyes was sitting on a stool beside a wooden shack that served as a security office, with a barrier that rose and fell to let cars into the dock. He was wearing a uniform, and there was a walkie-talkie clipped to his belt. As the Citroën pulled up, he lowered himself off the stool, barely glanced at Griffith, then walked around to examine Bond. "*Vos papiers, monsieur,*" he demanded. Bond flashed his passport through the window. Satisfied, the man lifted the barrier, allowing them to drive through.

"That's strange," Bond muttered as they continued forward. "He asks to see ID but doesn't ask us what we're doing here."

Griffith considered. "Maybe he doesn't care."

"Maybe he already knows."

The man hadn't, however, returned to his stool. Instead, he went into the shack, snatched up his walkie-talkie, and pressed the button to transmit. "It's them," he said. He spoke French with an Italian accent. "One of them is the American. The other is James Bond. They've just driven through." The man didn't know who he'd been talking to. He'd just done what he'd been told.

Meanwhile, the Citroën continued its progress across the empty harbor, driving along a flat concrete surface that was a road, then a storage yard, then a jetty. It stopped in front of a low brick wall. Bond and Griffith got out.

"Is this the place?" Griffith asked.

"Yes," Bond said. "This is the place."

He had seen it at once: the graffiti on the wall that had been present in the photograph. Now he could make it out in full. SOLIDARITÉ AUX MINEURS. Bond looked around. The fisherman and the boy were about twenty feet away at the end of the jetty. They had caught a couple of fish that lay in the dust. Bond saw the boy staring but knew there was no chance of being overheard.

He walked over to the water's edge and looked down.

This was where the dead man had been found. Bond remembered the photographs: the splayed arms, the three bullet holes. It was very likely, Bond knew, that he, too, would die violently. The thought didn't worry him. It could have happened already, while he was working for the secret service or during the war. There was, of course, a difference. Since Bond had been given his new status, the rules had changed. Death was now his business. He remembered M growling at him: *It was my decision to send an executioner.* That was what he had allowed himself to become.

Bond stared into the water and saw the reflection of himself. "He knew the person who killed him," he said.

"How can you be sure?"

"He came here for a meeting. There's no other possible reason. There's nothing here." Bond pointed in the direction of the two distant figures. The boy had turned to the older man and was whispering in his ear. "If anyone had approached, he'd have seen them. If he'd thought he was in danger, he'd have tried something. At the very least, he'd have turned and run. But he was shot in the chest and at close range. He just stood here and let them do it."

"You're right. But there is one other thing that might have brought him here." Griffith pointed toward a building on the other side of the water. It was an office, with three stories and three sets of windows identically spaced. Bond saw two large silver letters spelling out "FC" above the door. "Ferrix Chimiques," Bond said.

"Exactly. We're right on their doorstep. I don't think that's a coincidence."

"What time did you say we were coming?"

"Twelve forty." Griffith looked at his watch. "We ought to move—unless there's anything else you want to see."

"No. There's nothing here."

They walked back to the car and got in.

As they drove away, the fisherman and his son got to their feet. They were Corsican, but the boy's mother had been English. Age six, the boy had been struck down by meningitis, which had caused him to go deaf but which had left him with an unusual gift.

He could lip-read in three languages.

Now he repeated everything that Bond had said. The father nodded, patted his son on the head, and walked over to a telephone box, set back from the quay. He dialed a number. Like the French-African guard, he had no idea who he was talking to.

"His name is Jems. He is a friend of the Englishman who was killed. There are two of them, and they are going to the chemical company, Ferrix."

There was silence, then a click. The father hung up, then put his arm around his son. "*Ben battu, Paulu.*" Well done.

They walked off together, leaving the fishing rod and the two dead fish behind.

"THIS way, please."

The girl who had come down to the waiting room to collect them was slim and pretty, Bond thought. How old was she? Probably in her late twenties, although her china-blue eyes and straw-colored hair made her look younger. He could imagine her waking up in the morning and getting ready for work. She would probably have a two-bedroom flat, which she shared with another girl somewhere on the edge of Marseilles.

He followed her through a door and into an office with desks spaced out at precise intervals, men and women bent over typewriters. Nobody looked up as they passed, he noticed. They took a staircase to the second floor. Both Bond and Reade Griffith, walking beside him, were wearing suits despite the heat of the day. He hoped that he looked like a middle-ranking executive from a reasonably successful British company. The girl led them down a corridor and into a wide office where two windows framed an olive-skinned man who was sitting at a desk.

Bond looked through the windows to the extensive loading bay beyond. Men in overalls were shifting crates and oil drums, helped by forklift trucks that carried their loads into the open warehouses that surrounded them on three sides. More warehouses stretched out behind. The olive-skinned man stood up to welcome them. Andria Mariani, the managing director of Ferrix Chimiques, was smiling. Although the dark hair swept back over his forehead, the narrow eyes and aquiline nose had the effect of making him look both distant and disdainful.

"Good morning, Mr. Plover. And Mr. Howard, I believe. Please, will you be taking a seat. Coffee?" His accent was both French and Italian.

Bond and Griffith sat down. "No thank you, Mr. Mariani," Griffith said.

"That's good, then, Monique. You can go, please."

So the girl's name was Monique. Bond remembered the name he had seen on the back of the postcard at the Rue Foncet. He wished he had examined her more closely when she had greeted them. But she had already disappeared.

He forced his attention back onto the man sitting opposite him. "It's a pleasure to meet you, Mr. Mariani," he said. "As I'm sure my agent, Mr. Plover here, has informed you, I represent a corporation in London that has recently moved into the field of agronomy. We have acquired extensive farmland in the West Country, Wales and Ireland, and we need to buy large quantities of fertilizer and insecticide. I take it these are areas in which you operate."

"Mr. Howard, we operate at every area. Feedstock, fertilizer, medicine." He announced each word as if he had just found it in the dictionary. "Whatever you want, we can find it for you."

"Do you import from America?"

"From China, Korea, India, Vietnam . . . Many of our chemical product are from Asia. But also from America. Yes. Sometime."

"DDT?"

"DDT, sure. But there are better chemical now. Cheaper and more effective. You hear of toxaphene? Or maybe dieldrin." He was suddenly suspicious. "You know these product?"

"Of course," Bond replied smoothly. "Dieldrin is an organic chloride. It's developed in Denver, in America, I believe." He sighed. "And that's the problem, Mr. Mariani. Like everyone else in Great Britain, we have to deal with import quotas." He glanced at Griffith as if seeking his approval. "It might be helpful, actually, if we were able to, shall we say, obscure the country of origin."

Mariani's dark eyes flared. "Mr. Howard, this is a legitimate company. Nothing we do in this company against the regulation. Everything in white and black."

"My friend wasn't suggesting otherwise," Griffith cut in. "As a matter of fact, the paperwork is very important to us—"

"That's right." Bond picked up the cue. "My chairman is actually a stickler for detail."

"Stickler?"

"He likes everything written down. I'd be interested in looking at your accounts department and your billing systems. I presume that all happens here."

Mariani gestured vaguely. "Accounts on the floor underneath."

"Do you have many clients in London?"

Bond had changed the subject quickly. Griffith took over, going into details about quantities, costs, timings, export licenses, and logistics. The conversation was so ordinary that Bond had to ask himself why he was being so careful. The invoice that he had found in the Rue Foncet was in his jacket pocket. Why didn't he just bring it out and show it to the managing director? Wouldn't Mariani simply tell him what he wanted to know?

And yet Ferrix Chimiques was involved in some way with organized crime in the south of France. The copy of the invoice must have been stolen for a reason, and the man who had stolen it had been killed just five minutes away from where they were sitting. Bond had been told where the invoice department could be found. There were other ways to get the information he needed.

They finished. Mariani pressed a button on his telephone, then stood up and shook hands with both men. At the same time, the door opened and a second girl came in to escort them downstairs. Bond followed Griffith out of the room and back down two flights of stairs. They reached the main entrance, which had two glass doors.

Bond stopped suddenly and patted his jacket. "How very stupid of me," he said. "I've left my spectacles in Mr. Mariani's office."

"I will call up for you," the woman said.

"No need. I'll just run back up."

"We'll wait for you here." Griffith stepped in front of the girl to prevent her moving, and at the same time, before she could protest, Bond hurried back through the office and up the stairs.

He reached the first floor and found himself looking down a corridor with about half a dozen blank doorways facing each other on both sides. He noticed a red button—a fire alarm—set into the wall and, without a moment's hesitation, stabbed out with the heel of his hand. At once a bell began to jangle hysterically throughout the building. All along the corridor people appeared, streaming out of the doorways. Bond stood there as they brushed past him and down the stairs. He waited until the corridor was empty, then hurried forward in the opposite direction of everyone else.

He passed one empty room, then another. He heard the bang of a drawer, and a young man in a white short-sleeved shirt came rushing out carrying a sheaf of papers. Bond grabbed his arm.

"Le département des comptes. C'est où?"

The man pointed vaguely with his elbow, in a hurry to be away. The alarm was still echoing. Bond found the door that had been indicated and went in. He knew at once that he had come to the right place. The walls were lined with filing cabinets. There were two rows of desks, all abandoned with files left open and sheets of paper everywhere. Bond picked one up at random. It had the same format as the carbon copy, with an eight-digit number printed in the right-hand corner.

Bond drew the copy out of his pocket and memorized its number: 82032150. He had to find the original. He tried the nearest drawer. It was locked. He tried another, and this one slid open to reveal several hundred documents hanging in cardboard files. This batch ran from 00120206 to 00135555. He glanced at the dates and saw that they were four years old. The carbon copy belonged to a much more recent transaction.

He pulled open several more drawers before he found what he wanted. There was a clump of invoices, seven or eight of them, which had all been drawn up at the same time and which related to a single customer. The company hadn't been named but had the initials W.E. Quickly he found the one he wanted. The invoice had been issued to W.E. on a date nine weeks before, following the delivery of thirty gallons of a substance called acetic anhydride. He folded the sheet and slid it into his pocket. He slid the drawer shut, and at exactly that moment, the bells stopped. Bond straightened up and turned to see a matronly woman with bad skin standing in the doorway, looking at him with disgust.

"What are you doing in here?" she asked.

"I was looking for Mr. Mariani's office," Bond said innocently. "I think I left my reading glasses there."

"This is not an office. This is the accounts department."

"I know. I can see that. I was just about to leave." Bond smiled at her. "I hope there isn't a fire. What was that all about?"

"It was a malfunction. I will show you to the exit."

"Thank you. We can call up to Mr. Mariani from the reception desk. It was clumsy of me. I can't imagine how I forgot them."

"Please, will you come with me."

Bond followed the woman without saying anything more.

They had come to a set of doors.

And that was when three thoughts came to Bond. The first was that this was not the way he had come. The woman had led him further into the back of the building. The second was that he had dismissed her because she was stout and elderly. But although he had not spoken a word to her, she had addressed him in English, not French. She knew where he came from, which quite probably meant that she also knew who he was.

They were no longer alone. The third thought arrived too late for Bond to take action. A man had stepped out of a doorway behind him. He heard a footstep on the wooden floor and began to turn just as something flashed down in the corner of his vision. He felt it hit him hard on the back of the head, propelling him toward the woman, her dress becoming a world of blackness into which Bond folded himself, leaving consciousness far behind.

WHEN Bond came to, he found himself seated with his mouth gagged. His hands were securely tied behind him with some sort of metal wire, and his ankles were secured to the legs of the solid wooden chair on which he had been placed. His head was throbbing, but as far as he could tell, he hadn't been seriously hurt. Worse damage had been done to his self-esteem. He had allowed himself to be led into a trap, and now he was helpless and alone.

No. Reade Griffith was still in the compound and would come looking for him. The question was, would he arrive soon enough? Bond waited until he was certain that he was alone and then looked around him. He must have been taken to one of the warehouses he had seen from the office—somewhere on the edge of the complex, away from any witnesses. There were shelves on both sides of the room, with dozens of glass flagons, cartons, and packages arranged in long lines. Everything was covered in dust.

He heard a loud grinding, and somewhere out of his field of vision, a door slid open. It was followed by footsteps on concrete. The door slammed shut again, and he looked around to see four men walking toward him. A tendril of fear twisted through his stomach. He reminded himself that there were at least a hundred people working for Ferrix Chimiques, and quite a few of them must have seen him being brought here. It would be an extraordinary man who would rely, absolutely, on their silence.

That man stood in front of him.

Bond recognized Jean-Paul Scipio from the photographs he had seen both in London and in Nice. The photographs didn't do him justice. The actual physicality of the man—the amount of space he occupied—was breathtaking. He had taken his time as he crossed the warehouse, using a shooting stick to support himself. When he was facing Bond, he unfolded it and sat down. He rested his hands on his stomach, and Bond saw that he was wearing an assortment of rings—some gold, some silver, some set with precious stones—one on almost every finger. As he perched there, he looked for all the world like a cannibal king, one who had eaten his entire court.

Bond found himself staring into a face that had a strange babyish quality. It was utterly hairless, apart from two faint commas that were his eyebrows. Scipio was almost certainly bald. At close quarters the wig looked even less convincing than it had in the pictures, black and shiny, sitting lopsidedly on his skull. He had small pale blue eyes and a pursed, circular mouth with thick lips. As he moved his head from side to side, Bond noticed a dark mauve line stretching around his neck. This must be the scar that he had been left with when his throat was cut at the age of ten.

A second man stood just behind him, and Bond recognized him from the photograph at the Caravelle bar. This was Scipio's translator. He was a slender man, also bald. His face was dominated by eyeglasses that were two round discs held together by wire. He was expressionless, looking at Bond but hardly seeming to notice him.

And the other two men? They were dressed in black jackets and jerseys. One had a broken nose, disfiguring a face that had been ugly to begin with. Bond had seen their type before. They wore the blank faces of hired hands. One of them removed the gag from Bond's mouth. "*Bon dopu mezziornu*, Mr. Bond," Scipio said.

"Good afternoon, Mr. Bond," the translator began.

"*Sò quale vo site è perche site qui.*"

"I know who you are and why you are here."

Bond watched the double act with fascination. Scipio's voice was hoarse and high-pitched. There was something extravagant about the way he spoke. This was a man who had grown up in a world of vendettas and high drama, and he enjoyed acting the part.

But it was all to no purpose. The translator communicated in a way that was bland, matter-of-fact. Scipio might threaten his enemies with torture and death, but the translator would relay the words as if they were a weather report. "You are James Bond 007 of the British secret service," the translator continued. He had to adjust his sentences to keep up with the man who was speaking, occasionally backtracking as he struggled to find the right word. "It was a mistake for you to come here to the south of France. A friend of yours also came here, and attempted to impose himself on my . . . Mr. Scipio's . . . business affairs. He paid the price. Do your employers not understand that you have no place here? I have no interest in your country. But that is the arrogance of the British. You are a tiny island, but you still think you rule the world. You will not wake up to the fact that you are becoming irrelevant."

Scipio paused and ran a tongue between his lips. The translator was staring at him. "*Perchè vanu mandatu qui?*"

"Why did they send you here? Have I not made it clear that I have total control here in Marseilles—the port, the city, the police, the justice system? It is all mine!" He spread his hands to emphasize his point. "It seems that I must send a second message to London. And this time I am going to make sure they listen.

"You will carry that message. I could kill you here—I have only to give the order. But sometimes, Mr. Bond, there are worse things than death. This is what you are about to discover."

Even speaking was an exertion for Scipio, and he stopped to recover his breath. Bond chose that moment to answer back.

"We know who you are, Mr. Scipio," he said. "We know about your business here in Marseilles, but you may be surprised to learn that we aren't interested in you. You're just a low-level crook. I'm here for other reasons. And I should warn you that anything you do to me will be paid back tenfold. I would recommend that you run away and hide while you still can, although, looking at the size of you, I would imagine that might not be so easy.

"As for your remarks about my country, you wouldn't be the first psychopath to underestimate us. The last one ended up blowing his brains out in a Berlin bunker. We hanged all his associates. I'd get out now, while you have the chance."

The translator had been taken by surprise but had quickly begun converting the words into Corsican.

Scipio waited until he had finished, then began again.

"Bravely spoken, Mr. Bond. I have respect for you. In my country—in my original country—we expect our enemies to be courageous. Courage, as much as hatred, is the fuel of the vendetta. We will now put that to the test. I am going to send you back to your masters a different man to the one who is sitting before me. I am going to teach you a lesson. Carlo, Simone . . . *Appruntà ellu!*"

These last words were spoken not to Bond but to the two men who had been standing silently throughout the exchange. One of the men went over to the shelves and drew on a pair of thick rubber gloves. Then he reached up and grabbed a glass container with a transparent liquid inside. Meanwhile, his colleague had leaned over Bond and pulled his jacket back over his shoulders. Then he tore Bond's shirt open, exposing his chest and stomach. Bond watched as the first man walked over to Scipio, carrying the bottle.

"Hydrochloric acid." Scipio spoke the two words in English, and the translator repeated them before they continued in their separate languages. "It is also known as spirits of salt. One of the wonders of the human body is that we produce many quantities of hydrochloric acid in our gut, even though it has the ability to do us great harm. How much harm, you are about to discover, Mr. Bond. I would like, first, to give you a demonstration."

He nodded, and the man with the rubber gloves set the container down and opened it, being careful not to breathe in the fumes. The second man dragged a metal table across the floor. Then he went over to the shelves, chose an empty glass vial, and positioned it in the middle of the table. Carefully, the first man filled it with two pints of the liquid from the container. Even from where he was sitting, Bond could smell the chemical, and his eyes began to sting. When the vial was full, he screwed the lid back onto the container and carried it away. Bond could feel fear feeding his imagination.

"Show him!" Scipio instructed.

The man with the rubber gloves tilted the vial so that some of the liquid spilled onto the table. As it came into contact with the surface, there was hissing, and white smoke rose into the air. The metal bubbled and changed color, eaten away by the acid. Bond choked. For a moment he was blinded, but he could still hear the acid doing its work. Finally, the demonstration was over. The top of the table was pitted with holes. The chemical stink was in Bond's nose and throat. Inside he was screaming.

"I am certain you are a man with imagination," Scipio said. "You are not going to die today, Mr. Bond, but I want you to imagine that you return to London blind and disfigured. Your friends and colleagues will no longer be able to recognize you. It will be impossible for you to continue in your current occupation. You will spend the rest of your days in some sort of home, although I am told that the pain will never go away. In truth, it makes me sad to do this to you. You are a very handsome man. I admire good looks, especially in the masculine form. But as I have explained, I must send a message. Your people must learn to stay away."

Scipio stood up. He folded his shooting stick away.

"Wait!" Bond rasped.

Scipio made no reply. He simply nodded.

The henchman threw the contents of the vial into Bond's face.

Bond screamed. He felt the hideous liquid, ice cold with its first touch, splash into his face, his eyes, his bared shoulders and chest. At the same time, he jerked backward, overturning the chair and crashing down to the ground. The acid was burning into him. His chest and stomach were on fire. He was blind. He was . . .

. . . alone.

Scipio had gone. His men had gone with him. Bond was lying on his back with his arms trapped by the chair, his legs bent above him. He was covered in the liquid, but the pain had concentrated itself in the back of his head, where it had struck the floor. He was half out of his mind with the horror of it all, but he wasn't burning. His vision had cleared, and once again he could see.

It wasn't hydrochloric acid.

Bond had been through the worst agony he could imagine, but he understood now, just as Scipio had told him, it only had been his imagination. At some stage during the presentation, they had switched the vial, and it was chilled water that had been thrown into his face. The rest of it Bond had inflicted on himself, and even now, knowing the truth, he could still feel his system recoiling in shock. The sudden trauma might have killed an older man.

It had been a brilliantly conceived lesson in terror and power.

Later, much later, he heard the door grind open a second time and a man come hurrying in. Bond was still lying with his arms pinned behind him, his feet above his head.

"James?" It was Reade Griffith. The CIA man rushed over to him. "What happened to you? I've been looking for you all over. What have they done to you? Are you okay?"

"Scipio . . ." Bond was barely able to talk.

"He was here?" Griffith picked up the back of the chair, carrying Bond with it, tilting it back onto its legs. Bond's shirt hung open. "I'm going to have to find some wire cutters. Your wrists are bleeding. Hang in there. I'll be back in a minute."

Bond closed his eyes. For some reason Scipio had decided to give him no more than a warning. But what a warning! Bond found himself contemplating the sheer, cold-blooded brilliance of it. Bond knew that in the new world to which he belonged, it was vital to have the edge over his adversaries. If he didn't believe that he was stronger than them, he would never defeat them.

That edge had just been ruthlessly torn away. Sitting there, exhausted, Bond wondered how he would ever get it back.

CHAPTER 6

Shame Lady

LATER THAT EVENING, coming out of a hot shower with a glass of whiskey inside him, Bond felt better. He dried himself, got dressed, then wound a bandage around both wrists, concealing them beneath the cuffs of his ivory-white silk shirt. As he left the bedroom, he caught a glimpse of himself in the mirror and stopped to examine the blue-gray eyes, the lines of his jaw, the scar on his right cheek that he had come to accept as part of who he was. Just a few hours ago it could all have been taken from him.

He flicked the light off and went down to the Royal Lounge, where Reade Griffith was waiting for him. "I ordered bourbon on the rocks," he said as Bond took a seat. "I hope that's okay."

"Bourbon will be fine," Bond said.

A waiter brought the drinks over, and Bond lit a cigarette.

"So how are you feeling?"

Bond nodded. "Okay."

"Still going to the party?"

There was no need to ask. As well as the silk shirt, Bond was wearing a midnight-blue single-breasted suit with turnback cuffs, a charcoal grenadine tie, and black moccasin shoes. He looked completely relaxed. He lifted his glass, and the two men drank.

Although it had been left unsaid, they were both disappointed by the results of their visit to Ferrix Chimiques. W.E., the initials on the invoice, stood for Wolfe Europe, a subsidiary of Wolfe America, the company that Bond had heard about when he was in London. On the face of it, this was a significant development. The chemical import/export business was clearly connected to Jean-Paul Scipio and the Corsican syndicate. He might even own it. It seemed that Bond had found a connection to Irwin Wolfe.

But Reade Griffith had checked out the chemical compound Wolfe Europe had purchased, and there was a simple explanation for it. Acetic anhydride was used to convert cellulose to cellulose acetate—the main component of photographic film. "I don't get it." He sighed. "Your guy went to all the trouble to get the invoice. But it's meaningless! Wolfe has to buy his chemicals someplace, so he buys them from Ferrix Chimiques. What's the big deal?"

"The invoice could have been falsified."

"There were hundreds—thousands—of invoices in that place, James. You think they were all fake?" He thought for a moment. "Maybe you should talk to Monique."

"I'll see her tomorrow."

"And Madame 16 tonight?"

"I don't see why not."

"I'll tell you why not, my friend." Griffith lowered his voice. "Scipio knew who you were. He called you by your name and your number. There was only one person who could have given him that information. Her!"

Bond nodded, suddenly recognizing that there was a large part of him that wanted to believe in Sixtine. But all the evidence was against her. "They knew we were coming," he said gloomily. "They were expecting us. And for what it's worth, when I met her, I actually mentioned Ferrix Chimiques. I asked her about it."

"That wasn't too smart. She probably telephoned them the moment she left you."

"It does look that way."

Griffith jiggled the ice in his glass. He looked rueful. "I warned you about her, James. She's the spider in the web. She's living with Wolfe. She's met with Scipio. And now she's got you in her sights. Maybe I should tag along and hold your hand."

Bond smiled. "I think I can manage."

"Well, okay. But take care. We've had enough scares for one day . . . and I'm telling you, that lady scares me. Quite seriously."

Bond thought about the CIA agent's words as he drove past Villefranche and around the bay to the peninsula, which—though barely one square mile in size—had become the most elegant location in the world. There was something unassailable about the glamour of Cap Ferrat: the gardens and the walkways and the fabulous villas. At night, with the stars thrown across a black velvet sky, it was hard to imagine anywhere more perfect. Shame Lady was a brand-new construction, obviously built to impress. It sat in the wooded hills above the little port, rising up on white concrete legs. Huge square windows gave the occupants spectacular views of the coastline. It was embraced by the gentle curves of multiple terraces planted with olive trees, rose bushes, and tumbling ivy, but the main building was itself angular and hard. White marble steps led up to the front door. Two attendants with clipboards guarded the way. Bond was on the list. He was admitted.

The party was already in full swing. There was a jazz band playing, white-jacketed waiters somehow finding a way through the guests. Bond accepted a glass of champagne and sipped it approvingly, recognizing the delicate flavor of a 1934 Pol Roger. The guests chatted in French and English, plucking caviar on blinis, lobster tails and smoked salmon from silver trays.

He saw Sixtine entering the room from the garden, looking gorgeous in another Dior creation, this one pale pink, strapless, with a wasp waist. She was holding the arm of a man in a velvet dinner jacket and white evening shirt but no tie. Bond knew at once that this was Irwin Wolfe. He was not a large man, but he exuded confidence and control. He had a yachtsman's face, tan and chiseled by the wind. In his early seventies, he moved into the room with the ease of a much younger man. His eyes were pale blue but had a slightly glazed quality that suggested to Bond that he might be taking medication. He still had a full head of silvery hair. Together the two of them entered like film stars. Sixtine saw Bond and led Wolfe over to him. Bond noticed how close they were to each other, and a small part of him recoiled. Was he jealous? He had no time to answer the question. Suddenly they were in front of him.

"Irwin," Sixtine said. "This is the man I met at the casino. His name is James Bond, and he owes me 100,000 francs."

Wolfe held out a hand. "Nice to meet you, Mr. Bond." He had

a solid American accent. "What brings you to the Côte d'Azur?"

"Business," Bond replied. Wolfe was still clutching his hand with a surprisingly strong grip. "Import and export," he added.

"Oh, really? What, exactly?" The man was refusing to let go.

"Agrochemicals." Bond fell back on the same cover he had used at Ferrix Chimiques. "I represent a company that owns farmland in Great Britain."

"That's interesting." Finally, Wolfe released him. "So you met my baby girl in Monte Carlo?" He leaned over and kissed her awkwardly on the naked curve between her shoulder and her neck. She didn't try to push him away and seemed to enjoy his advances. "And I hear you gave her a good spanking!"

"Irwin, I don't know what you're talking about." Now she was coquettish.

"At cards, baby. At cards!"

Wolfe turned to Bond, suddenly serious. "So when did you get down here, Jim?" he asked.

"A couple of days ago." Bond felt the need to be polite and looked around him, trying to find something to say. "I have to congratulate you. You have a magnificent home."

"Oh, this little place isn't my home. I live in Los Angeles. I had this house built when I expanded my business into Europe. It took me two years to get the permission to build. Would you believe that? There was a little church up here, a run-down chapel that nobody used. It had been here for centuries, and that's about how long it took me to persuade them to let me knock it down. It was the same at Menton. I have a plant about twenty miles from here, and I said to the local authorities, 'You don't get around to giving me what I want, maybe I'll close down and take my business elsewhere.'" He rested his hand just above Sixtine's waist and jerked her closer toward him. "That quickly changed their minds."

"Irwin is in the film business," Sixtine explained.

"Sixtine here is fascinated by my work. She's always asking me about it. I can't understand why. I've never yet met a woman who understood technology." He lowered his hand to cup the curve of her bottom, and Bond was astonished that Sixtine didn't seem to mind. "That's the way I prefer it," he went on. "My first wife was good for three things. Boys. She gave me two sons. Boats. She was crazy about cruising. And bed." It was a formula he had used before. He challenged Bond not to be amused by it.

But Bond wasn't playing. "Are your sons here tonight?" he asked innocently. He knew the answer. A flash of something ugly glimmered in the man's eyes. "No. Both my sons are dead. They fell on the battlefield. In fact, they were taken from me on the same day."

"Oh. I'm so sorry."

"Don't be. Many Americans made sacrifices. I'd like to think where you Limeys would be right now if it hadn't been for us."

Sixtine sensed the atmosphere between the two men and cut in. "You mentioned boats," she said. "You should tell James about the *Mirabelle*."

"The *Mirabelle*!" Wolfe softened. "She's named after my first wife, and she's a beauty. Are you interested in cruise liners?"

"Very much so."

"The *Mirabelle* was built in your country, but I brought her down here to be fitted out. Twenty-four thousand two hundred and fifty tons, 680 feet in length. Fully equipped with all the latest technology from the anti-roll stabilizers to some sort of new-fangled funnel that stops smuts falling on the upper deck. She's set to make her maiden voyage."

"I'd like to see her."

"Then you should get your ass on board. But you'd better make it soon, Jim. We're weighing anchor Tuesday morning, eight a.m. We're allowing three weeks for the crossing. We could do it in half the time, but we're going to be dealing with any last-minute kinks, spending the first week just a mile off the French coast. It's a shame I can't invite you to make the trip with us. The mayor's going to meet us when we dock at the New York harbor. The vice president's hoping to fly in. We're going to have a party on board like you wouldn't believe. I've spent $1,000 on fireworks alone!"

Tuesday was four days away. "I'm sure I could look in before then," Bond said.

"Then why don't you arrange a time with Sixtine? She's going to be with me on the crossing. It wouldn't be a maiden voyage without a maiden, and it should be fun—just the two of us, with no passengers and five hundred and fifty cabins to choose from."

"Maybe you could come along tomorrow," Sixtine suggested.

"Sure. Tomorrow afternoon. How about teatime? You Brits like your tea, don't you! Let's say four o'clock."

"Four will be fine," Bond said. "Is she berthed in Marseilles?"

Wolfe shook his head. "No, she's here in Nice. Sixtine will make the arrangements." His hand was still resting on her obscenely. "Come on, honey. There are some people I want you to meet." He steered her away.

Bond stood where he was for a minute. He was still holding the Pol Roger, but suddenly he had no appetite for it. He twisted around and made his way out.

He was halfway down the steps when a voice called out his name. He turned and saw Sixtine.

Bond walked up to her. "Yes?" he asked coldly.

"Why are you leaving?" she asked. "You've only just arrived."

"It's been a long day, and I'm not really in the mood."

He might have left right then, but she held him with her eyes. "I want to talk to you. Come with me."

Without waiting for a reply, she walked into the shadows of the garden. Bond watched her for a moment, then followed. They came to a swimming pool surrounded by strange little plants with flowers that looked like pink dandelions. These were the shame ladies that Sixtine had described. Bond had seen them once in Jamaica and remembered being told that the leaves shrank when they were touched. That was why the name had been given to them. Sixtine continued walking toward a Japanese-style pavilion constructed at the far end of the pool. Inside, there were wicker chairs and cushions with floral covers. She threw herself down with her arms folded behind her. She glanced up as Bond arrived, but she had never doubted that he would come.

"Do you have a cigarette?" she asked.

Bond took out a packet of Du Maurier and handed her one. She looked at it disdainfully. "Canadian cigarettes named after a minor British actor. There's a place I go to in London. Morlands. You should give them a try. If you're going to pursue such a filthy habit, you might as well do it with style."

"To hell with you, Sixtine," Bond said. He lit her cigarette and one for himself. "Why did you invite me here? What do you want?"

She raised an eyebrow. "You're in a bad mood."

"You could say I've had a bad day."

"Have you? Do you want to talk about it?"

"I have a feeling you already know."

She didn't deny it. Instead, she blew out smoke and said, "You were looking for Scipio. Did you find him?"

"Yes."

"And?" Bond didn't answer, so she added, "I'm genuinely interested."

Bond turned on her. "I know who you are," he said. "I've seen your file. I know about the Kosovo papers. I know about some of the people who have been your victims."

"I prefer to call them clients."

"I'm sure you do. This may all be a game to you, but a friend of mine was killed—"

"You already told me."

"And I've been sent to find out who was responsible. Right now I'd say you're the most likely suspect."

"I told you. I never met him. Why should I want to get involved with the British secret service? I have my own reasons to be here, James, and although it might hurt your ego, you really ought to consider the possibility that they have nothing to do with you."

"Maybe you should let me make up my own mind about that."

"Maybe I don't care what you think."

"Then stop wasting my time." He paused and looked at her coldly. "Are you sleeping with Irwin Wolfe?"

If Bond had meant to insult her, he had succeeded. Her eyes flared. She stood up so that she was facing him, eye to eye. "What damned business is it of yours?"

"Are you?"

"What do you think?"

Bond couldn't help himself. He grabbed hold of her and pressed his lips against hers, holding her tight. He didn't know how she would respond. At that moment, he didn't care.

Finally, he released her. She took a step back. Her dark hair had tumbled across her eyes, which glinted with anger but also amusement. "Well, well, well!" she exclaimed. "The British spy can't get what he wants by consent, so he has to try force. Is this how you treat your women? I think I prefer Irwin Wolfe."

For a moment neither of them spoke. The jazz band had struck up another tune. It sounded a long way away.

"I invited you here because I like you and I'm interested in you," Sixtine said. "But you're going to have to take it one step at a time, James. Come to the *Mirabelle* tomorrow, and afterward we'll have cocktails and see if we can come to a business arrangement that satisfies us both."

"Is that all it is with you?" Bond asked. "Business?"

"Why else are we here?"

She brushed past him, and he watched her return to the house. Irwin Wolfe had stepped onto the terrace and was looking for her. Bond saw the two of them meet. The older man put his arm around her shoulders and swept her indoors. She took one look back as if trying to find Bond, and then she was gone.

BOND had been wrong about Monique de Troyes, the girl who worked at Ferrix Chimiques and whose first name and telephone number he had found on the back of a postcard. She did not live in a two-bedroom flat on the edge of Marseilles, but in a house with her parents in the neighboring town of Aubagne. But he'd been right about her age. She was twenty-seven. And she was pretty.

It had been easy enough to trace her address through the telephone number, and Bond was sitting in his car outside the house at eight o'clock the next day. It was a Saturday, so she would not be at work, and he hoped she had not gone away for the weekend. He had been waiting an hour when Monique finally appeared. She carried a basket, obviously on her way to the morning market. Bond got out of the car, closing the door behind him. The sound of it slamming shut must have attracted her attention, because she glanced across the road and then swerved away and began to walk quickly uphill. She had recognized him. Bond quickened his pace and caught up with her outside a chapel with two angels looking down on him, palms held up as if warning him to stay away.

There was nobody else in sight. Monique suddenly stopped and swung around. She was angry or perhaps afraid. Or both.

"What do you want?" she demanded, speaking in French.

"I need to talk to you," Bond said.

"I don't want to talk to you. Go away."

"I can't do that, Monique. I'm sorry. You knew a friend of mine, and I have to talk to you about him."

"Is this about Richard Blakeney?" It took Bond a moment to remember that this was the alias the dead man had used.

"Yes," he said.

"I don't want to talk about him. There is nothing I can tell you."

"You remember me."

"Of course. You came to Ferrix. You shouldn't have gone there." She clutched her basket as if she could use it for self-defense. "Please, monsieur. My parents have sent me to the market. I will get into trouble if I don't do as they say."

"Let me come with you."

"No! If I am seen talking to you, they will kill me. If they even knew you had come here, they would kill me."

"Nobody knows I'm here, and nobody is going to hurt you."

She looked up and down the street as if challenging him. But they were still alone, apart from the stone angels. She seemed to notice them for the first time and drew strength from them as if they were watching over her. She made her decision.

"I have to go to the market, but I will meet you afterward. There is a café near the station. It's called Le Papet. Wait for me there."

"Monique—it won't do you any good hiding from me."

"I have said I will come." Now there was anger in her voice. "I will be there in one hour." She turned and walked away.

The railway station at Aubagne is almost absurdly handsome. Painted a royal yellow with arched windows and ornate canopies, it could at a glance be the home of a retired ambassador or perhaps a small casino. It was built by an architect who believed in train travel, at a time when travelers enjoyed champagne and caviar on the Orient Express or listened to chamber orchestras playing Tchaikovsky on the Golden Eagle across Russia.

James Bond was sitting at a table just opposite with a view of the station clock that both told him how much time had passed and taunted him with the suggestion that Monique might not show up. The clock was showing twenty past ten when Monique finally appeared, crossing the road without the shopping basket she had been carrying earlier. She saw Bond and sat down opposite him.

"Can I get you a drink?" Bond asked.

"No, thank you."

"Don't be ridiculous. It's a hot day." He called to the waiter. "I'll have an Americano," he said. "With plenty of ice."

"And for madame?"

She hesitated, then relented. "*Un orange pressé.*"

The waiter swiveled around and left. He hadn't recognized Monique, but most of his customers were probably commuters.

"I don't know what you want," Monique began. "But I can't help you."

"You can start by telling me why you're so afraid."

"I already told you that." She looked left and right. All the other tables were unoccupied, but even so, she kept her voice low. "You wouldn't understand. You don't live here. But in Marseilles you have to be careful who you talk to and what you say—"

"Please, Monique. Don't waste any more of my time." Bond went in hard. "I know you were friends with Richard Blakeney. Maybe more than friends."

Her eyes filled with tears. But they were tears of indignation. "I didn't sleep with him! You are a pig to suggest that."

"But you were fond of him."

"I liked him."

"How did you meet him?"

She drew a breath, gathering her thoughts. "I don't even know who you are," she said. "You called yourself Mr. Howard when you came to the office. Is that your real name?"

"Does it really matter?"

"I suppose not. And maybe Richard also lied to me. I can see that the two of you are the same. Give me a cigarette!"

Bond held out the packet. She took one. He lit it for her.

"I met Richard about a month ago. He was at the station at Marseilles, and he said he couldn't find the right platform."

Bond almost smiled at the obvious pickup line. It wasn't one he would have used himself.

"He was also traveling to Aubagne. He seemed a nice man. He told me that he was working for an insurance company, and when we arrived, he asked me if I would like to have a drink with him. We came here. We sat at that table."

She pointed.

"He started asking me about Ferrix Chimiques, and of course I knew then that there was nothing accidental about our meeting. I should have told him to go away right then. It would have been better for both of us. But he was charming. He made me smile."

"What did he want to know?"

"He was interested in one of our clients, Wolfe Europe. He wanted to know what chemicals they had been buying from us. He asked me to look at the accounts and to bring him copies of any transactions that had taken place in the last six months."

Bond took out the carbon copy of the invoice that he had found in the Rue Foncet and unfolded it. "You took this?" he asked.

She examined it briefly and nodded. "I took fifty different invoices. I had to be very careful. I took four or five each time. He returned them all to me. Except this one."

"But what's the significance of this chemical, acetic anhydride? Wolfe Europe makes photographic film. It's part of the process."

"I don't know." She shrugged. "He didn't tell me."

The waiter arrived with the drinks. Monique had ordered fresh orange juice but seemed uninterested in it.

"What did he tell you about himself?" Bond asked.

"He didn't tell me anything, and anything he did say would have been untrue. He said he was working for an insurance company, but that was a lie, wasn't it? He's the same as you. You both want information. That's all. You don't care what happens to me."

"I do care what happens to you, Monique," Bond said, and meant it. "That's why I drove all the way to Aubagne. Nobody knows I'm here. After I'm gone we won't see each other again."

"They know everything!" Monique said. "I warned Richard when he asked me to steal the papers. But he didn't listen and they killed him. When I discovered that a body had been found at La Joliette, I knew it was him." She paused. "He said he was going to take me to Paris and London. But it was all lies. If he hadn't been killed, he would have gone away and forgotten me. Just like you."

They sat looking at each other. She hadn't touched her drink.

"Do you know who he went to meet the day he died?"

"No. He never told me anything." She stood up. "I have nothing more to say to you, Mr. Howard, and now I have to go back to my family. Please, leave me alone."

"Thank you, Monique. I'm sorry about Richard. You may not believe it, but I'm sure he cared for you. And for what it's worth, he was my friend."

"Do people like you have friends, Mr. Howard? I wonder."

She walked away from the table and crossed the road, heading toward the station. Bond waved for the bill. At the same time, he heard a car approaching. He knew at once that it was going too fast, and even as he registered the roar of the engine, he twisted around, dreading what he was going to see.

Monique was halfway across the road. She had stopped, freezing as she saw the black four-door Peugeot 202 Berline hurtling toward her. There were two men inside, but they were gone in a blur. Bond saw the car make contact. It had aimed for Monique quite deliberately. She was scooped up, twisting in the air. By the time she hit the tarmac, the car had traveled beneath her and was well on its way out of the town. Suddenly there were people on the pavement, coming out of the station, coming out of the bar.

Bond was up and running. He saw the car disappear around a corner and heard the scream of the tires. His own car was still outside Monique's house. There was no way he could follow them.

He reached the girl and knew at once there was nothing he could do. He had to fight back a sense of rising anger. How had they known? Bond had asked Sixtine about Ferrix Chimiques, but he had never mentioned Monique and he hadn't told anyone that he was coming here today. More than that, he had been careful driving out of Nice, making sure he hadn't been followed. Someone— the two men in the car—must have been watching the girl. They knew about the stolen carbon copy. The decision to kill her had already been made. It had just been a coincidence that Bond had been there to see it happen.

And what now? A police car had drawn up. Two uniformed men got out. Bond stood up and backed away, not drawing attention to himself. If anyone asked, he was just a tourist. He had nothing to do with her. He had just been passing by.

CHAPTER 7

Love in a Warm Climate

"IT'S GREAT TO SEE YOU, JIM. Welcome aboard."

The words grated in Bond's ears even as he took his last step off the gangplank and surrendered himself to the streamlined beauty and extravagance of the *Mirabelle*. Irwin Wolfe had been there to greet him, dressed improbably in naval whites complete with cap. Once again, Bond noticed the strange gleam in the man's pale blue eyes and wondered whether it was pain or fanaticism. For this was his creation, this floating world.

The *Mirabelle* was 676 feet long (Wolfe had rounded the number up) and eighty-five feet wide, with two propellers, each weighing twenty-eight tons and turning at two revolutions per second. The ship had three decks open to the elements: the sports deck, the sundeck, and the promenade deck. It was on the last of these that Bond was standing, with last-minute activity all around him.

Men were on their knees polishing the handrails and swabbing the decks. More men dangled over the side, cleaning portholes. An endless stream of supplies was being carried on board while a uniformed purser holding a clipboard shouted out instructions: "Midships, A deck 10. Forward, B deck 8. Forward, baggage room, R deck aft . . . And be careful with those!" This last command was directed at a team of workers carrying large cardboard boxes marked FEUX D'ARTIFICE, and Bond was reminded of the party Wolfe planned to throw once he arrived in New York.

There was no party atmosphere now. Instead, Bond was aware of a deadly seriousness. In just three days the turbines would hum into life, the propellers would turn, and the 25,000-ton vessel would slip its moorings and head out to sea.

"So what do you think?" Wolfe demanded. He waited, his eyes hungry for Bond's response.

"She's beautiful," Bond said grudgingly.

"The most beautiful ship on the seven seas!" Wolfe exclaimed. "What we've got here is simply the most luxurious way a human being will ever cross the Atlantic."

Before he knew it, Bond had Wolfe's hand on his shoulder and the two of them were walking toward the bridge as if they were old friends.

"We have just 200 first-class and 320 second-class cabins, although I could have fitted in twice that number if I'd wanted. But you travel on the *Mirabelle*, you get more space, your own private terrace, a separate bathroom, and proper beds. Why, if you book into one of our diamond suites, we'll throw in a Bechstein grand piano, a fireplace, a bar, and a personal butler to look after you."

Bond found it hard to focus on what the millionaire was saying. There was something about his voice—unctuous, self-satisfied— that Bond found almost repellent. The death of Monique de Troyes was still on his mind. To have gone from that to this in the space of just a few hours made him ashamed. He forced himself to look interested. He had to remind himself he was doing his job.

"I thought Sixtine was going to show me around," he said.

"Sixtine wouldn't be able to find her way around," Wolfe said.

"I thought this was the beautiful lady you'd come to see. The *Mirabelle!* If you want my advice, you'll leave that other lady alone."

"I didn't realize the two of you were so close."

"Close? Between you and me, Jim, I may have found me the next Mrs. Wolfe. I haven't popped the question yet, but give a woman a diamond the size of a ball bearing and you can be pretty sure of the answer. I'm going to leave it for the night we reach New York. Shame you won't be around."

Wolfe let go of Bond's shoulder and walked up to a man who had been waiting for them at the entrance to the first-class drawing room. He was also dressed in whites, which contrasted with his dark skin and jet-black hair.

"I'd love to give you the complete tour, Jim, but I'm a little busy right now. This is Dr. Borghetti. He'll take you into some of the main rooms. Then we can have that cup of tea and maybe Sixtine will join us." He turned to the doctor. "Take Mr. Bond into the main staterooms and show him a couple of the cabins. Then bring him to the Wolfe bar. Okay?"

"Right, Mr. Wolfe."

"I'll catch up with you later, Jim. Enjoy yourself!"

Wolfe left, walking back in the direction he had come from. Bond examined the doctor. He was, Bond thought, surprisingly ugly, with a fussy little mustache decorating an otherwise bland face. The color of his skin couldn't quite disguise the acne that had disfigured him as a child and left its mark around his neck and chin. Borghetti forced himself to smile. He spoke English badly.

"This way, please." The doctor opened the door, and for the next forty minutes Bond explored the sumptuous interior of the *Mirabelle*. They began on the upper decks: the dining saloon, the smoking room, the library, the lounges. Bond had never seen so much shining chrome and Lalique glass, so many fine Persian rugs and onyx tables. And yet without laughter and music, without women in long dresses and men in black tie, the *Mirabelle* had about as much allure as a furniture showroom. As they continued, Bond became aware of one peculiarity. The ship was equipped with an extraordinary number of fire extinguishers. Everything else was so exquisite that the ugly red cylinders really stood out, particularly as there were so many of them. Bond was surprised that the designers had been so careless. And why remind the passengers, so overtly, of the dangers of a fire?

The doctor was less than friendly as he guided Bond from area to area. From the passenger decks, they passed through a service door and down a series of staircases to the engine rooms. This was a completely different world of snaking pipes and cables. Every inch of space was taken up with the complicated equipment that would power this huge ship. A fifty-strong crew was going through a series of last-minute checks, calibrating the brand-new machinery. Eventually the doctor took him back to a bar that seemed to have been modeled on the Savoy in London—all dark wood and plush—and which the ship's owner had named after himself. Bond was relieved to see that the promised tea had not been served. Also, Sixtine had arrived. She was sitting in a velvet armchair, smoking a cigarette, looking as if she would rather be somewhere else.

"So what do you think?" Wolfe demanded.

It was the sort of question that could only have one answer. "She's magnificent," he said. Then he added as an afterthought: "You seem quite nervous about her."

"Nervous?"

"I've never seen so many fire extinguishers," he explained. "I suppose you must be worried about a short circuit or something."

Wolfe smiled without humor. "I'm not worried about anything, Jim. Every last detail on this boat has been thought out, and we've got the sea trials starting in three days to pick up any issues." He jabbed with a finger, making his point. "But when you've spent over $2 million on a project, it makes sense to protect your investment. I guess you wouldn't understand these things."

"I quite understand," Bond said affably.

"Irwin has bad news," Sixtine said in a voice that didn't sound too sorry at all. "He's canceling tea."

"That's right." Wolfe nodded. "I'm heading out to the plant at Menton. I have some business that needs taking care of."

"I'll come with you!" Sixtine spoke casually, but Bond got the feeling that somehow it mattered to her.

"That's not a good idea, honey. You'd only get in the way. I'll see you tomorrow."

"But you promised you'd take me out there, Irwin. You know I'm keen to learn about your work. And this is my last chance if you're leaving on Tuesday."

"I'm sorry." Wolfe gave her a thin smile. "It won't work for me right now, and anyway, I've already told you, there's nothing out there that would interest you. You really want to learn about film production, you can visit my plant in Massachusetts."

"But I'm here right now."

"Honey, let's not argue about it, okay?"

There was no point continuing. Sixtine stubbed out her cigarette and stood up. "All right, then. I'll go home and have an early night. The south of France isn't any fun without you."

Wolfe pulled her toward him, kissing her on the side of the cheek. "You mind showing my guest off the ship?" he asked.

"Of course," she said. "And don't worry. I'll make sure he doesn't set fire to anything on the way."

"Good to see you again, Jim." A handshake. "Next time you come to America, you know how to get there."

"I certainly do."

Bond and Sixtine left together, taking the gangplank down to the quayside of the port of Nice. Bond had walked over from the Negresco, but Sixtine had driven. A bright red two-seater MG TD was waiting for them on the forecourt with its hood folded back.

"Come with me," she said without looking at him. She opened the door of the little car and climbed in.

"Where to?" Bond asked, climbing in beside her. "Are you going back to Shame Lady?"

She shook her head. "No. I don't like being there on my own."

"Isn't Wolfe going to turn up later?"

"I like it even less when he's with me."

"Then where?"

She reached into the glove compartment and took out a pair of sunglasses, then turned the key in the ignition. Bond listened appreciatively to the throaty growl of the tiny 1,250-cc engine. "Let's make it a mystery tour," she shouted. "It's not very far, and it's going to be a beautiful evening."

She was right. The sun was already setting as they roared out of Nice, following the coastal road toward Cannes, with the Mediterranean a deepening scarlet on their left. They came off the main road at Antibes and dropped down the Boulevard du Cap until it reached the end of the headland. Here a narrow lane continued steeply downhill. Sixtine spun the wheel and drove through the open gate of a small old-style house with pink walls, tumbling bougainvillea, and a paved courtyard planted with lemon trees and olives. Without asking, Bond knew it was hers.

The house wasn't locked. Sixtine led him into a living room with French windows that opened onto a small garden with a swimming pool running its full length to one side. With the warm touch of the evening, everything smelled of pine and eucalyptus.

"Will you have a glass of Dom Pérignon?" she asked.

"I'll join you."

"Of course."

She put on a record. It was an Édith Piaf album, *Chansons Parisiennes*. Then she went into the kitchen, leaving Bond to admire the furniture—antique but comfortable—and the modern art. A moment later she was back, holding a bottle and two glasses.

"I've always liked Antibes," she said. "Nice and Cannes are already spoiled and overcrowded. In a few years' time they'll be impossible. When I'm here, I feel like I'm hiding from the world."

"I can't imagine you hiding from anyone."

"You'd be surprised."

"So why have you brought me here?"

"Why did you come?"

She looked at him, and he saw the amusement in her eyes. At the same time, he felt the desire that had taken hold of him the night before. He caught hold of himself. "I've had enough of this. Why do you have to treat everything like a game?"

"Because it is a game. Haven't you noticed?"

"For you, maybe. Not for me." He turned on her. "What are you doing in this country? You don't love Irwin Wolfe, so why are you with him? He's talking about marrying you, for God's sake!"

She threw her head back and laughed when she heard that. "Maybe I'll get a boat named after me. Can you see me as the next Mrs. Wolfe? The first one killed herself, you know. She threw herself out of the ninth floor of a building. He says she fell. But even he doesn't believe it."

She poured the champagne, but Bond shook his head. "Not for me, thank you. You asked me why I came here. Well, it wasn't to drink champagne with you. I want information."

"You're becoming tiresome, James. That's what you said the first time we met. And I told you: I don't give anything away."

He took a step toward her. "This time it's going to be different. You're going to tell me what I want to know."

"Oh, yes? And how do you propose to get it out of me?"

It was all the invitation he needed. He drew her against him, pressing his mouth onto hers. He could feel her against his chest and swept his arms around her, drawing her close. He didn't expect her to resist and was surprised to find both his wrists suddenly clamped in her hands. For a moment he stared at her, puzzled. Had he misread the signals? But then, with a mischievous smile, she lowered herself onto her knees, pulling him down onto the rug with her. Bond got the message. If this was going to continue, it would be on her terms.

Kneeling on the rug, locked in her arms, which were still warning him to keep his distance, Bond examined the deep brown eyes, the lips, the voluminous black hair. The years had given her an aura of experience and confidence that he found strangely attractive.

Slowly she nodded. The music had changed. He could hear "La Vie en Rose" around him.

Bond pulled her toward him.

Afterward, when they had finished, she stood up and walked out of the room, leaving Bond on his own. Bond got dressed and threw back his champagne, then helped himself to more. When Sixtine returned, she was wearing a satin dressing gown fastened at the waist. Her hair was wet. She had been in the shower.

"Well, if that's your interview technique, I have to say I like it," she said. She noticed his glass. "I see you've helped yourself."

"I hope you don't mind."

"Of course not." She found a packet of cigarettes and lit one. "I have some fresh fish and salad in the refrigerator, and I have a decent bottle of Puligny-Montrachet. Will you stay for dinner?"

"I'd like that," Bond said.

"You can lay the table—the one in the garden." She pointed. "The plates are in the cupboard."

She went into the kitchen. Bond opened the cupboard and found plates and cutlery. He carried what was needed outside, thinking it had been years since anyone had asked him to lay a table.

A few minutes later she joined him, holding the wine, which she held out for him to open. "I bought the house just after the war," she said. "I like to have as many properties as possible. I never know where I'm going to be."

"There are a lot of things I want to know about you," Bond replied. "But to be honest, I don't give a damn when you got this house." Suddenly he was disgusted with himself . . . this playacting. "Sixtine, a friend of mine was shot in Marseilles. And this morning a pretty girl was run over and killed in front of my eyes simply because she'd met the wrong man. You have a beautiful house, and this is a beautiful part of the world, but it's all been poisoned. Scipio and his men, Ferrix Chimiques, Irwin Wolfe . . . There's something ugly going on, and whatever may have happened between you and me, that's the only reason why I'm here."

She stopped and looked at him, and he saw that he had hurt her.

"You're right," she said. "I understand exactly what sort of man you are, James, and I know why you're here. But we have this moment together, so why don't we enjoy it. Let's have dinner together like two people who have found each other and who have just made love." She paused, allowing her words to sink in. "And then I'll tell you everything you want to know."

CHAPTER 8

Secrets and Lies

THEY HAD DINNER IN THE GARDEN with the swimming pool shimmering behind them and the stars crowding out the night sky. For a while they didn't speak. There was a part of Bond that was uneasy. As much as he now saw that it was inevitable they should have become lovers, he was worried that he had confused the situation. It was still quite possible that she was his enemy.

As if sensing what was on his mind, she leveled her eyes on him and said without emotion: "Do you still want information?"

"Yes."

"I thought we might enjoy the evening together."

"I'll enjoy learning more about you."

She considered. "What do you want to know, James? Was I responsible for the death of your friend? No. Or the girl this morning? I don't even know who she was. You asked me what I was doing here in the south of France. Why should I tell you? You know nothing about me, and unless it's connected to your work, you care even less."

"You're wrong." Bond lifted his wineglass and swirled the honey-colored liquid. "I want to know everything about you. Not just what you're doing here in France. You're obviously quite an operator. My office in London has a healthy respect for you, and I can see that you've enjoyed putting me in my place. But why don't we leave the games behind us now. If we're both on the same side, it seems crazy to have secrets from each other."

"If we're both on the same side . . ." She let the words hang in the air. "All right." She held out her glass, and Bond refilled it. "But if you betray me, I will never forgive you, James. More than that, I will make sure you regret it."

Bond said nothing. He waited for her to begin.

"You may be surprised, but I was born in New Zealand. My father was from France. He was an engineer, and he'd been invited down there to work on the main trunk line from Auckland to Wellington. My mother made dresses. I was there for the first five years of my life, and I remember almost nothing about that time except that I felt bored and trapped. I was glad when the work finished and my father announced that we would move back to Paris. How could I have known that we were going to arrive just in time for the outbreak of a world war?

"There were guns everywhere. The Germans were getting closer and closer—at one stage they were just fifteen miles away.

"By now my mother was working in a defense factory. My father got a job helping to build the railway from Montparnasse to Porte de Vanves. I didn't see either of them very much. I was looked after by a neighbor, an old lady who talked to her cats. In a way, those days made me what I am. I learned to be self-sufficient."

She fell briefly silent, looking into her wineglass as if it could provide some window into her past life. Eventually, she went on.

"On August 30, 1914, my mother was killed by a German bomb that fell onto the Rue des Vinaigriers when she was on her way home from work. It was a completely random event. A German pilot was flying a Taube. That's the German word for 'dove.' He dropped three bombs by hand. It was the third bomb that killed my mother. . . . As far as I know, she was the first civilian ever to be killed in an air raid. It was completely hushed up at the time. The French were worried about morale. My father only told me what had really happened a few weeks before the war ended.

"By that time, everything was over for him. He hadn't been able to cope after my mother died. He was drinking heavily. He didn't eat. I wasn't at all surprised when I came home from school one day to find the neighbor sitting in our empty flat. She told me he was dead. She said he died of a broken heart, but it's more likely that he killed himself. I never found out. What difference did it make to me? Either way, I was alone.

"When the war ended, I was sent to England. It turned out that

I had an aunt who lived in London, in Pimlico, and she agreed to take me in. I don't need to tell you very much about the next few years. I grew up. I went to secretarial college and started working for an insurance company in Knightsbridge. The girls there used to talk about the boys they were seeing, and I wondered how much longer I was going to be alone. And then I met Danny."

She reached for her cigarettes. She smoked Morlands, the brand she had mentioned. Her cigarette was slim and elegant, with a single silver band. She lit it, and the flame leaped up briefly.

"Danny Salgado—that was what he called himself," she went on. "We bumped into each other outside Knightsbridge station, quite literally, and he invited me for a drink. He was dark-haired, a few years older than me, expensively dressed. He had an extraordinary charm. I'd never met anyone like him.

"Danny told me that he was a business adviser. He was always traveling, and he always went first class. Later on I discovered he had three passports. I found out a lot of things about Danny but only when it was too late. He took me for dinner that night—to Kettner's in Soho. Everyone seemed to know him. He bought champagne, and when it was time to pay, he scattered five-pound notes like they were meaningless to him. 'Plenty more where that came from, Jojo,' he would say.

"Danny and I married, and I was very happy for the first couple of years. He gave me a generous allowance. We traveled together— to Cannes, to Vienna, to Rome, and to Malta. We stayed in the best hotels and went to wonderful restaurants. Danny was a gambler, and he took me with him to the casinos. He was the one who introduced me to *vingt-et-un*. He taught me how to memorize the order of a pack of cards and how to work out how many cards the dealer was holding just by glancing at his hands. I spent hours learning that, because I wanted to please him.

"My love affair with Danny ended pretty much the day I got pregnant," Sixtine said. "Although I didn't see it at the time. He was so happy when I told him. But he no longer felt comfortable with me. Suddenly he was traveling more. He'd often been away for days at a time, but after the baby was born—it was a boy, Julian—it became weeks. I never complained. I had been married to him for five years before I discovered the truth.

"I should have known from the start. Perhaps I had known and all along I'd just been pretending. There were the three passports, the different names. There had been telephone calls in the middle of the night, strange men who never announced their names arriving at the flat. And the money! Envelopes full of banknotes with no real explanation about where it was all coming from. He was a crook. I learned the truth from a Scotland Yard detective called Jack Travers who came looking for him and who took pity on me. Danny had started his career as a confidence trickster. No surprises there. He was what was called 'the roper' for a well-organized gang who worked in London. The roper is the one who pulls in the mark, which was exactly what he had done with me. All it takes is a lot of charm and plausibility.

"Recently, he'd branched out. He'd set up a racket forging National Health and Unemployment stamps. They were being printed in Poland, and he was selling them through gangs that he was meeting in different parts of London . . . the Hoxton Mob and the Elephant Boys. He was a familiar figure, hanging out at clubs and racecourses. It seems that everyone knew him. Except me.

"And I suppose it goes without saying that I wasn't the only woman in his life. Danny had girlfriends all over London. I'd constructed this little dream of being a wife and a mother when I was just a convenience. I'm not even sure why he married me, although later on I found out that Salgado wasn't his real name, so the whole marriage was null and void, part of the pretense."

The evening air was getting cooler. Sixtine drew the robe closer around her. Bond lit another cigarette.

"Don't worry," she said. "I'm not going to talk all night. You said you wanted to know everything about me. Well, I'll spare you that. This is the edited version. Do you want me to go on?"

"You can talk as long as you like," Bond said.

She drank the rest of her wine and pushed the glass away.

"I left Danny. We didn't have any confrontation. I simply took my son and went back to Aunt Lucy. She'd been expecting me. My old room was ready for me, and there was another room up in the attic for Julian. I'll say one thing for Danny. He still sent me money every week. I don't know whether it was for me, for his son, or just for his conscience, but I didn't have to go back to work. I never saw him again. It was better just to live with the memories.

"When the money stopped, I knew it could only mean one thing. I went back to Travers, and he told me exactly what I expected to hear. Danny had been shot dead by one of his gangster friends. In the last few years of his life, he'd allowed gambling to consume him and he'd been cleaned out by the casinos. I wondered how he'd found the money to send to me. Travers smiled when I asked him that. It seems he'd been dipping his hand in the till, stealing from his associates. That was what got him killed." Sixtine shivered. "Let's go back inside. I'm getting cold."

They went into the living room. Sixtine sat on the sofa, and Bond sat opposite, waiting to hear the end of the story.

"Another war was on the way, and part of me was glad," she continued. "I wanted a new world to explore. I was thirty years old when war was finally declared. Aunt Lucy had a friend who taught at Imperial College, and knowing that I spoke fluent French, he suggested I apply for a job at somewhere called Bletchley Park. It was all top secret, and I shouldn't be talking to you about it even now. I went for an interview, and the next thing I knew, I'd signed the Official Secrets Act and I was on my way to Buckinghamshire. Julian stayed in London with Aunt Lucy.

"I was at Bletchley for most of the war. I started in naval intelligence. My job was to look out for any words in French and German that might be of interest and put them down on cards for cross-referencing. I worked long hours, but I was very happy there. The work I was doing was important. I didn't have to think about the rest of my life, about Danny, about any of it.

"And then, in the summer of 1943, the same professor who had recommended me to Bletchley came calling a second time—only now he wanted me to join an organization I'd never heard of and which, he said, would put my life in danger. I knew at once that he wanted me to become a spy. He was talking about the SOE."

Sixtine shivered again, but this time Bond knew it wasn't because of the cold.

"I was recruited and sent to Scotland for training in field craft, weapons, demolition, night-and-day navigation, and all the rest of it. I was thirty-four by then, and I found it completely exhausting. Then it was off to Beaulieu for cryptography, weapons, escape and evasion techniques, Morse . . . I know you were in naval intelligence, James, so this is all probably very familiar to you."

"How do you know?" Bond interrupted. "When we first met, you knew my name and everything about me. How did you get that information?"

"You think I've been spying on you?"

"It's what I assumed."

"Well, you're wrong." She paused. "Irwin Wolfe told me about you. He even showed me your photograph and warned me to keep away from you."

Bond considered what she had said. He still wasn't sure if he should believe her. "That's very interesting. But you were telling me about your work with the SOE . . ."

She took the cigarette that Bond was smoking, used it to light her own, then handed it back. "I was given the code name of Sixtine and sent out for the first time at the end of 1943. My job was to join the Stockbroker Circuit as a courier, relaying messages in and out. Stockbroker had developed a method of sabotage, in which they'd hijack a locomotive and send it rushing down the tracks. Eventually it would crash into another locomotive or a building without any need of explosives. I was with them for three months, and it always struck me as funny. My father had been creating the French railway system, and here I was with the people who were destroying it. I wondered what he would have thought.

"I was sent into France three times, and on the third time, my luck ran out. I was arrested by the Gestapo one day after I parachuted into northern France and a week before D-day. Of course, I'd been betrayed. They knew I was coming."

Bond could see the memories tearing through her and reached out to hold on to her—but she shrugged him away.

"I'm all right. A lot of people were hurt in the war, and I was just one of them. But there was something that hurt a lot more, although I only found out about it later." She took a deep breath. "When I parachuted into France that third time, the Germans were waiting for me. I fell right into their arms. But it was only later I discovered that the SOE had been aware of this all along. They knew that I would be arrested, interrogated, and probably killed. There were whole networks—Stockbroker, Prosper, and many others—that had been infiltrated by the Germans. But the SOE were playing a double game. They didn't want the Germans to know that they knew. They wanted to distract their attention from the Normandy landings, and if that meant sacrificing people like me, then so be it. And believe me, I wasn't the only one.

"Yes, James, I'm still alive. But when I got back to England, and when I understood what had been done to me, how I had been manipulated, a large part of me died. It's still dead now."

She didn't want to smoke any more of her cigarette and stubbed it out, the sparks rising around her fingertips.

"That was when I decided I would never allow a man to tell me what to do again," she went on. "I would have no allegiance to anyone—and not to any country. I would go into business for myself. I kept the name, Sixtine, because it was also a number and it seemed right that I should set aside part of my humanity. It's something you and I have in common. They call you 007 because they know it will make it easier for you to kill brutally and without remorse. They have taken part of your humanity, too."

Bond didn't believe what Sixtine was saying. He knew there had been double agents within the Special Operations Executive. But he couldn't believe that there had been some sort of conspiracy running through the upper echelons of the organization, and he was tempted to argue with Sixtine.

He decided to stay silent. He had to see this through to the end.

"I don't think of myself as a number," he said. "I've already told you why I choose to do the work that I do. But there are two things I want to ask you. The first is, what happened to your son, Julian? You haven't mentioned him."

She made a vague gesture with one hand. "He's in the Bahamas. I have a house there, and he's happier away from me."

"And you still haven't told me what you're doing in the south of France. What about Irwin Wolfe? I know you don't love him. I imagine you don't even like him. What do you want from him?"

Bond waited. The entire conversation had been leading to this.

"I'll tell you," she said. "Because I don't want there to be any secrets between us and it may be that we can even help each other." She paused. "Irwin is a sick man. I think he's dying. He takes about a dozen pills every day, but they're not helping him anymore. The strange thing is, his illness only makes him more determined. He's developed a new product, which could make him another fortune—even if it's one he'll never get to spend." She paused. "Do you know anything about Technicolor film?"

"I know a little. I don't often go to the cinema. I've always found more interesting things to do in the dark."

She nodded. "I'm sure. Well, the basic process of Technicolor is very simple. The colors are divided into three basic components: red, green, and blue. The trouble is, it demands three separate negatives, and that causes complications."

She was businesslike, as if everything she had been saying for the last hour had been forgotten. Bond observed her with a sense of admiration he had rarely felt for a woman. Child, orphan, wife, mother, widow, secret agent, prisoner, and self-confessed criminal, she had managed to break down her life into separate compartments with a ruthlessness that had ensured not just her survival but her success. Bond had never met anyone quite like her.

"Multiply the negatives and you divide the light," she went on. "So you have to use a lot more lighting when you're shooting the film. And that makes it much more expensive.

"But Irwin, or the people working for him, has invented a type of 35-millimeter color negative stock that has a much wider latitude. It's good for indoor and outdoor photography. He calls it G-Vision, and it's going to put Technicolor out of business. Which is where I come in. There are certain people I know who want the formula. They've paid me a considerable amount of money to steal it."

So that was it: industrial espionage, as simple as that. "He produces this new film stock at his plant in Menton," he said.

"That's right. Or at least, that's what I believe. I've been cozying up to him, trying to get him to give me a tour, but Irwin has been completely silent about what he gets up to in his secret compound in the woods. He's leaving France on Tuesday morning, and without him here I won't get another chance. I even went out and took a sneaky look for myself, and you'd think he was manufacturing nuclear bombs the amount of security he's hired. There are two fences, the inner one electrified. He has armed guards on twenty-four-hour patrol and guard dogs. I can't say I blame him. He's sitting on something that could be worth millions of dollars.

"Today was my last chance. I knew he was going to Menton this afternoon, and when I met him on the *Mirabelle*, I really expected him to take me with him. It was what he'd promised."

"And if he had taken you in—what, then?"

"I'm good at improvising. Anyway, it looks as if I'm going to have to fall back on an alternative plan." She looked at Bond. "Meeting you could be exactly the break I need."

"You think I'm going to help you steal commercial secrets?"

"Why not? Maybe I can help you find out what's going on around here. You say this part of the world is poisoned. I agree. There's definitely something nasty in the air. Scipio may look like he's just walked out of a circus, but he's extremely dangerous. Trust me, you don't want to go after him on your own."

Bond was reminded of his confrontation with Scipio. Describing him as dangerous was an understatement. He was a monster.

"Why did you meet him at La Caravelle?" Bond asked.

"I already told you," Sixtine said. "Scipio heard I was in Marseilles. He knew who I was. He invited me to meet him, and there was no way I could refuse. He wanted to know that I wasn't up to anything that might interfere with his business."

"What is his business? From what I understand, he's given up narcotics."

"I have no idea. I didn't ask, and he didn't say."

"Did you tell him why you were here?"

"No. I led him to believe that I was a gold digger trying to get my hooks into Irwin's fortune. And he believed me. It fits with his view of women. I don't think he likes us very much."

She yawned, and Bond glanced at his watch. It was ten o'clock. "I should leave," he said.

"I was hoping you'd stay." She looked at him with laughter in her eyes. "I'm going to bed, and you're going to come with me. I'm sure you've had plenty of girls, James, but you've never had a woman and you've still got a lot to learn." He was about to protest, but she stopped him. "Don't say anything. We've talked enough. If there's more to be said, we can do it in the morning."

There was a staircase opposite the kitchen, and she climbed up with Bond following. The bedroom was small and pretty, with an antique bed and two windows leading out onto a terrace. She turned as he came in. "No more talking," she said.

It was only the next morning, as the sun came up, that they spoke again. Bond was woken by Sixtine slipping out of bed and padding barefoot out of the room. When she returned, she was carrying something in her hand. "I want you to have this as a souvenir of our time together," she said. "You can use it when you buy yourself some decent cigarettes."

It was a flat cigarette case made out of gunmetal. When Bond opened it, he saw that there were four words inscribed in the lid: FOREVER AND A DAY.

"I bought it for Danny," she explained. "On the day we got married, he said he wanted to be with me forever, but I told him that wasn't enough. I wanted forever and a day. I had this made for our anniversary, but he was dead before I could give it to him. So I want to give it to you."

"I thought you hated Danny," Bond said, closing the lid.

"Did I say that? No. How can I hate him? He's part of my story, and that story brought me to you."

Bond reached out for her, and as the first rays of the morning sun stretched across the wooden floor, she slipped into his arms.

CHAPTER 9

Down to the Wire

THE ROAD FROM MENTON is a gift to thrill-seekers. It climbs steeply through a series of hairpin bends with dazzling views of the Mediterranean Sea before plunging into the dense forests of the Alpes-Maritimes. It feels like nothing has changed here in a thousand years. Saracen fortresses, or the remains of them, still stand guard over rocky crags, and villages cling to hilltops. It's a world apart from the coast of the Riviera.

Bond and Sixtine had enjoyed a late breakfast in Menton. The sun was hotter than ever, and the mountains had thrown an overprotective arm around the little community, preventing any breeze from reaching its tightly packed streets. By the time they had finished their meal, they were glad to climb back into the MG and set off with the wind streaming over their shoulders.

Bond wanted to take a look at the plant where Wolfe Europe manufactured its new film stock, and Sixtine had agreed to take him. It was still hard to believe that Irwin Wolfe was involved in any criminal activities, but at the same time, he certainly appeared to be at the center of a web that stretched across the south of France. A British agent had been sent to look into the activities of the Corsican syndicates. He had been killed in Marseilles, close to a chemical company either owned or operated by Jean-Paul Scipio. Wolfe was a customer there. The link had been made. Scipio and Wolfe. Visiting the plant when it might not be possible even to penetrate the perimeter fence might seem like a waste of time, but it was a Sunday, the weather was glorious, and right now there wasn't anywhere that Bond would prefer to be.

The road took them through Castellar, one of the many *villages perchés*, where they were forced to slow down behind a donkey and a cart piled up with watermelons. "One day," Bond said, "I want to spend a week with you in a village like this. We'll sit in the sun and drink wine and pretend there aren't any bad people in the world."

"A week?" Sixtine looked at him scornfully. "You'd get bored in three days."

The donkey shifted forward. Seeing an opportunity, she touched the accelerator and sent the little car in a wide curve around it.

Still climbing, the road seemed to go into contortions as if trying to shake them from its surface. They almost missed the turning. There was a low sign with the letters w.e. and an arrow, but it was the lane itself that gave the game away. The bitumen was brand new, and the grass had been cut back to reveal the edges. Sixtine pulled into a clearing between two trees. The car, only a few feet from the main road, was completely invisible.

"We'll walk from here," she said. "If they hear the engine, they'll know we're coming."

Before they'd left Nice, Sixtine had driven Bond back to his hotel and he had changed into a short-sleeved cotton shirt, trousers, and nubuck saddle shoes. He'd chosen shades of brown and gray so that he would blend in with his surroundings. He had also picked up his Beretta, now tucked reassuringly into his waistband.

He nodded. "After you."

They set off, keeping a line of trees between themselves and the edge of the new lane. After about ten minutes Sixtine held up a hand and they stopped. "There it is," she whispered. "They're still working, even though it's a Sunday. I don't think they ever stop."

Bond looked through a gap in the foliage and saw a metal fence. It was about ten feet high, disappearing through the trees on either side of the lane. There was a solid-looking barrier that rose and fell electronically and, next to it, a two-story office and administration block made out of gray concrete with searchlights and radio antennae mounted on the roof. Two men were standing outside, both dressed in dark blue uniforms. Bond could make out the letters w.e. on their jackets. It was more like the entrance to a high-security prison than a manufacturing plant.

"The whole thing is shaped like a doughnut," Sixtine whispered next to him. "This is the outer ring. There's another quarter mile of woodland and then a second fence. That's the electrified one. The actual plant is in the middle."

"When did you come here?"

"Two weeks ago. Follow me. And take care where you tread."

They turned left, heading away from the lane and moving clockwise around the fence. Sixtine was looking for something, and after ten minutes she found it: a white cross scratched on a fir tree. The fence was right next to them, and she went over to it.

"This is where it gets interesting," she said.

Bond saw that the wire had been carefully cut at ground level. The join was invisible, but one section could be lifted up like a cat flap. The gap was just big enough for the two of them to squeeze through. Now they found themselves inside the inner ring, with the second fence somewhere ahead of them. The trees seemed even thicker here, the ground covered in nettles and moss.

Sixtine held a finger to her lips, and they continued forward in silence. After a few steps Bond understood why. Sixtine pointed to the trunk of a tree, and he saw a thick cable running up to a fan-shaped microphone. The entire wood had been wired for sound! Irwin Wolfe had taken security to extremes. They were lucky that there didn't appear to be any cameras.

They continued more slowly after that. Sixtine pointed at a thick clump of leaves, heart-shaped and a dark, bilious green. It was some sort of nettle, and he knew at once that it had no place in a European wood. Sixtine put her lips very close to his ear and whispered: "Gympie-gympie." Bond knew immediately what she meant. He had heard it once before at a briefing on jungle warfare in relation to Australia and Indonesia. Gympie-gympie. The most painful stinging nettle in the world. If the tiny silica hairs came in contact with your skin, within minutes you experienced pain that you would not believe possible. And here it was, growing just a few miles away from the quietest and most genteel resort in the Riviera. Bond had no doubt that it had been brought to France and planted deliberately to punish unwary trespassers, and he had to ask himself: Were such extreme measures justified simply to protect a replacement for Technicolor film? Plenty of industrialists kept secrets. Very few were prepared to maim or even kill to protect them.

With a sense of dread, he pressed forward. The forest had one last trick to play. Sixtine held up a hand, this time pointing down with the other. There was a tripwire, about six inches above the ground. Bond followed it, carefully separating the leaves with a stick. The wire was connected to a metal box that was fastened to a tree a short distance away. A miniature crossbow was attached to the side with a needle-sharp bolt pointing back. Anyone activating the device would have been crippled, shot in the ankle. He wanted to get out of there. Instead, they pressed on.

Bond heard the fence before he saw it—or rather, the 2,000 volts of electricity pulsing through it. They had emerged from the woodland. The ground had been cleared and trees cut down for about ten yards all the way around the compound, making it impossible to go any closer. They would be unprotected out in the open and all too easily seen. It didn't matter. From here they had a reasonably good glimpse of the hidden world of Irwin Wolfe.

The main entrance, with a barrier and a security block identical to the one they had already seen, was over to their right. The lane emerged from the forest and led to a wide concrete area with two jeeps parked next to each other and a water tower to one side. The jeeps were Willys MBs, used by the French army. On the other side of the wire, they could make out the first in a series of long rectangular buildings, set in straight lines. A watchtower rose up in the far corner with two men silhouetted against the sky, one of them scanning the treetops through binoculars. "Seen enough?" Sixtine whispered.

"Wait!"

Everything was wrong. Armed jeeps. Guards. Electrified fences. And there was something else. Studying the compound more carefully, Bond saw that it was split into two halves. A whole area was taken up with buildings that had been added more recently, constructed in a quite different style. They had no windows, and they were air-conditioned, with large steel boxes clinging to the woodwork and chimneys jutting out of their roofs.

Was this where the new film stock was manufactured? The lack of windows made sense. Undeveloped film would demand complete darkness. Bond detected a sharp chemical smell in the air. A door had opened, and a man came out wearing a white laboratory coat. Bond had brought a Minox subminiature camera with him and fired off half a dozen shots. He nodded at Sixtine. There was no point staying.

The two of them turned to leave.

They were no longer alone.

Three men stood facing them, dressed in khaki and carrying light machine guns. They had emerged silently from the forest, creeping up on Bond and Sixtine while they were watching the compound. They had the same dark features of the Corsicans who had surrounded Bond at Ferrix Chimiques. Bond's mind was racing. The Beretta was still in his trouser waistband, but he would be dead before he could reach it. He would have to try another way.

He lifted his hands in the air and smiled. "Good afternoon," he said, speaking in French. "I wonder if you can help me. My wife and I went for a walk in the woods, and we seem to have got lost."

The men weren't buying it. One of them, the leader, said: "Keep your hands in the air. You will come with us."

"I really don't think you need to be quite so aggressive." Bond was still playing the innocent tourist. "We were following the lane and took a wrong turn. You shouldn't be pointing those guns at us. I can assure you I'll be taking this up with the British consul."

One of the men had a radio transmitter and brought it up to his mouth. Bond realized that he had to act now if they were going to have any chance of getting out of this. If they allowed themselves to be escorted into the compound, it would be over. These men didn't work for Irwin Wolfe. He was sure of it. They must work for Jean-Paul Scipio. And Bond had been warned. A second confrontation with the gangster would be his last. His hand edged around behind his back, reaching for the Beretta.

"Keep your hands in sight!"

One of them had seen what he was doing. The muzzle of his machine gun rose, the single black eye daring Bond to continue. Bond froze. His fingers were only inches away from the Beretta.

And then something silver glinted in the air, shining out against the dark background of the woods. It traveled so quickly that it had found its target before Bond knew what it was. The man with the radio grunted and collapsed. The handle of a knife jutted out of his neck. The other two turned just in time to face their own death. Two more knives spun toward them. One of the men was hit in the throat, the other in his chest. Both crumpled and lay still.

Three more people stepped out of the woods. Once again, Bond's hand crept around, reaching for the Beretta, but Sixtine had seen what he was doing and issued a command. "Don't!"

Bond realized that he knew the new arrivals. He had seen them before. One looked like a schoolteacher, young, with thick glasses. One was short and overweight and could have been a businessman. The third was shabby and unshaven, standing lazily with a crooked half smile. The last time Bond had seen them, they had been sitting together playing *vingt-et-un* in the Monte Carlo casino. They were Sixtine's syndicate. But how had they got here?

The schoolteacher was examining the guards. He glanced up and spoke in English. "This one is still alive."

"Finish him, please, Marco," Sixtine said.

The survivor was the guard who had spoken to Bond. Marco calmly pulled the knife out of his chest and reinserted it in his throat. The guard's legs shuddered once. He made no sound.

"Are you all right, madame?" the businessman asked.

"I'm fine, thank you, Frédéric." Sixtine looked around her. She seemed completely unfussed by what had just occurred.

"We will need to get rid of the bodies," Frédéric muttered. "We can bury them, if you like, in the woods."

"No. I don't think we should disturb the ground in this wretched place. Find some of those bushes—the ones with the nettles—and throw them in there. With a bit of luck, nobody will find them until we've finished. Then go back to Nice. I'll contact you there."

"Would you like us to accompany you out of here, madame?" the third man asked.

"No, thank you, Georges. I can find my own way. Anyway, I have Mr. Bond to look after me." She turned to Bond and smiled. "Have you seen enough?"

"More than enough, I think," Bond said.

They left the three men to deal with the bodies and made their way silently and carefully back to the outer fence. Sixtine had marked the section that had been cut with another white cross on a tree. Bond lifted the flap for her as she crawled out. The two of them made their way back to the car.

"They followed us here," Bond said as they drove back down the hill. At last it was safe to speak.

"Actually, they were already here. I asked them to wait for me and then follow us into the woods."

"You didn't trust me?"

"I don't trust anyone, James. But that's not why they were there. The boys follow me wherever I go. They look after me."

"They were playing cards with you in the casino."

"Yes. Marco is actually very good at *vingt-et-un*. He could win on his own, but he likes to indulge me."

They reached Castellar after a few minutes and drove slowly through the narrow streets. This time there was no donkey to block the way. Bond thought about what he had seen: the old and the new buildings, the traps in the forest, the guards with machine guns. He knew that he had to go back. He turned to Sixtine.

"Last night you said you thought you'd found a way into the plant but that you might need my help."

Sixtine nodded. "That's right. But it's very high risk and we'd have to be completely on our own."

"Do you want to try it?"

"Absolutely."

"Then tell me."

IT HAD taken Sixtine two weeks to find the baker who supplied the canteen at Wolfe Europe and another two weeks to persuade him to help her.

Paul Rémy was a nervous man. He had inherited the business from his father and dedicated himself to his work, getting up every morning at four to begin the lengthy process of creating the baguettes, croissants, *pain de campagne,* and *fougasses* that would fill the window of his shop in Menton. When he had first been offered the contract by the film manufacturer, it had seemed too good to be true. But he had come to dread his visits to the factory in the woods. He did not understand why there had to be guns. He had been ordered to sign a confidentiality agreement. Why make such a big deal when all he was doing was delivering bread? To make things worse, this beautiful woman had suddenly appeared out of nowhere. She had offered him a huge sum of money to do something that would almost certainly put his life at risk. Why had she chosen him? He had been mad to speak to her at all.

The trouble was, Paul Rémy desperately needed money. He had fallen several months behind with the rent. Earlier that summer, one of the kneading machines had given up the ghost, and the cost of its replacement had been exorbitant. There was a full-time patissier who was threatening to resign unless he got a raise. Which was why, that same Sunday evening after their visit to the factory, he found himself sitting in the tiny apartment above the shop, sharing a bottle of wine with the woman who called herself Madame 16 and the Englishman she had brought with her. "What can you tell us about Wolfe Europe?" the Englishman asked. He spoke excellent French.

Rémy spread his hands. "Very little, monsieur. I see nothing. I come. I go." He looked the Englishman square in the eyes. It was time to assert himself. "I can take madame in the van with me. But that is all I can do. You must not ask for anything more."

Sixtine had promised to pay Paul Rémy 200,000 francs to drive her into the compound. The guards had grown used to seeing him and never searched his van. There was plenty of space to conceal somebody underneath one of the shelves that lined the back. Sixtine would cover herself with sacks. While Rémy went into the kitchen with his loaves, she would slip out and find somewhere to hide. That was what they had agreed, but now, it seemed, everything was going to change.

"This new plan is much better, Monsieur Rémy," Sixtine cut in. "You still have concerns that they will search your van even though they never have done so before. Then it's safer for you if you don't drive it. My friend will take your place. We will enter the compound at eight o'clock tomorrow morning. An hour later, at nine o'clock, you will telephone the police and say that the van has been stolen. That way, no blame will attach to you."

"How can he take my place?" Rémy squinted at Bond.

"There is a similarity between you . . . the same age, the same dark hair. Wearing your coat and with flour on his face, nobody will notice. I will be in the back of the vehicle, as we agreed. If we are apprehended, we will say we stole the van."

Rémy considered. "How can I trust you?"

"Why would I lie to you? This is easier for you, Paul. And since there will be two of us going into the plant, I will double the money that I offered you—400,000 francs. What do you say?"

Greed entered the baker's eyes as he repeated; "400,000 francs." The baker had never earned so much money. "If you'll agree now, I'll round it up to 500,000. All you have to do is to give us the keys."

The next day, early on Monday morning, wearing a herringbone worker's jacket and a cap, Bond sat behind the wheel of a Citroën H van, urging it up into the hills surrounding Menton. It was crude and uncomfortable to drive—Bond could barely push it above thirty miles per hour—but at the same time it seemed reliable. Bond hadn't shaved, allowing dark bristle to spread over his cheeks. He had also rubbed flour into his face and his hair.

Sixtine was beside him in the passenger seat. There was no point hiding yet. Only when they were in sight of the turn-off did Bond slow down and stop.

"If this goes wrong, get out as fast as you can," she said.

"In this van, that's not very fast."

"I know." She took out a gun, a custom-made Baby Browning with an ivory grip, checked it, and slipped it into her pocket. "Once we're inside—assuming we get that far—we're not going to have a lot of time," Bond said. "After what happened yesterday, Wolfe may well have racked up his security apparatus."

"Don't worry. I'm not going to hang around."

She slipped out. The van rocked slightly as Sixtine climbed into the back and swung the doors shut behind her. Bond pushed the van into gear and turned off down the lane toward Wolfe Europe.

He drove at a constant speed, passing through the green tunnel to the security barrier that he had seen the day before. Even as the Citroën H drew near, the first barrier was raised. The guards had recognized the van, and their eyes told them that the dark-haired figure hunched over the wheel must be the baker. Bond kept as much of his face concealed as possible. The lane continued through the wood with its deadly stinging nettles and booby traps although, looked at through the windows of the van, it seemed completely normal. Ahead of him the electric fence loomed with the second checkpoint. There were four guards here, and the barrier stayed where it was as the van approached. Bond sank into his chair, allowing the collar of his jacket to rise up. He rolled down the window and called out cheerfully, "*Bonjour!*"

One of the guards glanced at him curiously, then seemed to remember who he was and snapped out a command. The barrier rose.

"*Merci!*" Bond waved a hand and continued forward. He steered the van into the parking area beside the water tower. The jeeps, complete with guns and ammunition boxes, were still standing in the same parking bay where they had been the day before. One of them had its hood open and there was a man in overalls leaning into the engine. Nobody else was in sight. Bond got out. He opened the door and spoke quietly. "It's clear."

Sixtine rolled out of her hiding place. She and Bond picked up trays of baguettes and walked quickly toward the nearest building. This was the kitchen. Rémy had sketched out a map of the complex—or the parts that he knew—before they had left. Bond kept his head down. He could feel the shadow of the watchtower looming over him and wondered if he was being observed through binoculars. Hopefully, the trays would speak for themselves. He was glad when he reached the door and found that it was open. He and Sixtine moved inside.

The kitchen was industrial-sized. Bond and Sixtine set down their trays and continued forward without stopping. They passed through the dining room and into a corridor with whitewashed walls. Halfway along, Bond found exactly what he was looking for.

There were two washrooms and a changing area where the staff could take off their outer garments before they ate. Half a dozen white coats had been left hanging on hooks, and there were also square caps made out of white nylon. Without speaking, Bond and Sixtine slipped them on. Now, as they moved around the complex, they would look no different from anyone else.

They continued to the end of the corridor and passed through a double door into a much larger area, with at least fifty people, all wearing protective coveralls, attending to different machines. The room was in half darkness, which suited Bond well. It was impossible that he and Sixtine would be recognized. Even so, the two of them kept moving. There was a steel gantry overhead and internal observation windows made of thick plate glass. Everyone was being endlessly observed by white-coated figures with protective goggles and clipboards. Nobody was talking. The people here were as well regulated as the machines.

Bond saw a clipboard lying on a table and picked it up. In an instant he had turned himself from a worker to an inspector. He examined the stainless-steel panels, recording devices, platforms, ladders, and overhead pipes. Knowing the final product, he was able to make some sort of sense of it all. In one part of the factory, emulsion was pouring down from an upper level, coating a roll of cellulose at least three feet wide. The cellulose was wound onto massive cylinders and then directed into the next metallic beast, a drying chamber that howled and shuddered as it fed. Moments later the film base was regurgitated, cut into strips, then folded into rolls of yellow protective paper. All the time, the machines hummed. Fulfilling the day's quota was all that mattered.

Minutes later Bond and Sixtine emerged through another set of double doors into the fresh air. Here they were sheltered, out of sight of the watchtower. "What do you think?" he asked.

Sixtine shook her head. "There's nothing there," she said. "It's a classic film-production facility. Wolfe isn't doing anything revolutionary. In fact, half that equipment is five years out of date."

"Then let's try one of the new buildings."

They walked across the compound to the section that had been built more recently, keeping close to the walls. They came to a space that divided one section from the other and saw a warning sign: PERSONNEL AUTORISÉ SEULEMENT. Authorized staff only. Bond heard footsteps and froze, pressing back against the nearest wall. Two guards with rifles walked past just a few feet away but failed to see them.

They crossed from one zone to another, leaving any sense of safety behind them. In front they saw the first of the new buildings, with an unmarked metal door. Bond noted that it fitted flush with the wall and had no keyhole. He cursed silently. It could only be opened from inside. Just as he was about to move on, the door opened and a man came out, holding an unlit cigarette. Bond glanced at Sixtine who nodded. Together, they stepped forward. Sixtine reached the door before it swung shut. At the same time, Bond addressed the man, taking in the fact that he was Corsican.

"Do you need a light?" Bond asked.

"What?" The Corsican looked at him with dull eyes.

Bond hit him hard, twice. The man collapsed onto the ground, and Bond dragged him quickly inside. It had been the safest thing to do, but he was still annoyed. He had just put a time limit on how long they could stay here. Sooner or later somebody would notice that the man had disappeared. He would certainly come around in ten or fifteen minutes and raise the alarm. By then he and Sixtine would have to be on their way.

But for the time being, they were in. They continued down a brightly lit corridor, passing half a dozen fire extinguishers lined up together. Everything about his surroundings—the extraordinary cleanness, the smell of chemicals—told him that there was something taking place at Wolfe Europe unconnected to film. Ahead of him were two swing doors with little glass portholes.

"What is this place?" Sixtine whispered.

Bond didn't answer. He moved ahead and pushed the door open. And there it was in front of him. It was the last thing he had expected, and yet it made immediate sense: Irwin Wolfe and Jean-Paul Scipio and the *Mirabelle* and Ferrix Chimiques.

It should have been obvious from the start.

CHAPTER 10

Hell's Kitchen

EVERYTHING WAS WHITE: the walls, the work surfaces, the porcelain sinks, the protective clothes, the neon lights. The people employed here were a world apart from those working on the other side of the compound. They were phantoms, utterly silent, moving in slow motion among the test tubes and Bunsen burners.

Bond had walked into hell's kitchen. He could think of no other words to describe it. For this was the laboratory where Jean-Paul Scipio and Irwin Wolfe, in business together, had embarked on the mass production of high-grade heroin with an expertise and a sophistication that had never been seen before.

For the past twenty years heroin production in the south of France had been a cottage industry. There were tiny villages all around Marseilles where run-down farmhouses and villas had been converted into makeshift factories that could be closed immediately the moment the police got anywhere near. The conditions would be filthy, the operators often so clumsy that it was a miracle they could produce anything of value at all.

It took twenty-four hours to produce twenty pounds of pure heroin, and the process was fraught with dangers. If the morphine mix was overheated, it would explode. The fumes given off were enough to knock out an elephant, and a leak could kill everyone in the room. The purity of the finished product varied, and it would be cut and recut many times before it reached the street.

James Bond knew that this laboratory was unique. What he was seeing took heroin production to an entirely new level.

The room was large, filled with equipment that was expensive and brand new: vacuum pumps, electric blenders, venting hoods, and sophisticated exhaust systems. There were shelves stacked with syringes, suction pumps, funnels, and filter paper, and Bond guessed that every item would have been accounted for down to the last strip of litmus. This was a meticulous operation.

And there was the final product. Bond saw four women in white coats and gloves pack the fine white powder into bags. This would be the last stopping point on a journey that had begun in the opium fields of Turkey or Afghanistan. The morphine base would have been smuggled into Marseilles, probably in fishing boats, before being brought here. And where next? Bond thought he had a good answer to that question.

But it still made no sense.

The French authorities had been investigating, and M had sent two agents down to the Riviera because the narcotics supply had come to a halt. They had all been concerned that the criminal activity was being replaced by something else. But looking at the evidence in front of his eyes, Bond could only conclude that the supply line had been brought to a deliberate halt while tons of the drug had gone into production. The obvious conclusion was that Scipio was stockpiling it. But to what purpose?

Even as these thoughts stormed through his mind, Bond realized that he and Sixtine were in danger. They had penetrated the very heart of the operation. They had unmasked a criminal enterprise working inside a respected international business. Getting in had been one thing. Getting out would be another. Standing next to him, Sixtine grabbed hold of his arm. "This is crazy," she whispered. "Wolfe is sick . . . maybe dying. Why would he want to get mixed up in narcotics?"

"Later," Bond said. "We have to go."

It was already too late. A man wearing a white coat was walking over to them. Bond saw that he was some sort of supervisor. He stopped in front of Bond and Sixtine and pointed down. "*Vos souliers,*" he said.

It was as simple as that. Everyone in the laboratory wore protective covers on their shoes. Bond and Sixtine had their stolen coats and caps, but the man had noticed their feet were uncovered.

Bond was about to answer, but it was no good.

"*Vos cartes d'identité!*" the man demanded.

"*Certainement!*" Bond reached into his inside pocket as if about to draw out an ID card. Instead, he lashed out, his three extended fingers driving into the man's throat, cutting off the oxygen. Bond caught him as he collapsed and lowered him to the ground.

There was a moment of frozen silence while the work went on as before. But then half a dozen men came running toward him from all four corners of the laboratory, and a moment later every alarm in the compound began to shriek.

Bond turned to run, then thought better of it. He twisted around and, taking out his Beretta, fired half a dozen shots, aiming not at the men but at the machinery. Whatever happened, he wasn't going to leave this obscene place intact. The first bullets smashed glass vials, the next fanned into the circuitry of the blenders and the centrifuges, severing the electric cables. The result was exactly what he had hoped for. There were two or three blinding sparks as the machines short-circuited just as the liquid from the broken vessels came splashing down. He could smell the fumes he had released. What happened next was inevitable. As the laboratory staff screamed and scattered, a great mushroom of flame billowed outward. At once a sprinkler system burst into operation. A torrent of water cascaded down, drawing a curtain between Bond and the guards closing in on him. He fired off two more shots, emptying his gun, then left, pushing through the two swing doors.

Sixtine was already ahead of him. "The van," she said. As they reached the corner, a guard appeared, rushing toward them. Sixtine had her own gun in her hand and shot him. "Or one of the jeeps. There's no other way out of here."

"Right . . ."

"How are you for ammunition?"

"Empty," said Bond.

She grimaced. "Then maybe you should have thought twice before shooting the hell out of that lab."

They reached the next door and opened it cautiously. They were looking back out into the open air, and there were people everywhere. There must have been a protocol that directed all the personnel to head for some general assembly point when the alarm sounded. The pair could hide in plain sight. Moving at the same pace as everyone else, they would disappear into the crowd.

"Wolfe can't have known about this," Sixtine muttered as they pressed forward. "He's made a fortune out of film. Why would he risk everything to get into narcotics?"

"He can't *not* have known about this," Bond returned. "Hiding a heroin factory inside a film-production plant in the middle of nowhere . . . In a way, it's brilliant. But he must have cooperated."

"It would certainly explain why he never brought me here."

"And there's something else. . . ."

"What?"

"The *Mirabelle*—"

But before he could explain what he had worked out, there was a rush of three armed men pushing through the crowd and heading past them toward the laboratory. Bond broke off, and he and Sixtine separated, knowing instinctively that the guards were looking for two intruders. They would be safer walking apart.

It was only when the baker's van was in sight that they came back together again, and Bond saw at once that they couldn't use it. Someone must have noticed that it had been parked there far too long, and a guard carrying a machine gun was posted beside the front cabin, waiting for the baker to return. A short distance away, the man Bond had seen earlier was still working on the Willys MB French army jeep, but even as the two of them approached, he slammed the hood and wiped his hands on a rag. Bond made his decision. He just hoped the mechanic had done a good job.

Ignoring the van, he continued as if heading for the kitchen area, then at the last moment swerved to the right. The mechanic stared at him, aware that something was wrong. But too late. Bond grabbed the side of the jeep and used it to lever himself into the air, both legs lashing out, his feet slamming into the man's head. The guard at the van saw what had happened and shouted out, bringing his machine gun around. Sixtine shot him in the chest.

The sound of gunfire changed everything. The factory workers scattered, and now, finally, they were alone on the empty ground, making them an obvious target. There were three gunshots from the watchtower, spitting up the dust close to their feet. Bond leaped into the driver's seat of the jeep and flicked the ignition switch. Sixtine scrambled in beside him, twisting around to fire at two men who were racing toward them across the concourse. One of them went down. The other veered away and took cover.

Sixtine reloaded.

Another gunshot slammed into the door and ricocheted with a loud twang. Bond wrenched at the gear stick and spun the jeep into reverse. He drew a savage arc in the dust, maneuvered the gears, and sent the jeep hurtling toward the barrier and the way out.

"Get down!" he shouted.

There were two guards in front of him. They had come out of the concrete block and were emptying their pistols into the windscreen. Sixtine crouched down. His hands still gripping the steering wheel, Bond leaned sideways, taking partial cover behind the dashboard. The windscreen shattered. A second later the jeep hit the barrier, smashing it. Bond felt the vehicle shudder once and then again as it rammed into the two men, batting them away. There was another gunshot from the tower, the bullet tearing into the canvas seat behind him. But then they were away, speeding up the lane, leaving the broken barrier behind.

Bond and Sixtine straightened up. Bond had thought she might be shaken, but she looked exhilarated.

"We need to head back to Menton," she said. She looked behind them. The lane was empty. "If we go further into the hills, the road goes on for miles and they may be able to catch us. But there's not much they can do once we get to the sea."

She was right. The choice was between a corkscrew ride into the mountains or a fast run down to a busy coastal road with traffic, police cars, and plenty of witnesses. Bond cast his eye at the fuel gauge. It was touching red: The tank was almost empty. That was one twist of the knife he hadn't considered.

Branches and leaves raced past them in a jumble. With the glass shot out in front of them, the wind hammered into their faces, sending Sixtine's hair flying. She had reloaded her Browning and twisted around in her seat, ready to use it. But for the time being, they were still alone. The outer barrier and concrete administration block rose up ahead. Two more guards were waiting for them, but they were young and nervous. They had begun firing too soon, quickly emptying their guns, and could only hurl themselves out of the way as Bond slammed the jeep through the barrier and onto the last section of the lane. A minute later he reached the main road and spun around without stopping.

Bond was beginning to relax. Castellar, the first village, was only a few miles away. It was beginning to look as if they had made it to safety. What next? He would report to M that evening, and afterward the whole thing could be handed over to the French authorities. The plant would be closed down, Irwin Wolfe arrested. Finding Scipio might be more difficult, but that wasn't his business. Basically, he had done exactly what he had been told.

He might even ask for a leave of absence. Why not? He wanted to take Sixtine somewhere he would be on his own territory. Rome, perhaps. A midnight stroll along the Tiber and then . . .

"James."

He heard the worry in her voice and glanced in the mirror. He saw them at once, half a mile behind, already closing in. Not cars. Motorbikes. He had two or three minutes before they caught up.

He stamped on the accelerator, but the jeep was already doing the best it could. They had reached Castellar! The road swept them along, giving them no alternative but to follow the hill down into the village center. There were no turnoffs. They were hemmed in by olive trees on one side and a high stone wall on the other. The motorbikes were filling the mirror now. Black BMWs. Bond could make out the riders leaning over the windscreens.

No! There it was ahead of him, the worst bad luck. The wretched donkey with its cart filled with melons, the same one that he had seen the day before, once again blocking the way. Its owner was tugging at the reins, but the animal seemed to be in no mood to cooperate. Bond swore. He couldn't slow down, but there was no way around it. One side of the road consisted of houses packed tightly together. No alleyways. No openings. The other was barred off by a long line of metal bollards. The village was busy. There were women shopping, old men playing backgammon, children chasing each other around the tables. All it needed, Bond reflected bitterly, was a few baskets of geraniums and he could have made a fortune selling the postcard.

He slowed down. The motorbikes were right behind him. There were five of them in all: black and silver, as mean as hornets. Some of the riders had taken out guns, balancing them against the hand grips. He suddenly became aware that Sixtine had left her seat and was clambering into the back. Looking over his shoulder, he saw her jerk open the ammunition box and pull out a magazine clip. She rammed it into the gun and pulled back the cocking handle. Bond's hands tightened on the steering wheel.

Seconds later there was a burst of gunfire. The nearest two riders were blown out of their seats. People ran in all directions. The donkey whinnied and jerked forward, scattering the melons. Children were grabbed and swept into doorways. As Sixtine let loose with a second burst, Bond stamped down on the accelerator, swerving to avoid the tumbling melons. He heard screaming, but the whole village had become a blur. The shooting stopped. As Bond steered the jeep out of the other side of the village, Sixtine climbed back next to him.

"It's jammed!" she shouted.

"It did the job!" Bond replied.

It hadn't quite. Two motorcyclists remained, dropping back, but still not letting the jeep out of their sight. Bond was determined to lose them and took the first hairpin bend at breakneck speed, the wheels of the jeep almost leaving the ground. Before they'd had time to recover, he'd swung them viciously the other way, anticipating the next corner. The jeep rocked from side to side. The needle was now well into the red. Bond swore quietly. They must be running on fumes. He twisted the wheel, and they rounded the second corner and plunged down, the road steeper than ever.

The Mediterranean lay ahead of them, a dazzling blue that stretched out to the horizon. Bond gunned for it. He wanted to be out of the hills, perhaps out of France. If he could make it to the Italian border, there would be police in patrol cars. He wondered what they would make of an armed jeep riddled with bullet holes, trying to leave the country. Well, let them arrest him. Right now a night in jail sounded almost attractive.

"They're dropping back!" Sixtine exclaimed.

It was true. The two surviving motorcyclists seemed to have lost heart. The distance between them and the jeep had doubled. Even so, Bond didn't slow down. Two more bends and they would be down at sea level. They had got away with it!

"When we get into Menton, I'm going to buy you—"

"James!"

She had seen them carefully spaced out on the road ahead. He saw them, too. A dull shade of silver. They were shaped like pyramids but with four separate protruding spikes made out of steel. Each one was about four inches long. They were inspired by medieval caltrops, devices used to cripple horses, but when the Germans had dropped them on airfields and roads in the last war, they had referred to them as crow's feet. He recognized them only when it was too late.

He was already braking, but the jeep had driven over them and the tires exploded, the rubber torn to shreds. He lost control at once. The steering wheel spun uselessly in his hands. They were either going to crash into the hillside or be thrown over the edge of the cliff. Now it was in the hands of the gods.

"Brace yourself!" Bond shouted.

The jeep came to a corner and, unable to turn, launched itself into the air. For a tiny eternity they hung there, suspended in space. Bond saw the sea rushing toward them, replacing the sky. He felt himself tipping forward and pressed his hands against the steering wheel, pinning himself in his seat. They fell and they fell, everything silent now in the last moments before the end.

They hit the sea with all the force of a missile strike. Bond was aware of the water erupting around them. At once he was sucked under. The jeep that had saved them had now become an instrument of death, threatening to lock them in its grip as it sank. Bond tried to free his legs, but they were pinned under the steering wheel.

And what of Sixtine? She was no longer next to him. If Bond was going to die, he would die alone.

He bent himself forward and jackknifed over the steering wheel. He felt the blunt edge of the windscreen slicing into his stomach, his thighs, and then, finally, his ankles. He was free!

Bond began to swim, forcing himself upward. It seemed an impossibly long way. He kicked out six times before he broke through the surface, gasping for air. He looked around him. Sixtine was there. She had made it out. He swam over to her.

"Are you okay?"

She nodded, too exhausted to speak.

Bond turned around. They had left the road and driven off the cliff about thirty yards above them. Bond was surprised they had managed to survive. He guessed that the metal bodywork of the jeep had, at least to some extent, protected them. There was a ribbon of sand running alongside the foot of the cliff, but no swimmers, no one in deck chairs. Everything had happened so quickly, it was possible that nobody had seen it. They were on their own.

"Can you swim back?" Bond asked.

Sixtine was treading water. "I can't think of any other way to get there," she said.

They set off together. The beach was very close. It didn't take them long to reach the edge of the water and then to drag themselves onto the sand. For a moment they lay there, panting. Bond was relieved. It could have been a lot worse. The crunch of footsteps made him look up. There were two men, both of them dressed in leather jackets, holding guns. They had climbed off their motorbikes, leaving them parked on the edge of the road. From behind him came the sound of an outboard motor. Bond turned and saw a four-seat speedboat cruising toward them. It was manned by the two thugs he had encountered at Ferrix Chimiques. Carlo and Simone. Bond glanced at Sixtine and saw in her eyes what he already knew for himself.

It could have been worse. And it was.

CHAPTER 11

Number Four

IT WAS A TOURIST-CLASS CABIN for the class of tourist who didn't demand too much in the way of space and comfort. One day, more than 600 of them would discover the charms of the *Mirabelle*, the cruise liner that Irwin Wolfe had named after his first wife. There were two berths, one above the other, two wicker chairs, a chest of drawers, and a sink. The floor area was just big enough for two people to sit together. There was a porthole, but it didn't open and it wasn't big enough to provide much of a view.

It was less than twenty-four hours since Bond and Sixtine had been brought here. They had arrived separately. Scipio's two hired hands—Carlo and Simone—had accompanied Bond. Their presence had confirmed what he already knew. They worked for Scipio. Wolfe owned the *Mirabelle*. Scipio and Wolfe were in this together. But there was still something missing from the picture. This wasn't just a case of narcotics smuggling, even if the amounts involved were enormous. What was their common aim?

All night long the *Mirabelle* had been preparing for its departure. Finally, just before sunrise, Bond had been woken by a distant rumbling and a series of vibrations coursing through the cabin. He swung himself off the bunk and went over to the porthole. There was no view. He and Sixtine had been deliberately placed on the seaboard side, away from the port of Nice. It occurred to him that there were people looking for them. Sixtine's team would know that something was wrong, and Reade Griffith must surely have noticed that Bond had disappeared. Might he have alerted the CIA? Bond thought it unlikely.

And, anyway, it was too late. Looking out of the porthole, Bond saw that they were moving. Wolfe had told him the *Mirabelle* was going to weigh anchor on the Tuesday morning, and here it was, exactly on schedule. The ship would conduct a week of sea tests off the coast of France and then continue to America. And he and Sixtine were to be unwilling passengers, at least for part of the trip.

"We're on our way." Sixtine's voice came from behind him.

"It looks like it." Bond watched her climb down from her bunk.

"So what now? Maybe they'll throw a launch party. We might even get invited to the captain's table."

"It'll make a change from beans and potatoes." That was all the food they'd had so far, brought in by a scowling crewman.

Sixtine came over to him, and he put an arm around her. "Listen to me," he said. "Whatever happens, you have to survive. It may be that Wolfe has a soft spot for you. He was talking about marrying you only a few days ago. And Scipio knows who you are. He won't want to go to war with you. What I'm saying is, don't worry about me. If you can find a way out of this, you have to take it."

"Don't be ridiculous, James. For a start, Wolfe is a horrible man who doesn't care about anyone. As for Scipio, maybe I can talk him around—but I doubt it. No. If we're going to find a way out of this, it's going to be together. It seems to me our best bet will be to get to the radio room. I can get a message to my group, or we can send out a general Mayday alert. Otherwise, it's just going to be on deck and overboard, and let's hope it's not too far to swim!"

"They've kept us alive," Bond said. "There must be a reason for that. Maybe they need us for something."

Sixtine shuddered. "You may be right," she said. "But I'd prefer not to find out what it is."

It was another eight hours before they heard the lock being turned and the door opening. The same men who had brought them to the *Mirabelle* had come for them a second time.

"Out!" the man with the broken nose grunted.

"Which one are you?" Bond asked. "Carlo or Simone?"

"Just move."

"It would be nice to know your name when I kill you."

The two men led Bond and Sixtine out of the cabin and along a corridor that stretched out ahead of them with what looked like a mile of brand-new carpet, unused handrails, glowing lamps, and the countless fire extinguishers that Bond had noticed before. They went up the stairs and out onto the deck. Bond saw the coast of France and guessed they were at least a mile away. There was no chance of jumping now. He would be dead, riddled with bullets, before he had even reached the side.

A second staircase led up to the promenade deck, where Wolfe had greeted him when he first came on board. They made their way up and then back inside, through the dining room and into the ballroom. Here the carpet gave way to acres of walnut, and their feet tapped out a rhythm of sorts. Another door led into the Wolfe Bar that Bond had already visited. Wolfe himself was waiting for them, settled into a velvet armchair with a dark wood table in front of him, and two more chairs facing. Jean-Paul Scipio was sitting at the bar. His translator stood next to him.

"Sit down," Wolfe said. It was not an invitation. Bond chose one of the chairs opposite him. The American millionaire looked uncomfortable. He was wearing a gray flannel suit and a silk tie—it was all business tonight. Bond noted with interest that he was doing his best to avoid looking at Scipio. There was a sort of disdain, as if the Corsican gangster was a butler who had risen above his station by joining the family for drinks.

"Irwin . . ." Sixtine was crouching beside him, her eyes wide and tearful. "I don't understand what's happening. I was just interested in your work. That's all. I didn't mean—"

"I know who you are," Wolfe cut in. "According to Scipio, you're as crooked as he is. From the very start I wondered why you were getting so close and cozy, but I was happy to play along with it. Why not? You're an attractive woman. Well, you can put a sock in it now. I know your business, and I've got a good idea what you were up to. It's a damn shame, because I don't see how you can get off this boat alive, but we'll come to that later. For now, take a seat. What can I get you to drink?"

"I'll have a bourbon with a little water and ice," Bond said. "But before that, there's something you need to know. Miss Brochet has got nothing to do with me. We hadn't even met until a few days ago. Send her back to the cabin and you and I can say what has to be said. But leave her out of it."

"She's here and she's staying," Wolfe replied curtly. "I think the phrase is, 'She's made her bed and she can lie in it.'"

"I'm not going anywhere," Sixtine muttered petulantly. "I've been stuck in that cabin long enough, thank you." She sat next to Bond. "And I'll have a bourbon, too."

The barman started fixing the drinks. The translator was already whispering into Scipio's ear, repeating everything that was being said. Scipio gazed ahead, his eyes fixed on Bond.

"I guess you want to know what this is all about," Wolfe began.

"I know what it's all about," Bond said. "And so do my superiors. I think you'll find there's quite an unpleasant reception waiting for you when you dock in New York. American customs officials take a pretty dim view of heroin smugglers. Your business affairs must have taken a turn for the worse if that's the only way you can think of to make money—but that's not my problem. Wolfe America, Wolfe Europe . . . From now on it's going to be Wolfe Alcatraz. Your business is finished, and so are you."

To his surprise Wolfe broke into laughter. "Is that what you think?" he demanded. "You think I'm in this for the money? Do you have any idea how much money I have? I'm seventy-three years old. Even if I was in perfect health, I'd only live another ten or fifteen years, and as it is, I'll be lucky to have half of that."

He tapped the side of his head. "I have something inside my brain. The doctors call it an ependymal tumor, which strikes me as a fancy name for something that's growing where it shouldn't. The fact is, it's going to kill me. There's nothing I can do, no treatment I can buy. I'm a goner, and I might as well get used to it.

"It was diagnosed a year ago, and that set me thinking. I thought about the war and about the two boys I lost. It was a stupid, unnecessary war. A European war, not an American war."

The drinks arrived. "America didn't exactly enter the war," Bond said. "Your country was attacked on December 7, 1941. Or maybe your brain tumor knocked that detail out of your memory."

"I think I know my history better than you, Bond. Pearl Harbor was the end result of a series of hostile maneuvers by the United States that began when the Japs invaded Manchuria in 1931. Once again, it was none of our business, but our politicians didn't approve. So what did we do? We threatened them with a blockade. That led to them dropping out of the League of Nations, the second Sino-Japanese War, and eventually to the Tripartite Act with Germany and Italy. The Japs didn't become our enemy overnight. It was our aggression and interference that drove them to it.

"Anyway, Roosevelt didn't need an excuse to go to war. He'd been wanting it all along. He had said as much in his commencement address to the University of Virginia on June 10, 1940. A few months later he provided your country, France, and the Soviet Union with $50 billion worth of supplies. So don't talk to me about Pearl Harbor. It was a European war, but we threw ourselves into it long before December 1941.

"We're doing the same thing right now in Korea. You tell me, what has the North Korean People's Army got to do with us? But American soldiers are dying, leaving parents feeling like I felt when they told me my two boys had been cut down on the sand."

Wolfe was sitting rigidly in his chair, breathing heavily.

"I have been thinking about my legacy and what I can do to change the way my country is heading," Wolfe went on. "We are coming to the belief that we can solve all the problems in the world, and we don't see what's happening. We don't see that we risk becoming monsters! Look at Hiroshima and Nagasaki. Believe me, I have no love of the Japs. But I never thought I'd see a day when we would sit back and kill tens of thousands of people, including women and children, simply to assert our superiority.

"Something has to change. What the United States needs is a wake-up call, or what you might think of as an injection of common sense. And that is exactly what I am intending to give them.

"I will not tell you how I came to meet Mr. Scipio. Working in Marseilles, I was obviously aware of the Corsican syndicates and their power. I learned a great deal about the narcotics business, and it became clear to me that it's going to change the world. In fact,

I would go so far as to say that drug addiction is going to become the driving force of the twentieth century. People are going to get ill. People are going to need treatment. People are going to turn to crime. That's the future, but maybe it can become a force for good. If America is made to look after its own, then maybe it will reexamine its position in the world.

"On this ship are concealed more than 12,000 pounds of what is known as Number Four heroin—between 90 and 99 percent pure. I do not intend to make money from this consignment, Mr. Bond. That is why I laughed at your suggestion just now. Although I have paid Scipio a fair market price for his product, I am going to pretty much give it away. Of course, this will eventually bankrupt me. It is financial suicide. But I am dying anyway, and I have no friends and, thanks to Mr. Roosevelt, no family.

"Can you imagine the transformative effect that so much high-grade heroin is going to have on American society? I intend to create a nation of heroin addicts, Mr. Bond. A million future customers for Mr. Scipio."

Bond saw the translator whisper this last sentence into Scipio's ear, and the man's enormous face rearranged itself into a smile. Wolfe's plan was hideous, but whatever happened, Scipio would reap all the benefits. Wolfe had facilitated the manufacture of high-grade heroin. He had paid for it. And he had provided Scipio with a business opportunity that would last for generations.

"Soon the streets will be littered with victims. As the prices rise and the supply begins to fall, there is sure to be an unprecedented crime wave. The government will be forced to concentrate all its resources on its own backyard and will not have the money or the energy for another Omaha Beach. It will start trying to help its young people instead of killing them.

"In doing this I will have built a memorial to my sons. I will go to my grave in the knowledge that I have changed the future of American history so that other sons will be saved."

He fell silent. The translator spoke for another few seconds, catching up with the end of the sentence. Finally, it was over.

Bond glanced at Sixtine, who was sitting straight, her face pale.

"I have to say, it will make interesting reading in the *Lancet*," Bond said finally. "I wonder if doctors were aware that an ependymal tumor could cause the sufferer to lose every trace of his sanity?" He leaned forward. "You really think that by condemning hundreds of thousands of young people to the living hell of heroin addiction, you can make your country a better place?"

"I'm creating a tunnel. But it will lead them to the light."

"You're creating a self-destructive nightmare that will benefit no one except Fat Boy over there. It won't work, anyway. There were drug addicts all over America in the thirties and forties. It made no difference to the entry to the war. You're deluding yourself if you think any good is going to come out of it."

Wolfe got stiffly to his feet. "Then think of it simply as revenge for what happened to my boys," he said. He turned to Scipio. "I'm done with him. You can do what you like. Don't kill the woman yet. She and I still have things to say."

Scipio waited until Wolfe had walked out of the bar. Then he slid himself off the bar stool, transferring his enormous weight to his legs. The translator handed him his shooting stick. Slowly he took a few steps forward. The smile was still on his face.

"Meester Bond," he said.

SCIPIO rapped out a command, and his two men dragged one of the bar stools into the middle of the floor.

"May I ask you please to sit down here." This time the words were translated into English for Bond to understand.

Bond got to his feet. He didn't like the look of this, but he had no choice. He walked over to the stool and sat down. Scipio stood in front of him. The two of them were now the same height.

But before anything could begin, Sixtine spoke.

"Scipio!" she said. "You know who I am. You know how much money I'm worth. Listen to me now." She waited for the translator to catch up. "You have made a mistake working with Irwin Wolfe. He's dying, so he doesn't care what happens in the future, but he can still bring you down with him. If you will let Mr. Bond and myself leave, I will pay you 100,000 American dollars. There is also the heroin on this boat. Wolfe wants to give it away, but you could sell it on top of what he has already given you. Surely you can see that you have no need for Irwin Wolfe. Let us go. You're making the wrong enemies here."

Sixtine fell silent. The translator finished and stood there, waiting for what might come next. Scipio shook his head.

"*Innò. Sò Corsu!*"

"No," the translator explained. "I am a Corsican. In my country a man's word is his bond. Do not speak to me again, madame." The translator paused, and Scipio waggled an elephantine finger in her direction. "I warned you . . . you should stay away from this part of the world. It is regretted that you did not take my advice."

Scipio turned to his men and spoke rapidly in his high-pitched whispering voice. The translator listened in silence, then addressed Sixtine directly. "Mr. Scipio has given instructions for you to be dragged out of here and locked up if you speak again," he explained with a note of apology. "You will be hurt quite significantly." He turned to Bond. "He also wishes you to know that Madame 16 will be shot if you make any move at all. You must sit where you are and take what is given to you. Do you understand?"

"Please tell Mr. Scipio that I understand completely and that whatever happens to me in this room will be paid back tenfold. I work for serious people. They know I am here. You have already killed one of our agents. If you kill me, you will spend the rest of your life running." He turned a cold eye on Scipio. "Or in your case, waddling. I hope you know the Corsican for that word."

For once the translator looked discomfited as he repeated the lines. But Scipio was unconcerned.

"The last time we met, I also gave you a warning, Mr. Bond. Stay out of my affairs. To be honest with you, I was quite expecting you to ignore me. It may surprise you, but I was also very pleased. I hoped that you and I would meet again and that I would be able to do what I wished without restraint. We have arrived at that occasion. You interest me, Mr. Bond. You are young, good-looking, resourceful. You are not unlike the man who was here before . . . your predecessor. I killed him. I shot him three times.

But I never got to know him. This time it is going to be different."

Scipio glanced at his translator and rapped out a sentence.

"Mr. Scipio says he will kill your friend if you try to resist," the translator said.

"You've already told me that," Bond said. "But you seem to have forgotten that the man you work for wants her alive."

The words were translated.

"I do not work for Irwin Wolfe," Scipio muttered. He took a step forward so that he was close to Bond. Then Scipio reached out with two fingers and stroked the side of Bond's face. Bond recoiled in disgust. Out of the corner of his eye, he could see Sixtine sitting in the oversized velvet chair, strained and afraid. One of the guns was trained on her. The other was on Bond.

"Let me tell you what I am going to do to you, Mr. Bond." Scipio's voice was thick with pleasure. "I am going to change you. I am going to make you into my creature. We have almost a month together on this boat—more than enough time to break you. The way in which I shall achieve this is all around us. When I leave the ship at New York, you will follow me obediently as a dog follows his master. You will be a heroin addict, Mr. Bond. Even one week from now, there will be no need to secure you. You will spend every minute waiting for your next injection. You will come to me on your knees and beg me to give you what you need. And maybe, in return for your complete submission, I will.

"But this is what you must understand. This is what will destroy you and ultimately make you mine. You will not know what I am going to do, whether I will provide you with pleasure . . . or pain."

With a speed that took him by surprise, the fat man swung his fist through the air, crashing it into the side of Bond's head. It was like being hit by a battering ram. Bond was almost thrown off the bar stool. Scipio caught him with his other hand and then punched him again, this time in the stomach. Again, Bond was blasted backward. He had never been hit so hard. Scipio let go of him, leaving him gasping for air. Bond saw him clasp his hands, bringing the various jewels together. Then the bullets of flesh and bone became a blur as they came pounding once again into the side of his head. There was a burst of light, and he was propelled sideways, this time falling onto the floor.

It wasn't over. Taking his time, Scipio kicked him again and again. Unable to stop himself, Bond let out a groan and rolled onto his side. Scipio stood over him and stamped down. Bond not only felt his rib crack, he heard it.

"Stop it!" Sixtine called out. "You're going to kill him!"

Silence. Bond lay floating in a pool of agony.

He heard words but did not understand them. Scipio was talking, not to him but to his men, giving orders.

The translator crouched beside him and explained. "You are to be taken now to your cabin. Your friend will come with you also. The pain is over for the present. Mr. Scipio is going to introduce you to a type of pleasure which . . . he is sure it will be new to you and which you will never forget. Do you have anything to say?"

Bond swore. He could taste blood in his mouth.

Carlo and Simone jerked him to his feet. Bond wanted to fight back, but he was exhausted by the beating. There had to be a way out of this. Any minute now Sixtine's people were going to burst in. Bond looked around, half expecting to see knives spinning through the air. There was nothing. No last-minute cavalry.

The two men dragged him across the floor, back through the ballroom and dining room, out onto the deck, and finally downstairs to the cabin. He was thrown onto the bed, and at once Sixtine was with him, holding his head in her hands.

"James!" She was trying to hide it, but he knew she was afraid.

"Don't worry," he whispered. "We'll find a way out. . . ."

A third man came into the cabin, carrying a small Gladstone bag, which he set down on a table. Bond recognized the oily hair, the bad skin, the shabby little mustache. It was Dr. Borghetti, the man Wolfe had introduced as the ship's medic. He opened the bag and took out various items, laying them on the table. First there was a syringe. Next to it he placed a spoon, a candle, a ball of cotton wool, and a glass, which he filled with water from the sink. Finally, he removed a packet of waxed paper that he carefully unfolded. It contained a small heap of white powder.

"Could you get him ready, please," he said in English.

Bond could feel his strength returning and wondered if he could fight back. But as two of the men moved into the room, two more took their place at the door. He knew that resistance was hopeless.

As if reading his thoughts, Borghetti added: "I am sure you will not try anything stupid, Mr. Bond. Not if you care about the well-being of the lady. You must accept what is being done to you. It is the beginning of a life-changing journey. Your first experience of heroin. Soon your life will be unimaginable without it."

"One day I will kill you," Bond said matter-of-factly.

"I don't think so."

Bond was gripped on both sides. One of the men took his shirt-sleeve and ripped it apart so that it hung in two strands on either side of his arm. At the same time, Borghetti lit the candle. He tipped the powder into the spoon, then added some water, using the syringe to suck it out of the cup. He held the spoon over the flame, stirring the mixture with the needle until it had dissolved. Finally, he dropped a ball of cotton wool into the preparation and sucked it back into the syringe. He nodded at the two men. "You are about to leave the real world and find yourself in a very different one. Do not attempt to struggle. It will do no good."

It was impossible, anyway. The first man had clasped his arm, forcing it forward so that the bare wrist was exposed.

Borghetti came over to the bed.

Sixtine started to rise, but the man with the broken nose brutally pushed her back, aiming his gun at her stomach.

"Don't!" Bond said. He was speaking to her, not to Borghetti.

He looked down and saw the syringe with its hideous load drawing closer. He saw the needle touch his wrist and felt the prick as it penetrated the skin. Borghetti pushed further, finding the vein. He pressed the plunger. The heroin swirled downward, entering his bloodstream. The syringe was empty. Borghetti removed it. Sixtine cried out and, ignoring the gun that was being aimed at her, rushed forward and grabbed hold of him.

"It's done," Borghetti said. He blew out the candle and placed it, along with the syringe, back in his case. He left the rest. "He will be helpless for the next eight or nine hours," he said. "Even so, one of you should remain outside all night." To Bond he added: "I will be back tomorrow."

The two men released Bond, who fell back into Sixtine's arms.

Borghetti was the first out of the cabin. The others followed, and the door slammed shut. The key was turned on the other side.

Bond and Sixtine were alone.

SIXTINE had worked out what she was going to do. Long before the door had closed, she had set about her work.

To the men who were watching, it appeared that she had grabbed hold of Bond—a frightened woman who thought she was going to lose her man. In reality she had done more than that. The torn sleeve of his shirt was hanging loose, and even as Dr. Borghetti was collecting his things, she had grabbed hold of it, wrapping it around his upper arm, effectively turning it into a tourniquet. Now she tightened it further and tied a knot. "Don't move," she whispered. She touched her hand against his head. "I'm going to have to hurt you. It's the only way."

Borghetti had left his glass behind. Sixtine picked it up and smashed it against the wall. The piece that remained was jagged, shaped like a knife. Without hesitating, she picked up Bond's hand and stabbed the point into his wrist, where the syringe had entered moments before. Bond cried out as a jet of crimson blood spurted out, forming a gleaming pool on the floor.

She had worked out what she had to do, but there was no way of calculating it precisely. It would have taken fifteen seconds for the heroin that had been injected into Bond to reach his heart and disseminate through his system and enter his brain. The makeshift tourniquet had prevented that happening, and the deliberately inflicted wound would hopefully remove much of the poison from his veins. The trouble was that if she let him bleed too much, she might kill him. Too little and the exercise would be pointless. Looking down, Sixtine felt sickened. Already the cabin looked like a slaughterhouse.

"Try to relax, James," she whispered. "I'm going to take off the tourniquet."

This was the moment of truth. Sixtine untied the shirtsleeve, then tore the fabric free, pressing it down on the wound that she had inflicted. As blood flowed back into the arm, she kept the pressure firm and constant. Her aim now was to stop the bleeding. How much of the heroin might she have removed? Half of it? More? There was no way of knowing. All she could do was wait.

Meanwhile, the invisible army stormed the fortress of Bond's consciousness.

It was as if a heavenly chorus had exploded inside him. Everything Scipio had done to him was wiped away. Just a few moments ago he had felt Sixtine tying something around his arm, and there had been another bolt of pain as the glass had cut into his wrist. Why had she done that to him? He had forgotten. But it didn't matter anymore. The wrist was no longer connected to his arm. His entire body had fragmented, and he could feel each and every one of his molecules spinning gloriously in the ether.

I will provide you with pleasure . . .

That was what Scipio had said, but it wasn't even close. What Bond was experiencing went far beyond any pleasure he had ever known. For the first time in his life, he understood what it meant to be himself—and it was clearer, simpler, more certain than anything he could have imagined. He was the greatest spy who had ever lived. He was the world's most successful killer. He was James Bond 007, rewarded with the number that placed him above the law and turned him into someone people would fear and respect in equal measure. He was happier than he had ever been. Indeed, he was discovering real happiness for the first time.

The first effects of the heroin injection lasted only five or ten minutes, but to Bond it was a celebration that went on for eternity. After that he settled into a warm sense of comfort, aware now that Sixtine was holding him and knowing, also, that the two of them were prisoners and that he was going to be killed. But even that didn't matter. He drew Sixtine closer to him, reveling in her softness. It wouldn't bother him if he never moved again.

Hours, days, weeks went by, and then, quite suddenly, he felt himself sliding back down the hillside to normality. He had thought he would never feel pain again, but now it began to insinuate itself, starting in his wrist, then hammering all the way up his arm. There was something wrong with his chest. He turned sideways and cried out as the broken rib made itself known. His vision darkened at the edges, and he remembered the blows to his head. His mouth was completely dry. And someone was talking to him.

"You're coming out of it. It's all right, James. You're with me again. I'm looking after you."

It was Sixtine, speaking softly. Remembering the danger he was in, Bond felt his senses locking together.

"How long?" It was all he could do to bring the two words together in a question that made sense.

"I managed to get some of the heroin out of you, James. I had to hurt you, but there was no other way. And it's worked. I've bought us time. They said it would be eight or nine hours, but it's been less than three. What you've been through . . . it's been horrible. But you're going to get back your strength."

"I'm okay." But he wasn't. He turned his head and saw the blood, now dark and sticky, on the floor. "Going to be sick . . ."

Sixtine helped him to his feet and supported him as he stumbled over to the sink, where he stood for a minute, resting with his hands on the porcelain. He was finding it hard to breathe. He was sweating. The muscles in his chest and stomach were in spasm.

"How are you feeling?" Sixtine asked.

"Not good. Need time . . ."

"James, we don't have time. We have a window of opportunity. An hour, maybe two. You have to get yourself back together."

He nodded. "Ten minutes. Cigarette . . ."

She lit a cigarette for him, and he sat down on one of the chairs and took stock. He would be able to move but not run. Sixtine had badly cut the wrist of his right arm, and even if he managed to get hold of a gun, it would affect his aim. He was dizzy from blood loss. He could still feel the drug clouding his thoughts. He had become a liability. He would only hold Sixtine back.

As if sensing his thoughts, she spoke. "We're going to break out of here together. First out of this cabin, then off this boat. You and me, James. Don't you dare argue with me."

Bond nodded. "We can't just . . . swim," he said. He still had to keep the sentences short. "Too far out. And I want to stop them. All the heroin. Tons of it. Sink the ship."

"Sink the ship?" She stared at him. "How are we going to do that? Forgive me, but I forgot to pack a hand grenade."

Bond thought about the fire extinguishers he had seen at the Wolfe Europe compound. And there was something else. What was it? Oh, yes. The boxes being carried on board the *Mirabelle* when he had visited that first time, a century ago. And Wolfe telling him: *We're going to have a party like you wouldn't believe.*

Somehow it all came together.

"I have an idea," Bond said.

CHAPTER 12

The Dark Blue Sea

IT WAS SOON AFTER MIDNIGHT that the hammering began—and with it a voice from the other side of the door.

"Help me!" It was the woman. She sounded desperate. "Someone . . . please. He's stopped breathing. I think he's dead."

The two guards stationed in the corridor unlocked the door and went in.

The sight that met their eyes was grim. Sixtine was on her knees beside the door, her whole body limp, tears streaming down her face. Bond was lying prostrate on the floor. He seemed to have struck his head when he fell. There was blood everywhere. It was impossible to see if he was breathing, but it seemed unlikely.

"He fell!" Sixtine sobbed. "There was nothing I could do. He just fell and he lay there. You killed him."

Was he dead? One man stayed by the door, covering Sixtine, while the other continued into the cabin, moving forward to examine the body. In the blink of an eye, Bond rolled sideways, driving his fist upward in a savage blow that dislocated his opponent's jaw and smashed him into unconsciousness. The man at the door swung around, aiming at Bond, at the same time taking his attention off Sixtine. At once she seized hold of his arm and, dragging it toward her, bit hard into his wrist. The man howled and dropped his gun. Bond was already on his feet, rushing toward him. Sixtine jerked upward, twisting the man's arm behind his back. As he bowed down involuntarily, Bond kicked out, his toe cap slamming into the man's head. Sixtine let go, and he collapsed.

Bond stood, catching his breath. He was fighting back, but the situation was still almost hopeless. They were out at sea. There must be at least fifty crew members on the boat, and all of them were on Scipio's payroll. Sixtine was certain that their best course of action was to get over the side and swim for the shore.

Bond shook his head. "No. It's too dangerous. We don't know how far out we are. We might not make it."

"What, then?"

"Tie these two up. Then follow me."

Sixtine knelt beside the man who had been guarding her. She took his head in her hands and twisted it sharply, breaking his neck. Bond stared at her. "I don't have any rope," she said. "And we're running out of time." Before he could protest, she did the same for the second man. Bond was too exhausted to argue.

"So where are we going?" Sixtine demanded.

"Baggage Room. R deck. Aft . . ."

"Why?"

"Trust me."

Locking the door behind them, they slipped out into a long, empty corridor. He and Sixtine both now had guns. Bond had taken a weapon—and a shirt—from one of the two dead men. But he still felt very exposed. There was nowhere to hide. The entire ship was a vast network of interconnecting spaces, stairways, corridors, doors, and arches. They had no way of knowing what lay ahead. Thank God for Sixtine. She knew what she was doing. She was the most extraordinary woman he'd ever met.

They reached a stairwell and climbed down. Bond couldn't be sure after his brief tour, but he thought R deck must be immediately beneath the level where they had been held. Fortunately, there were plenty of signs to direct them, and sure enough the letter R was printed on the wall one floor down. They followed a second corridor almost identical to the one above. Their journey took them through a shop, a smoking room, a pantry, and finally a kitchen with knives hanging on hooks above the polished worktop. Bond would need those for what he had in mind. He went in and helped himself to a couple, slipping them into his belt.

Despite the ever present signs, the various sections of the ship looked very much the same in the half light. Bond knew they were heading aft, but there were dozens of doors to choose from. Which one was the baggage room?

He stumbled onto it at the very back, surrounded by offices for the ship's baker, the restaurant manager, the storekeeper, and the stewards. The baggage room was labeled, and it wasn't locked. He opened the door and turned the light on. And there it was, in front of him, exactly what he was looking for.

Irwin Wolfe had told him there was going to be a gala reception when they arrived in America and had boasted about the $1,000 he had spent on fireworks. As it happened, just as Bond had come on board the *Mirabelle*, he had seen them being delivered. There were about a dozen large boxes marked FEUX D'ARTIFICE stacked up in front of him. For a major display in the harbor of New York, some of the fireworks would be huge. They would be packed with explosive gunpowder, along with other chemicals.

Sixtine had worked out what was on his mind. Bond wanted to produce a single explosion, one big enough to sink the *Mirabelle*. "Okay," she said. "You want to make a bomb. But where are you going to put it? In the furnace?"

Bond shook his head. "That won't work. We have to smash the cooling water system . . . the inlet valve."

"Do you know where it is?"

"I can find it." Bond had served on ships. He had also learned how to destroy them.

"Will it work?"

"It might."

Sixtine stared at the boxes of fireworks piled high in the storeroom. "There's plenty of gunpowder here. But you're going to need some sort of casing."

"One of the fire extinguishers."

"Okay. But how are you going to get it open?"

"Wait here."

Leaving Sixtine in the baggage room, Bond went out into the corridor. A few moments later he returned carrying one of the many red cylinders that he had seen lining the ship's corridors.

"They've got too many of these," he explained. "There must be hundreds of them. And I saw the same models at Wolfe Europe. They've got to be how he's going to do it." All the time, he had been examining the metal surface—and with a smile, he found what he was looking for. The base, in its entirety, unscrewed.

Bond took out a bulging plastic bag and held it in his hand. He and Sixtine had seen dozens more of them being prepared in the heroin laboratory, and here they were, carefully packed into the shell, ready for the crossing to America. When they arrived in New York, nobody was going to search the ship. On the contrary, they were going to welcome it with a celebration and they were going to miss what was right in front of their eyes. Dirt-cheap heroin for anyone who wanted it. Bond felt sickened, remembering the tiny quantity that had been injected into him. He clawed at the plastic, tearing it and allowing most of the contents to cascade between his hands onto the floor. Then he threw what was left into the far corner.

"You're going to have to help me," he said, handing her one of the knives he had taken from the kitchen. "We need to cut open the fireworks. And we'll need a fuse—"

"It's one o'clock, James. How long have we got?"

"Your guess is as good as mine. Let's get on with it."

He and Sixtine tore the lids off the cartons, revealing the brightly colored fireworks inside. There were cannons, rockets, mortars, and zip-bangs, each one industrial-sized, fat boxes filled with explosive. Using the knives, they sliced them open. Bond had cut a piece of cardboard into the rough shape of a funnel, and he used it to pour the gunpowder into the empty fire extinguisher, packing it in as tightly as he could. The fireworks had come complete with one-minute fuses. He fed one into the nozzle, then screwed the base back on. What he had, he hoped, was an effective bomb. "How many of these are we going to need?" Sixtine asked.

"One should do." Bond looked at his watch. It was a quarter past two. Their work had taken them over an hour.

"Did you bring your lighter?" he asked.

"I have it here." She took it out of her jacket pocket. "They left it with my cigarettes."

"Very considerate." With an effort, Bond hoisted the fire extinguisher onto his shoulder.

"Let me take it," Sixtine said.

"No. I can manage." He grinned at her. "When this is all over, I'm going to take you to Rome. I'm going to take you to the Piazza Navona and buy you the biggest ice cream you've ever eaten, and then we're going to go back to the hotel and drink martini cocktails the way you like them and stay in bed for a week."

"I'll take you up on that," she said. "If we get out of here alive."

They went back into the corridor and made their way past the offices until they came to a staircase that led them down two more decks. Finally, they reached a door marked CREW ONLY and pushed it open. At once they were greeted by a waft of warm air that smelled of oil. The sound of the triple expansion engine leaped up in volume, accompanied by the whir of the ventilators.

This was the hidden world of the luxury cruiser.

There were at least three separate spaces: the engine room, the boiler room, and the generator room. But with so many pipes, so much machinery, it was impossible to tell where one ended and the other began. The entire area rose up through three decks, connected by wide metal stairways, gantries, and submarine-style hatches. Bond was standing on the uppermost level, his eyes already smarting as he made his way down, breathing in the fumes that leaked out of the twin Lobnitz & Co. boilers.

The *Mirabelle* was cruising off the coast of France. Had it begun the transatlantic crossing, there would have been forty or fifty people at work. Instead, the engine room was eerily empty with just a few figures in overalls absorbed in their work—and nobody noticed as Bond and Sixtine continued past the air pipes, the turbines, and the main condensers. Bond carried the fire extinguisher on his shoulder, hiding his face. Sixtine stayed close to him. They didn't speak. They had to look as if they knew what they were doing, do it, and then get out of there as quickly as possible.

But where was the bloody inlet valve? Bond knew that it would resemble an ordinary circular tap on a pipe about twelve inches in diameter. It would be connected to the hull, drawing in a constant stream of seawater that passed through the engine, removing the heat from the cylinder heads, the exhaust valves, and the turbochargers. If this had been a Corvette, he would have been able to go straight to it. But it was a brand-new cruise liner. Bond barely recognized half the machinery around him. He would need a great deal of luck if he was going to find what he was looking for.

"You do know where you're going?" Sixtine whispered.

"Of course. . . ."

He broke off as a mechanic brushed past them. Bond was tempted to ask him for directions—at gunpoint, if need be. But then he saw it. The inlet valve was stuck between two platforms in the bilge area, tucked away against the outer wall. Was it possible that the makeshift bomb would be strong enough to blast out the rivets and welding that held it all together? Bond doubted it, but it didn't matter. The valve was thirty feet below sea level. Roughly translated, that meant it was taking in water at thirty pounds per square inch. Break the pipe and it would be the start of a deluge that would sink the ship fairly quickly unless the hydraulic doors were closed immediately. And Bond had ideas about that, too.

The mechanic who'd just passed them had stopped. He turned around and examined them, a puzzled look on his face. "Who are you? What are you doing here?"

Sixtine took out her gun and shot him in the leg. The sound of gunfire was almost drowned out by the noise of the engines . . . but not quite. Pandemonium broke out all around them with engineers and crewmen running in different directions. Bond knew he had to act fast. He swung the fire extinguisher down and rested it between the hull and the inlet valve with the fuse trailing toward him. Sixtine handed him her lighter.

"Ready?" he asked.

She nodded.

"We have one minute."

"To go where?"

"The generator room." He lit the fuse.

Another man appeared. Bond looked up and was surprised to see Dr. Borghetti walking toward them, still dressed in his whites. What was he doing down here in the middle of the night? Perhaps one of the engineers had been taken sick, or he could have been on his way to check on Bond. Either way, it didn't matter. Sixtine shot him, quite deliberately, aiming for his stomach. She stood and watched as he crashed down in front of them, then began to writhe on the metal. There was an icy anger in her eyes.

"Just what the doctor ordered," she muttered quietly.

They had wasted precious seconds. As the fuse sparked and hissed, Bond and Sixtine backed away, making for the nearest ladder leading to a hatchway on the deck above. It was the fastest route to where Bond needed to go next. He had seen the generators when they had first entered the engine room. There was a fire axe on a wall, and he snatched it. That would come in useful, too.

They reached the ladder and climbed it. By the time they had made it to the next level, climbing through the circular hatchway, the bomb exploded beneath them. The blast was incredibly loud, echoing off so much metal. The inlet valve had been shattered. A huge snake of water was bursting out of the pipe, leaping ferociously into the engine room. A Klaxon had begun to sound, and a series of red lights were suddenly flashing.

Bond was still gripping the axe. He and Sixtine came to a complicated wall of electrical machinery with dozens of switches, valves, and gauges. Bond knew that this was the main switchboard. There were half a dozen master switches, each presumably controlling a different area of the *Mirabelle*. Using the blunt end of the axe, he carefully demolished every one of them. Half the lights in the engine room went out. The ventilators stopped working. All the dials on the switchboard swung to zero.

He had done what he could. It was time to go. His entire body felt like hell. He just hoped he had the strength for what would be the most difficult part. Scipio and his men must have realized what was happening by now. He and Sixtine had managed to creep in. They would have to fight every inch of the way out.

Still holding the axe, he ran back the way they had come, making for the bow of the ship. The corridors yawned emptily ahead of them. They were about halfway down when three of Scipio's men appeared, heading for the engine room. Bond's gun hand spoke, and two of the men went down. But they were replaced a moment later by more men behind them. The corridor was blocked. There was no way forward.

"Help me!" Sixtine had grabbed hold of a heavy fire door, which she was struggling to close across the corridor. Bond seized hold of it, and together they swung it shut. Bond slid the axe between the handles, effectively bolting it. Scipio's men were on one side. They were on the other. They had wasted time, and there was no choice but to go back the way they had come.

Something strange was happening. The *Mirabelle* was beginning to tilt. Bond realized with disbelief that his improvised bomb must have done more damage than he had thought. Perhaps it had blown a hole in the side, after all. And with the electricity cut and all the safety devices neutralized, there was nothing to stop the ship filling with water and capsizing. He and Sixtine had to find a way out, which meant getting onto the deck—and fast.

Quite suddenly, beneath them, there was an explosion, much louder and more ominous than the one Bond had caused. It was immediately followed by a shaking so violent that Bond and Sixtine were thrown against the walls and then to the ground. Bond was dazed, but he managed to work out what must have happened. Gallons of cold water had poured into the engine room, hitting the boilers filled with high-pressure steam, and this had caused the second, much larger explosion. Now the passageway was tilting more seriously. Bond could hear a mournful grinding. It was the sound of Irwin Wolfe's $2 million steamship tearing itself apart.

Bond and Sixtine got to their feet and clung to each other.

"Up," Bond said.

"And out," Sixtine agreed.

They came to the end of a corridor and turned a corner in time to see a horrendous sight. At the far end, about thirty yards away, a torrent of black water almost floor to ceiling was rushing toward them. A whole section of the *Mirabelle* had disappeared behind it. They could only turn and run the way they had come, aware of the flood that must be inches behind them.

Somehow they found another staircase and clambered up—but it still didn't take them to an outside deck. Another corridor, more doors. But no portholes, no way out. And somehow the water had already reached them. It was around their feet, rising incredibly quickly. Another corner. They hurried around and stopped dead in their tracks. It was the most bizarre thing Bond had ever seen.

Jean-Paul Scipio.

Bond suspected that after the first explosion, he must have hurried down to the engine room with his translator to see the damage for himself. The ship would have already been flooding at that point, the seawater rushing in through the broken valve. But then there had been a second explosion, perhaps cutting off the main staircase. He and the translator had been forced to take the ladder, and Scipio had got stuck. It was the only possible explanation.

That was what Bond and Sixtine were seeing now. The bald head was missing its wig. His shoulders and part of his chest had made it through. His arms were on either side of him, his palms under the water, straining to free the rest of him. But that was all there was. It was like a magic trick that had gone horribly wrong, a man cut in half. He couldn't go up. Nor could he go down. The water was all around him. In less than a minute it would cover his mouth, then his nose. He was watching himself drown.

Now he stared at Bond, his face distorted with fear.

"*Aiutatemi!*" he gasped.

"Help me," the translator translated.

Sixtine took out her gun and fired a single shot. One of the lenses in the translator's glasses shattered, and blood streamed out of what had once been his eye. She aimed at Scipio and pulled the trigger a second time, but the gun was empty.

"Leave him," Bond said.

They turned. The water reached Scipio's lower lip. He screamed at them. The water poured into his mouth.

Finally, the next staircase brought them out to the main deck. By now the *Mirabelle* was listing badly, and they had to fight to stop themselves from sliding into the sea. Behind them they saw lifeboats being lowered in a tangle of ropes. Bond wondered what had happened to Irwin Wolfe. He was tempted to find him. A part of him didn't want to leave a single one of them alive.

Somebody shouted. Even in the darkness, he and Sixtine had been seen. Black shadows without faces were making their way toward them along the sloping deck. He saw the white pinpricks of gunfire and seized Sixtine. Bullets ricocheted around them as they ran forward and jumped. The sea was still a long way beneath them. They were next to each other, trapped in midair, an easy target for the people firing at them. There was more gunfire. Then, finally, their feet broke through the water. Bond felt a fresh bolt of pain in his chest as the broken rib was jarred. He screamed and almost blacked out, but the water revived him. It was swirling all around, driving him upward. He let it carry him to the surface and broke through, gasping for air. He saw Sixtine close by, the moonlight reflecting in her hair.

"Are you okay?" He swam over to her.

"Yes." Her voice sounded weak. Bond guessed she had been winded when she hit the sea.

"We have to move. The ship's going down. We don't want to be caught in the suction."

Together they swam—twenty, thirty strokes—knowing that the farther they went, the more invisible they became. Scipio was dead. His men would be fighting for a place in the lifeboats. Surely no one would care about them anymore. They turned and looked at the *Mirabelle*. It was slanting at an impossible angle, a great, dying beast, sinking into its grave. They were still too close. Bond knew that when the ship finally disappeared, everything around her would be sucked down with her. He twisted around and saw the lights of buildings along the coast. Bond figured that the distance couldn't be more than a mile. He was in bad shape. His breath was coming in dagger thrusts. But with Sixtine's help, he was sure he could make it.

And what of her?

She was close to him, still and silent. "We can't stay here," he said. "It may take us an hour or two to reach the coast, but if we take it slowly, we should be okay. Let the tide take us in."

"James . . ."

She was going to tell him something that he didn't want to hear.

"If you feel tired, you can hold on to me," he insisted.

"I can't come with you, James."

The sea was suddenly icy cold. He put his arms around her and drew her against him. He saw the pain in her eyes. When he took his hand out of the water, he saw that it was covered in blood.

"You can do it," he whispered. "You have to."

She was strangely calm. "We beat them," she said. "There were so many of them, but we got away with it." She shuddered. "Something hit me when we went over the side. . . ."

"I can get you back. I can swim with you."

"No. You have to finish this on your own." Her voice was beginning to drift away. "I'm sorry, James. Don't be angry with me."

"I could never be angry with you."

She smiled. "It wasn't meant to be forever. But at least we had our day."

"Sixtine . . ."

"You must go now. You mustn't . . ."

She died.

He saw the moment when the life slipped out of her eyes. Still he held her. Behind him he heard a great cracking sound as what was left of the *Mirabelle* broke apart. It was beginning the final plunge. He knew he had to let Sixtine go with it.

He released her and watched her slide away, gently carried beneath the surface of the dark blue sea. Her hair billowed around her, and she looked serene, as beautiful in death as she had been when they were together. Finally, she disappeared from sight.

Bond uttered a single sound, something between a snarl and a sob. Then he turned and began to swim toward the shore.

CHAPTER 13

Death at Sunset

LIKE SOME GIGANTIC bird of prey, the Boeing 377 Stratocruiser came dropping out of the sky over Los Angeles, its wings stretching out and its wheels searching for the runway. It was midday, and the sun was at its most intense. The wheels made contact. As the plane reached Hangar number 1, an armada of little vehicles congregated from every direction: baggage tractors, container loaders, dollies, and service stairs. By the time the plane had reached its destination, it was surrounded. The door was unsealed, and a blast of warm air came rushing in. For the past twelve hours—the last leg of the journey from New York—James Bond had sat silently in the pressurized, air-conditioned stillness of the cabin. Now the noise, the heat, and the smell of the airport reminded him where he was and why he had come here. He could already feel the sweat patches underneath his shirt. His sense of discomfort was made worse by the bandages tightly strapped across his chest. The broken rib was already healing, but it would be a while before he was fully fit.

A week had passed since he had returned to London from the south of France.

M had been pleased with the way things had gone. "You've taken out the number one trafficker in the narcotics business, and you've sent five tons of his product to the bottom of the ocean. This will deal a major blow to the international syndicates, and with a bit of luck it will allow the Americans to get on top of the problem of heroin addiction. Once the war ended, they could have eliminated it altogether if they hadn't allowed themselves to get sidetracked. Maybe this will give them a second chance.

"You also achieved what you were sent out to do. When you confronted Scipio, he told you that it was he who killed our man."

"Yes, sir. He was quite clear about it."

"Then I'm very glad he's been dealt with." M always chose his words carefully. Violence and death were often part of his remit. But that didn't mean he had to articulate it, here in this office.

"I was wondering about Wolfe, sir."

"Yes. I'm afraid that part of it didn't work out quite as well as we might have hoped. He managed to get into one of the lifeboats, and they took him ashore. He was driven down the coast to Perpignan and slipped over the border into Spain. He was on a plane back to the U.S. before anyone could speak to him. Now he's resurfaced at his home in Los Angeles, and he's surrounded himself with expensive lawyers. Claims that he knew nothing about Scipio or the drugs or you, for that matter—and unfortunately, as to what happened on the *Mirabelle*, it's your word against his. The police raided the factory outside Menton, but he's pleading ignorance. According to him, it was all down to Scipio."

"So he's not going to be prosecuted?"

"I've spoken to our friends in the CIA, but they've been surprisingly unresponsive. They want to handle things their own way."

M's voice was bleak. He would not have enjoyed being cold-shouldered by the Americans after everything Bond had done.

"I did want to ask you about Joanne Brochet," M went on, a little softer now. "I understand that she was very helpful to you."

"Yes, sir. I certainly couldn't have got away with it without her." As he spoke, Bond's thumb pressed against the wound on his wrist and the bandage wrapped around it.

"And she died."

"Yes. For what it's worth, she died helping me, and I'd like to think you'll amend the records to show that she was never an enemy of this country. Quite the contrary. I learned something of her experiences during the war. We owe her a great deal."

"I'll see to it. And that son of hers, the one in the Bahamas. We'll make sure he's looked after."

Bond nodded, satisfied.

"Is there anything else?" M asked.

"I'd like to take a week's holiday, if that's all right, sir," Bond said. "The doctor patched me up, but the rib still hurts like blazes, and it'll be a while before I'm fully operational."

"Absolutely." M lit his pipe. "As a matter of fact, I was wondering if you might like to spend some time on the west coast of America. I've been thinking about Irwin Wolfe. We can't involve ourselves in CIA business, but I'll be damned if I'm just to sit back and do nothing. I wondered if you might like to have a word with him."

Bond thought for a moment. "Yes, sir. I'd like that very much."

M smiled. "It can't hurt letting him know we're not giving up on him, and at the end of the day all the lawyers in California won't protect him from justice."

"That's a lot of lawyers," Bond muttered.

"Just see what you can do. You might find it personally helpful coming face to face with him again. And I want you to understand that whatever results from such a meeting has my full sanction."

So there it was. M was giving Bond carte blanche. The visit would be unofficial. Bond could take whatever action he saw fit.

"You handled yourself extremely well, 007," M concluded. "You fully justified my decision to promote you to the Double-O Section. Enjoy your week off. You deserve it."

Loelia Ponsonby had made a call before Bond left and had spoken to one of Irwin Wolfe's assistants. Although at first there had been reluctance, a meeting had finally been arranged at the film mogul's Los Angeles home at seven on the evening of his arrival. Bond was surprised that Wolfe agreed to see him, but what did he have to lose? He was dying. And he would doubtless be protected.

At the airport, Bond presented the passport provided for him, made out under a false name. He made his way through customs, presenting himself to a young man in a gray uniform shirt.

"How long are you here for, sir?"

"A week."

"A business trip?"

"I'm seeing a friend."

"Oh. A special occasion?"

"It might be."

There was a car waiting for Bond at the airport, and he drove himself to the hotel he had booked. Once he had been shown to his room, Bond took a long, hot shower. Feeling refreshed, he wrapped a new bandage around his wrist, got dressed again, and called down to the valet to bring his car. Before he left, he opened the hinged compartment concealed in the base of his travel bag and took out the .25 Beretta that he had brought with him from England. He loaded it, slipped it into his back pocket, and left.

Sunset Boulevard runs from Los Angeles to the Pacific West, but there is a point where it stops pretending to be an ordinary east–west thoroughfare and becomes something quite different; the home of movie stars, moguls, and millionaires. Bond drove for about half an hour before he came to the address he wanted. He pulled up to the gate and got out of the car, noticing a camera trained down on him. He found an intercom box with a single button and pressed it. After a long wait he was connected.

"Yes?" The voice was distant, metallic.

"My name is James Bond. I have an appointment with Mr. Wolfe."

"Come in."

Bond heard a buzz, and the gate slid open, revealing a pink tarmac driveway beyond. He got back into the car and drove in.

He passed extravagant gardens and the obligatory tennis court, and there ahead was the house, built in the style of a Spanish hacienda. According to the records, Wolfe lived here alone—but even when his wife was alive, with a cook, a butler, a tennis coach, and half a dozen friends, it would have been surplus to requirements. How many bedrooms did it have? Eleven? Twelve? The walls were thick and white. There was nothing welcoming about this house.

Bond parked between a turquoise Buick Roadmaster and a black Pontiac Chieftain. The first car was more likely to belong to Wolfe, he thought. So what about the second? A bodyguard, perhaps. He walked to the front door and pulled the iron bell chain. He heard the bell ring out inside the house, but nobody came. He looked behind him and saw the sun sinking behind the trees. He rang a second time. Still nothing. Wondering if Wolfe had decided not to see him after all, he reached out and touched the door. It swung open. There wasn't a single sound coming from the building. If it hadn't been for the voice that he had heard on the intercom, he would have thought the place deserted.

He stepped inside, into a cavernous hall with wooden floors, exposed beams, a minstrel's gallery with a twisting rail. Ahead of him a grand staircase invited him up to the second floor. Bond went upstairs. He took out the Beretta and held it in front of him, knowing instinctively that there was something wrong. The silence was too oppressive. He did not call out. He had announced his arrival at the gate, and whoever had answered knew he was there.

He reached a carpeted corridor that stretched into the distance with candelabras overhead. Two floor-to-ceiling doors stood open at the far end—surely the master bedroom—and he made for them, with the uneasy feeling that he had become a player in somebody else's game. He stopped in front of the doors and pushed them wider open. No sound came from the other side.

He'd guessed correctly—it was the bedroom. Bond stepped into a wide chamber with high ceilings and windows looking out onto a swimming pool. The bed was a four-poster. It had an oak frame with a canopy that was a heaving sea of antique, mauve satin. It was, Bond decided, a nightmare of a bed—made more so by the man who was lying in it, a gun lying in his open palm, blood seeping out of the hideous wound in the side of his head.

Bond had got here too late. Irwin Wolfe had shot himself. That at least was the picture that presented itself to him. The dead man's eyes were still open, staring glassily into the mid-distance. He was wearing pajamas and a silk dressing gown. The sheets, stained dark with his blood, were bunched around him. If Wolfe had killed himself, who had answered the intercom?

The answer came a moment later as a hand with a gun stretched out from behind the door, pointing in his direction, and a gravelly voice said: "We really shouldn't make a habit of this."

Bond had raised his hands. Now he turned his head and smiled. "I was rather hoping we'd run into each other again. But I have to say, you've taken me by surprise."

"I'm the one who's surprised, James. What are you doing here?"

"Can I put down my hands?"

"Of course. Just don't hit me again."

The last time Bond had seen Reade Griffith had been over a bourbon at the Hotel Negresco in Nice. As the man stepped out of the corner where he had been concealed, Bond recognized the neatly cut dark hair and blue eyes of the CIA agent. He lowered his hands and slipped the gun into his jacket pocket. "I don't need to ask what you're doing here," he said.

"Supporting and defending the Constitution of the United States against all enemies foreign and domestic," Griffith replied, quoting the CIA oath. He grinned. "As a matter of fact, Wolfe asked me to come out to the house. Quite ironic when you think about it. He had this idea that he might need protecting."

"From me?" Bond sounded innocent.

"I can't imagine why."

"And you'd been given orders to take care of him." Bond glanced at the dead man sprawled out on the bed.

"Wolfe was an embarrassment. He was also an enemy of the country. We like to keep things tidy. This seemed the best way."

"Suicide."

"The easy way out." Griffith paused. "Out of interest, why did you want to meet him?"

"My people wanted to put pressure on him. I think the idea was to achieve exactly what you've accomplished."

"Then you owe me a drink."

"I owe you more than that. I was hoping to see you again. I'm sorry we didn't catch up before I left Nice."

"Yeah. I heard you killed Scipio and closed down his entire operation. That's quite an achievement." Griffith put his own gun away. Bond noticed it was the same U.S. Army Remington that he had carried at the Rue Foncet. "So where are we going to have that drink? There's a place I know down in Westwood. . . ."

"That sounds good." Bond thought for a moment. "But before we head off, there is one thing I wanted to ask you."

Bond took out his cigarette case and extracted a cigarette with three gold bands. This mixture of Turkish and Balkan tobacco had been recommended to him by the man at Morlands, the cigarette maker in Grosvenor Street that Sixtine had told him about.

"You were working for Scipio all along," Bond said.

He lit the cigarette.

Griffith frowned but made no attempt to deny the accusation. "I wouldn't put it that way," he said. "I was working for the CIA. But yes, that meant cooperating with Scipio. How did you know?"

Bond had been warned from the start. The report he had read in London had made it clear that the CIA had chosen to support the Corsican crime syndicates in return for their help combatting the communists in the Marseilles docks—even if Reade Griffith had denied it. But it had still taken him a while to work it out.

"When I first met Sixtine, she knew who I was. My name, my number, my recent history—everything. I assumed she must have got the information from her own network. But later on she told me that it was actually Irwin Wolfe who had warned her about me. So the question was, who had told him?"

"That wasn't me."

"No. But he was working with Scipio. So someone must have told Scipio, who had then passed the information across. And that person could only have been you. Nobody else knew I was there."

"I hope we're not going to fall out over this, James."

"Not at all. You were doing your job. And the truth is, I should have seen it. When you and I drove to the dock at La Joliette, the man sitting at security asked to see my ID. He checked me out, but he ignored you. He knew who you were. He had seen you before." Bond paused and blew out smoke. "We lost a man at La Joliette. I'm going to assume you were there when it happened."

"I didn't have anything to do with his death, and I'm sorry that it occurred." Reade Griffith shook his head, remembering. "The thing was, he'd worked out something of what was going on. The connection with Ferrix Chimiques, for example . . ."

"That was why he had the invoice," Bond said. "I have to congratulate you. You completely blindsided me on that."

"Did I?"

"It was an invoice for thirty gallons of acetic anhydride. You told me it was the principal component of photographic film."

"It is."

"I know. But as it happens, it's also used in the production of heroin." Bond had checked it out when he got back to London. He was annoyed with himself for not having done so before. He had allowed Griffith to spoon-feed him the lie.

"Your guy was smart, but he still got it all wrong," Griffith continued. "He decided that Sixtine must be working with Wolfe. It made sense. She was a major operator and they were practically living together. He needed information, and he decided he could get it from Scipio. After all, he'd seen the two of them sitting together in that café in Marseilles. He'd even taken photographs. He figured he could persuade Scipio to tell him what she was up to.

"For what it's worth, I warned him against it, but he asked me to set up a meeting on neutral ground. I said I'd come along just to make sure that everyone played fair, and that's why he wasn't packing a gun. I arranged the meeting at La Joliette . . . white flag and all the rest of it. I was genuinely trying to help. The only trouble was, Scipio hadn't read the rules. When he realized your guy knew too much, he took out a gun and shot him three times in the chest. It all happened so fast, there was nothing I could do."

"Scipio knew I was coming to Ferrix Chimiques. You told him."

"I also told him not to hurt you, buddy. That's why it was water and not acid in that flask they threw in your face."

Bond had worked that out, too. Scipio had almost admitted as much when they had met that second time, on the *Mirabelle*. He had said that he wanted to deal with Bond—"without restraint." Those two words had told Bond someone must have been protecting him when he was at the chemical factory.

"There's one thing I don't understand," Bond said. "Irwin Wolfe was planning a lethal strike on your own country. Was Scipio so important to you that you were prepared to go along with the consequences? Or were you planning to stop the *Mirabelle* when it arrived?"

"I knew nothing about the *Mirabelle*," Griffith said. "I didn't know what was going on in Wolfe's head. Scipio didn't tell me. But why would he? For him it was a new business opportunity. My government is very grateful to you, James. I hear you're being recommended for a Medal of Honor. You certainly get my vote."

"That's very kind of you."

Griffith glanced at the dead body. "Let's get out of here, James. And make sure you take that cigarette butt with you. We want to leave things nice and clean for the police and the paramedics."

Bond didn't move.

"You're not sore with me?" Griffith asked.

"There is just one other thing I want to know," Bond said. "Did you know that Sixtine and I were on the *Mirabelle* at the end?"

"No, I didn't. What happened to her?"

"She died."

"That's too bad."

"Yes, it is."

Bond's hand had slipped, casually, into his pocket. When he took it out, it was holding the Beretta. In a single movement he shot Reade Griffith in the middle of the forehead. The CIA agent stared at him as if in disbelief. Then he pitched forward.

Bond moved quickly. Lifting him up by the armpits, he dragged the dead man closer to the bed and left him there. He took the gun out of Irwin Wolfe's hand. Using a handkerchief, he wiped it clean, then pressed it into Reade Griffith's hand. He removed the CIA agent's gun and slid it into his pocket. Finally, he wiped his own gun with the handkerchief and placed it in Irwin Wolfe's hand, closing the dead man's fingers around the trigger.

When Bond had come into the room, he had been presented with the scene of a fake suicide, but he had transformed it into something else. Griffith had been sent here to kill Irwin Wolfe. He hadn't realized that the older man was armed. In the end the two of them had shot each other. The CIA would be suspicious, but they wouldn't be able to ask too many questions, not without admitting why he had been there in the first place. Nobody knew anything about Bond. They didn't even know he was in America.

He finished the cigarette he had been smoking and pinched it out. He slipped the butt into his top pocket, then wiped the ashtray clean. He took one last look around, then left. The police would arrive eventually, but by then Bond would be long gone.

He climbed back into the car, thinking about the man he had just killed. Reade Griffith had lied to him from the very start. He had been hopelessly compromised by his relationship with Scipio and had been blind to the consequences. Whatever he might say, he had been responsible for the death of a British secret agent. He had almost certainly told Scipio about Monique de Troyes, the girl who worked at Ferrix Chimiques, and had caused her death, too.

And it had been thanks to him that Sixtine had died.

Slowly he drove back to the gate. He knew that although he had been given a license to kill, it hadn't extended to this. There would be no official report. He would never speak of it again. He had committed murder. Pure and simple.

Ahead of him a sensor picked up the movement of the car, and the electric door swung open, revealing Sunset Boulevard on the other side. Bond drove out, leaving behind him the memory of what he had just done.

He felt nothing.

AfterWords

Anthony Horowitz is no stranger to writing about the legendary Agent 007. The author's previous book, *Trigger Mortis,* also focused on the famous spy. "I couldn't have been happier when the Ian Fleming estate invited me to write a second Bond. I very much enjoyed exploring what might have been Bond's first mission and imagining some of the forces that might have turned him into the iconic figure the whole world knows," Horowitz says.

Of course, continuing the legacy of popular characters such as James Bond and Sherlock Holmes—Horowitz is also the author of the Sherlock novels *Moriarty* and *The House of Silk*—is sometimes complicated. When writing about Bond, Horowitz attempted to stay true to creator Ian Fleming's intentions. However, he admits that attitudes have changed since the 1950s, and "some of the things Bond says or does would no longer be considered acceptable." Ultimately, Horowitz writes with the fans in mind, believing that "for a writer to come barging into the room and to trample on the things they love is not acceptable; it's unthinkable."

In addition to writing novels, Horowitz is a television screenwriter and is the creator of *Midsomer Murders* and *Foyle's War,* among other shows. For more information, readers can visit anthonyhorowitz.com and ianfleming.com.

THE
LAST
ROAD
TRIP

'Crocker could set his novels
in a paper bag, and still
have you hyperventilating.'
—Jacqui L'Ange on *King*, in the *Sunday Times*

Gareth
CROCKER

The author of *King* and *Journey from Darkness*

Chapter 1

JACK EVERSON BUTTONED UP his thirty-year-old suit jacket and slowly made his way to the front of the church. Reaching the pulpit, he straightened his tie before turning to face the funeral congregation. Every seat appeared to be taken. He cleared his throat and leaned in toward the microphone.

"I'm sure you're expecting me to tell you that Paul was a good man. To hear some stories from his life. Memories from our school days together, perhaps. But I'm afraid I can't do any of that. The truth is I hardly knew Paul at all. In fact, I rarely saw him around the estate and we seldom spoke for any real length of time. As many of you know, Paul was an intensely private man who seemed to prefer his own company to others'. This being the case, I'm sure you're wondering why I'm standing up here today."

As Jack surveyed the room, half a dozen heads nodded faintly.

"A few weeks ago, Paul asked me over to his house. As you might imagine, I was a little surprised by the invite. In any event, I accepted. It was late afternoon when I arrived. We sat out on his porch and enjoyed a few drinks. He was surprisingly talkative and, after a while, asked if I would consider doing something important for him. A favor. Before I could ask what it was, he announced that he was dying. Just like that. He didn't share the details of his illness, only that the battle was lost."

Jack looked up and caught sight of his three friends sitting together near the back of the church—Samuel, Elizabeth, and Rosie. His gaze remained fixed on them as he continued. "It turns out that Paul had heard about my plans to leave the estate next month and wanted to know why I was going. My answer appeared to strike a chord of some sort. He then asked if I'd be willing to stand up here today. To read out a letter he had written."

With that, Jack reached into his pocket and withdrew two neatly folded pages. He fished out his glasses and slipped them on.

"My name is Paul Edwards. Like most of us here, I was fortunate enough to live a life in which I managed to accumulate a certain amount of wealth. Enough to allow me the privilege of living in a place like this. There's no question that in almost every respect Stone Well Estate is an Eden for people who have worked hard and wish to live out the remainder of their lives in peace and comfort. For those of you who don't know, I came out here many years ago following the death of my wife. Her passing hit me so hard that I was convinced I would follow after her in no time at all. I realize that makes me sound like an old and sentimental fool. But it's the truth.

"And so I waited to die. The days blurred into weeks. And the weeks came and went. One Christmas became another. And another. For eighteen long years I waited. When I finally fell ill and discovered the nature of my diagnosis, I felt relief. My long wait was over. You see, I stopped living the day I came here. I made this place my prison.

"I know some of you are thinking, How can a retirement estate as beautiful as this be considered a jail? Others among you will know what I mean. Trust me when I tell you that prisons can be made out of just about anything. It was only once I got really sick that I began to see things differently. When I was young, retirement homes were for the frail. Folks who, for the most part, could no longer care for themselves. But looking around at the people of Stone Well, a very different picture became clear to me. I decided to do a little research. Do you know that the average age of folks in our estate is sixty-three? So what, I'm sure you're wondering, is my point? Well, I'd like you to know how sorry I am for not taking the time to get to know more of you. It's no excuse, but you see, I was always waiting to leave. Now I realize how wrong I was and what a waste I have made of my time here."

Jack turned to the second page. The church was so silent now he could hear his fingers sliding on the paper.

"I can see that some of you aren't so different from me. You're waiting, just like I've been. You have stopped living. I'm asking you not to make the same mistake I did. Sixty-three—hell, eighty-three—is too young to be waiting for the clock to stop. I can't tell you how much I regret these past years. If you're like me and you've come here for the wrong reasons, I urge you to do something about it. You still have time to make things right. I was given eighteen years—a damn lifetime—and I spent most of those days staring at the sky."

"Thank you, Jack, for agreeing to do this. I was so pleased to learn of your upcoming trip. I sense you have unfinished business of your own. I enjoyed our brief time together, and I'm sorry we never spoke more or shared a drink occasionally. I have a feeling that I missed out on a friendship that could've really meant something."

Jack was surprised by a surge of emotion that tugged at his voice.

"I know that life isn't a storybook. I know that some of our mistakes are too far gone to be hauled back. But I also know that my life would've been so much better if I had just been trying for something. And that, really, is the point of this letter. My final wish for all of you is that you realize, while you still have time, that it's the trying that matters.

"Here's to life. And here's to you. Thank you for listening."

WITHIN hours of the funeral, Jack was back in the water. He had lost count of how many laps he had done. At age seventy-one, he was still capable of swimming prodigious distances.

The competitive urge that drove him to swim internationally for a time had long since left him. He swam now because it was a form of escape, and he still savored the sensation of cutting through the water, the comforting rhythm and solitude. It was also the one place where he allowed himself to think about things that, out of the water, he knew were better left alone. Swimming was his way of connecting back to Grace.

He had met her a little over ten years ago. In a public swimming pool. He was stepping into the water just as she was climbing out. Without thinking, he offered her his hand. To his surprise, she accepted and, as she ascended the last few steps, favored him with a smile, which irrevocably changed his life. He returned to the pool twice a day for the next three weeks in the hope of seeing her again. He eventually spotted her swimming on the far side late one Sunday, and waited patiently. When she finally emerged from the water, he was once again standing there with his hand outstretched.

Within a week they were dining together. Within three months he had proposed. Ahead of a honeymoon in Cape Town six weeks later, they had married on Robben Island. With no family left to call on, their only guest had been the minister who presided over the service. Etched against a deep blue sky and the backdrop of Table Mountain, it had been a cool, windless day. A day of dreams.

In the years that followed, they continued to swim together. The pools changed with the seasons, but their routine seldom wavered. After almost eight years of a cherished marriage, they had even spent time in the hotel pool the day before Grace's operation. It was, as it turned out, their last swim together. Some days Jack wondered what hurt the most: that Grace had been taken from him so soon, or that they had met so late in life. After all, eight years wasn't a life together. It was a glimpse of one. And some days that weighed heavily. She had been gone for almost two years, but when he swam, it felt as though she were still in the pool with him.

"What lap's he on?" Rosie called out from across the pool.

Samuel Lightfoot sat back in his chair and cupped his hands around his mouth. "Thirty-seven at my count."

As Rosie labored around the top of the pool, she shot him an unimpressed look. "Thirty-seven? Why bother getting in the water?"

Sam felt a wry smile tug at his mouth. Rosie Banks traded in sarcasm and irony the same way that lungs traded in air—almost constantly. Standing five feet five and weighing north of 260 pounds, she waddled from place to place with all the elegance of someone whose legs had been denied the benefit of knees. While some on the estate badgered her about her weight, Sam let her be. He was very fond of her just the way she was.

Rosie lowered her considerable frame onto a deck chair. "Have I ever told you my view on exercise?"

"Not that I can recall," Sam replied.

"Well, it's like this. I figure our hearts are a lot like engines. Car engines. We all know that there are only so many miles to be squeezed out of any one engine. Right?"

Sam cocked an eyebrow but played along. "Right."

"So why the hell would anyone want to force their heart to burn through so many extra beats? Nobody ever extended the life of their truck by driving it three thousand miles a day."

Sam smiled and shook his head.

"If you ask me, the best way to look after your heart is to do as little as possible. One could argue, in fact, that I did a certain amount of damage to my heart just walking here."

Sam began to laugh. "Car engine? Really?"

"It's like competing against a child who has suffered brain trauma," she said, kissing him on his forehead.

They chatted for a while, until Jack climbed out of the pool to join them.

"Nice going," Sam said, tossing his friend a towel. "Close on fifty laps at least."

"He's being kind. You were dragging arse out there," Rosie interjected. "It was embarrassing to watch, if I'm honest."

"My apologies, Rosie. I'll put in more effort next time," Jack replied, running a towel over his head.

"You know, Jack, with your hair all wet you bear a striking resemblance to an older George Clooney."

"Is that right?"

"It is. Of course I'm not talking about the actor, but rather the homeless drunk who used to pound on my gate back in the day looking for free food and a good time."

Jack smirked but resisted any attempts at a witty comeback. Instead, he slipped on his shirt. He then leaned over the cooler box and handed a wine spritzer to Rosie and a lemonade to Sam. He took a beer for himself. "So where's Queen Elizabeth?"

"Probably polishing her cheekbones," Rosie suggested.

At seventy-four, Elizabeth Shaw was the oldest of the four of them. But only on paper. Her long brown hair seemed unaffected by the passage of time and shimmered with a vitality that belied her years. Her smooth skin and clear blue eyes suggested she was, at most, in her late fifties. And if she was not already fortunate enough, she possessed the sort of facial structure and slim body that marked her as a classic beauty. It helped, of course, that she had spent most of her adult life in London, far from the ravages of the African sun, heading up an international fashion house.

"There," Sam said, spotting her leaving the clubhouse.

As Elizabeth made her way toward them, Jack noticed that she was wearing a silk scarf despite the oppressive heat. It made her look like an old-school air hostess.

"It's unlike you to be late, Lizzie," Sam said as she joined them.

Elizabeth went around, kissing each of them. "Sorry. I was reading and lost track of time. How are you all? Good swim, Jack?"

"According to Rosie, not good enough," he replied. "What were you reading?"

"Just some novel."

She sat down beside Rosie, and they launched into a discussion.

Jack turned to Sam and frowned. Sam shrugged. He had also seen it. Something was troubling Elizabeth.

As Jack poured her favorite drink, lime and soda, Elizabeth turned to look at him. "You were wonderful this morning, Jack. Paul was right to ask you. It was a remarkable letter. You did it justice."

"You did," Sam agreed. "Everyone's been talking about it." He took a sip from his drink. "I think his message really touched people. It's a pity we never got the chance to know him."

Holding his beer aloft, Jack regarded his friends with a smile. "To Paul. Quite possibly one hell of a guy."

Jack knocked on the door. It was well after nine, and he knew there was a chance Elizabeth had already turned in for the night.

"Lizzie, it's me," he said when he saw the kitchen light come on.

The door slipped open, and Elizabeth appeared in a dark blue velvet dressing gown. "Jack. Has something happened?"

"Everything's fine. I'm sorry to call on you so late. I hope I didn't wake you."

"No, not at all," she said, waving a hand. "Come in."

"Thank you," he replied, and stepped into the entrance hall.

As usual, Elizabeth's home was impeccable. It looked as if it had been lifted straight out of an interior design brochure.

"Coffee?"

"If you're having."

Elizabeth headed into the open-plan kitchen. She flicked her coffee machine to life and reached for a set of designer glass mugs. "So, Jack, what couldn't wait until tomorrow?"

"I can see something's bothering you. So I thought you might want to talk about it. You weren't yourself at the pool this afternoon, and at dinner you looked a thousand miles away."

Elizabeth said nothing as she poured the coffee. She handed Jack his mug, and they sat down at the kitchen table.

"How is it that you can always tell when something's not right?"

"Probably because you're crap at concealing your emotions."

She smirked. "Even so. You're always first to notice."

"It's a gift," he replied, winking. "So, would you like to talk about it?"

Elizabeth thought for a moment. "I'm not sure."

Jack decided not to push. Instead, he sipped his coffee. After a while, he pointed to the couches in the lounge. "Those look new."

"They are."

"Comfortable?"

"Not bad. Better than what we're sitting on."

"In that case," he began, holding out an arm.

As they made their way through to the lounge, Jack turned to face Elizabeth. "If it's too personal, that's fine. I just thought you might want someone to speak to."

Elizabeth picked up a cushion, which she placed in her lap. "There are a few things on my mind. You're one of them."

"*Me?*" Jack said, surprised. "What have I done?"

"It's not what you've done, it's what you're *going* to do. Did you ever stop to think what your leaving means for the rest of us?" Before Jack could respond, she raised a hand. "We don't even know why you're going. It's all part of this big secret of yours."

"Lizzie. There's a good reason I haven't told—"

"Jack, I know you must have good reason for not telling us why you're going, and I can respect that. Even if it doesn't make much sense to me right now. Besides, that's not really the point. I'm just sad that you're leaving. All three of us are. Okay?"

Jack felt a stab of guilt in his chest. "Okay."

"Just tell me one thing, though," she said, locking eyes with him. "Will we ever see you again?"

He considered the question. "I really hope so."

"I guess that's something," she replied, offering a smile that didn't quite reach her eyes. "As for the other things on my mind, I suppose I may as well share them. I've been living with them for most of my life. Just remember you asked for this."

"I did."

"So, as you've probably worked out, Paul's letter really affected me. You see, there's this door in my life that I thought I had closed years ago. But after today, I don't know if that's possible anymore."

"What's behind the door?"

Elizabeth reached for her mug, cupped her hands around it, and stared down at the carpet. "My childhood home," she whispered.

"And that has bad memories for you?"

"How can I put this? It's like a . . . beautiful nightmare. As you know, my father was a landscape artist who brought us out to South Africa when I was still a girl. Obsessed with stars and desert plains, he bought a farm in Sutherland. We all fell in love with the place. Especially the night sky. It was the perfect space for him to paint and for a small family to flourish. It was particularly good for a sensitive child like me who, in the rough-and-tumble of London, had struggled to fit in with other girls. It was a magical place. For a long time I thought I would never leave. And that was fine.

"But as the years drifted by, something inside me grew restless. I was reading a lot of French literature, and I became obsessed with the idea of studying in Paris. As I got older, the barren landscape and wide-open sky that I once loved began to stifle me. For the first time, I was fighting with my parents. Bickering incessantly with the two people who meant everything to me. I said things that I'll never forgive myself for. Horrific things that weren't true. I just wanted to hurt them because I thought they were holding me back. I went from being a shy, happy child to a rebellious, disrespectful teenager. I opened a rift so wide that, eventually, my parents had no choice but to give in and send me to Paris."

A lone tear rolled down her cheek. "I'm so ashamed of who I was at that point. I was selfish. I didn't care what I said or did. All that mattered was getting to Paris. And then, just like that, I found myself standing at the airport six months after my eighteenth birthday. As you know, in those days international travel was a big deal, and I can still remember the imploring look in my mother's eyes as we parted. At the time, I didn't know what it meant. That insight would come years later. She was praying that her daughter would come to her senses and return to the farm. As for my father, he looked heartbroken. We were always so close, and I think he couldn't believe what I had turned into. I think he blamed himself."

Jack placed a hand on Elizabeth's arm. "You don't have to go on."

"I know," she replied softly. "But I've kept this to myself for long enough. Maybe telling you will do me good. So I went to Paris, and just as my parents had warned, it wasn't at all the place that I had read about in my novels. I loved the architecture and the history, but it was lonely. I couldn't speak the language well enough. I was soon very unhappy and homesick. But after the fuss I'd kicked up, I couldn't admit the truth to my parents. So I stayed. Eight months after I was gone, my mother fell off a ladder and hit her head. She was in a coma for twelve days and died a week before Christmas."

Jack closed his eyes but said nothing.

"I had no idea how to cope with her death. It seemed impossible. I rushed home as soon as I could. But I was a mess. I stayed with my father for a time, but as the weeks went by, I couldn't bear it anymore. My mother's death had all but destroyed him. There was nothing I could do to take away his pain. And so, unable to deal with what was happening, and with the memories of my mother haunting me wherever I looked, I made the second-biggest mistake of my life. I used all my savings to buy myself a plane ticket back to Paris and, not having the courage to face my father, left early one morning for the airport. I never even said goodbye. I just left a note and walked out of his life." Elizabeth looked up at Jack, searching his face for the look of disgust that she knew she deserved. Instead, she saw only kindness. "I left him, Jack. All alone on that farm."

"You were very young. You can't blame yourself for not being able to face your mother's death. What you did was perfectly under-standable given—"

"You haven't heard the rest of it," she said, sighing. "A few months later, my father suffered a major stroke. The farm's care-taker, a kind and wonderful man named Joseph Thobela, managed to get word to me. He helped look after my father during that time. I didn't have the money to come home. It took me a while to raise it from my aunt in London, and before I could get home to atone for what I had done, he passed away in his sleep." The tears ran down Elizabeth's face, and she made no attempt to wipe them away.

Jack leaned over and wrapped an arm around her.

"I loved them both so much," she managed. "I've never been able to come to terms with what I did."

Jack rocked her slowly. "What happened to your parents wasn't your fault."

"*I should've been there.*"

Jack thought of arguing the point, but decided to change direc-tion. "What happened after your father's passing?"

"I went to London to live with my aunt. I never went back to the farm. She arranged for Joseph to look after the place until we decided what we were going to do with it. That was a lifetime ago."

"Are you saying that the house is still in your family's name? You've had this Joseph guy looking after the place all these years?"

"It's absurd, I know. He's an old man himself now."

"Does Joseph stay on the property?"

"Not as far as I know. He has his own home nearby."

"So what's inside the farmhouse?"

"I think it's the same way it was when my father died. My aunt was there six years ago, and she said it was like a time capsule."

Jack shook his head. "If you never planned to return, why didn't you just sell the place?"

Elizabeth shrugged. "My father loved the place so much that selling it seemed like another betrayal."

"So Paul's letter has made you . . . what?"

"Reconsider things," she whispered, fiddling with her hands. "Maybe it's time I went back. To face what I did."

They were both silent for a while.

"Then let me take you," Jack said.

"What?"

"I'll drive you. I'm going to Cape Town anyway, and there's no way in hell you should do this by yourself."

"Hold on, Jack. I don't even know if— Wait . . . are you serious?"

Jack placed his hands on her shoulders. "Let me help you."

Elizabeth stared at him, tears slipping down her cheeks. "Really?"

"Really."

SITTING on the veranda with its elevated view of the golf course, Sam admired how the sprinklers sprayed liquid rainbows over the fairways. An early summer sky framed a clear, fresh morning. There were few places on earth that could compete with Johannesburg when the weather was just so.

"How beautiful is that?" he asked, almost whispering the words.

"Not bad," Rosie replied. "For a prison."

"Ah yes. Touché."

"As a matter of interest, why have you never played golf?"

Sam shrugged and reached for his orange juice. "I tried playing a couple times, but the game didn't do anything for me. I preferred just walking around the course."

Rosie was about to reply, when Jack and Elizabeth arrived at the table. As they exchanged pleasantries, Rosie glanced at Elizabeth's plate. It contained a slice of watermelon and a tablespoon of yogurt.

"Lizzie," she began, "please tell me you have a sparrow with a broken wing in your pocket."

"Oh, Rosie, this is more than enough for me."

"C'mon, that's ridiculous," she replied, throwing up her arms. "I've flossed more food out of my teeth."

Elizabeth pulled a face as she sat down. "That's some imagery I could probably do without."

"Do you know what else you're going to have to do without?"

"What's that?"

"Hair. Because that's what you lose when your body doesn't get the nutrients it needs. Your hair falls out in clumps. You think I enjoy eating this much? The only reason I do is because I'm on a strict hair maintenance plan." She ran her hands through her short brown hair in a seductive manner. "This doesn't just happen, you know. It's hard work. Sacrifice. Dedication."

Jack pulled a face. "Sometimes I wonder about you, Rosie."

"Thanks, Jack, but I'm not sure your private thoughts of me are appropriate breakfast table conversation. In any case, just imagine how boring your chats would be if I wasn't around? What would you talk about? The weather? Elizabeth's alopecia?"

"Well," Jack said, "this might surprise you, but Lizzie and I have some interesting news for once. News and a proposition. As you know, I was planning to drive down to Cape Town in a couple weeks. Lizzie and I have been talking, and she's decided that she wants to visit her childhood home in Sutherland. I've offered to drive her. The idea is that she can spend some time on the farm and, when she's ready, fly back to Johannesburg."

"So we were wondering," Elizabeth cut in, "if you two might like to join us. There's no rush, so we thought we could take our time. Maybe spend a couple of weeks making our way down the country, visiting small towns. That sort of thing. What do you think?"

Sam thought for a moment. "It sounds like a fine idea."

Jack turned to look at Rosie.

She clapped her hands together. "I'm in. Just so long as my hair nutrition needs are met. It sounds like fun. Besides, it's about time we busted out of this prison."

"Lizzie, if you don't mind me asking, does this have anything to do with Paul's letter?"

Elizabeth looked at Sam and nodded. "I should've done this a long time ago. I don't want to put it off any longer."

"What about you guys?" Jack asked. "Is there anything you might want to do on the trip? Somewhere you'd like to go?"

Sam shook his head. "Just coming along for the ride is good enough for me."

"Same here," Rosie agreed. "So when do we go?"

"Next Friday?" Jack suggested. "That gives us a good week or so to prepare. I only have to be in Cape Town by New Year."

They looked back at Jack, knowing that any questions around the mysterious New Year deadline would be glossed over.

Rosie hefted up her glass. "To our road trip!"

"Our road trip," they echoed, raising their glasses.

THE next few days sailed by in a blur of lists and road maps. Routes were discussed, articles on forgotten back roads and ghost towns pored over. While accommodation was sought out and notes taken, no firm bookings were made. It wasn't that sort of trip.

Jack spent most of his time making sure his old Chrysler Voyager would be up for the journey. While the car was in good shape in terms of miles on the clock, the old girl's tires would have to be pumped, her battery replaced, and the engine needed a service.

At the end of the week, once again, they were sitting around the swimming pool—all but Rosie. Jack was about to serve drinks, when he noticed Albert Brooks sitting in his wheelchair under the tree to their left. As usual, he was staring at the book in his lap.

"I don't think I've ever seen him without that birding book of his," Jack said.

Sam nodded. "I think with his condition it gives him a degree of comfort. It's like an anchor in his memory."

Elizabeth adjusted her chair to get a better look. "I hear they want to move him into frail care. I think they're worried that he's not going to be able to take care of himself for much longer."

Jack got to his feet. "Well, he's not in frail care yet." With that, he turned and made his way toward Albert.

Sam and Elizabeth followed.

"Albert," Jack called out. "It's good to see you."

Albert looked up, a dazed smile dancing over his lips. "Hello . . . good afternoon," he said, reaching for a name. "Jack."

"Do you remember Sam and Elizabeth?"

"Yes, of course," he replied, though his expression suggested otherwise.

They all shook hands. Jack pointed to the book. "I tried getting into the whole birding thing myself once. I enjoyed it for a while."

"Do you know that we have some fantastic birds on the estate? Johannesburg is awash with them." Albert threw out his arms exuberantly. "*Awash.*"

Jack saw that detailed notes had been written beside each of the six birds depicted on the page. "Do you have a favorite?"

Albert nodded. "*Ardeotis kori.* The kori bustard. The world's heaviest flying bird. The jumbo of the sky!" He flipped to a dog-eared page. And there, highlighted, was a photo of a kori bustard. Jack thought it looked like a bloated pigeon. It was a grayish brown bird with black-and-white speckles on its wings. "Why is the kori bustard your favorite?"

Albert began to reply and then frowned. "Sorry, I get a little . . . *lost* now and again." He pointed to his head. "Some of the marbles are falling out. It's the Alzheimer's thing."

"I understand, Albert. It's no problem. Have you ever seen one of these birds in the wild?"

"No. I've never had the privilege, I'm afraid."

Largely bald, with a wisp of gray hair trailing over the roof of his head, Albert looked forlornly down at the page.

Elizabeth lowered onto her haunches and placed a hand on his knee. "Where can they be found?"

"They're quite rare in South Africa. One's best bet is to search in the Kruger Park."

Elizabeth smiled at him. "It's not too late, you know."

"What do you mean?"

Elizabeth glanced up at Jack, and he nodded. "Well, a few of us are going on a trip soon. If you like, we could take you into the Park for a few days. Try to find your bird. What do you think?"

"You would take me to Kruger to find a kori bustard?"

"Absolutely," she said, smiling. "How does that sound?"

"It sounds . . . wonderful. Truly wonderful."

Sam placed a hand on Albert's thin shoulder. "We'll have a grand old time."

"Yes . . . yes, *thank you!* But what about my wheelchair?"

"It's no problem. We'll put it in the trailer. And if we need to carry you anywhere, Sam and I will manage," Jack offered, guessing that Albert couldn't weigh much more than a hundred pounds.

"I don't know what to say; that's the most—"

"Just say you'll come, Albert."

"Yes. Of course! Thank you. Thank you all so much."

"It's our pleasure," Jack replied. "How do you feel about leaving on Friday?"

"That depends," Albert replied, "what day it is today." He began to laugh. "I can't keep ahold of dates anymore." He hesitated. "I have no right to ask this of you, but I think I'm going to anyway. Might you have room for one more?"

Jack contemplated the question. The Chrysler would seat five comfortably, but six was possible. "Who do you have in mind?"

"My dog, Pilot."

Jack exchanged looks with Elizabeth and Sam. "I didn't realize you had a dog, Albert."

"Oh yes. An old black Labrador. Probably about my age in dog years. A wonderful animal. I miss him so much."

Jack wasn't sure how to respond. "Where's he now?"

"My son-in-law has him. Despicable man. He keeps Pilot chained up in his backyard. Chained up! Can you believe that?"

"Why does he have your dog?"

"I—I can't remember. I just know that he took him away from me. And I want him back."

"Do you think your son-in-law will give him to us?" Sam asked.

"No."

"Why not?"

"Because I convinced my daughter to leave him. He's a horrible man, and he never deserved her."

It was Elizabeth's turn to frown. "I never realized you had a daughter."

Albert looked down at his bird book. "She passed away."

"Oh, I'm so sorry, Albert."

He looked back at her, tears brimming in his eyes. "You'd really like Pilot. He's something special."

"Then we'll just have to go and get him," Jack offered, having absolutely no idea how they were going to do it. "Anyone who keeps a dog chained up doesn't deserve to own one."

JACK was sitting opposite Arnold West, the estate's general manager. "Come on, forget the fine print. How much longer can he possibly have?"

"Look," Arnold replied, shutting Albert's file. "Every resident, including you, Jack, has signed a contract stating that in the case of a severe deterioration in health, with no family to turn to, we reserve the right to make decisions on behalf—"

"Are you telling me that it would be in Albert's best interests if he were sent away to frail care to die? Rather than let him come out with us for a few days?"

"Jack, I've given you an insight into his medical status. Alzheimer's is the least of his problems. His heart is very weak. If something happens out on the road, he could be gone before you know it."

"Then so be it."

"Excuse me?"

Jack was running out of patience. "How old are you? Forty?"

"What's that got to do with anything?"

Jack stared back at him, waiting for an answer.

"I'm forty-two. What's your point?"

"My point is that you have no idea what it feels like to be where Albert is in his life. Nobody wants to die alone in a hospital ward. Albert is desperate to come with us. You've seen how he is with that book. He wants to find his bird. Let me do this for him."

Arnold rubbed his eyes. "You're being unreasonable, Jack. You're making me out to be the bad guy. My hands are tied."

"Your hands are tied? With what? *Red tape?*"

"These are binding contracts. I could lose my job."

Jack sat back and folded his arms. "So this is just about covering your arse, really. It's not about Albert at all."

Arnold bristled. "The decision's made. And don't try to go over my head. Albert will be moved to frail care in the morning."

Jack allowed himself a humorless smile. "I didn't see you at Paul's funeral."

"I couldn't make it."

"It's a real pity. He wrote a letter. There were some interesting things in it. He wanted people to try to reach for something in their lives. To go after what they still can. It's a good message."

"It's quaintly idealistic, Jack, but not exactly practical. Especially for people like Albert Brooks." Arnold checked his watch. "Listen, it's getting late and I'd like to go home. Talking in circles isn't going to change my decision. Tomorrow Albert will be admitted to frail care, and that's that."

Jack stood up. "You know, Paul described this place as a prison. At the time I thought he meant it figuratively. Guess I was wrong."

"Good night, Jack," Arnold said, pointing to the door.

Jack began to walk away. "It must be tiring," he said without turning around. "Playing God from behind that desk."

Chapter 2

"Wake up, Rosie," a voice whispered in the darkness.

Rosie stirred and rolled onto her back. She blinked and wiped her eyes. "*Jack,* is that you?"

"Or an older George Clooney, if you prefer."

Frowning, she fumbled for the lamp next to her bed. "What the hell are you doing in my room? It's the middle of the night!"

"Sorry, Rosie, but there's been a change in plan."

As she flicked on the light, three more faces smiled back at her.

"Morning, darling," Sam chimed.

Elizabeth held up her hands in apology. "They did the same to me."

"Am I dreaming? What's going on?"

"We have to leave now. Arnold won't let Albert come with us. He's admitting him into frail care in the morning. We have to get him out tonight."

"Get him out? What are you talking about? People can't be kept here against their will."

"They can if they're incapacitated and there's no family to turn to. It's in our contracts."

"You're kidding me!"

"Afraid not. I had it out with Arnold. He won't budge."

Rosie hauled herself into a sitting position. "What time is it?"

"Just after two."

"You realize I haven't been awake at two a.m. in more than twenty years?"

"Uh-huh, isn't it great?" Jack smiled.

Rosie scrunched up her nose. "Yeah, it's really amazing. We should do this every night." Reaching for her gown, she yawned and turned to Sam. "So what's the plan, Black Pimpernel?"

"It's quite complex. First, we're going to Albert's house and wake him. Then we'll climb in the car and drive out the front gate."

"You've obviously given this a lot of thought."

"Look, Arnold isn't expecting this," Jack added. "We should just be able to leave without any problem at all. So you're in?"

"Go fetch my bags, Claus von Stauffenberg. Let's get this show on the road. How the hell did you get into my house anyway?"

ALBERT sat smiling in the back of the car, hugging a small kit bag to his chest. His eyes shone through the darkness.

Jack adjusted his rearview mirror toward him. "You okay back there?" he asked, firing the Chrysler to life.

"More than okay, Jack. I feel like I'm ten years old."

"Glad to hear it. And . . . you're *clear* about everything?"

Albert nodded. "Arnold is planning to admit me into frail care, where I will be forced to stay and most decisions will be made for me. But if we leave tonight, there's nothing they can do to stop us."

"In theory," Rosie corrected him. "In reality, we may well be arrested for abducting you in the middle of the night."

"They'll never take us alive," Jack said, smiling at Rosie in the mirror. He shifted his gaze to Albert. "Ready to get out of here, Mr. Brooks? Find ourselves a bird?"

"Not just any bird," Albert said, raising a finger. "*The* bird."

"*The* bird," Jack agreed. "If I push it a bit, we could make it to the Park in time for a late breakfast."

"But we first have a stop to make. Yes?" Albert cut in, a note of concern in his voice.

"Don't worry, Albert. I haven't forgotten," Jack said, and turned to Sam, who was riding up front with him. "Got the address?"

Sam dipped into his jacket pocket and held up a piece of paper.

"You sure this is the house, Albert?"

Albert thought for a moment and then nodded. "I am. Mostly."

"*Mostly* will have to do."

Jack's eye was drawn to the digital clock on the dashboard. It was 3:17. "And so it begins," he whispered.

"DOES the place look at all familiar to you?" Jack asked, his eyes scanning the tall palisade fence that ended in eight strings of high-voltage electric wire. Unlike many of the neighboring homes, the house in front of them was shrouded in darkness.

Albert rolled down his window and leaned out into the night. "I don't really remember. It was a long time ago. But I'm fairly sure the address is right."

"So what's the plan, Jack? How do you want to handle this?" Sam asked, checking the street for movement.

"Well, maybe we should get Albert outside and let him call out to the dog. See if we can get the Labrador to come to us."

Sam nodded. "Makes sense. He'll have to keep his voice down, though."

As they climbed out of the car and stepped onto the sidewalk, Elizabeth held up her hands to quiet them. She pointed to the near side of the house. *"Listen,"* she whispered.

Across an expanse of lawn, the low sound of a dog's growl drifted toward them from the shadows beside the house.

With Albert still in the car, Rosie whispered to Jack, "Mr. Everson, what if we're about to kidnap the wrong dog?"

"The thought did cross my mind," Jack conceded. "But at least we've been told he's a black Lab. That narrows it down a bit."

Sam and Jack lifted Albert from the car and carried him to the fence. It was like carrying a child. Still, the sound of their shuffling was loud enough to make the dog growl. The animal was on the verge of a barking frenzy when Albert called in a whisper. *"Pilot . . .* it's me. We've come to get you. Can you hear me, boy?"

At once, the growling ceased and was replaced by another sound. That of a steel chain unfurling.

"It's him. Has to be," Elizabeth said.

They listened as the chain continued to rattle and scrape toward them. Moments later, an elderly black Labrador, his legs stiff with age, hobbled out into a patch of moonlight.

"Pilot!" Albert cried, and clasped the palisade fence with what little strength he had left.

Elizabeth held her breath, and Rosie draped an arm around her friend.

As Pilot saw Albert, his tail began to sweep wildly from side to side. He hurried forward, but the chain yanked at his neck and he fell awkwardly. Hurt, but undeterred, he got up and tried again. The chain caused him to choke as he fought against it.

Albert pushed his arms through the fence, holding his hands in a *Stay* gesture. "Pilot, wait there! We're coming to get you." But Pilot kept pulling against the chain, his legs trembling as they fought for purchase in the soft lawn.

"Let's get Albert back in the car," Sam said. "The dog's fixated on him."

Jack agreed, and they quickly lifted Albert back into his seat.

"How are we going to get over this fence?"

"Not over. *Through*," Jack said, heading for the trailer and returning with a crowbar.

Sam looked at the tool and then at the fence. "Could work, but it's going to wake the whole neighborhood."

Jack hunkered down. "I just need to pry off three of these struts." He positioned the crowbar between the first strut and the horizontal bar, then pulled back with as much force as he could muster. A sound like a steel cable being sheared in half rang out. Dogs from up and down the street lit up in a chorus of alarm.

"Dammit!" Jack whispered, gritting his teeth.

They waited for lights to come on inside the house. But the rooms remained cloaked in darkness. The barking died away.

"I don't know how we got away with that," Sam said. "But there's no way we'll get away with another two of those."

Rosie stepped forward. "We need a blanket to wrap around the strut. It'll muffle the sound."

"Great idea. I'll get one." Elizabeth rushed back to the car.

Returning with the thickest blanket she could find, she worked quickly to wrap it around the second strut.

Rosie sighed. "We must be out of our minds."

"Could be worse," Sam said. "We could be sleeping in our five-star retirement estate."

Jack pulled back on the crowbar. To their amazement, the sheared steel cable now sounded more like the dull thud of a telephone directory falling off a table.

"Rosie, you're a genius," Sam said, puffing out his cheeks.

Jack and Elizabeth repeated the exercise on the third strut; then Jack hurried to the trailer and returned with a bolt cutter. He squeezed through the gap and jogged toward the Labrador.

Albert called from the car. "He's a friend, Pilot. He's coming to get you off that chain, boy. You don't need to be afraid."

While Albert continued to speak soothingly to the dog, Jack lowered himself to his haunches and gently patted Pilot on the head. The Labrador looked up at him, his eyes dark marbles in the moonlight, and licked the side of Jack's arm.

Jack cut through the chain, then removed the collar. The poor dog had lived with it for so long that the skin was raw from the constant abrasion. Pilot hurried toward the fence, squeezed through, and managed to leap up into the car.

Some things didn't need to be seen to be felt. Already, Jack realized as he straightened to his feet, the trip was paying off.

At the first signs of daylight, Sam glanced over his shoulder. "They're all still asleep, Jack. Even Pilot," he said, reaching out and patting the Labrador. "I still can't believe we stole him."

"Stole? I like to think of it more as a daring rescue," Jack countered, his eyes fixed on the road. "And it felt pretty damn good."

"Can't work out why people chain up their dogs. I mean, why do it? With that fence, it's not like Pilot could get out."

"I don't know. Well, at least we've got the dog. For a while there, I thought he might not exist."

Sam hoisted up an eyebrow. "Clearly Albert isn't as far gone as Arnold makes out. Coffee?"

"Sounds good. Thanks."

Sam reached down for the thermos at his feet, then set about balancing two plastic cups on his lap. After he had poured the coffee and stirred in some sugar, he handed Jack one of the mugs.

Around them, the darkness was lifting. Streaks of navy and purple were starting to show. Through the murk, distant mountains took shape like the headless shoulders of giant men.

Sam lifted his mug toward the windshield. "To whatever this is that we're doing."

"I think they call it *living*."

"Or dementia," a tired voice broke into the conversation.

Jack turned and saw Rosie massaging her eyes with her knuckles. "Morning, Rosie. You're just in time for the sun's grand show."

"Yay," she groaned. "I can die now."

"Coffee, madam?"

Rosie shrugged. "What do you think?"

"Just a *yes* would've been fine."

"But it would've lacked flair." She yawned. "Get much sleep, Jack?"

"Not so much. Mainly because of the whole driving thing. Thought it best not to kill everyone."

"That's why you're our leader," she said. "Even Pilot is in awe of you." She stroked the dog gently on his cheek.

THEY were barely minutes out from the Kruger Park when Elizabeth clamped a hand to her face. "Oh, hell. You aren't allowed to bring dogs into the Park."

Sam looked at Jack and then across at Albert as the realization sunk in. "Elizabeth's right. Why didn't we think of this sooner?"

Albert's eyes widened with concern. "What're we going to do?"

"Take it easy. It's not like we're crossing the border with a suitcase full of heroin. I'm sure we can come up with something."

"I don't mean to be the voice of doom," Rosie added, "but I imagine they'll check the car? And unless Pilot has the ability to impersonate a spare wheel . . ."

"You're right," Jack agreed as an idea began to form, "but they won't check *us*."

Rosie pulled a face. "I know I'm fat, but you can't expect me to tape a Labrador around my waist."

"No one is taping anything to anywhere."

"So what's your idea then?"

"A bit of misdirection."

"Oh, really? Misdirection? That's a great idea, considering that we just happen to be a party of traveling magicians."

"Look, hear me out. That dress you're wearing—"

"It's not a dress . . . it's a *muumuu*. And before you say anything insulting, you should know it's the most comfortable thing I own."

"Fine. The point is that you could drape it over Pilot. If someone looks inside the cabin, we'll tell them you're not feeling well. I can't see some Parks official forcing you to get out of the car."

"I suppose it might work," Rosie said, brightening. "I'll do it."

Elizabeth was less convinced. "But what if they insist on searching the entire car?"

"It's a fair point. If we got caught with illegal weapons, we'd probably be looking at ten years. Maybe double that for drugs. I imagine it would be life without parole for an illegal Labrador."

"Oh, be serious, Rosie."

"Listen, bringing an animal into the Kruger Park is surely like smuggling a glass of tap water into the ocean."

"It's the parasites and diseases that they're guarding against," Elizabeth replied. "And they take it seriously."

"But what's the worst they can do? All that'll happen is that they'll turn us away. If that happens—"

"We'll go to the next gate," Jack cut in. "Deal?"

Elizabeth considered the argument. "Well, I suppose it's not like we have any better ideas."

"Which one's yours?" the Parks official asked.

"The Chrysler SUV. Over there," Jack said, pointing.

"Sorry to delay you, but it's procedure."

"No problem. I understand." Jack shrugged, trying to appear as casual as possible. "If you don't mind me asking, what do you guys check for anyway?"

The heavy man's uniform clung to him in the heat. "A few things. But mainly weapons for poaching."

As they headed for the car, the official picked up a long pole with a mirror crudely taped to the end of it.

"And that?"

"To check if anything's strapped under the vehicle. They use proper versions of these at embassies and government buildings to check for bombs."

"Oh, I see."

"Please unlock the trailer."

"Actually, it's already open. You can go right ahead."

The man lumbered forward and raised the large aluminum lid. Securing it to its support strut, he leaned over and began to rummage between the bags. Jack looked over his shoulder. Elizabeth, Albert, and Sam were sitting on a bench across the road.

When the official was satisfied with the trailer, he turned his attention to the car. "Please open the hood."

Jack reached through the driver's window and released the latch.

Once the engine bay had been checked, the man walked to the passenger door and slid it open. Noticing Rosie for the first time, he nodded toward her. "Ma'am."

"Hello there," she said meekly. "Warm this morning, isn't it?"

"Yes, it certainly is. Everything okay?"

"Wonderful. Thank you."

Preempting the question, Jack chimed in. "Rosie struggles with her legs. They swell up in the heat, and she battles to walk."

The man regarded Rosie. "It's okay, ma'am. I understand." He turned to Jack. "Enjoy your time in the park."

"Thank you. I'm sure we will," Jack replied. "Have a good day."

AFTER four hours of driving and almost an hour spent phoning travel agents, they managed to secure accommodation at a private bush camp on the banks of the Luvuvhu River. To get around the issue of keeping Pilot's presence in the Park a secret, Jack offered his credit card and booked all eight bungalows in the camp, seven of which were located firmly and sensibly on the ground. The eighth unit, however, was a luxury tree house perched proudly in the branches of an old baobab.

With Rosie and Elizabeth more than content to keep Albert company on terra firma, Jack and Sam claimed the tree house, enchanted by its storybook appearance. Made of wood, it fanned out around the tree like a large timber lily pad. It included a kitchen, two bedrooms—each with a four-poster bed—and a lounge that extended out onto an open deck suspended thirty feet in the air.

"You know a place is special when it surpasses anything your imagination could've conjured up," Sam said, sitting down on one of the deck's armchairs. He took a sip of his drink and looked out over the river that flowed, soft and gentle, in the fading light.

Jack's gaze settled on a distant speck as it wheeled and arced above the riverine trees. He reached for the binoculars on the table beside him. Twisting the dial on the lens, he squinted as the blurred image sharpened into feathers and wings. "That's really something," he said.

"What is it?"

The bird swooped down and landed on a bare branch that hung like a skeleton's arm over the river. "Here. Take a look."

Sam snatched up the binoculars and hoisted them to his face. Spotting a major bird of prey now would add icing to their cake. After a few moments, he sighed. "You're not as funny as you think. You know that?"

"What?" Jack said. "You got something against pigeons?"

AFTER dinner, they positioned themselves around the firepit and settled in for the night. Pilot was sound asleep at Albert's feet.

"And to think this time yesterday he was chained to a wall," Elizabeth said, bending to stroke the Labrador. The fire cast a rich amber glow over his coat.

"To be honest, I never thought I'd see him again."

"That would've been a great shame, Albert," Sam offered.

Albert made a point of looking at each of them. "I want to thank you all for bringing me along on this trip. I don't know what made you think to include me, but I really appreciate it."

"It's our great pleasure," Jack replied.

"Let's just hope we find that bird of yours," Sam said.

"That would be quite something." Albert nodded, wiping his brow. "But if we don't have any luck, so be it. At least we're out here and the possibility exists. That's glorious in itself."

"If we don't find it, it won't be for lack of trying," Jack replied. "Have you thought of mapping out the best places to search?"

Albert seemed almost embarrassed to answer. "I did that the day you invited me on the trip."

As Rosie imagined Albert poring over detailed maps, unable to contain his excitement, her eyes began to sting.

"You okay, Rosie?" Elizabeth asked.

"I'm fine. It's the smoke. You know?"

"I know," she said, smiling.

Above them, stars shone like torches. Around them, insects sang their forever song. And between them, flames swayed in a faint breeze.

"This living thing isn't half bad," Sam said, closing his eyes.

Chapter 3

THE FOLLOWING MORNING, Albert was already dressed and waiting in his wheelchair when Jack and Sam made their way down from the tree house. Jack looked at his watch. It was five thirty.

"Morning, Albert. You look like you're ready to go. How long've you been waiting?"

"Not long. Maybe an hour."

"You've been here since four thirty?"

"Uh . . . I guess so."

"How was the sunrise?"

"Difficult to put into words, actually."

An hour and a half later, they were on the road. Within forty minutes of setting off, they had seen elephant, giraffe, wildebeest, antelope, crocodile, and a family of hippos. The birdlife had been phenomenal. There had been eagles, vultures, storks, weavers, falcons, and more deep blue starlings than they could count—which had sent Albert into a sort of delirium. But so far, no kori bustard.

"So just how big are these birds anyway?" Rosie asked.

"The males can grow to four feet and have a wingspan of around two and half meters. They can weigh upward of twenty kilograms."

"Can you remember why this bird is so special to you?" Elizabeth continued, recalling their initial conversation.

Albert took a few moments to slip his mind into the right gear. "It's because of my father. When I was a boy, he told me that a kori bustard saved his life. As a young soldier he was part of an army convoy that got stuck in the desert in northeast Africa. The story goes that he and another soldier volunteered to walk for help but lost their way in a sandstorm. After a few days, they were out of water. My father collapsed at the bottom of a sand dune. When he woke, a kori bustard was standing a few feet away, watching him. As he moved toward the bird, it didn't fly off but instead began to walk away. He decided to go after it, and it eventually led him to a water source. He was adamant that it saved his life."

Rosie considered the story. "You don't think that maybe your father was hallucinating?"

"It's possible," he replied. "But I hope not. It's a good story."

Albert then stared out the window, his eyes tracking across an endless field of mopane bush. Suddenly a look of confusion drifted across his face. "You know something? This place looks a lot like the Kruger Park. Don't you think?"

A SHORT while after dinner, Rosie and Elizabeth helped Albert to his bungalow before deciding to call it a night. The heat of the day, coupled with the early start, had taken a toll on everyone. It was ten p.m. when Jack and Sam sat down for a drink on the deck of their tree house.

"Good day, wasn't it?"

Sam puffed out his cheeks. "Better than good. Quite close to magical, I'd say."

"I can't understand why I've stayed away all these years."

"I know. I was thinking the same thing this afternoon."

"I suppose that's what routines do to people. They make you forget about places like this. What it feels like to be here."

Sam nodded and gazed up at the moon. "Do you know what I resent most of my forty years as a lawyer? Not the cases I lost or the bastards I had to defend, but the time it cost me. I should never have ridden a desk for as long as I did."

Jack was about to respond, when Sam continued. "If I were an advertising man, do you know how I would sell this place? I'd get a top photographer to shoot this deck . . . and that moon," he said, pointing, "and at the bottom I'd just run the camp's name and telephone number. Nothing else. You wouldn't need any adjectives. Just a single photo."

Jack agreed, then took a sip of beer. "So listen, Sam, mind if I ask you a question?"

"Course not. What is it?"

"I just noticed that you weren't really yourself tonight. Pretty subdued. Even Rosie was struggling to get a rise out of you."

Sam shrugged and pushed back in his chair.

"Come on. What's going on, old man?"

"It's not worth talking about."

"How about we talk about it anyway?"

Sam continued to stare up at the moon. "It's this place, I guess. It gets you thinking, you know? About life. Things that've gone well. Things that haven't."

Jack had a good idea of what Sam was getting at, but decided not to go there. Instead, he bided his time, listening to the crickets.

"I've been thinking about Sarah mainly."

Jack nodded and sipped his beer. "I thought that might be it."

"It's been almost *nine years*," Sam said in a whisper.

"She still won't return your calls?"

"Calls, letters . . . she won't respond to anything."

"What about your granddaughter?"

"Never met Casey. Never even spoken to her. She's growing up, and it's all slipping through my fingers. I have one photo, but it's already a couple years out of date." Sam reached into his shirt pocket and withdrew the small photograph. It had been carefully laminated and placed in a plastic pouch.

Jack held it up. Casey was dressed in a children's costume—a shark suit—and was smiling from ear to ear. "She's beautiful. Ever thought of just arriving in London unannounced?"

"Tried that. Two years ago. I found out where Sarah worked but never made it past reception. They called up to her, but when she heard it was me, she refused to come down. I waited for three hours. Eventually security asked me to leave. And that was that."

"I'm sorry, Sam."

"Me too," he replied softly. "But don't give me your sympathy, Jack. I don't deserve it. Not a word of it."

"Look, I don't know what happened between the two of you, and it's none of my business. But I'm sure that whatever it is, it can still be fixed. It's just a question of—"

"I hit her, Jack," Sam whispered. *"I hit my own daughter."*

Jack turned to Sam as if he had misheard.

"I was a selfish drunk who didn't deserve to have someone as wonderful as Sarah in his life."

"Sam—"

"She'd been wanting to move to England to be with her new boyfriend. One night, I'd been drinking hard and we got into an argument. I kept telling her the guy was no good and that it wouldn't work out. She lost her temper and started shouting at me about my drinking. About how selfish I'd become, that I was holding her back from living her life. God help me, Jack, before I knew what I was doing, I slapped her with the back of my hand. I can still see the look on her face. It was like she was staring at a monster. And she was, Jack. *She was.* I'd do anything to go back and change what happened."

"It was a mistake, Sam. A horrible . . . *mistake*. When you're drinking you can't—"

"Don't, Jack. Please. Don't even say it."

Jack checked himself, then grasped for something else to say. "Does she know about last year? About the cancer?"

Sam shook his head. "No."

"She has a right to know."

"I've put her through enough. I won't *guilt* her into speaking to me."

"She's your daughter, Sam. She deserves the truth. Besides, you're in remission now. What's the harm?"

Sam opened his mouth to speak and then closed it again.

"What is it?"

"It's not over, Jack. The cancer's back. It's in my lungs now."

"Why didn't you tell me? You shouldn't be on this trip. You should be getting treatment."

"There's nothing they can do," Sam continued "So I figured a road trip was better than a hospital bed. If you think about it, Albert and I are in the same position. This is it for us, Jack."

Jack stared at his friend, numb. "I don't know what to say. I don't even know what to think. You don't *look* sick, Sam."

"I was a lawyer for a long time. I know how to play my cards close. Besides, I'm not in much pain. I'm sure that'll come soon enough . . ."

"But Sam—"

"There's nothing else that needs saying. I'm just glad to be out here. This is more than I could've hoped for."

Jack stared at his friend. "I'm so sorry."

"Don't be, Jack. Don't be," Sam said, and then turned to look at the moon once more. "Look at her. Isn't she something? Just a photo and a telephone number. I'm telling you."

After Jack had finally agreed not to tell the others, both men rose to their feet. Sam looked at him. "This trip is important, Jack. For all of us. Probably more than you realize."

Before Jack could respond, Sam thanked him for the evening and headed off toward his room. "I'll see you in the morning. Maybe we'll find that bird for Albert. The elusive kori bustard, rescuer of lost soldiers. That would be pretty sweet."

"It would be," was all Jack could summon.

For the next three hours he lay wide awake with his hands knitted behind his head, staring up at the thatch ceiling. The Sam he knew was not a violent man. He was a gentle, kind soul. Tolerant to a fault. In fact, he had never heard Sam raise his voice. He couldn't imagine him raising a hand against anyone—let alone the person he loved most in the world.

THEY were back on the road just as the sun was cutting through the tops of the trees. Swaths of yellow light lit up the dust on the Chrysler's windows. It wasn't even seven a.m.

"So why's everyone so quiet?" Rosie piped up, making light work of a shortbread biscuit.

Jack looked up at the rearview mirror. "Just trying to wake up."

Albert, sitting between Rosie and Elizabeth, was wired after three cups of coffee. "I'm awake."

"From what I've seen, Albert, you never sleep at all," Elizabeth cut in, smoothing out her silk skirt.

"I find it very difficult to sleep in this place. There's just too much happening all around us."

Rosie used her tongue to clean her teeth. "Worried you're going to miss something?"

"I suppose I am. Yes."

Jack glanced across at Sam, who was dozing quietly in the passenger seat. He was still struggling to come to terms with what his friend had told him. Trying to push it out of his mind, he looked over his shoulder. "So, Albert, how about a wager?"

"What do you have in mind?"

"I bet you any dinner you like that we find your bird today. What do you say?"

"Deal," Albert nodded. "Although it's a bet I'd be happy to lose."

Rosie wiped crumbs from her T-shirt, which read FAT PEOPLE HAVE FEELINGS TOO. HUNGER, MOSTLY. "That's not a fair bet."

"Why?"

"Well, because Albert will probably have forgotten all about the bet by lunchtime."

Elizabeth rolled her eyes. "I'm sorry, Albert. You'll get used to Rosie's wildly inappropriate comments after a few more days. Really, underneath that acerbic outer crust, she's all heart."

"Not true. I'm mainly made of *cholesterol*."

Albert beamed, despite the joke at his expense. He then looked down at Pilot, who was lying in the footwell beneath Elizabeth's legs. "And what's your name, fella?"

Rosie felt the smile slip from her face. "That's Pilot, Albert."

"Pilot?" Albert asked, confused.

"Yes. He's your dog. We, uh, took him from your son-in-law."

"My son-in-law? I'm sorry, but that can't be right."

"What do you mean? Why not?" Jack asked.

"Well, for one thing my son-in-law lives in Australia. And my Pilot died many years ago. I buried him myself. Cried like a child."

Rosie held out her hands as if to try to steady the conversation. "Albert, you gave us an address. We went to the house, and there was a black Labrador chained to a wall. Just as you told us there would be. You said that was Pilot."

Albert thought for a few moments. "Was the house surrounded by a large palisade fence?"

"Yes."

"I think that might've been my old neighbor. They used to have a Labrador named Bobby or Benny or something. They kept him chained up. Always hated that."

Rosie lifted a hand to her mouth. "We stole the wrong dog."

"What are we going to do?" Elizabeth asked softly.

"About what?" Albert asked.

Rosie stared back at him, incredulous. "About the dog, Albert."

Perplexed, he glanced down at the Labrador. "You mean Pilot?"

"Pilot? Albert, what the hell—"

And that's when he broke into a broad smile. He winked at Rosie. "You're not the only one who likes a good joke."

Chapter 4

As it turned out, Jack lost the bet. Not only were they unable to find a single kori bustard that day, but they failed to find any in the three days that followed. Jack knew that as far as Albert was concerned, the trip was already a success—something he would cherish for as long as his ailing mind could hold on to the memories—but he was becoming desperate to find the bird. Rocks, tree stumps, and anthills all started to look like kori bustards. Whenever they came across a game ranger's vehicle, Jack would flag it down and ask for advice. But so far, it had all come to naught.

They were driving over a bridge in the late afternoon, when Elizabeth reached for her binoculars. "Jack, can we stop for a moment?"

Jack eased the car to a halt at the end of the bridge. "What is it, Lizzie?"

Elizabeth stared into the binoculars, carefully refocusing the lenses. "I can see something in the riverbed."

They all turned toward the sandy vein that cut through the trees beneath them.

"I—I don't know. I think . . . I might've spotted one."

Albert leaned across Elizabeth and scanned the area with his own binoculars. At first he couldn't find what she was looking at, but he soon locked on to it. Partially obscured in a patch of shadow stood the distant, unmistakable form of a kori bustard. "*That's it!* I think it's a male. He's enormous!"

Using a third set of binoculars, Jack also homed in on the bird. It was too far away to see clearly, but it was there.

Albert kept the binoculars pinned to his face. "Oh, thank you, Jack. Thank you, everyone! This is wonderful. *Remarkable!*"

Jack was relieved that they had finally found what they had come to see, but something about the moment seemed wrong. In his mind, he had imagined a close-up experience. Not this. "Albert."

"Yes, Jack," he replied, his gaze still focused on the river.

"I don't think this is good enough. We're too far away."

Albert lowered the binoculars and looked at Jack.

Sam, reading his friend's mind, began to smile.

"What's going on?" Elizabeth asked.

At that point, Rosie also picked up the thread. "Jack wants to take Albert in for a closer look. On foot," she added.

Something flickered in Albert's eyes.

"I don't mind the risk if you don't," Jack whispered.

"No. I won't let you endanger your life for me. It's not—"

"Albert, listen to me. I'm going to take a walk down into that riverbed, with or without you. I'd rather it be with you."

"You're not being serious."

Jack clicked open his door. "Oh, I'm serious."

Sam nodded. "I'll help you, Jack. We'll do it together."

"This is absurd," Elizabeth said, her voice rising. "You three can't go out there."

Rosie shrugged. "No point arguing. Jack's got that look."

"We'll be fine, Liz. It's a dry riverbed. There's plenty of visibility on both sides."

"Yes, I'm sure the predators will be able to see you very clearly."

"This isn't a zoo. It's not like there's a lion behind every tree. We'll only be a few minutes."

Elizabeth glanced across at Albert and saw the one thing in his eyes with the power to disarm her: hope. She sighed. "Just make it quick."

Having hauled Albert into his wheelchair, Jack and Sam managed to roll him down the bank easily enough, but progress in the thick river sand soon proved all but impossible. So they each grabbed a side of the wheelchair and carried Albert toward the bird, which was perched on a log three hundred yards from them.

"Can I do anything to help?" Albert asked.

"Sure, lean toward Jack," Sam replied. "He's the fit one."

"Just enjoy the ride, Albert. Don't listen to the old man—he needs the exercise."

"This is remarkable," Albert said, trying to steady his words. "I can't believe you're doing this for me."

Sam looked at Jack. "That's the thing about our Jack—he's always doing things that you don't quite expect. But even by his standards," he said, swallowing, "this is something."

As they closed in, the great riverine trees arched above them. Albert looked up. "It's so beautiful," he managed.

A minute later, they had made it to within throwing distance of the great bird. Standing as tall as a five-year-old child, it craned its head toward them. Moving as slowly and as quietly as they could, they lowered Albert's chair into the sand and stood back. And watched as Albert Brooks fulfilled a lifelong dream.

Jack stared into the fire, mesmerized. For the first time since they had come to the Park, there were voluminous clouds in the night sky. They glowed a vivid orange, as if reflecting the flames at their feet.

"To our last day," Sam said, raising his glass. "And to finally finding our bird."

"Hear, hear," Albert followed, lifting his drink.

Elizabeth sighed and hugged herself. "I'm not sure I want to leave. It's so wonderful here."

Thunder rumbled through the trees, and a wind picked up. Pilot raised his head and sniffed at the air.

"Can you smell the rain coming, boy?" Jack asked, ruffling the Labrador's head.

"Jack," Rosie remarked, cocking her head toward the tree house, "with a storm coming, you might want to rethink your strategy of sleeping in a lightning conductor."

Before Jack could respond, lightning snapped into the trees ahead of them. Large droplets of rain began to fall. As one, they scrambled under the cover of the outdoor kitchen and stared out, through the fence, into the bush.

"This just caps it all off. I was hoping we'd see some rain," Albert said, inhaling deeply. "It's incredible! Can you smell it?"

"Yes. It smells like pneumonia."

"Oh, come on, Rosie! I know you're loving it as much as I am."

"Maybe not *quite* as much as you."

More lightning flashed, and as it did, Jack rose to his feet.

Sam was the first to notice the look on his face. "Jack, what is it?"

"There," he said, pointing toward the fence. "Look."

At first there was nothing to see but the rain and the night. Until lightning flickered again and the bodies of half a dozen enormous elephants lit up the bush. They glided silently past the fence, barely yards from the covered kitchen patio, like glistening gray ghosts, their tusks swaying gently.

"Would you look at that?" Rosie whispered.

HAVING left the camp well before dawn, they were nearing the exit to the Park when the sun broke over the horizon. Heavy grays and dark greens gave way to an explosion of color. Fever trees glowed like apparitions in the early morning light. Starlings twitched and darted in their sapphire armor, glistening as the light caught their wings.

Jack lifted his foot off the accelerator. There was no reason to rush. The open road could wait.

"So, about those elephants last night," Rosie said. "What I can't get over is how quiet they were. It was as if they were floating above the ground."

"Ever heard of an elephant pause, Lizzie?" Jack asked.

"A what?"

"An elephant pause. When arriving at a place where an elephant has died—even years after the fact—many elephants will stop walking and stand motionless, sometimes for minutes on end. The experts believe it's both an act of mourning and a gesture of respect for the life that's been lost. No other animal on the planet does it."

"That's beautiful," Elizabeth replied softly. "And sad."

Jack wanted to engage Albert on the subject, when he noticed that he was asleep, his head resting against the window. *About time,* Jack thought, convinced the man had been awake for days.

"You don't think this elephant pause business is just something the rangers cooked up to have fun with gullible Americans? Oh, look, that elephant's in, uh . . . *full pause.* You see, he's paying homage to a dead cousin. Oh, and there's another doing the same thing. And another. Wow, this must be an elephant cemetery. Want to buy a key ring?"

Jack shook his head. "Your cynicism is almost charming, Rosie. Almost."

Before further banter could ensue, Elizabeth asked Jack to turn up the air-conditioning. "I think Pilot's getting a little hot back here. He's quite restless."

Jack looked back and could see that the Labrador was agitated and beginning to pant and whimper.

"I'll open my window," Sam volunteered. "Maybe he needs air."

As a stiff breeze circulated through the cabin, Jack noticed that it was doing nothing to calm the dog.

Pilot began to bark at them, loudly and without respite.

"Pilot? What is it, boy?" Elizabeth asked.

It was only when Jack stopped the car and turned around that he realized what had happened. He felt something cold clutch at his chest. Everyone had turned to Pilot and was trying to calm him down. Everyone but his owner. Albert remained slumped against the window in a pause that Jack knew was permanent.

AFTER they returned to the estate, it took only a week to put Albert's funeral together. While Albert's attorneys handled his will and financial affairs, Rosie and Elizabeth took care of his personal effects. Jack and Sam dealt with the undertaker.

When it came to the service itself, Elizabeth volunteered to speak. She had grown extremely fond of Albert and wanted to share her recollection of him.

Reaching the pulpit, she steadied herself. "Some weeks ago, Jack Everson stood up here on behalf of a man he hardly knew," she said. "Today, I find myself in much the same position. I can't tell you a great deal about the life of Albert Brooks. I know he had a daughter who passed away some years ago. That he owned a successful property business. I can also tell you that Albert had a great love for birds and spent hours searching the trees on the estate, making notes in that book of his, a book he was seldom without. I take great solace in the fact that Albert had something in his life that he cherished so deeply. The best I can do is tell you about the last week of his life. And his search for his favorite bird."

As Elizabeth took the mourners through the final moments of Albert's life, her gaze kept returning to Pilot, who was sitting beside the bier that held Albert's coffin. The mournful look in the Labrador's eyes threatened her resolve, but she managed to get through the eulogy. When she was done, she walked over to the Labrador and kissed him on his head. He licked her cheek.

Sitting between Jack and Sam in the front row, Rosie wept.

ELIZABETH was first to ask the question. "So do we carry on?"

"I think so," Jack replied. He looked at Sam and Rosie, and they both nodded. They were sitting together on the estate's clubhouse patio, watching the sun go down over the golf course.

"I suppose the question is *when?*"

"Why hang around?" Rosie said, folding her arms. "I don't want to be here anymore. Let's leave tomorrow."

Jack waited for an objection, but none came. "Sam? Lizzie?"

"I think I'd also feel better out on the road."

"It just doesn't seem like there's enough air around here," Elizabeth added.

"Okay. Well, I guess if everyone's on the same page, then that's what we'll do. We'll head out tomorrow morning."

"Sounds good," Sam replied. "Where're we going?"

"Just *away* will do for now," Rosie said.

"We've still got some time to decide. Maybe we should just get onto the back roads and work our way south to Sutherland."

"Pilot will love it on the farm," Elizabeth offered. "There's so much space for him down there."

"Maybe we can stop off in—"

"*Hopetown*," Rosie interrupted Jack. "I'd like to go to Hopetown for a while."

They all turned to look at her.

"There's a place or someone there that you'd like to see?"

Rosie shrugged, her gaze fixed on the horizon. "Yes, Jack. Something like that."

Chapter 5

THEY HAD BEEN ON THE ROAD for barely two hours, but already Elizabeth and Rosie were sound asleep. Sam, sitting in the front passenger seat, was nursing a mug of coffee.

"Can we talk?" Jack asked.

Sam turned to look at him. "Sure. What about?"

"Your cancer."

"There's not really much to say on the subject."

"Still. Would you mind?"

He shrugged. "I guess not."

Jack overtook a large coal truck. "Do you have some sort of"—he hesitated, searching for an appropriate word—"timeline?"

"You mean when am I going to die? Nope. I did ask the question. I was expecting the standard six months, but they kept it vague. Could be as long as eighteen months or half that, was the best I could get out of them. Of course, that's the sort of thing I might tell a patient if I knew he had a couple of weeks to live."

"And treatment's really not an option?"

"Oh, it's an option all right. Just not one worth taking. Treatment could maybe buy me a few extra months. But what would be the point? I'd be sick to death half the time. No thanks. They can keep their poisoned drips. This is the way I'm meant to go out. And that's okay with me, Jack. I've made my peace with it."

"Do you at least have some pain medication?" Jack asked, and then added quietly, "For later."

"In my bag."

A light rain began to pepper the windshield. "Is there anywhere you want to go? I don't care where it is. Anything you want to do?"

Sam rolled down his window, let his arm hang out in the stiff breeze, and smiled. "Thanks, Jack. But I'm doing it right now."

"LET's do something crazy," Rosie suggested, yawning.

"Four geriatrics in a twenty-year-old van, driving between hell and high water on a lonely road—that sounds pretty mad right there," Sam replied.

"Yes, but shouldn't we be stopping in some one-horse town to cause a bar fight or swim naked in the river?" She rubbed her eyes. "Where are we anyway?"

"About half an hour outside Virginia."

"Oh, Virginia," she replied fondly, gazing out across the rolling fields. "It'll be especially beautiful this time of year. I mean it's always beautiful, but in summer it really pops. You know?"

Sam raised an eyebrow. "You've been to Virginia?"

"Don't be an idiot. Of course not. Nobody's ever been to Virginia," she replied, deadpan. "Is there any food in this rust bucket?"

Elizabeth handed her the cooler box, and Rosie quickly fished out a box of biscuits. She gave a biscuit to Pilot before dispatching two herself. "Sorry, guy. I get two because humans are more important than Labradors. And we have thumbs. Those are the rules."

Jack was pleased that Rosie was getting back to her old self. "Rosie," he called from the driver's seat, "we'll be in Hopetown in a couple of hours. Is there anywhere specific you want to stay?"

"How about the Four Seasons?"

"I doubt they take dogs."

"It's an old mining town, Jack. The place would offer a bed to the bubonic plague if it paid its way."

"I take it you've actually been to Hopetown before?"

Rosie was quiet for a moment. "Once. When the world was still black and white."

As THEY drove over the old bridge that led into Hopetown, Rosie turned to look at the Orange River, which flowed beneath them.

"It's pretty," Elizabeth said, rolling down her window. Pilot, sitting beside her, rested his muzzle on the doorframe. His nose twitched in the breeze.

"Not bad. Although they should've called it the *Brown* River."

Sam watched as the town grew larger in the windshield. After so many miles of arid landscape, he was relieved to finally have something different to look at.

"What's the name of this guesthouse?" Jack glanced at Rosie.

"Eureka."

"Eureka?"

"Eureka."

"Don't you mean *Eureka!?*"

"Not particularly."

As they turned into the main road that cut through the center of town, two things were clear. One, the town appeared to be running a little short on the hope that it boasted of in its name, and two, they would not be needing further directions to the Eureka Guest House. While the rest of the town presented itself in the character of most small Karoo towns—wide, dusty roads, tin-roofed houses, outdated shop fronts—their accommodation for the next three days looked as though it had been lifted out of 1980s Las Vegas.

Shimmering in the late afternoon sun, the guesthouse played on the fact that Hopetown had been the site of South Africa's first diamond rush. The knee-high wall that guarded the front of the house was adorned with football-size plastic diamonds, which at one point might well have been a brilliant blue-white but were now a dull yellow-beige. Some had cracked, and at least one appeared to have melted in the sun. The guesthouse itself was decked from ceiling to floor with strings of diamanté that alternated with fairy lights. On top of the faded blue tin roof was an enormous sign: THE EUREKA GUEST HOUSE—WHERE DIAMONDS ARE FOREVER.

Jack pulled up to the front gate.

As they stepped out into a heat so profound they seemed to be wading through something only marginally less dense than water, the front door swung open and two faces appeared, smiling a great deal more than seemed necessary.

Jack summoned up a smile of his own. "Good afternoon. We spoke on the phone. It's Bill and Margie, right?"

"Right!" Margie replied. "You remembered!"

"I'm good with names," was all Jack could think to say.

Margie was in her late sixties and painfully thin. Apart from some freshly applied lipstick, her skin was the color of desert bone. Her hair was pulled back into a tight bun.

Rosie gave Margie's floral dress the once-over and then whispered to Elizabeth, "Somewhere inside the diamond cake a window's missing its curtain."

Bill hurried forward and stabbed out a hand. "Pleased to meet you, Jack. Welcome to Hopetown."

He was blue-eyed and appeared to be approaching his eighties at a gallop. He wore short navy-blue pants, black sandals, and a vest that years ago might have been white but was now the color of weak tea. What remained of his hair was neatly trimmed, and he sported a pencil mustache. His eyebrows had come to resemble the wild, curled bristles of an old scrubbing brush. Thick and gray, they twisted flamboyantly up his forehead.

"And you are?" Bill asked, poking a hand in Rosie's direction.

"Amazed at the beauty of your guesthouse." She beamed, more cubic zirconia than diamond. "I'm Rosie."

Sam and Elizabeth then introduced themselves in a flurry of embraces, handshakes, and back pats. Even Pilot was hugged.

"You sure it's okay that he stay inside with us?" Elizabeth asked, looking down at the Labrador.

"Of course. We've had many dogs stay with us over the years. He's part of your family, isn't he?"

"He is," she replied, tickling Pilot under his chin.

Moments later, they were ushered into the entrance hall, a large, dark-wooded space, complete with buck and zebra trophies.

"So what brings you folks to our humble town?" The eyebrows twitched.

Jack exchanged a look with Rosie. "Nothing specific, really. It just looked like a good place to visit. We're heading to Sutherland and then on to Cape Town."

"Sutherland?" Margie exclaimed. "A lovely Karoo town, but, as you'll discover, not quite as charming as ours. Let's just say that Sutherland doesn't quite have the legacy. Or the pedigree."

Ah, Jack thought.

Sensing that a history lesson was in the air, Rosie was about to explain that it had been a long drive and that she desperately needed a lie-down, when Bill cleared his throat.

"Founded in the mid-1800s, I'm sure you know that this is where the world-famous Eureka diamond was discovered. Thus, of course, the name of our place," he said, offering a proud smile.

"The diamond was picked up by a fifteen-year-old boy in 1866," Margie chimed in.

"Twenty-one carats."

The bread-and-fishes act—no doubt trotted out many hundreds of times over the years—was now in full swing.

"But it was nothing compared to the diamond that was found in the region in 1869, by a shepherd."

Following his wife's cue, Bill lowered himself to his haunches and reached into a cupboard. He withdrew an ornately carved wooden box. Carefully he lifted the lid and took out what was clearly the jewel of the Eureka Guest House crown: another cheap, plastic diamond. "This is one of only fifty replicas," he said in awe.

Margie nodded solemnly and gazed deep into the pear-shaped polymer. "The magnificent . . . *Star of South Africa*."

Rosie bit her lip, wondering if their hosts were about to burst into song.

"A shade under eighty-four carats. *Eighty. Four. Carats*. Difficult to imagine."

Elizabeth leaned in for a closer look. "Spectacular."

"So, uh . . . who made the replicas?" Jack asked.

"Oh, we did. Every few years when we really like a guest, we give them one."

"When last did you give one away?" Sam asked.

Margie thought for a moment. "About six years ago."

Rosie slapped her hands on her hips. "Wow. Those are some standards you set. What did the recipients have to do? Invent time travel?"

"Oh, let's just say we look for certain special qualities."

Sam glanced at his watch. "Bill, Margie . . . if it's all right with you, might you show us to our rooms? It's been a long day, and I'm sure the ladies would appreciate some rest before dinner."

"Well, of course," Margie replied. "We can pick this up later."

After the diamond had been safely put away, they were led down a long passage. As their footsteps echoed on the sagging wooden floor, they passed a number of framed portraits. Each was of a diamond prospector, and each was accompanied by a less-than-quick story that Bill was only too happy to impart.

After half a dozen stories and several minutes stewing in the excruciatingly hot passage, Pilot squatted down and made known his feelings at being cooped up in the sauna-like corridor. Pleased with his offering, he barked to announce its arrival.

As they turned around and saw what Pilot had done, Elizabeth shook her head. Jack and Sam peeled away in embarrassment. But Rosie took it all in her stride. "So I guess we can kiss away our chances of getting that diamond then?"

THE NEXT MORNING, HAVING forgiven Pilot for his indiscretion, Bill and Margie had prepared a plate of sausages for the Labrador and a feast of bacon, eggs, tomatoes, mushrooms, and toast for the rest of them. While they worked their way through the mound of food—evidently they were the only guests—Bill picked up on the history lesson from the day before. He was threatening to extend his lesson to other towns when Jack said they needed to get going.

Rosie announced that she would not be joining them.

"You feeling okay?"

"I'm fine, Jack. Just a little worn out."

Elizabeth studied her, unconvinced. "Rosie. What's going—"

"Lizzie, I'm all right. I just need a few more hours' rest. Didn't sleep well last night. I'll see you this afternoon." Cutting short the discussion, Rosie headed for her room.

"What's that about?" Sam asked.

"I don't know. Maybe she is just tired."

Elizabeth shook her head at that. "Doubt it."

An hour and a half later, the three of them had explored just about all there was to explore in Hopetown. With little else to do, they parked beside a quiet sand road and walked down to the banks of the Orange River. Content to take in the dappled morning sun, they positioned themselves under a lone tree.

"So, anybody have the first idea of why we're in Hopetown?"

Jack looked at Sam and shrugged. Both men turned to Elizabeth.

"Don't look at me. I haven't the faintest. Rosie hasn't said a word about it."

Sam removed a shoe and sock and dangled his foot in the cold water. "She said she's been here before. Long time ago."

"Yes, but we know she wasn't born or raised here."

"She also said she'd only been to Hopetown once."

Jack thought about that. "Then the obvious question is what could've happened here in the space of a single visit that would make Rosie want to come back all these years later?"

"Maybe it wasn't something so much as someone?" Elizabeth suggested. "Perhaps she had a wonderful day here with someone she loved."

Sam removed his remaining shoe and slipped off his sock. "From what Rosie's told me, her marriage was a disaster from day one. Whatever happened here, I don't think happened with her ex-husband. And she doesn't have any brothers or sisters."

"Okay. So is anyone buying the fact that Rosie's taking a nap?"

Elizabeth looked up at Jack and shook her head.

AT DINNER, Rosie picked at her food, contributing to the conversation only when called upon. When she wasn't staring at her plate, she was gazing out the window, her mind elsewhere.

Jack's concern was mounting. It wasn't just that she was quiet. Her armor—her constant wit and banter—was no longer in effect. Whatever was plaguing her was strong enough to strip her defenses. And that, Jack knew, took some doing. He watched as she sipped her wine, her eyes tracking something through the window that only she was privy to. *Something from her past,* he thought.

After dinner, Bill and Margie cleared away the dishes and retired for the night. Before anyone could consider following suit, Jack suggested they go to the lounge for a nightcap. After drinks had been poured and everyone had settled onto various couches, he tossed a few logs into the fireplace, then rubbed his hands together. He was thinking of what he could say to Rosie to get her to open up, when she began to speak.

"My mother," she uttered in a low voice, "was not a good woman. She suffered from the kind of sickness that no doctor could get to. Certainly not back then, probably not today either. She was guilty of the most horrible things. I won't burden you with the sob story of my childhood—suffice to say that Abigail Banks pretty much put a torch to the first twenty years of my life. I'd like to tell you that I got over all the things that happened, that I managed to work through the issues and emerged happy and healed on the other side, but that's just not true. The way I speak, my weight, the things I do, well . . . it's pretty obvious, isn't it? It's all part of my big act. *The Rosie Banks show.* I don't blame my mother for everything, though. That would be too easy. I've allowed myself to wallow in self-pity for years. Allowed my weight to spiral out of control. Been quick to blame everything on her. After all, we never want to acknowledge our own failures. But I certainly do blame her for one thing. The worst thing she ever did."

Rosie began to circle the rim of her sherry glass with her index finger. "I loved my father very much. *Worshipped* is perhaps a better word. Unfortunately, his work required him to travel for long periods. When he was home, things were wonderful. Idyllic even. The minute he walked through the front door, my mother was a different person. She would change from being this aggressive, vindictive monster into just about the perfect wife and mother. It was like a lever had been pulled. The change always took my breath away.

"Anyway, whenever my father was home, I would try to spend every last minute with him. I'd follow him around the house. Help him with whatever needed doing. I used to spend afternoons in his garage while he tinkered with things. I considered telling him what Mother was like when he was away, but I was worried that he wouldn't believe me. Or, worse, that he would believe me and wouldn't be able to do anything about it. After all, it wasn't as if he could stay home to take care of me and forget about his job. We never had much money and relied entirely on his paycheck. I suppose, even as a child, I didn't want to add to his burden." Rosie paused. When she spoke again, her lips were trembling.

"I was nine years old when my mother handed me this," she said softly, reaching into her pocket. She withdrew an old, folded letter and placed it on the table.

Jack looked at the letter and then back at Rosie. "May I?"

She nodded.

He lifted the letter, carefully pried it open, and began to read.

"Abigail.

"It has all become too much for me to bear.

"For the longest time I thought I wanted to be a father. I thought it would complete our lives together. But I'm sorry to say that having Rose has only made matters worse. Part of the problem is that she's not the child I wanted. She never leaves me alone, and I simply cannot tolerate it anymore. She has also managed to force us apart to the point that I don't believe our marriage can be salvaged.

"I'm sorry, but I just can't do it anymore. I simply can't.
"Edward."

The room lapsed into silence.

"For the next thirty years I believed my father had left because of me. My mother told me that he had wanted a boy and that he often wished I had died at birth," Rosie said, pausing to take a breath. "Many years down the road, I was working hard at building up my clothing business when I broke down one morning. I had a close friend in the office, and the whole story just poured out. My mother's abuse, my father's abandonment, my running away from home at seventeen—all of it. It was only when my friend insisted on reading the letter that everything changed. I'll never forget the expression on her face when she was done. I think, in some ways, it saved me. She said that, given what I had told her about my father and all the wonderful things he had done for me, there was no way he could have written that letter. *Not a chance.* My mother must've been jealous of our relationship and was obviously mentally ill."

It felt like the air had been sucked out of the room. Tears rolled down Rosie's face. "The moment she said that, something inside me realized it was true. For my entire adult life I had been reading that letter as a nine-year-old child. As a person who wasn't able to question her twisted mother's authority. To bring reason to an absurd situation, to a letter that is ludicrous in the extreme."

Fending off her own tears, Elizabeth shook her head. "So what did you do?"

"I decided to try to find him. I wanted to find out why he really left and why he never saw fit to contact me again. No phone call. No letter. I waited years to hear from him, always praying that he would change his mind and come walking through our front gate."

Jack could hardly look at Rosie.

"Even though I now understood that my mother had written the letter, it didn't excuse the fact that my father had left me behind. I wanted to know why. I had to know what I had done."

Suddenly Sam pushed himself back in his chair. "Oh no, Rosie," he whispered. "Your father died, didn't he?"

Rosie nodded gently. "A week before my mother gave me that

letter. He was a mechanic—used to work on boats mostly—and had died at sea while trying to repair a fishing trawler. They were caught in a storm, and the boat went down. His body was never found."

Jack stood up and went over to Rosie. He was immediately joined by Elizabeth and Sam, who reached out a comforting hand.

"Is that why we're here? Was your father born here?" Sam asked.

Rosie shook her head. "Sometimes, when he knew he was only going to be away from home for a few days, he would take me with him. Once, when I was about seven, he had to travel down to Cape Town, and we stopped over here. Early the next morning, he woke me up with a surprise. One of his colleagues owned a truck and was kind enough to drive us out to the top of a hill just outside town. I had no idea what was happening, but as we climbed out, my father reached into the back of the truck and pulled out an old bicycle. He climbed on, lifted me onto his lap, and as the sun rose over the mountains, we started down this enormous hill. He said it was called Seven Mile Hill. Bill and Margie helped me find it yesterday. Back then it was still a sand road."

Elizabeth pressed a tissue to her eyes.

"As we rode down the hill, he told me to close my eyes and imagine that we were flying. I swear to God, I *was* flying that day. When I think back, I can remember it so vividly. I can feel my father's arm around my waist and the smell of his aftershave. How the cool wind made my face tingle. I'd give anything to be close to him again." Rosie looked up, her face drawn. "So, tomorrow before sunrise, I'd like to go back to that hill one more time. It would mean a great deal to me if you would all consider riding it with me."

Sam lifted Rosie's hand and kissed it. "Of course, old girl. *Of course.*"

"I was hoping you'd say that. I've arranged bicycles for us. They arrived late this afternoon."

Chapter 6

As Jack pulled over onto the shoulder of the road, first signs of daybreak were sparking on the horizon. While the edge of the sky was clear, heavy clouds had moved in overhead. Stepping out of the car, Rosie held out her hands and felt the kiss of a raindrop against her palm. She breathed in the fresh morning air with its rich, earthy fragrances. So often she had imagined coming back. Now that she was here, she was struggling to take it all in.

Jack walked over to her. "Sure this is the place, Rosie?"

"I am, Jack. Thank you."

Sam strode around the car and joined them. "So Bill and Margie are waiting at the bottom of the hill for us?"

"Yes."

"And they know why you're doing this?"

"They know some of the story. They've been so generous about everything. They're wonderful people. I feel bad about some of the things I said about them when we arrived."

Jack nodded. "Just think, weeks from now you'll be one of the stories they tell their new guests."

Elizabeth walked up behind Rosie and rested her head against Rosie's back. They stood in silence as rain began to fall and the sun eased itself over the mountains.

After a while, Rosie cleared her throat. "I think it's time, Jack."

He and Sam headed for the trailer. A short while later, they returned with the bicycles.

After Jack had checked everyone's brakes and made sure that Rosie and Elizabeth were comfortable, he walked his own bike onto the road. "You going to lead us, Rosie? Nice and easy."

Nodding, she inched ahead of them. She stared down the winding hill as the first rays of sun glistened on the road. "I can't believe we're doing this," she murmured. "It feels like a dream."

And then she released her grip on the brakes, and her bicycle began to roll forward.

For the first two miles they drifted cautiously down the hill, making their way through dips and around sweeping bends. When the road straightened and it was clear that they had at least another mile of simple freewheeling ahead of them, Jack moved up next to Rosie. She was, he saw, smiling and crying at the same time.

"Do you trust me?" he called out.

She nodded, the wind making slits of her eyes. "Of course."

"Then keep your bike steady," he said, and carefully maneuvered his bicycle closer to hers. With one hand, he reached out and took hold of her handlebar. "I've got you. Do you still trust me?"

"Yes, Jack."

"Then close your eyes and let go, Rosie. *Just let go*."

She glanced down at her fingers, then over at him, hesitant.

His voice trembled. "You didn't just come here to ride, Rosie."

Fresh tears filled her eyes. *"Jack . . ."*

"I've got you," he insisted.

Rosie let go. She shut her eyes and raised her arms to the sun and rain. And to her father who had once held her tight and made her believe that she could fly.

EARLY the following morning, Bill and Margie were seated on a bench in the front garden when Jack walked out the door.

"Jack, are you sure you don't want to stay for breakfast?"

"Thank you, Margie, but we've decided to get an early start."

"Heading straight for Sutherland?" Bill asked.

"Not quite straight. I think we'll take a more scenic route."

"It's Karoo country, Jack. All the routes are scenic."

Rosie and Elizabeth made their way into the garden. Rosie headed for Margie. She took hold of her hands and looked across at Bill. "Thank you for yesterday. I know how silly it must have seemed, but it was really important to me. More than I realized, actually."

"It was our privilege," Margie said. "We barely know all of you, yet it feels like we're about to say goodbye to lifelong friends."

Elizabeth embraced Margie. "I won't forget the last few days."

"Neither will we," Margie replied as Sam made his way down the steps.

"Morning, everyone," he said, and then pointed at Margie. "You know you were right about Hopetown. There really is something about this place. And it's got nothing to do with the diamonds."

"Thank you, Sam. This trip that you're all on, it's a very beautiful thing. More people should do it."

Elizabeth nodded. "We think so too."

As Sam and Jack loaded up the bags, Margie hurried inside and returned with a small gift-wrapped box. "This is for you, Rosie."

"Oh, Margie, I can't accept this. You've already done more for me than you know."

"You can accept it, and you will. Besides, the gift itself doesn't hold any real value. Just the sentimental kind. It'll be something to remind you of your time with us."

"In that case," Rosie conceded, "thank you."

Margie hugged her tight, then wrapped her arms around Elizabeth. "Have a wonderful time in Sutherland. Take care of yourself."

"I will. You too. I'll tell everyone about your special guesthouse."

After the last bag had been stowed away, Jack and Sam returned to the group. "Well, I guess that's it."

"Look after these ladies, Jack," Margie insisted. "They're precious cargo."

"Don't I know it."

After a final round of hugs and handshakes, they were all in the car and the Eureka Guest House was receding in the rearview mirror. Rosie opened her gift. Beneath the wrapping paper was a black box. As she lifted the lid, she didn't know whether to laugh or cry.

She fished out a large plastic diamond, one of the cherished replicas, and held it up to the morning light.

THE silence that settled over them as they drove was neither uncomfortable nor cloying. Rather, it was a time for contemplation of what had been and, for Elizabeth in particular, what was still to come.

Jack stared through the windshield but saw little of the empty road ahead. Instead, he pictured his late wife, Grace, swimming low in the sky. He watched as she cut through the water, her strokes elegant. When she reached the edge of the pool, he was waiting. "Don't you think that's enough?" he asked, wading up to her.

She winked at him. "No, I don't."

He drew his arms around her and whispered. "Grace, please. You really shouldn't be in the water."

"No, Jack. This is *exactly* where I should be. With you."

"But your surgery—"

Grace placed a finger across his lips. "We both know that after tomorrow I may never get off that hospital bed. So today, Jack, while I still can . . . I want to be in the water."

Jack pressed his forehead to hers. "Please don't talk like that."

"I'm sorry. I don't mean to upset you."

He cupped her thin face in his hands. "You are so beautiful."

"And you're such a bad liar. I know the cancer's taken whatever looks I once had."

"You're wrong. The cancer can't get to what I can see."

She smiled. Lifting her hand from the water, she rubbed his shaved head. "It was so sweet of you to cut off your hair for me."

"I wish it was me. The whole thing . . . *I wish it was me.*"

"Don't you say that, Jack Everson. And don't forget you have a promise to keep. You hear me?"

"That's not fair. What you're asking me to do is—"

"You gave me your word, Jack. Now tell me that you'll honor your promise. I need to hear it."

"I promise," he finally said.

At once, her frown blossomed into a smile. "Let's swim a little longer. Come on, swim with me."

It was after dark when they finally emerged from the water and headed back to their room.

In the end, Grace had been right on both counts. It had been her last swim. She never did make it off that hospital bed.

WITH SAM AND ROSIE SOUND asleep, Elizabeth leaned forward and wrapped a hand around Jack's elbow. "If it's all right with you, I'd prefer not to go to Sutherland today. I know I'm being pathetic, but I'm just not quite ready yet. Could we stay over somewhere else? I need another day to get my head straight."

Jack placed his hand on top of hers. "Actually, I was thinking of stopping over in Victoria West anyway. It's a small town about half an hour away. How does that sound?"

"Like a reprieve. Thank you, Jack."

"No need to thank me. And you're not being pathetic. I can understand why you're nervous. What you're doing is not to be underestimated. We'll get to Sutherland when it feels right to you."

They were quiet as Jack negotiated a steep curve in the road.

"So, Lizzie, I was doing some reading last night. There's an old cinema in Victoria West. Been around forever. Still running, apparently."

"Oh, Jack, I *love* old cinemas," Elizabeth replied.

"According to my little travel book, the place exists. I can't remember the name, though."

"Think it'll be open tonight?"

"There must be a good chance. It's Saturday, after all."

"I wonder what sort of films they show. Maybe the classics. *Gone with the Wind* or *Casablanca*. Wouldn't that be something?"

Before he could respond, Elizabeth forged ahead. "I don't care what's showing. I'd love to go. Will you come?"

"Of course. You should see your face right now."

Elizabeth clapped her hands together, thrilled at the prospect of watching an old film in a decades-old theater. "I hope it's open."

"It probably has fleas."

"Don't care."

Sam straightened up in his seat and rubbed his eyes. "What are you two on about?"

"Jack says there's an old cinema in Victoria West."

"I thought we were going to Sutherland?"

Jack slowed the Chrysler as they passed a cow grazing. "Change of plan, Sam. That's the beauty of a trip like this."

"Indeed it is." He yawned, then settled back into his seat, blinked twice, and, as if in sync with the old Labrador, fell right back to sleep.

"The man's a dog," Elizabeth remarked, a playful look in her eyes.

A part of Jack wanted to tell Elizabeth about Sam's cancer. To share the truth of what they would all have to face up to in due course. But he had promised Sam that he wouldn't. Not on their trip. And if Jack was good at anything, it was keeping his word.

THEY stood outside the two-story building with its blistered white paint and stared up at the sign. The sheet metal letters had been cut by hand. Unfortunately, the hand in question had not been blessed with any deftness. The letters were all of different shapes and sizes, attached at slightly different angles.

"Isn't that just brilliant?" Jack said, lifting up his arms. "The Hotel California. These small towns are something else."

"I'm not sure I get it?"

"C'mon, Lizzie, it's a song by the Eagles. You must know it."

"Oh, right," she said, nodding. "Something about a desert highway. Wind in your hair. And we're in the Karoo. Very good."

Sam turned to Jack. "And your guidebook claims that old Pilot here will be welcome?"

"Apparently. At the same rate as children under twelve."

Making their way inside, they saw a young man sitting slouched behind the front desk, an enormous set of headphones over his ears. He arched an eyebrow and summoned up an annoyed look.

"As charm offensives go, we're off to a shaky start," Rosie said.

As they reached the desk, the youngster slipped a stud-encrusted ear out of the headset. Although he didn't say anything, his blank expression implied that he deigned it acceptable for them to speak.

"Hey there," Jack said, reading the name on the desk. *"Henry?"*

"No," he sneered. "That's my stepfather. I'm Bradley."

"Right, Bradley," Jack continued. "So, do you have anything available for us? We'd like four rooms if possible."

Bradley's eyes traveled down to Pilot. "What about him?"

"He'll stay with me," Elizabeth replied. "If that's all right."

Bradley shrugged in the way unique to sullen teenagers. "Whatever." He sniffed and swept an arm in the direction of the key box. There were keys hanging from every hook. "There're *always* rooms available here because this place is a hellhole. In case you didn't notice on your way in, the whole town's a hellhole."

Having no desire to argue the town's merits or lack thereof, Jack waited a moment. "So how about those rooms?"

Bradley reached back and extracted four sets of keys. "No aircon. No showers. No television. But these probably suck the least."

After Elizabeth had filled out the paperwork, Bradley pointed them to their rooms. As they gathered their luggage, Rosie turned to the young man. "Can we check out any time we like?"

"Yeah."

"But we can never leave? Isn't that right, Bradley?"

"I don't get it."

"I know."

AFTER a short nap, Jack decided he could do with some exercise. Heading downstairs, he was pleased to see that Bradley was no longer at the front desk. Instead, his chair was now occupied by who he assumed was the boy's stepfather, Henry.

Before Jack could offer a greeting, the man was on his feet and around the desk. "Good afternoon. Welcome to the California."

"Fan of the song or band?"

"Both," he said, holding out a hand. Almost completely bald, he was tall with bright green eyes and a grip that was evidence of a life lived outdoors. "Henry Sidwell. Good to meet you."

"Likewise. Jack Everson."

"Hope my stepson gave you at least a half-decent welcome."

"Oh yes. He was fine."

Reading between the lines, Henry held up his hands. "I'm sorry about that. His mother dragged him out here six months ago, and, well, he hasn't quite forgiven us yet. We're a new family."

"Maybe you shouldn't hold your breath for too long."

"You're probably right. I'm hoping he meets a pretty girl in town. That would get us off the hook for a while. Anyway, I see that you're a party of four," he said, then glanced down at Pilot. "Four and a half. Are you here to unwind or just passing through?"

"Both, actually."

"Good. If there's anything you need, don't hesitate to ask."

"Actually, there are a couple of things," Jack began. "I read that the town has an old cinema. Is that right?"

"The Galaxy," Henry beamed. "Fifty-three years old. The most charming theater for a thousand miles in any direction. It runs every weekend whether there are customers or not. Unfortunately, you've come at a bad time. It's closed for some restoration work."

"Ah, that's a pity. My friend Elizabeth and I were really hoping to watch something tonight."

Henry's eyes narrowed as he thought for a moment. "I tell you what. Leave it with me, and let me see what I can do."

"Do you know the owner?"

"Very well. I'll have a chat with him. See if he'll open up for you."

"Only if it's not too much trouble. I don't want to—"

"I'm sure it'll be no trouble at all. What sort of film would you like to see?"

"Can we choose?"

"Yes, of course. There's a storage room behind the cinema with hundreds of old reels."

"Well, what about something classic? Please tell the owner that we're more than willing to pay for the privilege. Whatever it takes."

Henry nodded. "Leave it to me."

"Thank you," Jack said. He was about to leave, when he remembered the reason he was standing there in the first place. "Henry, is there anywhere to swim around here? A public pool maybe?"

"There was one, but I'm afraid it's fallen into disrepair. Water shortages saw to that about three years ago. However, there's a nice dam about two kilometers outside of town. It even has its own little island. Quite a special place, you'll find. The water's very clean."

Henry offered directions before looking down at Pilot. "There's something particularly wonderful about old Labradors, isn't there? What's his name?"

"Pilot."

The Labrador's ears pricked up at the sound of his name, and his tail began to sweep across the floor.

"How old is he?"

"Not really sure. Probably about my age."

The gray hair around Pilot's eyes all but twinkled in the sun.

"Is he yours?"

"Sort of. I'm one of the owners. The four of us . . . well, we kind of inherited him," Jack replied. "It's a long story."

"Sounds like a good one."

"Actually," Jack said, running his index finger along the bridge of Pilot's nose, "it's not half bad."

DESPITE the blistering afternoon sun, the dam was surprisingly cold. So cold that Jack struggled to draw breath at first. As he waded out from the shade of an old tree, ripples emanated from his arms, fracturing the calm surface. He noticed the island that Henry had mentioned. A bump of grassy mud, no larger than a tennis court, that rose a yard above the water. In the center stood a remarkable embellishment—a crudely fashioned sculpture of an enormous stick man. Painted white, the figure was five meters tall and looked as though it had been copied from a third-grader's chalkboard. The longer Jack looked, the more bizarre it seemed.

What the hell is it? he thought. *And why is it?*

Deciding that it was worthy of further investigation, he began to swim for the island. He was just getting into his stroke when he got the feeling he was no longer alone. Treading water, he turned around. Sure enough, Pilot was swimming out after him.

"Pilot! What're you doing?" he called back.

The Labrador barked, seemingly proud of his insubordination.

Concerned that the dog might soon run out of steam, Jack turned back and swam to meet him. But as he closed the gap, it was obvious that Pilot was no stranger to water.

He licked his chops and pulled up alongside Jack.

"Think you can make it to the island?"

Pilot snapped his teeth at the water and drank, mid-swim.

"I'll take that as a yes. All right, let's go."

Within a few minutes they were trudging through the thick,

sticky silt that surrounded the island. The place was empty save for the extraordinary wooden man.

As they moved toward it, Jack realized it was even taller than he had initially thought. The top of the figure was at least seven meters off the ground, and it was built entirely of wooden gum poles lashed together with rope. The legs were four gum poles thick, eight for the torso, while the arms—drooping down like old tree branches—were single poles bolted together. The fingers were made of bamboo. The neck was a sawn-off gum pole, on top of which sat an old beer keg. Although the paint had faded, Jack could just about make out the markings of a pair of eyes and a smiling mouth. It looked as if it had been thrown together, yet Jack could sense a certain warmth about it. Whoever had painted its face had done so to convey an expression of benevolence. Kindness, even.

Why had someone gone to the trouble of building something as peculiar as this on an island in the middle of nowhere? He was desperate to know the story.

An hour later, Jack was standing outside the hotel. Reaching down with his towel, he did his best to mop the mud from Pilot's legs and paws. When he felt the Labrador was clean enough, he straightened up and headed for the entrance.

"Good swim?" Henry asked, looking up from his newspaper. "Were you surprised by how cold the water was?"

"Absolutely. I'd say that was easily the second most surprising part of the afternoon."

Henry smiled and got to his feet. "Sorry, Jack. I don't know why, but I thought it better that you discover it for yourself."

He made his way around the counter and gestured for Jack to join him on the couch that looked out over the front of the hotel.

Henry considered how to begin. "It's a remarkable story. But it's not exactly light listening. I need to be up-front about that."

"That's all right," Jack replied. "I still want to hear it."

While Pilot settled down between the two men, Henry began. "His name was Klaus Drescher. German, obviously. In his forties. He owned a farm outside town where he lived with his young daughter. Nobody knows what happened to his wife. Some people believe she died years before, but I don't have any real idea. Anyway, Klaus was a shy man and spoke very little English. Over the years I hardly said more than a few words to him, and yet I found myself liking him very much."

Jack nodded and waited for Henry to continue.

"I can still see his little girl. Daniela," he said. "Klaus used to call her Danny. Beautiful little thing. Six years old. All blond hair and big eyes. She was always running or skipping at her father's side. Such a happy girl." Henry's gaze narrowed. "One day Danny gets very sick. Klaus calls a doctor and is told she has the flu. She's ordered to stay in bed, drink lots of fluids, that sort of thing. But after a week, she isn't any better. The doctor is called again, and once more, Klaus is told it's just persistent flu. Over the next few days, Klaus stays at her bedside, checking her temperature, making sure she's drinking enough, sleeping only when she sleeps. You get the picture. Then one evening, Klaus reads her an old German folk story about a magical white tree man who lives on an island. This tree man is some sort of healer and a protector of children. The story goes that any child who sees the tree man will be kept safe and cured from whatever illness is plaguing them. Of course, when little Danny hears the story, she begs her father to take her to see the tree man so that she can get better."

Henry shook his head. "Poor Klaus. He didn't have the heart to tell her that it wasn't real. So he did the only thing he could. He made it real. He went out and built the tree man for her."

Jack felt an ache in his chest.

"He got his neighbor's wife to watch over Danny for a few hours at a time. It took him four or five days, I think. When it was complete, he drove her to the dam to show it to her." Henry's voice faltered. "The neighbor found Klaus at the dam some hours later. He was sitting on the bank holding little Danny in his arms. But she was gone. Nobody knows if she ever got to see what her father had made for her. I really hope she did. You know? I really do."

Henry took a moment before finishing the story. "It wasn't flu. It was meningitis. The doctor who misdiagnosed her left town soon afterward. We never heard from him again."

"What happened to Klaus?" Jack said in a whisper.

"He took his own life the week after Danny's funeral. Left a note behind. Just one word: *Zu Hause*. Home."

For a long while neither man said anything.

"Nobody in town had the heart to take down Klaus's creation. In fact, every year a few of us head out to the island to paint it. We light a candle. Say a prayer. It just seems like the right thing to do."

Chapter 7

"IT's ALMOST TIME for your big date," Rosie announced, lying stretched out on Elizabeth's bed.

"You're hysterical. You know that?"

"You'd make a lovely couple."

"We're just friends, Rosie. End of story."

Rosie slipped her hands under her head and stared up at the ceiling. She watched as the ancient fan wheezed and wobbled, doing its best to cut through the last of the day's heat. "You're in that sort of twilight between friendship and a relationship. Even if you don't mean it to be that way. Nothing you can do about it. Not a thing. One can't control what the heart wants."

Elizabeth was unpacking her bag. "Excuse me?"

"I'm just saying there's something bigger than friendship between the pair of you. Even if you're too scared to admit it."

Elizabeth gathered her words. "I've never met any man more in love with his wife than Jack. What they had was very rare."

"I don't mean to sound callous," Rosie began, "but Grace is gone. She's been gone for a long time."

"Not to Jack she isn't. She's still very much with him."

"And if Grace had never been in Jack's life? What then?"

"Rosie, please. This is ridiculous. Let's change the subject."

"Okay," Rosie replied, holding up her hands in mock surrender. "Do you at least know what's waiting for Jack in Cape Town?"

"I don't."

"You haven't asked him?"

"No. It's none of our business. If he wants to tell us, he will."

"Aren't you curious? I mean what's the big secret? Why Cape Town, and why does he have to be there by New Year's Day?"

"Look, all I know is that he's had this trip planned for over a year. I couldn't even fathom a guess. And you shouldn't bother trying. It's Jack's business. Just like Hopetown was yours."

"Touché," she replied, and then decided to change tack. "Lizzie?"

"Uh-huh," she replied, unfolding a blouse.

"Mind if I ask you a personal question?"

"You always ask me personal questions."

"I know. But this one's more personal than normal. Are you nervous about Sutherland? About going home?"

The question caught Elizabeth off guard. She looked down into her lap and smoothed out her skirt. "Honestly? Yes, I am."

"Is that why we're staying in Victoria West? To buy you time?"

Elizabeth nodded.

"What are you so nervous about? Specifically, I mean."

There were a few ways Elizabeth could've answered the question. She went with her first thought. "Ghosts."

"Ghosts?"

"I left home on very bad terms, Rosie. And I never got the chance to make up for it. To tell my parents how sorry I was for the way things ended between us."

"We all have regrets."

"Not like this. I forced my parents to send me to Paris straight after I finished school. I was completely self-absorbed. So staggeringly foolish, it beggars belief. All I cared about was getting away. And before I had a chance to grow up, to realize what I was doing, both my parents passed away in the space of a few months."

"Oh, Lizzie, I don't think that—"

"To tell you the truth, I don't even know why I'm going back. Maybe to punish myself."

"Was it a happy home when you were younger?"

"More than happy. It was very special. I was extremely fortunate. Which makes what I did all the more unforgivable."

"Then maybe that's part of the reason you're going back. To reconnect with memories of when you were young. To touch and feel those times and places when everything was still good."

Elizabeth was suddenly struggling to draw breath. "I—I don't know. Maybe. I just wish there was a way to atone for what I did. To tell my mother and father how sorry I am."

"Come on, Lizzie, even if you were half as bad as you claim you were—and I seriously doubt that—they know how sorry you are."

"How would they know?"

"Because they're your parents and they loved you a great deal. Nothing you could've done as a teenager would've changed that."

Elizabeth whispered, "I broke their hearts when I left."

"No, Lizzie. I don't think so. What you're doing now . . . this is what's breaking their hearts. Put yourself in your mother's position. How would you feel if you knew your daughter had been torturing herself all these years? Wouldn't that hurt you? Wouldn't you want your daughter to be at peace? To know how much she was loved?"

Elizabeth tried to absorb what Rosie was saying. "But I—I don't think you can . . . you can't really—"

"Just think about it. Maybe it's time to lay it all to rest? You need to start forgiving yourself."

Elizabeth had never considered it from her parents' perspective in this way. "How did you come up with that?"

Rosie smiled. "I'm hugely insightful. What can I say? Fat people have superpowers."

Elizabeth stood up and embraced her.

"Enough of this. We don't want to ruin your makeup. You better hurry up and get dressed. Jack's going to be here in ten minutes."

Elizabeth wiped her cheeks. "Are you sure you and Sam don't want to join us?"

"Yes, I'm sure. We're both looking forward to an early night. This heat's exhausting. Enjoy your evening," she said, rising and heading for the door. "And whatever happens tonight, Lizzie, please don't do anything you'll regret tomorrow."

"What are you—"

"Don't get yourself pregnant, is what I'm saying."

Elizabeth reached for a pillow and hurled it at Rosie. "Just get out of my room," she said, unable to suppress a smile.

Rosie ducked to avoid the pillow, then reached for the door.

"Rosie."

She turned around. "Yes."

"Thank you."

JACK and Elizabeth stood on the sidewalk. The grand old theater loomed over them, adorned with thick tubes of resplendent neon light. A fluorescent rainbow flickered in a timed sequence up to the theater's name, THE GALAXY, which revealed itself in a starburst of dazzling silver and blue. The lights were so bright they glowed up into the night. The main sign was flanked by two smaller signs.

"Oh my word," Elizabeth said, pointing. "Look!"

The left panel read WELCOME, JACK AND ELIZABETH. The right panel carried the name of the film that was currently being featured.

"*Pretty Woman*. That's my . . ." Elizabeth whispered.

"Favorite film? Yes, I know. I'm incredible."

"Thank you, Jack," she said, kissing him on the cheek. "Thank you. This is wonderful."

"Don't give me too much credit. I just chose the film. Thanks for suggesting the detour."

Elizabeth returned her gaze to the theater's grand façade. "How can a place like this exist all the way out here?"

"There's more to this town than you know. Wait until I tell you about my afternoon. But that's for later. Let's go inside."

As they pushed through a pair of freshly polished brass doors, Elizabeth felt her breath catch. The theater's reception area was adorned, floor to ceiling, with a plush navy pin-striped carpet. A chandelier hung beneath a black ceiling pinpricked with small silver globes, intended to resemble stars in the night sky. The left side of the room was fitted with glossy wooden counters where patrons could buy their confectionery. Opposite was a glass ticket booth.

A grand wooden staircase led up to the black-and-gold theater doors. The scent of warm popcorn danced with Dean Martin as he sang "Everybody Loves Somebody."

"Jack, just look at this place."

Framed black-and-white movie posters were festooned across the room between old cigarette ads. Jack's gaze skipped to a series of neon signs announcing that the theater had STEREOPHONIC SOUND and THE BEST FEATURES IN ALL THE WORLD.

It took him a while to realize that they were completely alone. At least that was what he thought until a voice called out, "Evening, Jack. This must be Elizabeth. Welcome, both of you."

Jack turned and saw Henry sitting in the ticket booth. "*Henry?* Is that you?"

"Indeed it is."

"Where's the owner? Did he allow you to open for us? I'd really like to thank him personally. This place is unbelievable."

Henry strode out from the booth and bowed in Elizabeth's direction.

Elizabeth nodded back at him. "I'm guessing that you're looking at the owner, Jack. Good evening, Henry."

Henry smiled. "It's true. Sorry I didn't say anything earlier, Jack. I thought it would be fun to play it out this way."

"You're full of surprises. But how have you managed this?"

"I can't take much of the glory. My job here is simply to keep the old girl going. My father built the Galaxy. It was his pride and joy. After he passed, I stepped in and have been trying to keep the doors open ever since. As you might imagine, the place doesn't make much money. I can only run the lights for an hour or so each night. You wouldn't believe how much electricity it soaks up. But it's worth it. This is a special place. There'll come a time when I'll have to close the doors. But not yet."

Jack regarded Henry closely and could see how much it hurt him to acknowledge that the Galaxy was living on borrowed time.

"Henry, I don't think I've ever set foot in something quite as extraordinary as this. It really is something else."

"Thank you, Jack. Tonight it's the Galaxy's great honor to screen your favorite film, Elizabeth. We have a few minutes until the curtain goes up. How about a glass of wine?"

Inside, the theater was a vast, luxurious black chamber. Large curtains hung in front of the screen and on the walls—partly, Jack knew, to help with sound insulation but also to add a sense of drama to the room. The seats, numbering well over five hundred in an upper and lower tier, were upholstered in ornate navy and silver cloth. Each was fitted with a swivel headrest and a smooth wooden tray that unfolded out of the armrest.

Elizabeth said, as they took their seats, "Thank you for making this happen, Jack. I'll never forget tonight."

"Neither will I," he replied. "It's magical. It's a pity Rosie and Sam decided not to join us."

Elizabeth rested her head against his shoulder. As much as she had refuted Rosie's assertions, the truth was she had been in love with Jack Everson for the better part of a year. Until this moment, she had never considered saying anything. She knew how much he still loved his late wife and was determined to respect that. Sitting beside him now, with her face pressed against his warm shoulder, her resolution faltered. "You're a wonderful man, Jack," she murmured. "Thank you for bringing me on this trip."

Jack turned and kissed her gently on the forehead. "Thank you for coming, Lizzie. I couldn't imagine any of this without you."

Elizabeth was suddenly gripped by a deep yearning to let him know what was in her heart. The wine, combined with the enchanting setting, was stripping away her resolve to keep her feelings to herself. Before she even realized it, her lips had parted to speak. She had just whispered his name when the main curtain rolled up and sound boomed through the theater.

"What was that?" Jack asked, turning to her.

"Nothing," Elizabeth said. "Just looking forward to the film."

THE next morning at breakfast, after Jack had finished telling the story, there was a long pause before Elizabeth spoke. "I think that's just about the saddest thing I've ever heard."

"And this Klaus fellow took his life a couple days after the funeral?" Sam asked.

"According to Henry."

"I'd like to see it. This tree man," Rosie said.

"So would I."

Jack glanced over at Sam. "Actually, I was hoping you'd feel that way, because I was thinking we could do one better. Henry tells me that every year he and a few townsfolk head to the island to paint the tree man. And, as I saw yesterday, the fellow's looking a little worse for wear. You know how strong the sun is down here."

"You want us to paint it?"

"That's what I was hoping, Lizzie. Before we head out this afternoon."

"Yes," she replied at once. *"Yes."*

Jack watched as both Rosie and Sam nodded their agreement.

"Wonderful. Because Henry's offered to take us. He has a small boat."

"When?"

"Actually, Sam, the paint's already in the car. I was thinking we could go out now."

"That's our Jack," Rosie said, draining the last of her coffee. "Always one step ahead of us, and always on a crusade."

"I don't think this quite qualifies as a crusade."

"Oh, come on, Jack. We're even boarding a boat for this one. We should all be wearing tunics, helmets, and blue paint on our faces. "When you think about it, we're like Pensioner Vikings."

"And she's back." Jack smiled.

AN HOUR later, they were standing in the thick mud on the edge of the island, staring up at Klaus's extraordinary creation.

"He did this on his own? In a couple of days?"

Henry turned to look at Rosie. "We're still trying to work out how he managed it. We think he used some kind of rope pulley system. He was a very clever man. Built his farm by himself."

Pilot stared up at the tree man, barked softly, and then began to wag his tail. Jack leaned over and stroked the Labrador's neck.

"I can't imagine what it must be like to lose a child," Elizabeth replied.

Picking up on the significance of her words, Jack glanced across at Sam, who was gazing at the sky.

Henry clapped his hands together. "Well, we should probably get started. Before it gets too hot."

"I'll start unloading the equipment," Jack offered, and headed for the boat.

For three hours they labored over every inch of the structure. Henry had brought quick-drying paint, which allowed them to apply three coats. To reach the tree man's head and upper torso he had attached a large paintbrush to a series of telescopic metal poles that were wired and taped together.

When they were finished, Jack mopped his brow and walked over to Henry. "Thank you for allowing us to be a part of this."

"I'm the one who should be thanking you. I've told this story to quite a few guests over the years, and nobody's ever offered to get involved like this."

"Maybe it's just because we have a little more time on our hands than most other people."

"No," Henry replied, shaking his head, "that's not it. Time is normally the one thing people have in abundance when they come out to a town like ours."

As they gathered together, Rosie leaning on Lizzie's arm from the exertion, Jack reached into his pocket and handed Henry an envelope. "Henry, I'd like you to have this. It's a small gesture to help you to keep the Galaxy going for a little while longer. It's a special place. Elizabeth and I will never forget it."

"Jack, this is very kind, but I can't accept your money."

"I'm afraid you don't have a choice," Sam cut in. "Not if you know Jack the way we do."

"Just accept it," Rosie added. "If you don't take whatever's in there, Jack will tear it up or throw it away. I've seen him do it."

Conflicted, Henry looked at the envelope. He decided that he would first see the extent of Jack's generosity before deciding anything. But, before he could open the envelope, Jack reached out a hand to stop him. "I have only one small condition, Henry. I want you to wait until we're gone before you open it. And once you've opened it, I want your word that you'll make use of it."

"Jack, I really don't—"

"Your word. Please." Jack locked eyes with Henry.

"Why are you doing this, Jack?"

"Because I want to. And because I have the means to."

Henry thought for a moment. "We hardly know each other."

"I'm not sure that's true."

Henry rubbed his fingers across the envelope. Feeling that it wasn't particularly heavy, he decided to give in to Jack's wishes. He was loath to admit it, but a few extra notes could come in handy if they helped to keep the Galaxy going for another month.

"All right, you have my word. Thank you. I hope this isn't overly extravagant."

Jack thought about the check in the envelope and shook his head. "It's not," he said, shaking Henry's hand. *Not really.*

Chapter 8

THE FINAL STRETCH OF ROAD leading to Sutherland swept its way through valleys and knolls that rose and fell. The stubby grassland combined with a paucity of trees meant that they could see for miles. The effect this had on the sky was nothing short of astonishing. It wasn't merely above them—it was everywhere, painting blue every window in the car.

"So this is what they mean by *big sky*," Jack said quietly, scanning the horizon. "Lizzie, you've undersold the place."

"By a lot," Rosie added, staring out over the fields.

"Just wait until it gets dark. That's when it really catches your breath. Whatever you've heard or read about, it won't come close. Especially when the moon sets."

Sam looked over at her. "The moon?"

"The moon's obviously very beautiful in its own right, but it throws too much light in the sky. It detracts from the stars. You have to wait for the moon to set to truly experience the Sutherland night sky. Normally an hour or two before dawn. When I first saw it, I started to cry. Makes you believe in a God."

"Who were you with that first time?"

Elizabeth turned to Rosie. "My father. I couldn't have been more than fourteen. We camped out the whole night. Spoke for hours. I told him things that I don't imagine many teenage girls tell their fathers. I often dream about that night."

"Sounds like a great memory to have in your locker. Where was this? On your parents' farm?"

"No. It was at an abandoned drive-in on the edge of town."

"Sutherland had a drive-in? In those days?" Sam asked.

"Well, not really. Someone had built a large sheet metal screen and a small building to house the projector, but nothing came of it. It was very early days for drive-ins, and projectors must've been terribly expensive. Which is a pity. Not that the town would've been able to support the drive-in for long. There just weren't enough people. Anyway, it was the ideal setting for my father and me. Perched on a hill, with an uninterrupted view of the sky."

Jack breathed in deeply. "What is it about these small towns and their big ambitions?"

For a while they drove in silence. A few minutes later, they drifted past a rusted sign welcoming visitors. Jack turned to look at Elizabeth. "Here we go, Lizzie. You ready to come home?"

"I don't know, Jack. I hope so."

"There it is," Elizabeth whispered.

The old farmhouse appeared into view. Set at the foot of a small hill, it was a squat, stone building with a green corrugated iron roof. To the right stood a circular stone building that had lost much of its thatched roof to the passing years.

"What's that second building?" Jack asked.

"My father's studio," she replied. "I believe some of his paintings are still inside. Joseph offered to have them shipped to me years ago, but I couldn't face them."

Joseph Thobela was the elderly handyman who, over the years, had done what he could to keep the farm from slipping into ruin. Many of the jobs that needed doing were beyond him, but he still worked diligently to keep the property maintained—evidence of which was clear to see as they pulled up to the main house. The window frames had been freshly painted, and the old front door shone with a new coat of varnish. A square of manicured lawn was bordered by vivid white and yellow wildflowers. A lone tree to the left of the house offered some shade from the punishing heat.

As the car drew to a halt, Sam reached out his hand to Elizabeth. "You okay?"

Elizabeth gripped his fingers tightly and nodded.

Stepping from the car, she turned toward the old tree as if under its spell. Stretching out a hand, she gently caressed the bark. "A swing," she uttered. "There used to be a swing."

She shut her eyes, and as she did, she could almost feel her father's hands on her back, gently pushing her in the swing.

"I don't think I can do this. It's too much. What was I thinking coming back here? I must've been—"

Jack hurried over to her. "Take it easy, Liz. You can do this. We're all here for you. There's no need to rush. We'll take our time . . . *together*. Maybe we should just wait outside for a while longer. How does that sound?"

She took a calming breath. "Okay. That sounds good."

Jack ushered her to a wooden bench. She had only just sat down when the front door opened and an elderly black man stepped out. Despite the heat, he wore an ancient sports jacket that was thinning at the elbows. His polished shoes and freshly ironed trousers were complemented by a Humphrey Bogart–style hat. Seeing Elizabeth, he removed his hat and patted down his gray hair. "Miss Bethy?"

"*Joseph?* Oh my God. Joseph!"

A broad smile parted his straggly beard. Elizabeth rushed over to embrace him. "We're a few days late. I'm so sorry. I should've let you know."

"Not at all. I'm just glad you're here now."

"I don't know how to thank you for all that you've done for me. For my family. All these years."

Joseph reached for her hands. "I only wish I could have done more. There are many things I can no longer do. I'm sorry—"

Elizabeth leaned forward and kissed him on the cheek. "No, Joseph. I'm the one who's sorry. I can't believe it's taken all this time for me to come back. I'm so ashamed."

"Don't say that, Miss Bethy. I know how difficult it was for you when your mother and father passed. It was a horrible time."

"But it was a *lifetime* ago."

"Some things aren't touched by the years."

"Oh, Joseph, there are so many things I want to speak to you about. I have so many questions."

Before she could ask any of them, Jack stepped forward.

"Oh, I'm sorry, Jack . . . everyone. Forgive me. This remarkable man is Joseph Thobela. He has worked with my family his whole life. He's been caring for the farm since I was a girl."

After the introductions, Joseph turned the rim of his hat through his fingers. "Are you ready to see your home again, Miss Bethy?"

"I think so," she replied. "But let's go slowly, Joseph. Okay?"

He smiled. "Since I've passed eighty, everything I do is *slowly*."

A TIME capsule. That was how her aunt had described it. And while she was right, Elizabeth thought, she was also wrong. The place certainly did look much the same—uncannily so—but unlike something trapped in stasis for decades, the house had not been left to gather age and dust. It had been cleaned and cared for. The wooden floors were polished and shone in the afternoon light. Threadbare as they were, the tablecloths and curtains were clean.

Struggling to keep her emotions in check, Elizabeth made her way through the entrance hall and into the sitting room. The old oak dining-room table, where they had spent so much time together as a family, still seemed to anchor the house in the way it always had. Trying not to dwell on the empty chairs that surrounded it, she turned toward the kitchen. "Does the stove still work?"

"Yes, it does. It's a good stove."

Elizabeth nodded and headed into the kitchen. She had barely made it over the threshold when she stopped. Ahead of her, she could see her mother—or at least the memory of her—standing at the sink, arms elbow deep in soapy water. She was humming a tune, as she always did, and Elizabeth hummed along with her.

She looked around the room. The old counters, the ancient stove, and even a small table where she used to do her homework were still present, like old friends. She turned to Jack. "It feels like they've just stepped out for a few minutes. That they'll be coming home anytime now. Can you feel it?"

There was a pleading in her voice that made the hairs on his arms rise up.

From the kitchen they moved into the lounge with its grand fireplace. Elizabeth smiled. "My father used to read to me right over there," she whispered, pointing to an expanse of floor. "At night I'd fetch a blanket and the pillows from my bed and I'd stare into the flames. He had such a kind voice. Sometimes I wouldn't even listen to the story. Just the sound of his words. It was wonderful."

Rosie stepped forward and rubbed her friend's back. Sam slipped his hands into his pockets and lowered his head. He knew what it was to read to a child.

They continued on through the rest of the house. Finally she was standing outside her old room. She was about to step inside, when Joseph took her hand. "Miss Bethy, your father asked me to keep two of the rooms just like they were. The room where he made his paintings and your room. Do you understand?"

Elizabeth nodded and pushed open the door. While the rest of the house had kept up with the passing years, this was not the case in her old room. Everything had been left precisely the way it used to be. Her closet doors were still splayed wide open, the chair in front of her desk askew as though she had just stepped out to make a sandwich. On the bed, a suitcase lay with its lid flipped open.

And that's when it hit her. The room had been kept exactly as it was on the day she had left for the airport. Which is why almost all her clothes were missing. And why, lying on the desk, was a vintage brochure for the airline that had carried her away. She stared at it for a long while before finally surrendering fully to the decades of regret and remorse that had so blighted her adult life, and the sobs took hold of her.

After an early dinner, Elizabeth retired to one of the spare rooms at the back of the house and fell asleep almost at once. Such was their concern that Jack took it in turns with Sam and Rosie to watch over her during the night.

As THE sun peered over the horizon, Sam looked out the window and shook his head "I don't know, Jack. Maybe we should call a doctor. She's been sleeping for a long time."

"It's just the stress of coming home. Her body needs to shut down for a while. To reset itself. She'll come around soon."

"I think so too," Rosie replied. "I'm sure she'll wake up any time now. There's no need to panic."

"Maybe we shouldn't have come. There's no closure for Lizzie here. It's just fresh pain on top of old pain," Sam suggested.

"Perhaps that will change," Rosie said. "Once she settles down a bit, I think she'll be able to focus on all the good years she had in this house. And that will give her the peace she's looking for."

"I think she blames herself for things that aren't her fault."

They all turned to look at Jack.

"Sure, her parents were sad to see her go, but that doesn't mean they felt she had abandoned them. I'm convinced that most of Lizzie's guilt is misplaced. I just wish there was a way of proving it."

"A way of proving what?" Elizabeth asked. She was standing in the doorway, wrapping her silk gown over her shoulders.

"*Hey.*" Jack smiled. "How're you feeling?"

"Better," she said, smiling faintly. "I'm sorry about yesterday. I lost control. I feel terrible that you had to see me like that."

Rosie was about to tell her that yesterday had, in fact, been almost two days ago, but thought better of it. "There's no need to apologize, Liz. We get it."

"How about we get your mind on something else? Like breakfast."

"Thanks, Sam. Maybe a bit later. So what were you talking about before? When I came in?"

Jack scrambled for an answer. "The stars."

"The stars? What about them?"

"Well, after what you told us in the car, I figured we should stay up one night and see them for ourselves."

Elizabeth mulled it over, then said, "I agree. Maybe we can find the old drive-in. If it's still there, of course."

"The old drive-in? Think that's a good idea?"

"It's one of my favorite memories." She glanced at Rosie. "If you can put up with my tears, I think I'd like to go back there."

While Jack was still trying to work out if it was a good idea or not, Elizabeth continued. "Let's do it—the sooner the better. I think I need to get out of here for a while. What about tonight?"

Jack knew that her words might have been phrased like a question, or even a suggestion, but they were neither of those things.

"Whatever you want, Lizzie."

"I THINK it might be up here," Elizabeth suggested for the third time in half an hour. Large plumes of dust tumbled across the Chrysler's headlights, obscuring the view ahead.

Sam reached out and turned up the music. Springsteen's "Working on a Dream" was playing. For the first time since arriving in Sutherland, some of the heaviness had lifted.

When the song ended, Elizabeth leaned forward and tapped Jack on the back of his head. "So when were you going to mention to me that I pretty much slept for two days?"

"Didn't think it mattered," Jack answered. "Besides, we knew you'd work it out before too long. You're smart like that."

"I've never slept for that long. Not even close."

"It was your body's way of protecting you," Jack offered. "How're you feeling now?"

"Quite peaceful. I'm looking forward to this evening."

Rosie pressed her face to the window and looked up. "I don't mean to ruin the moment, you two, but have you looked at the sky?"

"It'll clear," Elizabeth assured her.

"Don't you think it's uncanny that in an area that gets about as much rainfall as the sun, we have an enormous cloud hanging over us? On the one night we come out to see the stars?"

"It'll be wonderful if we have a decent downpour. Nothing cleans the sky like summer rain. It'll pass. Trust me. And then you'll have the show of your life. Something you'll remember forever."

As they crested the hill, Jack flicked on the wipers to clear the dust from the windshield. He squinted through the gloom as the headlights washed over what was, he suddenly realized, the dilapidated face of a one-time drive-in.

"It's still here," Elizabeth whispered. "I don't believe it."

Rosie unclipped her seat belt. "It's like nothing ever changes in this place."

Elizabeth replied under her breath, "Just the people."

Less than an hour later, their rudimentary campsite was set up. While they didn't have tents, they had a few mattresses and blankets that they placed in a semicircle around a log fire. The idea was to keep the fire going until the moon set, after which they would extinguish the blaze. If, of course, it wasn't raining.

Rosie looked up at the clouds as thunder bellowed around them. "Well, the important thing in a storm is to get to the top of a hill and strategically camp next to the most obvious lightning magnet for a hundred miles in any direction. A rusty drive-in screen, preferably. It's in all the safety manuals."

And then, as if on cue, the rain began to fall.

The downpour lasted for hours. With little else to do, they sat swathed in blankets in the car, the sound of the rain rendering any conversation all but impossible.

When the deluge finally relented, Rosie shook herself awake and opened the door. Stepping out into the night, the first thing she realized was how clean and fresh the air felt. Her second observation seemed to trap that air in her throat. The night sky was utterly transformed. The clouds were gone, and the stars were no longer stars; they were bright silver nailheads pinned to a black dome.

Elizabeth took her hand. "This," she whispered, "is nothing."

As the moon slipped imperceptibly toward the horizon, Rosie checked the time. It was almost quarter to four. They had been lying on their plastic-coated mattresses for the better part of three hours, submerged in blankets that were just about fending off the cold. The fire had dwindled to a latticework of glowing embers.

Sam rolled onto his side. "I feel like I'm in a car commercial."

"A car commercial?" Jack repeated, his eyes closed.

"You know the one. A bunch of university kids go on a road trip in a brand-new car where they do all sorts of absurd stuff that never happens in the real world. Like sleeping on the hood of their car or playing football with homeless kids on the side of the road."

"I h-hear you," Rosie agreed, shivering. "Except if we were really in that ad, my boobs would be hanging out and we'd be giving each other high fives every three seconds for no discernible reason."

"We would also spontaneously break out into dance," Sam added. "And we'd never stop smiling. Ever. I used to hate those commercials. They reminded me of how I was wasting my life."

"That *wasted life* of yours made you a wealthy man."

Sam shrugged. "It cost me too much. Far too much."

Rosie was about to reply, when Elizabeth interrupted them. "It's starting to happen."

Jack opened his eyes and noticed that the moon had been reduced to a chalky white glow on the horizon. As the darkness intensified, he peeled away his blankets and rose to his feet. "It's like the sky's on a dimmer switch," he said. "Would you look at that."

"Just hold on," Elizabeth replied.

"For what?"

"You'll see."

Jack was trying to work out how the sky could possibly look any more extraordinary, when it happened. As the last of the moon's glow faded to nothing, the stars came alive. They changed from flat silver nails to pools of liquid crystal that glistened with color.

"*Oh my God*. That's impossible," he said, his words hushed with awe. "Where are those colors coming from?"

"It's called scintillation. It happens as the starlight is refracted through the atmosphere. The darker the sky and the brighter the stars, the more they change color. My father used to call it *starworks* . . . you know, like fireworks."

"It's *incredible*," was all Jack could say, his fingers laced together behind his neck. "Look how they're flickering."

The deep black sky was now pulsing with color, oscillating and twinkling like a jeweler's mat daubed with gemstones.

Sam spoke as if in a trance. "I think it's time."

"Uh-huh," Jack replied. "For what?"

Sam did not respond. Instead, Jack heard his shoes shuffling on the gravel. As he turned to see what Sam was doing, a broad smile lit up his face. At four a.m., on the top of a rain-soaked hill outside Sutherland, sixty-nine-year-old Samuel Lightfoot was doing for real what was so often faked in Television Ad Land. He was dancing for the pure joy of it.

JACK watched as Elizabeth stared through the kitchen window, eyes fixed on her father's studio.

"Morning, Lizzie. Did you get some sleep?"

Elizabeth spun away from the window. "Morning?" she asked, recovering quickly. "It's afternoon already, Jack."

"So it is," he said, glancing at his watch. "That's what happens when you screw with your body clock and stay up all night."

"Was it worth it?"

He looked at her. "Worth it? Last night was one of the most remarkable evenings of my life."

"It's delightful, isn't it? Especially when you're not expecting the stars to do that."

"It wasn't just the stars. It was that we were there together. All four of us. So few people get to do what we did last night."

All four of us, Elizabeth thought, thinking for a moment of Albert. She reached for her coffee. "You're right."

"And you seemed to cope well."

"With every hour that passes, I'm feeling more positive about things. Can I make you some coffee?"

"Actually, that'd be nice."

As Elizabeth switched on the kettle and reached into the

cupboard for a clean mug, Jack moved toward the window and peered out. "Do you have the key for the studio?"

"Joseph gave it to me yesterday."

"Been inside yet?"

"No," she replied, biting her lip. "Whatever I feel for this house, Jack, I feel even more for the studio. I spent so many hours there with my father. He would set up an easel for me, and we would paint together until it was dark. I was never happier. I just don't know if I'm up to it. I don't want Rosie and Sam to see me break down like that again."

Her choice of words both surprised and flattered him. "You don't mind if I see you like that?"

A look of alarm flashed through her as she considered what she was implying. "Things just feel different with you . . ."

Jack kept his eyes on her. "Would you like me to come in with you?"

"Only if you wouldn't mind."

"Of course not. When do you want to do it?"

"Tomorrow morning? After we've all got some decent rest."

"I'll be there," he said, accepting the coffee mug from her.

"There's something else. I know that my father wanted me to have some of his paintings. His final work."

Jack trod carefully. "Okay."

"He was very talented, Jack. When I look at his work, I can see him. It's difficult to explain, but I feel such a powerful connection to him through his art. I'm just worried that it'll be overwhelming."

"I understand. But you'll have me to lean on. That's got to count for something, right?"

Without thinking, Elizabeth stepped forward and wrapped her arms around him. *More than you know,* she thought.

"You're something else, Lizzie. You know that?"

Elizabeth pulled back from their embrace. "Why, when we talk, does it always feel as though you're on the verge of saying goodbye?"

"It doesn't feel that way to me."

"Jack, I know it's none of my business, but is there anything you can tell me about what's waiting for you in Cape Town?"

"I just . . . I made a promise that I need to keep," he offered, his eyes suddenly serious. "A long time ago."

Elizabeth stared back at him. She wanted to ask more. But something held her back. Instead, she squeezed his hands.

"So listen, you're not going to believe this, but Rosie's keen to go for a walk this afternoon," Jack said, changing gears. "I've noticed a change in her—she seems more energetic. Want to come along?"

Elizabeth considered the offer, then shook her head. "Joseph's coming over in a while, and I have so many questions to ask him. He was with my parents through everything. This is one thing I need to do on my own. But I appreciate the offer. Enjoy your walk."

Jack thought he detected a sudden coolness to Elizabeth's mood. "Sure you're okay?"

"I'm fine, Jack," she replied. "See you this evening."

ELIZABETH watched as Joseph removed his hat and sat down at the dining-room table.

"Thank you for coming to see me, Joseph. I appreciate it."

"Of course, Miss Bethy. I know how many questions you must have. I hope I can answer at least some of them for you."

She nodded, grateful for his kindness. "Joseph, do you remember what my parents were like after I left? And I don't want you to try to make me feel better. I just want the truth. Please."

"Your mother was upset for a long time. Your father, well, he turned to his painting for comfort." Seeing the pain in her eyes, Joseph leaned forward. "But do you understand *why* they were sad?"

"Because I . . . I abandoned them. I was terribly selfish. Come to think of it, I never even said goodbye to you."

"Oh, Miss Bethy. Is that what you've been thinking all these years?" Joseph regarded her. "Your parents were sad. But not for the reasons that you think."

Elizabeth blinked. "I don't understand. What are you saying?"

"I'm saying that your parents weren't upset because of the *way* you left. They were just sad that you were gone."

"I'm not sure I see the difference—"

Joseph held up a hand. "Your parents understood that you were young and had your heart set on doing what you felt was right. They were just worried about you. It didn't change how much they loved you." He spoke with such quiet authority that Elizabeth didn't know how to respond. "Your mother was a wonderful woman. She spoke to me about your life overseas. She told me about your letters and the things you were doing. She was so proud of how you were making a life for yourself. She cried a lot for you, Miss Bethy. But they were good tears."

"B-but I never got the chance to tell them how sorry I was for the things I did. I never expressed how much they meant to me," she stammered, raising up her arms. "I just wish that—"

"Just because you never say the sky is blue doesn't mean that it isn't. Do you understand? A mother knows. A father knows."

Elizabeth had spent so many years persecuting herself that she never even considered the possible flaws in her argument: that perhaps her parents understood that she was young and impetuous. That maybe they just missed her.

She rose up from the table and walked over to Joseph. She kissed him on his forehead. "I'm so sorry I never said goodbye to you," she whispered, her tears slipping onto the collar of his white shirt.

He placed a calloused hand on top of hers and gently patted it. "In my culture," he whispered back, "we never say goodbye."

Chapter 9

THEY HAD JUST SAT DOWN at a small, nondescript restaurant on Sutherland's main road, when Jack remembered he hadn't switched on his mobile phone for some time. As he searched his pockets, a waiter arrived to take their order.

"Just a lime and soda for me," Jack said, thumbing the power button on the ancient Nokia. "And a bowl of water for him, if that's okay?" he added, glancing at Pilot, who had slumped down under Rosie's chair.

While Jack's phone powered up, Rosie and Sam placed their food orders. As the waiter headed for the kitchen, Rosie sank back into her chair and dropped a hand onto Pilot's head. "Whose genius idea was it to go for a walk? In the bloody desert no less."

"To be fair, it's not quite a desert," Sam countered, using his handkerchief to mop a line of sweat from his brow. "It's a semi-desert. And I think you'll find that the walk was your idea."

"Oh, thank you, Sir Samuel Attenborough. Maybe later you can lecture us on the deserts of the world. That would be such a treat."

Having been fully resuscitated, Jack's phone issued a shrill chirp.

He punched in the number for the voice message system and lifted the handset to his ear. A voice informed him that he had one new message. There was a click and a slight hiss of static.

"Jack, this is Henry. I've opened your envelope, and, well, I obviously can't accept it. Have you really just given me a check for . . ." He trailed off, seemingly unable to verbalize the amount. "This is ludicrous. I can't possibly take this. Please phone me back."

Jack pressed END CALL and brought the phone down to his lap. He accessed the messaging option and typed a short note.

HI HENRY, I'M AFRAID I MUST INSIST THAT YOU ACCEPT THE MONEY. PLEASE USE IT FOR THE PURPOSES WE DISCUSSED. Jack lifted his head for a moment, thinking of what else he could type that would convince Henry to use the money to keep the Galaxy going. And then he had it. YOU GAVE ME YOUR WORD, HENRY. YOU HAVE TO STAND BY YOUR PROMISE. He clicked SEND and watched as the witchcraft that was mobile phone technology spirited his words from the screen.

ELIZABETH looked down at the key in her hand. The morning sun glinted off the studio's windows. She moved her hand toward the door and slipped the key into its lock.

The old door creaked open on hinges that had not been tested in some time. She pushed inside, and Jack followed closely behind her.

The studio was a single open space accentuated by a high-beam roof and a flood of natural light. The back wall was fitted with wooden benches, upon which an array of painting supplies was stacked. Buckets, canvases, tubes of paint, sketch pads, acrylic pots, jars full of paintbrushes, and an assortment of aprons. But what stood out most were the seven large easels positioned in a half circle around a lone stool. They seemed like sentinels standing watch over the room, draped in loose folds of white cloth.

Elizabeth's gaze shifted from one easel to the next. "They're all still here. I can't believe I'm looking at them."

She drifted to the middle of the semicircle and dropped onto her knees. Not bothering to ask what she was doing, Jack lowered himself down beside her. Her eyes homed in on the easel in front of her. She pointed at its stout wooden legs. "When I was young, I used to sit at my father's feet while he painted. One day, he gave me some paint of my own and told me I could decorate the legs if I liked." She held her hands to her mouth and began to cry.

Jack noticed that the legs were covered with faded dabs of flowers and trees. Patches of sky. Dogs. People. He could imagine Elizabeth as a small child, sitting at her father's feet.

After a while, she moved over to a bench where a brush lay beside a dust-covered palette smeared in globs of different oils.

"Joseph told me that my father had his stroke here in the studio. While he was painting." She picked up the paintbrush. "Whatever he was working on . . . he never got the chance to finish it."

She brought the brush up to her nose, breathed in its scent, and set it down again. "When Joseph told me there were paintings here that my father wanted me to have, I didn't think I'd ever be able to look at them. So many times I've tried to imagine what they are."

Jack reached out and took hold of her hand.

She smiled. "This is it, Jack. The last thing I have to face. And then maybe I can start to breathe again."

"Why don't you turn around and let me pull away the covers. I'll tell you when they're ready."

Elizabeth nodded and turned to face the windows. She closed her eyes and listened as the cloths were removed.

When Jack was done, he stood back and regarded the seven paintings. "Turn around, Lizzie," he whispered.

Slowly she did as instructed, then opened her eyes. At first she struggled to comprehend what she was looking at. Smudges of vivid color danced in her vision, until, finally, they pulled together.

She lifted her hands and pushed her fingers through her hair.

The seven paintings weren't seven paintings at all.

They were one painting, spread across seven canvases.

It was the memory of a father and his young daughter, huddled together under a vast amphitheater of stars. Between the stars and the ground lay the sketched outline of an old drive-in screen whose metal panels were peeling like the curled petals of a desert flower.

As THE days led up to Christmas, a sense of tranquility and purpose settled over the farm. Seemingly energized by the pure air, the four of them set about returning the farm to its former glory. They painted walls, cleaned floors, and repaired the thatch. Careful not to overexert themselves, they made time for long lunches and dinners at which Joseph and his wife, Gloria, were often present.

When Christmas Eve finally rolled around, most of what they wanted to achieve had been done, and they sat down to a feast.

Sitting at the head of the table, Elizabeth looked around the room and felt more at peace than she had in years. To her right sat Jack, Sam, and Rosie. To her left, Joseph and Gloria.

She stood up and placed a hand on her glass. The light conversation fell away, and everyone turned to look at her.

"I'd like to say a few things." She was met with nods and smiles. "Firstly, I want to thank you all for so generously helping to breathe new life back into the farm and for getting me through a very difficult homecoming. I want you to know how much I appreciate everything that you've done for me. Joseph and Gloria, I'll never be able to thank you properly for all your hard work over the years. Whatever money has been paid to you, it hasn't been enough. Not even close," she said, knowing that she would soon make amends for that. She then lifted her glass. "To Joseph and Gloria."

"To Joseph and Gloria," the room chorused.

Elizabeth turned to her three friends. "What do I say to you lot? To the people responsible for helping me to heal a wound that I thought was beyond repair. For the first time in so many years

I can look beyond this. I can't begin to tell you what that feels like."

Rosie blew her a kiss.

"I also have an announcement to make. I've decided that I won't be returning to the estate. For what's left of my life, I want to wake up and fall asleep on this farm. I think it's right that I come back now. Of course, you are all welcome to stay with me. Nothing would please me more. But we can speak about that in the days to come. For now, I just want to tell you that I haven't felt this good in a very long time. Thank you and Merry Christmas."

As one, everyone stood up from the table, taking turns to embrace her. Elizabeth's eyes were drawn to the crackling flames of the fireplace on the far side of the room. For a moment she could picture her father reading to her younger self cocooned in a blanket.

Sitting on her favorite armchair—one that Jack had just repaired—Elizabeth's mother turned to her and smiled.

"ARE you sure, Rosie?"

Rosie nodded. "But only if you are."

"Oh, of course I am! It'll be wonderful to have you here. I was hoping you'd want to stay."

"Maybe I can plow the fields and lose some of this weight."

Elizabeth pulled a face. "We don't have any fields. And you're perfect just the way you are."

"Thank you, Lizzie, but this isn't the Miss America pageant. You don't have to lie for the cameras."

"I'm not," she insisted. "But if you want to live a healthier life, I'll support you all the way. Even push you along."

"You might have to," Rosie warned, winking. "In a wheelbarrow."

She rubbed her hands together. "So listen, Jack's asked if Sam will accompany him to Cape Town. I'm not sure why Jack wants him there. I just thought you should know."

Elizabeth considered the news. "Think they'll come back here when they're done?"

"I think Sam might, but I'm not sure about Jack. There's something about him at the moment. He's not himself. Whatever this Cape Town thing is, it's serious."

"I know."

"And he still hasn't said anything?"

Elizabeth frowned. "I asked him again, but he wouldn't give me a straight answer. I didn't have the heart to push him. He hates to speak about his personal life at the best of times."

"Do you want to know what I think?"

"Of course."

"I think you should give him a reason to come back here."

"Like what?"

"Like the fact that you're in love with him."

"No," Elizabeth replied, shaking her head.

"No, you're not in love with him? Or no, you won't do it?"

"It's not the right time."

"What are you talking about? It might be now or never."

"I'll tell him if he decides to come back."

Rosie sucked in her cheeks. "That's one hell of a gamble. You realize he might not return?"

"I do," she replied, looking away.

"Can I tell you something that you're probably not aware of?"

She nodded.

"Jack Everson loves you. Whether he knows it or not. He loves you, Lizzie."

Jack's final days in Sutherland slipped by like the last embers of a glorious summer. Trying to make the most of what little time remained, he had spent a weekend at Joseph's home helping to erect a new roof. When he wasn't working, he could mostly be found sitting out on the veranda at the back of the farm, watching the sun set. The hours spent there, often on his own, were both precious and painful, inspiring and suffocating.

As the date of his departure crept closer, he withdrew into himself. It wasn't that he had consciously made the decision to retreat from the group but rather that some instinctual part of him knew it was the right thing to do, as much for their benefit as his own.

Hefting his suitcase out into the morning sun, he wasn't at all surprised to see that both Elizabeth and Rosie were already beside the car, waiting for him. Sam was loading his bags into the trailer.

"You can't stay for one more day?" Elizabeth asked.

"I'd really like to, but I need to get to Cape Town in good time."

She nodded, unable to conceal her disappointment.

Jack was thinking of what he could say to her, when he noticed Sam turning to Rosie.

"Look after yourself," she said to him. "Try to stay out of jail."

"It'll be tough, but I'll do what I can."

Rosie lifted onto her toes and kissed him on the cheek. He offered her a smile that conveyed so many of the things that they would never say openly to each other. Then he walked over to Elizabeth. "Take care, Lizzie. I'm so glad you've chosen to stay on at the farm. It's absolutely the right thing for you."

She rested her head against his shoulder. "Please be safe, Sam. And let us know when you get there."

"Will do," he replied.

Jack lifted his own bag into the trailer and shut the lid. Turning to Rosie, he opened his arms and closed them around her.

Emotion slowed her words. "I hope whatever's waiting for you in Cape Town doesn't keep you there for good."

Not certain how to respond, he dipped his chin in acknowledgment before kissing her on the top of her head. He then moved over to Elizabeth, and for a while, neither of them said anything.

"I hope that whatever this is . . . it stops hurting you."

"You don't have to worry about me, Lizzie. Everything's fine."

"You're a horrible liar, Jack. It sits badly on you."

He summoned up what he hoped was a smile.

"I want you to know that this trip of ours, well . . . you have no idea what you've done for me. For all of us."

Jack wanted to say something worthy of the moment but knew that his words would fall short. Elizabeth looked at him, and, for a second, he sensed there was something else she wanted to say. But then her face changed and the moment was gone.

"I arranged a camera from Joseph," she finally managed, pointing to the table behind them. "I want a photograph of us together."

"Of course," he said, nodding, studying her.

Retrieving the old Canon, she positioned it on the trunk of the car, then ushered everyone in front of the tree. Once the timer was set, she checked the viewfinder, then took her position between Jack and Rosie. She tried to hold back her tears. *"To life,"* she whispered.

As BRUCE Springsteen fought to be heard above the hum of the tires, Sam finally spoke. "So how're you doing, Jack?"

Lost in thought, Jack blinked and then glanced at Sam. He seemed to have forgotten that his friend was sitting beside him.

"All right, I guess."

"Really? Sure about that?"

"Pretty much. Why?"

"Well," Sam replied, shrugging, "I was just wondering about it, considering that we both know you're far from all right."

"And you know this . . . *how?*"

"Couple of reasons. For one, whatever game your mouth's playing, the rest of your face isn't in on the act. Especially your eyes, Jack. They're telling a completely different story."

"That so?"

"Then there's the way you've been acting these last few days. Always heading off on your own. Going to bed early. It hardly takes a genius to work out that you've been avoiding us."

"Fine. You win, Sam. I haven't been myself. What do you want me to say here?"

"I don't know. But given that you've asked me to come with you to Cape Town without so much as a stitch of information, maybe the least you can do is admit that something's wrong and not treat me like some stranger who doesn't know you."

The Chrysler lifted over a swell in the road. "I'm sorry I haven't told you about Cape Town. I just assumed that you understood about that. I really need you to respect my wishes—"

"You're missing the point. I don't have a problem not knowing what your big secret is. What I don't respect is you telling me that nothing's wrong when something clearly is."

Jack felt a spark of anger flash through him. "Fine. Point taken. I apologize. Now how about we drop this?"

"In a minute. First tell me something. How do you think things went at the farm this morning? I mean the way things ended."

Jack threw him a bemused look. "What do you mean? It was difficult. Obviously." Jack sensed that he was being led into a trap but was too tired to try to think his way out of it. "We were saying goodbye. It was sad. Which made it *difficult*. The end."

Sam feigned surprise. "Was it difficult saying goodbye when you left the farm to help Joseph with his roof?"

"What?" Jack asked, his patience running thin. "Of course not."

"It wasn't difficult because you knew you were coming back."

Jack opened his mouth to reply, then closed it again. *So that was the trap.* "You're saying that this morning was tough for me because I know I'm not coming back?"

"Bingo." Sam sighed. "And that's why you've been avoiding us."

"Listen to me. You don't understand. This isn't what you think."

"I'm going to ask you one last question, Jack. Are you sick?"

"No. Not at all. But it's ironic that you should ask that of me. How about we talk about your health?"

Sam held up his hands as if to suggest that it was open territory. "If it so pleases the king. Go right ahead."

"Why don't you tell me the real reason you haven't gone for treatment?"

Sam pulled a face. "I've told you this already. It's too late."

"I don't believe that."

"You calling me a liar?"

"You know what, Sam? This is long overdue." Jack stood on the brakes, and the Chrysler snaked to a halt. Without offering another word, he flung open his door and stepped out into the middle of the desolate road. "What you told me before . . . it doesn't add up."

"Oh, this should be good," Sam said, following him into the road.

Jack held up a finger. "*One,* you've hardly lost any weight over the past few weeks. *Two,* from what I've seen around the farm, you're as strong as you've always been. *Three,* nothing about what I see in front of me looks like a man at the end of his life."

Sam's face drew tight with anger. "The cancer's back! I wasn't lying to you."

"*I know it's back!*" Jack yelled.

"Then what's your point?"

Jack took three quick strides toward him and waved another finger in his face. "I know what last-stage cancer looks like. I sat at my wife's side and watched it tear away at her. Hour by hour. What you have . . . *is not last-stage cancer!*"

Sam shook his head, trying but failing to look wounded.

"You told me there was no hope. That's crap. You could've chosen to have treatment, but you didn't. I want to know why."

Sam lifted his hands to his head and glared back at Jack.

"Come on, Sam. Tell me I'm wrong. Tell me I'm dreaming."

After a long moment, Sam looked away. He lowered his arms and headed back to the car. "We're done here."

"Really? You're going to walk away because you don't like what you hear? Why can't you just admit—" Jack pulled up midway through his sentence as the truth occurred to him. One moment he had none of it. The next it was right in front of him, clear as the midday sun. "This is about your daughter."

Sam was reaching for the door, when he withdrew his hand.

"She never forgave you," Jack whispered. "And you never forgave yourself. This is your way out. I'm right, aren't I?"

In the silence that fell between them, Springsteen sang distantly—and not without pain—about a wrecking ball.

"Damn, Sam," was all Jack could say.

Chapter 10

JACK STRODE UP TO THE WINDOW of his hotel room and stared out over the beach. On a clear day he would be able to see right across the bay to Table Mountain. It was a sight that drew travelers from all corners of the world. But this was not one of those postcard days. From his vantage point, all he could make out of the Atlantic were the dull ghost heads of the breakers as they pitched and fell through a veil of mist and rain.

He slid open the window and rested his elbows on the frame. Inhaling the familiar smell of the ocean, he shut his eyes for a while and journeyed through a raft of childhood holidays, impromptu adventures as a student, and, finally, inevitably, to his honeymoon with Grace. He had thought that coming back to the hotel where they had consummated their love would have brought him closer to her. But everything about the place had only served to make him feel more alone, more left behind. His mistake had been not realizing that what he felt for the hotel had nothing to do with the bricks and mortar and everything to do with the person he had once shared it with. Without Grace, it felt like a mausoleum.

Jack was at least grateful that he had been able to mend his relationship with Sam, despite all the things that had been said. Time—and life—were short and better spent on good terms.

He remained distraught about Sam's decision not to fight his cancer. But the more he thought about it, the more he came to settle on an uncomfortable truth. Who was he to question another man's decision on how to live—*or not live?* Especially at their age.

He lowered his gaze and watched as a few diligent souls set about stringing colored lights over the pergola of a beach restaurant beneath him. In a few hours, the promenade would be a hive of activity. As he imagined the crowd milling below the colored lights, he could picture his younger self at one of the tables, drinking too much. He wished he could have a conversation with that young man. He would tell himself to become a better person—*fast*. To live with more thought and regard for those around him. More than anything, he would tell himself that one day when he met a woman named Grace and she complained about pain in her stomach, he must take her to the hospital at once and not rest until she was being given the best treatment possible. Because nothing else in his life would ever matter as much.

THERE WAS A KNOCK AT THE door. Faint at first, then more insistent.

Blinking away the heaviness in his eyes, Jack looked at his watch and realized he had been asleep for more than three hours.

"I'm coming," he groaned, pushing himself up off the bed.

Patting down his shirt, he pulled open the door. Sam was standing in front of him, two large brown bags under each arm.

"Oh, dammit. I'm so sorry, Sam. I fell asleep."

"Figured as much. Don't worry about it," Sam replied, shaking his head. "Seeing that it's New Year's Eve, I thought we could do something a little different tonight."

"What did you have in mind?"

"It's probably better just to show you," he said, glancing down the passage.

"Do I need anything?"

"Just a jacket. I've got everything else."

"I really don't feel like dealing with crowds tonight," Jack said, shutting his door.

"Good. Neither do I," Sam agreed, walking past the elevator and heading for the stairs.

Curious now, Jack followed behind him as they ascended to the top floor of the hotel. When they reached what appeared to be a locked door, Sam turned. "You're not the only one who can organize things, you know." With that, he pushed open the door and stepped out onto the roof of the hotel. Ahead of them sat two deck chairs separated by a cooler box brimming with drinks.

Sam held up the bags. "I thought this might be a good place to usher in the New Year. A few cold drinks accompanied by pizza."

Jack slipped his hands into his pockets, a smile drifting across his lips. "That would be just fine, Mr. Lightfoot. Just fine."

"TIME?"

Jack looked at his watch. "A couple of minutes to midnight."

Sam nodded, sipping at a tall bottle of lemonade. He looked out across the bay and shook his head at the sheer beauty of it. The lights of Cape Town glimmered fiercely against Table Mountain. Flashes of gold, green, and crimson pulsed from half a dozen ships anchored in the bay.

"This is a great ending, isn't it?" Sam asked.

Jack glanced at him. "Yeah, Sam, it is. It's the perfect ending."

"I want you to know that this trip of ours has been . . . well . . . kind of magnificent."

Jack nodded in the darkness. "I'm just grateful that you agreed to come along. It wouldn't have been the same without you."

"That's the beer talking."

Jack's mouth curled into a smile. "Not a chance."

They were quiet for a while, until Sam shifted in his chair. "What do you think Rosie and Lizzie are doing right now?"

Jack had been thinking the same thing for some time already. "Don't know. But I'm glad they've got each other."

Sam nodded and raised his bottle to the sky. "To Rosie and Lizzie. Two of the best."

Jack hoisted up his own bottle. "Rosie and Lizzie."

For the next few minutes they contented themselves by listening to the muted sounds of the revelers beneath them, the music pulsing softly through the concrete at their feet.

And then, all at once, people began to shout a countdown.

"Ten . . . Nine . . . Eight . . . Seven . . . Six . . . Five . . ."

Jack reached over and held out his hand to Sam. "To a beautiful ending, old man."

Sam gripped Jack's hand and shook it hard. "Damn right."

"Four . . . Three . . . Two . . . One . . ."

People began to cheer, cries of "Happy New Year!" ringing out. A kaleidoscope of fireworks lit up the night, exploding around Table Mountain and from some of the ships. There was a wonderful energy to the moment, but sadness as well. Jack was trying to sort through his emotions when something remarkable happened. Large paper lanterns, the size of box jellyfish, soared up from the promenade, high into the night. By the heat of their candles and on the current of a shared wind, they drifted as though connected to one another, following a tide.

ELIZABETH ANSWERED HER phone on the third ring. *"Jack."*

"Morning, Lizzie. Did I wake you?"

"Not at all. I've been up for an hour or so already," she lied, sitting up in bed. "I'm so pleased you called."

"I just wanted to wish you and Rosie well for the New Year. Did you have a good evening?"

"Yes, it was quiet but lovely. We had dinner on the patio. I don't think we actually made it to midnight, though. How about you?"

As Jack took her through his evening with Sam, she could hear that all was still not well with him.

"Those lanterns sound wonderful," she heard herself say.

"They're spectacular, but pretty dangerous. You just need one of them to land in a dry field," he said, then stopped himself. "God, listen to me. I sound a thousand years old."

"Oh no, you don't," she replied. "You sound wonderful."

The words were out before she could catch them. She closed her eyes and bit down on her lip. A second passed. And then another.

"Sorry for phoning so early."

"You can call me anytime, Jack. You know that."

Another pause.

"Is everything okay?" she ventured.

"Everything's fine, Lizzie. How're you doing?"

I'd be so much better if you were here, she thought. "It's getting easier. Little by little."

"Good. I'm glad."

Worried that he was going to end the call, she reached for the first question she could find. "So how's the weather?"

"You know what it's like down here. If you don't like the weather, just wait twenty minutes."

She smiled. Suddenly she wanted to tell him that she could no longer sleep soundly, knowing that he wasn't under the same roof.

"I've been thinking a lot about your father's canvases. I'm so glad you got a chance to see them."

"All thanks to you," she whispered.

"Lizzie, that's not what—"

"I know, Jack. But it's the truth."

Uncomfortable, Jack tried to deflect the attention. "Anyway, for your father's sake, I'm really thankful that his daughter got to see his most important work. That it wasn't in vain."

Elizabeth stared into her lap, tears stinging her eyes. "Dammit, Jack. Only you can make me cry like this."

"I'm sorry, Lizzie. I didn't mean to make you emotional—"

There was a sudden impatience in her voice. "Is it nearly over, Jack?"

"I'm sorry?"

"This thing of yours. Is it almost done with?"

Jack nodded slowly. "Yes."

"And then what?"

He considered the question. "I don't know."

"What kind of answer is that?"

"It's all I've got right now. I'm sorry."

There was a lull before Jack spoke again. Elizabeth already knew that her curt tone had put paid to any further conversation.

"I'm meeting Sam for breakfast. It's probably best I get going."

"I'm sorry. I didn't mean to sound so harsh."

"Not at all. It's perfectly fine. Really. You have every right to be irritated by all of this. I really am sorry."

"Send Sam my love, will you?"

"Of course," he replied. "And take care of yourself, Lizzie."

"I will. You too, Jack."

As JACK headed for the dock, face downturned, the hood from his jacket pulled over his head, it was obvious that the weather was getting bad. Not only was it raining hard but a strong wind was buffeting the yachts and fishing trawlers, causing them to bob harshly against the harbor walls.

Jack headed straight for the offices that controlled the tourist boats. His heart sank when he realized all but one were closed. He noticed a lone man huddled over a desk and knocked on the glass window.

"Yes?" the man replied gruffly, clearly annoyed by the intrusion.

"Sorry to disturb you," Jack said, opening the door. "I was just hoping that you're going out today."

The man, middle-aged with a shaven head, frowned. He pointed out the window. "In this? Not even the fish want to be out in this."

Jack took a step closer to the desk. "I'm afraid it's terribly important that I get on a boat today. If it's a question of money—"

"The thing about money is that it's pretty useless when you're at the bottom of the ocean."

Annoyance prickled up Jack's spine. "Isn't that a little over the top? It's not that bad out there."

The man glared at him. "When it looks like *that* in the harbor," he said, "it's five times worse out on the open sea. Now listen, I've got work to do. Why don't you come back in a couple of days? Maybe the weather will have cleared."

"A couple of days? What about this afternoon?"

The operator flashed an insincere smile. "You're not from around here, are you? This weather isn't going anywhere today, trust me."

"Is there no one else who could take me?"

"None of these boats or their skippers will go out in this. Now, please. I think it's time you—"

"*Listen*," Jack snapped. "You don't understand. It has to be today."

Now the man looked more nervous than annoyed. He reached for his phone. "I don't know what's wrong with you, mister. But I want you to leave my office. I'll call security if I have to."

Ignoring the threat, Jack placed both hands on the desk. He leaned forward in frustration. *"It has to be today."*

As JACK pulled into the hotel parking lot, he could recall almost nothing of his drive back from the harbor. Shaking his head in a futile attempt to clear his mind, he climbed from the car and stepped out into the rain. On autopilot, he made his way to the hotel's rear entrance. Once inside, he headed for the emergency stairwell, unwilling to share an elevator with other people, particularly groups of high-spirited holidaymakers.

Reaching his room, he sat down on the bed to gather himself, to prepare for what was to follow. He had been waiting so long for this moment that now that it was upon him, it hardly seemed real. The silence drummed in his ears. He was aware of beads of sweat needling through his skin. He still had almost two hours to wait.

He fished out his phone. Taking his time, he drafted two text messages, one of which was to Sam. Then he slipped the phone into his pocket, lay down on the bed, and waited.

SAM struggled to hold on to his umbrella, such was the strength of the wind and rain at his back. He could just make out the vague outline of a man sitting on the bench where the promenade met the beach. *This is madness*, he thought.

He cautiously made his way toward Jack, mindful of his footing on the wet bricks. "Jack!" he called. "What are we doing out here?"

Jack, staring out over the storm-tossed sea, didn't even turn to look at his friend. His hood was pooled uselessly around his neck, and water streamed down his head and face. "Have a seat, Sam."

Sam frowned. "You're scaring me. What is this? Is this the thing? What you've been keeping from us?"

"What? Sitting out in a rainstorm?" He shook his head.

"Can't we go inside and get something warm to drink?"

"I'm afraid not," Jack replied. "Today. At this moment. We have to be here. Right here. Nowhere else." He turned to Sam, and what had been a stern look softened. "Besides, there are worse places to be than sitting out here watching all this. Don't you think?"

Sam looked into his friend's eyes, searching for some insight into what was happening, but found nothing. He had no idea what he was doing sitting in the pouring rain, but it suddenly didn't matter. If Jack wanted him there—then that's where he would be.

"I don't know what's happening, Jack, but I'll stay here with you. Whatever this is. For however long you need me."

Jack's gaze was locked on to the sea. He nodded.

They sat watching the rain and the waves, surveying the ships as they pitched and swayed in the bay.

Sam was trying to imagine what it must be like out on the ocean in this weather when he became aware of footsteps behind them.

He turned around and, blinking through the rain, saw a woman's coat, long and tan. The woman was holding a yellow umbrella over her right shoulder, leaving her left exposed to the deluge. She was angling the umbrella to keep her daughter dry—a child no older than seven or so, clinging to her waist.

As Sam attempted to make sense of what he was seeing, Jack leaned over and whispered, "I'd rather regret the things I did, Sam. Than those I didn't. I hope you understand."

Sam turned to Jack and then looked back at the woman. His eyes widened, and his lips parted. He felt himself stand up.

"Dad," the woman uttered.

"*Sarah?*" he managed, before glancing down at the child.

She nodded.

"*C-Casey?*"

Sam stepped toward them. Struggling to contain his emotions and not wanting to scare Casey, he dropped to his haunches. "H-how are you, Casey? You are so very beautiful."

The girl, wearing a beanie and swathed in a heavy pink jacket, met his eyes. She looked up at her mother. "Grandpa?" she asked softly, pointing at Sam.

"*Grandpa,*" Sarah agreed, in tears.

Casey looked back at him and then, without another word, let go of her mother's hand and ran toward him. Sam spread his arms, closed his eyes, and waited for the embrace he had been dreaming of for so long. And then, impossibly, his arms were around his granddaughter and there was nothing he could do to stop the sobs from cutting through him. As he wept, he felt Sarah's body lean over him, the warmth of her face pressing against his.

"*How?*" was all Sam could manage.

Sarah kissed him on the cheek before pointing to Jack. "Jack wrote to me. He told me everything."

Jack stood up. Then he hunkered down next to Casey.

Casey grinned at him, her arms still wrapped around Sam. "My grandpa," she said.

"Yes. Your grandpa." Slowly Sam maneuvered to his feet. He traced a hand across his daughter's cheek. "You're really here."

She nodded and placed a hand over his. "I'm sorry it took so long."

"No. No . . . *I'm* the one who's sorry." Overwhelmed, he turned away and looked at Jack. "I don't know what to say to you."

"I do," Jack replied. "Promise me you'll get the treatment."

Sam felt his lips tremble. "Yes," he nodded, and then again. *"Yes."* Unable to contain himself, he hugged his girls again.

"You should go back to the hotel," Jack finally said.

Sam nodded, but then frowned. "You're not coming?"

Jack slowly shook his head. "You guys go."

Sam thought of trying to convince Jack to join them but decided that he would no longer second-guess his friend's decisions.

Jack held out his hand. "Hell of a trip, old man."

Sam smiled, pushed Jack's hand away, and embraced him. "Hell of a trip, Jack."

Sam watched as his granddaughter sipped at her hot chocolate.

"Are you okay, Dad?" Sarah asked, placing a hand on his wrist.

"I'm sorry. I just can't believe you're both here."

"I wanted to come and see you so many times. I'm so sorry I never had the courage to follow through."

A waiter arrived with their coffee order. "I want you to know something," Sarah whispered. "I forgave you a long time ago. I don't know why I stayed away so long. I think part of me was ashamed at leaving you the way I did. For condemning you for a moment that I know you regret, that *wasn't you*. I'm so sorry."

Sam was about to interject, when she held up a hand. "Please, Dad, let me finish. Jack sent me two letters. In the second he wrote that you'd never forgiven yourself for what happened between us. And so I want to stipulate the one condition I have for us becoming part of each other's lives."

"Anything," he whispered back.

"You have to forgive yourself. Do you hear me?"

Sam looked into his still trembling hands. "I'll try."

Sarah leaned over the table to kiss him on the cheek. "Will you come back to London with us? Just for a few weeks, and then we'll figure things out from there. Would you consider that?"

Sam didn't even have to think about it. "Of course."

Visibly relieved, Sarah looked down at Casey. "Grandpa's coming home with us. How does that sound?"

Casey looked up from her drink, her lips smudged with chocolate. "Grandpa can sleep in my room."

Sam felt a laugh rise up in his chest. "That sounds like a plan."

Feeling fresh emotion pressing at the back of her eyes, Sarah tried to lighten the conversation. "This friend of yours, Jack, he's quite something."

"You have no idea, Sarah. I look forward to telling you all about him. He's the best man I've ever known."

She nodded. "I must say, I don't understand why we had to meet by the bench, though. Jack's instructions were very explicit. He texted me when I landed this morning, saying that we would meet at the end of the promenade, whatever the weather. I'm just wondering why we couldn't have met in here, in the hotel."

Sam, his mind still dazed, tried to consider the question. What *was* so important about meeting out there?

Jack had known how bad the weather was long before he had sent Sarah his final message. Why did—

And then, all at once, he understood why.

"Stay here," he managed, running for the door.

He shouldered his way past a young couple standing in front of the door that led out onto the promenade.

"Hey!" an annoyed voice called out. But Sam was through the door and out into the rain before the man could even turn around. His arms and legs burned with each stride. The end of the promenade was barely two hundred yards away, but it felt much farther.

As he neared the bench, gasping for breath, he saw that Jack was no longer sitting there. Dread rushed through him.

Hurrying on down a series of slippery wooden stairs, he looked through the haze of mist and rain but could see nobody on the beach. And then he saw what appeared to be clothes strewn at intervals leading to the water's edge. A rain jacket. Shoes.

Running hard, he kept going, charging into the waves. Gasping at how cold it was, he stared out across the churning water. He caught sight of a vague figure striding ahead of him. "Jack!" he screamed, the wind sapping the strength from his words. "Please!"

But Jack kept going.

Scrambling for purchase in the soft sand, Sam pulled himself forward in the water. He leaned back, filled his lungs with air, and reached for one last cry. *"Jaaccck!"*

This time Jack stopped and turned around.

Sam continued deeper into the water until they were barely thirty yards apart. The choppy sea was up to his chest now, but Jack was standing, waist-deep, on a sandbank ahead of him.

"What are you doing?"

For a moment Jack said nothing. Then he held up his hands. "I tried to get a boat."

"What are you talking about?"

Jack pointed to the ocean. "I had to get to Robben Island today."

"Why?"

"Today's the day, Sam."

"What's so special about today? What are you talking about?"

Jack looked toward Robben Island in the distance. "We got married on Robben Island. When Grace got sick, I took her back there. She knew she was dying and was worried that I wouldn't want to live on without her. She was right. So she made me promise that I would come back to the island on our tenth wedding anniversary." His voice started breaking up. "That's today."

Sam suddenly felt sick. "Jack. No. Don't do this. Please."

"I'm sorry. You have Sarah and Casey now. This is how it's supposed to be."

"For God's sake . . . *Don't do this*. You'll never make the swim," he insisted, grasping for the words that would keep his friend from ending his life. "We'll find a boat to take you there. I'll come with you. I swear. We'll do this together. *Today*."

Jack looked out over the ocean and shook his head. "There aren't any boats. It doesn't matter anyway."

"Why not?"

"Because," he replied, shrugging, "don't you understand? I was never coming back from the island. I promised her I'd return for our anniversary. I never promised to carry on after that."

Sam felt his stomach clench. "She wanted you to live, Jack. That was the point of getting you to come back. Please, think about—"

"What? What should I think about, Sam? How about what *I* want? What about that?"

"There are other reasons to carry on," Sam offered, but knew at once how anemic his words sounded.

"I'm already gone, Sam. Go back. Go home to your family. And I'll go to mine. I'll see you," he said, and then slowly turned away.

Knowing he had lost him, Sam squeezed his eyes shut. Through the cry of the storm, he listened as Jack's body cut through the waves. Finally there was nothing but the sea and the rain.

Chapter 11

STRUGGLING FOR BREATH, Elizabeth placed her hands on her knees and looked down at Pilot. "We're almost there," she huffed. She turned her gaze to the top of the hill, noticed a cluster of rocks ahead, and at once, another memory pinged to life. She and her father had picnicked up there every now and then. She could imagine him kneeling on a blanket, unlatching his old army bag. "Watermelon," she whispered. "There was always watermelon."

Feeling her spirits rise, she ran a hand down Pilot's back. "C'mon, let's get up there."

A few minutes later, she stepped onto the uppermost rock and sat down. Pilot moved in beside her, tongue lolling. She poured some water into her hand and smiled as his tongue tickled her fingers.

Looking down at the farmhouse as the afternoon sun reflected off its roof, Elizabeth felt a wave of emotion surge through her. Just as it had when she was a girl, the house looked different from up here—like a doll's house or some sort of cake decoration.

Her phone vibrated. She reached into her denims, surprised that there was coverage on the hill, and smiled when she saw who it was. "*Sam*. How're you doing?"

"He left a bag n-next . . . the bench, Lizzie," came the fragmented voice through the phone.

"Sam? You're breaking up. Say again. What's going on?"

". . . left him out th-there. Alone—so stupid. And he just . . . into the w-water . . . Swam . . ."

Elizabeth stood up. "Sam, you're scaring me."

There was a moment's silence, and when he spoke again, she could hear that he was in tears. "Coastguard's looking . . . him, Lizzie. B-but . . . too late. I know . . . he's gone. *Gone*."

"What do you mean *he's gone?* Sam?"

"Jack's dead, Lizzie."

Elizabeth began to shout into the phone. "Sam! You're not making sense! Jack can't be dead. That's impossible. What's going on?"

"Sorry."

"Sam?"

". . . sorry, Lizz—"

And then the connection was lost.

Elizabeth stared at the phone, unable to draw breath.

Jack couldn't be gone. What was Sam talking about? What water did Jack go out into? It wasn't true. *Please*. Jack couldn't be gone.

THE pain in Ezra Fall's back was getting worse, exacerbated by the inclement weather. He was beginning to wonder how much longer he could do his job. Compacted lower vertebrae was the fancy term his doctor had used. Too many years on his feet was the plain truth of it. He would have to keep going for as long as he could. Which was fine by him because he loved his job.

He had just fetched his old grass broom and was about to sweep away the wet leaves that had blown into the corridor when he received a message on his phone. His youngest son's school shoes had been stolen while he was playing football with friends.

Leaning on the broom, Ezra sighed. There wasn't money for new school shoes. There was barely money for food. He would have to sell his father's record player. He had been facing up to the fact for weeks, and now the moment was upon him. He typed his reply. DON'T BE ANGRY WITH HIM, OLIVIA. I WILL GET HIM SOME SHOES. TELL HIM IT IS ALL RIGHT. I KNOW HOW HE WORRIES. SEE YOU ALL TOMORROW.

He slipped the phone back into his overalls, then set about mopping up a pool of rainwater.

When he was done, he tried to stretch out his back. As he lifted his head, he could make out the familiar livery of the coast guard's main recovery boat out on the water. Some poor vessel, probably a fishing trawler, must have run into trouble.

It was almost eight p.m. What little light the sun still had left would be gone within half an hour, making a rescue in the dark that much more treacherous. He whispered a prayer for those in peril.

Despite his money troubles, he was again lifted by his duties. *Yes,* he was on minimum wage. *Yes,* he was just a cleaner. But he was a cleaner on Robben Island, where Nelson Mandela had once been imprisoned, a symbol of hope for millions across the world.

His eyes floated over curves of land and silhouettes of rock that were as familiar to him as the faces of his own children. And that was when he saw the pale figure of a shirtless man, sitting near the water's edge.

"MISTER," Ezra called out as he climbed down the rocks.

The man remained perfectly still, staring out over the sea.

Cradling the blanket in one arm, Ezra nearly lost his balance. Riding out a fresh wave of pain, he steadied himself and then continued toward the stone bench. Wary of the stranger, Ezra shifted his position so that he could see the man's face. "Mister?"

Jack's head turned toward him, but his eyes remained focused on the water.

Instinctively aware that the man—close to his own age—was of little threat to him, Ezra stepped forward and wrapped the blanket around his shoulders. Mercifully, the rain had eased to a faint drizzle. He waved a hand in Jack's face. "Can you hear me?"

The movement of Ezra's hand seemed to break Jack's trance. "I'm sorry," was all he could say. His throat was dry and cracked from the saltwater.

Ezra dipped a hand into the front pouch of his overalls and pulled out a thermos. He poured some of its contents into a cup and handed it to Jack. "It's not very hot, but it'll help."

Jack took hold of it. Shivering, he lifted it to his lips and drank.

Ezra refilled the cup before deciding it was safe to join Jack on the bench. "Ezra Fall," he volunteered.

"Jack. Jack Everson."

Ezra pointed to the sea. "How many others were in your boat?"

"I'm sorry?"

"I saw the coast guard out on the water. Your boat must've gone down. How many others were there? Or were you alone on board?"

Jack looked back at him and shook his head. "No boat."

Ezra realized that the man must be in shock. "Forgive me, Jack, but you must've been on a boat. How else could you have got here?"

Jack looked down at the bench and gently ran his hand across its smooth surface. "I married my wife here. Right here. It was a beautiful morning." He looked at Ezra. "I loved her so much."

Ezra's frown deepened. It was clear to him that Jack was in a bad way. He reached back into his overalls and grabbed hold of his phone. "We need to let the coast guard know you're here. I'll get you some help, Jack. Maybe they've already rescued the others."

As Ezra searched for the emergency numbers on his phone, Jack whispered, "I wasn't planning on making it. I was just going to stop when I got tired. But I kept thinking of her."

Ezra could only shrug. He had no idea what Jack was trying to tell him.

"You asked what got me here."

"Yes, I did."

"Wanting to live," he said. "Wanting to try for something."

Dropping his chin to his chest, Jack closed his eyes. The last face he saw, before exhaustion swept him away, was that of the woman who had kept him swimming in a storm-tossed sea that would have claimed most men half his age. A woman at the top of a hill, at an abandoned drive-in, bathed in the glow of a star-filled sky.

Epilogue

Twenty-three months later

JACK PEERED OUT THE WINDOW of the hotel lobby. "It's starting to snow again. Should we call for a cab?"

Elizabeth glanced at Rosie. "I don't mind. What do you think?"

Rosie, now almost two years into an unlikely walking addiction, shook her head. "It's only five or six blocks. Let's walk."

Jack reached for the hotel umbrellas that were propped up in front of the reception desk. He held open the door, and they headed out into the gentle snowfall. As they crossed the road, Jack reached for Elizabeth's hand.

"Snowing in London," Rosie remarked. "It's a cliché."

"But a good one," Elizabeth replied. "I used to have a snow globe of Buckingham Palace when I was growing up. Dreamed of coming here for years." She looked at Jack and knew that he hadn't heard a word she had said.

He caught her eye and blinked, as if to clear his mind. "Sorry, Lizzie. What was that?"

She squeezed his hand. "Nothing. Just making conversation."

Abandoning further attempts at small talk, they walked the rest of the way in silence. When they finally passed through the old gate, Jack was not surprised to discover that the church was almost full.

Just what was it about Sam that people so responded to? He had lived in England for only a short while, and yet every face that Jack saw carried the wounds of Sam's passing.

Seated in the front row, Sarah turned around and smiled warmly through her tears. Elizabeth and Rosie waved in return.

Elizabeth's gaze wandered to the girl sitting beside Sarah. It took her a moment to realize that she was looking at Casey, Sam's granddaughter. She was at least a foot taller now, and her hair had been braided with bright beads. "Look how much she's grown up," Elizabeth whispered.

Before Jack could reply, Sarah gestured to the minister as he took his place at the pulpit. After a short prayer, he began to speak. "Friends, we always want more time. Time to do the things we promised ourselves when we were young. To say the words that need saying. But so often our time runs out before we get the chance. Our deepest regrets are always the things we leave between ourselves and those we hold most dear to us. Our thoughts. Our fears. Our love."

The minister looked out over the congregation and raised a finger in defiance. "But not today." He straightened his glasses. "In the short time I knew Sam, I was constantly astounded by how openly he spoke. A surprising fact when you consider that Sam came from a guarded generation that cherished privacy. To tell you the truth, Sam inspired me to be more open with my own family. With my children. It's a debt I'll never be able to repay.

"It's remarkable to think that just two short years ago most of you had never met Sam. The fact that he's had such an impact on your lives in such a short space of time is testament to the man he was. Friendly, generous, kind, always there to lend a hand. I could go on for a long time about Sam, but I know that's not what he would've wanted. Instead, my job here today is straightforward. I'm here to see that his final wish is fulfilled."

The minister signaled to a young man sitting to the right of the pulpit. The man stood up and walked behind a curtain. He returned wheeling out a large television. As he switched it on, Sam's smiling face appeared on screen.

"Oh God," Elizabeth whispered, bringing a hand to her mouth.

Sitting in his hospital bed, tethered to a cluster of drips, Sam smiled into the camera. "Hello, everyone," he began. "I suppose there's every chance that I'm speaking to an empty church right now, but I hope that's not the case. Because there's one last message I'd like to share with you. Something I learned too late in life. I'd like to pass it on." Sam cleared his throat. "If you're living with regrets—things that you've put away in a box but that maybe keep you awake at night—I want to tell you that you still have time to make things right. I know that life isn't a storybook. I also know that some of our mistakes are too far gone to be hauled back in. That maybe you've lost things that will remain beyond your grasp. But I also know that my life would've been so much better spent if I had just been trying for something. My final wish for all of you is that you realize, while you still have time, that it's the trying that matters. Maybe it's all that matters."

Sam's eyes glistened. "Before I came out here with Sarah and Casey, I was fortunate enough to go on a remarkable journey with four friends. A thousand-mile road trip that led me to my family. I could try to put into words how grateful I am for that trip and how much it has changed the remaining days of my life, but I think my words will come up short."

With that, Sam pulled away the blankets that covered his legs. Moving to the side of the bed, he took a moment to steady himself before pushing up to a standing position. He wheeled his drip stand to one side and winked into the camera. Casey stepped into view and placed a small music player on his bed. She pressed a button, and Bruce Springsteen's "Working on a Dream" began to play.

Just as he had once done at the top of a faraway hill, in the company of his closest friends, Samuel Lightfoot danced one last time.

AfterWords

South African author Gareth Crocker was born in Johannesburg in 1974. He first appeared in Select Editions back in 2008 with his debut novel, *Leaving Jack*, and then again in 2014 with *Journey from Darkness*.

A prolific writer, Crocker's career began early, at age nine, when he "discovered that young girls were fond of rhyming couplets." He wrote love poems on behalf of his "poetically challenged" male classmates, contributing to what he refers to as the most lucrative writing period of his life. Crocker offers this advice to other young aspiring writers: "If you truly believe you have the game to get published, do not stop trying."

Prior to becoming a novelist, Crocker worked as a reporter for many years before joining a top South African PR and publishing firm—or, as he puts it, selling his soul to the corporate world.

He has recently added screenwriting and directing to his list of talents through his work on *Jongo*, the first African superhero series. Crocker says of the TV program, "We wanted to showcase the beauty and dynamism of the continent and of South Africa in particular. So much focus is placed on the problems Africans face. *Jongo* emphasizes all that is wonderful and positive about this great continent."

Crocker lives in his hometown of Johannesburg with his high school sweetheart turned wife and their two children, three cats, and four dogs.

The condensations in this volume have been created by Trusted Media Brands, Inc.,
by special arrangement with the publishers, authors, or holders of copyrights.
With the exception of actual personages identified as such, the characters and incidents
in the selections in this volume are entirely the products of the authors' imaginations
and have no relation to any person or event in real life.

ACKNOWLEDGMENTS

Page 177: © Axel Dupeux. Page 321: Deanna Leach. Page 465: Jon Cartwright.
Page 575: Courtesy of the author. Jacket and title page image: Shutterstock/Serhii Zavalnyi.

The original editions of the books in this volume are published and copyrighted as follows:

Past Tense, published at $28.99 by Delacorte Press,
an imprint of Random House, a division of Penguin Random House LLC
© 2018 by Lee Child

Hope on the Inside, published at $15.95 by Kensington Books,
an imprint of Kensington Publishing Corporation
© 2019 by Marie Bostwick

Forever and a Day, published at $26.99 by Harper,
an imprint of HarperCollins Publishers
© 2018 by Ian Fleming Publications Limited and The Ian Fleming Estate
James Bond and 007 are registered trademarks of Danjaq LLC,
used under licence by Ian Fleming Publications Ltd.

The Last Road Trip, published by Penguin Books South Africa,
an imprint of Penguin Random House LLC
© 2015 by Gareth Crocker

The volumes in this series are issued every two months.
Readers may receive this service by contacting us by mail, email, or company website.

In the United States:
Reader's Digest Select Editions
PO Box 50005, Prescott, AZ 86304-5005
bookservices@rd.com
rd.com

In Canada:
Reader's Digest Select Editions
PO Box 970 Stn Main, Markham, ON L3P 0K2
bookservices@rd.com
rd.ca

Some of the titles in this volume are also available in large-print format.
For information about Select Editions Large Type, contact us at
PO Box 433031, Palm Coast, FL 32143-3031 or selt@emailcustomerservice.com.